STARMASTERS

STARMASTERS

by
Gérard Klein

Starmasters' Gambit
adapted into English by C.J. Richards

The Day Before Tomorrow
adapted into English by P.J. Sokolowski

The Mote in Time's Eye
adapted into English by C.J. Richards

Foreword by Robert Silverberg

Introduction and bibliography
by Jean-Marc Lofficier

A Black Coat Press Book

Acknowledgements: The publishers should like to thank Gérard Klein, Lindsay Ribar at DAW Books, Robert Silverberg, Kate Wilhelm and Manchu.

Published by arrangement with DAW Books, Inc.

Table of Contents

Foreword

By Robert Silverberg

Gérard Klein, in his capacity as the editorial director of France's superb *Ailleurs et Demain* series of science-fiction books, has brought many of my novels to French readers in unusually handsome editions. In his capacity as critic he has written several thoughtful and insightful essays about my work. And he has been my friend for close to fifty years, ever since our first meeting in New York. I am often in Paris, have visited him in his extraordinary Left Bank apartment, and we frequently have met for lunch or dinner. So—since we have had a close professional and personal relationship for nearly half a century—I am not exactly qualified to offer an objective analysis of his place in the world of science fiction. But I could, if necessary, call almost any member of the French science-fiction world as a witness when I testify that he has been for many years a central, even dominant, figure in that world, whose contributions to the literature of what the French call "*anticipation*" have been enormous and vital.

Klein's most visible contribution to science fiction has been *Ailleurs et Demain*, emanating for many years from the prestigious publishing house of Robert Laffont at a rate of half a dozen or so titles a year. These were trade paperbacks of great beauty, bound at first in glittering metallic covers, no two alike in design, until eventually it became impossible to obtain the distinctive cover stock that made the series immediately identifiable, and a more conventional, though still attractive, format was adopted. The series began in 1969 with a translation of Fritz Leiber's *The Wanderer*, and continued, year after year, to bring French readers the most distinguished contemporary science-fiction novels, most of them, though not all, American or British: a brilliant roster of books that reflected Gérard Klein's discriminating taste as a reader and as an advocate for the best in science fiction. I need only mention a few highlights of the *Ailleurs et Demain* list to demonstrate what I mean: Brian W. Aldiss' *Helliconia* trilogy, John Brunner's *Stand on Zanzibar*, Ursula K. Le Guin's *The Left Hand of Darkness*, Philip K. Dick's *Ubik*, Gene Wolfe's *The Fifth Head of Cerberus*, and a host of other memorable novels by such writers as Frank Herbert, Philip Jose Farmer, Gregory Benford, Norman Spinrad, and Arthur C. Clarke. (As I noted above, he published a good many Silverbergs, too.) Nor did he ignore the best work of the French science-fiction writers, such people as Philippe Curval, Michel Jeury, André Ruellan, and Stefan Wul, whose books, if only they were known in the English-speaking world, would be fitting companions for the novels of Dick, Aldiss, Le Guin, Wolfe, and the rest.[1]

If the *Ailleurs et Demain* line had been Klein's only accomplishment in science fiction, it would have provided him a place among the great editors of the field. But he has also been a critic, producing, over the years, a host of deep-ranging essays and introductions that examine the role and function of science fiction and set forth the guiding principles that have shaped his long career. Very few of these essays, alas, have been translated into English—a couple of them can be found on the Internet, but most remain available only to Francophones. Nevertheless, the importance of his critical work is well enough known internationally to have brought him, in 2005, the most important honor in the field of science-fiction criticism, the Pilgrim Award, given annually for lifetime achievement in the field of science-fiction scholarship.

But there is also Gérard Klein the writer of science fiction, who has practiced what he preached and done it very well. His first stories appeared in 1955, when he was eighteen, and by 1977, when he seems to have abandoned short-story writing, he had had some sixty stories published. Once again, very few of these are available in English: our loss, though we have collected three of them here. There were also a good many novels, and, again, four have been translated into English, three of which are republished here. The best of these, alas, is not among them because of copyright problems -- the wildly inventive *Les Seigneurs de la Guerre* of 1971, which carries its protagonist through a startling series of adventures worthy in their intricacy of A.E. van Vogt. John Brunner, no trivial writer himself, produced a fine translation, published in the United States in 1973 under the title of *The Overlords of War*. Would that it could have been included here. But the other three are worthwhile contributions all the same.

And I should speak also of Gérard Klein the man: very French indeed, by which I mean a serious thinker who is also debonair, fluent in several languages, and eloquent—in all ways a most appealing figure. He was trained as an economist and, having made a deep study of Marxism, leans toward the left-center in matters of politics and economics. Since my own leanings in these areas are somewhat in the other direction, we have had a few lively but always amiable disagreements over such matters, usually discovering as we talk that we are not really very far apart. An economist and philosopher he may be, but the essential Gérard Klein is primarily a man of letters. His Left Bank apartment surely contains more books per cubic meter than any other place in Paris, the Bibliothèque Nationale included. The building he lives in dates from the sixteenth or seventeenth century, and that it is still standing despite the weight of literary matter

---

[1] Michel Jeury's *Chronolysis* (now out of print) and André Ruellan (writing as "Kurt Steiner")'s *Ortog* have been published by Black Coat Press. (*Note from the publisher.*)

that Klein has imposed on it is a tribute to the architectural skills of its ancient architect. (Now that he is in his eighties Klein, no longer taking an active role in the Laffont science-fiction series, spends much of his time at his second home on the north shore of Brittany. I have not been there, and so I'm not able to say whether it is as crowded with books as is the place in Paris, but my guess is that it is gradually approaching the same critical mass.)

The remarkable career of Gérard Klein, as editor, writer, and critic, is without parallel in the annals of French science fiction. That so little of his best work is unknown in English-speaking countries can only be regretted; and here, long overdue and not really sufficient, is a volume that takes one step toward remedying that lack. May it be followed before long by others.

Robert Silverberg

BIBLIOTHÈQUE

MARABOUT

GÉRARD KLEIN

le gambit des étoiles

Sur l'échiquier des tourbillons interstellaires
un homme joue sa dernière chance

Introduction

By Jean-Marc Lofficier

Gérard Klein was born on May 27, 1937. His family lived in the 4th arrondissement of Paris, then moved to Blois for the duration of the War, then returned to Villemomble, a then-affluent suburb of Paris after the War. He later graduated from the famous Institut d'Etudes Politiques and from the Sorbonne University's Institut de Psychologie.

Klein was the first in a new wave of post-WWII French science fiction fans to be inspired by American science fiction and become a writer. He began to publish a series of Ray Bradbury-influenced short stories in the genre magazines *Fiction* (the French edition of *F & SF*), *Galaxie* (the French edition of *Galaxy*) and *Satellite* as early as 1955, when he was only 18. Three years later, most of these were collected in *Les Perles du Temps* [The Pearls of Time] in the prestigious *Présence du Futur* imprint of publisher Denoël.

After publishing two minor space operas under pseudonyms, Klein set out to write his first major novel. It turned out to be the A.E. Van Vogt-influenced *Le Gambit des Etoiles* [Starmasters' Gambit], published in 1958 by the *Rayon Fantastique* imprint, a joint venture of publishers Hachette and Gallimard. *Le Gambit des Etoiles* established Klein as a major new talent, and from that point on, he remained one of the best loved science fiction authors in France.

Klein followed up *Le Gambit des Etoiles* with the popular "Argyre saga," describing the future history of Man's conquest of the Solar System. This trilogy was written for the more popular *Anticipation* imprint of Editions Fleuve Noir.[2] The books were originally published under the pseudonym of "Gilles d'Argyre," a subtle joke by Klein about his desire to make money at writing, *Argyros* meaning silver in Greek. It is also the name of a Martian plain. The first novel, *Chirurgiens d'une Planète* [The Planet Surgeons] (1960)[3], described the terraforming of Mars by the enterprising Georges Beyle. The second, *Les Voiliers du Soleil* [The Solar Sailors] (1961), featured Beyle, now linked to a giant computer and residing on Callisto, defeating an alien invader from outside the Solar System. By then, Mankind had begun to colonize the outer planets. The third, *Le Long Voyage* [The Long Journey] (1964), saw the messianic Beyle return one last time to turn a terraformed Pluto into a starship that left the Solar System to

---

[2] For more about Fleuve Noir, see our introductions to Kurt Steiner's *Ortog* and G.-J. Arnaud's *The Ice Company*.

[3] It was heavily revised and rewritten by Klein in 1987 and republished as *Le Rêve des Forêts* [A Dream of Forests].

explore other star systems. Beyle was last mentioned, briefly, as a legend, in *Le Sceptre du Hasard* [The Scepter of Chance] (1968), a far future political thriller in which Earth is supposedly governed by intelligent computers.

Other notable works of the period included yet another Van Vogtian time-thriller, *Le Temps n'a pas d'Odeur* [The Day Before Tomorrow] (1963) for *Présence du Futur*, and *Les Tueurs de Temps* [The Mote in Time's Eye] (1965) for *Anticipation*, which reprised the chess theme of *Le Gambit des Etoiles*. Klein also published a collection of more literary-minded stories, *Un Chant de Pierre* [A Song of Stone] in 1966. During that time, Klein developed a reputation as an economist. In 1963, he joined the French Caisse des Dépôts, a publicly-owned savings and loan company. Among notable career achievements, he designed a popular new savings plan.

In 1969, Klein, who, by then, had become a renowned genre critic and essayist, became an editor at publisher Robert Laffont, where he launched a prestigious science fiction imprint, *Ailleurs et Demain*, which is still in existence today. There, he published his next major new novel, *Les Seigneurs de la Guerre* [The Overlords of War] (1971), and an excellent short story collection, *La Loi du Talion* [The Law of Retaliation] (1973).

Les Seigneurs de la Guerre was a more sophisticated version of *Les Tueurs de Temps*, a complex space-time opera incorporating challenging philosophical implications. Its hero, Colson, was a lone warrior caught in a future war who found himself thrown back and forth between two segments of time separated by 6000 years. The prime movers were the mysterious Gods of Aergistal, omnipotent chess players who lived a complex hyperlife (infinitely replaying their own existence) at the end of time, and had built a simulated battlefield where all the various wars of time could be waged again. Their goals were both simple and complex: war was to be abolished, war was to be understood, but war was also to be preserved, in case the universe needed it someday. War was depicted as a negative, yet indispensable, factor in human evolution, virtually a biological imperative. It is interesting to note that Klein declared in an interview that a large part of *Les Seigneurs de la Guerre* had been written during his military service during the French-Algerian war and heavily influenced by it (1960-62).

Since then, Klein has devoted all his energies to his work as editor and anthologist. In particular he has been the leading anthologist of a 36-volume "Grande Anthologie de la Science-Fiction" published by the Livre de Poche imprint between 1973 and 1986. Klein has won numerous genre awards including the 1974 Grand Prix de la Science-Fiction Française for one of his short stories ("Réhabilitation" included in *La Loi du Talion*), and again in 1987 for another short story, "Mémoire vive, mémoire morte" [Live Memory, Dead Memory], which also won the Rosny Award, and the 2005 Pilgrim Award. It has since been collected in an eponymous collection released in 2007

Jean-Marc Lofficier

STARMASTERS' GAMBIT

CHAPTER I
The Recruiters

He was thirty-two years old and his name was Jerg Algan. Most of his life had been spent on the Earth, where he'd roamed over the planet. He had glided across the seas on rickety hydrofoils, flown over whole continents in obsolete planes left over from the last century; he had sunbathed on the beaches of Australia; he had hunted the last lions in Africa before the desert plateau had tumbled into the ocean.

His achievements had been negligible. He had never left the Earth. He had traveled through the stratosphere. Between trips, he lived in Dark, supporting himself doing odd jobs as it was possible to do in large cities.

Dark was, in fact, the sole remaining city on the Earth. It had a population of thirty million and was the last resort in the entire galaxy for men of his sort. So long as they went quietly about their business, the Psychological Police left them alone. By virtue of its situation and antiquity, Dark, despite its small size, had become one of the most important ports of that section of the galaxy. Here, trafficking in all sorts of commodities was unrestricted. All the known species, and some unknown as well, could be bought; even forbidden imports, presumed to be dangerous, could be procured. All the drugs concocted for humans, as well as for other breeds, were obtainable in Dark. It was rumored that even slaves were available. Dark was the never-ending scandal of the galaxy.

Algan had had his ups and downs. He couldn't remember ever working more than three months at the same job, nor having sold the same commodity twice. He had never had any run-in with the Psychological Police, but that hadn't been entirely his doing.

He was now looking for something else to do: a chance to explore a corner of the Earth as yet unknown to him. There were still a few unexpected opportunities to be found in the section of the old stellar port which handled only the traffic for the near planets: perhaps he'd run into an old crank on his first visit to the Old Planet who wanted to visit ancient ruins; or get his clutches into an obsessive hunter consumed with the ambition of adding a Terrestrial rabbit to his trophies; or, best of all, find some lost member of a scientific expedition who, between a couple of drinks, would pay to find out what he knew about the customs of the inhabitants of the Earth.

Algan went into Orion's Sword, a tavern whose very name caused, quite unfairly, a shudder to run through the high-minded. He sat in the darkest corner and ordered a drink. He slouched at his ease, never taking his eyes off the door. Orion's Sword, which gave the place its name, swung over the entrance. It was a long shiny stem of steel, sharp as a needle, antenna-like, decorated with curious sparkling moldings. Had it really served as a weapon, millions of years ago, in another world? No one knew. It could have been just an artifact.

The bar was still almost deserted and surprisingly silent. Even the zotl presses seemed muffled.

Algan clinked some silver on the table.

"One zotl," he said.

The sight of the heavy pistons crushing the hard root as it slowly lost its color, while the juice foamed out, gave him almost as much pleasure as drinking the amber liquid. Zotl root was one of the few legal sources of drugs in certain sections of the galaxy. Its effect varied with the individual. Sometimes it produced sensations of power. Its effect was comparable to kinesthetic frenzy, the nervous mental state which is the result of the crossing of nerve ends that makes sounds visible and colors audible.

Algan slowly drained his glass. Every time he drank zotl he had the same vision: a gray desert under a low green sky spangled with the iridescent outlines of moving rocks, which regrouped themselves to the rhythm of the ages. Distant, invisible suns played strident music. It was a peaceful spectacle, outside of time.

When he opened his eyes again the bar was half-full. There were men from every corner of the universe: merchants from Rigel wearing their metal shirts; tremendously tall, thin navigators from Ultar moved clumsily, hampered by Terrestrial gravity; small Xiens with blond hair and speckled eyes; bald men from Aro with pupil-less eyes deep as wells, under bulging foreheads, their complexions livid, almost greenish.

Dress and colors varied: some were bright, some gaudy, some dull. Weapons had a nightmarish quality about them. Orion's Sword proffered a small cross section of the sort of carnival that undulated through Dark when a fleet of merchant ships sailed into the stellar port.

Accents ran the gamut from guttural to musical, but everyone there spoke the old space language, a bastard mixture of all the languages of the Earth.

Someone sat down next to Jerg: a sturdy Earthling with a deep tan and a paunch filled with the good food available in this galaxy.

"Would you like to do some traveling, Mack?" the man asked, looking at Algan.

"It all depends where," replied Algan, guardedly.

"Take your pick; you can go where you like. A zotl?"

"I'll take the zotl anyway," said Algan.

14

They drank and remained silent for a bit.

"There are many beautiful worlds in space," said the fat Earthling dreamily.

"Are there?"

"Young man, when I was your age I had already been to about fifty planets. But maybe you have too...? You're between expeditions, aren't you? Space isn't an adventure anymore, is it? Another zotl?"

"I've never left the Earth," Algan said slowly, "and I don't want to. There's nothing like this green Earth; you can have all those worlds whirling about in space... Thank you for the zotl. But it takes more than a zotl to put out the sun, as the saying goes. Isn't that right?"

"Sure."

They were silent for a moment. Algan scanned the small weasel eyes deepset in fleshy slits. There was a gleam in them that he did not like.

"I suppose you're a trader."

The Earthling gave a coarse laugh.

"You can call it that, young man. I'm a sort of trader. Business is a bit tight on Earth at this moment, isn't it?"

Politeness was absolutely essential in space and in ports. Jerg Algan understood the value of caution, so he had cultivated exquisite manners, and the better part of good manners consisted in the art of never baldly asking questions.

"Yes, rather. Goods are getting scarce."

The fat businessman again laughed coarsely. Jerg chose to join in. That made the fat Earthling laugh even more. His eyes kept disappearing behind fleshy folds of fat. Algan suddenly stopped laughing.

"Are you looking for something on Earth? I know it like my pocket. Perhaps I can help."

"Perhaps you can. A zotl, my boy?"

Algan disliked the familiarity of the fat man's tone, but the zotl excused it. Looking inwardly at his dream, soaring over a gray desert, he could hear his companion's clucking noises crashing down like a sudden darkness, smothering the song of aerial suns.

"Sure, you can help me, my boy. Just sign this and you'll see new places."

"Where are you going?" asked Algan thickly.

"Where duty calls," came from the depths of a fold of fat. He felt something damp on his fingertips, and then was aware that they were being crushed on a hard surface.

"Is he ever plastered!" said a strange voice. He opened his eyes. Someone placed between his fingers a cylinder made of something soft. He didn't know what it was. He was flying between pearly cliffs under a low green sky.

"Write your name, chum," said an affectionate voice which he could see being written in the clouds in a flowery script. "You want to travel, you're dying to travel. Write your name."

Large luminous stones were writhing to the rhythm of unstable millennia, like tentacles trying to put out the light of the whole universe.

"Sign, chum; one more try."

He tried to pull himself together, to make his fingers hold the little cylinder. He began to write, but it was difficult because his half-shut eyes could perceive the colors only as sounds.

"One more try."

He stuck out his tongue and began to drool. Someone took hold of his arm and said:

"OK."

Algan dropped his hand; it was so heavy he thought his arm was going to come off. He felt himself falling between endless pearly cliffs, dragged down by the leaden weight of his right hand. Then he fell forward. His fingers drummed on the hard surface of the table. His eyes, riveted on the iridescent glass, perceived an increasingly intense and strident sound. He was plunging into a pearly well, down, down into green water under a green sky; it was like a pearly cylinder with a green floor and a green ceiling which were coming closer and closer. The pearly wall was now only a narrow strip between those green areas, nothing more than a thread. Then the well exploded.

He sat up suddenly, lights still flickering in his eyes. He instinctively touched his armpit with his right hand; then he snorted like someone coming out of the water.

There was no one next to him. The fat Earthling with the sausage-like fingers could well have been a dream.

He raised his hand and snapped his fingers.

"A drink."

He emptied the glass in one gulp and felt better. He got up and tried to walk. His legs felt as though he'd been lying down for centuries. He had drunk too much zotl. He felt around in his pockets and left a handful of coins on the table, and then he went toward the door. Someone greeted him as he went by and he responded with a weary gesture. He was stumbling and as he was about to fall steadied himself by clutching the doorknob.

The thick damp air of Dark engulfed him as he went out. He blinked several times.

Painfully, he walked along the badly lit street. His feet slithered along pavements worn down by thousands of boots, but his well-trained eyes unconsciously searched the dark comers. Dark was a safe city but only up to a point, and it was better never to find out what that exact point was.

He had no place to go. He thought of spending the night in some section of the old town, a place where one could lean one's back against a comer and doze, hand on pistol butt.

The lights of the Old Stellar Port guided him. He wove in and out of doorways, followed dark passages between houses that were older than the port itself, avoided openings that were too well-lit. He occasionally stumbled and made use of the brief lights from outgoing ships to pick his way along.

A sudden noise made him prick up his ears.

"Now," a voice shouted.

Several men jumped him. He had not seen them approaching and tried to fight his way out of the fog clouding his mind. Just as they were about to grab him he slipped to the ground, then ran between their legs. It worked. He started to run, trying to see who had attacked him.

His boots echoed on the pavement. He couldn't hope to shake off his pursuers. An open doorway in this section of town would be almost as dangerous as the street. His only real chance was to come upon a patrol of the Psychological Police. But the police seldom ventured out at night in the Old Stellar Port, not because they were concerned with their own safety but because there was actually no need for them. The inhabitants of the old town did not ask for the protection of the Psychological Police and the Psycho left them pretty well alone. This was the result of an ancient tacit understanding which gave the people of the ten puritan planets a chance to criticize the vices of the Old Planet.

Algan's right hand went up to his armpit and he caressed the sheath of his radiant. Murder was a serious matter, not to be committed except under extreme provocation. Explanations to the Psycho about legitimate self- defense would fall on deaf ears.

He looked over his shoulder and saw that his attackers were very close. They ran almost noiselessly. He could see four shadows. Perhaps others followed. In any event, the struggle was over even before it had begun unless he used his weapon.

Swerving suddenly, he turned into an adjoining alley which led to the Stellar Port by an enormously wide staircase. But he knew he would never reach the bronze doors. He heard his pursuers laugh. Goaded, he went faster. For one second he thought he'd shaken them on the winding stone staircase, but there was no place to go. He could only leap from step to step, fleeing between those blind walls, under a thin ribbon of sky and stars, trying to figure out who they were, why they wanted him, and where they were now.

He was rapidly getting winded. His right hand touched the radiant in its sheath. Perhaps he ought to stop and fight. Or was he nearer the port than he thought? They didn't give him time to choose. They shot first. They didn't want to kill him, but a large sticky ball hit him in the nape of the neck while steely strips furled themselves around his legs. He fell forward, his hands groping for the ground. He tried to roll up in a ball, bouncing from step to step along the walls and at the same time reaching for his radiant. But the blow on his neck was paralyzing him and more strips fettered his arms. He managed to pull out his radiant and squeezed the trigger. Nothing happened. He squeezed the butt against the palm of his hand, but there was no shot. As he sank into darkness he felt the butt of his weapon. It had no loading clip.

17

He flung the weapon away and it bounced from step to step. Then hands ran over him.

"That's him."

"OK. Go to it."

A cupping glass was put against his right ear. The thin ribbon of sky and stars began to revolve and turn green while the dark walls became lighter and lighter, taking on a pearly gray hue.

"Good night," he mumbled and fell asleep.

He was drifting on a pearl-gray cloud and wondered what he was doing there. He woke up, and at once felt for his pistol; it was gone. Then he realized that he was lying naked on a cot in a windowless, white-walled room.

He pushed himself up on an elbow. He had to sort this out Algan dimly remembered having been in a fight the night before. Perhaps the Psychological Police had picked him up. He did not like the idea. Unless he had been wounded and been brought to the port hospital for treatment. Yet he was feeling in splendid form.

As he thought the situation over, he realized that the room looked exactly like the ones in the Stellar Port which he had occasionally visited. There was nothing intrinsically worrisome about it, except that it seemed to have no aperture: no door, no window, and no trapdoor. He was not unduly concerned; since he had got in, he would certainly find a way out. On the other hand, the theft of his clothes was decidedly irritating. But was it really a theft?

He tried to recall the last thing that had happened to him. As he unconsciously rubbed his head behind his right ear he suddenly remembered that he had been given the bell treatment. That in itself was more worrisome than the loss of his clothes. As far as he knew only the police used those instruments and they were so well-guarded that an ordinary gang of thieves would not have access to them. He undoubtedly was in the hands of the Psycho.

Algan was reassured with the thought that if they had wanted to kill him they could have done so much more easily when he was unconscious.

He lay back on the cot and waited. He needed more information to plan either defense or escape. And if the Psycho was out to get him, they had at least five charges against him; he did not even have to open his mouth.

The wall facing him lighted up and became transparent. He could see the Stellar Port now. In the back, among the high prows pointing skyward, at the very end of the huge cement plain, gleamed the great bronze doors which separated order and space from the chaos of the city.

The wall on his right opened up like a piece of cloth being torn.

"Get up and go down the hall," a voice said.

He did so. The feebly lit corridor closed behind him. It was a one-way passage.

He reached a small, totally dark room. As he was trying to get his bearings he felt something warm winding around his arm. He put up no resistance. He felt the slight sting from the hypodermic needle. Then a gentle rain fell on him. Heat from invisible rays dried him off. The wall in front of him opened again and he went down a wide brilliantly lit corridor which led to a small room. There were clothes hanging on the wall. Algan noted that they were a navigator's outfit.

"Get dressed," said a voice.

He quickly donned the clothes, uttering not one word of useless protest, and set forth down another corridor. The building seemed to be made of some kind of malleable material which lent itself to partitioning into vacuums. Then, suddenly, the walls of the long winding corridor sprang open and Algan stopped, blinking; he seemed to be suspended over space, afloat, in broad daylight, three rocket-lengths above the port. Or so he thought. Actually he was in a large room one whole wall of which was an enormous window that opened on the working part of the port. As his eyes became accustomed to the light he looked around him. A man in a blue shirt was seated behind a huge white desk. He seemed to be waiting.

"Good morning," he said. "Go ahead and admire the port. It's as good a beginning as any."

Algan did not immediately answer. He was, actually, fascinated by the port and the huge ships but he also did not know what to say. This was his first visit to the Stellar Port. People like him were ordinarily kept out.

"I'm ready to talk now," he said quietly.

"I'm glad you're taking it like that," the man in blue replied. "Usually I have to do so much arguing with people who come here for the first time that my job becomes almost unpleasant. Please sit down."

Algan settled into a large white chair.

"I'm listening."

The man in blue looked somewhat embarrassed.

"I thought you'd have some questions."

"Well, I'm hungry," said Algan.

He was in no hurry for explanations. He was enjoying the chair, the rug with its complicated pattern, the magnificent white desk, and especially the view of the Stellar Port.

"Just as you like," said the man in blue and he pushed a button.

He watched Algan eat, without a word. When Algan had finished, he got up and faced the bay.

"What's your name?" asked Algan, "and why am I here?"

"One thing at a time," replied the man in blue. His searching gray eyes scanned Algan's face. "My name is Tial, Jor Tial. I don't suppose that means much to you. You seem resigned to your fate."

"What fate?" asked Algan coldly. He hoped his nervousness would not show through.

"A marvelous fate," said Tial, with a sweeping gesture that encompassed the room, the port, and the rockets.

"The conquest of space."

"You're joking," said Algan. "I'll never leave the Earth."

"Come, come," said Tial, "don't talk like that. Did you or did you not sign up?"

"Sign up?" echoed Algan.

He suddenly understood. He had been had by a recruiter. The fat Earthling of the night before had gotten him drunk to extort his signature and now he was committed to space, to any planet whatever, after an interminable cruise on a broken-down ship. Anger flooded him. He had heard stories of this, in the Old Port, but he had never paid any attention to them. When anyone disappeared from an old section of Dark, no questions were asked; the missing person was just as likely to turn up a year later, rich enough to buy half a continent on the Old Planet, as he was to simply vanish into the thick air of Dark.

"I see that you follow me. Perhaps some of the details escape you? I can read you the contract. Usually the signatories accept it, hmm... let's say, trustingly. They don't even bother to read the provisions. But I can assure you they are worth it."

"It's against the law," said Algan. "I'm not going to knuckle under. There's still some justice on the Earth."

"Of course," said Tial. "And there are judges who can determine whether or not a contract has been properly executed."

"It was extortion," said Algan. "I assume I'm not telling you anything you don't know.

"The judges would be very happy to hear about this. Extortion, you say. By the use of force? Are you quite sure?"

"There's no question of force; I was drugged."

"Against your will?"

"Not exactly. And anyway, you know better than I what happened. All I want is a fair trial; I'll bring charges."

"I should be delighted to give you some advice before you do anything," said Tial.

He spoke coolly and evenly. Algan thought to himself that his case must be weak.

"I presume you admit you drugged yourself. You claim someone took advantage of your condition to make you sign this paper. Is that correct?"

"Not quite," said Algan. "A man offered me several zotls. He seemed anxious to have me drink with him. I didn't want to be unfriendly. Then the stinker took unfair advantage. I suppose he gets something out of this smalltime deal."

"You willingly accepted this... drug, didn't you?"

Algan agreed.

"You admit having taken more than enough to lose control."

"I don't see what you're getting at."

"Just this: drugs are illegal. Losing control is illegal. I'm willing to believe in the existence of this man. Can you bring him to me? I imagine that the Psychological Police might try to find him for you, but you know that its policy is not to interfere with the people in the Old Port. People like you. Within certain limits, of course. So, do you prefer to be arrested by the Psychological Police for drug abuse and be judged by a jury freshly recruited from the Puritan Planets or will you accept the terms of the contract? I imagine the jury would sentence you to a few years of hard labor on a new planet. There isn't much sympathy, you know, for drug addiction among the inhabitants of the Puritan Planets. Wouldn't you rather spend ten glorious years in space, at government expense, being handsomely paid? You like adventure, I think. Don't look back, look forward."

"Very clever," said Algan. "I suppose everyone is in on this: the Psychological Police, the port authorities, the space program, and even the government itself. I just say 'Good-bye,' and leave."

He got up, his eyes never wavering from the distant lights that shone on the prow of a ship. Beyond the bronze gates the city spread out on the hills, a teeming, disorderly city made up of multicolored cubes piled up haphazardly—the city which he would not see again for ten years. A now inaccessible city. Dozens of light-years of space and emptiness already lay between him and Dark— hundreds of suns, the possibility of shipwrecks, of unexpected dangers, of unknown, hostile and powerful beings.

And behind the city were the green oceans and the green plains of the Earth, the inscrutable ruins of its civilizations submerged by a tide of moss, invaded by the great northern glaciers, its cities dead and their secrets forever lost. There couldn't, Algan said to himself, there couldn't be in the universe two planets like the Earth. Something welled up inside him, a need for revenge; it was a seed that was to grow during the years spent in emptiness; it would explode one day and destroy this port, this cold inhumanity of the Galaxians. For a long time he had believed that the Galaxians were coldly unconcerned with the inhabitants of Earth. He would see to it that they paid when their time came. Only it was too early now, much too early.

"I've been kidnapped," said Algan in a strangled voice. "I've been kidnapped. I did not come here of my own free will. You'll admit that."

"OK, if you want to quibble, you've been kidnapped. Officially you were picked up by a squad of the Psychological Police and it was only because of your contract that you were brought here. Under ordinary circumstances you'd have been tried. But the police officials generously agreed you were entitled to celebrate your departure and they were willing to look the other way. Of course, if you lodge a complaint, they will have to speak up. Believe me, they would rather not."

"If the people of the galaxy knew how pioneers are recruited," said Algan, "if only they knew!"

"Lots of people do know, but the word of an inhabitant of old Dark does not carry much weight in space. I'd bet they'd laugh at you if you told your story. Unless they beat you up when they learn where you come from. The people of the galaxy take a dim view of backward people like you."

Algan leaned against the large window. He was consumed with fury. He wanted to hurl himself through the glass onto the porcelain ground a thousand feet below. He wanted to see the ships explode and bum and sailors run in every direction, to see the port in ruins while the city, in the shelter of the large bronze gates, looked on peacefully.

Space was a prison and he knew it. He was going to roam for ten years in this prison. Rage and anxiety welled up inside him. He could see in his mind's eye the shining gates of the old free city, hear the rumblings of the ancient and savage life on Earth.

"I know just how you feel," said Tial, "I've seen others, but none quite like you. Most of them scream, shout, threaten, and beg. But at the end of three months they feel at home in space. I hope you will, too. Frankly, I'm not sure you will. I hope that somewhere else, on another world, you'll find something similar to this city. I think this one will be very different when you come back in a thousand years."

Algan turned slowly. His eyes shone. One thousand years. It was the fall, the flight into time that he dreaded most; he had never wanted to talk about it. Ten light- years there and one thousand years here. The port would be unchanged, but the city would have disappeared.

"I'll be dead when you come back, that is, if you want to see the Earth. And everyone here will have forgotten me. I hope you will no longer hate me then. In any event, it will not matter in the least. There will be other men, and they will be doing the same simple and difficult things. Sometimes I say to myself that we are lost, not so much in space as in time. Two thousand five hundred years ago, when men first started their voyages of exploration on the Earth, in ships that were wind-propelled, the distance from one place to its antipode was almost as insurmountable to the explorers as the walls of a cell are to a prisoner. Yet now we roam amid the stars. But we are still prisoners of time, more than ever."

"Stop it, stop it."

The sound of those years going by was like the sound of grains of sand tapping against the sides of an hourglass. This was senseless. One thousand years. Glaciers could spread, oceans rise or dry up. The people he knew on Earth would be dead. In the new worlds, everyone lived alone, worked, traded within his own time span. Ships came in and left with the flow and ebb of the years. On the Puritan Planets marriage was forbidden by law because of its immoral consequences; one month of traveling made a son older than his father.

This was understandable. Men were thrown like grains of sand against the stars. They were so weak, so alone.

But he, Algan, was the product of the old Earth. This couldn't be happening to him. He couldn't accept it. His universe was a limited one along a curved horizon; it held lifelong friendships, an old family house, and the land of his forefathers.

"A backward, bestial point of view," sneered the people on the Puritan Planets.

Maybe. Maybe they were right. Maybe man had to change, broaden his views to keep up with his new environment, the galaxy; much of it was still unexplored after five centuries of space history.

But this was the Future, and like all the inhabitants of ancient cities, like the inhabitants of the Earth who were universally despised, Algan felt himself to be a man of the Past.

"I don't like all the methods of the government," Tial said gently, "but in some ways I think they are good. I, too, am a man of the Past, in my way, which is different from yours, because I wasn't born on this planet. I'm trying to understand you. I know that after me there will be other men who will deal more harshly with the people from the old cities; these men will no longer know anything of the glory of the Earth. I want you to realize this. People like you, Jerg, are condemned for at least one thousand years. One thousand years in this world. When you come back there will be no one who can understand you. But perhaps some of the new planets will have a history by then. A history that is different, slower-moving, more peaceful than the Earth's, but a history nonetheless. As yet, there are so few of us in space. There are more inhabitable worlds in the galaxy than there are men. Our empire is so fragile. That's why we are forced to send out, so far away, even those who don't want to leave their world. We are spread awfully thin. Try to understand, Jerg."

I have one thousand years to destroy this, Algan thought. *One thousand or ten; it comes to the same thing.*

A long vibration shook the port. A spaceship was rocketing up from a fiery pad. The sky seemed to darken as the ship rose majestically into the atmosphere. When it reached a height of one thousand kilometers, in an almost total vacuum, its reactors would go out and its nuclear propeller would take over. It would speed up almost to the velocity of light—and time for its passengers would come to a stop—and then it would leap into lateral space and there, motionless, during its crew's long sleep, it would drift, outside of time, carried along by one of the great currents of the universe toward its distant and perhaps still unexplored destination.

"A pleasant trip, Algan," said Jor Tial.

"Thank you," Algan replied coldly. But his eyes were not on Tial's; they were searching the sky.

CHAPTER II
The Stellar Port

There were as many invisible threads crisscrossing the universe as there were possible trajectories for a ship. These threads made up something like a canvas and each knot in the canvas was a world, a port. The oldest of these stellar knots, the one from which had sailed the first ships in quest of unimaginable worlds, was the port of Dark. It had been like a spore explosion in those heroic times. Expansion had slowed down in the course of centuries. Not that all the worlds had been explored or that all the explored worlds were inhabited, but because humanity was thinning out. Whole systems were inhabited by only a few families. The most densely populated planets had less than a hundred thousand inhabitants, although there were a few cities in the galaxy with a population of over fifty million.

It was a time of paradoxes. Not the least of these was the vastness of these cities and the deserted planets. But the traffic of a port, because of its size, required the presence of ever-increasing numbers of men. Machines had been the beginning of a solution. There had been cities of a hundred million inhabitants spread over an entire continent during the heroic times, when for one single man in a spaceship ten thousand men were required on the Earth for the maintenance and repair of the port equipment. But the machines had made it possible to send forth most of the inhabitants of the cities to conquer new worlds. The most ancient cities, like Dark on the Earth, Tugar on Mars, Olnir on Tetla, were only shadows of the gigantic capitals they had once been. Those had been and still were, though widely separated, times of conquest and glory. A man could be his own master, but his life was not worth very much.

Sometimes an entire stellar region sank into silence. It might be a century before the fate of its inhabitants was known. Sometimes they had disappeared altogether and the planet would be classified as dangerous. At other times it was only that they had given up all technological civilization and had simply neglected to turn on their transradios. Sociologists would study these neoprimitives with great interest when their attention was not taken up by the number of worlds and societies which grew up, lived, and died.

Humanity flocked into space, but it also became lost in Time. The planets themselves did not experience the passing of time at the same speed: this varied according to their density or the rate of speed at which they revolved around their axes or their distance from the center of the galaxy. And those segments of space trips which took place at the speed of light presented odd chronological pit-falls to travelers.

History, as a continuous passing of time, no longer had any meaning. During the five centuries of conquest, as measured in Earth time, history had been a sort of fibrous matter in which it was difficult to discern cause and effect. Wars no longer had any meaning. The central government, whose seat was on a giant planet near Betelgeuse, was an effective and lasting symbol both in space and time, a symbol of unity which local authorities called upon. It seemed as though the rays of the enormous red star which was visible from one end to the other of the human galaxy carried far and wide the will of central authority. Actually the governing planet did not revolve around the red giant but around a lesser, neighboring star, but the frightened or surprised looks of those who feared or admired the center of the largest human civilization turned instinctively toward Betelgeuse. Its name was whispered as if the brilliance of that star were indeed an indication of the power of its neighbors.

However, had new cultures and civilizations grown up on each planet, the central government could not have lasted nor kept up its influence.

But that distortion in time, experienced by all human societies which depended upon intersidereal voyages, had prevented the rise of individualism. There was a traditional loyalty throughout the galaxy to the central government in Betelgeuse because its very endurance represented the only security in these times of permanent dislocation.

The central government sent its officials, its researchers, and its pioneers into all the know worlds of the galaxy. When they came back, bringing information that was already centuries old, the men in Betelgeuse who were responsible for the destiny of the galaxy were no longer there. The very names of those who had made the arrangements for their trip were, more often than not, forgotten. But it was immaterial. Data piled up in the giant memory banks of the computers of Betelgeuse; plans that were to be put into effect five hundred years later in some distant section of the galaxy were drawn up to the last detail.

In order to survive, Man had to know the galaxy well. The greatest risk he ran was overlooking danger. He had to get used to the idea of danger without ever forgetting its presence. A frighteningly large number of the early explorers had died either because they had not seen the threat to their safety or because they had been too panic- stricken to react defensively. The task of the central government was to set up a training program that would insure the survival of the largest possible number of explorers.

At first Algan thought that he would not survive the training program. Before he had even left the port, while he was working in huge caves, he thought he'd never again see Dark. But the biologists and psychologists had carefully worked out their programs to conform to the limits of human endurance. Space itself has little to do with those limits.

The tests dealt with both the physical and mental endurance of the trainees.

The first time that Algan was tied up in a large armchair he thought it was funny. By the end of the third minute he was yelling: "Let me out of here. Stop the machine."

But they went right on while he damned them. They knew how Algan felt because they too had gone through it. They also knew what was Algan's only hope of escaping madness in certain situations, and were aware that later he would consider these conditions pleasant and restful compared to what was still to be endured. They hoped for his sake that they had not made a mistake when they had examined him.

Algan felt as though he had fallen into an endless dark space where not a single star shone. He kept falling. His stomach turned over. His heartbeats, regulated by the chair's electrodes, sped up.

Algan yelled: "Let me out. Stop."

He kept falling. It was a simple fall, but into the void. There was nothing to catch hold of, to claw at. He was conscious, every moment, that he was going to crash on an immense dark body which he sensed was just under him. But the end of the fall, delayed second by second, never came. He thought he'd gone blind.

At about the fourteenth minute he stopped yelling because his throat had become too dry to let out a sound. He knew he had just crossed the limits of the universe. He knew now that he would go on falling. There was no longer any point in his being afraid because something worse than fear had taken its place in his mind.

At about the sixteenth minute he felt as though he had become a mere point. He tried to remember the time when he had had hands and legs he could move, but it was too long ago and too unreal.

At about the eighteenth minute, he thought he was swelling up.

Being a point of expansion was an intolerable sensation. He felt as though he were occupying, as he kept falling, an infinite amount of space, and all the while his nerves were being stretched in every direction.

At about the twenty-first minute he felt himself exploding. Countless particles of himself flew about beyond imaginable space. He became an infinitely stretched fog. His mind tried to follow each of those particles and to hold them, but he wore himself out in vain; he could not do it. Then he gave up.

There was no longer anything coherent or ordered about Algan. He was nothing but chaos and confusion. Something less than half an hour of total falling had been too much for him. He felt destroyed, disintegrated. With what little consciousness remained to him, he understood that the universe was hostile, and this understanding restored some strength to him. A core of intelligence, supported by this last recognition, began to reorganize his scattered memories, his old experiences. A flicker of hatred began to bum in his brain. Suddenly the fall seemed unimportant to him. He slowly found the path back to his own nerves. Hatred was forcing him to discover, deep down within him, new reserves of strength and equilibrium.

This was what the experts had wanted. There were several ways of achieving the same result. Some trainees had survived the tests, centuries earlier, with nothing but their enthusiasm for new worlds to support them.

In others, fear alone had acted, forcing them to find within themselves defenses against it.

But the paths of darkness had led Algan to other regions, around other bends. Had the experts been able to read Jerg Algan's mind they might have felt less complacent.

For at the very moment when he reached the core of his being, hatred took over every ounce of his energy. His nerves obeyed. His glands poured out complex secretions into his veins.

At about the thirty-sixth minute he rediscovered himself through his hatred. During the last five minutes he had learned more about man and the universe than he had during the preceding thirty-two years of his life.

He relaxed, allowed himself to fall. He suddenly came out of the night.

When they rushed forward to help him as he staggered from the great chair, they neglected to notice, just before he fainted, the cold glint in his eyes.

The big armchair was the end-all of the art of illusion. Its electrodes took the place of the real world and could conjure up any imaginable grotesque or terrifying universe. Simplified versions of the chair were in use in auditoriums on some of the planets. On others, or sometimes on the same ones, the chairs became instruments of torture. They were used in all ports to test pilots and pioneers.

The chair was the result of three centuries of research on the nervous system. It made possible the control of every fiber, the linking or unlinking of a multitude of synapses. For complex nervous systems it was the sole existing treatment—that is, if the patient survived.

The chair constituted a universe in itself. There was a legend that the great Tulgar himself, who had built the first chair according to specifications made ten centuries earlier by his brilliant precursor Bergier, had committed suicide after trying his creation because he had found no other use for it except as a potential paradise or hell, both of which were inextricably entwined. Scarcely one century later, at the beginning of the conquest, someone remembered Tulgar; the chair which was the repository of all the wonders and horrors of the universe was found in the attic of a university.

Algan learned to fall, without flinching, into darkest night and still retain his awareness of the immensity of space.

Hatred was his lifeline. Because at first he did not know on whom to concentrate it, the feeling was a rough and shapeless, but vital one. Then he began to hate the port, that alien element which had been imposed on the Old Planet, and to think up, in a cool detached manner, the means of destroying it. But his cold anger was soon transferred to those who had built the port. It was during his second week of training, when he was feeling as though he had spent at least ten

27

years in the subterranean regions of the Stellar Port, that he decided to destroy the central government.

Conquering stars and strange new worlds meant nothing to him. All he knew was that it had taken brute force to detach him from the Earth. He decided to become the cog that would slowly and methodically cause the breakdown of the great human machinery that had been set up to conquer the stars.

After he had learned to control the night and his descent into it, he was sent off alone on worlds that were either hostile or different from anything he had ever known. One day, he flew down and hovered over an enormous shiny surface. He suddenly found himself stretched out on the ground, unable to move. He knew he had to get up and walk, but he was glued to a huge metal sphere larger than the Earth. The heavy black sky, studded with stars, seemed to crush him.

Painfully he got up on his knees. The air was dry and icy, so dry and icy that it burned and tore his lungs.

Algan knew he had to walk in a given direction, but he couldn't even move, let alone take a step. He was engulfed, drowned in fear, yet he could see nothing anywhere that would account for the terror that paralyzed him.

The fear was within him. He was alone. He had never before been afraid of solitude. He had traveled, alone, across enormous distances on the oceans and continents of the Earth. But that solitude was nothing compared to what he was experiencing here.

He had learned, as the technicians who were in charge of his training had intended he should, that the only survival possible in a strange world is group survival; death for a single individual was inevitable.

But the lesson did not stop there. One had to learn to survive alone, if one happened to stray off, temporarily, from the rest of an expedition.

He started to creep along the icy surface. Some unknown force was spurring him toward a particular point on the horizon. Trying to slow the rhythm of his breathing, he dragged himself forward along a few hundred yards. Just then the entire surface of the planet tipped and he was thrown forward, slipping faster and faster. His hands feverishly sought something to cling to, but there was nothing. He finally let himself slide along the smooth plain, his hands in front ready to break a possible shock.

His fall accelerated. He saw the sky slowly change and the color of the plain grow lighter. The polished steely surface slowly became luminous. At the same time an enormous red sun rose on the clear horizon.

He knew he was falling toward that sun and that nothing could save him. The red sun seemed glued to the horizon. But just as Algan was drawing near, it climbed up and floated amid the stars, eclipsing the nearer ones, devouring the night.

Then the wind bore him off.

He was blown about like a straw by the gentle breeze that brushed the polished plain which was now growing red. Then a storm blew up and began to roar. He was lifted up into the air, helpless to control his course. He flew over the surface of the planet and had the impression it was flying past him at a dizzying speed. He saw a huge dark shape looming up on the plain, which appeared to be sending out shapeless tentacles toward him. He tried to cry out, but he had no breath left.

Then he realized that it was only his shadow, that he was passing under the giant red sun.

He was climbing. The storm bore him so high that he could see the entire planet; it was like a disk unbelievably large and concave, rather like the inside of a bowl. Then the wind suddenly died down. He could no longer breathe. He was at the same height as the stars and as his lungs collapsed, his heart gave out, his blood ebbed away; he knew that he was going to die as he flew over the frontiers of emptiness.

He made an effort. He tried to escape from that deadly balance. But his reflexes were gone; his mind was blank.

He rolled up into a ball, then violently stretched. He began to hate the red sun which had started to disappear behind the steel disk. And suddenly he plunged.

Algan had the impression of a closed trap. He could get back to the ground and crawl again and rediscover the red sun and be swept up by another cyclone, or by the same one on its way back. He began to fume with rage as he fell uncontrollably, damning the chair, the technicians, the port, the Earth and Dark, space, interstellar ships and, above all, the central government of Betelgeuse.

I'm nothing but a toy, a puppet, he said to himself, I'll get the one who is holding the strings.

There was nothing here for him to attack or destroy. But behind that hostile and cold facade of the universe someone was watching.

Someone who was laughing at his vain efforts.

Someone who made fun of men.

Someone who set the stage.

I'll get him, Algan said to himself. He noticed that he did not want to die.

Not in this desolate icy world. Not before he had destroyed this odious set-up.

He found himself again on the icy surface, in darkness. The red sun had disappeared.

He began to crawl with a cold determination. He saw another sunrise, this one blue, surrounded by fog and circled by three smaller revolving suns whose colors changed with their positions.

A shadow loomed up on the horizon and slowly grew bigger.

He crept along faster. Was it a new stage set? A new trap? He broke out in a fine sweat. The ground seemed to warm up, the closer he came to the shadow.

The steel grip which had clutched him loosened. He got up on his knees and slowly stood up. Stretching to his full height, he scanned the horizon, then turned around. The multiple shadow cast by his body, from the light of the midget sun and from its satellites, was the only interruption on the plain.

He began to run.

There was a city stretching out the edge of this world. A dream city. Its crystal towers dominated the steel plain; its high walls looked like luminous cliffs defying cold and the night of the desert. Ancient bridges connected the palaces which stood silhouetted against the black background of emptiness.

There were people inside, a whole population ready to welcome him and celebrate his arrival. Flags were flying from turrets. Festival music rang in his ears.

He began to shout and dance with the intention of alerting the watchman on the turrets of his presence. He stopped, expecting some sound: the crack of a pistol shot, the noise of a rocket opening in the sky.

Nothing. No one.

He began to run again. He was filled with a terrifying premonition. There loomed before him, under the cold light of the blue sun, the high bronze gates of the city. A blurred memory stirred within him. These gates were not unknown to him. The high wall was very near. He hurled himself against the huge doors which were ten times his height, and he beat on them steadily. The bronze gates resounded like great gongs.

No one. Nothing.

He pushed forward with all his might; surprisingly, the huge bronze doors slowly gave. He slipped through the crack he had made.

I've done it, he thought. I've done it.

He walked out in the shadow of the huge porch, then continued forward under the cold light of the blue sun, onto a huge deserted square enclosed by tall white polished walls. Opposite him were the high towers and a building so tall that it seemed to touch the stars.

Silence.

I've seen this before, he thought.

He stepped onto the middle of the square and looked all around. No one.

He began to laugh. He remembered. He had come back to the port from which he had set forth thousands of years ago and now everyone had died, the planet was dead and so were the stars. He would never leave the Earth. He was the last man on a cold planet.

Algan wiped the sweat from his forehead. He dropped to the ground, stretched out on his back, and looked at the blue sun and its satellites that were slowly shrinking in the sky.

It isn't true, he thought, and he closed his eyes, trying to find the dark and to fall into a starless space. In a way, he found a certain peace. He began to hate, coldly and methodically, and filled space with a myriad stars of hatred.

He felt better.

It was then that they woke him up.

The training program in the underground of the Stellar Port lasted five weeks. Algan lived alone the entire time as part of the training. He saw only the shadows of the technicians, who never spoke a word to him. Thanks to his reflexes, he managed to survive a species of mental night, haunted by the adventures he had in the chair: he was parachuted onto water planets and swam for hours on the surface of oceans saltier than those of the Earth; dragged himself through countless marshes; climbed sharp cliffs; crossed chasms; balanced on an almost invisible cord; jumped down from terrifyingly high peaks; was slowly swallowed up by moving sands; was blinded by burning suns; was smothered by storms; was asphyxiated by clouds of red sand; was crushed by spongy soft rocks that were sickening to the touch.

Then, toward the end of the fifth week, when the look in his eyes had hardened, their sockets deepened and the experience of ten years in space could be read in his emaciated features, he was allowed to come up to the surface.

It was only then that he discovered the Stellar Port. He lived in the huge building under the control tower that challenged space with its antennas. He roamed at will among the rockets, questioned pilots, sailors, and explorers. He gradually discovered what mark man had made among the stars.

The stars stored up incalculable wealth and almost infinite sources of power. They were heaven and hell combined, just as the chair had hinted. But, inhuman though they were, the stars were the universe, a glittering irresistible prize which men repeatedly tried to ensnare in the web of their voyages.

The names of the ships evoked foreign lands. Their shapes varied according to whether they came from the edges of the galaxy or from its more central regions. Only the black outmoded ships of Betelgeuse remained unchanged; their powerful engines still enabled them to give chase to any stellar craft or to reach any inhabited world.

The contents of the storehouses came from all the corners of the galaxy. The scent of zotl roots embalmed one area of the port while piles of Aldragor's weightless furs, quivering in the lightest breeze, filled another area. There were transparent cages filled with splendid or repellent animals awaiting their fate: giant spiders with bodies as shiny and pink as a human skull, vampires with red wings, amphibians from Zuna in shapes that were changeable and vaguely nauseating, animated stones from Alzol, which sparkled like braziers enclosed in a block of changeable glass.

Algan learned to tell where the sailors came from by their accents, the color of their skin, the shape of their skulls, and the color of their eyes. He soon learned to tell a ship's year and model from its hull. Some of the hulls had been built on the Earth itself, four centuries earlier, at the beginning of the conquest. They were still plowing the cold currents of space.

31

Algan spent days on end walking along the lookouts on the battlements, discovering anew the old city as it looked from the Stellar Port. It seemed oddly distant, alien. He felt almost as though he had just landed from a ship and was seeing, for the first time, the teeming city with its apartment houses stacked close together and its narrow, sordid little streets. He knew he would not go down into the city again before his departure. The Stellar Port was ns remote and distant as a ship; he might just as well have already left the Earth. The Stellar Port was like a foreign growth on the city, a meteor from the sky, deeply bedded in the planet but barely tolerated. Algan knew he belonged to the old city and looked upon himself as a prisoner of the port. It was not a pleasant impression.

"You're a strange man," the psychologist told Algan.

They were both looking down from the top of the giant tower at the constant movement in the port: the arrivals and departures of the throbbing little cargo ships which kept communications open with the other cities of the Earth and made possible the launching of heavy rockets.

"I suppose there were a great many men like you when the conquest started. People who liked their own planet and who saw in the conquest of space only an infinite extension of their own world. The problem is finding out what our civilization can do with people like you."

"I did not ask it to do anything with me," Algan said dully.

"I know that," replied the psychologist.

He looked up and scanned the heavy clouds in the sky. "But your views are not very important. Men make up a large body in space. Do you think the opinion of one small cell is of any importance?"

With a faraway look he considered the irregular piles of the old city.

"Your thinking is outdated," said the psychologist. "It may once have been valid. I don't know. But man is now faced with problems he never had before. Old ways of thinking must go."

He turned his light, cold eyes on Algan. His bald pate shone.

"A certain amount of freedom, a certain amount of power. That's an equation. And the solution is a new way of thinking. It is starting, you know, in all the ports of the galaxy, in the heart of the remotest jungles, on board the shabbiest ships. It is no longer a product of time or of history; it is the result of little skirmishes against space and of a great interdependence of men, beyond time and space, from one end to the other of the inhabited portions of the galaxy. A ship left a distant planet three years ago in relative time, fifty years in Earth time, and its movement may well determine your fate even though its trajectory was determined before your birth. One is powerless in the face of these things. Probably the first medusae which were agglutinated to form a multicellular body felt the way you do, although on a different scale; they must have felt desperately diminished, imprisoned. But the process was their only means of becoming less dependent upon their environment and of conquering oceans, then the land,

and finally of becoming what we are. If you'd been a medusa you would probably have tried to kill one of those multiple beings. I am assuming that right now
you'd like nothing better than to destroy this embryo humanity, still rough-
hewn, still in the process of growing. That's why you interest me. I don't expect
to win you over. But you belong to a species that is rare nowadays: a rebel.
There are perhaps a few million rebels in this world; we send them out as pioneers into space. There was a time when your kind ruled this world. It was a
time of poverty and wars. But it was also a period of glory. Our glory is different. It is the result of the effort of trillions of men, millions of sailors, thousands
of scientists. Do you know what is being done right now in Betelgeuse? The
editing of a galactic encyclopedia. It is something like a memoir of the entire
galaxy, which will be added to as more discoveries are made... Can your mind
encompass such an undertaking?"

"Leave me alone," said Algan.

Toward the end of his second week of freedom, he ventured into the high
tower that dominated the port. Doors opened readily for him. The electronic
eyes that operated them must have been given his description and that of all the
other explorers so that they could go about in the port, wherever they wanted,
learning its layout, which was roughly the same as that of all the other ports of
the explored areas of the galaxy. Algan seldom ran into his future companions.
He avoided them as much as possible. Most of them were the sort to whom he
would never have spoken in Dark unless armed with a loaded weapon at the
ready. However, here they seemed inoffensive and disoriented, even more lost
than Algan. They spent day after day in their own quarters, playing and quarrel-
ing, but not daring to fight. They would feel more at ease in the new worlds,
axes in their hands and weapons in their belts, fighting a defined and visible
enemy.

As he slowly climbed long inclined planes, propelled by the gentle push of
the anti-gravity fields, borne along on an invisible and insubstantial platform,
Algan could understand the attraction that places like Dark had for the galaxy. It
was a carefully tended human reserve, an artificial one perhaps, from which,
when the need arose, the government of Betelgeuse drew men accustomed to
living like wolves and settled them in little known worlds. Algan was, willy-
nilly, nothing more than a cell in the galaxy. His hatred was strengthened by this
thought even as he was busy admiring the huge passages that led to the top of
the great dungeon.

Viewed from the inside, the top of the tower seemed to float in space. Its
walls were huge windows that looked out on the sky and on the hustle-bustle of
the port, but the windows made of one-way glass imprisoned the light. Seen
from the outside, the tower looked like an opaque structure without openings
that might have been massively carved out of a mountain, then dropped on the
ground. From the inside, it looked like a fragile glass and micro- crystal metal

construction, as soft to the touch as old velvet. But it must have been incredibly strong. A lost spaceship crashing into it would probably not have shaken it.

The control centers of the Stellar Port, which were at the top of the tower, directed the commercial traffic and coordinated the activities of the black ships of Betelgeuse.

Algan went through a door that led to the transmitting station of the tower. Even before the partition had opened, he knew what he would see. Although it was his first visit to this section of the port, he unerringly found his way through the labyrinths of corridors and wells. He knew that any information he might need had been hypnotically engraved in the lower levels of his memory. It was always information of a practical nature. He did not know how the gates and the awesome installations that he had discovered worked, but he knew how to use them. The technicians who had taught his subconscious cared little whether he understood. All that mattered to them was that he fulfill certain requirements.

Algan had often wondered how many technicians themselves understood the working of the port. Perhaps no one on Earth understood. Perhaps they were secrets jealously guarded by Betelgeuse, and perhaps that was one explanation for the surprising unity of the human galaxy beyond the oceans of space and the abyss of time.

The transmitting station was in the shape of a well whose walls were covered with small alveoli connected by a spiral staircase leading right up to the topmost dome. Each alveolus was staffed by a technician who manned the instruments, received and transmitted messages. All the voices from distant space could be heard. Beyond the galaxy of stars, beyond the galaxy of ships and men there existed another stellar complex made up of separate sounds: scattered information, signals blinking in space, breaths, voices, murmurs.

These voices assailed him as he wound his way up the staircase and passed by the alveoli one by one. The voices were toneless, deep, tense, disembodied, and expressive of some acute suffering undergone beyond space and time; they were the voices of larvae crawling along the lowest strata of emptiness, hopelessly imploring some unimaginable salvation. They were the voices of another age in time, of another world.

As he looked at the calm faces of the technicians, Algan tried not to hear those distant, tortured, distorted, heavily vibrant voices: those harsh cries, those metallic shrieks, and those sinister hisses.

Words.

He could understand words. They told the position of ships; they spoke of new planets situated at ten years of Earth travel time, of formulas, of names, of dates now meaningless; they gave arid, meticulous reports; they reported calls for help that had been moaned far from any human ear—all this mangled, diluted in time.

Time.

Time which was quick here and slow there, depending upon the movement of the ships, of the planets. Time, variable and misleading, the destroyer of information; time, which could transform a warm human voice into an almost toneless, shapeless sound barely audible against the crackling background of the music of the spheres; that song of exploding stars, that grinding of particles, projected by another galaxy, which continued their unending voyage through emptiness, setting antennas in motion once every million years.

Time.

Every planet, spaceship, star, fragment of the universe possessed its own time and completed its orbit at its own speed. The transradio, alone, denied time by challenging space. It made possible the transmission of infinitesimal quantities of energy by passing through complex dimensions which shortened the longest paths of the universe but which would not have allowed the passage of spaceships, or even the smallest grain of matter, without profoundly altering them.

The transradio worked on the same principle as interstellar ships but much more roughly.

Spaceships could not travel faster than light, but there were shorter paths in space than those uncovered by optical telescopes. These plunged into the very heart of the universe, following the shortest curves, and could shorten to one year a trip that could have taken one century. But there was one drawback. The more the path was shortened, the worse was the quality of the transmission. The more complex the dimension chosen for the transference, the more the ship was altered upon arrival, sometimes to the point of annihilation. Therefore, scientists had sharply defined the margin of security. The paths from one star to another, although shortened, still remained tremendously long. But these were no problems to the transradio. It could follow a line in space which reduced distances to almost nothing. It mattered little if a message was modified on the way, if the information it contained was altered or cut down, so long as its content remained intelligible upon reception.

In this way, the transradio could connect different kinds of time, contradictory spans of time: Earth time, the velocity at which spaceships traveled, and the variable speeds of planets orbiting around their suns.

This explained the alteration of the voices. One minute spent on a ship that was approaching and decelerating was the equivalent of three minutes spent on the Earth, so the voice became slow, deep, spectral, drawn out like soft dough. The only messages that were comprehensible were those transmitted from a point in the universe which was moving at a speed plainly comparable to that of the Earth. But there were often considerable differences, especially in the case of the fast spaceships which traveled at almost the speed of light. Then a single word could be drawn out for one whole hour, the movement of distant, almost unimaginable lips was slowed down to a virtual stop. At times it took a week, or a month, for information to reach its destination. Codes were devised to avoid these inconveniences. The transmitting ship could record its message and send it into space via transradio at an accelerated rate of speed. And if this method turned out to be inadequate for Earth transmission, there were machines that were attuned to the grunting of human voices and, after a long session of listening, turned them into normal voices, comprehensible to a human.

Time.

With each step he took in the port, Algan came upon the mark of time. And he began to suspect that man was starting to colonize time, as, slowly, he had colonized space.

As he climbed toward the tower dome that opened to the skies, he realized that in less than a month there would be no trace of him left on the Earth except as one of those deep, warped voices emanating from a ship.

CHAPTER III
Along the Paths of the Void

Algan closed his eyes and stretched. His fingers unconsciously clutched the arms of his chair. It was his first voyage into space and yet, without ever having landed on, nor even seen the moon, Mars, Venus, Saturn, or Jupiter, he was going to take a great leap into space, a leap that would take him to the stars. He looked over the ready- room. There was nothing remarkable about it: there were only rows of chairs in which the explorers sat, pale-faced and drawn. They ignored one another.

Algan turned his head and examined his neighbor, a redheaded young man with square shoulders and a normally suntanned complexion which, for the moment, was livid. He was muttering something. Perhaps a prayer?

The shadow of the massive high tower was thrown on the large screen that was clear as glass. A voice intoned numbers and letters. It was a calm, cold voice, somewhat bored by this tedious work, that enunciated syllables with a touch of preciousness. It was the last voice from the Earth that Algan was to hear for a long time.

He was surprised that he was not paying more attention to this fact. Then he realized he was quivering with suppressed excitement. It was, after all, a departure. And this one was no different from others he had made in hydroplanes leaving the last ports of the Earth to plow the oceans.

Perhaps, after all, he would like the worlds he was going to discover.

But he knew he would never feel about them as the

Galaxians did, nor even the people of Betelgeuse. The Galaxians looked down on them. One world was much the same as another and all epochs were the same. The only things they considered important were the space they occupied on Earth, the amount of air they breathed, and the seconds during which they lived. As for the people of Betelgeuse, they looked upon these worlds in a purely proprietary, manner, their only interest being to get everything they could out of lands they would never visit. They all denied, systematically, the immensity of space. For them, space was only a series of problems to be solved, one by one.

A red light went on over the screen. Then the outline of the high tower became blurred and darkened. The light went out. There was no vibration, no dull and prolonged throbbing, none of the things Jerg had, in his ignorance, anticipated: no sudden crushing into a chair that had abruptly become hard, no wailing of engine nozzles, and no grinding of metal. There was only another voice enunciating numbers and words, carefully mounting syllables and seemingly bored by this monotonous work.

Nothing. They were on their way. On the screen, stars trembled. Then, after they had crossed the last limits of the atmosphere, they merely shone, immobile, with a steady light unlike their apparent twinkling from the Earth. They were on their way.

Algan got up from his chair. He went cautiously down the passage, a prey to an indescribable fear brought on by the lessening by one-third of the force of gravity he had been used to during his thirty-two years on the Earth. The gravity which was the same as that of all the ships that plowed the galaxy would be maintained during the entire trip, but the fear inside him would diminish.

He went up to the big screen. Then he turned around and looked at the astronauts as the ship sailed through space at a speed steadily increasing outside the solar system, outside the orbit of Pluto, toward their faraway destination, and said:

"Which star are we headed for?"

They looked at him, apparently dazed, without replying.

Algan sat down and scanned the faces of the three men who were with him in the cold, nickel-plated room: Paine, an old space navigator, with a pale, deeply lined face; Sarlan, the redheaded young man who had been his neighbor at takeoff; a short, squat, pop-eyed man with a thick neck whose name Algan did not know. They were not a bad-looking group. They were conscientiously trying to imitate Paine's gestures and, as a start, tried to keep their eyes off the screen which showed a black sky on which only a few stars were visible.

"Which star are we headed for?" asked Algan.

Paine began to laugh.

"Worried, already, Jerg? You've heard too many stories about monsters on distant planets. In a year or two you'll complain about not having seen enough of them."

"What difference do you think it will make to us?" said Sarlan in a bored voice. "One world or another. At the point we've reached ..."

The short, stocky man said nothing.

"We're headed for the middle of the galaxy," said Paine. "That's where there's the greatest concentration of worlds in space. That's where our best bet is for finding one suitable for humans."

"Let's have something to drink," said Sarlan in an unsteady voice.

Paine opened a cupboard and took out a bottle and glasses.

"To our departure," said Algan.

They drank in silence, avoiding one another's eyes. Their eyes were fixed on the shiny metallic surfaces of the walls. They looked somewhat uneasy.

Then Paine gave a small smile.

"You're not going to live in this cage all the time."

He ran his finger over some knobs. The light suddenly went out. One of them dropped a glass and it bounced with an echo on the flexible floor. Algan backed up until he could feel the reassuring cold wall. He put his hands out, ready to ward off an attack. His pupils dilated in an effort to catch the slightest ray of light. But he was floating in total darkness, in a silence punctuated only by the whistling breath of his companions. He remembered old reflexes and fears and ways to overcome them.

Then the light came on again, at first creeping hesitantly along the cold end of the spectrum, then gradually increasing as it outlined the quivering contours of shadows, then bodies, then the metal clasps and buckles of their space clothes; it finally shone on the light in their eyes.

They could feel a strong breeze. They were waking up in an immense forest. Trees, centuries old, with emerald green leaves, swayed to the rhythm of the wind that blew around and over them. Somewhere in the bushes flowed an invisible spring.

Algan turned around. His hands felt the invisible surface of the wall. They were prisoners in an indiscernible cage and that forest which stretched out beyond imagination was illusory, unreal.

"So what they tell us about ships is true," he said. "Ships are magic places."

"Don't be afraid," said Paine. He was grinning as he leaned down and looked for the glass. His fingers closed over the goblet through tufts of grass.

"Don't be afraid," repeated Paine. "It's only a trick. You weren't warned so that the surprise would be greater, but it's only a trick. Just see what man can make out of a cold bare cabin. The sea, mountains, depths, and heights are within reach."

During the first years of space exploration astronauts would go mad from boredom and monotony. Then psychologists devised total, perfect illusion: the transformation of the world into a series of stage settings, into a game. It was possible to plunge amid the stars or walk between ruined columns of palaces that had died thousands of centuries before on other worlds. As long as the trip lasted, you were a god. But you got used to it. You would look upon these ghosts of trees or waves only as a necessary antidote to claustrophobia. Man was born under open skies and no matter what he did, the immensity of those spaces weighed more heavily on him than a leaden cage. He could not escape empty skies for long. They stayed with him.

Empty illusion, thought Algan as his hands felt the cold surface of the walls. Empty illusions for undiscerning eyes. He remembered the old forests of the Earth and the long hunts, the weariness that would creep up his cramped limbs as he waited for his quarry, the wild chases, and the feel of icy torrents on his shivering skin.

They sat on a mossy bench, old pewter tankards in their hands. They were in a dream, actors in a dream of their own, one that was drawn out for the length of the trip— months—as the ship went through space in search of new planets.

"What star are we headed for?" Algan asked for the third time.

"The young stallion is already champing at the bit," said Paine, laughing. "Well, I've already told you we were heading for the center of the galaxy. But our first stop will be Ulcinor, one of the Puritan Planets. If any of you wants to stay, I imagine it can be arranged. But it's seldom that anyone decides to do so after a few days spent on one of those hellish worlds. You'll see why."

"And then?" asked Algan.

"Don't be in such a hurry. The worlds to which we're going have no names as yet; only numbers. I don't even know them. Maybe they'll be named after you, Algan, if you're lucky enough to be killed during the trip. Algan wouldn't sound too bad. But there's plenty of time. Right now we have nothing to do except tell each other stories or read or smoke to while away the time. After you've visited a few inhospitable worlds you'll wish that these moments could have lasted a little longer."

Algan got up and took a turn around the room. He could distinctly hear the sand squeak under his boots. The forest disappeared near the entrance and he could see the door, but if he moved off a few steps all he could see was the wide expanse of trees.

He stretched out on the grass, closed his eyes, and felt the warm rays of an illusory sun caress his skin, but his hands slipped on the smooth surface of the ground.

"Why are we going after these impossible worlds?" he asked dreamily.

His words seemed to him to dissolve in the silence. The others were listening to him silently. He went on.

"We're being sacrificed for many reasons. What good will it do? Isn't there room enough, in the worlds that have already been conquered, for everybody, for a long time to come?"

There was something in their silence that he did not like, a shade of distrust, a faint smell of fear. It was a question that ought not to have been asked. He knew it and he raised his voice on the last words.

"It's Betelgeuse that decides," Paine finally said. "But you mustn't say things like that, son; it won't do."

"I want to know," said Algan. "I just want to know. I want to be sure that what I do will be of use to someone or to something."

"What difference does it make? You're asked to do something, do it! Is there ever anything in life that is of any use? Don't ask so many questions. It's a bad habit acquired on the old planets."

Paine was looking at Algan without a trace of impatience; his pale eyes looked empty, barely friendly. Algan wondered if there was anything behind those eyes except an absence of worry, an arid serenity, and a slow erosion caused by time and the stars. He looked into Sarlan's eyes. The young man seemed frightened, but in his expression there lurked a tinge of admiration for Algan. Algan stretched his legs on the moss.

"It doesn't really matter," he said calmly. He was thinking of Betelgeuse, of that formidable and discreet government that spun the destiny of the stars and time.

Each new attempt to straighten out the tangle of space had only served to highlight its infinite complexity. With abstract and simple spaces as a starting point men gradually, in the course of ages, went on to geometric concepts that were increasingly difficult to formulate. One of the basic tenets of the idea of space was the geodesic line, that line which, in a given space, was the shortest path between two points. But real space was a multiple entity which postulated a large number, if not an infinity, of geodesics. Thus as the legendary Bergier discovered even before the conquest had begun, in order to connect two points in space one could plot several paths which in their own way were the shortest, in the sense that each one allowed only a predetermined amount of information to pass. This simply meant that, though they had no relation to physical reality, some of the paths were shorter than others. However, that shortcut might be offset by a more pronounced alteration of the body or the message traveling along that path. Certain geodesics, although seemingly ideal at first glance, were therefore unusable for ships because, at the start of the trip, the ships would undergo alterations fatal to their crews.

The first ships just followed the paths of light at a speed appreciably slower than that of light rays. Voyages in those days were almost interminably drawn out and the temporal distortion was almost nil, so accidents were rare.

Then there followed rapid progress. On the one hand, the speed of ships increased to almost that of light, which increased the time warp; as a counterbalance, a general theory of geodesics was formulated at the same time as the invention of the mathematical instruments required to calculate the laws of probability governing the alteration of bodies and messages along these new paths.

New ships soon made use of the extraluminous paths. The latest improvements of accelerator-meters made it possible, at the same time, to give up the old-fashioned method of triangulating from the stellar sources of electromagnetic waves. A ship could at last determine with satisfactory precision its absolute position by its calculated coordinates, its speed, and the curve of its direction. A certain number of unavoidable accidents were statistically foreseeable, but within an acceptable margin. All the same, these were negligible compared to the other risks that the ship ran. Most of these risks came from the men themselves. Homesickness and boredom, magnified by fright and loneliness, gave rise to a nervousness that made sharing close quarters unbearable. Psychologists worked out acceptable conditions. Engineers tried to produce them. A quick solution was generally found. Geniuses were essential in a period of such feverish discoveries and grandiose projects. They were found, trained, and put to use. Some of them, pressed for time, did not hesitate to use drugs which stimulated their mental efforts, but also destroyed them after an alarmingly short lapse of time. But it was a period of grandeur and enthusiasm.

41

The vest canvas uniting the stars was woven over the years. Ships carrying astronauts left the cities of the old planets and flocked to new worlds. New centers were created. The human population increased phenomenally within a few centuries, but the total number of humans was still laughably small with respect to the number of habitable worlds. There sprang up new myths about that enormous space which was apparently impossible to populate. New religions were practiced side by side with the old ones. Historians and sociologists liked to emphasize the absence of any serious conflict. Actually, the war that was being waged was against another enemy: space.

Some utopias were successful; others failed. It was a period of multiple and changing worlds. It was then that the first meetings with the Puritan worlds were set up. It was also at this time that the power of Betelgeuse became first a determining one, then an undisputed one. It started on an economical level, then became solely political, as frontiers were pushed back by human expansion.

Certain plans were carried out successfully. Some attributed this evolution to the natural and general progress of humanity; others attributed it to haphazard forces that nonetheless had a statistically foreseeable result; still others attributed it to the schemes of one man or several men operating behind the scenes.

This latter group, although they did not know it or interpreted it in a wholly different context, were very nearly right.

Jerg Algan opened his eyes. A fresh breeze caressed his face. It was still night. Stars were shining in the sky and two russet colored moons were slowly orbiting around one another. The cries of animals could be heard in the distance. It was a long musical sound, a strangely comforting one.

Jerg Algan raised himself up on an arm. The forest was still. The moss looked damp although the morning dew had not yet fallen.

There was no one near, not a trace of equipment, tents, or men. He automatically felt for his weapon. It was not there. Nor was his hunter's radiant in his belt.

"Where is the safari?" he grumbled.

He could barely remember what had happened. They had spent all of the previous day wandering amid the ruins that the man from Betelgeuse had been so eager to visit. They had penetrated, but not very far, into the forbidden section in order to hunt mutating animals, remains of the last Earth war. They had finally settled for the night in a clearing some distance from the native camp the smell of which was unbearable.

Again Algan heard the distant howling. He had never heard such an animal cry. There was something wrong in this forest, something about the light. Were there really two moons on the Earth? Or was it somewhere else? Scattered memories jostled each other in his mind.

He got up from his bunk and took a few steps. He noticed a man on another bunk and leaned down to look at him, but he did not recognize him. He had never in his life seen such a face, deeply lined and pale, so pale that it seemed made of moonlight.

The moon. He remembered. There was only one moon on the Earth. He was not on the Earth.

He was in the middle of space.

He shook the sleeping man. His memory turned up names, faces.

"Where is the safari?" he shouted at the stranger.

Then he sat on the edge of the bunk and put his head in his hands.

"Oh no, no," he said.

Something came up inside him, began to bum behind his eyes. He knew it was anger, and something more.

"Come on, son, stop worrying," said Paine in a voice thick with sleep. "We've been gone only two months and we'll soon be on Ulcinor."

"I was ... I was somewhere else," said Algan. "I thought I hadn't left. I was in the deep forests of the Earth."

"I know," said Paine. "I've seen others like you. For a long time I was homesick for my town. It was a high, proud city, perched on an alabaster column, in a world you'll never see, and which I'll never return to, on the other side of the human galaxy. I was free there, in a way that no one here can understand anymore. It doesn't matter. Worlds pass by, but men come and go, as the saying goes, you know. Come on, let's wake up Nogaro and go down to eat something."

Nogaro was a thin, brown, silent man with black eyes deeply set in a narrow face. His fingers were surprisingly long and his movements showed more agility than strength. But on the Earth or on any of the other planets, in ancient cities where the Psychological Police were not all-powerful, he could easily have passed as a dangerous man.

Nogaro shared Paine's and Algan's living quarters. He asked no questions, said nothing. Although he looked much younger, he appeared to know as much about space as did Paine.

The ship's technicians seemed to be superstitiously afraid of him and Algan knew that Nogaro had access to certain sections of the ship which were normally forbidden to astronauts.

While they were eating their rations in the refectory, Algan tried to get Paine to talk about Ulcinor, all the while watching Nogaro's reactions. Paine had only hinted at his knowledge of the Puritan Planets.

"You'll see when you get there," Paine answered once again. "All I can tell you is that their city is pretty dismal and that they wear curious masks. You'll get one when you leave the ship. But they're good tradesmen."

"I'd like to ask you a question, Paine," said Algan. "Has anyone ever escaped from the Psycho? Did anyone ever get back to his native planet?"

"What for?" asked Paine. "Only men from the old cities would ever get such an idea into their heads. Life in space has its ups and downs. But life on a planet isn't always a bed of roses either. Betelgeuse knows better than you what's good for you, isn't that right?"

"Are you quite sure?" said Nogaro.

"What did you say?" asked Paine, startled.

"I was asking you," said Nogaro, "if you're really sure that Betelgeuse knows better than you what is good for you?"

Nogaro's voice was deep and muffled; it sounded remote, as though it had traveled over barriers and been carried by some strange echo along invisible cracks.

Algan leaned forward and stopped chewing in order to hear better.

"I don't know," said Paine slowly. "I'm just a sailor. I navigate through space and I grow older. Decisions are made over there, in Betelgeuse. I can't tell whether they're good for me or not. When I'm asked to explore a new planet, I go. I never know who the inhabitants will be nor what will grow there, but I do because I always have, I suppose, just like my father before me. We're not the kind of people who own land here and there and who feel rooted to their planet. We are free men and we leap from one world to another."

"Good," said Nogaro. His thin lips, drawn into a smile, revealed long teeth. "And you, Algan, what do you think? What do you think of Betelgeuse's policy?"

Algan laid his hands flat on the table and breathed deeply.

"I hate Betelgeuse," he said calmly but loudly enough to be heard at the neighboring tables. "I hate everything that comes from Betelgeuse and I don't trust its policies."

Heads turned toward him. Silence spread.

"May I ask why?" asked Nogaro.

"I come from old Dark," replied Algan, "and I'm not ashamed of it. I'm a man from the old cities and all I asked was to be left alone. What's the good of occupying new lands when we can't even settle the ones our ancestors plowed!"

The men at the tables closest to theirs were listening openly. Some looked at Algan with fear and disgust; others, less numerous, with a shade of admiration.

"It's a long story," said Nogaro. "I'll tell it to you some day but not now, not here. We must be powerful, Algan, extremely powerful, if we want to keep our empire. I, too, am a man from the old cities, Algan. I know how most people feel about you. Shall we join forces? We're both somewhat alien to this world, although in quite different ways. Perhaps our respective oddnesses will be complementary."

"OK," said Jerg Algan, and he remembered other friendships in a world that was now remote, which had been sealed in the barrooms of old Dark or on the hunting fields of the free Earth.

Nogaro had an astonishing mind, Algan thought soon after this exchange. He knew the history of the human galaxy backward as well as an endless number of stories about each of the worlds of which it was made up. He gave the impression of having roamed through space since time immemorial. Unlike Paine, who kept telling the same stories, Nogaro could move easily from one story to another. The breadth of his experience was unbelievable. His only real enthusiasm seemed to be space and exploration but he spoke of the worlds as though they had been infinitesimal molecules that slid about within a restricted place. He was mad, Algan said to himself, mad from having looked too long at something too vast for man; but his madness was both grandiose and contagious. The problem that seemed to be haunting Nogaro was the problem of nonhuman races. He said that in the course of his wanderings he had met only races which differed little from the human species and that had attained only a primitive technological level. Yet some of their characteristics were strangely common-place, so much so that he had decided to discover a race that was completely nonhuman, completely different. Old sailors' legends had led him to believe, he claimed, that such a race did exist. He would play with questions anyone on board who had traveled along any unusual routes.

Nogaro taught Algan that the human galaxy did not form a monolithic block and that the authority of Betelgeuse was not undisputed. There were rival-ries aggravated by distance. But time was working for Betelgeuse. Rebels would disappear while the red star continued to shine in the sky. Betelgeuse had not only time on its side but knowledge as well.

Nogaro said that Betelgeuse was like a spider crouching in the middle of its web, watching the little drops of light that were the stars, taking note of a tremor here, a quiver there, and waiting, secure in its everlastingness and in its strength; never pushing, but waiting, spinning threads to catch rebel feet. And it was, said Nogaro, who had set himself up as the interpreter of the rumors rife in the human galaxy, an infallible spider, because it was mechanical, soulless, and immortal. It consisted of enormous machines which, from their concrete strong-holds surrounded by human servants, wrote the history of the planets according to an inexorable logic. And men accepted their power because they were ma-chines; cold, dispassionate, beyond the reach of human ambitions and human imagination. Men accepted them as they accepted the rivers and mountains and space itself, even more readily because their own breed had built them in times so remotely in the past that they were becoming mythological.

Perhaps that was a tissue of lies, thought Algan; perhaps Betelgeuse was only a monstrous lie. Perhaps these machines had existed only in the imagina-tion of a dynasty powerful enough to impose its rule for centuries, protected by immense walls of space and by bottomless pits of time.

And where did Nogaro belong in this canvas, Algan wondered. And how did he himself fit in? And what was the role of all those who had conquered, explored, and died, without ever knowing exactly what their function was as they leaped from one square to another on this cosmic chessboard?

What was Paine's place, with his naïveté; and Nogaro's, with his cynicism, his cold, shrewd eyes, his calculating silence, or his sharp tongue? What was Jerg Allen's place, a man from old planets and old cities, from free, anarchic worlds which looked back into the past rather than forward into the future, sifting, in ancient dust, glories that were past instead of victories to come?

Was there a place for them? Were they not superfluous? Were they simply nothing, just ashes in the great human brazier that devoured space? Algan spent the last days of the journey, before the landing on Ulcinor, in the ship's library, but he learned nothing from the films, tapes, or books. Perhaps, after all, the world was simple, and therefore Algan hated it. Or perhaps it had a hidden face, a secret, that had to be uncovered, which was reality, or a fragment of reality, and Algan hated it because it crushed the lives of men by means of myths.

Perhaps there was no one, from one end to the other of the human galaxy, who any longer knew truth. Perhaps no one had ever known it. But Algan's mistrust, as he studied the films and the books and listened to the tapes, was that of the hunter uncovering a hidden trail, who has caught the scent of a quarry that is either stupid or dangerous. And he could find nothing as he went along, but he knew that animals and men can move softly without snapping twigs or stirring up the air.

Perhaps Nogaro was right. Maybe salvation would come from another race, a nonhuman, different race that could bring the weight of its experience. Or perhaps destruction would come from that other race. But the salvation and destruction of this civilization were intermingled in Algan's mind.

Algan's interest in the Puritan Planets grew as they approached Ulcinor. He knew little about them—just legends and gossip picked up in the dives of the old city of Dark, gloomy stories and a black reputation, but no precise facts. The abyss of space and time dulled the force of events. It was difficult to pass on traditions when everyone was isolated in time. And sailors disliked telling stories they considered dead. Sometimes explorers were more talkative, but they were seldom well-informed. Betelgeuse probably preferred this way. Betelgeuse intended to be the principal and, whenever possible, the only bond between the various universes.

Three hundred local years earlier, when explorers had first reached the planets which were to become the Puritan worlds, they had run into harsh and even hostile conditions which had molded their personalities. In addition, they had been the first genuine models of the Galaxian civilization. Before their arrival, the conquest had been undertaken by men from the Earth who were still steeped in their own world, but the explorers of these new worlds were mature men who had spent most of their lives aboard slow spacecraft that traveled through the outer reaches of the galaxy. They knew all about time warp, they couldn't even conceive of a world ignorant of it, a world that had only unchanging time. They felt like foreigners on the Earth, for they had been contemporaries of people who had died, one or two centuries earlier. They were looking for a new world in which time would have a new value, in which men's lives would be less dependent upon the lives of their contemporaries and more on the lives of men to come. They discovered ten such worlds, orbiting neighboring stars. They left their imprint upon them, deeply enough to last for centuries.

Then other societies were created elsewhere in space. The reason for the creation of the Puritan worlds became meaningless, because the mentality of Earthlings had almost disappeared with the years. But the Puritan worlds, bastions of a tradition, probably the only one in the human galaxy except for that of Betelgeuse, survived, complete with their rigid organization and morality, their religion and strange customs which excluded foreigners. The ports which Betelgeuse built on the Puritan Planets, like the ones they had built on all the inhabited planets, were soon abandoned. Engendered by space and its effects upon man, the Puritan worlds soon began to distrust anything new and worrisome that man might bring.

Distrust is perhaps a narrow form of wisdom. In any event, the currents of space carried an embittered Jerg Algan to the shores of the Puritan worlds.

CHAPTER IV
The Puritan Planets

The name of the planet shone in letters of fire on the tall bronze gates of the Stellar Port: Ulcinor. It was an old-fashioned name, a light, musical one that trailed ancient myths, cloudy and disquieting memories, a name that rang out loud and clear but was also hemmed in by disturbing rumors.

As Algan went through the gates, he saw the suburbs; at first all he could see were the roofs through which narrow streets wound like narrow trickles. Then in the distance he could make out the colossal shadows of the new city. He was to be free for many long days, free to come and go on the planet, but not to leave it. He knew that the government of Betelgeuse was most reluctant to lose a new recruit; he also knew that he would doubtless prefer life on board stellar ships to that on Ulcinor, if even one- tenth of the legends told about the dismal Puritan worlds was correct.

Before entering the city he slipped his hands into long black gloves and covered his face with a dark mask. It was equipped with light filters for the nose and ears to allow the passage of sound, air, or smells; the mouth was covered; only the eyes and forehead were in the open.

Algan had been warned never to go without the mask. Going out barefaced was tantamount, for the Puritans of Ulcinor, to a crude insult, to a deliberate act of indecency; the penalty for violators was a heavy one, even if he was protected, as an explorer, by the all-powerful administration of Betelgeuse.

Algan roamed about the old streets through which no vehicle now traveled. Behind those monotonously white walls that had split and cracked under the extremes of heat and cold of countless seasons, he could only sense a larva-like activity. He liked that. It reminded him of the Earth. The Puritan worlds were among those most violently opposed to the Earth's way of life but he liked the idea of finding a history and a decadence comparable to those of old Dark.

He remembered what Nogaro had said to him before he left the ship: "The Puritans are so afraid of growing old that the weight of their fear instantly aged them." It was true; he understood it now and once more admired Nogaro's strange mind: the Puritans had wanted to create a deathless civilization. Rigidly conceived, from its very inception it had borne the weight of the curse: it was doomed to sclerosis.

However, as he went on, the streets began to exhibit more liveliness. The Puritans had started out as merchants and they had never forgotten it; they had been explorers ready to grab what they liked in new worlds if only to sell it on the rich planets. Consequently, all the goods necessary for trade in the human galaxy could be found in their ports.

Algan soon came across men who were no longer furtive shadows, but were obviously important people, dressed in dark velvet, black or dark blue, depending upon their status, and whose masks gleamed with bright stones. Shops were full of luxury items, unostentatiously displayed: antique polished wood from Atlan, light silky furs from Aldragor, or the products of native crafts: brightly colored shawls, glass blocks enclosing multidimensional and kaleidoscopic views, bronze plaques engraved with hieroglyphics, crystals in strange colors and shapes, glass bees, giant lifelike insects with powerful stingers.

There were no limits to the wealth of the human galaxy, and its best products were assembled here on Ulcinor.

Jerg Algan felt lonely as he leafed through old books written in an unknown language or felt the softness of a piece of fabric. He was lonely as he seldom had been on the Earth. For the first time in his life, he felt lost in the midst of a new, upsetting world, friendless, without even a guide to show him the way, to protect him. And he was not free.

He tossed the fabric back on the counter, to the annoyance of the shopkeeper whose greedy eyes glinted inside his mask. Greed was deemed a virtue on this planet where human feelings were classed as vices. The inhabitants of Ulcinor assiduously cultivated cupidity.

Under the pile of fabrics, painted canvases, and embossed leather books, Algan noticed an old chessboard. He swept the materials aside and examined it. The sixty-four squares seemed to be made of two kinds of wood, one blue as the night, and the other rosy as a delicate complexion. There was nothing unusual so far. But each of the squares was finely engraved. These curious markings drew Algan's attention.

The precision of detail and freedom of design were remarkable. It was almost impossible to believe a human mind could have conceived them. They were not sufficiently plain to have been intended as a decoration, nor was there any indication that they bore any relation to the game of chess.

Yet they stirred up vague memories which intrigued him. He had heard about signs like these, on the Earth, that had something to do with a very old science or, more precisely, with a religion... no, he remembered now, it had to do with a superstition called astrology. Some of the signs etched on the chessboard looked like certain of the symbols which had been used to designate parts of the sky and groups of stars at a time when men believed their fates were written in the firmament.

But the other signs did not look like anything that could have been imagined by a human mind. There were arabesques, some geometric in character, others consisting of interlacings of fantastic figures, but unrelated to any human endeavor. There was no apparent connection with chess. The whole thing was rather like one of those mystical squares occasionally wrought by painters or engravers of antiquity.

49

Algan lightly touched the chessboard. It may not have been wood for the material it was made of showed a finer grain than even the finest fibrous wood. But it was not an ordinary synthetic either because the play of light on the dark and light squares revealed an unusually complex chemical structure.

He was surprised at how small the chessboard was. His two hands could almost completely cover it.

His curiosity began to fade. He said to himself that it must have belonged to some spaceman who had strayed on the planet by chance. Nonetheless he beckoned to the shop owner, who came up eagerly. Nothing in the shop was his; the inhabitants of Ulcinor considered it immoral to sell anything owned by them, but, paradoxically, acquisitiveness was considered a duty.

"Where does this come from?" Algan asked casually.

"It's a very old chessboard," said the shopkeeper. His yellow eyes glistened. "Very old. Maybe a thousand years old. Maybe ten, maybe more. Interesting. Are you a collector?"

"How could it be ten thousand years old?" asked Algan. "The conquest of space is more recent than that. What makes you think that the chessboard is that old? Are you trying to cheat me?"

But as he said it he didn't really believe it. He knew that Puritan shopkeepers were thoroughly honest; they never claimed that their products were better than they actually were; only, at times, they just did not mention flaws.

"It's older than any of us," the shopkeeper said. He stroked his mask. "It's older than this city. Believe me. It's extremely interesting. No one knows its date. It could be worth a fortune. But I have to sell it. Business is bad."

"Really," said Algan, smiling. "How much are you asking for it?"

"Let's not discuss the price, sir. At least, not right now. We both love beautiful old things, don't we? Look at this chessboard. Can you tell me what it is made of? There are old legends...

"Tell me first where the pawns are; then you can tell me your old legends."

The shopkeeper threw him a suspicious look.

"The pawns?" he repeated. "There are no pawns. Not with this kind of chessboard. I thought you were an expert. Did you at least notice the designs on the board?"

"Then how is it played?"

"No one knows. I told you this chessboard is very old, undated. There is no one now who knows the rules of the game. Boards like this were around long before man learned to move pawns in sixty-four squares."

"Where did this one come from?"

"I don't know, sir. A spaceman brought it to me to sell one day. He came from the worlds that are on the outermost edge of the human galaxy. I don't quite know where he found the chessboard. He didn't tell me. But I know these boards are very old. Not very rare, sir; we've seen lots of them in Ulcinor. Not very rare, but very old. Long before man came."

"There were other civilizations in the galaxy before that of man?"

The shopkeeper looked at him sadly.

"How can I answer you, sir? I don't know any more than you do. Explorers, among whom were my ancestors, as well as yours probably, discovered intelligent races here and there, human or otherwise, but never one that was wholly civilized or that succeeded in leaving its native planet. But I believe... I believe, sir, that we are not the first to go to certain planets. I believe that *They* are watching us. I believe that *They* are waiting for us. Maybe *They* made these chessboards."

"Who are *They*?" Algan asked curtly.

"Who knows? Who knows? Certainly not a poor Ulcinor shopkeeper who hasn't made three trips away from his planet. But there are tales, strange tales."

"What sort of tales?"

"Do I dare speak? These are not supposed to be mentioned. But I can see that you're a friend and that you would give me a good price for this old and valuable board."

"All right," said Algan.

"Then follow me," said the shopkeeper. Algan looked around. An animated crowd pressed against the shop windows; noiseless, long black cars went down the streets. But all this activity was carried out in such complete silence that the atmosphere was sinister; the dark masks and clothes only added to the general gloom.

Algan went through the low narrow doorway into the back of the shop; it was nothing more than a narrow hovel in which were piled up unimaginable riches: furs of incredible warmth and quality, finely engraved metal objects.

The shopkeeper sat down on a pile of furs and motioned to Algan to sit in a tall leather armchair which plainly had come from the Earth. The light was somewhat dim, but Algan's eyes soon became accustomed to it and his gaze roamed over the little shop.

"I see you like my place, sir," said the shopkeeper. "It quite warms my heart."

He leaned over toward Algan, giving him a conspiratorial smile, and said:

"Do you like zotl?"

"It's a long time since I've had any," sighed Algan. "But I thought that in the Puritan worlds...?"

"Oh, one makes compromises, sir," said the shopkeeper. "We have a saying: Facades count only for those who do not go inside. It's a very old saying. Don't you like it?"

The shopkeeper took a zotl root from a shelf and slipped it into a small zotl squeezer which looked like an inoffensive bit of statuary. He waited until the hard root had lost its color and the juice had run all the way down. Then he poured the amber liquid into tall silver goblets.

"Wait," he said. "Don't drink right away, I want to show you something. I know that I can trust you."

His tone of voice had changed imperceptibly. It had become less obsequious, less commercial; it had become more precise, more positive. The shopkeeper intended to be obeyed and Algan wanted to know what he was leading up to.

"Place the chessboard in your lap, sir; put your right hand over the squares, like that, each finger in a square. It doesn't matter which ones. Now listen to me:

"We see all kinds of people on a planet like Ulcinor and usually people trust us because we have the reputation of being incorruptible. Our customs are not always properly appreciated, and our intolerance, albeit justified, is often held against us. However, on the whole, foreigners trust us, and believe me, that's pretty rare, in space. So they tell us things that even Betelgeuse, in its mighty pride, does not know.

"You don't like Betelgeuse, sir, don't try to tell me you do. I could tell right away from your clothes that you are an explorer and that you come from the Earth, and I know how Betelgeuse recruits explorers on the Earth, even if the central government doesn't boast about the methods. Well, we too have good reasons for disliking Betelgeuse.

"For three centuries now, our influence has been restricted to the worlds you call Puritan, even though there are countless uncolonized planets in space. Betelgeuse wants our men, but not our society. She's afraid of us and keeps us from expanding.

"So we listen carefully to the stories travelers tell us and we are always on the lookout for some secret that will give us a hold over Betelgeuse. Someday we'll find one. We know, for example, that in certain worlds there are ruins more ancient than man."

He stopped talking and his deep-set yellow eyes scanned Jerg Algan's expressionless face.

"You are not surprised?" he asked.

"I'd already heard something of the sort," said Algan.

"Could be; or perhaps you're good at hiding your feelings...? Perhaps I ought not to have spoken so soon. Never mind. I know you hate Betelgeuse as much as we do.

"Now, listen. A number of expeditions have discovered and photographed colossal ruins on the planets bordering the human galaxy. Unfortunately none of those expeditions has come back."

"An accident?" Algan asked. His voice betrayed none of his surprise.

"They just simply disappeared. Perhaps they were destroyed. That's what Betelgeuse thinks. Or perhaps they just left. That's what we think."

"Left?" said Algan.

"Just imagine those ruins as being some sort of a gateway to everything you can conceive; imagine that those expeditions set forth, trustingly, into new universes and that they were never able to get back."

"Absurd," said Algan.

"No doubt, no doubt," replied the shopkeeper. "But men did come back a couple of times. Oh, not straight back, and usually under different names. Betelgeuse never saw them again even though they had sworn loyalty to her years earlier. But we found them. They had something to sell and they offered it to us."

"What had happened to them?"

"Nothing. You mustn't think I'm trying to hide the truth from you, but nothing had ever happened to them. Their stories were, for the most part, surprisingly similar. They had been left behind by the main body of the expedition, usually to keep an eye on the campsite. But no one ever came back to relieve them. So then they fled, taking with them anything of value in the camp, sometimes after having taken a few snapshots."

"We have all those snapshots. Those ruins really do exist."

"They're too ancient," said Algan.

"Do you think so? After all, the expeditions did vanish."

"All right, but what connection can there be with this chessboard, and why are you telling me this?"

The shopkeeper's black silk mask creased so markedly that Algan could see he was smiling.

"Put your fingers on the board, sir, either hand, each finger on a square. Good. Now drink your zotl."

Algan lifted up his mask and slowly emptied his glass. He was racked with homesickness. He could remember the Earth and the shady barrooms of Dark and the imaginary land that the zotl conjured up. A gray desert under a low green sky, iridescent and changeable rocks. Distant and invisible suns vibrating like harp strings. But this time the zotl did not affect his ganglia and he neither heard colors nor saw sounds.

He felt as though he were on the chessboard and as though he were nothing but a pawn in a white square; he could not see the edges of the board. He was rigid, perfectly still, his eyes fixed in space, his stiff arm holding the glass. He was no longer himself. He was traveling on the chessboard.

An irresistible force propelled him. Then the squares around him began to change and grow larger. He could see stars shining in the darkening sky; he flew briefly over a green stretch, then went down vertically and landed gently in tall undulating grass.

The grass reached up to his shoulders, but he forgot about it as he looked around because, under that lavender sky studded with a gigantic blue star, the black polished walls of cyclopean ruins glistened.

It was a wall. But he started to shout. He saw it crack, collapse, and then it crushed him. It was only a dream, but he fluttered his eyelids. The wall was too big, too smooth, too unbroken to have been made by humans; too black also. It was not perfectly vertical, but clearly slanted, leaning over Algan's landing place. That was what had made him think that the wall was collapsing.

Then Algan looked up toward the sky and tried to decide which sun it was, but he suddenly felt a weight at the end of his arm. He blinked and saw the masked face of the shopkeeper over him.

"What is it?" he said, even before putting the goblet down on the table.

"How do I know? I wasn't with you," the shopkeeper replied.

"You knew what was going to happen to me. You told me to put my hand on the board. Zotl never sent me there before."

"Probably not," said the shopkeeper. "Well, now you know as much as I do. You can be sure that there really is such a place, just as you saw it. Those walls have been falling, for thousands of years, toward the section of the ground on which you were standing. Was the sun in the sky blue, red, or still yellow?"

"It was a large blue star," said Algan.

"That's the most usual. You see, there are many factors that affect these visions. The vegetation, for example, or the color of the sky or the sun, but the walls never change. These colossal fortresses appear in all the worlds that have some connection with this chessboard and with zotl. Heaven only knows what treasures they contain."

"Or what weapons," said Algan.

They were silent for a moment, then looked at one another.

"An hallucination," said Algan.

"Probably," said the shopkeeper, "an hallucination that kills."

Why did you never send out an expedition?"

"Because of Betelgeuse," said the shopkeeper. "Ships and technicians are only for Betelgeuse. You know how few men there are. But we've learned quite a lot anyway, as you can see. Yes, quite a lot."

"And now," said Algan somewhat uneasily, "Tell me why you've told me this."

The shopkeeper's eyes closed almost entirely.

"You were interested in the chessboard," he said. "I thought you were really interested; was I wrong?"

"No," admitted Algan, "but there must be another reason."

"We Puritans like to spin yams," said the shopkeeper. "We also like to hear them. Imagine for a moment that you see something, or even only hear of something, of a large black slanted wall, for example. You may be sure we'd be so glad to know more that it would be worth a great deal to us to hear about it. A very great deal."

"I'm only an explorer," said Algan. He hesitated to say yes. He wasn't sure he could trust the shopkeeper and was afraid of a trap. "I don't even know where my first trip is going to be. I couldn't be of much help to you."

"Who knows?" said the shopkeeper. His eyelids were fluttering as though he were transmitting in Morse code a secret message to some invisible assistant.

"Who knows? Perhaps tomorrow you will be traveling, free, among the stars. Whatever happens to you, don't forget us."

"I'll bear it in mind," said Algan. "And how much do you want for the chessboard?"

"Nothing," said the shopkeeper. His voice was heavy with regret, as though he were committing a sin too burdensome for his conscience, which was precisely the case.

"Nothing," he repeated. "It's a present."

'There is more to this than meets the eye," Jerg Algan said to himself as he walked through the streets.

Nogaro had been right on almost every score. The human galaxy was not a monolithic bloc, but a kind of yeasty mass pulled in every direction by different ambitions. Perhaps one single shock would suffice to topple the power of Betelgeuse. The idea appealed to Jerg Algan.

But what really surprised him was the interest in nonhuman races that Nogaro and the shopkeeper had shown. This interest must have sprung from information that he, Algan, did not have. It could well be related to the instability of the power of Betelgeuse over the galaxy, or to some intelligence that could endanger her. The Puritan worlds fully expected that the discovery of the black stone fortresses would give them victory over Betelgeuse. They probably knew more than the shopkeeper had been willing to tell Algan. But what was his, Jerg Algan's, role on this gigantic stage set, he wondered uneasily as his fingers ran over the smooth surface of the chessboard.

There was no immediate answer.

Each of the trails he mentally explored was a dead end.

Ulcinor was a planet peopled with shadows, tall black flames that sped along the streets.

The place was filled with black-masked figures in flowing capes that shielded their wearers from probing looks. The animation in the streets had something furtive about it, as though the inhabitants of Ulcinor, in striving to look Eke sexless ghosts, had ended up by acquiring the habits of timorous specters. The cars in the streets were long and black, and the windows on their outsides were mirrors that reflected passersby. They rolled by silently, smoothly, at a fast and steady speed. There was something funereal about them; even the chrome glistened somberly.

No one carried weapons. This surprised Algan, who had always seen the men in Dark wear all kinds of radiants in their belts. The sense of security here was such that no one would ever have thought that speed and skill in self- defense were necessary for survival.

Ulcinor was a world of enduring solid traditions. The Earth, too, had once had them, Algan knew, but now— and he realized for the first time with poignant certainty—it held only chaos and decomposition.

The new city surprised Algan. He saw now that Dark, despite its splendor, was nothing but a city from the past in the process of decay. Here the huge black and white buildings were taller and more majestic than those in Dark. There were towers stretching toward the sky that could have crushed, by their sheer weight, even the tower of the Stellar Port of the Earth.

But boredom and anxiety seemed to have taken over. It was a cold city, peopled with shadows that had forgotten their human destiny, who whispered to one another instead of speaking out, who ran silently in the shelter of walls. It was already a dead city, muffled in the shroud of its silence, just like the thousands of faces behind their masks.

The idea of the ancient Puritans had been that each man, confronting an immense but not inaccessible universe, was and ought to be quite alone, that he had to count only on himself or on the mathematical laws calculated to insure his protection or his survival. Spaceman could no longer be the man of a particular epoch or a particular world. He had to be detached from everything and be interchangeable. He had to be colorless, odorless, almost invisible, and nearly inaccessible.

In the space of a few hundred years he had, in effect, achieved just that. At least in the Puritan worlds. One could leave Ulcinor, then come back a century later and find it unchanged. The streets were always the same, the black and white facades barely feeling the breath of time along their surfaces. The men behind their, masks might have changed, but there was no way of telling.

Jerg Algan remembered the men and Women of the Earth, their strong resonant voices, their brightly colored and occasionally original clothes. Here, he was able to recognize the women only from their long hair floating in the breeze and their slender figures. But their features, lips, and cheeks were hidden behind smooth unchanging masks and their supple bodies disappeared under the full, dark cloaks.

This was the world of the future, Jerg told himself as he stared at the bare, blind facades which on Earth would have had a wealth of light, windows, curtains half-opened like eyelids on the serene warmth of welcoming rooms. His hands in their long black gloves shook with anger. His lips quivered with anxiety and nervousness under his mask of featherweight silk.

Would space produce a different kind of future: one that had been engendered in worlds immemorially old or still to come?

No one knew, Jerg Algan thought, as he walked through the wide streets of Ulcinor, checking the length of his stride and trying to look like everybody else.

He felt a hand on his shoulder. He turned quickly and noiselessly. His hand instinctively reached for his belt. But there was no weapon there, no sheath.

"I gather that you are taking an interest in antiques and shopkeepers." Nogaro's voice, muffled but clear and slightly ironic, reached him.

"How do you know?" Algan replied curtly.

"Never mind. I hear all sorts of things. Have you seen the roofs of Ulcinor? Believe me, they're worth seeing. Come on. I want to have a talk with you. We'll be less likely to be disturbed up there."

Nogaro took Jerg Algan by the arm. They went through the gate of an enormous building and crossed a number of white rooms. There was a crowd of masked figures milling about. At the end of this corridor Algan saw an enormous spiral staircase that seemed to be revolving on itself. He realized, when they set foot on it, that it was an escalator.

Algan had never seen one like it on the Earth.

"Don't bother to tell me what the shopkeeper said to you," Nogaro said. "I know. I just want to warn you about a number of strange things that will certainly happen to you."

Jerg Algan looked at Nogaro.

"Do you think there's any truth in all that?" he asked. "Do you really think that there exists in space another, more ancient civilization than man's?"

"I'd like to feel sure about it," Nogaro replied evasively.

"The chessboard and the zotl?"

"I don't know any more than you do."

"Those lost expeditions?"

Everything the shopkeeper told you about is true except what he said about Betelgeuse. Betelgeuse knows, as much as the shopkeepers do, neither more, nor less; just as much. And Betelgeuse, just like the merchants, would like to know more. Perhaps she will learn it from you. Who knows?"

"I'm only a spaceman. I don't even know in what world I'll be living next year."

"Who knows?" repeated Nogaro. It seemed to Algan that he was smiling under his mask. "Perhaps tomorrow you'll travel, free, among the stars. Perhaps tomorrow you will be leading an expedition."

A point in Algan's mind froze.

"The shopkeeper has already told me that," he said slowly. "Now, you. It looks as though I'm the least informed about my own future."

"You could well be, my friend," Nogaro said in a tone of cold finality. "Betelgeuse and the shopkeepers are cooking up something for you."

Algan became pensive. The escalator had taken them up to the top of the building. He looked up and saw a transparent cupola above. Black dots which he identified as spaceships could be seen in the sky.

Nogaro went on: "Betelgeuse might let you use a high speed ship. Oh, just a small one. Just a simple launch that one man could handle alone. In that way you could get to the distant skies in which the black citadels are located. But, as Betelgeuse would prefer not to have this known, she could ask you to take over a ship by force in a Stellar Port—Ulcinor, for example. It's been done before. And it would be easy enough to do. You've no idea how careless the port authorities are. So, you'd set forth in that stolen ship, and after a long voyage of exploration you'd bring back some interesting data. You would then become the object of a long struggle for power between Betelgeuse and the Puritans. Do you see?"

"I'm beginning to," said Algan. "But why did they choose me? And why are the Puritans giving me information that will be useful to Betelgeuse if I leave?"

"This is where things begin to get complicated. As far as Betelgeuse and the Puritans are concerned, you're nothing but a pawn. But as soon as one side has chosen you, the other one will take an interest in you also. You'll probably never know which one did so first, but that doesn't matter.

"Let's assume that you're not just an ordinary spaceman, not even among those that come from the Earth. You're able to survive alone in a hostile environment. But in addition you hate both Betelgeuse and the Puritans. You hate the present-day world. You would like to find, somewhere in space, the means of destroying it. You'll try hard to find those means. That's enough. Betelgeuse and the Puritans hope to discover, through you, a means of destroying the power that worries them: for the Puritans, the central government; for Betelgeuse, the Ten Planets. The information given you by the shopkeeper is of no importance. Betelgeuse already has it. It was given to you for the sole purpose of allaying your suspicions."

They were now directly under the cupola. The city spread out before them, all around the Stellar Port, just like a game of black and white dominoes lined up in even rows along a flat table. An enormous black ship carrying the colors of Betelgeuse whirled, like a giant insect, around the Stellar Port. The sky, above the city, was covered with the white wake of ships taking off.

"So, space is not large enough for Betelgeuse and the Puritans to coexist," said Algan.

"No," whispered Nogaro, "or rather, it's too big and there are too few men to permit either of the two powers to share. Perhaps the situation would change if men were to find a powerful ally in the skies. But so far they have discovered, along the line of thinking races, only primitive types who may have been failures of History and Time."

"Who are you; anyway?" Jerg Algan asked. "How do you know all this? For whom are you working? For yourself?"

"No," said Nogaro. He looked away, toward the city. "All of this is interesting, but I think I ought to tell you that I represent Betelgeuse."

CHAPTER V
All the Stars in the Sky

All the stars in the world were shining in the Ulcinor night, Algan thought, and it was virtually impossible to believe that beyond that haze of suns there existed other clouds of fire and other orbiting and perhaps inhabited worlds.

He had left his room noiselessly and was now on the patrol path formed by the top of the thick walls that surrounded the Stellar Port. A radiant hung on his belt and he was wearing an air pilot's uniform. From the high wall he could look down on the city and the port esplanade. The air was fresh, the sky clear. He could see the lights of distant suburbs, miles from the center, shining like little islands of stars, like galaxies detached from the firmament and squashed on the ground.

The port itself was only a kind of white desert surrounded by walls and bathed in light, darkened here and there by the black outlines of ships headed toward the zenith. One of these ships, one of the small fast going units of Betelgeuse's inspection service, was waiting for him.

It made a small slender shadow at the southernmost points of the port, a thin black spindle with all its lights out. This was Jerg Algan's destination.

He was about to play an odd sort of game: hijack the ship, with the secret cooperation of the port patrol. He was to take the aircraft, ostensibly pursued by the whole of Betelgeuse's space force, to Glania, a tenth-rate, sparsely settled world, but with a brand-new Stellar Port. Glania was only the first lap of his journey, but a necessary one.

Glania was at the very border of the human galaxy, on the edge of the troublesome regions of the center of the galaxy. And it was on Glania that one of the two or three survivors of the lost expeditions now lived.

Glania, an invisible planet in the starry sky.

Algan carefully went over the contents of his pockets. He was not supposed to take with him anything that would give away his identity in case he failed or died. But he did not know against whom these precautions were being taken. Perhaps Nogaro really believed in the existence of other races and did not want to leave anything to chance. Perhaps he did not want to indicate to possible invaders the way to Betelgeuse. Or perhaps he was afraid of adversaries that were nearer or more human. He could not figure it out. There was only the chessboard which filled one of the ample pockets of his flying suit. It was his sole clue, the only beginning he had of a possible trail.

He told himself that he was like a hunter who does not know what his prey is to be, nor even the location of his hunting ground. He looked at his watch: two minutes before eleven. On the dot of eleven he would swing into action.

59

The night was calm and silent. The city glowed quietly in its cold lights. The blades of a distant helicopter occasionally beat the air with a sound of rustling silk. The high towers outlined against the night sky were like vertical rays of light. Algan started the countdown. There was no point in doing it, but his lips had begun counting before he'd become conscious of it.

Five. Four. Three. Two. One.

Nothing happened. It was precisely eleven o'clock.

He waited a moment, undecided, then started to run noiselessly along the watchman's walk. He went down a flight of stairs like a cat. He had exactly thirty seconds to reach the spaceship's launching pad: every thirty seconds an electronic beam swept the entire port.

It was an invisible and undetectable beam, but if in its trajectory it alighted upon anything unusual, an alarm was set off. Normally it explored the port haphazardly. Theoretically it was impossible to avoid it because no one could tell which section of the port it would sweep. But every thirty seconds, at least, it lit up every portion of the port, searched all the shadows, and touched the smooth hulls of the ships.

But on that day, between eleven and eleven-ten, at thirty-second intervals, the sweep of the beam was not to be left to chance. It was to follow a plan, an ostensibly disorganized one, which would allow him sufficient time to cross the esplanade by jumping from zone to zone without touching off the alarm. Jerg Algan knew the program by heart.

He counted the seconds as he sped down the interminable staircase leading from the watchtower walk. He was three seconds ahead of schedule when he reached the Stellar Port. He forced himself to be motionless. Three. Two. One.

He started to run as fast as his legs would carry him, toward a dark, distant point and he thought that from the top of the tower he must have looked to anyone watching like a sort of black ant dragging itself along the surface of a plain as smooth as glass. He reached a zone of shadows and caught his breath. This time he was ten seconds ahead of the beam and he had to wait for it before dashing out once more onto the esplanade.

He was a perfect target, he thought to himself as he darted out once more. In theory, no one was to shoot him. In theory.

The tall black prows of the ships loomed up larger and larger. He was in a hurry to reach the shelter of their shadows even though any comfort he derived from them would be psychological. The shadows might have enabled him to escape the eyes of men, but not those of the machines.

He had thought it a queer idea when Nogaro told him of Betelgeuse's plan. Why not, he had asked, leave during daylight, aboard a ship of Betelgeuse's fleet? Why this absurd and dangerous masquerade? Was it to deceive the Puritans of the Ten Planets?

"No," Nogaro had replied in his chilly voice. They would know as soon as they had heard of Algan's escape where and why he had gone.

It was because neither Betelgeuse nor the Puritans were willing to admit, before the whole of the galaxy, that they were worrying about hypothetical civilized races possibly living in unknown worlds beyond already explored regions. The reasons were purely political. How can we justify a refusal of a spaceship to the merchants of Ulcinor, men from Betelgeuse said, if we send an official expedition to look for the black citadels?

"If I'm caught, will I be prosecuted for piracy?" Algan had asked.

"Of course," Nogaro had replied. "But you won't be caught. Unless you want to be. If that happens, you'll be well-escorted to Betelgeuse. You might escape from there."

"It's a dangerous game," Algan had commented.

"No doubt," Nogaro had admitted. "But you are free. Do you prefer space or new lands to colonize?"

"Space," Algan had said unhesitatingly.

He was now crossing a strange forest: a metallic grove of ships; the rectilinear branches of the trees around him were antennas. Some of his hunter's instincts were aroused.

Perhaps I ought to have refused, he thought. How can I serve Betelgeuse, which I hate?

The answer was deep-seated. He was a hunter. He belonged to that breed which, from the beginning of time, had been used as mercenaries. He was a mercenary.

He liked to hunt—any quarry; his long outings on the depopulated Earth had had no other purpose.

There was still, among the stars, a place for men of the old world. Algan's place was analogous to a grain of sand set in a piece of machinery to be sabotaged, or like that of a ferret sent into a lair to flush out quarry.

The place of a knight on the chessboard.

Leaping from star to star.

Trying to stop a hostile king.

The black king who ruled over the galaxy.

He began to run wildly among the tall shells of the rockets. A breath of wind sang along the shiny steel plates.

He barely heard the sound of his own footsteps, but he thought he felt on his body the warmth of the detective beam.

Then he noticed a sound and he stopped suddenly, melting into the shadow of a huge ship. He strained to listen. He thought he heard the various clicks that fill the innards of ships: the growling of their motors, the hissing of electrons running along copper wires. The ground seemed to be vibrating underfoot.

But it was only a human step, the regular hollow beat of heels on the concrete of the esplanade.

An enemy, Jerg Algan thought, but immediately rejected the idea. A special patrol? Or, more simply still, a technician making a last-minute checkup of a ship ready to take off?

This was more dangerous than the detective beam or the maneuvering of the Ulcinor merchants. It was that unforeseeable trap that opened up suddenly underfoot during a hunt in the forest.

Algan counted the seconds. He had to start running again or the detective beam would find him in the shadows.

He slowly went around the enormous hull that was giving him temporary cover and saw, slightly to one side, the small ship that had been assigned to him. But to reach it he had to cross a zone of light, pass between two rows of ships that were as still and as threatening as sleeping monsters.

He straightened out and darted forward after his shadow which was clearly outlined on the ground ahead of him, seeming to point the way.

"Who goes there?" a voice cried.

He didn't stop, did not look behind. He merely speeded up.

"Who goes there?" the voice repeated, with less assurance this time. "Show yourself or I'll sound the alarm."

As he ran Algan tried to figure out where the voice came from. The man must have been working on one of the ships along the lighted way that Algan was following. He could not help but see him and if he had not been warned to ignore certain comings and goings that were to take place that night in the Stellar Port of Ulcinor, this was going to be the end of Algan's expedition. He would never travel amid the stars.

He thought quickly. He stepped between two ships, thus abandoning the lighted path. He knew that by doing this he might be picked up by the beam, but it was a risk he would have to run. The several seconds that it took him to go around one of the ships seemed interminable—the ship had taken on mountainous proportions. Then he slipped into the shadow of the next ship in the row and he came out again onto the lighted path.

He could hear the footsteps, which were still at some distance, speed up. The man was not afraid of coming out into the open. It was certainly a guard or a technician. The control machines knew that he must be in the port and were not concerned about his presence. And if it was a guard, he was armed and trained for a manhunt.

Algan suddenly saw him. Or, rather, his shadow. It was only a minute spot compared to the mass of ships around him, but it made his heart beat faster. He drew slowly near. He knew that he could not reach his ship without being seen.

There was only one solution. He deplored it, but he could see no alternative.

Slipping into the dark shadow of the metal ship, he struck it with his finger, making a musical sound in the silent air of the port.

"Who goes there?" the voice cried out, coming toward him.

It must have been a technician. A guard would never have made the mistake of giving away his position by calling out loud.

Algan moved quickly. He struck the hull again. The resonant vibrations ran along the sheet metal. It would have been impossible, even for a trained ear, to determine exactly where they came from.

Then he saw the man walking toward him, but unseeing, blinded by the bright light, still hesitating to sound the alarm. He stepped out of the shadows. The man made a gesture of surprise that was his undoing. He was a technician who had not been trained for fighting. He thought not of giving the alarm, but of defending himself. Algan's fist crashed into the technician's stomach and the side of his other hand came down hard on his neck. The technician fell soundlessly.

Algan dragged him into the shadows of the ship. The alarm might go off in thirty seconds.

Without looking back he hurtled into the lighted alley lined with massive, still, metal giants and crossed the deserted, luminous plain. He ran up the gangplank of his ship, fled down the runway, disregarding the noise he was making, and rushed into the pilot's seat.

The ship was ready. Its generator was purring gently and all the lights on the instrument panel were green. He could take off at once.

Systematically, Algan began to push all the buttons. The doors of the ship closed. Then metal safety belts came out of the chair and wrapped themselves around Algan's body.

The ship was outfitted for fast flying and fully equipped with safety devices.

"Good-bye," Algan murmured, glancing at the screens that showed the Stellar Port.

He pushed the starter button. One microsecond later he saw most of the lights in the port go on. He thought he heard the shrieks of the sirens. Then a leaden weight fell on him, and on the screen the lights of the port merged.

He could barely move his arms, but he managed to put his hand in the large pocket of his spacesuit and, smiling, gently touched the polished surface of the chessboard.

The long quest had begun, but for the time being he could sleep. For many long weeks it would be up to the countless controls that made up his ship to carry on.

"Have a pleasant trip," said Nogaro. Algan started. But the voice went on and Algan realized that it was a recording.

"I can only assume everything went all right since you got off into space without a hitch. I hope everything will continue to do so. I want to give you some advice about your future job.

"First of all, a warning: don't try to outwit Betelgeuse. We could find you even in the farthest corners of the galaxy if we wanted to. We know you don't like the central government. You may be sure Betelgeuse sent you on this strange mission because we're convinced that we can get from you what we want, even against your wishes.

"Don't take this as a mark of unfriendliness. On the contrary. Betelgeuse needs her rebels more than her followers.

"A piece of advice: when you reach Glania, don't try to land in the Stellar Port; you would instantly be captured. Your description and classification as a pirate have now been transmitted to all the receiving stations by Betelgeuse. We had no alternative, as otherwise our sincerity might have been questioned. Never forget you are a free agent. Betelgeuse will deny, categorically, anything you say about your connection with the central government.

"So, land somewhere on the planet, not too far from the Stellar Port, and go on foot to the city, which surrounds the port. You won't have any trouble with your rocket in crossing the detective barrages. Security, on those distant planets, is very lax, and we'll see to it that it is even more so in the month to come. Contact the man we told you about but don't tell him who sent you.

"After that, well, you're free. We'll try to show you, when you come back, that the new world that is being created is as good as the old ones.

"We trust you.

"And never forget, Jerg Algan, that I'm your friend. If the need arises, say that I sent you. My name is known here and there in space. It might help.

"See you, Algan."

See you. That postulated all sorts of improbabilities: that Algan would return from his trip to the ends of the galaxy; that Nogaro would still be alive when Algan went back to Betelgeuse, despite the time warp, despite the frightening extension to the speed of light of the seconds spent in space.

"See you, Nogaro," Jerg Algan muttered unconsciously.

The lengthy trip in space consisted of going through a dark tunnel, of coming close to marvels without being aware of them, of defying time and death as one heard their approach in the clicking of the gears. It consisted of waiting, blind and oblivious to cold and space, of being a prisoner in the center of the whole universe, sleeping with eyes open, of drinking and of eating without appetite, reading without curiosity. The whole experience was both normal and miraculous.

All things vacillate and crumble in the space that separates the stars. Even after centuries of interstellar navigation, men still preserve the reflexes and habits of that species that has never freed itself from the Earth.

The psychological problems that arose during the course of the various phases of the conquest were solved less easily than many technical problems.

Personnel technicians responded to the challenge of the stars in two ways. At first they tried to modify man, to change his thinking, to free him from his fear, in short to have him consider as normal the oddest distortions of time and space. They tried to imprint data upon his subconscious which he could grasp intellectually. They finally succeeded in forging for him a sort of armor by sub-jecting him, without risk, to the most disconcerting experiments. The training was painful, but the game was worth the candle; it was the apprenticeship of the stars.

But this did not satisfy the psychologists. They knew that it was not enough for man to Adjust to his conditions. They wanted to arrange things so that man would carry with him everywhere his ideal environment, in the image, at first, of the Earth, then, with the passage of time and conquest, of other worlds. So they transformed the heavy spaceships into gigantic machines that created illusions that would fulfill the need for security of the conquerors. They recreated, inside the spaceships, landscapes of the Earth, forests, fields stretch-ing out of sight, a sun floating in the sky, starry nights. They had at their dispos-al the powerful magic of light. The grass in its field, the clouds in their skies, the mountains outlined against their horizons, were only illusions. But these were the illusions man needed.

However, the exploration ships which were light, quick, and maneuverable had none of these refinements—a great loss to Jerg Algan, who was on his way to Glania.

He floated through silent space in such a steady light that he began to feel he was plunged in darkness and he also felt, while the long hours passed, as though everything that made up his individuality was dissolving inside him. His memory no longer kept track of time; it gradually became impossible for him to put a date on a past event. Sometimes all that was needed was a gesture to put him in touch once more with reality and to become himself again. But reality was so depressing that he would take refuge again in the world of sleep.

The machines looked after the ship as well as after him. G-meters with del-icate gears kept the ship on course. Computers charted the safest and most eco-nomical course.

Time passed.

Days and weeks of space time; months and years of Earth time. Algan, half-asleep, dreamed of days spent on the Earth and was unable to sort out the good days from the bad. He thought of the thirty-two years of life, the dust of centuries which would cover the Earth when he returned. He thought about Be-telgeuse and her infernal power and grandeur, of the Puritans of the Ten Planets and their undermining schemes; about the beginnings of various civilizations scattered about in the human galaxy, which hoped to survive and to develop and which in turn looked forward to imposing their rule upon the whole universe despite the absurdly small number of humans scattered like sand on the face of the stars.

He thought about all the things that could happen, all the things men might accomplish; the stars they would relight, the worlds they would displace, or that they might someday create, the tremendous energies they would unleash, the beings they would meet, the other galaxies they would people, the unimaginable universes to which they would emigrate after the suns on the face of this universe had gone out one by one. He thought about everything that had been accomplished and was still to be accomplished, those planets which would never again be what they had been before the coming of man, and all the other dark diamonds of the night which were lost in the depths of their spatial solitude, awaiting the arrival of stellar ships; he thought about the men who would do these things because they had to be done, because other men had prophesied them and had wanted them done even before the nearest stars had been reached. And he told himself that they too would be torn between their memories and that strange wave, that thirst for conquest that would spur them on.

He wondered what sense all this made and decided it made very little. The only sense it did make was that man was actually doing these things; and, conversely, man made sense only because he was turning his dreams into reality.

It made sense only because it was painful. Each leap forward, each new conquest was a new birth. And every birth was painful.

Long, long ago, Algan thought, man had known periods of dormancy during which he had made no progress, when he had even lost the ground gained during the preceding eras. For a while, he would settle into comfortable immobility and allow himself to be sucked up into the quicksands of habit.

Long, long ago. For the conquest of the stars was a rebirth for the whole of humanity. And it was to be followed by an infinite number of other rebirths, perhaps even more painful ones, or other rejections of the past. One could not simply be content to be born, nor could one refuse to be born.

Man had to go on, he had to explore the huge new world that opened up before his eyes, his fingers, and his virgin mind.

The history of the species was roughly repeated in the history of each individual. There was the prelogical mentality of the infant, then the apprenticeship of logical thought. Then came the adolescent's attachment to his native planet. The final stage was contact with space, with its attendant distortions of time, its pulling away from the past. In the same way the whole of humanity had been prelogical, then logical, but so closely bound by its conditions of life that emigration to other worlds had seemed almost sacrilegious. The final progression was to the stars.

Humanity was in the process of becoming stellar. It still had reflexes of fear, of distrust, like those of the adult who leaves home for the first time, and forever. It had not solved some of its inner contradictions. Was it neurotic? Perhaps the human species in its infancy had undergone such shocks upon coming into contact with reality, and was still so bruised from that contact, that the slightest deviation from the norm aroused in man's innermost being an instinctive desire for flight. Humanity had almost learned to shed its fear of space, but it still had to master its terror of time. The Puritans had solved the problem by denying its existence, by refusing to ascribe the slightest importance in their lives to time. Betelgeuse had skirted the difficulty by toting up, in the course of the years, the experiences of dead men.

Jerg Algan thought that perhaps man would grasp time as he had grasped space. He might someday send emissaries into the future with the sole aim of directing certain great projects to be carried out over several centuries. Emissaries willing to give up their country, whose sole family would be all of humanity, past and future, and whose sole country would be the universe.

And the weeks went by.

About one light-year away from Glania, the ship began to lose speed. At that distance, the sun of Glania was only a luminous dot impossible to distinguish in the fog of stars which filled that section of the sky. But its diameter increased rapidly, as Jerg Algan studied all the data about Glania that the ship contained and all the information Nogaro had left for him about the man he was to look up.

Glania was the only planet revolving around that sun. Stars having only one planet were quite rare in the galaxy, at least in the explored regions, because most of the suns were either planet-less or had a complete system of planets. But this no longer held near the center of the galaxy, for the probability of the destruction of a certain number of worlds increased with the stellar density.

The ship got into orbital position for the planet. The computers traced out a landing trajectory that might lead possible detectors on Glania to mistake it for a large meteor. Jerg Algan picked out, with the help of maps, a plain near the Stellar Port for his landing. Low hills would permit him to conceal his ship and it would take only a few days to cover on foot the distance to the Stellar Port. Then, if all went well, he could return to his ship and plunge more deeply into space toward the center of the galaxy.

He saw the planet grow larger on the screens. It was a rose-colored world, just as the Earth is essentially a green one.

It was no doubt partly because of the vegetation, but even more because of the relative proximity of a red star which probably, during the greater part of the year, lighted up the nights in Glania.

The metal straps once more came out and wrapped themselves around Algan. For the second time he ran his hands over the controls and got ready to feed data to the computers. These would be analyzed and the best course chosen.

The ship plummeted toward the surface of the planet in order to escape, insofar as possible, the beams of detectors sweeping the skies. It penetrated with a whistling sound into the planet's atmosphere; its propellers went into action, braking its speed suddenly. But it had been built to withstand shocks of that kind and complicated adapters went into operation to soften, for Algan, the impact of deceleration.

The ship came to a stop a few yards from the ground. Then it went down slowly as if held by ropes. It finally came to rest, crushing under its bulk some of the pink vegetation and mossy bushes that covered the plain as far as the eye could reach.

Algan looked at the screens. The ship dominated a pink plain that turned to violet toward the horizon. Night was closing in; the white light of day was yielding to the red light of night. Nothing moved. It looked as though there were no forms of animal life on this world, as though only a primitive vegetation subsisted there.

The reports he had read had indicated this. He got up and opened the door. He gathered into a knapsack some rations, first aid supplies, some tools, and slipped the chessboard into his pocket.

Glania was quite the opposite of a deserted world, even though it gave the impression of being a desolate planet, he thought, as he was about to go out the door. There was not a single rock, a single place that was not covered with the pink moss that seemed to be everywhere on this planet. He wondered whether, if the carpet was thick, it would seriously hamper his walking. He was thirty-five miles from the Stellar Port. On Earth it would have been a short distance, but perhaps he had been wrong to think in terms of his hunting days on the Old Planet.

He began to go down the steps, when he was startled by a dull roar. A strong wind pinned him against the side of the ship as he felt it give way. Then he understood. The ship was keeling over, disappearing into the ground.

That dull vegetation concealed a moving terrain. He paused to think. He could try to get back at the controls, start the engine, and attempt to free the ship from the bog. The maneuver would be dangerous but not impossible.

But he hesitated too long and the decision was made for him. The ship suddenly oscillated as though tossed about by a stormy sea and the wind caught Jerg Algan and flung him from the craft. He fell, painlessly, onto a heavy carpet of moss. He sank into the vegetation as if on a feather bed. He struggled, found himself on firm ground, and stood up.

The ship keeled over completely and sank between two clumps of pink, spongy, tall grasses, noiselessly, as though swallowed up by an invisible maw.

It's prow stood up, for a short time, then disappeared completely as Algan looked on, stunned and despairing. There he stood, adrift on the surface of a mud planet, unable to make up his mind whether or not to set out for the port.

He was alone, without weapons, friends, or maps, with a three weeks' supply of food, a compass, an old chessboard and vague information of the existence of a Stellar Port thirty-five miles away.

Was this what Nogaro had intended? Or had he slipped up somewhere? Had he thought the ship light enough to be borne on the surface of the planet?

It no longer mattered.

Before it had even gotten under way, Algan's mission turned out to be pointless.

Algan's progress was easier than he had anticipated. He managed to clear a way for himself between the tall clumps of moss which the red star in the sky was now tinting a blood red.

The gusts of wind died down. The succession of days and nights seemed to produce gigantic atmospheric tides every evening and morning.

He walked a number of miles, then felt exhausted. He chose a place where the ground appeared to be particularly firm. The air was soft and warm. He stretched out, tried to forget the red light on his eyelids, and fell asleep.

CHAPTER VI
Accursed Worlds

As Algan lay back with his eyes closed, on soft purplish moss, he convinced himself that the fabric of space was made up of the broken woof and warp of matter and light, facts and causes. And because he, Jerg Algan, had occupied at a given moment, a given place in space at the crucial and decisive moment of his birth, because he had grown up in a world that was known as the Earth, in a civilization that measured the universe in terms of light- years, and among men who were in the process of becoming too dissimilar to understand one another, what had happened had to happen, to him; it couldn't happen to anyone else and nothing different could have happened to him. The idea of this narrow destiny was a strange one, but it was a final conclusion; there was, in time and space, a narrow passage labeled Jerg Algan, which he would follow for the remainder of his life and, however long he lived, he would never be able to get off that track which had been inscribed in the stars.

It was a confused, upsetting thought. Never, since he could remember, had he couched it in such precise and succinct terms. He had always had, in varying degrees, a sense of freedom, but this was vanishing. He now knew that he was nothing but a pawn on a chessboard similar to the one in his pocket, but an infinitely larger one, and those who were moving him about were pawns also, even though they were probably not aware of this; and so on ad infinitum. He had often felt in the past, while hunting in the great forests of the Earth, the tight bonds between hunter and hunted that make death of the one as inevitable as that of the other. These bonds were made up of the forest, the paths, the wind, the scents, the stars, the whole universe, but they remained strangely indefinite, almost imperceptible. The quarry was vaguely and instinctively aware of them; the hunter found himself dwelling on them mentally, knowing and doubting, too ignorant about the final structure of the universe to dare venture a decision.

But now he found he was both the hunter and the quarry and that the hunting field or the chessboard was really the entire universe, in each square, a planet, or a star, or another galaxy.

And the point of the game was simply a question.

What is man?

And there was another question, which was somehow a part of the game, of the setup which had been written in the stars from time immemorial.

Was there, in space, something other than man, sufficiently different from him not to be human?

No one had ever been able to answer this, neither bearded philosophers poring over their scribblings, nor white-coated scientists peering into their microscopes or scanning their instrument panels. No one had ever been able to answer because the time for answers had not come.

But now it had. Two huge armies, or perhaps only the populations of two anthills, had come within touching distance, but without knowledge of one another. The shock was imminent. All that was needed was the displacement of one pawn to set off the battle.

Perhaps the pawn's name was Jerg Algan.

Or perhaps he was not that important? Perhaps on the periphery of the two dark empires large numbers of pawns or guards stood ready to hail one another or slaughter one another? Perhaps his quarry and a hunter were lying in wait for him somewhere in this new world and they were as ignorant and as uneasy as he was?

He got up and shook himself. The track he had made had almost disappeared during the night. There was nothing left in the moss and pink vegetation except a sort of purple scar which would remain in the vegetal skin of the planet for a long time to come. He wondered what was happening to his spaceship. He supposed that it was sinking into a living abyss between heavy pulsating masses, slipping along spongy tree trunks.

He collected his gear and set out. The night was red and the feeble light from the distant crimson star threw a bloody reflection on the plain. He easily cleared a passage for himself between the clumps of vegetation. The ground underfoot was spongy but firm enough to support his weight.

He managed to go in an almost straight line. From time to time he checked his compass. He calculated he was roughly twenty miles from the small astral port. The lightness of his pack would enable him to reach it in ten hours or so.

His fear had left him long ago. His nerves and muscles had gotten back into habits picked up during his long outings through the wild and deserted sections of the Earth. The night was fresh, but his clothes protected him from the cold. Every once in a while he heard a muffled cry, a kind of long, monotonous lamentation, but he had not yet seen any form of mobile life and the plant life had shown no hostility toward him.

This plant life seemed to be of an extremely elementary type, of the kind that must have been on the Earth millions of years before the appearance of man and similar to those on Terrestrial type planets, crude models of what was to come later.

Jerg Algan was unable to fathom the reason for the dissemination in space of all those laboratory cultures. Perhaps they were intended to produce some form of conscious life after a tremendously long lapse of time; or they could be failures. Perhaps the game was being played on such a colossally large chessboard that the less important rules of the game escaped a mere human.

The wind came up and the mossy bushes bent and moaned under its touch. The wind was part of the game insofar as it hindered or helped Algan's walking, insofar as it delayed or hurried a meeting which could be decisive for the future of the human race.

It propelled Algan forward. It lifted him and bore him in the air, like a spider hanging on its thread, far above the red plain populated with blurred, quivering, blood-colored masses. The wind roared in Algan's ears and carried him along in the dense air just as a river carries a twig.

But the training Algan had undergone in the port of Dark preserved him from fear. He did what he should: he began to swim in the icy air. Then, suddenly, he fell.

The red plain was divided in two by a gigantic fault. Algan clearly saw the two cliffs which edged a deep valley.

He beat the air with his arms and succeeded in getting upright. His movements became coordinated and he managed to control his fall. He fell onto the ground and landed in a moss bush from which he was able to extricate himself. The edge of the chasm was a few yards from where he had fallen. The city, naturally, was on the other side.

He sat on the edge of the cliff and looked at the sky. The red star dominated the firmament, eclipsing the weaker light from the other stars which were so numerous that the entire sky seemed plastered with them. The nearness of the center of the galaxy was perceptible, and here the stars were so close to one another that the night hardly differed from the day in quantity of light; only the quality was different.

There was nothing to do. The crevasse was an enormous obstacle, as enormous as a river for an ant. He had reached the outer edge of one of the squares and the next square was inaccessible. He had come all this way just to make that discovery.

He leaned over the edge of the precipice and saw at the very bottom the moving trunks of trees quivering in the dense air like Earth algae quivering in a sea current. Then he looked up and saw, on the opposite side of the break, the other cliff, shiny as a silver wall, gleaming under the fire of the red star. Colossal pillars, columns of cyclopean temples whose roofs had disappeared, covered with tufts of violet vegetation, stood between those high walls.

The wind had died down. And this sudden calm caught his attention. There was something in this fault that was stronger than the wind or which controlled a current of air able to balance the strength of the wind which had carried him at first. He remembered that he had started to fall just as he was flying over the edge. He felt something warm on his face, but he could see nothing. He ran his hand over the cold surface of the cliff and had the impression he was dipping his fingers into a liquid. Suddenly he understood.

The banks of the crevasse were as bare of vegetation as the edges of a river and the moss that covered the bottom of the valley behaved like the algae of the Earth: because it had the same texture and was subject to the same conditions. This enormous fault was a river. But, on this planet of low density, where weight counted little and where the air was so thick, it was nothing but a river of gas, an invisible serpentine that had dug its bed, in the course of ages, in the crystalline crust of the planet.

It was, Algan realized, a river of gas even denser than that of the air of the planet, a gas that probably could not be breathed, but that might carry him, provided that he made the necessary movements and that the current helped. He pulled out a handful of moss on the edge of the cliff and threw it into the invisible current; it sank slowly, as if held by a string, drifting toward the red stillness below.

He readjusted his gear, tightened the straps of his knapsack, and slid along the side of the cliff, clutching the crystalline brink. He felt as though he were diving into a lukewarm liquid; then he sank and the current bore him along. His lungs filled with a heavy, thick, viscous gas and he suffocated. He made a few desperate efforts and suddenly surfaced. He breathed the air deeply. The current carried him along without his needing to swim at all. Although his own bodily density was greater than the gas in which he was immersed, the surface tension kept him from sinking. But he was as powerless as an ant carried by a river or stuck in a drop of water.

He looked down and saw, more than a thousand yards below, through a blood-colored fog, the open petals of quivering algae. Then he heard a hissing sound that soon changed into a deafening roar. Without being able to see anything, he was dragged into a whirlwind and before he had time to dive to escape the maelstrom he sank and lost consciousness.

His head hit something hard and his fingers weakly clutched a rope. He pulled himself up and filled his lungs with air. His ears were pounding. He heard shouts and saw, right against him, a dark bulk which hid the further cliff from him. He was conscious of calls uttered in a human voice; he heard the sound of bare feet running along a deck; he felt himself being hoisted and put down roughly on a hard surface. Hands ran over him. He tried to speak but when he opened his eyes the red star in the sky shone brutally in his face and everything around him became dark and silent.

It was day and with the dawn the storm that had agitated the surface of the gaseous river had died down. Jerg Algan walked from one end of the deck to the other. The crudely built ship, hewn from the spongy and light trunk of a pink tree was about one hundred yards long and Algan could see why. The difference in density between the wood of the trees and the gaseous current was so slight that a very large submerged bulk was required to carry even a light load. The ship merely followed the current. It had no sort of motor and more or less held its course by means of enormous sails, submerged in the gaseous river. The prow reared majestically above the invisible surface and plowed through imperceptible waves while in her stern there was an around-the-clock lookout perched in the crow's nest.

A ship of this sort was quickly put together. Her builders had to abandon her at the end of the voyage because it was impossible for her to make the trip back against the current.

The sailors of this strange ship were deeply tanned men from the center of the galaxy. They did not pay much attention to their involuntary passenger. They were talking in a language unknown to him, probably an offshoot of one of the numerous tongues spoken in the

galaxy out so ancient that even an experienced linguist would have been unable to make out any of it.

There were about ten of them on deck, but every once in a while Algan could hear sounds of laughing and singing from the hold and he decided this must be a team of hunters or perhaps miners who, at the close of their season, were going to the Stellar Port to peddle their meager wares.

It was difficult to tell where they came from. They could have been the remote descendants of the passengers and crew of a ship unable to leave the planet because of an unrepairable breakdown; or perhaps their ancestors had been explorers purposely abandoned by Betelgeuse in the hope that they would start another civilization. They appeared to have sunk back to an almost primitive level, but their manners were still civilized. What little they knew about their ancestors' past and of the civilization of the galaxy made a queer mixture in their minds. They did not seem unhappy. In its own way, this planet was hospitable and these men had rediscovered the way of life of those civilizations, now almost totally forgotten, which had once swarmed over the continental surfaces of the Earth and had dispersed to the Pacific Islands.

But the new Pacific of the civilization under the rule of Betelgeuse was the whole of space: the enchanted isles or the legendary cursed lands orbited in the dark about the multiple suns of the galaxy.

The analogy was senseless, Jerg Algan realized, as he lay stretched out in the prow of the ship on the spongy wood of the deck, turning over and over again in his hand the small chessboard with its delicate etchings and symbols of the universe, gazing at the sinuous banks of the invisible river, noting that the slow waves of the surface that lapped lightly against the high hull were like a mist.

The analogy was senseless because the scattering of the ancient civilization of the Pacific had been determined by chance and by History whereas this one was man-made. Men had been left behind on new worlds, purposely, so that History could be molded. Behind this cold-blooded concept of the conquest of the galaxy stood Betelgeuse. Betelgeuse which, not content with having given man control of the universe, intended to have him control human History as well: hence control the future.

A sudden cold fury filled Jerg Algan. His hands, resting on the polished wood of the chessboard, began to shake. All his former rancor against Betelgeuse returned tenfold. But he could now see that his hatred had taken on new dimensions. He was only a pawn, but he belonged to the opposition; he was on the other side of the chessboard, wherever that might be. Betelgeuse was not only his enemy, it was also the adversary in the cosmic game.

The lookout gave a prolonged yell, and Algan, afraid of some trick, half sat up. But all he saw was a huge net of vegetable fibers blocking the entire width of the gaseous river, caught here and there on the enormous rocky bolts that stood out in the valley bed like trunks of dead trees. Beyond that were the tall white buildings of the Stellar Port that rose from the lavender tangle of the grassland.

The men rushed out on deck and pulled up the heavy center board. The ship slowed down gradually. Her prow finally got caught in the nets and stopped, almost in the middle of the river, seemingly afloat in midair.

Ropes were connected to her sides and dragged by invisible tugs; she was pulled to shore. She came alongside the silver cliff, just below the buildings of the Stellar Port, and the men ran forward along the winding track made by thousands of bare feet going between the river of gas and the village.

The chalky white face, creased by hundreds of wrinkles, slowly turned toward Algan. The old man sat in a shapeless heap in a metal armchair that must have been rescued, long ago, from the smoking remains of a ship.

His half-open eyes roamed over the muddy courtyard, bounded at one end by a cabin of sorts made from the spongy wood of the forests of the planet and on the other by thorny cactus hedges imported from the Earth. These green plants stood out strangely against the pink and lavender vegetation of the planet

Above the courtyard and the cabin, the Stellar Port loomed silently, rearing its tall white bulk toward the stars, the silhouette of a watchman. The carcasses of spaceships showed through here and there amid the invading vegetation; their dismembered keels evoked the obsolete contours of ships dating from the first period of the conquest.

The old man's thin, dry lips moved soundlessly. Then they began to let out, one by one, in weak and muffled tones, unknown words. Finally, very slowly, as though they were pushing against a heavy weight, they formed words Algan could understand.

"It's been so long, so long," the old man said.

He stopped and lifted his right hand from his knees, stretching it out to Algan. In the light of day it looked almost blue, and its skin was so parchment-like that every vein, tendon, muscle, bone in it was clearly visible.

"I have forgotten the words," the old man said. "It's so long since I've spoken this language. They're only children here, you know, children ... you have to talk to them like children."

"I come from the Earth," said Algan in a low voice, afraid of seeing the shape crumble into dust if his voice shook the air too loudly.

"What?" the old man shouted in a sharp voice, leaning forward and seeming finally to focus his yellow, rheumy eyes on the visitor.

"I come from the Earth," Algan said, more loudly.

He took a step forward and stayed there, right in the middle of the court-yard, his feet in the mud. He undid, with a shaky hand, the straps of the bag containing his equipment, inspecting the cabin and the green, incongruous spots made by the cactus.

"The Earth is no more?" the old man said. He was obviously groping for words and Algan thought he might have expressed himself badly.

"The Earth is no more," the old man repeated. "The radio mentions only Betelgeuse nowadays."

He closed his eyes and nodded his head as though approving his own memories.

"I can remember a time," he said, "long, long ago, when Betelgeuse was just a colony and the Earth was strong and powerful and we were proud pilots. Yes indeed, proud pilots. We used to hop from one world to another in those days; we were intoxicated and never tired. We needed constant change, that's why we're still alive.

"But, you see, we were unimportant. No, not really. Those who remained on the planets we had discovered were important. They died, but before dying they had become rulers, merchants, technicians. We were only hotheads who leaped from one world to another without ever stopping to catch our breath, and we lived it up. We saw the others grow old and die; at the return of every trip, we found that the sons of our friends had taken their fathers' place and we went off again and the years piled up. But the Earth ... there is no more Earth. I never saw the Earth again. It's finished now, as I am. I'll never see it again, you know."

His eyes blinked and he put his hands on the arms of his chair.

"Who are you, my boy?" he said. "I've never seen you around. You're a spaceman, aren't you? I thought so right away. You don't talk in that damned jargon that they use here, but I have almost forgotten the nice old language of the ships."

"I come from the Earth; my name is Algan, Jerg Algan. I was told on Ulcinor that you could give me some information."

Algan was surprised by the coldness of his own voice. He could feel, growing within himself, more and more clearly, a being whose icy lucidity frightened him. He dropped his bag on the ground and opened it. He took the chessboard out of it and placed it under the old man's eyes. He leaned down toward the wrinkled face, intently watching any change of expression.

The old man laughed bitterly; Algan shivered.

"They wouldn't believe me, oh no, they wouldn't believe me and they left me to rot in this damned world, and now they're seeking me out because they are afraid, because the Times are drawing nearer and the Masters are grumbling, because they are discovering the Accursed Worlds one by one. It was quite an expedition, wasn't it? Complete with a young skipper and brand-new ships. And this is all that remains, an old fool on his damned planet.

And not even a ship from the Earth to make an occasional stopover."

He looked up and stared hard at Algan. There still remained in his eyes an icy look that must once have been unbearable, which had gradually hardened in the light of countless suns and in the contemplation of the ghastly blackness of hopeless space.

"Who are you," he asked in his cracked voice, "that you should have in your possession the chessboard of the Masters? During the course of my long life, I've seen it just three times. Once, it was the one you have, or one exactly like it, and the other two times I saw it etched on the black walls of those damnable citadels. 'Who are you? Get out, leave me in peace. I've run away all my life from that memory. Or are you one of their men? Have you come to take my soul, as you did from all the other poor spacemen you buried alive?"

"I'm just looking for information," said Algan, simply. "I've come from Ulcinor where I found this board. I'm looking for some weapon to destroy Betelgeuse. I wasn't able to land in the Stellar Port of this planet because my spaceship was brought down in your sky even before I had time to land. I ended up in the underbrush and I walked for miles and miles. I was rescued by humans and I know that they won't talk or if they do that Betelgeuse will pay no attention to their gossip. I'm counting on you. You can call the men from the Stellar Port and have me arrested, but I think you'd first like to hear what I have to say."

"Perhaps," said the old man. "Perhaps." His head nodded gently on his shoulders. "I believe you. I, too, had to run away, once. I believe you. I'm going to help you. I can't do much, but I'll do it. You've gone through space; so did I. That's enough. What is it that you want?"

"I want to know exactly what happened to you from the moment the expedition you took part in disappeared, how you survived, what you said to Betelgeuse, what you told the Puritan merchants. They are the ones who told me I'd find you here and that you are the only man who can help me."

"They know everything I know," said the old man. "They already knew everything when I was still traveling among the stars, let's see, about fifty, sixty years ago. They know more about me than I know myself. You'll learn nothing from me since they're the ones who sent you... But I can at least tell you the story, since you have the chessboard."

And as he talked, Jerg Algan listened, standing in the middle of the muddy courtyard, under a sky that was changing gradually from lilac to pink, between two barriers of green cactuses incongruously growing on this planet. As he listened, his fingers toyed with a chessboard of almost unbelievable antiquity, probably made by a breed in conceivably older than mankind and immeasurably better informed.

"We had ventured forth," the old man was saying, "toward the center of the galaxy. You know that the galaxy looks like a wheel and that the Earth is situated on a relatively exterior part of this wheel and that, from time immemorial, interstellar travelers have been tempted by the idea of reaching the mathematical center of the galaxy, the spot where space undergoes the most extraordinary distortions and where the stars are so numerous that the whole sky seems like a golden dome.

"We had a glorious takeoff in fifteen ships; we had a new captain and a crew of scientists, technicians, and astronauts like me, all bursting with pride. In those days, everyone hoped to be another little Christopher Columbus and believed in an Eldorado. But, young as we were, we all had had some experience, and we knew that most of the worlds that man discovers are frighteningly alien and hostile, so we took plenty of precautions.

"We had been cruising for at least one year and we had gone a considerable way toward the center of the galaxy, when we began to feel that we were entering a stellar region quite different from all the ones we had gone through up to then. Our instruments were no longer giving us exact information. And our charted positions, although we had verified them carefully, sometimes were inexact. The physicists who were taking part in the expedition classified all these inconsistencies and told us there was nothing to worry about. They even worked out what would be the conditions of the new space in which we were traveling so we stopped talking about it. We were all prepared to encounter the most extraordinary things and these barely decipherable variants in infinitely small decimals did not bother us.

"And yet, we ought to have suspected something, for it was the signal that we were coming into someone else's bailiwick. At that point we were well beyond the present human galaxy, closer to the center of the galaxy than any other expedition before us had been or has been since, to my knowledge.

"We crossed, in a layer of several light-years, a zone of eight dead suns or planet-less ones. Not one of our astronomers was able to explain this formation, but we thought no more about it. I now know that we had crossed a boundary and that we had reached an area about which the less said, the better.

"We finally discovered a star surrounded by planets. We explored them all and on the sixth one away from the sun, we discovered a black citadel.

"Oh, no one penetrated its secret. It was so large we could see it from the top of the sky, as we were circling the planet in our orbit. We zoomed down on it through the clouds and as we landed our spaceships crushed a large section of the jungle which covered the planet. We had not intercepted any message and the citadel appeared to be deserted.

"Having landed at a respectable distance, we started toward it. It was a planet of the Earth type, with, however, a greater force of gravity, which made it more difficult for us to walk. We painfully cut a path through a damp muggy jungle. The tremendous walls of the citadel loomed larger and larger as we approached.

"There was complete silence. It had probably been uninterrupted for thousands, perhaps millions of years. At least, so we thought. Our steps faltered somewhat. We jumped every time a twig cracked under our boots and our hands kept feeling for the butts of our weapons.

"We could see those high walls outlined against the sky; they were of such an enormous height that they had hidden the sky from us and threw into almost total darkness the landscape over which they loomed. We ventured as far as the foot of those tall, polished onyx cliffs which looked as though they might at any moment collapse on us, for they were planted at an angle and hung over the surrounding terrain.

"I noticed, when I was very close to the wall, that at about three times a man's height, there was an etching as fresh as if it had been done the day before, although its age was probably incalculable by our means of reckoning. It was a large-scale model of your chessboard."

"And the expedition vanished?" Algan asked. He was by now sitting on a pink log which he had gone into the cabin to get. He saw the walls of the Stellar Port slowly becoming luminescent as night fell and the brightness of the red star which was beginning to tint everything blood-colored became more definite.

"No," the old man said, "not that time. On that day, we went back to our ships to talk over the situation. The astronauts wanted to get out as quickly as possible. They could remember old legends and, although they didn't believe them, they were ready now to reconsider them. But the scientists and the only historian in the group were beside themselves with joy and were worried sick at the prospect of missing such an opportunity. In the long run, the point of view of the astronauts, who had the captain's ear, prevailed. We left the black octagonal citadel, higher than the highest mountains of the Earth, but we had marked on our maps the location of this planet with the very clear idea that we would come back after we had made a superficial exploration of that stellar sector.

"Barely a month later we landed on an absolutely dead planet, a world of emptiness and silence, one of those wandering rocks which used to terrify spacemen; it was a purely superstitious terror in any event, since the use of radar made it possible to avoid them and since they didn't get in the way of space exploration any more than did the other worlds. We had seen, from the top of our orbit, the second of these citadels.

"You see, our minds were blown. It was the first time that man had met any trace of another life in space, the hope of another civilization, and this civilization was, or had been, interstellar. There was no possible doubt. No two different breeds could have created, all the while unbeknown to the other, two such enormous and similar citadels, so visibly defying the laws governing the universe.

"We landed hastily. We built a station. We unpacked, our tractors. There was no need, on this planet, to fight off the jungle and, despite the absence of any atmosphere, our work was easy.

"I myself personally went around the citadel, in a tractor. And I noticed the sixty-four squares of the chessboard, carved in stone so hard that not even our sharpest tools could knick it.

"Was it a symbol or the key to the mystery? We kept asking ourselves that question and speculated endlessly. We looked up chess in the ship's library and we found out that all of the civilizations of the Earth, scattered throughout time and space, either had known it in the past, or knew it at that time; that in some of them the game had taken on religious or magic significance and that it corresponded strangely to certain characteristics of the human mind.

"We wondered if perhaps, behind those high slanting walls, there lay the mystery of the origin of mankind and of the secret of the origin of life.

"On the twenty-fifth day of our presence in that world, after more than fifteen months of space travel, the high gates of the citadel opened. They unveiled a world of light and interlaced curves such as we had never dreamed of and which no poet on hallucinogenic drugs had ever evoked.

"Small search parties ventured forth into the depths of the citadel. They returned, staggered by the dimensions and incomprehensible layout of the corridors of that labyrinth.

"It was then that we made a capital mistake. We decided to send the entire expeditionary force to explore the citadel. The scientists had been most pressing in their request and the astronauts had stopped believing in any danger.

"I was left on the outside to guard the gates. I served as a clearing house for messages. The hours went by. I was dozing off in my spacesuit in spite of the drugs I had taken to stay awake, when I saw the high black gates, which were slanted just like the walls, silently close. They were only huge slabs, each engraved with the chessboard signs, which pivoted inside the citadel and which sealed hermetically the space that had remained open for several days. My earphones registered feebler and feebler signals; then nothing. I leaped into a tractor and made off at top speed toward the landing pad and the rockets, but suddenly a bolt of lightning shot across the sky and the landing pad and rockets exploded, lighting up, with giant flames, the entire horizon of the planet. I stopped the tractor, jumped off, and started to run. I had gone scarcely a few yards when, despite the lack of atmosphere, I heard a tremendous noise and an iron grip picked me up and threw me on the ground, just as a smoking crater opened up where the tractor had been."

"And that was all?" Jerg Algan asked.

"Almost all," the old man said. His voice had grown stronger as he talked and his words, many of them archaic, were spoken more and more easily. His eyes now shone serenely. The bitter irony which had filled them at first had disappeared.

"Almost all," he repeated. "For five days I waited for death because I had at most only a few weeks' supply of oxygen and food; then men came out of the sky and rescued me.

"But they were not from the Earth, nor from Betelgeuse, nor from any known world; their spacecraft were different from ours, their design less advanced than ours, as a matter of fact, and they didn't understand the language I spoke any better than I understood theirs."

CHAPTER VII
On the Other Side of the galaxy

"Men?" asked Jerg Algan.

"Men," the old man repeated, nervously twisting his bony hands. "You can believe me or not; you may think I'm crazy. The people from Betelgeuse did and they sent me into exile here; or you may listen to me silently as did those Puritan merchants from Ulcinor who never even paid up one-quarter of the sum they had promised me. But I was rescued by men. They weren't even very different from us. Their ears were small and pointed, their skins very pale, they were smaller than we are; they moved faster and more gracefully, their language was unbelievably complex, from what I could understand, and they were, by temperament, less inclined to be active than we are, but they were unmistakably men. Do you know how I learned to communicate with them? You'll never guess, not in a thousand years. You'll never work it out even though it was entirely and absolutely logical. By playing chess. That's all. You see, the king, the queen, the pawns, can be given other names and take on other shapes, but the moves are the same everywhere, and the possible combinations of the sixty-four boxes are infinite, almost as infinite as the universe itself."

"Where did they come from?" Algan asked. His heart was thumping violently and his voice had become harsh. He suddenly felt the accumulated weight of fatigue, but he struggled to keep his eyes open and to keep his wits about him.

"From the other side of the galaxy," the old man said quietly. His features had relaxed and his hands were now quiet in his lap. "You probably won't believe me," he went on. "You probably think I'm an old fool who has a fixation after twenty years of exile. I can't prove anything. But, after all, you came to get a story, didn't you? Use it as you like."

"I believe you," Algan said softly, feeling the evening breeze on his neck. Three pink moons were rising above the Stellar Port; he had not noticed them the night before. Then he noticed that they were only the reflection, on the low-flying clouds, of the powerful projections of the tower.

It was impossible not to believe what he had heard; he couldn't help but trust an old man looking back on his past, who had witnessed a unique and incredible occurrence. But nothing was unbelievable anymore; the limits of the possible had definitely been pushed back by ships traveling through space at the speed of light; the world had suddenly expanded way beyond anything human experience had encompassed, and all that space left free in the minds of man belonged to the marvelous, to the fantastic. There had been similar periods in human history when new lands had been glimpsed in the Occident by navigators; doubt then had also been wiped out. Then, once the lands had been conquered, men had lost the feeling of intoxication. But in the sky there would always be lands to conquer and mysteries to solve.

Unless the new planets were already inhabited.

"It makes no difference to me, whether or not you believe me," the old man said in a voice that had suddenly grown tired and quavering. "They were men, just like us, that's all I can tell you, and they came from the other side of the galaxy. They were born under the same conditions as men on the Earth, and they didn't need to tell me the story of their species. I saw that I already knew it. You see, it was the story of mankind, with some differences, to be sure. Nature had been more generous to them than to us. Their development had been appreciably lengthened, stretched out. But it had been a steadier one. You see, they were less aggressive than men are, and they made fewer mistakes in the course of their history, not a whole lot less, just enough so that they didn't have to start their civilization all over again every few centuries. Their language was different from all those spoken by mankind, much more adaptable, but also much more complicated than man's. It seemed to me that they never had what we call a Tower of Babel. And their whole thought processes and even the makeup of their vocal systems were so different that I would be hard put to repeat a single one of their words; they never succeeded in pronouncing some of the Earthly phonemes.

"But this does not constitute a real difference. All this exists or has existed on the Earth and all men are men. And they were men also. And, like us, they wondered why they were men."

"Chance," whispered Algan. "The galaxy is so huge."

"Maybe," the old man answered in a low voice. "Maybe. I've never quite known what chance is. But I don't believe that chance is responsible for the simultaneous development of several human races in different parts of the galaxy nor for their coming into contact with one another at the precise moment that they learned to navigate, more or less skillfully, between the stars. And I have better reasons still for not believing it... Wait a minute.

I'm thirsty. Would you go into the cabin and get the metal canteen, which is on the table, and two glasses which you'll find on a shelf above the door. I can't talk very well when my throat is dry."

Algan got up and put the chessboard on the pink wood chopping block he'd been sitting on. He crossed the courtyard, conscious of the sloshing sound his boots made in the puddles which the light of the red moon had turned into an alarming shade of blood red. He had to duck as he went through the doorway and he hesitated in the pink twilit room. A thick layer of dust lay over most of the room. The removal of the chopping block had left a clean circle on the floor; two paths, one leading from the door to the rough-hewn wooden bed and one from the bed to the table, were equally clean. Algan pondered on the passage of time.

But the years that had passed here were nothing to those that had vanished in space and which provided all the old man's memories. He had been born at about the same time as some of Algan's ancestors, so long ago that no one on the Earth remembered their names. They probably had not left even a trace in the dusty archives of the Old Planet or on the gravestones of the cemeteries in Dark. He had spent a long time traveling between the stars and the span of his life had stretched out frighteningly. He was nothing more than a kind of fossil, washed ashore by the currents of space into this dirty and wretched cabin. He had, along with thousands of others, defied time and he alone had survived, but time, at last, was catching up with him.

In its own way.

It was inscribed in the dust which covered the floor and the furniture, which lay thickly over a piece of crystal wrenched from some unknown mountain, over the skull of a fabulous animal, over an ancient gun hanging on a beam in its dried-up leather holster.

The shiny metal canteen lay on the table. Algan grabbed it. From the shelf over the door he picked out two glasses that the dust seemed to have spared.

"Thank you," the old man said. "I have a hard time getting about now. Two years ago I still hunted in the forests around here, but that's all over now. Everything comes to an end, doesn't it? Even space."

Algan cautiously sipped his drink; it was smooth and sweet.

"They didn't come exactly from the other side of the galaxy, but their native land was so far away that the stars with which they were familiar are lost to us in a cloud of suns; charting them would be meaningless, even to our most learned astronomers. As a matter of fact, the expedition that rescued me was even farther from home than ours was. I told you that their spaceships were of a less advanced design than ours, and slower. But the passage of time didn't have the same meaning for them as for us, at least, not exactly the same. They didn't care whether they spent their entire lives on a spaceship or in their own world. They thought, somewhat like the people of Betelgeuse, in terms of continuity and of centuries. But that's neither here nor there.

"You know that the galaxy has been arbitrarily divided up by our cartographers into four quarters and into three hundred and sixty sectors, like a wheel. You know that the human galaxy is contained within the first four sectors. Well then, their home was in the twelfth sector, starting from the Earth's, at a distance from the center of the galaxy that is at least half the distance that separates the solar system from that same center. All this merely to point out that they lived in a region incredibly far away, even for a fast spaceship.

"But they weren't all that surprised to find me. I rather thought they'd been expecting to. They had strange beliefs: one of them was that there were other human populations, in even remoter sections of the galaxy, that around the star which is at the center of the galaxy, there are a series of human settlements separated by tremendous spaces, that these spaces are in the process of being colonized and are gradually merging with one another, thus beginning the formation of a gigantic chain around our suns.

"These may have been nothing more than legends. I never was able to find out whether they had really found other groups of humans that had reached a level of interstellar civilization, or whether these were only nebulous prophecies which the passage of centuries had shrouded in mystery. And when I spoke with the people of Betelgeuse about that human crown surrounding the center of the galaxy, they laughed in my face.

"But I'm positive that the men who rescued me knew something about the men of the Earth, or did know once, and then forgot in the aftermath of one of those upsets with which history abounds. They also maintained that there were no such human groupings in the regions closer to the center of the galaxy, that those regions were, in some way, forbidden territory; they said that they belonged to the Masters who created us. But they didn't know any better than we do why those hypothetical Masters had created us. They didn't even know whether those Masters were still alive or had died. The only thing they believed was that They had planted seeds in certain regions of space for a particular, secret purpose, and that during all this time They had waited for some plan, unknown to mankind, to go into effect and that at times, They had acted, but without mankind's being aware of it.

"You can look upon this as just a hodge-podge of legends, which is what I did for a long time. But I have come to believe that there are, a little everywhere on the periphery of the galaxy, human groups that are quietly beginning to explore their own stellar space. That's all I can tell you.

"After a long trip, they deposited me on a planet of the colonized Marches. I walked to a stellar port and managed to get myself repatriated in a roundabout way. One fine day I tried to sell my information to the Puritans, but Betelgeuse heard about it and when I had told members of the Psychological Police Force what I have just told you, they laughed at me and sent me into exile here. But I know that the Time is coming."

"I see," said Algan, "but haven't you some sort of evidence?" His voice shook with weariness and irritation.

"Not a shred," said the old man. "Or rather, yes: I am alive. What more do you want?"

"Why didn't they make themselves known? Why didn't they go on as far as Betelgeuse, as far as the Earth, since they had reached the borders of our empire?"

"They weren't interested. That was reason enough. They said that things had to be allowed to happen, that contact, then, would have been premature. I told you. They were never in a hurry in any of their enterprises."

"Is that all?" asked Algan.

"Nearly all. Except for this: we had in common with them (one) the fact that we were all men, hardly different from one another, (two) the chessboard

85

with the sixty- four squares, (three) zotl. Their flora and fauna were different from ours, not basically, but their evolution had been very different, almost the opposite of ours, and yet just as logical. But they had the same zotl, which they got from the same plant, like ours, with roots buried under feet of rock. And like ours, it did not grow on their native planet. We discovered zotl only after having explored worlds other than the one on which our kind originated. It was the same for them.

"You see, I think that in space there are three things to be found: first the chessboard, which is probably more ancient than man; then man himself, along with life as we know it; and last, zotl, which man in each case discovered only at a precise stage in his development. I believe that all three things are interrelated and that they have only just been brought together, here and elsewhere, and that there are correlations between them that we're only just beginning to perceive. It's up to you to discover them."

The old man looked up and stared at the red star that lit up the night. His dry lips were quivering and the hands on his knees were shaking. The last breaths of wind had died with nightfall. He got up, leaning on a cane.

"Come in now," he said to Algan. "Let's eat and rest."

Algan listened to the slow and irregular breathing of the old man. He had rolled up in a blanket and was lying on the wooden floor, his knapsack used as a pillow, and had waited unsuccessfully for sleep to come.

His gaze roamed over the wooden ceiling, in the red light of night. His nerves were on edge. The silence was total, marked only by the light, familiar, reassuring sounds of the night and the old man's breathing.

He could not sleep. He was thinking.

It could be that there was nothing, in all he had heard, but unverifiable facts and legends. It seemed most likely. Almost certainly so.

On the other hand, there was space, its extent, the myriad worlds which dotted it, and the possibilities it held; there were also hundreds of questions as old as man that had never been answered. But that wasn't all. There were other things.

There were those rumors which circulated throughout the galaxy, of the expectation of the discovery of another thinking breed, human or nonhuman, that was not the result of a series of mutations of an Earth breed, like the men of Aro whose eyes had no visible pupils.

There were many other considerations as well: Nogaro; the curiosity and interest which the people of Betelgeuse as well as the Puritans on Ulcinor and on the Ten Planets showed in the tales brought back by their explorers; the conviction shared by Nogaro and the shopkeeper of Ulcinor that space held certain secrets that man could not fathom.

There was the chessboard.

There were also the proximity of a silent, invisible army, the moving of pawns on a cosmic playing board, the rivalry between Betelgeuse and Ulcinor about what might spring out from space. There was Jerg Algan, with what he knew and what he did not know; his hopes, the problems he was to clear up. There were two or three expeditions that had been completely destroyed, the strange visions produced by zotl, the immense black citadels which the Puritans believed in and which the people of Betelgeuse seemed to know about.

The solution to the problem might lie in Betelgeuse. Perhaps it lay in the electronic memory banks of giant computers, in archives. It might even be that Jerg Algan was a red herring chosen to mislead the Ulcinor Puritans.

But there was the chessboard and its sixty-four squares; its general look of a double-entry table; its incomprehensible figures and its almost infinite possibilities of mathematical combinations.

Was it a symbol? The symbol of the universe?

But was it only a symbol? Jerg Algan wondered, staring at the window, feeling on his back the unevenness of the floor and on his skin the damp coolness of the night.

Or was it a reality, a key, a sort of plan; or perhaps a door that would unlock the mystery of the black citadels, placing them at the service of whoever could gather the scattered pieces of the puzzle and fit them together?

Slipping his hand under his head, he rummaged in his knapsack and took out the chessboard. With his thumb he stroked the cold, smooth surface of the wood. The chessboard was a key of greater antiquity than man and had waited patiently throughout all the human civilizations for men to learn how to use it. And perhaps the citadels scattered in space were as numerous as those grains of rice which the king in the legend promised to the inventor of the chessboard: one grain on the first box, two on the second, four on the third, continuing in a geometric progression until the sixty-fourth box would have contained more rice than the whole Earth could have produced.

Or was the chessboard a plan of space, with the trajectories followed by the pawns always representing a simple visualization of certain privileged trajectories? Or was the game of chess a roundabout way of preparing man's mind for certain tasks? And perhaps the outcome of certain games was only the result of certain problems posed by certain infinitely complex spatial coordinates.

For the problems which the chess game posed were primarily geometric, spatial, and topologic ones. These were complicated questions having to do with itineraries to be followed while avoiding the destructive effect of certain pawns placed in strategic locations.

In the middle, for example.

Was the chessboard really made of wood? he wondered as his fingers lightly touched the soft polished surface without being able to feel even the slightest space between the squares, as there certainly would have had to be if the board had been made of pieces of wood stuck together.

He had assumed from the very first that the chessboard had been carved from one or several kinds of very finely grained wood. He had thought of wood because nearly all the old chessboards he had seen on the Earth had been made of it.

He began to think that no piece of wood could have been kept in such a fine state of preservation for so long.

Unless the chessboard was a forgery, a crude trap.

He rejected that thought. The Puritans as well as the people of Betelgeuse had extremely precise scientific means for estimating the age of an object, even if forged in metal, and they would never have been fooled. And what possible reason could they have had to take advantage of him, Jerg Algan, a man from the Old Planet, a rebel against Betelgeuse, a lone wolf lost in the Marches of the human galaxy?

And then there was zotl. Zotl and the chessboard.

Zotl, that strange drug which was in no way harmful, which affected the nervous system and enabled it to perceive certain otherwise incomprehensible realities.

Psychologists said they were illusory, dangerous, traumatizing. But, countered mathematicians and physicists, the universes which could be explored by drinking zotl were perfectly logical, much more so than a man's dream; they were as logical as the universe itself.

Kinesthetic delirium the psychologists retorted. Just a crossing of nerve fibers. You see what you ought to hear and hear what you ought to see.

Neurologists took no interest.

The chessboard and zotl.

Zotl was a door that half-opened on incomprehensible worlds. And the chessboard was like a pass, a plan which flowed you to take your bearings and to glimpse certain worlds that were comprehensible and quite real.

Zotl and the chessboard.

They complemented each other, like a lock and a key, so long as there was a man's hand to slip one into the other, and to push open the door.

But the man had to do more than just take a quick look into the room that had been unlocked; he had to enter it boldly.

Boldly.

There were the chessboard and Jerg Algan.

He got up suddenly in the pale light which bathed the room, and shook the old man.

"Wake up," he shouted, leaning over the wrinkled gray face.

"What is it?" mumbled the old man, sitting up and blinking his eyes.

"Get up. I'll explain. I need your help."

Algan watched him slip into a worn and patched astronaut's uniform.

"The sun isn't even up," quavered the dry, trembling lips.

"It doesn't matter. I can't wait any longer."

"So?"

"I've been thinking about what you were saying. I need some zotl to try an experiment. Have you any?"

"No. What use would it be to me?"

"Do you know anyone on this planet who has some?"

"Zotl roots don't grow here. And the people are poor. They can't afford that luxury. No, I don't know of any."

The old man opened the door and they went out. The courtyard was just as muddy and dismal as it had been the night before, but the ending of the night cast an enchantment over it. The surrounding jungle looked as though it were being devoured by flames; the house itself seemed to be consumed by an imaginary, cold brazier. But the high buildings of the Stellar Port rose like blocks of ice, even in the heart of the deep red night.

"Hold on," said the old man. "Maybe the port commandant. You'd have to go see him. Perhaps there is a cargo of zotl in the cellars of the Stellar Port. Maybe he drinks it. I doubt it, because he comes from one of the Puritan worlds. But I don't quite see how you're going to talk him into letting you have a little zotl even if he has some. What can you give him in exchange? Anyway, tell him I sent you."

"All right," said Algan. "I'm on my way."

"It isn't even daylight yet. Wait a bit."

"There are no days or nights in stellar ports," Algan said, "and I've already waited too long. I want the captain to remember my visit. Good-bye."

"Good luck," the old man said, but his voice betrayed doubt and distrust. He watched Jerg Algan close his knapsack and move off along the steep path which led to the high bronze gates of the Stellar Port, between the wretched hovels which made up the only street of the little town. He shrugged and went back to his cabin.

"You can't go in. Not at this hour of the night. And besides, you're an alien."

There was a steely air about him in his uniform of supple metal. His unmoving fingers rested on the buttons of an instrument panel; he could unleash all the fires of hell around the gate. His eyes shone like polished glass. His helmet gleamed like the nugget of a fabulous metal. He was, in his unruffled obstinacy, immortal and invulnerable. He was the representative of Betelgeuse and he knew that the whole might of Betelgeuse was at his command.

"I am a free citizen of the galaxy," Algan said loudly. "I have the right, night and day, to enter stellar ports."

"In theory, yes," the guard said in his icy voice. "But here, at night, even the leaders sleep. You ought to do the same. You can speak to the captain tomorrow."

"I act only under his authority," Algan said. "You haven't the right, on your own, to forbid me entry into the port."

"I see you know the rules," the watchman said with the shadow of a smile. "Very well; if you can prove that you're a free citizen of the galaxy I'll let you in."

"I am a human," said Algan. "That ought to be enough."

The guard shook his head.

"You're a foreigner. Where did you come from? You're not native to these parts." His voice dragged condescendingly over the word native. "And you've never come to the Stellar Port. There aren't that many visitors to this forsaken hole; I'd have noticed you."

"That's immaterial," Algan said. "How do you know that a patrol ship from Betelgeuse didn't leave me on some sector of this planet that your detective beams don't cover. Didn't your screens register the approach of a ship?"

The guard's expression changed slightly.

"Maybe," he said. "Maybe. But even if that were so, I've had my orders. I could be punished for not obeying them."

"I don't think that your commandant will do so if you let me in. If you don't, I guarantee nothing."

The watchman closely looked over Jerg Algan once more. The rumpled and dirty clothes, the unshaven face, the fatigue in the stranger's eyes were not reassuring.

"Nogaro sent me," Algan said abruptly.

"Nogaro? Where did you hear that name?" The guard's voice had become commanding.

"He sent me. That's all."

"Nogaro," the guard said thoughtfully. "I thought he'd died. OK. I believe you. But I'm going to call the commandant and he'll decide himself whether he'll see you now or wait until morning. I wash my hands of the whole affair."

He pushed a button and the high bronze gates, on which were inscribed in enormous letters the name of the planet, Glania, opened and admitted the stranger who stepped in alone, onto the enormous deserted esplanade of the port and went off toward the luminescent tower.

The commandant's back was resolutely turned to Algan as he looked at the sky through the great bay window at the other end of his office. The light of the rising sun darted along the thickets which bordered the eastern horizon and the black aerials of the port stood outlined against the sky that was still a dark red; they were like the overly symmetrical branches of calcined trees.

The commandant was small and brown but, with age, had become regrettably portly and his disposition had soured. He wore a wide leather belt and gazed longingly at the Stellar Port, empty of spaceships, and at the sky, empty of any messenger from Betelgeuse.

The hours sometimes dragged on Glania.

"You have a proposition to make?" he said unpleasantly. "Let's hear it. I'm listening."

90

"You don't even know who I am," Algan observed. "That's immaterial."

"Let's rather say we'll discuss that later."

"I'm waiting," the commandant said.

His hands, which he had been holding behind his back, began to move. The first clear rays of the sun overflowed from the horizon and the light and the color of the sky began to change. Every night and every morning, the contest between the red light of night and the white star of day was renewed. The white sun was a huge spider which spun, on the whole surface of the sky, a web of rays which almost instantly spread over the entire horizon and the faraway deep red star which seemed to grow pale and to flee was invariably caught.

And every night it was the other way around. Legends were beginning to take form in Glania, about this continual struggle between night and day.

"I've come to offer you the means of attracting Betelgeuse's attention to yourself," Algan said slowly. "Maybe even to get a couple of promotions, or to have you transferred to a world closer to the center."

"Well?" replied the commandant. He began to laugh, but it was a hollow sound. He stopped abruptly, turned around, and looked Algan up and down.

"What the human galaxy needs most at the moment," said Algan, "is a means of interstellar transportation that is almost instantaneous. The gadgets we use to increase the speed of our spacecraft are no longer adequate. I believe that the central government of Betelgeuse would show its gratitude to the man who could invent a new procedure."

"You, for instance?" said the commandant icily.

"Who' is immaterial. Let's say that I am now in the experimental stages. Let's say that I need a product I cannot obtain here. Let's say that you have some. Would you be prepared to let me have a small quantity so that I can go on with my research? I would be extremely grateful to you, as would all of the galaxy."

"What do you need?" the commandant asked, staring into the distance, beyond Algan, beyond the walls of the room, beyond even the planet, into a world of dreams to which only the commandant held the key,

"Some zotl," Algan said softly.

The commandant's eyes at once lost their faraway look and focused on Algan. He placed his hands on the desk and leaned over toward Algan. Then the blood rushed to his face and he started to laugh so hard that tears rolled down his cheeks.

"Zotl, my boy," he said when he had quieted down. "Is that all? Are you quite sure that's all? But, first, what makes you think I have any? Are you crazy? Asking me, with a cock and bull story, for zotl. Zotl to travel among the stars. Let me tell you that lots of people have tried to get drugs from me; some even tried to steal, but this is a new one. You really believe your story, don't you? You're paranoid, just paranoid."

"Zotl is not technically considered a drug," Algan replied coldly.

The commandant stopped laughing.

"I've had enough of you," he said. "Now get out."

"Zotl is not a drug," repeated Algan, "and if you have some, I'm prepared to pay you for it. It's a perfectly legal transaction. Only the Puritan worlds look upon it as a narcotic, even though they have never been able to prove any harmful effects. But here we're in a world completely controlled by Betelgeuse. You're allowed to sell me zotl if you have any, and I think you do. And Betelgeuse will show you her appreciation some day."

The commandant's eyes resumed their faraway look.

"I do have some zotl," he said. "I take it, sometimes. The days drag by in this forsaken land. It's not illegal. You know that, if you're a secret agent from Betelgeuse. I ought to have suspected something of the sort."

"I'm not a secret agent from Betelgeuse," Algan said. "I'd rather tell you before you discover it for yourself. I've never even set foot on Betelgeuse. But I need zotl and I'm ready to pay ten times its price. Let's put our cards on the table, shall we?"

"OK," said the commandant. "Have you any money?"

"No."

The commandant became visibly irritated.

"You're crazy."

He reached for a switch concealed in the moldings of the desk.

"Don't do that. I said I didn't have any money on me, but not that I couldn't dispose of a considerable sum. As a matter of fact, I represent a considerable sum. I need about twelve zotl roots. Set your price."

The commandant thought for a moment. It was a huge sum.

"About five hundred unities."

"I'll offer you five thousand. My name is Jerg Algan. And there's a price on my head. Five thousand unities, in fact. An even exchange. You can check in your latest bulletin."

They looked at one another for a while without speaking. Then the commandant broke the silence.

"I suppose you're under the impression that you've covered every contingency. But what would you do now if I detained you without giving you the zotl?"

"That's easy. The money put on my head will be paid only to the man who has taken me prisoner. The offer does not hold if I give myself up to a representative of Betelgeuse. So there can be two versions of my capture.

Either you caught me after a rugged chase and you get the reward. Or I state that I gave myself up and you get nothing."

"They won't believe you," said the commandant, biting his lips. "They'll believe me sooner than you."

"Sure," said Algan. "But they'll believe the evidence of a lie detector even more. Then I'll be forced to tell the truth. They'll believe me only when I say that I gave myself up. And you'll be prosecuted for perjury. On the other hand, if you accept my conditions, I'll never have to go through a lie detector test. The law allows a criminal to refuse the detector even if he is heavily incriminated. I have nothing to lose."

"How do I know you won't double-cross me as soon as you've been arrested?"

"You can't know. My word is as good as yours, that's all. I've been open and aboveboard with you in the hopes that you'd understand that my word is good. And, after all, there would be no point in my double-crossing you. It's Betelgeuse that's paying, not me. You run some risk, but it's worth it, believe me."

"Five thousand unities," the commandant said quietly. "It's almost the price of a secondary planet. Damn you if you really are a secret agent from Betelgeuse."

"There's a price on my head," Jerg Algan reminded him. "You can check."

"All right."

The information about him flashed on the screen. Ships' positions, signals, warnings, then the rhythm slowed down and the film stopped abruptly on a picture. Jerg Algan's.

The portrait was startlingly lifelike. It must have been taken on the Earth, in the port of Dark, while Algan was undergoing training. Yet it no longer completely corresponded to reality. It was an image of the past. Algan's face was now harder, browner; his eyes were deeper, more brilliant.

Instructions followed. A detailed description, the charges leveled against him, a picture of the ship in which he had fled, and the amount of the reward offered to any citizen of the galaxy—be it a civilian, a soldier, or an officer—for his capture. And, in red letters: To be captured alive. Under no circumstances to be shot. Probably not dangerous.

"They really seem to want you," the commandant merely said.

"Much more than you think. They need me as much as I need zotl. And for the same reason."

"OK. Follow me."

And as he walked behind the commandant, Algan reflected on the information given in the bulletin. The men from Betelgeuse had not mentioned the charges they had leveled against him nor the threats they had made. They alluded only to the theft of a ship, and in mild terms. But that had not been the real crime, if crime there had been, since they themselves had given Algan the opportunity to take over a ship. The truth was that they wanted to be sure that Algan would be returned to them as soon as he had discovered something and before the Puritans could grab him.

They had loosed Algan into space much as a ferret is loosed into a burrow, cages being placed at all the openings in the hopes of catching him after he had flushed out the quarry.

But there was one opening they had overlooked.

"There's obviously no point in trying any monkey business," said the commandant. "As you probably know, no weapon will work in any part of the Stellar Port, unless I give the order, locally, to do away with the inhibiting field. Furthermore, my guards would swing into action at the faintest out-of-the-way sound. Let me add that never, in the long history of the human galaxy, has a gang of criminals, even in large numbers and armed to the teeth, succeeded in capturing the Stellar Port."

"No point in harping on that," said Algan. "I didn't come here to fight."

They went through a door which shut silently after them. A section of wall pivoted, revealing a deep recess which contained a deluxe zotl press and a sizable pile of roots. Algan whistled.

"I owe this setup to my predecessor," said the commandant. "He was recalled to Betelgeuse, one fine day, because of some obscure matter of trafficking. I found this long after he had gone, quite by accident. Legally, it's mine."

The tone of his voice showed he was on the defensive and that he was still not sure that Jerg Algan was not a secret agent from Betelgeuse.

"Put a root in the press," Algan said.

He took the chessboard out of his bag and put it on a low table. He placed an armchair facing the table, sat down, and lay both his hands on the chessboard, each finger in a square. Then he took his hands off and examined the fine engraving, the figures etched by a diamond stylus eons ago. They appeared—or was it an illusion?—to be trembling. He tried to think of something besides what he was going to do. He had no idea what was going to happen to him. But it didn't matter. Given his situation, this was the only solution. If it was a solution. He watched the zotl root being crushed by the heavy piston, and that reminded him of the Earth, Dark, and the shopkeeper of Ulcinor.

Only a few days had gone by since his departure from the Stellar Port of Dark, at least, a few days for him; he had traveled from one end of the galaxy to the other at almost the speed of light along very short routes, but on the Earth, perhaps whole decades had passed.

And his friends were dead.

He stared at the half-full glass the commandant had put before him and pushed it aside.

"Squeeze another root," he said. "Double the dose."

"You're risking insanity," said the commandant.

"No," said Algan, "that's a myth. I know what I'm doing."

"I hope so," said the commandant.

He was eyeing the chessboard suspiciously.

"What's that?"

"I'll tell you later," Algan replied wearily.

The second root vanished under the piston.

He had no way of knowing what the optimum quantity of zotl was. He had to experiment. Nine chances out of ten he would fail.

Unless, behind his back, without his knowledge, someone was pulling the strings of the puppet he knew he was.

He emptied the glass and placed his fingers on the chessboard, haphazardly.

Or was someone guiding his fingers?

He saw the commandant staring at him, unbelieving; he saw his eyes widen. He saw the commandant's lips move to form a cry.

Shapes and colors quivered and became fuzzy.

"Good-bye," he said in a last gasp.

Then he disappeared.

And the chessboard with him.

CHAPTER VIII
Beyond the Dead Suns

It was a gray, unstable universe, fuzzy, imprecise, made up of changing curves and constantly changing orbits. Then, gradually, certain lines became clearer. Straight lines. And gray clouds emerged from definite areas either lighter or darker. Lines separated the areas. It was a chessboard.

Algan tried unsuccessfully to move. He wasn't supported by anything. In the first moments he had been conscious of falling, then that feeling had vanished gradually as the contours of the immense chessboard on which he was became clearer.

He was a pawn on the chessboard and he was traveling along certain complex trajectories, skipping from square to square. His skull hurt agonizingly. He didn't know why he was jumping from square to square, but he told himself that there must be some reason, that he knew the reason, but that he couldn't remember it: it was deeply engraved in his subconscious.

He had a headache, as if he had been making a concentrated mental effort. He had instinctively made some calculations based on certain data, but he didn't know how he had done this. He had used the result of his calculations, but he did not know why he had to skip from one square to another on the chessboard.

Or perhaps his calculations, his migraine, and his unplanned moves on the sixty-four squares were all related. Algan remembered number sixty-four as a relatively low number. How could the chessboard be so enormous if it was made up of only sixty-four squares? He was struggling in a cotton-like fog; memory had fled; there was nothing around him that he could understand.

"What's my name?" he asked aloud. But the sound of his voice never reached his ears. One problem filled his mind. Which square should he move into now? He thought hard. Then suddenly, his mind cleared; portions of his brain which had been inactive until then stirred. He had the feeling he had won a victory, but he did not know over what.

The solution came to him. He started moving again on the chessboard.

"What's my name?" he wondered again.

It was a rhetorical question. He had not the faintest idea what a name was. All he knew was that he was faced with a number of problems that took the form of ideal moves to be made in a game of chess.

There was no meaning in a name. Only the solving of ideal itinerary problems had any meaning.

Sixty-four squares were not much, but the number represented a colossal quantity of possible itineraries, obstacles to be avoided or overcome. This required a no less colossal amount of calculation.

The human mind functions, partly, like a calculating machine, he thought. It solves the problems put by ...

By whom?

By no one.

By me, Jerg Algan.

He had solved the problem and he knew who he was. Jerg Algan. Thirty-two years old, a rebel against Betelgeuse. A human. A refugee who had just escaped from Glania by means of the chessboard. He was on a mission.

He had a frightful headache.

I drank too much zotl, he thought. I must have had the D.T.'s.

The gray shapeless fog which surrounded him parted. He suddenly started to float in the heart of a black universe interspersed with lights. Space.

He had solved the problem of the chessboard. He had left Glania and traveled through space. He had extracted the root of the equation: man-plus-chessboard-plus-zotl.

And he had not lost his sanity. He had come into contact with reality once more. Could he be sure? He was floating in the heart of a black space sparsely sprinkled with stars. The fear of falling gripped him. But the reflexes which had been inculcated in him during his training period on Earth allowed him to regain his self-control.

He was not really falling. When his eyes had adjusted, he saw that he was resting in a huge, black, hard, cold armchair in front of a table made of the same kind of material, on which the chessboard lay. His fingers were resting on squares. The air was cold and serene, alive; there was a whiff of countless ages. He looked up and saw stars shining in a black sky; they were few, reddish, extinguished and reflecting the light of other stars, or in the process of dying; but much farther in space luminous regions shone, distant agglomerations of suns that were difficult to tell apart.

He sniffed the air and decided that it was perfectly safe to breathe. As he considered the blackness of the sky, it seemed to him that he was suspended in emptiness on a planet that had no atmosphere, that there was nothing between his eyes and the dying braziers burning in space.

But, he thought, it was possible that an invisible dome, perhaps a purely energic, unsubstantial one, in the depths of the ocean of space contained an air bubble capable of sustaining life. It was possible that his visit had been preordained and that enormous citadel in space had been built solely with his future presence in view.

It was an odd idea. It seemed inconceivable that a fabulously ancient breed, which more than likely was nonhuman, could have built, a little everywhere in space, gigantic stopping places for the sole purpose of helping the human species to conquer the stars. Unless this breed had itself been a human one and that the machinery it had built in ancient times was of such a degree of perfection that it was still in operating order.

He got up from his chair and walked around the enormous circular room. It was lit by a gray light which did not prevent the rays shed by the stars from being visible.

The walls of the room were bare and black. And in one precise spot, exactly opposite the armchair and the table on which lay the chessboard, Algan discovered, etched in the wall, a chessboard in each of whose squares were incredibly delicate etchings.

These intrigued Algan. They were the same ones he had seen on his own chessboard, but they followed a different sequence. He crossed the room, picked up the chessboard, then compared the two.

There was no difference. His memory could have failed him, but he doubted it. The figures on his chessboard had moved. This could mean that the chessboard was a reflection of the universe and that each change of position of the images represented the solution of a problem. It could also mean that there existed a relationship between the universe, or between the galaxy anyway, and the chessboard, and that any change in the chessboard corresponded to a displacement in space.

Was it an almost instantaneous displacement, or did it spread out over a period of time? He could not tell. All he knew was that as far as he was concerned an extremely short period of time had elapsed during the trip. He felt his face with his hand and noted that his beard had not grown much. But had the Earth grown older? That was the question. Had thousands of years passed over Betelgeuse while he was traveling over that distance; or was it only ten seconds? If he ever returned to the human galaxy, would he be dealing with Nogaro, or with his distant descendants who would not even know his name?

There was no exit from this room. Yet the chessboard engraved on the wall could be a lock. He put his fingers at random over the squares, for he had no precise question in mind. His fingers had barely touched the middle squares when he became aware of a light, crystal-like sound and a small section of the wall directly under the chessboard pivoted.

He hastily stepped aside, unsure about what might pop out. All he saw, in the opening, on a black pedestal, was a gray globe.

He went up to it and saw that the globe was a sort of vessel filled with an amber-colored liquid—the liquid extracted from a zotl root.

So, the black citadels really were the key to the problem of man, chessboard, and zotl. Zotl plunged man into a trance which made it possible for him to glimpse other universes, other worlds, along new directions, and the chessboard made it possible for man to move in space toward those worlds.

To move directly, without having to make use of all the costly and slow paraphernalia of space transport, and stellar ports scattered on hard-won planets.

Perhaps the black citadels were the infinitely more advanced equivalent of stellar ports. And just as Betelgeuse was the spider in the web encompassing the stellar ports throughout the human galaxy, there must be in the heart of the galaxy an alien and ancient intelligence lying in wait, which made decisions and moves, all the while watching over the men who dared to venture out in its labyrinth.

But he did not know into which part of the galaxy he had been transported by the effect of the zotl on the chessboard. Judging from the scarcity of stars and the blackness of the sky, it might be that the huge and dead world in which he was at present was situated on the edges of the galaxy. The suns which he could see appeared to be dying. But he remembered what he had been told, on Glania, by the old pilot, about that string of dead suns which a lost team of explorers had met on the way to the center of the galaxy.

An incredible amount of energy had probably made an obscure furrow in space, long, long ago, perhaps even before the appearance of life on the Earth, and had accelerated in incredible proportions the process which controls the aging and dying of stars. Therefore the center of the galaxy was surrounded by a desolate barrier of midget white stars and purple suns which marked the boundaries of forbidden territories. He was far less removed from the center of the galaxy than he had feared. But this proximity itself made no sense if he thought about it in terms which he was accustomed to using. It took light more than fifty thousand years to travel the distance which separated the center of the galaxy from the outer edge of the huge constellation of suns. Astronauts in their spaceships, moving about in the stratosphere, could have done so in a fraction of the time that they actually took. But that was still too long. He realized for the first time how silly words used in the human galaxy were.

Men had conquered only one province in space, one suburb of the galaxy; only a few thousand planets had been explored—yet there were millions of stars that surrounded them. He shivered. His earthbound assurance, his human self-sufficiency suddenly evaporated. He was unable to remember the glory and power of man. All he could now see on the screen of his mind was the incredible, multitudinous swarm of sparks that made up a cluster of stars. He was overwhelmed by the size and complexity of the problem. He closed his eyes. But it suddenly occurred to him that he had something just as complex as the galaxy itself, his mind, and its neurons, which could make innumerable associations. The universe posed almost unlimited problems, but humans had at their disposal an instrument capable, consciously or unconsciously, of solving them. They had been given an instrument and the means to use it. He had to know how and why.

He took the globe in both hands and drank the zotl. The liquid cooled his throat. He crossed the room, sat in the armchair, placed his fingers on the chessboard, then scanned the sky. The stars became blurred and changeable.

The transition this time was much easier than the first time. He did not have a feeling of being tom apart and the migraine which had been oppressing him vanished. He floated for a while in grayness while cerebral centers of which

99

he was unconscious coordinated the movements of his fingers on the chessboard and the displacement of his body in space.

He was moving at random. His goal was to find some indication of the nature and provenance of the makers of the chessboard and of the black citadels. He was hoping that by jumping from world to world he would at last reach the end of an immeasurable trip: the place from which had come the builders, or the Masters, as the old pilot on Glania had called them.

But there were millions of suns and planets in the galaxy and there might be almost as many black citadels. Perhaps this was a hopeless journey.

The citadels were all alike, he soon noticed, and the room in which he found himself at the end of each trip was always round and topped by an invisible cupola, but the starlight that filtered through the cupola and the colors of the sky were always different.

Once he thought he was at the bottom of the sea because the color above was so low and green. He could not see the light of any star, only the steely gray light of an enormous sun. The planet was so large that he could make out the line of the horizon through the cupola, above the black walls of the room. He looked fixedly at low blue hills whose immobility was worrisome; there was no movement anywhere. It was an inchoate world on which life had not yet begun, perhaps because it could not support life. It was an alien world, enclosed within its walls of clouds.

He left it for a shining rock that was moving through star-hung skies. He thought he must be approaching the center of the galaxy because the stars were so numerous there. They appeared to touch, to crush one another. The sky was golden and the sparse dark places looked like black stars that had irradiated from the night. Another time he saw ruins stretching out under a dark red sky afire from the proximity of a giant red star. Those ruined palaces had not withstood time the way the black citadels had. They must have been the work of a lesser breed, comparable to humans, who had hoped to compete with the power of the Masters. Or perhaps these beings had committed suicide in a fit of bloody madness. It was a drama that Algan was unable to reconstruct. In any event, oddly-hewn stones in geometric shapes, stretched up toward a flaming sky forming a circle around the citadel.

He began to move about with greater and greater ease within the restricted area of the chessboard. He did not yet know how much control his mind had over the sixty-four squares and the curious designs with which they were decorated, nor which portion of his brain was being used, but he did not much care. He was now able to move all over the galaxy. He even found that he could land on a planet at a place other than the top of the black citadel, that he could regulate his flight in the stratosphere and get back into normal space or land in the middle of a star, or on the surface of a deserted world and then, in a split second, take off for one of the black citadels. Whenever he traveled there was a kind of protective screen between himself and danger from the outside. He felt that he was simultaneously in normal space and outside of it.

While he traveled, he never felt hungry, thirsty, or tired. He was situated outside of time. He felt fulfilled as he never had before. He was at last performing the task for which he had been created. He was the master of the stars and space, more powerful than the men of Betelgeuse or the Puritans of Ulcinor and the Ten Planets. He was doing what none of them had even dared dream of.

Worlds of ice and worlds of flame, diamond planets and sand planets, marshes and deserts, clouds heavy with storms, luminous fogs, crystals aligned in infinite rows along plains of purple mud, stormy sterile seas—these were what he saw from the unchanging domes of the black citadels. He began to wonder whether the citadels were not giant spacecraft—or a single spaceship—which he was trailing along with him in his journey over the chessboard of the universe.

The worlds he visited were nameless, inhuman ones, which could never be colonized, but they had a beauty that was more pure, more austere, more vibrant, than any he had read about in the books about the conquest of space. On these light was refracted, surfaces distorted by the pull of tremendous gravity. But the conditions prevalent inside the black citadels were always the same.

His eyes had their fill of giant stars floating in the sky like balloons of fire that were larger even than Ras Algheti or the Auriga Epsilon which had been the admiration of the astronomers of the heroic age. Once when he had completed an incredibly long journey, at the end of a cascade of suns and planets and had reached the central regions of the galaxy, he discovered new wonders, a space whose multiple curve was visible, an unbearable blaze of colors, stars orbiting around one another, bumping into one another like balls. Space itself, filled with gas and dust, seemed luminous. He saw ringed stars; he saw, shining in the distance, globular cumuli each of which represented more stars than man had conquered and which were only a drop in the bucket of the galaxy.

His regard and admiration for the builders of the black citadels increased even more when he realized that he was traveling not only in space, but in time. The light of the stars in the center of the galaxy, which he had seen on the Earth, had been traveling for thousands of years, yet he now saw those suns as they had been just a few years before. The builders had erected a civilization in proportion to the universe, as immeasurably vast in relation to human accomplishments as the whole of the stellar parts was in relation to an anthill.

And they were dead, he told himself.

For a long time he was unable to find any trace of them. The empty rooms did not contain the slightest clue; it was as though they had been only waiting-rooms, abandoned long ago, or as though they had been built for a purpose that had never materialized.

But all that changed as he came closer and closer, by means of an irregular spiral, to the center of the galaxy. A presence, a vague scent floated in the air, suggesting a recent passage, a trace, nothing that was as yet visible. Algan noticed that increasingly the black citadels were located in gigantic worlds that were surrounded, to judge from the color of the sky, by an atmosphere consisting of hydrogen.

Once, a long vibration shook the tiled floor of the room. Algan waited, but nothing more happened. Hours passed in silence and he felt fatigue slowly and dully engulf him. He left without having heard the vibration again. He was not worried about being lost. The very idea of getting back to Earth seemed unnatural.

But there were more and more signs that indicated the end of the journey. He had thought that he'd been placing his fingers at random on the chessboard, but actually—he realized—he was solving problems mysteriously put to him.

Then suddenly he found himself in a room of a different kind. Its black walls had wide doors set in them. He rushed out and saw a golden sky and lavender-colored fields that were not unlike those of the Earth; there were low hills outlined against the horizon. He felt on his skin the warmth of thousands of suns. Fatigue overwhelmed him and he dropped onto the purple grass. It felt soft and cool.

He knew he had reached the world he'd been looking for, that he had reached the end of his journey. He raised his head a fraction of a second before hearing the voice.

"Greetings, robot," said the deep, musical voice, in Algan's language.

"I'm not a robot," protested Algan. "I'm a man."

"In our language," asserted the voice, "man is a synonym for robot."

CHAPTER IX
Betelgeuse

The room was huge and bare. An ashen light oozed from its solid walls. Eight men were seated around a glass table, talking and drinking. Their clothes seemed to be woven of silver; on their fingers rings shone with gems. Whenever they stopped talking silence reigned, a heavy, deep silence unbroken by any sound or vibration.

The room was located three hundred yards below the surface of a world near Betelgeuse. Two hundred and fifty yards of solid rock and fifty yards of steel separated it from the floor of the Government Palace. These were the eight men who held the fate of the human galaxy in their hands.

"You're still a young man, Stello," said a brown man with deep-set black eyes. "We know all about that kind of uprising. We don't believe in using force. Time is on our side."

"All right," said Stello, who was sitting to the right of the man who had just spoken. "But we've had three cases of mutiny in less than a week. That ship off Olgane whose crew, led by their captain, is openly engaged in the most objectionable sort of traffic; that station on Oldeb V which refuses to admit our agent and, last of all, that expedition on the outer Marches which is refusing to leave the world we had sent them to explore. Don't you think our fleet will soon abandon us either to devote themselves to looting or to settle on that paradise that is said to exist somewhere in the galaxy? Some positive action must be taken about the fleet."

The seven men dressed in silver turned toward Stello. There was an odd gleam of amusement in their eyes. They all appeared to be in the prime of life and yet time had left imperceptible marks on their foreheads and on their slender white hands.

"I shall vote no," said the man with the black eyes. "Not because the use of force frightens me. But because destruction is futile and brutal. No, believe me, Stello, any fears I may have about the future of the human galaxy come from something else. You are inexperienced. We have known other periods. We have seen entire stellar systems secede. And time has always brought them back to the fold. There are ways of dealing with this other than sending a war fleet. And how do you know that it wouldn't be a good thing to have the crew of a ship settle on a distant planet? Their descendants will come to us for help and protection."

"Perhaps," said Stello, putting down his glass on the crystal table. His eyes scanned the faces of the others, lingered on their cold eyes, their thin lips, and their high, intelligent foreheads.

"We have unlimited means at our disposal," said Al- brand, whose hair had been tinted silver by time. "And yet, Stello, we are curiously unarmed. We maintain order in the galaxy, we are the most powerful tyrants human history has ever known, but space and time protect with an almost invincible barrier those we want to strike down. I don't know what label will be given to our period in history. Perhaps it will be looked upon as a strangely perverse epoch, or a singularly free one. I hope we'll be judged only by our intentions. We want man to rule the galaxy."

"We're well aware of this," said Olryge in his icy voice. His red hair and his eyes that sparkled like rubies were a familiar sight on many a ship of the Betelgeuse fleet. "And we also know that you are quite content to rule this empire of the galaxy, even if you are not entitled, as were the kings, emperors, or dictators of the past, to glory and to the hurrahs. I've known you for almost three centuries and we have talked a great deal about your mission. Are you growing old?"

"Be quiet," whispered Albrand, his fingers trembling with rage, but his features impassive. "I am not so ambitious as you. I'm quite satisfied to be an administrator. All I want is the welfare of mankind. I don't care about the honors."

"You'd sell us all down the river to bag the title of all- powerful master of this galaxy."

"You're judging me by yourself, Olryge."

"Stop it," said the dark-eyed man. "Can't you see that the worst danger lies within ourselves, within this group? Have you learned nothing during your long lives? Whether it be ideals or ambitions that rule you, can't you keep them under control? Can't you understand that, faced with the immensity of the space that we have to conquer, we are all equal? We ourselves, the Machines which fill the Government Palace over our heads, and those of our people who are traveling here and there in space are the secret rulers of the galaxy. It is our impetus which has enabled mankind to forge ahead so fast. And yet you'd destroy all that with your quarrels. Come, Albrand, I can remember when you never spoke of anything but peace and you, Olryge, remember your dreams about the power and the freedom you wanted man to have."

"We're far from it now," said Stello. "Sometimes I wonder whether we've accomplished anything at all, whether the secret power we wield makes any sense, whether the anarchy that prevailed at the beginning of the conquest was not better than this iron rule which logic forces us to maintain."

"You've certainly done a complete about-face, Stello. A few moments ago all you could talk about were punitive expeditions, repressive measures, and now you're full of doubts," said the black-eyed man.

"I don't know. I'm always afraid our empire will crumble. Shall I outlast it? But I know that wouldn't make any sense. My existence depends entirely upon it; I live only for it. I am less master of my fate than the lowliest of the spacemen I met when, years ago, I made the rounds of our conquered territories.

The very thought robs me of my sleep. I think about all the stars we have con-quered and about the sparse population on them and about the ease with which those bonds could be severed and about the whole human structure that could just drift off. At times, I say to myself that it is just one huge body of which we are the head, our agents are the eyes; the body is gradually dying and we, the Immortals, remain. I think we could not survive the destruction of that body. And fear breeds violence, doesn't it, Olryge?"

"You've been reading too many early philosophers," grumbled Albrand; the others remained silent, plunged in thought.

"There's something in what Stello says," interjected Fuln, as he put his thin, slender hands on the cold table. "We are the masters, yet we would be powerless without those few million Immortals who travel all over the human galaxy, and without those electronic brains that process the data we give them and which are even more indestructible than we are. Sometimes I wonder whether we are not all of us the slaves of those Machines, whether they have always waged their own wars without regard to us."

"You're living in a dream world!" shouted Albrand. "The Machines put forth suggestions; we make the decisions. Billions of humans believe that their existence depends upon decisions made by Machines. But think back to the first Immortals who began this work, long before you were born; they decided to hide behind Machines and to rule secretly because they knew that men would be more willing to obey orders given by a mechanized ruler than those given by men, even immortal men. The Machines of Betelgeuse have become the symbol of the continuity of the human galaxy, but we are in fact that continuity."

"Perhaps," said Fuln. "Perhaps. But on what do we base our decisions? On the basis of data provided by the Machines. Let's suppose those data are careful-ly selected. Let's suppose those Machines are themselves controlled by some-one? One of us?"

"It's an old, old problem," the dark-eyed man said gently. "I've never been to a meeting where the question did not come up. And no solution was ever found. The problem for the Immortals is that experience has made them suspi-cious and yet they want to be sure about everything. But that's impossible."

"Never mind who makes the decisions," Stello threw in. "We are moving toward a goal. That's the problem."

No one said anything.

"We'll never reach it," Olryge said gloomily.

They looked at one another and waited.

"Do we really want to reach it?" asked the dark-eyed man. "When the cen-tral government was set up near Betelgeuse and the Immortals took it over, the precise goal, which was kept secret, was to turn the human species into a breed of Immortals able to take on the entire universe and to conquer, in time, or in spite of time, the farthest reaches of space. Has that goal been altered?"

"No," they answered in chorus.

"But is this what we really want? Do we still want it? Do we still want the whole of the human race to be like us? I'm not sure. I think something has happened that the founders of the central government did not foresee. Mankind was developed in space like a gigantic organism, as Stello was saying just now, whose every planet is a cell and whose head is Betelgeuse. And we are glad, in some ways, to provide that organism with goals and directives. We do not want it to dissolve, not even to produce a higher form of organization. We do not want it to die because we'd die with it. We are trying to keep it alive, such as it is, as long as possible."

"All right," said Olryge. "But do I need to remind you why our goal was not immediately realized? The end result required that certain secondary goals be reached first. Immortality bestowed upon the entire species would have imperiled the future of mankind. Our predecessors were afraid of overpopulation, famine, war, and I don't know what else. The human galaxy wasn't large enough at the time and mankind not sufficiently mature. Are they now?"

"We can't be sure," the black-eyed man said with a smile. "We'll never be sure. We only know that we have conquered or explored a huge number of habitable planets, that there are still others; that mankind is only a tenuous veil stretched among the stars and that our conquest will not last unless we can soon call upon large numbers of people."

"Is mankind mature?" Olryge repeated.

"We could discuss it to the end of time, and we still wouldn't know," the dark-eyed man said. "It was decided, once, that the Immortals were immortal and the rest of humanity was not. I'm not sure this arrangement would be feasible nowadays, yet we continue to use the same criteria whenever the question of recruiting new Immortals arises. It was also decided that immortality would remain a secret, the best kept secret. But can we keep it forever? Wouldn't it be better to let it out before someone else does?"

"What do you mean?" Stello asked.

"We have kept our immortality secret only at the cost of Draconian measures and because the time warp, resulting from trips made at the speed of light, has shrouded our existence in mystery. But can we keep it up? I doubt it. Just imagine what would happen if another group of Immortals were to show up in the midst of the human galaxy and wanted to challenge our power."

"Humanity, as we know it, would die," said Fuln.

Their faces, normally so impassive, became anxious. "We've overcome all crises of this sort," said Olryge.

"So far," the black-eyed man went on. "But how much longer can we keep it up?"

"What do you suggest?" Albrand asked.

"Immortality for the whole of the species."

No one spoke. Stello drained his glass. Olryge's fingers began to twitch nervously.

"I vote no," said Olryge. "There is no danger yet."

"Are you sure?" countered the black-eyed man.

"Before I believe in it I'll have to see the danger with my own eyes. The galaxy is secure. All our data confirm this."

"The Machines process our data. Have you already forgotten what Fuln was saying just now?"

"Figments of the imagination."

"Are you really sure?"

"We have no enemies we know of."

"We have masses of them, Olryge. Where have you been? Have you forgotten, among others, the Puritans from the Ten Planets?"

Olryge laughed.

"Ghosts. We brought them completely to heel over fifty years ago. They learned on which side force and history were."

"Perhaps fifty years is long enough to forget. Don't argue, Olryge. You're wrong to think always like an Immortal. Don't forget that ten years is a long time in the life of a man and fifty years stretches over several generations. I'm not sure that we, Immortals, could stand defeat as well as simple humans do. You'll notice that whenever a wave of humanity is crushed, another rises to take its place; we, on the other hand, never forget the lessons we have learned. Our defeats are final. Men's are as transitory as their lives. Ulcinor has never forgotten its old dream of hegemony. They have recently tightened their regulations pertaining to aliens. They have of late been in something of a turmoil. Sometimes they remember things we have forgotten. They hope, whereas we calculate. It doesn't take much more to topple an empire."

"Their power is nothing compared to ours."

"All right, but that wasn't true yesterday, or, rather, fifty years ago. It could grow again."

"We'll stop them again."

"Perhaps this time we'll lose."

"Nonsense."

"I expected that from you, Olryge. We must realize that we are neither omniscient nor omnipotent, and that we could be beaten. And I should prefer that that defeat not extend to the whole of the human galaxy. I should like to have Immortality bestowed upon all mankind. Oh, I don't expect to win you over, Olryge. You remember what Stello said a little while ago, about his fear of seeing the humans whom we rule, die. You feel the same. We all share the same fear. But if we must go, let us do so by choice.

"Let's let mankind rule the entire galaxy," pleaded Stello. "We have years and years, if not whole centuries, still before us, before we reach the outer limits of that island of space."

"We'll reach them, if the time is granted us," said the black-eyed man. "We probably would have to make men immortal in order to accomplish this, because there aren't enough of them. But let's leave that aspect of the problem aside for now. I just don't believe that we will have the time. We have enemies inside the human galaxy. We may have some outside it."

"I don't understand," Stello, Fuln, and Albrand said in chorus. The others merely opened their eyes wider.

"Let's assume that, in spite of all our efforts, the Puritans were to discover the secret of immortality. That would be disastrous, wouldn't it? All our plans would become obsolete. And, weak though the Ten Planets are, they could successfully stand up against us within a hundred years. Especially if they threatened to give away our secrets. Up to now, the Puritans have made use of only the best known substitute for immortality—travel through space. They sent out some spacemen to cruise at the speed of light during a few months or a few years, and when they came back from their journeys, decades or sometimes centuries had passed; in this way contact with the past and the future was constantly maintained. The men of the past could force their descendants to carry out plans made centuries earlier. But those men just led the lives of men. They died too soon. And now they are aiming at something else, at a more positive form of immortality. Toward a continuity between the past and the future which looks very much like ours."

"Where would they get it from? Their laboratories have been destroyed. Their scientists led along false scents."

"Have you never wondered, Stello, why this secret of immortality remained a secret so long? There was a time when no secret of this sort could have been kept, no matter how closely guarded. That time was not so long ago, but do you know what lies between that time and ours? Space, nothing else. We've been able to keep the secret because there is, between worlds, an immense barrier of space. And nothing can travel through space without our explicit consent. That is why it is difficult to reach or leave Betelgeuse. There have been, from time to time, vague rumors, but there are so many legends careening about in space that they were soon forgotten.

"But space, which is our ally, can also become our enemy. It isolates us, but it also isolates other worlds and other secrets. And it could be that the Puritans received the promise of outside help and that that is the source of their hope."

"Help from outside the human galaxy?" said Fuln.

"Just that. Does the name Jerg Algan mean anything to you?"

"Almost nothing," said Stello. "But I think he is an important factor in the Puritan mythology."

"They called upon him when they were fighting fifty years ago," said Albrand. "But I seem to remember he died about two hundred years ago."

"I'd like to be sure," said the dark-eyed man. "The Puritans are all stirred up because they say Algan has come back."

"They're looking for something to back up their legends," Olryge said.

"Perhaps," said the black-eyed man. "But Jerg Algan was seen a few days ago on Betelgeuse."

"You pay too much attention to legends. You're just a dreamer, Nogaro," said Olryge.

Nogaro's dark eyes scanned the gray walls of the subterranean chamber. The shiny tiles were inscribed, in tiny characters that time would never erase, with the names of all the Immortals. Hardly a thousandth of the surface of the walls was covered with inscriptions. The whole of the past history of the human galaxy was summed up in those names and on those walls. But there was a fair chance that there would be no future history for the Immortals.

"Try to convince me, Olryge," said Nogaro.

Betelgeuse. Jerg Algan came out of the frozen darkness of space, blinked, and recognized his surroundings. He stood opposite a huge glass wall covered with mathematical symbols, behind which the eyes of giant computers opened and closed. He was in the very heart of the Governor's Palace; above his head there floated a large red sphere, symbol of Betelgeuse ruling the human galaxy.

The room was empty. The first time he had visited it, it had been full of people and he had come in through the great door, along with travelers from a thousand different worlds, in order to admire the Machine upon which their lives depended. But this was his second trip to Betelgeuse, and the Masters had sent him to the very heart of the problem.

Night must have fallen on the only inhabited planet in the system, the one on which were the Government Palace and the Machine. It was impossible to tell from the light because for centuries neither light nor heat had varied in the great hall of the palace. But this room was empty only at night after the great bronze gates had been closed. They were stronger and larger replicas of the gates that enclosed, from one end of the human galaxy to the other, the white fortified walls of the Stellar Ports.

Detectors might already have picked up Jerg Algan's presence in the great hall; the Machine might already have made a plan of defense. But Algan was unconcerned. He looked down at his feet and examined the floor tiles. It was strange that during all the centuries that had passed since the Government Palace had been built, no one had taken any interest in the particular design of the black and white flagstones.

It was a chessboard. Sixty-four gigantic squares.

In each of the squares there were designs, that were almost imperceptible, which looked like the fine scratches that time, chance, and the feet of travelers might have made on the vitreous tiles.

Algan did not bother to make them out. He had already studied them during his preceding trip. He had other things to worry about! Hatred and triumph were jostling one another in his mind. And something else.

Loyalty.

During his first trip to Betelgeuse he had come to a deserted place at the end of one of the parks that circle the city. He had come out of the night, his eyes still reflecting the cyclopean splendors of the center of the galaxy, and he had seen, spread before him, the largest of the human cities. And whatever his faith in the genius of the Masters, he realized that the city stood up well in comparison with the black citadels and the wonders, buried in the depths of the stars, which he had seen. Betelgeuse represented the greatest success of human madness and genius. Government ships had brought here all that was best in the human galaxy.

Algan relaxed. Two centuries of practice had taught him to go through space effortlessly. He filled his lungs with fresh air. He sniffed the smell of grass and damp earth. He got up and slid noiselessly between the trees, toward the city.

He looked like a human. And yet he was not entirely human. The Masters, who, long, long ago, had created men, had changed him, improved him somewhat. His heartbeat was slower than that of men, consequently he was less prone to fatigue. He could vary his metabolism, and survive a long time under difficult conditions, or cause any wounds to heal quickly. He was impervious to germs and viruses. And even death had passed him by. He was immortal.

He saw the domes and the spires of the city between the trees, as the pink vapor of the morning rose under the heat of the red sun. Spaceships went across the sky from time to time or rose from the neighboring Stellar Port. Their design had scarcely changed. Their performance may have been better. But this was not what surprised Algan. The real surprise lay in Betelgeuse and in everything that Betelgeuse contained.

He had traveled bodily, in time. Two centuries had elapsed since he had left the human galaxy. Two centuries on the Earth and almost two centuries for Betelgeuse, if one took into account slight variations in time. But all sorts of people had been traveling in space since there were spaceships able to travel at the speed of light.

However, few people ever reached Betelgeuse. Betelgeuse, which, on a human scale, seemed to be situated outside of time.

Algan was going slowly along the walks of the deserted park. He didn't care whether anyone noticed him. It was unlikely that he'd be recognized. So, at least, the Masters had decreed. He was wearing the same clothes he had worn when he left Glania. But there was little likelihood of his being noticed, for one saw the most extraordinary outfits on Betelgeuse.

He noticed strange plants in the park. They were green. Green plants. He hadn't seen a tree for almost two hundred years. He remembered that the founders of the central government of Betelgeuse were born on the Earth, a long time ago, and that they were still homesick for their native planet.

He tried to remember Dark, and the plains and oceans of the Earth, his friends, the jungle, the jumble of dirty streets, the fights, the warmth of a butt in the palm of his hand, the sweat of a hot day, and the icy breath of a winter night.

All that was over and done with.

It's unbelievable that all this once existed, he thought. Dreams.

The sand crunched underfoot. This nerve-racking noise had not changed; it was a sound that reminded him of waiting, of long walks along the seashore, and of hunting in the deserts of the Earth. The sand had not changed in two hundred years. It was always the same, on whatever planet. Sand was what remained after palaces and mountains had collapsed. But he, Jerg Algan, had changed.

Dark and the Earth, Ulcinor and the Puritans, had been submerged in the bituminous fog that the sound of wet squeaking sand underfoot evoked. He had once wanted to see humans again, to walk through the maze of streets in Dark, or to browse in the small shops of Ulcinor among tall, masked figures.

He had done it. He had leaped from one point to another in the galaxy; they had never been real journeys, like the one he was undertaking now in Betelgeuse; those had been visits, strange experiences which could have been exciting.

But which hadn't been.

Dark was nothing but a rathole at the end of space, and Ulcinor a bear's den. Worlds and cities had altered in two centuries, but not to the point where he couldn't recognize them. The change was in himself.

He was now, and he knew it, a spaceman. His cities were the stars that shone in the sky. He felt a vague pity for men burrowing into their houses at the bottom of the oceans of cottony atmosphere that surrounded the habitable planets. He had heard, during his brief stay on Ulcinor, that his name had taken on a somewhat symbolic meaning for shopkeepers of the Ten Planets, but he did not trouble to find out whether he'd been recognized. The problems of humans no longer interested him. He was a spaceman and proud of it. He was not one of those astronauts who cross the great voids in a steel hull, blind, terrified, and paralyzed by the thought of the many dangers lurking. He was a true spaceman, able to follow the paths of outer space, to leap from one square to another on the chessboard of the stars, to solve the finicky problems of trajectories and to checkmate the opponent's King: Betelgeuse.

He was—and he had recognized it proudly—a pawn on the chessboard of the stars. A pawn of the black king who ruled over the galaxy. He found it hard to remember the period when he had been on the other side. It was so long ago, so confused, so unreal.

He had at that time been a human.

Now, he was a Robot.

The light from the cupolas and spires of the city shone softly through the branches of the trees. But the massive outline of the central Government Palace dwarfed them all. Algan reached the outer limits of the park without having met a single human being. Suddenly he was in the city; his footsteps rang with a new sound on the road and he was in contact with humans once more. He saw them hurrying along; in their faces joy, sadness, disgust, fear, old age. They filled him with pity.

He thought of the cities that were going to perish, of the spaceships which would be stopped in orbit, of deserted roads, of faces which were going to become expressionless, and of the bodies that would become immortal. It might take years before all this took place, but years no longer meant anything. The age of cities, spacecraft, and humans was over. And now he knew that it was what he had always wanted, what all humans had always wanted, that that destructive fury they had manifested in every period of their history was only the confused anticipation of the time to come when neither life, nor cities, nor ships, nor stellar ports, nor the heavy, costly, crushing organization of human powers, nor time, nor death would have meaning anymore. It was soothing, strange, to think of all those beings still bubbling over with life, as if they were superannuated and dead, reduced to dust; and yet he was forced to because that was what was going to happen.

It had already happened at other times, in other places, in other portions of the galaxy and in other galaxies. The age of provinces in space and the age of man had ended. They had thought themselves masters, albeit always conscious of their shortcomings, their inadequacy; they had proclaimed themselves the final product of the universe, but they were only the means to an end, robots.

He must not, he thought, let his face be too void of expression, or his walk be too unconcerned. He might attract attention.

He mingled with the crowd and followed the wide avenues to the Government Palace. There were magnificent apartment buildings along the way. He recognized how splendid they were, but only, he said to himself, as a paleontologist recognizes the strength of vanished species and the perfect articulation of their limbs, none of which, however, prevented them from dying.

The gigantic square in front of the Government Palace was in itself almost as great a wonder as the stars, as the countless worlds in space, or the constructions of the Masters. Moving roads furrowed the vast metal expanse like rivers of silver. There were colossal statues, on crystal pedestals, of human figures molded in the same indestructible bronze as had been used to make the gates of the Stellar Port. Their calm gaze looked confidently into space, seeming to watch over the continual activity of spaceships plowing the skies. They were as high as mountains and their hands, raised toward the immense sphere of the dazzling star, looked big enough to shelter a spaceship. Farther along the way there were strange pieces of sculpture—abstract ones, knot-works of curves and light which represented man's idea of the universe, complicated, mathematical, elusive, and hostile structures, splendid in their colored multiplicity. On the way to the palace of Betelgeuse, Algan, carried along by the gentle motion of the moving roads, saw etched in glass and metal, complex symbols that depicted man's conquest of the universe. The processes regulating the birth, life, and death of stars, those which controlled the dance of electrons or the perpetual overlapping of waves were inscribed there. Here, man's admiration was equal to his understanding and art sprang naturally from knowledge.

But it was, Algan told himself, a last twig on a dead or dying tree. It was time for man to discover what he really was.

Going through the gigantic gate he closed his eyes unconsciously as he faced the enormous sphere of red fire representing Betelgeuse, which floated above the crystal cupola. It was shining high overhead, but its brightness was such that for an instant he thought that it was plunging toward him. He pulled himself together and saw, below this midget sun, a bright ring of white lights which he recognized as a replica of the galaxy.

He smiled. Men had thought for so long that they would rule the galaxy that they had become accustomed to the idea of a future victory and thought they had achieved it.

The moving sidewalks stopped at the entrance to the great hall. Algan went forward onto the huge black and white tiles, each big enough to hold a fairly large spaceship and he saw before him the crystal wall which separated visitors from the Machine.

Everything in the great hall had been contrived to impress visitors. The palace had been built centuries before, when the central government had been located on the third planet of the ones that rotate around Betelgeuse. From the very start of that remote time, it had been singled out to store the archives of the human galaxy and the Machines which process the endless data.

Countless visitors had gone through the great hall which was a meeting place for the world of the conquered stars and the mysterious and abstract one of the Machine; where the past and the future crossed. All kinds of people came: barbarians from remote lands, scholars from ancient worlds, astronauts plowing the frontiers of space, soldiers from Betelgeuse who wanted to take a look at the sanctuary for whose defense they were responsible, architects filled with awe by the pure, immense lines of the crystal vault, merchants wanting to see the Machine which assured order in the empire; men of all breeds and colors, size and intelligence, wearing the most exotic or the most ordinary clothes. There were footsteps that echoed with assurance on the tiles, and others that shuffled along the cold floor; people drank in with their eyes the high metal pillars, jostled one another like a swarm of ants, put questions to the Machine and listened with unflagging interest to the answers it gave.

For the miracle of the Machine was that it knew everyone and everything and that it answered every question. It was a miracle, repeated daily, one of secondary importance which the less complicated portions of the Machine were programmed to deal with, but it served as legendary and tangible evidence that the Machine governed with unerring fairness.

Historians claimed that since the very beginning of time there had been Machines to help men make decisions, by defining for them the nature of alternatives of the problems to be solved. The Betelgeuse Machine was merely the logical result of the invention by man of a long series of devices to aid the memory. But, the historians continued, this one had been devised to replace man rather than to help him, in order to insure that the government of the human galaxy would have a continuity which human frailty would not have made possible, men seemed to accept its decisions more willingly than they would have accepted orders from other men.

A small section of the Machine could be seen behind the crystal wall which divided the great hall in two.

Some of the tourists thought that the mass of giant tubes, memory banks, revolving cylinders, sparks, screens, and copper wires were all that the Machine consisted of. Others, either less naive or more knowledgeable, suspected that there was more to the Machine than met the eye, that it occupied more space than there was room for in the great hall of the palace, that its data were piled up in dark underground vaults and that its decisions were worked out far from human eyes.

Data came pouring in from the entire galaxy; it did not matter how recently for the Machine was the past, the present, and the future.

Some wondered whether the Machine was not merely a screen, a part of the decor behind which a tremendous power was concealed, but they generally did not dare to ask that sort of question out loud. Least of all would they have asked the Machine.

Algan shouldered his way through the crowd hurrying along the black and white squares. When he was near the crystal partition, he saw the cells through which the Machine could be questioned. They were famous throughout the human galaxy. Children on remote balls of mud dreamed of some day coming here, questioning the Machine and getting an answer. But many grew up, aged, and died without ever realizing their dream. It was probably because so few of the billions of inhabitants of the planets had come to Betelgeuse and seen the Machine that the Government Palace kept its magic aura.

The cells had been dug out in the crystal partition. They were alveoli with mirror-like facets. There were hundreds of such cells all in a row at the foot on the glass partition.

Algan went into one. Facing his image, he looked deeply into his own eyes. The Machine's motto was: "You must seek the answer in your innermost self."

All the sounds of the world were stilled. He was alone with his image at the bottom of a luminous space; he saw a long, thin face, bony features, and bright, cold eyes. He had never before seen himself quite like this. Nor had he ever heard his heart beat, nor felt his breath like this. He moistened his lips and started to speak; but then waited uncertainly for the Machine to ask him a question. Suddenly he understood that there was no Machine, that it did not exist, that there was nothing except his reflection and that only his reflection would answer.

He could almost see what a human's reaction would be.

"Well, what do you want to know?" asked the Machine.

The voice was flat, without overtones.

Algan thought. He decided to ask a routine question, one which millions of men, dead or alive, had uttered, convinced, deep down, that they were profaning an oracle.

"What obstacle must I overcome?" he asked.

"Loneliness," the Machine answered unhesitatingly.

Was it the usual answer to that question, or had it given Algan the answer suited to his case?

Loneliness. He had not thought of it for a long time, nearly two centuries.

"My name is Jerg Algan," he said. "Do you know me?"

There was a pause.

"Yes," said the Machine evenly. "You were born on the Earth. You ought not to be here now."

"No, of course. Can you tell me where I've come from?"

He knew that that question was going to cause confusion and fear in Betelgeuse. He waited a moment.

"No. I don't know. Wait a minute. I'm going to check up."

"Don't bother. Just try to find out where I'm going."

He smiled at his reflection and suddenly disappeared.

For the second time he was in front of the Machine. But it seemed to be asleep. The crystal partition was almost completely dark. Only a few tubes were blinking. The mathematical symbols etched in the surface of the glass shimmered gently.

Hatred and triumph jostled inside him, for the last battle was near. He started to walk unhurriedly toward one of the alveoli of the Machine.

CHAPTER X
Through the Crystal Wall

"Two hundred years," said Stello.

"Yes, two hundred years," Nogaro repeated.

His face hardened. He put his hands on the table and stared at the seven men.

"He must be immortal," said Stello.

"I think so," said Nogaro.

Silence. Suddenly they were afraid. Afraid of a stranger over two hundred years old who had appeared with no warning from space, alone, empty-handed.

"Didn't he take a long trip on a spaceship?" Albrand asked. "A few years spent at near the speed of light could perhaps ..."

"No," said Nogaro. "The Machine is positive about this. He disappeared about two hundred years ago in the region of Glania, a small planet on the border of the central regions."

"He was never seen again?"

"Never. Fifty years ago, some of the people from Ulcinor who had been imprisoned at the time of the Puritan repression claimed they had seen him. But this was never confirmed."

"Could the Puritans have put him in a state of hibernation in order to use him as a weapon at the right moment?" Olryge asked.

Nogaro shook his head.

"How did he get to Betelgeuse?" asked Voltan, one of the oldest of the eight, older even than Nogaro. "Does the Machine know?"

"No," said Nogaro. "All it knows is that he did not come on a spaceship. At least, not on one of ours. Human spaceships, I mean."

They were all silent again. They felt something in the air stretch and vibrate. Everything they had accomplished in centuries past was evaporating, dissolving, disappearing in the frightening uncertainties of the future. For the first time they were afraid of what was going to happen.

"Outside help," grumbled Olryge, his eyes flashing. "You were speaking of it just now."

"It's the only logical solution," Nogaro replied coldly. "I am the only one of us who knows Jerg Algan. He was already a strange man two hundred years ago. I wonder if now, after all that time, he's even human."

He made a face, not that he was afraid, he was just simply consumed with curiosity. He knew why Algan had left, he knew that he had been successful. What had he found in the center of the galaxy?

"Tell us what you know, Nogaro," said Stello.

116

Nogaro turned and stared at him. Shall I tell them? he wondered. Shall /
tell them that I acted on my own initiative, two hundred years ago, thereby possibly endangering the whole of the human galaxy? Shall I tell them that I'm sure
I was right because there are problems more important than the well-being of the
galaxy? Or shall I say nothing and let them flit from one theory to another? Does
the Machine know?

But whether he decided to speak or be silent, he thought, nothing in the future history of the galaxy would be changed. Someone had to do what he had
done. As to what Jerg Algan had discovered and what had become of him, that
was another story.

"Do you think he has transmitted his secret of immortality to the Puritans?"
Stello asked.

"I don't know," Nogaro said. Lines of fatigue were suddenly etched on his
face. It had been a good life, all these years, asking questions, making decisions,
learning. It had been good, then weariness had set in, a heavy, gray weariness. It
would still have been good, he thought, if the world could have remained quietly, peacefully, the same.

A kind of terror began to grow inside him. Am I that old? he wondered.
Have we condemned men to immobility, the galaxy to stagnation?

"I don't know," he repeated. "Do you imagine this is of the slightest importance now? I spoke about the Puritans a little while ago only to get your attention. But can't you see that their agitation doesn't mean anything anymore?
Can't you see that the problem is no longer ours, that our ships are useless?
Can't you understand? Another race, another civilization, which is immortal, is
at our gates, able to travel in space without our knowing it...

"Perhaps that will be good for us. Do you see now why I am asking immortality for the whole of the race?

"I stick to my vote," said Olryge. "Our power is tremendous, intact; we
have not yet been attacked. We're still in control here."

"I wasn't thinking of war, Olryge," said Nogaro. "There are other forms of
competition."

"Who was this Jerg Algan?" Voltan asked in his deep voice.

"Two hundred years ago, or perhaps a bit less," said Nogaro, "when I was
not yet a member of the Council, when I wasn't even on Betelgeuse, I met Jerg
Algan. I was only an Envoy, one of the millions of Immortals who are the
watchdogs of Betelgeuse on the remotest worlds, who listen and transmit, who
are the eyes, ears, and hands of Betelgeuse. Shortly after our meeting, he disappeared. I had made friends with him. He was about thirty years old, had spent all
of his youth on the Earth. He had just been picked up in the port of Dark and
recruited under the usual circumstances. The first time I saw him was on the
ship that was taking us to Ulcinor. I was favorably impressed by him. He was
energetic and persistent, intelligent and sad. I think I'd have liked him to be one
of us. He hated Betelgeuse for he was, you see, a man of the old planets for

whom the past was more important than the future and who called a spade a spade. The name of Betelgeuse for him was synonymous with tyranny.

"At that time I was looking for someone to carry out a plan I had made. I looked over Algan's credentials and found them satisfactory. The same problems existed then as today, only circumstances were different. We kept looking for traces of another civilization. There was some evidence that pointed to an interesting zone in the general direction of the center of the galaxy. I was carried away by the idea of sending an expedition there, and I still am. But the Puritans on Ulcinor were watching us closely because they were afraid we'd find the means of wiping them out financially. They had information that I lacked. I arranged things so that it would look as though Jerg Algan was being sent by both sides, which is probably why the merchants of Ulcinor and the Ten Planets boasted about his support.

"We had already sent several expeditions to the center of the galaxy, but they had all failed. A couple of them even disappeared altogether. Extraordinary tales began to make the rounds of the galaxy. I thought it was high time they were stopped.

"But I was only an envoy and I hadn't the power to put Jerg Algan in charge of an entire expedition. To do this, I'd have had to get the Council and the Machine to agree and that would have taken too long. I decided to have Algan steal a spaceship. I knew that the Stellar Port authorities would do what I told them to and so, when we landed on Ulcinor, I made the necessary arrangements.

"One night, Jerg Algan slipped out of his sleeping quarters, knocked out a technician, stole a rocket, and left. I knew that he headed first for Glania, where he hoped to find the beginning of a trail that I had indicated. And there he vanished. He was on the border of the central regions of the galaxy, and suddenly he disappeared."

"Under what circumstances?" Stello asked.

"No one knows," replied Nogaro. "No, no one on this side of the galaxy knows. He lost his ship when he landed on Glania, probably as the result of clumsy handling, and he started on foot toward the planet's Stellar Port, which he reached; the evidence on that score is positive. He had an interview with the commandant of the Stellar Port, but never came out of the commandant's private apartments. Or if he did his destination was unknown."

"And what did the commandant have to say about that interview?" Olryge asked.

"Not a word. He committed suicide. He had allowed a prisoner to escape and I suppose he went to pieces. Just think: a man with neither ship, food, nor special information who suddenly disappears from an almost deserted planet and who literally vanishes in space."

"Could he have died in some dark corner of Glania?" suggested Albrand.

"No," said Nogaro. "I had a thorough investigation made. There was no trace of him on the planet. Nothing except some fingerprints on a glass that had contained zotl."

"Where was the glass?"

"In the commandant's office. The investigators found it after the suicide; they made a note of the fingerprints, just as a matter of routine, and they discovered that they belonged to a human named Jerg Algan. But they never realized the full import. I found out about it much later."

"Zotl?" said Fuln. "The commandant was stoned. Perhaps he killed Algan to avoid discovery."

"No, drinking zotl was not illegal at that time. It was outlawed only a century and a half later, when we felt obliged to keep in check the economic power of the Ten Planets."

"A strange story," said Voltan. I don't like stories that are that strange. Nothing good ever comes of them. But does any of this mean anything? Are we worrying about nothing? I don't believe one man can endanger the human galaxy even if he is immortal. Those days are over. I've seen dangerous men, very dangerous men, but in the past; not nowadays. No, not nowadays."

"What will it take to make you believe it and begin to worry?" shouted Nogaro. "You're too old. We're all too old. Nothing frightens us anymore. We no longer believe in danger."

What is to be, will be, Nogaro thought. We've done what we could. Men will now have to make out as best they can. If only / knew what was going to happen to them! Then he thought of Algan. One man, lost, alone in a forest of suns, attaining immortality, and what else? Was the center of life in the center of the galaxy?

"I have nothing more to add," he said. "I am asking you to set into motion as quickly as possible our plan to achieve immortality for the whole of the human species. I hope it is not too late."

He looked at them, one after the other, and he read on their faces which had been furrowed by time, fear, worry, weariness, habit, boredom.

"You know my answer," said Olryge exultantly.

"I can't," said Stello reluctantly.

"I don't think the time has come," said Albrand.

"No," said Fuln.

"No," said Aldeb, Voltan, and Luran in chorus. They seldom spoke, buried as they were under the weight of memories, crushed by experience.

"Perhaps you're right," said Nogaro. "I hope so. I hope you're not making a mistake.

"We hope so too," they said.

"Is the discussion over? Shall we bring the meeting to a close?" asked Olryge.

119

"As a matter of fact it would be better to stick to the decision you've made," said Nogaro ironically. "You might do even worse."

Albrand stirred.

"Perhaps we ought to look for this man, this Jerg Algan," he said.

"He's out of our reach," said Nogaro.

"The Machine?"

"The Machine knows nothing. Do you suppose that I am not consumed with curiosity to find out what lies outside the human galaxy?"

"Don't take it that way, Nogaro," said Voltan. "After all, you're the one who unleashed the danger that you say threatens us."

"I did, and it had to be done," said Nogaro.

"That is beside the point."

"It makes no difference," Olryge exclaimed. "The voting is over."

Voltan turned toward him.

"Don't be in such a hurry, Olryge. Eternity stretches before you. I'd like to ask Nogaro one or two questions."

"I'm listening," said Nogaro.

"What were those stories you mentioned just now?"

"I'm not sure I ought to speak of them here. After all, they were only stories."

"Let's have them."

"Well, they mentioned an empire on the boundary of ours, giant citadels; but we never saw anything. They mentioned the Masters, but they never came; they mentioned a chessboard and the origin of worlds, but they were only stories. I listened carefully for a long time, I believed some of what I heard. Nothing ever came of them, or almost nothing."

"Almost," said Voltan. "You call it nothing; immortality."

"They told of what had existed before man and what would happen after him," said Nogaro. "They were heavy with curses. They said we had taken a wrong turning. They dealt with whom we might meet in the center of the galaxy."

"Whom?" sneered Olryge.

"The creators of men," answered Nogaro." The Masters of the stars that dominate the galaxy, from the top of their sun palaces; and that was where I sent Jerg Algan. And when he returns, you may be sure he will have been sent by them."

"Who am I?" he asked.

"Jerg Algan," the Machine replied.

"All right," he said.

He was staring at his reflection which was moving at the end of a luminous space, in dreamlike fashion. He couldn't keep his hands from shaking. He was now near the end of his quest. The stars and the Masters, space and time, had brought him here, right into Betelgeuse, into this palace which was the repository of the whole history of humanity. He was now face to face with the Machine in which rested all human hopes.

It had been an awfully long quest. And suddenly, just as the Machine had predicted, loneliness swooped down on him like a bird of prey. There had been so many years. He had crossed the threshold of time alone, and alone he had survived. The universe, he thought to himself, would never have for him any savor except that of ashes and of the past, and bright as were the stars, they could never pierce the thick fog of time past.

Mankind, he told himself, had, through him, achieved one more quest, an ancient, encompassing, definitive one; in a few hours, in a few days, all humans would have in their mouths that same flavor of ashes as they thought of their useless exploits.

He wondered what would happen to the Machine, to the palace of Betelgeuse, the gigantic statues that adorned the esplanade, the agile spacecraft that hovered over the ports, whose prows had plowed so many different gulfs, whose hulls had reflected the rays of so many different stars.

"Do you want to ask me another question?" asked the Machine.

He did not reply at once. He looked at his reflection and thought he was at last finding his identity after a long search. So that was he, with that thin, somber face; fine, pale lips; bright, dark eyes. And those long, slender fingers would belong to him for an immensely long time. He wondered if the Machine ever thought itself beautiful, if the humans who had built it had also endowed it with an aesthetic sense, if it enjoyed its own brightness, the blinking of its lights, the green lightning flashes that made it quiver. Then he asked:

"Who are your masters, Machine?"

This question had hung in the air for a long time; it had burned his lips, his tongue, and now he could ask it, in peace.

"Men, Algan," it replied unhesitatingly.

Can a Machine be untruthful? he wondered. Can it lie? Then the answer came automatically. Men can lie.

"No," he said to his reflection.

The reflection did not waver.

"Listen to me? Machine; do you want me to tell you the truth? You're nothing. You're nothing but a piece of scenery. You might at least admit that. I want to see your masters, Machine. At least, tell them so."

"I cannot answer you," said the Machine.

Its voice was still flat, expressionless, even. It was a curious experience, Algan thought, to question a Machine and to fault it. But, unlike humans, a Machine knew how to lie. It would never contradict itself and it was impossible to make it take a lie detector test.

It was in some way better and worse than men, more absolute. It was hypocritical because men had made it so, but since hypocrisy had been built in, it became a quality; it was nothing but a possibility; that precluded any moral judgment.

Was it the same, by definition, for humans? Algan wondered. The Masters had never mentioned it. Yet, somewhere there was a difference. The Machine did not lie to achieve its own ends; it lied because, on some points, it had been built not to tell the truth. Men lied systematically in the hopes of attaining personal ends. Men were off the beam.

He wondered whether a machine, out of gear, would succeed in lying for its own ends. It was hard to imagine, but not, perhaps, inconceivable. It could happen, he thought, if the Machine were caught in a dilemma such as failing to follow certain directions, and as a result, being threatened with annihilation.

Perhaps the Machine would destroy itself. Or perhaps it would admit to the cause of the conflictive situation and would solve it by adopting an attitude that did not conform with reality. A neurotic attitude.

Humans were forever plunged in a conflictive atmosphere. They existed in order to attain a certain object which they were prevented from attaining. Some of them, when the pressure of the conflict became too strong, committed suicide; their instinct for self-preservation—that is, one of the rules which had been imposed upon them— vanished. Others sank into a neurotic state. But the equilibrium of everyone was threatened.

And that explained the history of mankind, those thousands of years of murdering, lying, looting, swindling, warring, and that thirst for conquests and victories, that passion for power.

Men were Machines out of gear.

"Listen to me, Machine," he said. "You'd better answer me."

He could not help talking to it as to a human. He struck his fist against the cold surface of the mirror. He heard a weak vibration which was stilled almost immediately. He could do nothing against the Machine, at least, not that way.

"I cannot answer you," said the Machine.

"I have a message for your masters, Machine. Give it to them. Tell them I want to speak with them. Tell them that I come from the center of the galaxy. Tell them that I was sent by Nogaro, if they remember his name."

"Men are my masters," the Machine repeated.

Suppose the Machine is telling the truth, he thought. Suppose it had been built so as not to know who is really giving it directions. He himself did not know. The Masters, likewise, did not know—or at least did not appear to be interested, which was why he had been sent. But he found it difficult to believe that humans could for whole generations have concealed their power behind so perfect, so efficacious a mask.

What if they refused to see him, to hear him out?

"I'm going to ask you a question, Machine."

"I'm listening."

"How did I get here, to this planet?"

"I don't know. Wait, I'm going to check."

He waited a few seconds.

"You already asked me that question a little while ago," said the Machine. "Why do you want to know?"

"I only want to show you, you don't know everything, Machine."

He wondered if the Machine's mechanical brain could understand his reasoning.

"No mechanism, no being can claim to know everything," said the Machine. "Their function is not to know everything. It is to remember. It is to learn. I must ask you a question. How did you get to this planet?"

"By means of the sixty-four squares," said Algan.

"I see," said the Machine. "I'm missing a lot of data, but a number of possibilities emerge. There could be other Machines like me in space."

"Could be," replied Algan evasively.

"The chessboard is one of the weak points in my reasoning," said the Machine. "I can ascribe certain values to it, but none is predominant."

"Does the problem interest you, Machine?"

"Nothing, in the human sense of the term, interests me. I was made simply to solve a number of problems. That's one of them."

"I know the solution, Machine, and I've come to give it to your masters. Tell them so."

A few seconds went by. This last attempt might fail and he would have to find other means of carrying out his mission. He had hoped that the Machine would serve as a link between him and the hypothetical masters of the human galaxy. But he was no longer sure.

"I know of no other masters than men," said the Machine. "I cannot solve the problem you have put to me, man. However, my instructions provide for such a contingency. I don't understand them, but I'll follow them. You may be right and maybe some particular men from among all men are my masters. But I can find no evidence of this in the circuits I know. I am going to try to analyze my subconscious ones."

A conflict, thought Algan. Here at last is a conflict. The Machine is programmed to remain ignorant of certain factors even though it has stored an outline of these factors, and now it seems that the solution to certain problems that it must solve according to basic instructions is impossible because it has neglected this programming. I wonder whether its inventor made provision for this.

It was exactly the same for men. They knew certain things, but they were incapable of remembering them consciously and expressing them verbally. Result: conflict, suicide, or neurosis.

"You will have to solve the problem by yourself, human," said the Machine. "I cannot help you. My instructions are merely to let you pass."

"Is this the first case of its kind?"

"The first in my memory bank."

Was it possible, Algan wondered, that the Machine had several facets, several faces, that its memory bank was multiple and compartmented? Was it possible that one part of its huge construction was used to answer humans while another was used by the hypothetical masters of the human galaxy? Was there somewhere a central coordinating place where the final decision was made? Or were the several conscious parts of the Machine separated by ill- defined, gray, unexplored zones?

Could it be that the masters themselves controlled a fraction of the Machine without the knowledge of other centers of the Machine?

"Good luck, human," said the Machine.

Algan's reflection shivered. The surface of the mirror trembled much like an expanse of water over which, suddenly, a breath of air is blown. Then, at the end of the luminous space, a black spot appeared which absorbed all of the light, spread, and gradually devoured Algan's reflection. The blackness now covered almost all of the mirror, conjuring up an unplumbed depth.

It was a door.

He stepped forward and found himself, with no transition, in the night. He put his hands out, then on the sides, but his fingers encountered nothing. He was in the middle of a huge, dark plain.

"Forward," said the Machine.

He concentrated.

Perhaps it was a trap. He was ready to throw himself a million miles away if there was the slightest danger. He knew that he was stepping into a region which few men knew of and which the Machine itself had probably never explored, even though it was located inside the palace. He remembered something Nogaro had said about Betelgeuse. It was, he had said, a gigantic spider spinning its web in time and space, hooking its thread to the stars.

He was going into the spider's parlor. He remembered the trapdoor spiders of the Earth, dragging themselves along into curious holes in the soil that were lined with silk and closed with a hinged lid. A hinged glass. A mirror.

The ground fell away underfoot and pulled him down. He had no way of telling how fast he was moving. All he knew was that he was going where he wanted to. Just as he'd been doing for two hundred years.

He came out suddenly into the light. It seemed to emanate from the walls of a corridor which stretched out of sight and which must bury itself in the colossal mass of the palace.

The moving belt which had been carrying him came to a stop. He had to walk the rest of the way. The builders of the palace had not wanted it to be fully mechanized. They knew that under certain conditions machines can become dangerous. Algan examined the walls. They were finely polished and made of a hard, cold, white substance. He told himself that he was only crossing to the other side of the real walls of the palace.

Walls hundreds of yards thick.

The palace was a veritable stellar fortress. Its builders had had war in mind. They had thought of men, but also perhaps of other adversaries, more powerful ones, from the stars.

Jerg Algan smiled. He was the equivalent of an invading army and he was sure to win.

The builders of the palace had heard too many stories in their childhood about sidereal fleets invading a planet or about fantastic weapons, bombs capable of destroying half a planet. They had never envisaged attack from one single man.

He walked on faster, the sound of his footsteps on the hard floor echoing sharply. It seemed to him, at times, that the clear sound of his heels came from ahead as if an invisible walker were preceding him. The color of the light gradually began to change. From white to ashen. Even the walls became tinted with gray. He remembered skies in the center of the galaxy which he had admired, star-studded firmaments which were tinted in the same ashen light, the color of an extinguished fire but which still preserved, for a long time, the intensity, the calm magic of flames.

At last he came to a series of large rooms and he knew he was on the other side of the palace walls. The palace probably had other entrances, less complicated ones, but this one had been built to impress possible future visitors, whoever they might be.

A double row of huge triangular pillars supported a rounded dome. The sound of his footsteps was absorbed by the floor and he felt as though he were burrowing into silence.

He remembered having read once, in some old books when he was still on the Earth, descriptions of buildings similar to these rooms, samples of a now defunct style of architecture. These were nearly as grandiose as the black citadels. In some fields, he thought, men had almost equaled the Masters; but what was the result of tremendous effort for men was only a game for the Masters.

He suddenly came upon a room that had no exits. It was smaller than the ones through which he had just come, and it was empty. He looked around, unable to see any trace of an opening in the walls. Then he noticed a circle engraved on the floor, in the middle of the room.

He had barely stepped into it when, as he had expected, the circle opened up and he fell into darkness.

He was falling slowly without feeling any of the disagreeable effects of a fall. He wondered how deep the well was. He tried to touch the sides by stretching out both arms, but he couldn't.

Was he, he wondered, the first man to go down this passage? Abruptly his feet were on solid ground again. A luminous ray stood out on a black wall facing him. It widened rapidly, and, blinking, he saw a large hall with bare walls, filled with an ashen light.

His heart beat faster. He saw a large, round crystal table in the middle of the room. There were eight men, seemingly dressed in silver, sitting around the table. He walked toward them. Their faces were strange, etched with lines of fatigue.

They watched him silently.

His glance came to rest on one of them and memory stirred. He couldn't believe his eyes. Yet he knew those deep-set dark eyes, those intelligent, somewhat bitter features.

He started to talk.

CHAPTER XI
The Chessboard of the Stars

"Nogaro."

"I was expecting you, Jerg Algan," said Nogaro.

Algan stood in front of the table and stared at the redheaded man whose eyes shone like rubies, and the man smiled.

So, Algan thought, these were the men who ruled the human galaxy. He wondered what had happened to the merchants of Ulcinor. The Masters had told him to pay no attention to them. Then he looked again at Nogaro. There was only one possible solution. Nogaro was immortal. All these men were immortal. That was why they ruled the galaxy. The merchants of Ulcinor had imagined another sort of continuity in time based on traveling at the speed of light and on time warps, but these men were completely and genuinely immortal.

They were almost as powerful as the Masters, he thought. Then the idea vanished. Nothing was comparable to the might of the Masters. He remembered certain facts which had surprised him in the past, about Nogaro's activities and about his influence. Now he understood.

"And so you are immortal," said one of the men, leaning forward.

"Just like you, Nogaro," said Algan. "That explains a lot."

"More than you think, Algan," said Nogaro. "It explains the stability of this civilization, the first to withstand the upheavals of history. We are somewhat like the brain cells of an individual, something that remains alive as long as the individual does, as long as this society. And we are well hidden, Algan, just as the brain of a man is hidden inside his skull. But you finally found us."

"After a long detour," he said.

"Why do you feel the need to explain all that to him, Nogaro?" Olryge said. Why not question him instead? I don't suppose he sought us out to hear our story."

"It may be useful for him to know it," said Nogaro.

"And you kept your immortality a secret all this time!" said Algan.

He felt rancor sweep over him. The hatred he had borne for so long inside him became mixed with something colder, less precise.

"And so you succeeded?" Nogaro asked.

"Yes."

"You reached the center of the galaxy?"

"I reached it." He saw the eight faces focusing on him and a sort of nausea invaded him. His mouth felt dry.

"And you've come back. After two hundred years. Why?"

"I have a message for you."

He disliked the feeling of those looks on his skin. He had forgotten men, and now he saw them, face to face, with no pleasure.

"From whom?" asked Nogaro.

"I have plenty of time; we all do. You'll find out everything."

"Don't try to play games with us," said Albrand. "You successfully carried out a long and dangerous mission, for which we are grateful to you. But don't try any games."

Algan started to laugh.

"I won't," he said hoarsely.

"You're changed, Algan," said Nogaro. "What's happened to you?"

"Yes, I've changed," said Algan. "I am immortal now. But you weren't concerned about that when I left. You weren't concerned then about any alterations that I might undergo. You used me, didn't you?"

"I had no choice. You were willing."

"I don't hold anything against you. I bear you no grudge. I might have once. But not now. I'm even grateful to you. In a way that you cannot understand."

"I think I understand, Algan," said Nogaro. "I too have lived a long time. And I was, and still am, your friend." "That no longer matters. Things are going to change, you know."

"Immortality," said Olryge.

Algan shot him a curious look.

"Immortality and lots of other things."

"How did you manage to travel in space?" Olryge inquired. "You had a spaceship, didn't you? A spaceship faster than ours? None of our detectors could pick it up."

"I had no spaceship," said Algan. "And you'll hear how I managed. Don't worry. I came to tell you."

He paused. "To tell you and all other men."

No one spoke. The eight immortals looked at one another.

"The human galaxy will collapse, if you do," said Stello. "Do you understand?"

Algan nodded.

"Don't think we'll let you do it," said Olryge. "Don't think you've won, even if you are immortal."

"Do you think I'm acting alone?" Algan asked. "Do you think my life is of any importance in what is about to happen? I've only come to give you a friendly warning. That's all."

"Is it an ultimatum?" Voltan asked.

"Did I set any conditions?"

"And so the legends were true," said Nogaro.

"They were not inaccurate," Algan replied. "They just didn't tell the whole story."

"The chessboard?"

"I'll tell you everything; I won't hold anything back," said Algan. "You'll master the chessboard just as I did. That's what I've come to tell you. You and all men."

"Men are not yet ready," said Luran. "As soon as they are, they'll get their immortality."

"What for? Immortality and the chessboard are unimportant. What is important is what I'm going to tell you." "We're listening."

"It can wait. Have you no questions? Important questions?"

They looked at one another again. Algan could detect a vague fear in their eyes.

"And so, there is a form of life in the center of the galaxy," said Nogaro.

"Yes."

"And a civilization?"

"Yes."

"More advanced than ours?"

"That depends upon what you mean by civilization and by life. Life and civilization to you signify forms of organization inscribed in space which alter in time along a predetermined course. What exists over there is very different from what you can imagine."

"Are they ... hostile?"

"Do you mean hostile toward humans? Why should they be? Why, then, send me to you?"

Olryge got up and leaned down toward Algan, supporting himself by his hands on the crystal table.

"You're an enemy," he said. "You were human once. But they have changed you. You're nothing but an empty shell inhabited by a stranger. You've come among us in order to destroy us. But we won't let you."

He slipped his right hand into a fold of his clothing and drew out a slender stiletto which he brandished at Algan. A golden beam flashed out from the point of the weapon and touched Algan's chest.

"No," said Algan. "Those who sent me armed me against this sort of an attack, You can't do anything to me. I, on the other hand, could grab your weapon and turn it against you. I thought you were more intelligent. I thought the years had brought you experience. You're unbalanced. But don't worry. We'll cure you."

"Perhaps you would be good enough to tell us now why you have come back?" said Stello.

"Perhaps I could," said Algan. "Only I wonder if you're ready to hear what I have to say. First, I'd like to tell you what I've done: I've looked at space, with naked eyes; I've stared at stars in all their brilliance, the galaxy in all its extent and splendor; I've plumbed depths you've never dreamed of; I've listened to the music of hydrogen; I've seen light and time flow about me like the waves of an

129

endless river. All this will be yours, too. When I experienced that, I realized that man had been created not to live in the dark dens he keeps building on muddy planets nor to take refuge in steel and glass spaceships, terrified, cowed by the idea of the universe around him; I realized he was meant to conquer the universe, but empty-handed and not just for himself."

"For whom, then?" Olryge asked loudly.

"You'll find out later," said Algan. "And everything I have seen and experienced will be yours also. But in order to get it, you'll have to learn a number of things."

He noticed their hands begin to tremble on the crystal surface of the table. He saw their expressions tense up and their eyes shine.

"The first part of my message is simple and can be stated in a few words. But I'm afraid it's going to take you a long time to accept it."

He stepped back and took a deep breath. He felt the deepest recesses of his lungs fill with air. He was pervaded with a tranquil sadness.

"Just one sentence," he went on. "Men are robots."

He heard Nogaro murmur:

"I knew it. I'd always thought something of the sort." "And those who sent you are our ... builders," said Stello with some difficulty.

"If you like. Imagine a race that does not think in terms of years nor centuries nor even millennia, but in terms of millions of years, for whom the birth, life, and death of a star represent a duration of time comparable to that of an individual for humans. Imagine that their hub lies in the center of the galaxy. Imagine that they want to stretch out and fill the surrounding space ... no, not that ... imagine rather that they want to stretch a web of life, a web of warmth and intelligence on surrounding emptiness, that they want to connect those distant points that shine in the dark, that they want to accomplish what we have called the conquest of space. They could use spacecraft like ours, but they could also make use of other means, more in keeping with their concept of space and time. So they decide to use machines that will enable them to travel through space, machines that can make their own complicated calculations that displacement of this sort would require.

"Imagine, therefore, that they conceive a plan, spread out over millions of years and calculated to guarantee control over the whole of the galaxy; that they realize the plan slowly but surely, with unruled meticulousness and a total disregard for the passage of time. This race of beings moves slowly and ponderously through space in order to fit together the pieces of the puzzle, somewhat the way men have sown, a little everywhere in space, fragments of their own civilization in order to reconstitute an entity which was known as the human galaxy.

Just imagine that long, long ago this race decided to build machines, and in order to do so, scattered, on thousands of worlds, the seeds of life and conditions suitable for the development of that life, as well as other things that will turn out to have been necessary. And that they waited, for a very short time by their reckoning, but an exceedingly long time by man's reckoning, for these seeds to burgeon into life. Imagine that this race watched over the development of these sources of life, scattered around the center of the galaxy which it occupied; that it saw all kinds of forms of government succeed one another, as provided for in the original plan; that it witnessed a great number of failures caused by infinitesimal divergences in the conditions originally set forth; but that, broadly speaking, the project was developing according to plan. Imagine that in these multiple testing grounds, life as we know it was developed, that multicellular forms won out over protozoa, that animals derived from plants, that mammals succeeded the great reptiles, in a gradually more complex sequence of increasingly delicate links leading to the machine destined to insure the control of space to this race of the Creators. Imagine that man appeared, one day, not just in that one place in the galaxy, but in thousands or perhaps even millions of places, and that this story which seems interminable, measured by our standards, lasted barely more than a second when measured by their race's concept of time.

"Imagine that men then developed at an increasingly faster rate, still in accordance with the plan which had provided for shorter and shorter periods of time between succeeding stages of growth; that men began to conquer, clumsily at first, with the imperfect means at their disposal, the space around them: first of the world which bore them, then beyond that world. That they grabbed, here and there, whole portions of the galaxy, still ignorant of what they really were and why they existed, not knowing that beyond the huge abysses of space, other experimental stations had given results much like themselves. At last, the final stages of the schedule are reached: the abysses of space that separate the various human empires shrink from year to year to the point where soon there remain only thin gaps of the unknown that could easily be bridged by random expeditions or because men are eager to get to the very regions from which the Creators came, that is, the center of the galaxy. Then, one fine day, a man, a machine, a robot, reaches these regions and the plan is completed. The huge organization built up in space by this race is now going to begin to function. Distances will be abolished; humans will find their true function.

"But will they accept it? That's the problem. Infinitesimal variations in the unfolding of the plan could have made men forget certain data, neglect others, build up a disorganized but autonomous civilization.

"Men are machines, but machines that are somewhat out of kilter. They will need to be repaired, taught what they have forgotten, given the immortality required to solve the problems caused by the vastness of space.

"And by a strange irony of fate, or of the plan, these men were driven by their own problems to build machines that were quite inferior to those built during millions of years by the Creators, but the power and intelligence of man's machines was considerable. Thanks to these machines, they've been able to resolve many problems. Except one.

"Who they were, where they came from, and why they always turned out, in the end, to be unhappy and maladjusted; why they continually wished to leap from one world to another, leave yesterday behind to get to tomorrow.

"But all that was needed was for one of them one day to reach the regions controlled by the Masters; then everything would fall into place. After a brief delay the plan will now finally be fulfilled. Men are going to be able to solve the problems for which they were created; there will be no more neuroses.

"What kind of problem is involved? A problem for which they are particularly well-equipped. A problem which all their civilizations learned to master more or less perfectly. One which appeared to be gratuitous, although actually it touched the very essence of things."

Algan paused.

"The game of chess," he said. "Naturally, men are equipped to solve problems other than those that arise in the game. They must survive as individuals and as a species. They were created to keep themselves in good condition and to proliferate. They are almost perfect machines. The Creators showed admirable ingenuity. They could have invented machines that were more effective in a given field, which functioned faster or with a smaller margin for error, or were longer-wearing: but they would have had to choose. They preferred a sort of synthesis, a machine that was self-sufficient, able to act independently of the exact problem that was put to it, that was capable of moving about, of repairing itself within certain limitations. In some men secondary attributes took over, but they all are able, in varying degrees, to play chess. In order to make the best possible use of men, the Masters need select and train only the most gifted ones, then reject the others, the criteria used being the same as men themselves used when they built their little machines.

"And those dormant attributes of man, those which he had hardly used, can be stimulated by certain drugs. Zotl, for instance.

"The plan, millions of years old, which is in the process of being completed, was based on three things. On certain rules of physics, which make it possible to move through space and which is symbolized by the chess game with its sixty-four squares and its billions of possibilities. On man, who makes it possible to solve the problems arising from movement in space, purely mechanical problems, which the race that occupies the center of the galaxy prefers to leave to others. And finally on zotl, that strange drug which is essential to the new attributes of man as air or food are to his vital functions. Through an admirable economy of means, the Masters have arranged to have man and zotl be part of the same experiment, or of similar ones, which we call life. Through the use of zotl the Masters can control men in the conquest of his new attributes. They placed him on worlds other than the ones on which men were born. This was done so that men would not discover prematurely the secret of their origin and of space travel. The Masters wanted man to be ready, wanted him to have built a civilization in space, just like yours. That was when zotl was made available to him.

"The game of chess is a symbol. I myself discovered by using one of those antique chessboards that can be found in the human galaxy, that each time a chess problem is solved, there was a move in space. This is not magic. Man is properly equipped for travel among the stars, but he has to know how to use the equipment. The squares in the chess game represent a certain number of necessary coordinates. For instance, eight squares represent eight dimensions. The solution to a chess problem corresponds to the solution of a problem of travel in space, and, as soon as the itinerary has been set, the human body, that most perfect of all spacecraft, plunges amid the worlds, and follows an almost invisible trajectory at tremendous speed. There is nothing incomprehensible about that. The Masters made use of the techniques that we discovered much later and which are used on ships. But they used them almost perfectly.

"They built, millions of years ago, tremendous black citadels which are the magnified equivalents of our stellar ports. They scattered throughout the galaxy chessboards that had been set up. Then they waited. Until now. The plan is almost completed. The Masters are going to be able to travel in space, explore the farthest reaches of space. Their web stretches from star to star. And humans are going to leap from one point of the universe to another."

"This is inhuman," said Stello in a different tone of voice.

"I wonder," said Jerg Algan. "Do you think it more human to reserve immortality for a small number of the privileged? Do you think it human to strengthen one's power by using men who have been recruited by force? Do you think it human to die wretchedly in the bottom of some poisoned bog on some lost planet under pretext of enlarging the human galaxy? I think, on the contrary, that we are going to become truly human, that we are at last going to accomplish what we were created for. We are all spacemen, but until now all we've done was to fight space. Tomorrow it will truly belong to us."

"We shall no longer be our own masters," Olryge cried out.

"Have you ever been, except in your dreams? Or were you so because your power crushed millions of men?"

No one spoke. Nogaro's glance wandered over the walls. Thousands of names, he thought. Thousands of names of immortals, a chain now broken. Was it to be regretted?

"The chessboard of the stars," he said. "The black citadels. So, it was all true."

"It was all true," Algan answered. "Somewhere in this planet, a few hundred yards under you, there is a citadel buried under heavy layers on lime and alluvium. You might, by chance, have discovered it. But was it chance that you did not, in fact, do so? Was it by chance that the floor of the great hall in which the Machine is located is an exact reproduction of the chessboard? Was it by chance, also, that you sent me on an expedition to the center of the galaxy; that

133

one of the shopkeepers gave me an antique chessboard? Sometimes I wonder. The Masters did not tell me."

"A huge network of citadels," Nogaro whispered as in a dream. "And our conquest is pure waste. Those millions of men died in vain. What a mess. And we thought we were so great."

"The time of the mess is over," Algan said gently. "And I don't think we've lost any of our greatness. I believe, on the contrary, that we have at last achieved it. We made a detour, a much longer one than my trip. As for the network of citadels, that huge spider web spread over space, there is no absolute need for it. It will be very useful at first. Then men will learn to travel alone along the wide paths of space."

"It doesn't matter," said Nogaro. "Whatever happens, I'll go with you. I want to see the center of the galaxy. I want to be present when the human species is transformed."

"Men, robots," said Stello. "I can't get used to the idea."

"You'll have plenty of time to do so," Algan said with a smile. "All the time in the world. When you're moving from star to star."

Olryge brought his fist down on the crystal table.

"You're nothing but a gang of traitors," he shouted, "and those who sent you, Algan, are nothing but a bunch of cowards. Oh! I can just see them. They sent you in the hope that we'd give up without a struggle, that we'd put ourselves in their hands lulled by enticing tales. I don't believe your story."

"No one is asking you to believe anything," Algan interrupted.

"We won't let ourselves be taken in," roared Olryge. "What our ancestors predicted has happened. We're going to have to fight. I, for one, am not complaining. This is war, Algan, and well win. You can go tell that to your Masters. We're not afraid of them. They won't enslave us simply because they occupy the center of a galaxy that belongs to man."

"There will be no war," Algan said coldly.

He walked up to the table and looked at each one in turn. Suddenly they felt themselves floating in the air while a long vibration shattered the walls of the subterranean room. Their bodies were almost weightless. Olryge gasped. Luran's hands began to shake. Nogaro remained impassive and Stello's eyes grew round with surprise.

"The pull of this entire planet's gravity has just been altered," Algan announced. "They can do that. They can wipe out a star in a second. They would rivet your ships to the ground. There will be no war. Do you think for one moment that men will follow you, when immortality and the stars are given to them?"

"But who are they?" Nogaro asked. "Do they look like men? What are they like? Are they eternal?"

"No," said Algan, "they are not eternal, although their lifetimes are greater than even the entire span of human evolution and history. They know they are

134

mortal. And you know them. Men have always turned to them... They are the stars."

He was silent for a moment, turning over in his mind what he was going to say, scanning their faces, in which he read fear, skepticism, or a strange relief. He could feel the words he was going to speak forming themselves in his head. He had carried them a long time inside him, when he was traveling in space, when he was touching comets and nebulas, when he was exploring man's garden, the universe. His eyes never left their faces as he told them who the Masters were. The stars.

He told them what the stars were, points of light clustered in huge groups which streak the skies like drops of milk dotted on an immense, cold black space; he told them who the Masters were.

They were the stars, or rather something living on the stars, something that was born, lived, and died with the stars, that had appeared a few billion years ago, in the great explosion of atoms, in the shock of billions of particles flung one against another; it was something that had grown slowly in the center of the galaxy, until it had become a core of consciousness and conscience that yearned to throw light and warmth on the icy emptiness.

He told them about the loneliness of the stars, the extent of which men could neither understand nor conceive: they could only try to imagine it, that determination to link the stars with bonds other than light. He told them that the great plan which had been formulated millions of years ago had only just begun and that, beyond the visible stars, there existed others and that they, men, would be like the intelligence, the conscience, the blood of the stars circulating in the veins of space, unceasingly pushing back chaos, and the cold of darkness. He told them that there were other galaxies and other universes and that men would explore them until the stars were extinguished one by one, and that beyond that frozen death of the universe they would perhaps continue to carry the torch of a glorious stellar existence.

He described for them the beauty of the worlds whirling about in space—which none of them had ever really seen—the splendor of double or triple stars, the magnificence of the skies in the center of the galaxy, where stars touched and worked together to achieve the great goal that had no beginning and no end.

He explained to them that now for the first time man was capable of dealing with the universe; that he could throw himself into the night and know that so long as he could see the light of one sun, he was safe.

He told them that the stars themselves did not know where they came from, but that they were content to be and to perform their task; that they sometimes thought that their relationship to other, greater beings was the same as men's relationship to them, that perhaps they constituted oases of privilege in the universe; that perhaps they were taking a glorious but silent part in an even greater, and to them, incomprehensible struggle.

He told them about the other men they would meet, about the strange and wondrous worlds they would put into contact with one another, bringing here the flame of life, their knowledge, and the message of the stars; that they would be the eyes and the ears, the voice and the hands of the suns. There was no lack of dignity in serving the stars, he concluded.

He waited and at last read in their faces something that might be understanding.

He told them of the surprising world of crystals, of gases and vapors in space, of the ceaseless movement of atoms in time, and of the tireless combinations of matter.

They were only children, he said. They had to learn again to look at the sky through the eyes of a child. A sky in which multitudinous burning and palpitating spheres would shine. And, abruptly, suddenly, they crossed the threshold of the wide open gates to space and entered, with their eyes still unseeing, the infinity that spread beyond.

THE DAY BEFORE TOMORROW

I

Wherever there is self, there must be conscience.
—Dr. Lagache

On Altair, the great black rectangle emitted a somber light, at the limit of visibility. The time engineers were preparing an expedition, the third in less than a year. The older ones remembered a time when expeditions had been less numerous. If they had had a taste for reflection, they would have been disturbed by this new frequency of time explorations. But their job was not to ask questions, and they scarcely thought about it On Altair, they were very precise as to the prerogatives of different specialties.

The job of the time engineers was to adjust the multitensors of a Horowitz space with a precision exceeding the sixteenth decimal. Part of the result could be attained with the aid of machines. But for the rest, Altair had to rely on their competence.

It was considerable. Indeed, much more considerable than the risks involved in the operation. And these risks were themselves enormous considering the quantities of energy employed in the operation. One does not manipulate with impunity forces capable of breaking the stable equilibrium of a time and space. Most of the inhabitants of Altair II, the only inhabitable planet of the system, believed that an error on the part of the time engineers would only mean the loss of a team, the probable death of seven men. They dreaded that eventuality because they were human, and death for them was a rare and unpleasant thing. Also because they knew that each of the men who composed a time exploration and action team was worth an immense sum, doubtless the fortunes of two or three of the most powerful planets of the Federation, which gathered no less than six thousand planetary systems under the authority of the Arque. But they did not know the truth. Only the Arque and the members of his council knew it, with the time engineers, evidently. The time engineers knew that an error on their part would mean either a possibly catastrophic change in the future of Altair II, and consequently of the rest of the Federation, or a cataclysm capable of destroying at least a part of the galaxy and of spreading like a wave to the ends of the universe. But the time engineers committed no error. They had never envis-

137

aged the possibility of committing an error, nor the course of action to take if an error were committed. Others were responsible for doing that and would set to work if it were necessary. On Altair II, roles were very precisely defined and very carefully distributed.

The time engineers juggled with the inmost structure of the universe. It is not possible to express in words the action of flexures on a Horowitz space. But when the time engineers had to explain their job to a layman, they would use an analogy. "Imagine," they would say, "that the universe were a kind of goldbeater's skin balloon and that we were on a point on its internal surface. By employing considerable energies and applying them in a well-determined direction, we could distend the goldbeater's skin to create a tiny opening through which we could project something outside. If the deformation were too slight, that something might be caught in the skin's thickness so that nothing could dislodge it. If the deformation were too great, the skin would be permanently pierced, and the balloon would either slowly deflate or explode."

At this point in their explanation, the time engineers would eye their visitors. Their expectation was rarely disappointed. The visitors who came from the central worlds of the Federation and wore rich garments, sometimes even the badge, of the Arque's personal servants, would pale despite the assurance of the time engineers. The visitors would regard the black rectangle which communicated with the absolute Beyond as they would a malevolent beast. They would hesitate to decide which of the two catastrophes was the more terrifying: the brutal explosion which would reduce the subtle architecture of the universe to a dust of elementary constituents, or the slow leaking which would empty the universe of its space, its matter, and its time, as a pin prick deflates a balloon. Between the death of a soap bubble and the end of a child's balloon, they could take their choice. They didn't like to think about it. But as proud men, sure of their power, which was that of humanity, that of a galaxy more than two-thirds populated, whose ships already ventured to other stellar islands, they liked even less knowing that the apparently tangible and solid universe which contained them had not much more reality or solidity than a soap bubble or a goldbeater's skin. They didn't like the comparison because they believed it diminished them. They didn't like to see the time engineers manipulate such forces. But they also knew that it was necessary. To assure its power, the Federation had to dominate time and, in doing so, to become conscious of the fragility of its support, the universe. The danger was the condition of the Federation's security.

Surveying their visitors, the time engineers inwardly shrugged their shoulders. The danger had less reality for them than the flexures, which were the most abstract concepts that man, aided by machines, had been able to construct after centuries of mathematical labor. The time engineers knew that the great black rectangle was neither matter, nor space, nor time, but was only a door, an abstraction materialized. On one side of the door extended a continuum which contained billions of galactic clusters, a number of galaxies a billion times greater, and a number of stars a billion times greater yet, each star composed of billions of particles. On the other side of the door—nothing.

At least, nothing intelligible. Nothing which would constitute a datum on the nature of the absolute Beyond. One could say, so to speak, that the door opened into primeval chaos, into the negation of space which had preceded the first moment of the universe, the first atom of the universe, whose explosion had given birth to it. And that was why the door which opened to the outside of the universe permitted the attainment of any place whatever, of any moment whatever in the universe— under certain conditions. These conditions imperatively limited the possibilities for voyages in time and space; but they were nevertheless flexible enough to include an enormous scope with respect to the duration of human history.

That was why the time exploration and action teams plunged into that emptiness, through the door, faced that negation, the absolute Beyond, to reappear on other worlds in the past or future.

To act upon time. To modify the past or the future. To assure the power, menaced by time, of the Federation, which had decided to abolish chance.

The seven men of the team came into the room. They seemed scarcely human, their equipment deforming their silhouettes. The detectors, the arms, the apparatus they carried would permit them to survive in virtually any circumstance—at the heart of a sun as well as in the gulf of space separating galaxies. They could challenge any adversary. They were capable of destroying a world, of facing a heavily armed fleet. Their Ordzian ray detectors theoretically would permit them to see through a mountain. Their field manipulators rendered them capable of displacing themselves at very high speeds to any altitude above a planet. Their symbiotic complexes could insure their nutrition and respiration from any base material. Thanks to their machines, they had the power of the mythological gods.

But their most useful, most formidable weapons were still their nervous systems, and the knowledge and training which they found indelibly stamped upon themselves. Even naked and abandoned in unfavorable circumstances, they had more chance of survival than almost any other beings populating the galaxy. This was the result of the innate capacities for which they had been chosen by the selectors, and also the fruit of long labor accomplished on their bodies.

They were ready to confront almost any situation, any danger—all those, at least, which man had encountered in the course of his voyages. Their conception of the world excluded defeat. Taken alone, each was almost invulnerable—and they were seven.

Seven who many times already had faced together time and its snares. Seven whom the selectors had chosen because they formed a coherent team, a single cell. Seven who, once more, were going to pass through the door and transform the future of an obscure world, so that the Federation could live, so that its power would not be put in question in a distant future.

They were Jorgenssen, the co-ordinator, Arne Cnossos, Mario, Livius, Shan d'Arg, Erin, and Nanski. Jorgenssen theoretically commanded the team, but in reality it needed no leader. It functioned by itself, like a well-oiled mechanism.

Yet none of the seven was specialized. It was the rule among time exploration and action teams to have members with equal dispositions for action in all fields. At the beginning of time travel, teams had been composed of complementary specialists, but the results had proved disappointing, sometimes catastrophic: a specialist feels ill at ease when forced by circumstances to leave his own domain.

Few envied the teams their status as non-specialists. Though they had varied and extensive knowledge, they could not pretend to compete with a specialist in any particular field. Each of their abilities, taken alone, was mediocre; the whole was unique. But those of the Federation who could appreciate this polyvalence were rare. To the majority, proud of being specialists, the members of the teams were freaks. The teams kept to themselves their secret bitterness, their impression of not quite belonging to the civilization whose future they assured. They kept to themselves the richness of their experience; their faces set, they rarely expressed a feeling through their compressed lips. They didn't feel completely at home except in an environment of absolute strangeness.

The seven went toward the black rectangle; the time engineers left the room. The seven, following a complicated maze drawn on the floor, penetrated the rectangle. A bluish light enveloped them, dancing over the polished surfaces of their apparatus.

An orange-tinged line bounded the rectangle. The seven were leaving for the past, for a planet which they had never seen, whose name they probably had never heard before they had been assigned their mission the day before.

For it was the rule never to inform team members much in advance. They were always ready to leave. They didn't know who made the decision to send them to a particular world, to a certain time, but they cared little. They received precise instructions and executed them.

The darkness of the rectangle mounted like a mist about the men's legs; it engulfed them little by little. Then everything turned white. The intensity of the white light was such that it would have irreparably burned the retinas and optic nerves of an unprotected observer.

When the light diminished, the black rectangle and the men had disappeared. The door in the universe had closed again, and the men had left for Ygone, a planet in the constellation of the Sphinx, whose history they were to change.

The day before, Jorgenssen was in the studio of his friend Aran, on the planet Igor II. He watched the artist in the process of creating a new sculpture. In a transparent block moved colored forms—very pale, like the smoke of a cigarette spreading out on still air, or the spiral forms of a drop of ink falling through a glass of water. Aran specialized in certain spatial combinations and grayed tones. His works ornamented the richest homes of the Federation.

"I like what you do," said Jorgenssen. "Often, I'd like to imitate you. You're a happy man. You can see your work transforming itself under your hands."

The artist raised his head and smiled. "I sculpt in smoke," he said, "you sculpt in time. Isn't that more important? I live in my dreams; you act Isn't that better?"

Jorgenssen, without responding, let his gaze drift to the heart of the crystal mass. Its abstract contours evoked anguish, and beyond the anguish, peace—a joy that he could scarcely conceive. He appreciated the effect Aran's work had on him without explaining it; but he would have liked to have understood. He stared at his hands. They were strong and bony, skillful; but nothing similar had ever come from them. They knew how to handle a weapon, but they had never traced a delicate contour. Sometimes Jorgenssen thought he liked coming to watch Aran work because his friend was successful at what he, Jorgenssen, had secretly desired to do.

Jorgenssen was a tall, thin man, with very clear eyes and a skull entirely shaved. His face was gaunt and hard, his cheek bones slightly prominent. The lines at the corners of his thin-lipped mouth indicated a certain lassitude. He was satisfied neither with himself nor with the world in which he lived. He liked his strange profession because it allowed him to escape his destiny. He asked himself questions, but he would have preferred the tranquil certitude he read on Aran's face to the skeptical responses that he came up with.

"I wonder," he said finally, "I wonder if what we're doing is right. Civilizations grow up on certain planets. Specialists decide that at a particular stage in their development they might endanger the Federation. Then we arrive on the scene. We intervene so that their history will be different. Oh! we're as discreet as possible. But our interventions make all the difference between disaster and success. The worlds we leave are condemned. They will never grow, they can never become rivals of the Federation. No, I don't sculpt time. I sterilize it... I limit it... I amputate it."

"You shouldn't think like that," said Aran in his mild voice. "I too—in my works, I eliminate certain possibilities, often with regret. But to keep them would injure the equilibrium and, finally, the beauty of the whole. The Federation controls time because it's the most powerful. It keeps order in the galaxy. It prevents war. Isn't that worth a dead civilization here and there in space?"

"I don't know," replied Jorgenssen with a gesture of impatience. He had the habit of speaking frankly to the artist, since he knew he risked nothing with him. In other places, his remarks would have made him a suspect of the Arque's agents. Turning slightly, he looked outside. On the other side of the circular bay stretched a grand landscape which an uninformed stranger would have thought wild. But this was an effect of the gardener's art. Mountains in the distance rose almost to the sky, and a mauve forest descended their slopes to mid-height, where it was replaced by an immense green prairie crossed by three water courses. Groves of trees adorned the expanse of high grass. A small valley dotted with flowers surrounded Aran's home on three sides. As light, nimble animals went in a single rush from one edge of the prairie to the other, the red sun, invisible at the moment, tinted the sky rose and covered the peaks of the mountains with purple. It was a perfectly peaceful landscape; contemplating it relaxed the mind. It seemed so natural—and yet there must have been nothing, or almost nothing, upon which it had been established. Not even the mountains, perhaps.

"I wonder," Jorgenssen resumed. "I've seen lots of things. I've learned plenty about the history of many worlds. I've probed their pasts and predicted their futures—to destroy them. I've seen all of them change, or try to. Only the Federation is immutable for time immemorial, immobile, unchanged. Why?"

"You know what the Arque says: The Federation is a mature, balanced civilization. It doesn't need to change. It's strong enough to avoid crises, the aging and death that await ephemeral civilizations. It's stable because it's strong."

"I know," said Jorgenssen. "But is the Arque right? Doesn't he defend his power? Everything in this universe changes, even the stars, even your creations. Only the Federation stays apparently equal to itself. And this stability—it's us, the time soldiers, who give it to the Federation, by bringing in the fresh skins of younger worlds."

Aran's fingers exerted light pressures on the walls of the transparent solid, and the pressures were transmitted to the colored spiral forms within. Aran's movements had an extreme precision. They guided the work toward its ultimate end, they disciplined chance. Abruptly, Aran stood erect again.

"I'll give you my opinion," he said. "I think the Federation is wrong. I think it's wrong to control time. Maybe the Federation's stopped aging, but it's also stopped living. I don't think we have the right—even to insure our lives—of distorting the future of other races. We ought to let them live, let them grow, welcome the novelties new societies bring us. Do you know that my art has existed for centuries, and that it's been perpetuated without the least change? Don't you think I sometimes could be weary of always repeating the same works and of being incapable of creating new ones? Because I'm a specialist. There are specialists for everything in this galaxy—even for art. Do you know I often envy your being able to escape this always-repeated perfection? The Federation may include thousands of inhabited worlds. Nevertheless, it has a musty smell. Sometimes, when I contemplate the sky, I feel myself imprisoned. And then

I resume my smile and my work, I recover the happiness of my specialist's job."

A musical tone was heard.

"I'm here," said Aran.

"I address myself to Jorgenssen," said a masculine voice, trenchant as a sheet of metal.

"I'm listening," said Jorgenssen. He knew the voice. He knew what was going to come. A kind of joy came over him, as the muscles of his hands contracted.

"A new mission is entrusted to you," said the voice. "You will leave tomorrow for the planet Ygone. You must effect a rectification of history. Return to Altair as soon as possible."

"Tonight," said Jorgenssen.

"Splendid. Good evening."

Jorgenssen turned to Aran. "Ygone—I've never heard that name. A rectification of history... the usual euphemism."

"There's the answer," said Aran. "The Federation doesn't tolerate competition. Its right is that of the strongest."

"I'm free to refuse," said Jorgenssen, "but I'll go. It gives meaning to my existence, as your sculptures give meaning to yours."

A child appeared in the vale; it was Aran's daughter. She was playing with a red football, a pure marvel of technology. The football contained complex mechanisms which permitted it to go around the child and to escape her at the moment she thought she had it. The difficulty of the game could be regulated. From time to time, the football committed an error and allowed itself to be approached. The little girl would burst out laughing and give it a kick. The ball would roll away, then return.

It was a game several centuries old, but which always met with the same success.

The day before, Arne Cnossos was fishing on the planet Hydra. The sea was his only passion, to the point that he knew the marine flora and fauna of a hundred planets better than the pisciculturists themselves. His glider scudded over the crests of the waves. It was an apparatus that he had conceived and realized, with the aid of robots, and that offered certain perfections: for example, the two slender aerials which the pilot could raise from the hull and which supported a transparent sail. From old books, Arne Cnossos had discovered that for thousands of years human civilizations had used the wind for motive power. Then the secrets of that navigation had been lost, but he had re-invented them. He loved to struggle alone between the wind and sea. For entire days, he would disconnect his motor cell and let himself drift at the pleasure of the sea breezes. At such times, his small boat would not be stabilized, and he would rock with the waves. This had given him at times an inspired conception of the sea.

Between time expeditions, Cnossos usually lived on Hydra, one of the rare inhabited planets of the Federation which was entirely covered by an ocean. The single sea contained in its depths several cities whose principal resources were tourism and the cultivation of algae; but Cnossos avoided them, not putting into port except when he was obliged to lay in supplies. He was a man who loved solitude.

Above all, he loved to descend into the depths of the sea, surrounded by that luminous density, to explore the submarine landscape, the cliffs of fossil coral, to observe the multicolored fish, and sometimes to hunt the giant species. But unlike the tourists, he did not practice slaughter. Each of his trophies represented a combat He had fought a great annelid of the depths in an unfathomable trench. Afterwards, despite the strangeness of his life, a certain respect surrounded him on Hydra.

On that day, his glider, which bore on its prow the name of an almost forgotten work, The Odyssey, advanced through a fog. The horizon was close, gray, circular. The detectors sounded the mist and the water, scanning for the possible approach of another apparatus and sounding the sea's depths. Arne Cnossos dreamed.

A strident tone pulled him out of his daydream.

"Cnossos," called a woman's voice impersonally.

"Yes," he said.

"You will leave tomorrow, for Ygone. Return to Altair."

"Fine," he said simply.

He pressed a button on the control panel. The sail folded up, and the long, telescopic aerials silently drew back into the hull. The motor cell propelled the vessel forward. It flew almost on the water's surface, scarce parting the waves with a quickly obliterated wake.

Mario loved music and mathematics almost as much a women, and these three centers of interest led him to travel a great deal. The day before his departure for Ygone, he had succeeded in reconciling them in the region of Procyon. A festival of synthetic operas had taken place on the planet Enguerrand III, and there he had met a splendid blond singer. He was dark and thickset, with extraordinarily piercing eyes and a convex forehead; he was not handsome, but he fascinated. He knew it and used it.

He had come to the teams rather by accident. He had been born on one of the central worlds, of a powerful and wealthy family, close to the Arque's. From the time of his birth, his career had seemed all cut out for him—but he hadn't liked the ways of the Federation's rulers. He had roamed the galaxy for some time without a definite end, devoting himself to mathematics tournaments here and there, having love affairs, and cultivating his taste in music. Then, even this had wearied him.

He had no specialty and did not consider choosing one; his fortune sheltered him from every pain, except the boredom which, at thirty, had begun to engulf him. At that time his family had offered him several posts, which he had refused. Then one night, by accident, he had met Jorgenssen and had become his friend. Two years later, Jorgenssen, having scrutinized him, asked him to join the teams. Mindful of his freedom and scarcely believing in the need to defend the Federation, which he hated, he had hesitated. But he had followed Jorgenssen, and he had taken a liking to his new job. Its danger made sense.

When he returned to his place that evening, he noticed the anxious expression of Ora, the blond singer. She remained leaning against a marble pillar and the smile had deserted her lips. Mario instantly understood what that meant He took her into his arms and asked, even before kissing her: "A mission?"

She nodded without saying a word. He put his hands into her blond hair, but he felt no regret. A feeling of experienced triumph spread over him anew. He already felt far from Ora.

"Ygone," she said. "I don't even know where it is. I haven't found a trace of it in the atlases. It must be a small, unimportant world on the border."

"It must have some importance," he said, "for us to intervene."

She looked at him, her eyes open wide. He could feel the softness of her body against him.

"You'll come back, won't you?"

"Yes," he said in an uncertain voice.

Nothing was less certain. No one could tie down Mario—no one, except perhaps the teams.

The day before, Livius roamed the outskirts of Shangrin, in search of friends, or a fight, or a splendid achievement to do. Livius was an adventurer. It was the taste for risk and violence which had led him to the teams. He concerned himself little with intellectual considerations, but relied on his reflexes. He was born on a poor and populous world, and doubtless would have devoted himself to piracy or to questionable dealings if the selectors had not offered him a better destiny. He had left his native planet without a thought of returning and spent his spare time in the great cities of the old worlds without being much concerned with his reputation. He knew his function protected him from the Arque's agents, and sometimes abused this—his quarrels with the police were notorious. On his better days, he would be content with smashing a few robots—he would say this put a little excitement into his dull life. He had no family and chose his companions from day to day, without regretting it. The sudden appearance of his tail, bent, and bony silhouette, and of his scarred face, which he obstinately refused to have restored by the biosynthesizers, would always provoke tumults of acclamation in most of the Federation's taverns. He liked this success though he despised those who gave it to him. He considered himself a wolf, and only reproached himself for his acts of pity.

That evening he was bored. He had planned to steal a ship from the stellar port, defying the heavy guard of robots, and go with some companions as near as possible to a sun, just for the excitement of danger. But suddenly, he considered the childish vanity of it. He had time on his hands. A crisis was approaching. And during these dull days, he thought vaguely of joining an extragalactic expedition or returning to his native world. Even the soft hands of Shangrin's women were at that time powerless to pull him out of his melancholy, and he refused to let himself be approached by a psychologist Certain agents of the Arque, whom he had recognized as such, had had to pay for it Once he had killed one, but the scandal had been suppressed. The Arque's agents were unpopular and easier to replace than a member of a team.

A sharp sound came from his pocket. He stopped and took out his transmitter.

"Livius?" asked a robot

"Speaking," he said in his low, rough voice.

"You are free to accept or to refuse the mission which is assigned you," said the robot with its customary precision. "If you accept, you will leave tomorrow for Ygone."

"Who will command?" asked Livius.

"Jorgenssen will be the co-ordinator."

"I'll go." Livius's face lit up. "Blessed be Arcimboldo Urzeit!" he said in a low voice.

"I beg your pardon?" asked the robot.

"Nothing," said Livius. "I was thanking a certain Arcimboldo Urzeit."

"I know of no living person who has that name," said the robot 'There was a historical personage by that name who lived five centuries ago. Dr. Arcimboldo Urzeit founded the mathematics of flexures and proceeded to the first practical experiments in time travel."

Robots always seemed very proud to exhibit their knowledge. This often irritated Livius. He regretted that the cyberneticists had thought it well to give them a minimum of consciousness.

"I spoke of him," the man said, thinking with sardonic joy of the confusion he had created in the robot's circuits.

The robot remained silent for a moment, then recovered its spirits. "I am registering your agreement. May the grandeur of the Arque be eternal!"

Night fell over Shangrin. With respect to universal time, he still had nearly twenty hours before returning to Altair. He watched the artificial moons take fire in the sky. The streets, arranged in more than twenty-four levels, formed an inextricably tangled and glittering skein. Intoxicating scents descended from hanging gardens; a heavy commercial ship, all lights extinguished, floated like a black shadow, gigantic and lenticular, above the stellar port.

"Let's go down to drink a last seghir to the health of good old Dr. Arcimboldo Urzeit," Livius said aloud, readjusting the transmitter.

Passersby turned around, but he paid no attention to them. They were only specialists.

Shan d'Arg maintained that he came from the Solar system, the mythical cradle of humanity. Strange to say, the civil government agreed with him. He claimed that his family had been distinguished in former times on Sol IV, which was then called Mars. He had participated in two extragalactic expeditions, in the struggle against the crystals of Capella, and in the extermination of the calculating insects of Sirius, who, after a mutation, had found means of leaving their home world and threatened to spread throughout the galaxy. The affair would have been adjusted by the time action teams, if it hadn't been discovered that the mutation had occurred after the intervention of one of the teams. Rather than run an even greater risk, the Federation had preferred to hurl millions of robots and some war-hardened men onto the contaminated planets. In principle, the men were condemned; but Shan d'Arg had survived, for he was more cunning than the insects themselves. He had yellow skin and narrow eyes. Anthropologists considered him a rare case because he exhibited the almost pure characteristics of an ancient race. In the course of galactic expansion, the early races had become mixed to such a point that the somatic differences had been effaced. Then, new differences had appeared as isolated societies established themselves on new worlds. A sun's rays, the composition of air, the intensity of gravitation, and climatic conditions formed a race in the long run. But Shan d'Arg's traits were due to nothing in his own environment: he reproduced almost exactly those people who had inhabited half the Earth even before the beginning of interplanetary navigation.

Shan d'Arg, smitten with history, always had on his lips the names of forgotten battles and heroes, and spoke of the antiquity of the Solar system as a blessed era when people passed their time fighting joyfully and passionately. He would have liked to wield with them the sword, the axe, or the submachine gun. He knew how to use a hundred obsolete weapons. At certain times, on decadent planets, he had indulged in duels and tournaments, but would return disgusted with them. He did not share the vulgar taste for murder that made the champions of Tanatos, which certain people called the Planet of Assassins, the heroes of the populace.

The day before his departure for Ygone, he waited at home among his armor and his books, his magnetic memoirs, and his instruments of death, reaped from a hundred planets. Not holding back any longer, he had called Altair.

"I'd like a mission," he had requested briefly.

"One leaves tomorrow," responded the robot, "for Ygone. But the selectors had not planned to call you. Nevertheless, if nothing is against it, I can put forward your candidature."

"Do it," Shan d'Arg had ordered in a dry voice.

He had waited impatiently for the response, busying himself with polishing the edges of his blades, which he never left in the care of a robot. The response had come. He had filled his lungs with air full of a metallic odor.

"I'm ready for you, Ygone," he had said.

The day before, Erin, a red-headed, taciturn giant, went on foot through the difficult mountains of the country of Timorg, on Zephion VI. The bluish halo of an energy helmet protected his face from cold and allowed him to breathe air under normal pressure although he was at a high altitude. He advanced on a black surface, as smooth as glass, on which he would have slid hopelessly without the suction-cups he had. He slowly approached a rock pinnacle that rose like a tower from the mountains, under the slap of a violent wind. The fatigue of a day's march was beginning to weigh on him. All day he had seen the light automatic apparatus of tourists, who would soar high above the mountains or wheel at ground level, sweeping at frightening speeds through the crevasses or circling the peaks like insane bees. He paid no attention to them. Previously, he also had flown over such landscapes, but now preferred to those rapid cruises the effort of a slow discovery, the weight of fatigue, and the victory of a difficult conquest He only took the minimum equipment.

From the heights of mountains, he experienced a sense of power and of peace. Often he had sailed through space, brushed past suns, approached planets to see them pass from the size of a pin head to that of an enormous sphere which would fill a whole screen—and on which would appear the faces of continents, the shadows of mountains, and the lights of cities, like golden studs. But nothing was as worthwhile as standing on a peak, to belong to a world and at the same time to be suspended between the earth and sky, in the silence, gazing on a well-known road, at once distant and near.

On no world had the mountains belonged completely to man. It was because the tourists basically feared the mountains that they took such liberties with their apparatus, confident in the security their instruments gave them. Erin also feared the mountains, and respected them. He had an intimate knowledge of why, in the most remote antiquity, they had been made the dwelling places of the gods and were approached with prudence and humility.

He knew, for example, that a cliff a thousand meters high was infinitely more terrifying than a million kilometers of space. Space destroys distance, abolishes vertigo, suppresses depth, lays out stars like so many points on a black table. The tourists who flew over the mountains did not know the sum of mystery and fear which could be concealed in a fissure invisible to the sky, a sheer wall, a tottering rock, an overhang filled with shadows. Erin's flesh had learned it; he had had to contact the things.

He was preparing to camp for the night at the foot of the rock pinnacle, when the shrill tone of his transmitter sounded under his helmet

"Erin," he said simply.

"A mission on Ygone. You will leave tomorrow with Jorgenssen."

"Good," he said. He glanced at the rock pinnacle. He would return later. It would wait. It had waited a million years or more to be conquered; it could wait longer.

"You will return to Altair tonight"

"Impossible," he said. "I'm in the mountains of Timorg —at least two days' march from the closest living things.

I've no autonomous apparatus. At any rate, it'll take several hours to come and find me now."

"It is annoying," said the voice.

"There is a solution," said Erin in his heavy, slow voice, which could resound like an avalanche going down the side of a mountain. "Send a ship. It could come to take me from the mountains of Timorg directly to Altair."

"I will try," said the voice.

Erin waited several minutes. He knew what the reply would be. The Federation was never niggardly when the members of teams were concerned. The co-ordinators of navigation would divert a patrol ship.

There was no answer. The decision of the co-ordinators had been instantaneous. Having come soundlessly from space, the enormous shadow of a patrol ship materialized abruptly above Erin. The man was drawn into the ship's hull by an aperture that opened like an eye. He scarcely had time to get to his feet before the patrol ship had left the Zephion system.

Nanski was a man of space. The day before his departure for Ygone, he was navigating among the asteroids of a little-known system on board his small scout ship. His crew was confined to his wife Nelle and his two sons. Though they had scarcely emerged from childhood, they already were perfectly capable of confronting a neutrino storm.

They were searching for a wreck lost there several centuries earlier—in a time when interstellar navigation in normal space was still in full vigor—which Nanski hoped to repair and take back to the sort of spaceship museum he had assembled over the years in the Tlon system.

Nanski knew the Federation's equilibrium was founded on the traverse-materials, which allowed the transportation of goods and people almost instantaneously from one world to another, whatever the distance separating them. He knew that the decline of classical space navigation was a logical development, a normal historical process. He knew that the Federation was slowly but surely becoming nothing but an immense city spread out over half a galaxy, and that its inhabitants were losing a little more each year the sense of the enormous distances extending between two stars, because it was only necessary to pass through a door to move from one solar system to another.

But he refused that negation of space for himself. As Jorgenssen liked to ask himself questions, as Mario revered music and Livius violence, as Cnossos adored the sea and Shan d'Arg the noise of arms, as Erin braved mountains, Nanski existed for space.

Time was another thing. For Nanski, time was a new way to discover space.

It was Nelle who received the call from Altair. She feared for her husband every time he left on one of those expeditions, about which he spoke little, though he had no secrets from her. She dreaded less a precise danger than the reality of knowing he was far from her, tempted perhaps not to return, despite his love for her, by a new experience of space, by fresh distances, by a younger civilization still rich in ships. She had never entirely understood Nanski; he was an unfathomable man, expert at riding comets. One day he might, on a silent call, depart forever toward other shores of the void. That was a risk she had taken fifteen years before in marrying him. She carried it within herself without ever expressing it, and each new mission of Nanski's revived her anguish.

She told Nanski in two words. He stared at her with his piercing eyes, which looked through people and things and often seemed to be hallucinating.

"What will we do? Can I leave you here?" he asked.

"We can pursue the search. You won't be long."

"I don't know," he said. "You ought to return to Tlon. We'll come back later."

That was all. Never had she tried to dissuade her husband from following a team. In a flash, the scout ship left normal space and re-entered it near a world equipped with traverse-materials. Nanski kissed his wife and left the scout ship, then crossed the atmosphere like a shooting star in his autonomous apparatus and set himself down beside the Planetary Center for Interstellar Voyages. It was night. The enormous dome of the Center gleamed like an eye in the soft light of artificial moons.

Thus, all seven at almost the same time—in terms of universal time—used the doors of space and returned instantaneously to Altair, to the same large entrance hall. On the worlds they had left, they had skirted the checkered crowd of travelers, heard the calls, the conversation of an innumerable people who never slept quite soundly because the days and nights changed with the rhythms of thousands of planets. All seven had come from scattered points in the galaxy, experiencing the marvel of the traverse-materials invented nearly a thousand years earlier, during an era when the Federation did not exist and when the Arque himself was still in the limbo of the future.

Of the seven, only Jorgenssen and Nanski perhaps knew for different reasons, exactly what the traverse-materials represented for the Federation. And only Jorgenssen could come to ask himself whether, perhaps, such a web communication was not beginning to create in time, between centuries, a network which would assure unity of the galactic city, rich in thousands of world—a unity not only in distance, but also in duration.

II

The year? 3161.

The place? The planet Ygone, rotating about a nameless yellow sun of the most common type.

Jorgenssen told himself that he would be born two hundred and fifty years later, dozens of light years from there; but he did not succeed in persuading himself of it completely. He existed in the present—it was simply inconceivable that on his native planet, he did not yet exist, that his forgotten ancestors would still be living. He knew it was true, even though it was incredible.

"First article of the Principles," recited Jorgenssen, hardly moving his lips: "Time travel is not possible if it does not accompany a translation in space sufficient that there will be no interference in the causal network of the universe."

It was a physical reality. Certainly, the first Principle did not express the truth exactly; it was content to approach it. There was always a certain amount of interference about a voyage in time. But if the distance in space between the point of arrival and the point of departure were large enough, the interferences and their effects could be ignored.

Logical, thought Jorgenssen. If it were possible to return to his own past, to the past of his own world, the variations introduced into that world's history by his unseasonable return would create all sorts of paradoxes. Writers during the first era of time exploration had played with these possibilities. They had imagined a time traveler's killing one of his ancestors and thereby ceasing to exist himself, and, because of that, finding the fatal voyage impossible to accomplish, and therefore resigning himself to existing, and so forth.

But reality did not admit paradoxes. It was not possible to return to one's past and change it—or, if it were possible, in order to overcome the resistance of the continuum, it would be necessary to consume a dreadful quantity of energy, the quantity precisely necessary for the creation of a new universe including the transformations produced in the causal network.

Reality allowed time travel under certain conditions. Between two worlds far distant in space, there exist relatively few causal relations. Everything happens as if it were a matter of two distinct universes—everything... or almost everything. It was therefore possible, by means of an expenditure of energy corresponding to that almost, to travel into the past of distant worlds.

The second article of the Principles: "The causal network of a given world may be symbolized by a cone with its point turned toward the past and base toward the future. First conclusion: The farther one travels into the past, the more one introduces interferences into the global structure of causality and the greater the quantity of energy necessary for the voyage. Second conclusion: The farther away in space a world is from the point of departure, the farther back into the past of that world it is possible to travel. Third conclusion: For a given expenditure of energy, the point in the past of a world which a time traveler can attain is a function of the distance of that world from the traveler's point of departure."

That was why Altair had been chosen. The worlds surrounding Altair were securely held by the Federation. The teams generally intervened farther away, either toward the center of the galaxy or toward its extreme edge.

"In two hundred and fifty years, I'll be born," Jorgenssen repeated in a low voice. "I already know the Federation's history for some three hundred years into the future. After that, I know nothing. But maybe at this very moment, there are in the galaxy time travelers who come from a distant future and who know what will come after us, after the Federation—beings born of a civilization for which we're only barbarians. If only we could meet them... if we could know the future... know what will come from this voyage to Ygone!"

The third article of the Principles was formally opposed to it: "Any voyage into the future or, by extension, any communication with the future, would necessitate a quantity of energy greater than that which has been developed in the continuum since its creation. In fact, the position of the time traveler is by no means defined in relation to an absolute system of reference, but in a way strictly relative to his point of departure. Likewise, the alterations and interferences in the chain of causes and effects can only be evaluated from the point of departure."

The third article was the simplest. Purely and simply, it amounted to an extension to time structures of principles of relativity which went back to the greatest antiquity—the expression of which had been attributed by some to Pythagoras and by others to Einstein. The slight difference had little importance and doubtless nothing would ever allow it to be determined.

Ygone was an inviting planet. They had arrived, all seven of them, in a clearing bordered by giant fungi. There was no trace of animal life. The earth was red, the sky blue. The sun warmed gently. The air was soft, impregnated with a light scent of water.

Nanski and Mario were busy setting up the time buoy that would permit them to find the door again and, subsequently, to regain their century and Altair. The others silently looked around, on the alert; but there was no trace of tension on their faces.

Nanski and Mario finished camouflaging the buoy. When they had finished, it looked like a rock. A native could have passed nearby twenty times without noticing anything. If he had taken it into his head to touch the thing, he would have received a slight electric shock, and if he had persisted to the point of trying to carry away this singular rock, he would have found it immovably anchored to the ground, weighing dozens of tons. All he could have done was to build an altar around the rock and make it a place of pilgrimage. That was obvious.

"Dalaam, the city we're supposed to operate on, is about ten kilometers north of this clearing," said Jorgenssen to his men, gathered around him. "A trail that leads there and descends the cliff overlooking the city passes quite near here. But we'll avoid it. We'll try to keep out of sight as much as possible."

He stopped an instant and critically examined the equipment of the six. He had already inspected them at least three times before leaving Altair and he had confidence in them, but the least oversight could make all the difference between success and failure.

With a dry report, a fungus spewed a cloud of spores into the air. At the sound of the explosion, the men had scattered in all directions, weapons in hand. They put away their weapons and returned slowly. Above the fungus floated a purple mist, which reminded Jorgenssen of the spiral forms of Aran's sculptures.

An ironic smile played on Mario's lips. "Already nervous, eh! What will it be like in a week?" The others ignored him.

"We'll reach Dalaam on foot," said Jorgenssen. "It's still the best way to be discreet and explore the country. You're not to use your weapons and protective screens except as a last resort. In case we're separated, we'll meet again here. The first to arrive are to wait for the others at least three months. After that delay, they'll be free to return to Altair. But their return will break the connection with Ygone and it'll be almost impossible to reestablish it. The late-comers will be prisoners on this world."

They agreed. That was an eventuality they had all considered at one time or another. It had even happened that members of certain teams had voluntarily remained behind. This was absolutely forbidden because it introduced considerable disturbances in the causal net; but the Federation had scarcely any recourse against those who vanished in time.

Jorgenssen had said what was necessary. He forced a smile. "I don't think," he said in a too-familiar tone, "that this expedition poses great problems. It's going to be a real picnic."

"No squabble in prospect?" asked Livius, his face tense.

"I certainly hope not. The natives are supposed to be peaceful."

"But in four or five centuries they might put the Federation in danger?" Mario inquired.

"I suppose so, if their technology progresses rapidly.

I don't know much more than you. The predictors are concerned with those questions. They tell us the operations to carry out without giving us details. How a world like Ygone could someday threaten the Federation totally escapes me."

"Maybe we'll find out," said Shan d'Arg. "But according to the information we were supplied, these are deplorably peaceful people. Their language is very rich, but it has almost no words on the subject of weapons. They don't even know what war is."

They started to march. Shan d'Arg and Livius went ahead; Jorgenssen and Mario followed. Arne Cnossos covered the right flank and Nanski the left, while Erin protected the rear.

They advanced among the giant fungi for a long time. Twice they changed direction to avoid the trail. It was a simple road of beaten earth, full of ruts. Shan d'Arg hissed between his teeth to express his contempt. "These are the people the Federation fears!" he growled.

"More than one world has made rapid progress," retorted Mario. "And the Federation isn't taking any chances."

"I thought that they'd at least reached the level of atomic energy—that they were beginning to launch ships into space."

"You can't judge a civilization by an empty road. And you know very well their technology is primitive. Or have you remembered the briefing so badly?"

"I still have a good memory, the Arque be praised, but I don't see what we've come to do."

"Don't try to understand. It's not our job."

"But it is," Jorgenssen prepared to protest. If we don't try to understand, who will? The specialists? Certainly not. Maybe we're the only ones who can reason about things in general, as they appear, because we don't see reality through the distorting prism of a specialty. But he was silent. They had already debated that subject a hundred times.

Crossing the trail for the second time, they almost found themselves face to face with a native riding a local mount. The native was human in appearance. He was old and fat, and the elongated shape of his skull emphasized his decided baldness. He wore a kind of short tunic which left his dangling legs bare. His mount had a flat head and two triangular eyes, a long, saurian neck, a short, very dark-blue coat, and six curiously articulated legs. It was difficult to tell at first glance whether the animal was viviparous, or oviparous, or whether it had a means of reproduction as peculiar as its appearance. The native was obviously mammiferous. It was improbable that a course of evolution independent of Earth's had yielded such a clearly human result. The civilization of Ygone had certainly been born of a spaceship wreck; the survivors of a ship in distress would have multiplied rapidly on such a pleasant world.

The seven crouched on the ground, under cover of the fungi. The animal turned its head to the right and left, but did not stop. Its rider seemed particularly pleased with himself. He gazed at the sky with an expression of beatitude and doubtlessly would not have seen the seven men even if they had crossed the trail in front of him. The emissaries from the future could see that the animal's eyes moved independently of each other. Then the native rambled away nonchalantly.

"He's going to Dalaam," whispered Jorgenssen.

"A merchant, no doubt," said Livius.

"There's no commerce on Ygone," corrected Mario.

"That's what the briefing said. But there are no planets without commerce."

"There's Ygone," Mario insisted.

"I'll have to see it to believe it," retorted Livius. "Those briefings are supposed to be completely accurate, but half the time they're wrong. Don't you remember, then, about that affair near Mizar? They'd decreed the technology of the natives wasn't above the L— level. Actually, it was near a good D. But the natives preferred to live in thatched huts instead of hovels of reinforced concrete, steel and glass."

"The mistake was corrected," Mario said simply.

"We corrected it—just in time."

They resumed their march. The fungi became sparser and their height diminished. Soon, they were scarcely taller than a man. The seven began to take precautions.

On the horizon, they could see the edge of the plateau. Very far away, on the other side of the gigantic fault, the top of a cliff emerged from a light fog. Dalaam was at the bottom of the canyon, still invisible.

The sun was already low on the horizon when they reached the edge of the cliff. Ygone rotated on its axis in one hundred eighty-two standard hours, so they would have to get used to long days and nights. They had made a long detour to avoid the trail. The terrain was now completely open. Behind them, a reddish mist floated above the fungi. The wind lazily dispersed it.

The attack surprised them completely. They didn't even have time to throw themselves to the ground. They felt more than they saw the orange-tinted flash fall on them; and the torrid heat of a furnace engulfed them. But their instruments were quicker than their reflexes. Their energy shields started to work before the radiation had attained a dangerous intensity. The antennae of the detectors rose with a light clatter from the helmets and began to turn, searching for the originating point of the heat ray.

The attack lasted scarcely a hundredth of a second.

Livius, his face wicked, pulled out his weapon.

"Calm down," cried Jorgenssen, "you don't even know where they are!"

They all glanced briefly at their detectors. The needles turned easily, to the same rhythm as the antennae, but did not stop in any direction. Yet a weapon of the power which had been used against them would require a huge generator, containing a great deal of metal, emitting intense radiation—in sum, easily detectable. The detectors remained uncertain.

They did not even know in which direction to protect themselves. In principle, the energy shields could protect them from nearly any attack, but it was hardly prudent to use their reserves before having fought, much less to tempt the unknown enemy to strike a decisive blow.

"This could mean several things," said Shan d'Arg, the weapons expert. "Either we haven't been the object of any attack, but simply of an hallucination

155

that for a hundredth of a second also affected our detectors, or else the projector used against us is more than thirty kilometers away, which is just about inconceivable. Or again, our adversaries have equipment of the same type as ours—extremely compact and almost undetectable. This last hypothesis is hardly less fantastic than the others. These weapons exist only in very small numbers in the Federation. They're restricted to the teams and to some space-exploration patrols. And, of course, a technological level of A+, that of the Federation's best worlds, is needed to make them."

"Let's look for cover," said Nanski, visibly uneasy. He was a brave man, but the ray's sudden appearance had shaken him. It was the last difficulty he had imagined in taking the road to Ygone, and it was the first used against them. Besides, he hardly shared the fine confidence of the others in the technological superiority of the Federation. At times, in space, he had come upon incomprehensible machines, whose antiquity and origin were unknown; they had given him cause to reflect. There had surely existed in space, and perhaps there existed still, civilizations at least as technically advanced as the Federation.

"What's the use?" said Jorgenssen, eying Livius, whose violent impulses he feared. "Our shields protect us, and the enemy won't have any trouble finding us, wherever we go—while we don't know either where he is, or who he is."

"There's good reason to think he belongs to this planet and knows why we've come," said Arne Cnossos slowly. "No one fires on strangers without warning, even if they're strangely rigged out. And only the inhabitants of this planet could have an interest in destroying us."

They sat down in a circle on blocks of stone. The energy shields formed peculiar, luminous halos around them.

"There must be a traitor on Altair, then," decided Livius. "Someone who's sold them weapons and information about our mission."

Mario began to laugh. "You keep company with too many crooks not to see things the way they do. It could just as well be that the inhabitants of Ygone made the weapons themselves."

"And our information was wrong to assign them the level L?"

"Maybe. It could also be that Ygone's evolved very fast. From when did the briefing's facts date? From fifty years ago? A hundred years? The time exploration teams have only been around a few decades. For certain worlds, that makes a difference."

"There's another implication in what you say, Mario," Nanski muttered through compressed lips. His face was suddenly gray, his features tense. "They also know how to travel in time. They can travel in time on their own world—and that's how they know why we've come."

They all protested at almost the same time.

"Childishness," murmured Erin.

Jorgenssen restored silence. "You had something to say," he said, turning toward Nanski.

The astronaut agreed with a nod. His hands shook slightly. He breathed deeply. His lips opened, but he still hesitated to speak. "A possibility," he said finally. "No one here seems to have any idea of it—that our adversaries don't come from Altair and don't originate on Ygone either. It could be that they represent another interstellar civilization."

"Imposs..." began Livius, but the word stuck in his throat. He stared at Nanski, then looked at the others, one by one. He could read skepticism on their faces and, just underneath, fear.

It was inconceivable, and yet it was a terror they all had had for a long time, Jorgenssen told himself. And it was proper that it was Nanski, the man of space, who expressed it. None of them could really admit that there was in the galaxy another interstellar civilization besides the Federation. Yet on each expedition they had asked themselves the question: This time, are we going to meet the ultimate enemy, the one that will destroy us and, through us, will reach the Federation?

An enemy from space... or else from time.

"We've got to decide on a plan of action," said Jorgenssen. "Our instructions anticipated that we would destroy a certain number of key points in Dalaam and submit a determined number of natives to the appropriate psychological treatment. But the situation is entirely new."

As co-ordinator, he had to take responsibility for the group. In normal times, each member of the team knew what he had to do; but now they found themselves in a crisis.

Suddenly, they felt isolated and lost, despite their arms and their power. The Federation could do nothing for them. They had to succeed and survive alone.

He gave them his instructions; then they resumed their march. They had adopted a new formation, spreading out over several hundred meters. Their voices crackled in each others' ear phones. From time to time, they scanned the forest of fungi extending behind them.

They reached the edge of the plateau which overhung the canyon, more than a thousand meters deep. Mist lingered at mid-height, blurring details.

Slowly, they drew nearer each other again, creating a defensive formation. The detectors' antennae did not cease to turn. Nothing.

Jorgenssen stretched out just at the edge of the cliff and looked down. Erin, right next to him, stood with his feet firmly anchored a millimeter from the void.

Dalaam, according to the maps, was below them, at the foot of the wall. For a moment, Jorgenssen looked for the city without seeing it. He had expected to find buildings, streets, vehicles, a certain amount of activity; but he saw nothing but a blue and orange forest, broken by clearings. The trees were enormous. Some of them must have been three hundred meters high.

Jorgenssen adjusted his binoculars. The distance seemed to vanish; the trails of mist ceased to be troublesome. Jorgenssen had the impression of hovering at a height nearly level with the tops of the trees. Something white, which stood out clearly from the trees and the ground, held his attention: a building. Then he spotted another, and still another. He saw the city take shape, little by little.

It mingled with the forest, but was not merely sheltered by the forest; it was mixed with the forest and was part of it. Jorgenssen had no doubt that the natives had cultivated the forest within their city. Besides, there was no other forested area in the canyon. The briefing had given no description of anything like it. It described a normal city, characteristic of a society of farmers and cattle-raisers. When the survey had been made, the trees had not existed.

How long did it take a tree to reach three hundred meters in height? Jorgenssen wondered. Five hundred years? A thousand years?

He adjusted his binoculars again. Now he could see through the forest's dense foliage. Looking down at ground level, he was really in the city. He discovered an extraordinary thing: There was no city.

He stood up again and made a sign for Mario to approach. "What do you think?"

The other shrugged his shoulders. He was chewing a nutritive tablet. "If it weren't for this sun, the terrain, and the vegetation—which correspond to our information —I'd say we're not on Ygone," he replied. "Almost nothing fits."

"And this city," said Jorgenssen. "It's at the place indicated, all right, but... but it's not really a city!"

"And then," said Mario sarcastically, "what's a city?"

Yes, what's a city? Jorgenssen asked himself as he tried to understand the absence of order among the little white buildings scattered at random in the shelter of the trees. A way of living in common? A sufficiently important mass of buildings arranged according to a plan, and including monuments and public buildings?

He had seen cities on more than a hundred planets: underground cities, lofty cities that rose tier after tier on dozens of levels, submarine cities, and even space cities, primitive cities of wood, and ultra-modern cities of steel and glass. They all had at least one characteristic in common—the network of streets, like a web, like a system of capillaries.

Dalaam had no streets—at most, paths that erratically connected one building with another, leading toward no center. There was no subterranean circulation either; the detectors would have indicated it. There was practically no traffic. From time to time, they could see a native walking on a path, disappear into the denser shade which surrounded the tree trunks, and after some time reappear, or even not reappear at all. Generally, the native would be empty-handed and the purpose of his trip would remain perfectly obscure.

Dalaam had no monuments either, nor anything which resembled an official building, a community house, nor a city hall, nor a factory, nor a stable. And there were no routes which could be used for bringing food produce and other kinds of products from the outside. There were no fields, either around the city or under the trees.

Jorgenssen asked himself how many inhabitants the forest could shelter. His instruments did not permit him to see the interiors of the houses clearly, since the walls were too thick, or else it was too dark inside. He made a quick estimate. Just below him, he could count about fifty buildings which could shelter five or six natives. The forest was several dozen square kilometers in area. Dalaam might include five hundred thousand people, perhaps a million. The briefing said twenty-five thousand inhabitants —the most important city on Ygone—twenty-five thousand inhabitants engaged in farming, cattle-raising and hunting... no commerce... and no trees.

The briefing was wrong.

Jorgenssen stood up again. The sky was perfectly clear; the sun had scarcely moved. What was happening on Ygone was completely incredible. But the reality was stronger than the briefing.

They all felt the ground move under their feet a quarter of a second after the detectors warned them. They hastily scattered from the edge of the cliff. The vibration increased. It jolted their ankles.

Jorgenssen knew what was going to happen. He signaled the others to run for it But Cnossos was too slow. The fissure opened in the ground before he had had time to get far enough from the abyss. The whole edge of the cliff swung into the void.

"Infrasonics!" yelled Mario, and they all could hear him on their ear phones.

Cnossos fell with the enormous mass of rock. When he had reached a sufficient speed, his degravitation chute worked automatically. He found himself again above the canyon while the rocks hurled down into the depths. The sound took a long time to reach their ears. They rushed forward to the new edge of the cliff. Miraculously, the avalanche had spared the forest—miraculously, or skillfully.

Cnossos floated in the air at mid-height like a spider at the end of its thread. He operated the controls of his apparatus, mounting again quite gently and coming to rest next to his companions. He was smiling, but his face was white.

"This time, it was a narrow squeak," he breathed.

They all congratulated him at the same time. The second attack had been as brutal and unpredictable as the first Jorgenssen, anguish gripping his heart, wondered how many times, how many attacks of this kind would be necessary to make them give way. None of them was mentally equipped for this kind of war, except perhaps Erin, with his silence and impassive nerves.

He suddenly realized Mario was saying something that seemed to surprise the others. He ceased contemplating the enigmatic forest below, buffeted by a breath of wind, and listened to Mario.

"... haven't run real risks," Mario was saying. "Up to now our protective systems have been perfectly equal to the task. If our adversaries really knew our ends and means, I doubt they'd try to kill us. Instead, I've the impression it's a matter of warnings. Something like, 'Leave this planet, or else we'll make life intolerable for you.' I think they simply want to frighten us."

Mario's voice was sharp and plain, like his person. Jorgenssen saw that it acted like a cold shower on the others. He himself felt his dread diminish. Neither he nor the others had been really afraid. Their common anguish had another cause: things were happening which they could not explain, which did not square with their information. They could not comprehend the situation. For emissaries of the all-powerful Federation sent to a world of the thirty-sixth order, it was a frustrating impression.

Jorgenssen began to observe the city again. Certain matters became a little clearer. It seemed the low buildings formed groups of eight or twelve houses connected by paths. The groups, in turn, were connected by more-or-less erratic roads. This rather distantly recalled a social plan, or even, Jorgenssen told himself, the organization of living cells.

The activity of the natives remained incomprehensible: most of the time, they walked around with their arms dangling, very relaxed, and appeared completely ignorant of what work was. There did not seem to be specialists among them, even on a low level. In fact, there didn't seem to be any trades at all in Dalaam.

But how did the natives live? Where did they get their food? Who gave them their silken tunics?

They seemed perfectly free and happy as far as Jorgenssen could judge through his binoculars from the height of more than a kilometer.

Was Ygone, perhaps, after all, the closest approximation of paradise to be found in the galaxy? The reason invoked by the offices of the Arque for the "rectification of history" on Ygone was "the aggressive and bellicose tendency of its inhabitants." This did not tally with what Jorgenssen could see of their activity. But the reasons the Arque gave officially were rarely the true ones; they served more or less to assuage the consciences of the members of the teams. In reality, the only reason the Arque knew was the service of his own power.

The principles of the "rectifications of history" were very simple. In the earliest times, teams had chiefly intervened materially, physically destroying beings and cities, if not entire planets. After centuries, their action became more subtle. The teams acted upon the collective "psyche" of a society. They would inject into the unconsciousnesses of a certain number of individuals ideas, opinions, "archetypes"—to return to the mythological vocabulary—which would at the end of several decades end by penetrating the collective unconscious. Then wars would break out, or civilizations, previously flourishing, would begin to stagnate and decline without anyone knowing why. The germ of their own destruction would have been injected decades before by the time action teams, but

160

they wouldn't know it. That germ was usually only a tiny thing, a new symbol which would develop, growing profusely like a sort of social cancer, sometimes giving birth to a religion or a myth which would lead its adherents into a fanatical and murderous crusade. It was the ultimate, pitiless, invisible weapon which the Federation used in the long war it carried out against its future rivals.

Pointed at Dalaam, it was a criminal weapon, Jorgenssen told himself, considering the tranquil and happy life of the Dalaamians. In a carefully sealed metallic box, which at the moment rested in one of his pockets, were the hypnotic recordings which would permit him to implant the destructive ideas in the minds of certain natives. He wanted to seize the box, throw it away, and watch it fall toward the gigantic trees; but he felt incapable of accomplishing this action. After all, he had been extensively and minutely conditioned to remain loyal to the Federation.

He asked himself what could put the others to the proof: Mario would have to be conscious of the problem, but would only smile at it; Livius would obey without questioning, being only aware of the immediate suspense of the others; Cnossos remained an enigma—his features rarely allowed an emotion to leak out. The others cared only about the exploit; its end remained foreign to them.

Mario touched his shoulder. "What are we going to do?"

"That's what I'm asking myself," said Jorgenssen. He reflected quickly. There was a solution which would momentarily resolve everything. The problem was to find out whether the others would accept it.

"Well go back," he said quickly. "We'll return to Altair. We'll retreat. There're too many new elements in this business. I'm not at all sure the plan furnished me will still work. The hypnotic recordings could very well yield completely unexpected results on the natives— doing more harm than good. The natives are perhaps even capable of defending themselves against suggestion. I can't take the responsibility of an eventual failure."

He knew he was lying and was trying to lie to himself. He wondered whether this showed on his face. He tried to read on Mario's smiling features whether the other understood the problem that troubled him.

"That means the natives have won for the moment," said Mario. "We leave their future in peace. They've succeeded in disturbing our minds enough to make us hesitate."

"The natives or someone else," replied Jorgenssen gently.

"You believe Nanski's theory?"

"I don't know," admitted Jorgenssen. "If it's based..."

Mario breathed deeply. Despite his external casualness, he was himself disturbed. "I see," he said finally. "I think your decision is perfectly wise. I support it on my part. It's for the people of Altair to decide."

Jorgenssen sighed. On that side, at least, the cause was gained—for the moment.

Above their heads, the sky was as empty and lustrous as the interior of a shell; there were no birds on Ygone.

Livius, obstinate, repeated the same thing for the third time. "This has never happened. Never has a team retreated."

"Inexact," said Jorgenssen in a cold voice. "One hundred twenty-seven years ago a team returned without accomplishing its plan because it was unanimously decided that the probability of success was nil. That's what I'm asking you to do today."

Mario, Cnossos, and Nanski went over to his opinion. Livius protested. Erin remained silent. Shan d'Arg, his face devoured by a tic, hesitated—weighing his taste for risk against his old loyalty to Jorgenssen.

"We'll be the laughingstock of the Federation," said Livius.

"That's better than leading it to its doom."

'I'm not afraid—not me!" Livius insisted. "It takes a little more to frighten me!"

Nanski grimaced in anger. "Shut up," he said in a hollow voice. "We've proved a hundred times we aren't cowards. The only fear that troubles me is making a mistake."

Shan d'Arg intervened. "I'm a man of war, Livius. I never take to my heels without cursing myself. But Jorgenssen is right. It's not just a question of ourselves. There's the Federation—and the natives."

Jorgenssen's features relaxed. There was one more point Erin would accept the opinion of the majority; only Livius still had to be convinced. "You can stay here, Livius," decided Jorgenssen. "You can carry on your war all alone, or you can bow before the majority. You have the choice."

He sensed immediately that he had made a mistake. His words had exceeded his thoughts under pressure of his anxiety. "We're going to withdraw, Livius," he added. "We're going only to seek new directives. We must inform the Federation of the presence of well-armed adversaries here—and of everything that's changed. But we're not giving up. There's a time for everything, for retreat and conquest."

Livius played with his weapon, his head bent. He glanced in the direction of Dalaam. The trees still concealed an unfathomable reality. He thought of all his past expeditions: of the empire of semi-intelligent lizards they had sent reeling on Bania, the jungle planet; of the crystal mathematicians they had rendered insane on Lomire; of the humanoids of Usal. Each time the problem had been simple, concrete. Here, nothing was plain. It annoyed him to flee before this mystery.

"Agreed," he said finally. "Let's go." Bitterness was visible on his face.

The spores of the giant fungi which had fallen on the ground formed a thick carpet of reddish dust. The men marched in silence, their antennae turning on their helmets, weapons in hand, eyes and ears on guard. In Jorgenssen's pocket, the little metal box tossed about. Dalaam had won, but its inhabitants seemed to know nothing about it.

"We've fallen on an entirely original society," said Mario. "It seems to have no organization, no government, no economy—nothing centralized. And at the same time, they seem capable of defending themselves. I wonder what would've happened if we'd tried to destroy the forest."

"I think we'd have failed," said Jorgenssen pensively.

"I think so, too. The city seemed so calm, its residents so unconscious of our presence. But at the same time, a kind of force emanated from the forest. As long as I looked at it, I felt uncomfortable," Mario said.

"Me, too," said the others, almost at the same time.

"Do you think they're trying to influence us psychologically?" asked Nanski.

"Maybe. The detectors haven't reacted. At any rate, we're in principle immunized against a hypnotic operation or any kind of subliminal suggestion. No, I rather have the impression the forest contains something extremely precious, living and powerful, that we haven't the right to destroy. Just a hunch, nothing precise."

"I felt it, too," said Jorgenssen.

"I've never known anything like it," Mario continued.

"Except maybe listening to certain symphonies. The impression of finding yourself at the brink of a new and unknown world with a heart you can't penetrate, to which you can never belong—I think Livius's anger has no other cause."

Livius marched alone, apart A detector suddenly roared in their ear phones and they instantly froze.

"Over there," whispered Livius, indicating a point between two giant fungi.

A form moved in a red mist of spores. It was human, but indistinct, as if an energy shield protected it. They began to run silently, scattering and trying to surround the unknown. Jorgenssen lost sight of the others; but thanks to the detectors, he knew exactly where they were.

'Take to the air?" asked Livius, his voice trembling with excitement.

"No. No. Stay on the ground."

Perhaps it was only a native watching them, but that didn't explain the detectors' long silence. The native had not been surprised, Jorgenssen thought; he had let himself be surprised voluntarily.

If it was a native.

The first volley passed over their heads, like a white lightning-flash. It decapitated a dozen fungi, which crackled ominously. Shreds of purple smoke rose into the sky. The radiation shields automatically engaged, protecting the men.

"Don't shoot!" yelled Jorgenssen into his microphone at the same moment the second burst of energy flashed out. It lashed Livius at full force. The adventurer's shield rudely turned white and almost immediately became transparent again, having played its protective role.

The seven did not stop running. They crossed two clearings. Then the fungi became less numerous, and they penetrated an area of fallen rocks. Most of the time, they lost sight of their quarry, but their detectors continued to indicate the direction clearly. The team gained ground.

"Altitude?" yelled Livius.

Jorgenssen hesitated. They could activate their antigravity units and fly over the rocky labyrinth. Their vulnerability would be sensibly increased, but the odds were high the unknown did not have weapons sufficiently powerful to endanger them. On the other hand, they would become immediately visible and would give away information about their tactical possibilities.

"Go ahead," said Jorgenssen finally.

He almost immediately heard Livius's cry of fury. "My unit doesn't work! Try yours."

Instinctively, Jorgenssen pressed the tiny button on his belt. But instead of rising vertically, he remained glued to the ground. He looked for the others. No one rose.

"Inhibiting field!" cried Mario. "They're really powerful." A touch of satisfaction came into his voice; he appreciated the situation as a gamester.

Almost immediately, he fired. The discharge of energy was moderated, just sufficient to stun a man. He hit his moving target, but the unknown didn't stop running, disappearing behind a rock.

"The shields!" yelled Nanski in a desperate voice.

Jorgenssen glanced toward Mario, who was running in front of him. The usual halo no longer protected the man. Jorgenssen couldn't see his own energy shield, but he didn't have to look at the control dial he wore on his right wrist to know that he, too, was no longer protected.

The unknown enemy played with them like a cat with a mouse.

Yet he wasn't really trying to destroy them. Since he could bring down the shields that protected them—and that implied a superior technology and a practically unlimited quantity of energy—he could have killed them from the beginning. He obviously preferred to try to terrify them. Was it, perhaps, pure sadism? Would he finally destroy them after proving that none of the weapons they were so proud of could disturb him?

"Stop the pursuit," ordered Jorgenssen.

"I have him!" crackled Mario's voice in the ear phones.

Mario fired twice. Jorgenssen couldn't see him, but he heard the slight hiss of the shots.

"I got him," said Mario.

But there were new bursts of shots, and one of them passed so close to Jorgenssen that it blinded him for an instant He fell flat on the ground, then got up again and began to run desperately in the direction where Mario had disappeared. He was little concerned with the others. Climbing over a heap of rocks, he discovered a ravine and let himself slide to the bottom. It was silent He was dizzy for a moment. The detectors* needles went wild. He knew what it was to be lost. Suddenly, he remembered a summer night on Igor II, years and years before, when he had been lost as a child. Although the planet was peaceful and he knew nothing threatened him, noises had taken on a frightening intensity. He hadn't stopped walking until daybreak. His father had found him walking along a river. He hadn't said anything; they had returned in silence.

Jorgenssen shook off his memories. Laboriously, he scaled the other side of the ravine. Rocks again. He hoisted himself onto the highest one. The other men remained invisible, and the ear phones mute. He paused, listening to the blood beat in his veins. No reason to be afraid. If they'd wanted to kill you...

Suddenly, he saw Mario in a crevasse. He signaled to him, but the other didn't see it. In silence, Jorgenssen approached. The stones rolled under his feet. He suddenly felt the heat of the sun, for his suit no longer protected him.

Mario was staring at something Jorgenssen couldn't see, something on the ground, behind a rock. Jorgenssen didn't have to ask Mario to know he had reached a crisis. The co-ordinator caught up with him, but Mario didn't turn his head. Jorgenssen had to push him aside to see, in his turn, what Mario was contemplating with such intensity.

The significance of what he saw did not strike him immediately. A man lay dead on the ground, behind the rock. The discharge had killed him; no robot surgeon could have revived him, since the burst had practically cut him in two.

The man wore the uniform of the teams, but that was nothing. The worst was that, in all respects, he resembled Mario.

Their stride was heavy.

"Are you sure we're going in the right direction?" asked Jorgenssen.

Erin nodded. Since the detectors no longer worked, their only hope was to find the spatiotemporal buoy again. They would be lucky if they could activate it. They already would need a lot of luck to retrace their steps without making a mistake. Although they had kept their useless weapons, it would have been just as well to throw them away. Fatigue bit into them, and sweat streamed down their helmets. They were as vulnerable as children, Jorgenssen thought

Without defenses—naked as worms opposite a faceless, immensely powerful enemy—as unarmed as the inhabitants of Dalaam seemed to be.

The idea struck Jorgenssen. He repeated it mentally: We're as unarmed as the inhabitants of Dalaam. That was perhaps one of the keys to the mystery, the result the invisible enemy desired. For years and years of varied missions they had faced adversaries who hadn't had the least chance of resisting them. They had operated well-protected by their energy shields, their helmets, their suits, exuding cold or heat at will. A cocoon of apparatus protected them unceasingly. They could fly over continents and seas, communicate with each other through mountains, constantly know where they were in relation to the others, in relation

165

to the buoy, a city, or any point determined in advance. They had had confidence in themselves and in their weapons. They had been like gods.

Not here. Not now. Here and now, on Ygone, they were naked and unarmed. All your life, thought Jorgenssen—and with him Arne Cnossos, Erin, Nanski, Shan d'Arg, Livius, and Mario—machines interposed between reality and you, Sometimes, for sport, you left them behind, you faced reality—the sea or the mountains, or that terrible killer man can be. But always you felt machines near you, ready to help you, to spare you any suffering, fatigue, or annoyance that you hadn't wanted, desired. Never have you known what a real combat is. Machines would fight for you, in reality, and you had the impression of controlling them. Machines would fight for the Federation, and you... you had the impression of existing at the price of an illusory danger. But not here, not now.

The people of Dalaam know what real combat is, thought Jorgenssen and the others with him, in silence, heads lowered, fighting against thirst (the water regenerating systems no longer functioned), heat, and weariness. The people of Dalaam know it and they're teaching it to you, whether you want it or not. And maybe they're right to teach you, but you, no doubt, will never know it. Maybe they simply want you to go down to them, to the false city, and want you to live with them under the trees, searching for that mysterious and precious thing that must be hidden there.

They had left the body of Mario number two behind, burying it in an unalterable bag after a quick examination which left no doubt. It was Mario, even though Mario marched with them at the moment It was the exact double of Mario—even the fingerprints, even the scars. The instruments which would have permitted them to examine the inside of the eye no longer worked; but they had no need of that ultimate proof. They knew what they would have discovered: absolute identity.

Perhaps an extremely thorough study would have revealed certain differences at the cellular level or, if it had been necessary to go that far, at the molecular level, but there was no reason to. There are no two identical objects in the universe. But at a precise time and place, there had existed two identical Marios—except for one detail: one of the two had fired more quickly than the other, and killed him. Yet, the identical weapons of both were not set to kill. Now the Marios had ceased being identical. One of them rotted tranquilly in his bag; the other fought against thirst and fatigue.

With which of the two did I leave Altair? Jorgenssen asked himself, avoiding a glance at Mario. With which did I talk about Dalaam? Was it with the one that's dead? And is the one who goes with us a false Mario, who fired on us, who's killed one of us? Or else is it the other way around? Did we win a victory over the enemy? Did we destroy a shadow sent to mislead us?

The problem was insolvable. That was the reason they remained silent. It was possible that the Mario who went with them was an enemy, and they didn't want to give him any information he could use. Mario had not debated Jorgenssen's decision; its necessity was evident

On Altair, the time engineers, and above all, the selectors would decide—if the team succeeded in regaining Altair.

Jorgenssen caught himself wishing that they hadn't come there. A new idea sprang up in his head: Perhaps their adventure on Ygone had been nothing but a setting destined to facilitate the introduction to Altair, in the time citadel of the Federation, of an enemy agent, a spy anxious to penetrate the secrets of time travel. But this explanation was questionable. The invisible enemy had given proof of his power, and Jorgenssen had no doubt that he would have been able to introduce himself in a more discreet manner on any world of the Federation.

Yes, he said to himself. But maybe not in any year. Is the invisible enemy maybe trying to go back to the source of our interventions in time to act in his turn on the Federation's future?

Nothing was certain, and above all not the direction in which they were marching.

"I don't recognize the terrain," said Jorgenssen. "I saw that bunch of fungi on our left when we came. It should be on our right."

Erin shook his head obstinately. "We still have an hour to go," he said. "Maybe two. But we're going in the right direction. Look at the mountains."

They had to rely on his habit of locating himself by the mountains. If they missed the buoy, it could take ten years to find it again, since the fungus spores had covered their tracks.

An hour to think without a halt, thought Jorgenssen. He tried to think of Aran's sculptures and to recollect exactly the subtle contours he had seen his friend shape. They were made in the image of time, in the image of their destiny, in the image of Ygone. The touch of a finger on the exterior was sufficient to transform them.

III

Erin raised his arm and Jorgenssen recognized the spot. Night was quite near. It would last ninety-six hours. On Ygone, the nights equaled the days, and such a long night meant a considerable lowering of the temperature. Their energy generators no longer worked; their suits were no longer air-conditioned. They could well die of cold if they didn't succeed in returning to Altair.

The clearing where they arrived was just in front of them. Livius and Cnossos tried to run, despite their exhaustion. Shan d'Arg maintained his long and elastic stride.

"Halt," shouted Jorgenssen.

They stopped.

Jorgenssen passed one hand over his forehead. He didn't like what he was going to do. "Mario," he said in a voice he strained to make hard, "throw down your weapon. Unbuckle your belt. You can keep your helmet."

Mario slowly turned on his heels. He froze like a statue and, after a moment, smiled. His face was gray with dust, his eyes ringed with shadow.

"I understand," he said. "You distrust me. You can't be sure I'm not an enemy."

"I can't take the chance."

Jorgenssen stood straight again, his right hand caressing the stock of his dead weapon. The light of sunset kindled red reflections on his face.

With a weary gesture, Mario let his weapon fall at his feet. He undid the magnetic clasp of his belt and watched it slip to the ground. With it, he lost even the symbol of his past power—his energy generator, his antigravitation unit, his nuclear grenades, his symbiotic complex.

Of all this, nothing worked any longer. It was nothing but dead weight. Yet it was also the badge of the limitless power of the Federation's envoys. Or rather of the power that found its limit on Ygone. Jorgenssen corrected mentally. He understood what Mario was feeling, if he was still theirs.

"Livius," he called.

"Yes," said the adventurer, grimacing slightly. Sweat ran down his hair onto his forehead.

"You have your dagger?"

It was an unnecessary question; Livius never parted with it. He was the only team member who knew how to use such a primitive weapon well. Even Shan d'Arg would not have attempted to challenge him with a knife. He threw it as well as he handled it

"Sure," said Livius.

"You'll guard Mario," said Jorgenssen, who avoided looking at one of the two men. "At the first suspicious move, you kill him. You understand—repeat it."

Livius's regard moved to Mario, then to Jorgenssen, then returned to Mario.

"At the first suspicious move, I kill him," he said in an expressionless voice.

The others listened, silent. Their boots were red with the dust of spores.

"We're going to try to get back to Altair," said Jorgenssen. "The buoy is just in front of us. You understand I wouldn't want to take a chance. If the real Mario is dead, if the one we have with us is only a copy and if his weapon began to work again at the exact moment I activated the buoy, if he killed us and went back to Altair alone, then...." He let his voice die.

"I understand," said Mario. "I'd do the same in your place. I don't have any way to prove to you who I am."

No one among us can really prove who he is. Jorgenssen thought suddenly. Sweat beaded on his forehead—cold. No one among us. At one time or another, each of us was alone. Maybe, in the rocks back there, there's a body of Livius and another of Cnossos and another of Nanski, and another of... I can't trust anyone. I only know who I am.... Or am I wrong? About myself?

He kept his reflections to himself, painfully swallowing his saliva. "You go first, Mario," he said.

Mario turned around and began to walk mechanically. Livius picked up the weapon and belt, and followed him, as the others got under way slowly. To the left, the sky reddened like an infernal conflagration. Only the peaks of the mountains still glowed.

The spatiotemporal buoy, camouflaged as a rock, awaited them in the center of the clearing. A wave of relief came over Jorgenssen, who suddenly felt the same impulse as Cnossos and Livius, and was on the point of starting to run. He had feared never finding the clearing again, or finding it empty.

He advanced toward the false rock. He ran his hands over the rough surface and felt a light electric shock, as his boots only insulated him imperfectly. With the ends of his fingers, he searched for a tiny, winding channel in which to press a hidden contact. The electric sensation he had experienced disappeared suddenly. His fingers frantically probed the tiny trough.

"Livius," he said in a voice he strained to control, "give me Mario's weapon."

He caught the object Livius threw him. Grasping the weapon by the barrel, the man struck the rock with the stock, at the point of contact. Something, perhaps, had jammed.

The weapon rebounded with a distinct noise. Jorgenssen struck harder. His muscles hurt. He wanted to hear the hard and clear voice of the man of Altair. The rock gave way. A thin, sharp fragment flew into the air. Enraged,

Jorgenssen struck the stone with angry blows: splinters were scattered in all directions, sparks shot out

Powerless, Jorgenssen turned to his men again. He didn't have to say anything to them. The buoy would always be there, in a way; but they would never return to Altair. The buoy disguised as a rock, for some incomprehensible reason, had become a rock.

Mario must have understood, because he broke into an insane laugh. They had been played for fools all down the line. They'd tried to hide the buoy, and their unknown enemy, with diabolical humor, had cut off all roads of retreat by doing better yet—by entirely transforming the buoy into stone.

They were prisoners of Ygone. Soon, they would be prisoners of the night. And the enemy, perhaps, had slipped into their ranks.

The trunks of the fungi burned with a clean flame. Livius had succeeded in lighting a fire by striking the stock of Mario's weapon against a stone. Twenty times the sparks had been lost, but at last the little pile of dry spores had consented to embrace them.

The seven regarded the flames with a kind of amazement Except for Livius and Erin, it was the first time they had seen fire.

Instinctively, they had seated themselves in a circle around the fire and warmed their tired limbs. Livius was playing with his dagger, watching Mario stealthily and humming a tune of his native planet.

Here we are, thrown a thousand years into the past, mused Jorgenssen, to the age of fire. For the first time, we're really making a voyage in time... a thousand years... no, ten thousand years, or a hundred thousand... before the first rocket had left Earth... to the time man fought bare-handed against the ferocious beasts of prehistoric times... or against man.

The trunks of the fungi crackled as they burned. For the seven, it was a new sound. Only Livius seemed at ease. Erin's mask was impenetrable. Mario, as if exhausted, stared at the fire without blinking.

Ninety hours of night yet, thought Jorgenssen, his throat dry. They had drunk the water their symbiotic complexes contained. If they survived until dawn, they would have to search for a spring, which they would perhaps find in the canyon near Dalaam.

More than fire and their destitution, another thing brought them nearer to their distant ancestors, Jorgenssen decided: suspicion. Now they distrusted one another. They no longer knew what was hidden behind the faces of friends beside whom they had once fought. The hunters of primeval times must have looked at each other thus during the terrifying nights, always waiting to see a neighbor's weapon fly in the direction of their skulls. Cooperation and trust had been the work of innumerable centuries.

It was fragile work, founded on an impression, perhaps an illusion, of knowing others, of being able to predict their acts, their violence as well as their fidelity.

It was a limited work as well. Confidence did not reign between different civilizations, even in the thirty-second century, nor between different centuries.

Suspicion's the reason for our presence here, thought Jorgenssen abruptly; and this idea illuminated the night in the heart of which he debated with himself. We act because the Federation's suspicious of the futures of other worlds. The strongest or most intelligent primitive hunter tried to kill his neighbors for fear they might unite against him and kill him. The Federation does nothing different. The Federation, the union of the most powerful and most civilized worlds of the galaxy, doesn't think otherwise, doesn't act otherwise, than a primitive hunter.

And the distrust which now hung over the seven like a morbid shadow, the distrust which weighed upon Mario more heavily than chains, was nothing else but the reflection of the same distrust which the Federation demonstrated with regard to other civilizations. They feared Mario might be a stranger, an enemy, because they couldn't imagine a stranger might be anything else but an enemy, because they had come to Ygone as secret antagonists, like thieves, and deep within themselves they expected to be treated as thieves. And what had happened had been right.

In all areas, the inhabitants of Ygone, perhaps the natives of Dalaam and, in any case, whoever they were— the mysterious adversaries who had put them in this critical situation—had paid them back in their own coin. The seven had arrived with the idea that the Dalaamians could do nothing against them; and here it was that they themselves had been reduced to impotence. They carried the suspicion and anxiety and also the hate of the Federation; and now it was turned against them.

For us, Ygone's been nothing but a mirror up to now, thought Jorgenssen. What we've seen here of such frightfulness, was nothing but our own appearance. If we'd come with empty hands, hearts full of friendship and trust, asking the people of Dalaam what they knew of life, if in exchange we'd offered them.... What could we have offered them... our power? Theirs overwhelms ours.... If we'd come simply with our problems, our lives, our futures, with the idea of understanding instead of destroying, what would've happened?

No answer. There would never be an answer unless he went to ask the people of the forest-city. After all, they didn't try to kill us, which we would've done in their place. They threatened us with our own weapons, they hit us with our own fear. And there's no doubt they'll continue. They don't force us to do anything. They're content to turn our own weapons against us, to plunge us into our own problems.

There was only one solution. It was clear as fire, burning as fire, frightening as fire. It cut the night which surrounded them as decisively as fire.

Jorgenssen decided to speak. He had to make an effort. His jaw had contracted while he reflected, and the muscles under his chin formed a painful knot. He swallowed his saliva and attempted to speak. This would be the first step toward re-establishing trust. The inhabitants of Dalaam would understand, perhaps, if they were listening.

"Put away your dagger, Livius," said Jorgenssen. "And you, Mario, forget what I had to say. I was wrong. I believe you're one of us. I think the other Mario, back there, was only an artificial body intended to mislead us... no, not exactly to fool us, but to point out a new direction. Up to now, we've been on the wrong track." "You're crazy," said Livius. "You want us all to be slaughtered. We have a small enough chance of getting out of this if we're careful."

Shan d'Arg's eyes turned away from the fire. "I'm not as impulsive as Livius," he said, "but I don't understand you either. Why this change of attitude?"

"I've come to understand certain things," said Jorgenssen. "I could be wrong, but I'll take the chance. I'm asking you to take it with me. It's worth it."

"What chance?" Nanski's voice was brusque and tense. Jorgenssen avoided the question.

"I'm going to leave for Dalaam. I'm going down to the city. I'm going to try to contact the natives, because I have to know what's happening. I'm sure the answer's in Dalaam."

"You can't," said Cnossos. "The regulations forbid contact with the natives. Altair... "

Jorgenssen threw a trunk into the fire. A fountain of sparks went high into the air. "Altair!" he interrupted. "Which of you can show me Altair in the sky. In what century in Affair's history are we? Do we have only one chance to get back to Altair and to our time? Do the men of Altair still trouble themselves about us?"

He stood up. His shadow danced behind him. I make a good target, he thought. / wish it were even bigger, so the Dalaamians, if they're watching us in the dark, would know I'm not afraid of them, would know I know I haven't anything to fear from them.

"Altair and its rules, the Federation and its laws, are no more than words for us," he resumed. "Nearer to us, there's this world, there's Dalaam. I have to go there to find out what's happening."

'To spy on the natives," said Livius skeptically.

"No, not to spy on them. I'm going without trying to hide myself. I've got questions to ask them."

"Never has a team..." began Cnossos.

"I know. But a team's never been imprisoned on a world before either. This had to happen. In a sense, I'm glad it happened to us and not to others."

"Why?"

Jorgenssen hesitated. "I don't know. I can't tell you— not yet I know I'm right. Later, maybe, you'll understand."

He couldn't explain anything to them. Just then, he had had an intuition that the answer was in Dalaam—a sudden, fragile intuition—and he had to leave before it vanished entirely, before he could retract his decision because of doubt. They had to take the same road as he. They were less prepared for it, and that was why he had grasped the true nature of the situation before the others. Or perhaps Mario had understood before him, and that was why the dead double...

A shudder went through him at the thought of the depths of the possibilities opening before him. He didn't dare to sound them, for he still didn't have the courage to get involved with them. Suddenly, he was afraid. "You're sick," said Cnossos. "You're shaking."

Jorgenssen shook his head. "I've never been more lucid."

"You'll get yourself killed. The natives will murder you!" "They could just as well do it here. You understand, I suppose, that we still wouldn't be alive if they didn't want it that way. Just now, before we arrived in the clearing, I ordered Livius to watch Mario for fear that he'd kill us and return alone to Altair and that he'd carry on war back there. But it was stupid. If they'd wanted to kill us, they could have done it at any moment—from a distance, without endangering one of their own.

"At a moment they could've chosen, they could've killed us and replaced us with doubles as perfect as Mario's—but living—at the exact instant we would've taken the road to Altair. Nothing protected us anymore."

"Instead, they cut off our every means of retreat," said Cnossos.

"Because they wanted us to go down to their city, because they wanted to meet us. I don't think they've any hate for us... maybe only curiosity. I should've seen it from the beginning, when I saw their city. But I only thought about our mission, about their destruction." "And now?" said Cnossos.

"Now I want to meet them."

"And you forget the Federation. You're ready to tell them why we've come, to betray the Federation's secrets, your weapons, maybe what you know about time travel?" "Maybe. Besides, there are no more secrets, neither weapons, nor time travel. Only us and them."

"I won't let you do it. In your own interest Jorgenssen. A co-ordinator can be relieved of his powers, if circumstances require it. The good of the Federation comes first, the welfare of the team after that. The personal ideas of the co-ordinator come far behind."

"You're wrong, Cnossos; you're completely wrong. You don't see that there are no more weapons, no more apparatus, therefore no more team. You don't see that what gave force and cohesion to the team was its technology, its great technical power. And there's nothing left of it, there's nothing but men, and each must face reality, solve the problem, alone. Cnossos, don't make things more difficult. I swear to you, I know what I'm doing."

"I don't believe it," said Cnossos. "I don't know what's come over you, but now I distrust you more than Mario." He got up in one bound, leaped over the fire, and, like a flash, was on Jorgenssen. He held his weapon by the barrel and the force it carried would have at least stunned Jorgenssen if he hadn't seen it coming and turned it aside. The stock of the weapon glanced off Jorgenssen's cheek and struck his shoulder violently. Jorgenssen grimaced with pain. He drew back quickly and put himself on guard. He regretted having removed his helmet. Instinctively, he wiped his chin dry; blood flowed from his cut cheek. He bent in two to break the shock of Cnossos's foot, but, despite this, the blow caught him in the pit of the stomach and a violent nausea seized him. Making an effort to breathe, he flung himself forward. His right fist hit Cnossos's chest with a dull thud that sickened him. With the edge of his hand, he tried to reach Cnossos's throat. Cnossos dodged, and Jorgenssen met only empty air and, thrown off balance, fell forward. He rolled over, then regained his footing. The reflexes of hand-to-hand combat, practiced a thousand times, returned to him little by little. His body fought for him, while his mind was strangely detached from the battle. He thought: Now we're really fighting each other like primitive hunters, with our hands, with our claws, like animals.

He heard the other panting for breath and the sound of blows. Cnossos stumbled. Feet together, Jorgenssen jumped on the hand holding the weapon. Cnossos's fingers were crushed against the barrel. With a kick, Jorgenssen sent the weapon flying out of reach.

Cnossos caught him around the waist, crying to the others, "Help me! Help me! Take him!" But the others didn't move. They watched the fight with set faces. Cnossos and Jorgenssen rolled on the ground next to the fire. Jorgenssen was underneath. Cnossos's hands closed around his neck. Jorgenssen knew Cnossos was fighting to kill. He didn't try to loosen the vice of Cnossos's fingers, but set himself firmly, launched out backward, and sent Cnossos flying over him. Cnossos released his hold, passing like a shadow over him.

Jorgenssen opened his eyes. No weight pressed his chest anymore. He could breathe freely. He got up slowly, his whole body aching. Then he heard an appalling, inhuman noise, and it seemed he had always heard it, but he didn't know where it came from.

Cnossos screamed. He had fallen into the fire. Cnossos burned. The others never moved.

I've won, Jorgenssen thought, wiping dry his chin. I'm a great hunter. At the same time, he turned around and rushed into the fire. He seized Cnossos by one arm and pulled him out, then carried him a little farther away and let him fall. Jorgenssen breathed slowly and heavily, hearing Cnossos's uninterrupted groaning. He saw Shan d'Arg get up at last and go toward Cnossos and, without a word, take from his belt a glass phial and tear Cnossos's clothes with Livius's dagger and salve his burns with the phial's contents.

Jorgenssen stood up, his legs nerveless. He regarded his immense shadow stretching out in the direction of the invisible cliff, in the direction of the city. He looked at Cnossos and saw that the helmet had protected the man's face, and saw the crushed, inert hand, which Shan d'Arg's adroit fingers examined gently. He vomited, shaken by spasms.

"This won't be anything," said Shan d'Arg. "He's not too bad."

"Why didn't you interfere?" asked Jorgenssen.

"It was your fight. Each one has to solve his own problem—you said it. You won. If Cnossos hadn't gotten up, I would have defied you."

Jorgenssen remained silent a long moment, recovering his breath. He threw his belt away, picked up Livius's dagger and began to tear up his clothing. "And now?" he asked.

Shan d'Arg responded without raising his head. "You're free to go to Dalaam. You've won. I couldn't fight you after the effort you've just made."

"Strength prevailed," said Jorgenssen, his mouth full of blood, sarcasm and despondency in his voice.

"Not strength," said Shan d'Arg. "It was a fight between men. You've won, that's all."

Jorgenssen regarded him pensively. Laboriously, he succeeded in understanding. Shan d'Arg knew more than he about combat, about victory and defeat. There was certainly truth in what he said, but Jorgenssen succeeded only in catching a glimpse of it. The issue, for Shan d'Arg, was not whether Jorgenssen or Cnossos had been right; the issue was that Jorgenssen's point of view was contrary to the principles of the team. It was necessary that someone fight Jorgenssen and in some way carry the team's colors. But, since Jorgenssen had carried the day, Shan d'Arg's conception of honor prevented him from questioning the conclusion of the fight. He wouldn't fight against an exhausted man. For him, it would have been a vile action. In defeating Cnossos, Jorgenssen had, in his eyes, earned the right to follow his own laws.

That was a very ancient conception of things, Jorgenssen thought, a conception perhaps older than fire. In Shan d'Arg it had remained intact It existed in a latent state in each of them, and it was that which had led him to pull Cnossos out of the fire instead of running away. In itself, it constituted an answer to the question he had asked himself concerning the primitive hunters and their mutual suspicion. A form of confidence can be born out of combat, also.

'I'm going,' he said. "I'll find my way... I can find it by the stars."

"Agreed," said Shan d'Arg. "Wait a minute."

He opened one of the boxes hanging from his belt and took from it a small plastic bag half full of water. He held it out to Jorgenssen. It was what remained of the reserve of his symbiotic complex.

"Take it, you'll need it. You've lost blood. The wound isn't serious, but dress it just the same. I still have enough water for Cnossos."

"And you?"

"We're going down into the valley tomorrow. We'll find a spring. We have to find one."

"Thanks," Jorgenssen said simply. He couldn't refuse. Looking at the fire again and at the four others who seemed to come from a nightmare and who glided like shadows toward Cnossos and Shan d'Arg, he turned and took several steps in the direction of the cliff.

"I'm going with you!" shouted Mario.

"No," said Jorgenssen without turning around again. "Later, if you really want to, you'll come. But now, I have to go alone." This ran through his mind: / fought alone, I have to go there alone. Each one has to find out for himself the reasons for going to Dalaam.

He picked up his belt, fastened it, and attached Livius's dagger to it. Hereafter, it would be less a weapon to him than a tool. He would have an absolute need for it.

"Good-bye," he said in a voice so weak that they certainly didn't hear it

He lengthened his stride and plunged into the moonless night. Only the stars shone in the sky. Some time afterward, the sky became darker and large drops of rain refreshed his body.

When Jorgenssen awoke, he was surprised to find nothing but the night surrounding him. Then he consulted his watch; he had slept fifteen hours. The night would continue nearly sixty hours more.

He unfastened his belt. With Livius's dagger, he cut the straps from which hung boxes full of apparatus, weapons, and provisions. Then he tried to slash his clothing, but the synthetic material resisted. He persisted because he wanted to go down to the city dressed like the natives, without weapons and without tools. He decided to save his watch, although it only seemed to work erratically.

Arms and legs bare, he felt better, liberated. He passed his hand over his face and his fingers glided over the uneven surface of coagulated blood and the stubble of his beard, which was beginning to grow.

He carefully arranged the things he was leaving behind in a pile. The natives would take possession of them, perhaps. Then he picked up his lamp, scarcely larger than a finger. Formerly, it had been capable of lighting up to a distance of a kilometer, but now it scarcely gave more light than a candle. He wondered why it shone at all. Perhaps the inhibiting field which had put their apparatus out of order hadn't worked completely on its mechanism; or perhaps their mysterious adversary had decided to leave them one chance in the opaque night. It was too soon to tell.

He studied the descent of the cliff toward Dalaam, then decided to use the trail.

He discovered in going toward the cliff, which was quite close, that it was marked by weakly luminous pebbles. This was sufficient for him to orient himself without risking the loss of the trail. The Dalaamians must have used it sometimes at night.

The road turned into a narrow defile, and only a few stars remained visible above his head. The road descended rapidly, making him break his stride. On the right, the high wall ended abruptly. He guessed at the abyss whose contour was traced by the phosphorescence. The darkness there was as profound as that of the sky, but more disturbing: no light, no star chanced to break it.

He walked for some time, listening to the pebbles roll under his feet. The trail was easy. It was good to advance this way on a mild night, along a vertical cliff whose summit was invisible. The abyss itself had nothing hostile about it, but only offered the attraction of the unknown.

Jorgenssen, approaching the edge of the road, saw in the depths a very pale, diluted glimmering begin to arise, like a cloud of opal floating in the canyon. As he progressed, the contours of the cloud became clearer. It included areas of various luminosity and darker zones which formed a net with faint knots. Soon he recognized the cloud for what it was: the city, Dalaam at night.

But the light had nothing artificial about it; it didn't come from any particular place. Even at Jorgenssen's altitude, it was easy to see that the light did not come from under the trees, but was mixed with the forest. It came from the trees themselves. Immediately, he made the connection with the luminous pebbles bordering the trail. In the subsoil, there must have been substantial quantities of phosphorescent material, and the trees must have been able to concentrate them in their trunks and leaves, so that the forest lighted the city.

This was a new aspect of the close symbiosis which seemed to exist between the city and forest. Jorgenssen wondered whether the trees had been naturally luminous, or whether the natives had developed a special species. In the latter case, they would possess a surprising mastery of the secrets of genetics—one mystery more to add to the dossier of Ygone.

Viewed more closely, the forest was a luminous sea where a light wind gave rise to slow undulations. The dark network corresponded to spaces where the trees were less dense, or to the points of contact of the leaves of several giant trees.

Jorgenssen penetrated into the luminous cloud. The round, immense leaves formed a vault over his head. Without transition, the road also became luminous. Jorgenssen didn't know the reason for several meters, then he perceived that he was walking on wood. The road ran along an enormous branch whose curves it embraced. After two or three turns, it led to a large opening made in a gigantic trunk.

Jorgenssen hesitated. The opening was one of the gates of the city. No guard, no security device was visible. The only sound he could hear was that of the wind in the leaves. The natives were sleeping, or else were devoting themselves to their incomprehensible activities. After a moment's hesitation, Jorgenssen went into the tunnel. After all, he had come to enter the city with his head high and hands empty. That resolution supposed that he would accept some risks.

The tunnel turned and descended into the tree's interior. The light coming from its walls, curved ceiling, and floor was everywhere the same. He could scarcely discern the darker veins of the perfectly polished wood, and on the ground, traces of footsteps. Two hundred meters farther, the tunnel emerged from the tree. The road again went along a main branch, even more enormous than the first, and inclined toward the ground. The tree, growing so close to the cliff, must have been the largest in the forest. The ground was still invisible. The depths of the forest were plainly darker than the kind of luminous roof of interlacing foliage. At night in Dalaam, this nearby sky shone unceasingly.

The road divided. At the fork, one of the branches— the smaller one—led upward again; the other descended. Jorgenssen decided on the latter. He was eager to get back on the ground and discover the city. He tried to estimate his position in relation to the cliff: he must have been nearly half a kilometer away from it. The reach of the branches was alarming. Later, he was to discover that they were held up in several places by less important trees, or, more exactly, that the forest was composed of a small number of tree "families" connected to each other, and that these families corresponded to the sectors, to the "quarters" of the city. But at the moment, he was content to marvel.

He reached the ground almost without noticing it. For several meters he followed the road, which had ceased to be luminous and which wound among weakly phosphorescent plants. Then the road disappeared.

Confounded, Jorgenssen stopped. Half a dozen narrow footpaths left the road in all directions and lost themselves among the Cyclopean trunks. He didn't know which to take. Finally deciding on the path to the left, which turned farther away from the cliff, he went forward for some time, watching carefully, and at last found a low, one-story dwelling, built of large stones, with an almost flat roof. The interior seemed dark. A door of luminous wood closed a porch, just opposite the path.

There was not the least sign of life: no noise, no smoke, nor any trace of humans or animals. Leaving the path, Jorgenssen walked around the building at a respectful distance. He crossed another path which led to a second house of which he could only see a section of wall among the trunks. This corresponded to the arrangement he had studied from the top of the cliff with the aid of his Orzdian ray binoculars.

He returned to his starting point and hesitated. He could have gone up to the door and knocked. If there had been someone there, he could have tried to explain himself in the language of Ygone the mnemonicians had taught him before his departure from Altair. If there hadn't been anyone, he could have explored the house and rested there.

But the man was afraid his appearance might frighten the residents. He knew too little about the Dalaamians' behavior. Stretched out on the ground, sheltered by one of the trunks in the high grass, nearly invisible from the path as from the house, he watched the door and waited for a long time. He lost the sense of passing time and must have slept for several minutes two or three times. Each time, he again found an unchanged landscape and the building as silent as before.

He began to suffer from thirst. On the way, he had drunk all the water Shan d'Arg had given him. Now he sucked some sugar-coated capsules of food concentrate which relieved his exhaustion. His face had stopped hurting, but his whole body still ached from blows.

The slight grating the door made in opening awoke him. A form glided out. He blinked to see better. It was a woman, a very young woman, without a doubt, just a girl. As far as he could determine at a distance, she was completely human: her blond hair was cut short, she wore a light, Dalaamian tunic, she was lithe and had a nice figure. She could even have passed for beautiful; but hers was a natural beauty, almost wild and yet calm, singularly remote from the unusual and sophisticated beauty of Federation women.

She carried a sort of pitcher cut from the luminous wood. Without hesitating, she took the road and passed very near Jorgenssen without seeing him. He watched her go, then got up with a bound, and followed her.

He thought she was barefoot, but saw the impressions of sandals in the dust. At a bend around a trunk, he suddenly lost sight of her. He quickened his pace, thinking she had distanced him, but came to the crossroads again without having overtaken her. After slowly retracing his steps and inspecting the edges of the road, he noticed an inconspicuous path which turned from the trail and led to an enormous trunk. He raised his eyes, but his gaze was stopped at thirty meters up by the luminous vault of foliage supported by the gigantic branches.

Jorgenssen resolutely went toward the trunk. The path went around it. The grass had been newly trampled down, and he was sure he had found the young woman's track again.

He was just about to go past the cavernous opening in the trunk without seeing her. It was the movement of her tunic in the interior that caught his eye. He risked a glance. The young woman was doing an incomprehensible task as she sang. When she was finished, she filled her pitcher and returned.

Jorgenssen jumped to one side, thinking she had seen him. He went around the trunk and crouched in the grass, but saw her go away tranquilly in the direction of the low house, with her full pitcher in hand.

He remained stretched out on the grass for fifteen minutes. Then he got up again and cautiously approached the opening in the tree. The interior was luminous, as he expected, but surprisingly, it did not seem that the cavity had been cut in the tree. There was no trace of a notch or seam in the superficial tissues of the tree. Neither was the tree hollow like a dead one. It seemed to have grown naturally around that cavity.

Jorgenssen entered by the round opening. The room was much more spacious than he had expected—and empty. For a moment, he had thought it might serve the Dalaamians as a dwelling or storeroom, but there was nothing in it. Yet, in the center, creases of wood formed circular vats. One of these overflowed with a colorless liquid; another was filled to the brim with a sort of creamy pulp. But what impressed Jorgenssen most was the third one. Plants were growing there—plants, or more precisely, fruit.

The pouch in the thickness of the tree naturally served to protect its fruit. The flowers and fruit of this plant species did not grow on the branches. This must have posed delicate problems of fecundation, maturation, and later on, of seeding; but the evolution of plants on Ygone had had to resolve them under existing conditions. The idea occurred to Jorgenssen that this method of plant reproduction could have been imposed on the trees by the natives. Perhaps they had entirely created a species to serve their needs: they would thus easily reap the products of the trees. On the other hand, the vats suggested hydroponic cultivation. The truth must have included all these elements.

Jorgenssen wet one finger with the colorless liquid and put it to his lips: no taste. It was water, and it was fresh. He filled his hands and drank, threw some on his face, and felt better. The water level in the vat did not seem to go down.

He tasted the pulp. It was lightly-sugared and had an almond taste. He didn't dare eat any of it, since he didn't know enough about the flora of Ygone. He had already taken a sufficient risk in drinking the water.

A kind of euphoria filled him. He had discovered why the Dalaamians didn't cultivate the earth and had no commerce: the trees furnished the nourishment they needed.

And also their tunics. Just beside the last vat, the wood appeared creased, but this was only an illusion. A thin piece of plant tissue was in the process of separating from the trunk. Jorgenssen felt it: it had the suppleness of very fine dressed leather.

The scent of vanilla floated in the air. He filled his lungs with it. He felt secure in the heart of the tree. Suddenly, his state of exhaustion returned. He stretched out on the ground and decided to sleep.

Sleep took possession of him almost instantaneously. He never knew at what precise moment the dreams began.

IV

In his dream, he walked in the middle of a crowd, but the people did not see him. For them, he had no reality. Neither could he distinguish them with any precision, since he was moving too fast. Sometimes, he attempted to slow down, but in vain. The crowd, filled the streets of a city. He went through narrower and narrower descending streets. Soon, although it was broad daylight, he walked in semi-darkness, because the walls were so high and close. He tried to lift his head toward the sky, but his muscles did not obey him. He experienced a keen annoyance.

Suddenly, he emerged into an immense and empty public square, ringed by staircases descending toward the center of that circular arena. He sensed the square itself was full of people, but he couldn't see them. He experienced greater and greater difficulties clearing a way for himself, though he saw nothing.

Then he saw, in the center of the square, a sculpture which he hadn't noticed at first. It was a sphere, set on a large pedestal. Maybe a symbol of time, he thought. At the same time, the sphere had another meaning which he had known, but could no longer recall. The sphere was not uniform. On the near side, it bore the outline of a face. He remembered having already seen those features, but without being able to give them a name. He went toward the sphere with the intention of examining it.

A silhouette loomed from behind the sphere; it was so intensely luminous that he couldn't see details. It was a tall man, wearing a strange uniform. His skull shone as if entirely shaved. In his dream, Jorgenssen knew that the new arrival would prevent him from reaching the sphere, and would even try to kill him. He wanted to run away to hide. He knew he could do nothing against his adversary. But he couldn't retreat either, for the crowd blocked all paths of escape. It drove him hack toward the sphere.

He began to run, hoping to outdistance his enemy. The square became an arena. But the open space contracted unceasingly. Then it came to him that if he could touch the sphere, he would be saved.

He ran as fast as his legs would carry him; his breath was short. But he didn't have the ghost of a chance. The enemy abruptly reared up between the sphere and him, nearly touching it, aiming a weapon at him.

Jorgenssen looked his adversary in the face—until then blurred, it suddenly became clear. He recognized it feature for feature.

It was not like the image in a mirror; it was himself. He knew he was going to die, like Mario, by the hand of his double.

He stirred in his sleep. The dream stopped, then began again. Each time, he knew he had already found himself in an identical situation, but he didn't know where or when; it seemed incredibly old to him. And the dream always ended the same way. In each dream, he had a little more longing to know what would happen if he had been killed, if the situation had come to a conclusion, but each time the dream was interrupted at the last moment, and he found himself half-conscious again. In each dream, he was a little more exhausted; the scene gained in clarity and horror. He knew that in the end, he would really be killed.

Hands shook him. He refused to wake. He felt someone carry him away.

An impression of freshness. Jorgenssen opened his eyes. The light of day fell from a narrow window onto the smooth wooden floor beside him. He heard a voice speaking in Dalaamian—a feminine voice, very young, slightly muffled.

"You've come back from afar," said the voice. "What an idea, to be asleep in a tree! Whoever you are, you could've died of it, if I hadn't found you."

Jorgenssen's mouth was dry. At first, he could only emit a croak. He swallowed his saliva. He had a headache. He sat up on his elbows and recognized the girl: she was the one he had followed... the night before. Was it really the night before? It was day. Therefore, those things had happened at least forty hours ago. Had he slept all that time? What had become of the others?

He discovered he was completely naked under a supple counterpane, probably of the same origin as the tunics. He wondered what the Dalaamians had done with his clothes.

"I'm thirsty," Jorgenssen tried to articulate.

She brought him a wooden cup full of water. He drank avidly.

"My name's Anema," she said.

"Jorgenssen," he said. "I... I come from very far away."

"I know," said Anema. "You weren't born on this world, it seems. Don't worry. It doesn't matter."

"How do you know?"

This was not how he imagined his first interview with a Dalaamian.

"Do you think a resident of this city would be in your state? Look at yourself!"

She handed him a metal mirror. He made an instinctive gesture of revulsion. His image recalled an erased memory which didn't quite succeed in rising to consciousness. His face in the mirror appeared extremely emaciated, his features drawn. It was the mask of a man who had seen something dreadful, more terrifying than death itself.

Anema put the mirror on a low table which seemed to grow out of the floor. Jorgenssen examined the table; it did grow out of the floor—it was part of it, a sort of excrescence of the tree. He wondered why the Dalaamians didn't live in houses entirely "produced" by the trees. For a time, his mind suggested no answer to the problem. Then a solution came to mind: The trees had to breathe, they must have filled the atmosphere of their cavities with all sorts of poisons. The Dalaamians never stayed there for long, but he had remained for hours. The hypothesis was plausible. He tried to explain it to the girl.

"I've been poisoned," he said. "Asphyxiated."

She shook her head. "No," she replied. "The trees can do no harm. They wouldn't have poisoned you."

"Just the same, trees don't have will," he said. It was a difficult concept to state in Dalaamian. The language of Ygone could be singularly imprecise about certain things— or too precise. Its words did not coincide with those of the galactic language.

"No," she said. "No, not exactly... She had a reflective air.

"All the same," she said, "one could say that... yes, in a certain way, the trees do will the things they do. They agree to give us what they give.... But I don't know very much. I'll have to ask my third father about it. He's very good at that. He's studied the relations between the trees and us a lot. He says he isn't sure whether we're still beings distinct from the trees."

Jorgenssen made a mental note of the expression third father. It didn't exist in the language of Ygone the linguists had taught him. Even the language seemed to have changed on Ygone. He understood some of Anema's words only by breaking them up and going back to their roots. The language of Ygone expressed a conception of the world extremely different from the Federation's. Just how different, it was still too soon to decide.

Anema removed the counterpane with a quick, natural movement. Jorgenssen turned scarlet; good society in the Federation had other customs. He controlled himself and maintained a supremely detached air while the girl took a balm and massaged it into the muscles all over his body.

"When you were brought here," she said, "your muscles were as hard as wood. I'd never seen a body so contracted. Your bones might even have been broken if they'd been more brittle. I even thought you might remain paralyzed. But now it's much better."

Jorgenssen was not of that opinion. He had the impression that his body had been broken on a wheel.... An unpleasant memory lingered at the edge of consciousness.

"But what's made me so sick," he asked, "if the trees can't do any harm?"

The response came immediately—dreadfully. "Yourself," said Anema. "You must detest yourself terribly to have come to this. You've all but killed yourself. The evil is within you."

She talks like a psychoanalyst, he thought. Is it a coincidence? She seems to think I'm neurotic to the core. Weighing the idea, he didn't like it. For the Galactic

Federation, he was relatively normal; but norms change from one society to another, and since his discovery of Dalaam, at the top of the cliff, he had constantly acted in a way totally aberrant in his own eyes.

"You must sleep now," she said. His stomach turned at that idea. She put her hand on his forehead. "You're going to sleep."

"I'm afraid to," he said. "I don't want to sleep."

She opened her eyes wide. "You remember the dream?"

183

"The dream? What dream?"

"Too bad," she said. "If you'd remembered the dream, you would've been almost cured. Someday, you must go again into the tree to recapture the dream. The trees can't treat someone as sick as you at one time. And you've received a massive dose. The first time, a few minutes would've been enough."

He didn't understand a quarter of what she was saying.

"I was sick?" The trees are able to treat people? What does that mean?"

Anema's expression suddenly became grave. "They're things you know from childhood," she said. "The trees help you understand yourself. But I forgot, you're a stranger,"

"Explain it to me."

"I don't know if I should. Maybe it could hurt you. You've suffered a very great shock. You've almost discovered who you really are... and I only know the rudiments. My third father knows almost everything there is to know about it."

"Try!" he implored.

She closed her eyes and concentrated. Then she began to speak in a slow, monotonous voice, using simple words. "Every human being," she said, "has several beings within himself. They're not exactly beings, but, instead, parts of his personality. When the being is very young, the parts are more-or-less ignorant of each other. Later, they can fight each other or cooperate. One of these parts has direct contact with the outside world; the others have less, or none at all. There're some that are blind and deaf and deprived of will and logic. Sometimes, as in your case, these are held prisoner by the others. They try to escape. They make enormous efforts to free themselves, in order to dominate the others. And the others use up a lot of energy to hold them back. If the straggle is too hard, the personality could explode like a rock split by freezing. Then the person is insane."

"I see," he said. He thought, The conscious and the unconscious. The conscious that suppresses certain elements of the unconscious, that, nevertheless, rise to the surface in devious ways and put pressure on the conscious. If the pressure's constant, there's neurosis. If it cracks the fragile conscious, its psychosis... insanity... frenzy...

"There's the environment also," she said, "relations with people. You can't really accept them unless you're healthy-minded, unless you accept yourself completely. The trees help us do this. The trees are able to bring the different parts of the personality in contact with each other. We leave children in the trees for some time each day, so that they'll learn to really be themselves. My third father says the trees play a very important part in our civilization. He says it's thanks to them that Ygone is a privileged world in the galaxy. He says we're almost alone in knowing happiness."

She hadn't used the term galaxy, but another, more vague one which signified all worlds. There was also in the word's root the idea of a community and of a city, exactly as if she had considered each of the worlds of the galaxy as the equivalent of one of their own quarters. The import of the word remained obscure to Jorgenssen. He chose to translate it by galaxy, but he would wait to thoroughly examine it.

"I don't know how the trees do it," she said. "They give us dreams. When you remember your dreams, you're adult, well-balanced. I remember my dreams very well. My third father says I'm remarkably well-balanced for a girl my age."

She seemed very content with herself, but there was no trace of vanity in her voice. Vanity, Jorgenssen thought, is a neurotic feeling based on a feeling of superiority, and, finally, on the denial of the rest of the world.

The Federation bursts with vanity. The Federation's profoundly neurotic. He corrected himself immediately— in relation to Ygone. He felt better, refreshed. He thought he would be able to sleep in peace. He had never experienced such calm.

"The trees belong to everyone," she continued. "I believe they communicate the dreams of different people among themselves, perhaps all of them. My father says they're much less differentiated, much less individualized, than we are. But he also says that only the superficial part of our personalities make us much different from each other. He says that, at bottom, we all have much in common, that this comes from the society we live in and also from the trees. But he says that profound things make one society much different from another, perhaps more different than two beings in the same society, on the superficial level, but that, still more profoundly, there're things common to all societies—and that perhaps someday, we'll be able to reunite them, with the help of the trees."

She's talking like a sociologist now, mused Jorgenssen, as he sank into sleep. Her voice became distant. She was surely not yet twenty years old and she spoke with authority, in a simple vocabulary, of problems that some of the Federation's most subtle minds, more or less secretly because the Arque disapproved, were struggling to resolve. He had had a tendency at first to charge her with magical ideas because she believed in demons within man capable of rendering him sick or insane, and in the intervention of the trees to dispel them.

But on the verge of sleep, Jorgenssen felt there were great truths in what she said—perhaps even the solution to his old and tormenting inquiry into the meaning of the Federation and of his own life. He had never felt his mind so clear. Gently, he descended into the depths of his body and felt good despite the diffuse pain he was always experiencing. The obstinate question of how the trees acted remained. Did they perhaps fill the air with drugs all the same, or was it perhaps necessary to find a more fantastic explanation? Was a kind of telepathy established between the people and the trees? Had he perhaps been threatened with destruction by the diffuse memory of the trees, full of traces of all the dreams they had seen spring up and unfold in their midst? He recognized he was still refusing to admit that he could have wanted to destroy himself and plunged into a sleep as deep and calm as the depths of the sea.

This time, the third father was at his bedside when he awakened. Anema stood close beside him. Seeing the man, Jorgenssen wondered whether the natives of Ygone were really human in origin, for nothing in his face was really extraordinary, but the whole gave an impression of strangeness. His head was enormous and his eyes grandly remote, testifying to a strange attention coupled with an amused calm. Even the man's posture evoked, at the same time, unusual suppleness and strength. He controlled his body perfectly, but it was evident that this cost him no effort.

There was in his movements a harmony like that of a wild animal, minus the fear and aggressiveness. Despite his training, Jorgenssen felt awkward before him. He read in the other's eyes that the same difference existed between them on the mental plane.

Jorgenssen suddenly noticed certain things about Anema which hadn't struck him at first. She was too supple, too lively, without appearing nervous in any way. Her eyes had the same almost inhuman calm as those of her father. The same amused gleam alone tempered the coldness of their reflection, otherwise as sharp as those of precious stones.

Had a mutation perhaps occurred on Ygone... by accident... or perhaps were the inhabitants of Dalaam the result of a genetic experiment, like the trees? Jorgenssen felt more and more strongly that there was another face to things, that Ygone represented nothing but a square on a colossal chess board, that of the universe, that the inhabitants of the city of trees, with their strange customs, were only pawns maneuvered by other beings, more powerful and until then hidden... and he himself was nothing but a pawn of the Federation.

Troubled, he avoided the man's eyes. It seemed impossible that this man could be a mere pawn. Never had anyone better incarnated freedom for Jorgenssen—freedom without anguish... no one, except, perhaps, Anema.

"You're better," said the man. "What are you going to do?"

The question took Jorgenssen unawares. The man's voice was grave, poised without constraint. "I... don't know," Jorgenssen stammered. "I'm thinking of living in this city for a while."

"You're free. You can stay as long as you like. But I don't know whether you'll want to stay here long. After all, you'll decide yourself."

Jorgenssen wanted to protest that the life of the Dalaamians would suit him perfectly; but he contained himself in time, understanding what the man had meant He hadn't wanted to frighten him nor to suggest that he would be unwelcome—simply that it could be disagreeable to live in a city where one knew less about the world and about oneself than a small child. It would be to find oneself in a position of unacceptable inferiority. Jorgenssen gave the man an understanding look.

"I am Daalquin," said the man. "That's at the same time a name and a function. I believe the little one has begun to explain certain things to you but I don't know whether she's done well or poorly. She decided freely in terms of your situation. You may ask me questions if you like, but I suppose you will better understand how we live by observing us. I know you're full of curiosity."

He paused and added in a voice tinged with irony, "Here, nothing is hidden, but everything is not always easy to understand when one has different customs."

"You seem so happy, so relaxed," Jorgenssen said impulsively. He put his hand on his head. His hair had grown. Still, it was hardly more than a few millimeters long. Suddenly he envied the man's thick, black hair. His usual custom of shaving his whole head seemed absurd.

"We have our problems," said Daalquin, "but they are real problems."

Jorgenssen bit his lip. He pulled back the counterpane. "I can get up." It was an assurance and a question at the same time.

"If you like."

Jorgenssen sat up on the bed and carefully put his feet on the floor. He stood up. Feeling more steady than he had expected to, he walked around the room. He glanced through a narrow window and saw a footpath disappearing among the giant trees. Only then did he notice he was stark naked.

"I'd like some clothes," he began. He knew his embarrassment was completely ridiculous to Anema and Daalquin.

"I'll go get you some," said Anema. She took a tunic and various accessories out of a chest. Jorgenssen got dressed with her help. During this time, Daalquin put various cups on a table. Jorgenssen drank and refreshed himself.

"I'd like to ask you a rather personal question," he said hesitatingly. "I hope it won't offend you. But Anema spoke to me several times of her third father. I suppose she meant you. I wondered what the expression meant Biologically, uh...."

Daalquin broke out in laughter and Anema echoed him. Jorgenssen smiled politely, without understanding.

"Our society is a little peculiar," said Daalquin, "at least in relation to yours, such as I can picture it to myself. Naturally, I'm certainly making errors. But your society seems to me still strongly characteristic of the heritage of your predator-hunter ancestors. It combines individualism and slavery. It resolved this particular conflict by means of specialization—an aberrant solution which can't be maintained long without danger."

Jorgenssen lifted his eyes from his bowl. Daalquin spoke without the slightest respect for the Federation's enormous power. Although only the native of an unimportant planet which the Federation's fleets could reduce to powder in less than a minute, he discussed the Federation's problems as if it were a matter of a mere ant hill. Yet, as unpleasant as it was, his diagnosis was far from wrong. In a few sentences, he began to give a foundation, a sense, to the old malaise of Jorgenssen.

"The individual is jealous of his freedom," said Daalquin, "but at the same time, unity can only be maintained by coercion. As a result, whatever is not the individual, he takes as more or less hostile. It's very difficult for him to surmount that wall of hostility to reach another individual. This has implications on the personal plane."

He leaned toward Jorgenssen, who thought he read a sort of pity in Daalquin's eyes.

"You believe the entire universe envies your power," pursued the Dalaamian, "but, at bottom, we're rather sorry for you. You are a race of recluses. The logical consequence is that you are theoretically monogamous, on the family plane, and practically speaking polygamous. I might go as far as to say that for us it's exactly the contrary, but you would misinterpret my thought."

He reflected a moment, staring into space, his fingers playing on the surface of the table. It was the first sign of nervousness that Jorgenssen had noticed on his part. Anema, stretched out on the floor, supported on her elbows, looked at one and then the other.

"The human being," Daalquin finally resumed, "is very complex on the affective plane. He depends enormously, above all at the beginning of his life, but later as well, upon those who surround him. He cannot be completely himself except thanks to them. Naturally, in the actual state of things, he cannot have very strong affectionate ties with a multitude of persons. But he can very well love several equally and at the same time. Thus, he enriches himself more than if he had chosen only one, and, in doing so, enriches the others also."

Jorgenssen began to catch a glimpse of the truth, through the obvious efforts which Daalquin was making not to shock him. He had the impression of being a child to whom one explains discreetly, for the first time, the mysteries of life.

"Our families are complex and changing wholes," said Daalquin. "They generally include six or seven, rarely more than a dozen, people. There exists a sort of network of bonds among the men and women, the parents and children. In your terms, I have, in a certain sense, several wives; but in return, they have several husbands. The system is not closed. Each is free to withdraw at will, or to enter the group if he finds a partner. On the other hand, there are very intimate affective relations among the different groups. Certain people easily pass from one to another. But the group of families is extremely stable, much more than your couples, and those you call fickle play an extremely important role in our society. I hope you understand me."

"I see," said Jorgenssen. In a certain way, he thought, the network of roads he had seen from the top of the cliff denoted that subtle equilibrium of families, those at once multiple, stable, and changing relationships. Dalaamian society was in large part founded on love, physical as well as moral—an old dream of humanity. It was normal that the social organization of Ygone did not rest on coercion.

"And jealousy?" he said. He had to search a long time before finding the corresponding word in the vocabulary of Ygone. In his mouth, it sounded obsolete in a way.

Daalquin repeated it twice, as if he were trying hard to grasp its meaning. "Jealousy, jealousy... it's a sign of incapacity, isn't it? The trees cure it."

He left his seat and went toward Anema. He sat down on the bed beside her and ran the fingers of his right hand through the girl's hair. There was nothing ambiguous in his behavior; his affection for Anema was simply and clearly paternal.

"The children," he said, "are raised by all the 'parents.' They certainly don't lack affection. With time, they choose the family members they prefer, who are not necessarily their biological parents. I'm not Anema's first father, but her third, that is to say, I've helped her grow from adolescence. Her first father helped her to enter life, the second helped her through childhood. Do you understand?"

Jorgenssen nodded his head.

Encouraged, Daalquin concluded, "She'll be even more beautiful than her mother. I sometimes regret not being her biological father. That's one of the great problems of our society. Theoretically, the division of the human species into two sexes permits all possible genetic exchanges. But a considerable time would be gained if a child could combine the traits of several of his parents, for example, of a mother and several fathers, only retaining the favorable factors. This is a problem that we shall resolve someday, perhaps."

Here's one of the real problems he accuses the Federation of not realizing, Jorgenssen thought. It was the idea of a biologist, of a eugenicist, of an expert desiring to master nature. But the warm and enthusiastic tone of Daalquin was incompatible with that vision of things. In the secrecy of their laboratories, the Federation's experts might well produce monstrous ideas and perpetrate crimes against life, but not this man. This man loved life too much, in all its forms. He was searching only to make it more lively still, to make it sing higher and stronger. The society of Dalaam, Jorgenssen decided, was not a Utopian society, a stable paradise set in its perfection, but a perpetually changing world on the road of progress. Its problems were those of the future, and not the sole and unique problem of eternally maintaining a present fixed in the image of the past.

He had a shocking intuition of what the Federation could have to fear from a world like Ygone. For the Federation, a woman like Anema was a danger, a mortal peril. She could come into any of the homes of the proud patricians of the Archy, and immediately eclipse the Federation's most beautiful bodies. She was not merely more perfected; she had more reality. She was.

Jorgenssen felt old scars revive in him. What Daalquin had said was true: he belonged to a race of recluses, used to facing the entire universe in silence and, finally, in sadness. He did not venture to sustain the direct gaze of Anema. A sudden flush came into his face.

He would not have known how to speak to her. He had the cultivation of a thousand worlds behind him, and all the finesse of a galaxy; yet he remained as mute as a fish in the face of this girl with golden hair.

"Would you like to ask me other questions?" asked Daalquin, tearing him away from his thoughts.

"No," said Jorgenssen, placing his heavy hands on his knees, which the tunic left bare. "No, not for the moment I'd like to think."

"Fine," said Daalquin. "We'll see you again later. I must go to confer with the trees. They are teaching me remarkable things." His ample lips smiled mischievously. In one supple movement, he reached the door, opened it and went out.

Jorgenssen, his mind empty, vaguely anguished, looked at Anema.

For four days on Ygone, he visited Dalaam, sometimes alone, sometimes in Anema's company. Sheltered by the forest the city showed itself to be almost always the same, and yet free of any monotony. The natives generally paid little attention to him, but proved themselves friendly and hospitable. They never asked questions, but some at least seemed to guess Jorgenssen's origin, and to be better informed about the Federation than he was about Ygone. However, nowhere did he see instruments capable of intercepting the Federation's messages. The technology of Ygone seemed nonexistent—unless there was a hidden face to things and a whole area of reality that escaped him.

The people's existence was simple. They seemed to take from the trees nearly everything necessary to their lives. They spent their time walking, discussing interminably, thinking, and practicing various art forms, much simpler, moreover, than those current in the Federation. Once, Jorgenssen felt he had fallen upon something different. He saw a man seated on his doorstep drawing symbols on a plant leaf. Doubtless it concerned mathematics; but Jorgenssen did not recognize a single one of the symbols. They gave him the impression of extreme simplicity, but he knew that in this field one mustn't rely on appearances. Such great simplicity could result from a high level of abstraction and actually reflect considerable difficulty.

The man seemed absorbed in his work; but abruptly, he lifted his head and surveyed Jorgenssen with a smile. Jorgenssen, embarrassed, stopped reading over his shoulder and walked away, but he felt he had discovered something. Trying to engage Anema on the subject, he soon realized that the question didn't interest her, and that she knew almost nothing about it. She did try to tell him the man was attempting to describe the way Dalaamian society was evolving from the unconscious interaction among the families, but this scarcely enlightened him. Anema's passion was biology and, as far as Jorgenssen could understand her explanations, genetics. She had, it seemed, devoted herself to some surprising experiments, "with the collaboration of the trees." Yet Jorgenssen never saw her with a laboratory instrument in her hands. There must have been, after all, other means of exploring reality besides the mechanical, brutal methods in favor with the Federation's experts.

Dalaamian civilization seemed almost exclusively oriented toward the life sciences. In the domain of physics they apparently had profound concepts, but the matter scarcely interested them. It was easy to see the reason: the very structure of their society forbade great development in physics, which required a whole technology, and, hence, extensive specialization. They had preferred freedom to knowledge; or rather, they had chosen other paths of knowledge— deliberately. The Federation had evolved, in a sense, under the pressure of historical necessity; but Dalaam seemed to grow and live at the will of its residents. Its civilization was the product of a conscious effort and not of an obstinate, limited, and silent travail of a human ant hill struggling toward an unknown end.

The city had no organization. Certain of its residents, however, filled offices in the general interest, which they had freely chosen and which they changed from time to time. This absence of collective organization expressed itself in the design of Dalaam, as Jorgenssen had seen it from the top of the cliff. There were only two or three public squares—which seemed to date from an earlier period in the history of Ygone and whose origin was uncertain, even for the Dalaamians, who gave only vague answers to Jorgenssen's questions. However, these squares seemed to have great importance for them. Fountains played there. The Dalaamians came together at certain times and drank, with a kind of respect, the water which came from the earth instead of being distilled by the trees. The Dalaamians adored water. In all their homes it flowed, hot or cold, into basins where they would bathe at any hour of the day or night. Jorgenssen did not succeed in understanding how the houses were supplied nor how the water was heated. The explanations Anema lavished on him made use of a vocabulary which was almost totally unknown to him. He had to be content to suppose the benevolent trees intervened there also.

He found the first of these public squares accidentally and had the shock of his life. Its circular form, its flagstone pavement slightly below ground level, which was reached by three stairways running around its circumference, reminded him of something; precisely what he could not determine. A pedestal, struck directly by the sun's rays, dominated the fountain. It supported a stylized bust, whose features recalled the faces of the Dalaamians. Seeing that face, Jorgenssen stopped, confounded. He recognized it. He had already seen it on Altair, in the Federation, on numerous worlds; but he could not remember exactly under what circumstances, nor the name of the model. He only experienced the impression of finding on that isolated world, a familiar element.

He turned toward Anema. "Who is it?" he asked.

She remained pensive. "It's the foremost man," she said.

The significance of this term was not clear. It could have meant that, for the Dalaamians, this was a representation of the first man, or else of the most important one; for the two concepts, of time and importance, were intimately bound together. Jorgenssen could gather nothing more from Anema.

Every day, he realized a little more that, despite appearances, he was foreign to her and to the other Dalaamians: he did not share their view of the world, and he knew infinitely less about mankind in general and about their society in particular. Once, Anema said it to him, in a way which flattered him at first, but overwhelmed him afterward: "I find you fascinating."

She looked at him with the greatest seriousness, although the habitual glimmer of amusement had not left her eyes. He surprised her; he had not hoped for such great success.

"I don't understand you half the time," she continued. "I don't know what you're thinking. The people of Dalaam... even if I don't know them, I know what they think, I know what they love, I know who they are—but not you. You're a stranger. It's marvelous."

All Jorgenssen's enthusiasm evaporated at once. I am a stranger and that's why I interest her. I'll never be anything else but a stranger to her, an object of curiosity. She wants to know how I think and that's why she stays close to me.

She felt something had offended him, so she began again immediately. "I must hurry to understand you, because soon you'll be like us. The trees will help you. If you like, you can lead the same life as we do. There're still all kinds of exciting things you haven't discovered." Jorgenssen rebelled. "No," he said. "No. I'll leave soon." "You're free," she said, "but why?"

He shook his head. "I have to go back to the place I came from. I have to find my friends again. I'll never be anything but a stranger here."

"Is that so disagreeable?"

He avoided her eyes.

"You always detest yourself so much," she said. "The trees did almost nothing for you. You don't really want to go, but you try to do yourself harm by thinking of your leaving. Can't you really see things as they are?"

She approached him and took his head in her hands, gently forcing him to look at her. "You're a child," she said. "Why do I have to tell you these things? There can't be anything between us now. Later, maybe... I don't know. But don't you see that with all this anguish you have inside you, all this hate, it's as if you belonged to a different species..."

"As if I were an animal," he clipped. The idea had already grazed him.

"You're being silly. It's not your fault! Your society... the trees..."

He drew back a step and pushed her away without rudeness. For an instant, he might have failed to let her go, he would even have been able to cry, but that had passed. Again he felt as hard and sharp as a metal tool, tarnished by anguish, heavy with an internal lump, a flaw diminishing its toughness. "I'm going," he said.

"As you wish."

192

He never again brought up the subject with her. He came to walk beside her and take her by the arm; he even came to kiss her before his departure, but she never again mentioned what had passed between them that day. And he knew that she was right, in every way. He detested himself.

And the face on its pedestal was an additional enigma, one more interval separating him from Anema. Is it a sort of Adam, or a kind of god, or both at once? But that did not correspond to anything he knew of Dalaamian thought. And there was that irritating impression of déjà vu.

The statue's features were rather heavy, fleshy, but they flashed with intelligence: they did not depict an. abstract man. The forgotten sculptor who had— at the time when Dalaam had still been a stone city, a classic city—raised the bust, had had in mind, with no possible doubt, a particular man.

Impulsively, Jorgenssen approached Anema again. He was a head taller than she. Bending slightly toward her and breathing her fragrance, he wanted to destroy the distance which separated them. But there was nothing to be done. In Jorgenssen's world, the die was cast from the world's first instant. The games were over; the distance was doomed to continue.

It would subsist even if he brushed against Anema, even if he could smell the fragrance of her skin and of her hair —a scent that had surprised him at first because Federation women effaced their fragrance, or smothered it under the weight of sophisticated perfumes. Anema's was a fragrance of life, that of a warm and living being, and not of a stiff object.

He saw a boy about seven or eight years old emerge from a footpath and cross the square running, kicking a ball—a simple ball of wood—in front of him. He directed it very skillfully with his feet, and Jorgenssen was reminded of Aran's daughter who also played with a sphere. But the difference between the game Aran's daughter played and that of the Dalaamian boy reflected the difference between the two worlds. The value of the girl's ball lay in its complexity, its internal mechanism. The value of the wooden ball was nothing, or rather, it rested entirely with the Dalaamian boy; he gave it the significance he wished.

A sphere. Jorgenssen's gaze went from the ball, rebounding on the stairs, to the bust raised above the fountain. Somewhere there was a connection between those two forms, a connection hidden in the uttermost depths of himself. If he found it, he would be freed, he was sure, and the rest would be given to him also. He put his hands on Anema's shoulders.

But he would never find it. He had no chance of finding it. "Let's go," he said.

For hours they had talked—Jorgenssen, Daalquin, Anema, Daalna, her mother, Burquin, Loordin, and Sineva, who were all part of Anema's family. They had talked of the Federation, of Ygone, of the problems of man and his future. On many points, Jorgenssen had remained silent. He regretted it inwardly, for they seemed more frank with him; but he could not renounce all at once his old loyalty to the Federation. He still could not repudiate his past. Neither had he dared to tell them for what precise reason he had come to Ygone, but had spoken vaguely of exploration, of studies.

Now they had all gone. Only Daalquin and he remained in the dim room, sipping an intoxicating liquor Daalquin had poured into cups of black, polished wood. It was a real pleasure to caress the wood's smooth and malleable surface and to watch the watery reflections on the alcohol.

"Well," said Daalquin, leaning toward him across the table, "what do you think of Dalaam? Do you think we could be a great peril to the Federation?"

The question caught Jorgenssen entirely unawares. It was the first time he had been questioned so directly. Until then, the Dalaamians' tact had permitted him to remain vague.

He did not answer directly. "Dalaam is an oasis of happiness in the galaxy," he said. "And I believe your society is entirely different from the Federation's."

"I'm going to ask you a question," said Daalquin. "You are free to reply or not. When you came here, you were full of fear, hatred, and anguish. You were intoxicated with it. Moreover, you have not truly ceased to be so. But with respect to us, at least, are you reassured?"

"I don't know," said Jorgenssen. "I understand you so little."

He had just lowered his guard. Until then, his relative silence might have passed for assurance. Now, he appeared before Daalquin as he really was, scarcely more than a child; and he could not even have the consolation of thinking that on Altair, Daalquin would have felt as lost as he did on Ygone. Nothing was less certain.

"Your friends, in any case," said Daalquin, "seem not to have stopped fearing us. They wandered for some time around the city, and they are now camped near the outer gate, at the fork in the road descending toward the river. I don't see very clearly what they propose to do, perhaps attempt a surprise attack on the city to 'free' you, for they think, I presume, that we're holding you prisoner here." Jorgenssen gasped again: that answered a question he hadn't dared to ask since his arrival in Dalaam. He had thought, more or less, that the other six members of the team had been unperceived.

"You're afraid of something?" he asked. "Do you want me to rejoin them and reassure them? Do you want me to ask them to return here with me?"

"They wouldn't follow you," Daalquin said categorically. "They seem to have a strange conception of us. I don't believe they could do us great harm in the present state of affairs, but they envisage our destruction with the greatest sang-froid" He spoke calmly, as usual, as if it were a matter neither of the destiny of his city, nor of the worst enemies of his people. "I think they must be considered insane," he said further, after a moment's reflection.

"Then almost the whole population of the Federation would have to be considered crazy, too," Jorgenssen was on the point of saying; but he contained

194

himself. "You've shown them great demonstrations of power," he said. "It's normal for them to fear you."

Daalquin's voice hardened. "We gave you no demonstrations of power. Without intervening, we allowed you to undertake all that you wished. We knew, nevertheless, that your mission on our world was purely and simply to destroy our civilization. But we have done nothing to defend ourselves, firstly because we didn't believe you could seriously endanger the equilibrium of our society, and secondly because we have at our command no weapons we could oppose to yours, at least, to those you carried on your arrival."

"You put them out of order," Jorgenssen accused in a toneless voice. "I'm not blaming you—but you attacked us several times; you apparently killed one of us, or at least put in our way a corpse resembling him in every detail; you broke our instruments; and finally, you prevented us from regaining our world by destroying the object that connected us with it."

Daalquin appeared profoundly surprised. "We did nothing of the kind! You may not believe me, but I can assure you, we have done nothing of the kind."

"Who then?" asked Jorgenssen. "Is there another civilization on Ygone? Is there another power besides yours?"

"There isn't any," said Daalquin. "But there was one, and there might be one, perhaps."

"In time?"

"In the past and perhaps in the future. You know, we don't concern ourselves much with physics. You know much more than we about the nature of time, even if you haven't deemed it wise to speak." He had a fleeting smile while saying these words. "What we know of time, we draw from our knowledge of beings and of our society. Within beings, there are constant relations between the past and present. At a certain stage of maturity, of mental organization, the present and even the image of the future react with the past, striving to control it, to discipline it; and in return, the past protects the being against the repetition of certain situations."

He paused. "I believe it's the same for societies at a certain stage. They more-or-less begin to control their development. As far as I know, your Federation has attained that stage, but has taken a neurotic course."

"You... you know we travel in time?" said Jorgenssen. He let his cup drop. It rolled onto the floor and the liquor was spilled; the uniform floor seemed to absorb the liquid instantaneously.

"Yes," said Daalquin. "In fact, we knew it well before you came. We've waited for this crisis a long time. Our tradition contains the expectation of this kind of event."

"A prophecy," said Jorgenssen.

"Yes, if you call the predictions of your astronomers prophecy. I don't know how you make voyages in time, but I know that the Federation systematically controls the past to assure itself the uncontested rule of its future. It's possible that our civilization has already done as much in the past or will begin to do it in the future, and that your mysterious adversaries belong to our present no more than you do. In any case, with respect to you, I don't believe they've acted as the Federation would have in similar circumstances."

"You're not sure?" asked Jorgenssen.

"Absolutely not. I envisage yet another possibility, but it will not please you."

"Tell me."

"Agreed," said Daalquin pensively. "There exist only two powers in the world at this moment, yours and ours. Your adversaries could belong to the past or future of one or the other. Perhaps your strange enemies have not been other than yourselves."

Jorgenssen stood up, violently angry. "It's impossible!"

"I said, perhaps" Daalquin replied. "But that possibility seems to me more likely than the other. Recall how much you hated yourself when you arrived here, how you were on the brink of destroying yourself in the heart of the tree!"

"You're lying! I was asphyxiated, poisoned!"

"You're free to believe what you wish. The possibility I proposed perhaps does not correspond to reality. But one thing is certain: the Federation has no greater enemy than itself. You have no greater enemy than you yourself. Be reconciled with yourself and you can live here or anywhere in the universe, in peace. We have no other secret."

Daalquin stood up and went to the door. He opened it, and, as if moved by a regret, said before leaving: "Farewell." But Jorgenssen did not reply, nor even hear him go. Seated with his elbows propped on the table, his head buried in his hands, he fought against a monstrous interrogation, a black shadow which rose from the depths of his being.

After a moment, he began to pace up and down in the room. Then, not being able to stand it any longer, he went outdoors. It was night. The scene was exactly as it had been at his arrival. He had to know more. His conversation with Daalquin had posed more questions than it had resolved.

He took the little road which wound among the plants. The trunks and the sky of luminous foliage shed a soft light. The group of trunks made a kind of luminous and circular horizon, at once distant and near. "A forest is a circumference whose edges are displaced and whose center is everywhere," he mused, paraphrasing a formula which had served in distant antiquity to qualify the Deity, then, a long time afterward, the universe itself.

He came to Daalquin's small house and knocked gently at the door. Inside, someone replied. He entered. Daalquin was there with Sineva. The pale light rising from the floor enhanced the woman's beauty and the contrast between her long, black hair and her white skin. Daalquin and Sineva must have been working on a piece of art, for Jorgenssen could see sketches scattered on the table.

Symbols covered them, as did some extremely clean lines. For the Dalaamians, art and knowledge were not distinct.

"I'm sorry about what happened just now," said Jorgenssen.

"It's unimportant," said Daalquin. His eyes sparkled.

"I'd like to ask you still another question—just one," said Jorgenssen. "I hope you'll answer it. Afterwards, I'm going away."

"I'm listening," said Daalquin. He leaned against the table and threw back his head.

"Here it is. I'd like to know where you come from, how your civilization appeared on Ygone. I can't believe it developed spontaneously, and the new city is not very old. Another city preceded it that didn't live in symbiosis with the trees... another ordinary city. And at that time the earth was cultivated on Ygone and there was trade, maybe manufacturing, at least, to a certain degree. How did you arrive at this point? What's your history?"

Daalquin turned toward his wife. "But he's progressed!" he said. "He's becoming intelligent. He's beginning to grasp that one can't understand things without going back to their origins. I think we'll accomplish something."

Sineva laughed, and that relaxed the atmosphere. Her laugh had nothing mocking, ironic, or cruel in it; it was a rich, joyous laugh. Jorgenssen wondered how old she was. At times, she seemed hardly older than Anema, and yet, she belonged to the generation of Anema's parents.

"I'll answer you frankly," said Daalquin. "If you'd had the courage to ask sooner the questions which intrigued you, we could have replied better. But you didn't wish to. You were persuaded that we would try to deceive you... exactly as the Federation would have done with strangers."

"It's true," said Jorgenssen, without anger.

"I'm going to disappoint you," said Daalquin. "Concerning our origins, we know scarcely anything. It's one of our greatest problems. We have no written history, at least not for the period which goes back more than a few dozen years... nor documents. Everything is as if erased. And our tradition furnishes us with only a few elements."

"What is this tradition?" asked Jorgenssen.

"The whole of what we know in a collective sense," replied Daalquin. "Essentially, it goes back to a period certainly prior to the creation of this city. It contains nearly all we know of the physical universe, of the other worlds of the galaxy, of the Federation, of time, and of many other things which we can't easily investigate directly. It helps us orient ourselves in the universe and foresee crises. Oh, it's not a matter of religious revelation or a group of obscure texts with multiple meanings. It's a perfectly scientific account of things, appealing to reason, not to faith, except for a small number of truisms which we otherwise have every reason to believe well-founded: for example, the existence of a Federation," he concluded smiling.

"I see," said Jorgenssen. "It's as if your ancestors had decided to record their knowledge, once and for all, and to devote themselves to other pursuits and to another way of life; they set up the tradition to balance your society, which is uniquely oriented toward living things."

"Exactly," said Daalquin. Suddenly, he appeared upset.

"But there's a danger," said Jorgenssen coldly, his feet planted firmly on the floor, his arms crossed. He began to see a crack open in the perfect edifice of Dalaamian society. "This tradition is a fixed whole, decreed once and for all, while reality changes. You will not be able to transmit abstract knowledge indefinitely. And the tradition certainly doesn't account for all reality. You condemn yourselves, at least in certain areas, to the halting of all progress."

Two wrinkles appeared on Daalquin's forehead. "You would be right," he said after a moment, "if the tradition were immutable; but it's not. It changes. Almost no one is aware of it in Dalaam, but I know it, and so does Sineva. And it's something incomprehensible. New knowledge enters the tradition and replaces the old."

"But that's impossible! You make no investigations in those areas, you have no instruments, you don't leave your world, you have no contact with other planets."

"That's also what I tell myself," confessed Daalquin. "But I'm certain the tradition changes. Oh, almost imperceptibly. You see, the children learn it in two ways, first by what the adults tell them and through our books, and then by the instruction of the trees, which is half-hypnotic. That's part of their education. I'm convinced that from one generation to the next, the tradition evolves. Thus, our society remains stable. We make no effort to conquer the whole domain of knowledge, and yet it is given to us and the tradition is regularly redeemed. This means our society is not as closed as we thought. It communicates with the outside, but we don't know how. This disturbs me. It's always dangerous to depend on an unknown source."

"As unknown as our enemy," said Jorgenssen.

"I've already made the comparison—it does not reassure me."

"And you maintain what you said just now?"

"As a possibility, yes. Reality is complex. It may include apparently contradictory elements."

"I imagine you've got a theory about this unknown power," Jorgenssen said slowly. "A theory that takes all the facts into consideration."

"I have several... but none which would be completely satisfactory."

"I'm listening," said Jorgenssen.

The situation's turned around in a flash, he thought with satisfaction. The assurance of the Dalaamians hid, then, a problem as profound as his own. They were ignorant of their origins; they did not know what power presided over their destinies.

"The first possibility best agrees with our way of thinking," said Daalquin. "It implies the existence of a sort of collective entity—unconscious—which our particular society and the action of the trees might give rise to, and which would be capable of knowing reality without passing through the medium of our consciousness. Up to a certain point, there exist functions of that order in each human being. It may be that we've succeeded involuntarily in rendering them collective. All of Dalaam could be, under those conditions, considered a single living being, a species of superlife in which we each would be a cell, not only socially but even organically. I can't even imagine the potentialities of such a superlife, but I believe it would have nothing to fear even from an organization as powerful as the Federation.

"The second possibility pleases me infinitely less. It's based on the idea that we depend on an exterior power which furnishes us, more-or-less without our knowledge, the intellectual materials we need, and protects us in such a way that we may pursue our investigations. It's more, or less, fantastic than the first, depending on one's point of view."

"A power that could have created Dalaam," said Jorgenssen, astonished, "that could erase the traces of the past, furnish Dalaam the means of being an original society, that could have planted the trees, founded your way of life, established your program of investigations... a power at once exterior to Dalaam and to the Federation, and unknown up to this point."

"Exactly," said Daalquin. "I prefer the first hypothesis, but I can't put aside the second. Moreover, they don't exclude each other entirely."

Jorgenssen put his hands to his face. He had not progressed a single step. The most complete obscurity still surrounded him. The problem he had hoped to solve by exploring Dalaam remained intact.

"I'm going," he said abruptly. "I've got to rejoin my friends before they try something. I want to protect this city."

"Against whom?" said Daalquin. "Against the Federation?"

For the first time, Jorgenssen sensed harshness in his voice.

"Let him go, Daalquin," said Sineva in her warm voice. "He'll return. The day he accepts himself, he'll return. Here he's found something he no longer hoped for. You'll come back, Jorgenssen, and the trees will help you find the way to Anema."

"Farewell," said Jorgenssen.

Once outside, he oriented himself effortlessly. He finally knew where to go, though he didn't know what he would do when he got there. Going down the road leading to the river, he found the team again at the angle of the valley. Afterwards, they would go together.

V

Wherever there is self, there must be conscience.
                                                Dr. Lagache

At first he saw Mario's silhouette standing out clearly on the horizon. The lookout-man made no effort to hide himself; but he was not inattentive. Even before Jorgenssen came out of the grass which hid him, Mario had turned in his direction. Jorgenssen raised his hand, in order to be recognized.

"Greetings," Mario said simply.

Only then did Jorgenssen see the massive shadow of Erin quickly leave its place.

"Someone?" asked Erin.

"It's Jorgenssen," said Mario.

Jorgenssen had expected more emotion. After all, he had disappeared for more than four hundred hours, the equivalent of sixteen universal days.

"The others are sleeping?" he asked in a hushed voice.

"Yes," said Mario. "Should I wake them?"

Jorgenssen made a vague gesture. "No, not for the moment. First, tell me what you've been doing."

He saw that in the darkness, Mario shot him a curious glance. Doubtless he hoped for a description of Dalaam, but he would have to wait. Jorgenssen did not feel ready to make a report on the city of luminous trees. All he had seen and heard ran together in his mind.

"We wandered for some time," said Mario. "We finally found a spring. Otherwise, we would have risked drinking the river water. Then we made a circuit of the city, but didn't dare follow you. We discovered something I'll tell you about later—something very important. But I have to tell you right away that the team's atmosphere's changed.

The men have become silent, anxious. It's time we found a way of getting out of this fix."

"I haven't brought back..." began Jorgenssen, when something came to mind. "How's Cnossos? Does he hold a grudge against me?"

"He's healed," said Mario. "I don't think he holds a grudge.... To tell the truth, I don't know. Each keeps his feelings to himself right now. Only Erin seems unaffected by what's happening. He never was very talkative."

'They distrust each other?"

"Not exactly. They're asking themselves questions." Mario's voice seemed almost pleased.

"I see," said Jorgenssen. He felt he was going to have to speak of Dalaam, of Daalquin, and of Anema, but he remembered in time Mario's first words. "You've found something?" he asked.

"I'll show it to you," said Mario.

He withdrew in the direction of the sleeping men. Jorgenssen saw him bend down and pick up an object. Then Mario returned. "Your belt," he said, handing the object to Jorgenssen.

"I don't need it anymore."

'Take a look at the detectors," said Mario.

Jorgenssen bent over the tiny dials. The indicators were faintly luminous, scarcely readable, but he saw nevertheless that one of the indicators appeared stuck in an abnormal position. He tapped the apparatus in hopes of making the needle move. It fluctuated and returned to its original position. "The mechanism's out of order," he said.

"It hardly works at all," said Mario, "but it indicates something just the same. You know what that means."

Jorgenssen straightened up. "But it's impossible! There couldn't be a spatiotemporal door near here."

"That's what we thought, too. We searched anyway. And we found it. There is a door... six or seven kilometers from here, in a sort of moraine."

"You didn't see..." Jorgenssen's voice trembled, "what's on the other side?"

"We haven't ventured to. We wanted to find you again first."

So, thought Jorgenssen, there is indeed a connection between Ygone and the outside, and a stable connection. Little by little, the pieces of the puzzle were falling into place. He fastened the belt and sat down on the ground.

The serene stars sparkled in the sky of Ygone. To the left, the city was a luminous haze.

"We've got to go through it, Mario," he said. "We've got to take the risk. We have to know where it leads... and we've got no other chance to leave this world. Now, I'm going to tell you what I've seen in Dalaam."

That took several hours. Four or five times, Mario, who said nothing, handed him a flask. At the end, Jorgenssen, exhausted, fell silent. He remained so for some time, listening to the sounds of the night, then he stretched out and, without realizing it, fell asleep. Alone, a pensive Mario went to awaken Shan d'Arg, who was supposed to relieve him.

"We've got to destroy Dalaam," said Livius forcefully. "Ah, yes," retorted Jorgenssen. "And with what?"

"I don't know," said Livius. "But we must be able to find a way. You've said they don't have weapons, that it's not them who attacked us."

"I'd like to be really sure."

Mario intervened. "Even if we still had the means, it's by no means certain we'd be allowed to destroy Dalaam. What we should first try, is to find out who protects Dalaam, who's checked us."

"Exactly," said Jorgenssen. "The chances are nine out of ten the answer lies on the other side of this door."

In silence, they contemplated the black rectangle which stood out clearly against the ochre surface of the ground. On all sides, heaps of rocks cut off the view. Day had finally dawned. The sky was unblemished, and a brisk wind made them gasp.

"I don't like the idea of taking my chances in there," said Shan d'Arg. "It looks too much like a trap. We don't have anything anymore—no weapons, no shields—and we could find ourselves facing enemies, or else on a world deadly to us. A trace of poison in the atmosphere is enough, or a temperature too high or too low, or too much solar radiation."

"We have to take the chance," insisted Jorgenssen. "We don't have the ghost of a chance to leave Ygone otherwise. And we have to find out who pulls the strings."

"Say, 'I have to find out,' " Livius flung out. "What are you getting at? What do you want to find?"

Jorgenssen shrugged his shoulders without taking his eyes from the black rectangle. There was no trace of apparatus; at least it hadn't been hidden in the ground. Hence, the generator had to be on the other side of the door.

"I don't know," he admitted. "I'm not even anxious to return to Altair. I only want to understand this world. I want to know who made Dalaam."

"I've got another idea about your intentions, Jorgenssen," said Livius. "I've thought a lot about everything you've told us. You're afraid we might stay on Ygone and put your city in danger, heh! You want us to leave this world as soon as possible. You've changed sides—no more question of defending the Federation, no more question of doing the noble work of the teams, the rectification of history, and all that claptrap, even if we have to do it with our fingernails. No, you took a stroll in that city and you've come back talking about those savages as if they were geniuses or demi-gods."

"I don't know," said Jorgenssen in a very low voice. "Before, I believed in the Federation; I believed in the role of the teams. Now, I think I was mistaken. I don't believe the Federation has the right to do what it's doing. I think we're criminals."

"You let yourself be taken," clipped Livius. "I've hung around a little everywhere in the universe, and I've found only one law—force. The Federation's probably facing the most formidable enemy in its history, and you think only of how to keep your hands clean, of solving your petty personal problem."

"Shut up, Livius," hissed Shan d'Arg between his teeth. "I've got confidence in Jorgenssen. He's better than you. I'm going through the door with him."

"I thought you hated the Federation, Livius," said Mario, "and now you defend it."

Livius grimaced in anger. "When I'm in the Federation,

I hate it. That's my right. Look at yourselves, then, all of you. You hate it too, but you refuse to admit it to yourselves. You detest it because you're different, because the others, the specialists, don't entirely accept you. Why does Cnossos love the sea, and Erin the mountains, and Nanski space, and Shan d'Arg war, and you, Mario, music and pale babes? Why does Jorgenssen torment himself with questions he keeps secret but that you can read on his face? The Federation's rejected you all. Me—the Federation treated me like a rat, until I had enough strength to tear what I wanted from it. Yes, when I'm in the Federation, I want its ruin. But as soon as I'm outside, in space or time, I'm the Federation's man. It made me what I am; it gives me power. Inside its walls, I'm a wolf. Outside, I'm its watch dog."

Daalquin was right, thought Jorgenssen. Hatred and suspicion—neurosis. "Stay, Livius," he said in a weary voice. "Stay here. We don't all have to go through the door. But I don't want you to try anything against the city before I come back."

This time, thought Jorgenssen, the team's broken up. It's the beginning of the Federation's fall, a very small crack in a tiny piece. But slowly, inexorably, the whole vast mechanism is going to deteriorate, jam, and finally fall into dust. Everything will have begun on Ygone, the dismal planet.... No, everything began on Altair. Everything began the day before our departure. Who were we? What were we doing? What were we thinking about? Already, for two and a half centuries, the question has been settled, since we're in our past.

"I'm going with you," said Mario.

Jorgenssen remembered Mario's appeal when he had left for Dalaam. He smiled. "Good," he said. "Who else?"

"Me," said Erin and Shan d'Arg at the same time.

"Agreed. The others stay. Livius will serve as co-ordinator. You'll wait for us in the vicinity of Dalaam. If you need provisions, don't hesitate to ask the Dalaamians. Good luck."

Livius remained unmoved. "Good luck."

Nanski and Cnossos avoided Jorgenssen's eyes.

"There's a man in the city named Daalquin, Livius," Jorgenssen said then. "If we don't return, tell him I tried to probe Ygone's past. He'll understand."

Livius didn't reply.

The four men turned toward the black rectangle and plunged into the darkness, floating for an instant in nothingness. A heavy and odorous heat enveloped them, like the breath of a wild beast.

They had passed through the door, finding themselves in a jungle.

The air was laden with the fragrance of spices. The jungle was an explosion of plant life, a fabric of tropical creepers imprisoning the moisture, a mat of trunks and foliage. The ground was glutted with water. In the half light, giant flowers rocked on stems as big as ropes. Instinctively, the four men moved closer together.

The clearing was clean, as if someone had taken a razor and scraped it of all vegetation. A carpet of moss covered the ground, except at the black rectangle. Again, there was no trace of machinery. The jungle surrounded the clearing like a wall.

Second stage, thought Jorgenssen, raising his head. The light of an enormous, probably blue sun filtered with difficulty through dense clouds.

"We're certainly not on Ygone," said Jorgenssen. "In accord with the principles, we've been displaced in space as well as time. The problem is to find out where we are and in what year."

It appeared to be nearly insolvable. Even if they'd been able to see the sky, there was only one chance in a million they would be able to recognize any constellations. As for the date, it probably no longer had any meaning. The universe has no present, properly speaking. One cannot define a date, a year, an hour, except in relation to a world. The images which come from distant stars emerge from the past. A world's present is only a sharp point of time which sinks into the past as one regards it from farther away in space.

Second stage, Jorgenssen repeated to himself, and we're a little more lost, a little farther from Altair and the Federation, a little more ourselves, abandoned to ourselves, alone, forced to decide. Is it really the second stage? Mario's false death—hadn't that been the first, and the disappearance of our weapons the second, and the visit to Balaam the third? But had there been intermediate stages that escaped us? All this formed a kind of labyrinth in which someone wanted to get them involved, Jorgenssen was sure. That was why he had confidently ventured through the door. He wanted to reach the end of the labyrinth, even if he would have to spend the rest of his life there, because the end of the labyrinth coincided with the answer to all the questions.

All at the same time, they examined their detectors, which still functioned as poorly as on Ygone, for the inhibiting field existed on this world also. Yet the detectors indicated something—weakly, but clearly, as if someone had wanted to leave them a sign, a means of following the trail. The detectors indicated the presence of a spatiotemporal buoy in a definite direction. The distance was immeasurable, certainly more than twenty kilometers, and probably less than seven hundred. Between the two, there was sufficient latitude.

Shan d'Arg pointed this out calmly.

"At any rate," said Mario, "we can't stay here. We might as well start walking."

They had confidence in themselves again, verified Jorgenssen. That was what counted; it was more important than all their dead weapons. They wanted to go to the very end, to find out. They formed a team again, diminished but coherent. Yet the team's goal had changed. That had been, with no possible doubt, the intention of their adversaries.

"It's not going to be easy," said Erin, staring at the jungle. They could hear animal roaring in the distance.

They advanced toward the green wall in good order. Close up, the apparent continuity of the vegetation disappeared; it was possible to slip into the cracks, to creep into the vegetation's fissures.

"We need axes," sighed Jorgenssen.

Normally, they would have opened a way through the jungle with their rays; the water-gorged trunks would have been calcinated instantly. The energy shields would have protected the men from any attack. But now, they had to adjust to the jungle and take chances.

Jorgenssen took the lead. It was an exhausting march. Ceaselessly, they would have to return on their track, would try a new approach, would discover they had stumbled into a thicket too dense to cross, would return again, would move forward by crawling and climbing, and would avoid contact with insects as large as a hand, which might have been venomous.

After two hours, the jungle's nature changed. The ground was dryer, trees taller and farther apart. At ground level their enormous roots intertwined. The men advanced in almost total darkness. They frequently glanced at the hesitant needles of their detectors, for fear of losing the buoy's direction.

The heat was oppressive, almost suffocating. Once, they had to make a detour of nearly a kilometer to avoid a veritable river of insects meandering among the tree roots.

Were they really insects? The men didn't linger to resolve the question.

"Life," said Jorgenssen. "Life in the raw, a constant, ruthless struggle. The largest trees soak up the light and heat of the sun. Fungus devours the trees, and insects attack the trees and fungus indifferently."

"It would only take a few days for a pioneer ship of the Federation to clear this world," said Shan d'Arg, "and make it a garden. That's civilization!"

"Our civilization," said Mario, sponging off large drops of sweat about to fall into his eyes. "What would the Dalaamians think of it?"

"I don't think they could conceive of such a jungle," said Jorgenssen. "They've no other experience except of a world to their measure, civilized and human."

"Maybe," said Mario, undecided.

A sinuous fault cut the jungle in two. They thought it was a road, but when Jorgenssen moved onto the smooth, green surface, he sank up to his shoulders in water and mud. He uttered a cry. The others pulled him out of the stream. Through the narrow chinks between the trees, they could see a sky heavy with clouds tinged emerald by the sunset.

Jorgenssen, streaming with water, shook himself. He put his hand on his face; his fingers left long trails of slime.

"Lucky," he said, "we came on it."

The others looked at him without understanding.

"We're going down in there and follow it, swimming or walking on the bottom. We'll gain kilometers."

"This stream could be full of poisonous animals," said Mario.

Jorgenssen shrugged his shoulders. "One more risk to run. We may run more there" His features had contracted. "Let's go."

He jumped first into the mud. After a moment's hesitation, the others followed. They stuck as close as possible to the edge of the stream. They were up to the waist in mud and water and advanced with difficulty, but they advanced.

"We march until it gets completely dark," said Jorgenssen.

But darkness did not come entirely: two enormous, orange moons mounted the sky, their light caressing the stream's pale, sea-green surface. Now and then, the noise of large animals tearing foliage resounded in the thick of the jungle. The stream's water cleared as they progressed, the muddy bottom giving way to sand. They advanced more easily but had to struggle against a light current. From time to time, they stopped to rest.

"When I think,' said Shan d'Arg during one of these halts, "that normally we would have flown peacefully over this jungle at two hundred meters altitude, without running the least risk, like lords of creation, and that instead we're crawling in the guts of the planet!"

Under his mask of mud, Jorgenssen smiled broadly. "We don't need machines anymore. We can do all right without them. We're tougher than we thought."

"What distance have we covered?"

"I don't know... ten or twelve kilometers."

"I feel like I've done fifty," said Mario.

"It's worse than mountains," added Erin.

Weighed down by fatigue, Jorgenssen felt more calm and lucid than he had ever been. Soon, a distant rumbling sound struck their ears. They recognized it several hundred meters farther on: the sound of a waterfall.

"Our road ends," said Mario.

The stream rounded into a basin bounded on one side by a semi-circular cliff from which the torrent fell, and on the other by the high wall of jungle vegetation. At the foot of the cliff, almost under the waterfall, there was a light—not a fire—a steady, cold, electric light They launched out swimming across the stream, regained their footing on the other side of the basin on pebbles, and painfully lifted themselves onto the bank. The two moons shone peacefully in a finally clear sky.

They deployed themselves without saying a word, according to the old formation, encircling the light. Then, silently, like shadows, they closed the circle. Almost immediately, they discovered the buoy and the cabin.

The spatiotemporal buoy was an ancient model which they had never seen; but it was impossible to be mistaken about its nature, since no one had tried to camouflage it. Time had simply half buried it in the sand. At its summit blazed the beacon that had attracted them: it could have burned for an eternity. The visible surface of the buoy bore no indication of its date. Its controls were intact, but the signs on the dials were incomprehensible, for the symbols were unknown to Jorgenssen and his men.

They turned toward the cabin. It was a metal shelter, apparently very ancient. The door was ajar. They rushed in. The only room was bare and empty. The men plunged up to their knees in accumulated dust. On the steel table, by the uncertain light of their dim torches, they saw a metal medallion attached to a steel chain, a medallion quite similar to those they wore, giving their names, home worlds, and dates of birth, and which were made of a nearly indestructible metal.

Jorgenssen turned the medallion over. Faintly luminous letters gleamed in the obscurity and revealed a name:

ARCIMBOLDO URZEIT

It was an incredible name... a mythical name... the name of the scientist who had made time travel possible in the distant past of the Federation.

Next to the medallion, almost buried in the dust, lay a book with a bronze binding. Jorgenssen seized and opened it. The leaves trembled and remained an instant suspended in the air. Then, like a fine ash, they crumbled, flew up, and fell again in a brittle snow. On the inside of the bronze binding, an unskilled knife had engraved the mythical name: Arcimboldo Urzeit.

But the scientist's notes had disappeared forever.

The circle closed upon itself. In the course of their temporal peregrination, they had fallen upon the initiator of time travel.

"Incredible," Mario let out, "that Urzeit should come here before us!"

"Sure and certain," said Jorgenssen. He saw the pieces of the puzzle fall together. Urzeit had passed through Ygone; he had tried an experiment there. Perhaps he had even been the source of Dalaam, the new Dalaam. He had arranged in the continuum a certain number of doors permitting him to watch his experiment unfold at a distance. But why, two hundred and fifty years later—or how many years, Jorgenssen wondered, for he couldn't tell in what century they were—hadn't the archives of the Federation preserved any trace of Urzeit's experiment?

The question crossed Jorgenssen's mind like a lightning bolt. Why was the character of Urzeit so vague, so imprecise? Why did they know so little about him? After all, five centuries did not constitute such a great length of time.

The lives of much more ancient individuals were known in their smallest details. Yet about Urzeit's there remained only anecdotes, probably inexact, and suited only to give luster to a legend and monumental works. Had this perhaps been the will of Urzeit himself? Had he perhaps knowingly made mischief? Or had one whole aspect of Urzeit's work been systematically done away with, passed over in silence by the Arque? Had not Urzeit himself seen the danger of that colossal power, time travel, put in the service of the Federation? Had he not been liquidated by the Arque? And hadn't the team been sent to Ygone precisely to destroy all traces of Urzeit's experiment?

The Federation had failed. If Urzeit was really the founder of the new Dalaam, he had given the city sufficient defenses to resist the team's activity. But the Dalaamians claimed to be completely ignorant of those defenses. Or else they lied... or else... Jorgenssen forced himself to go right to the conclusion of his thought.

Or else Urzeit himself, or some of his followers, defended Dalaam— against the Federation, against the invaders from time.

Jorgenssen put his hand on his forehead. He began to tremble. If his supposition was correct, the Federation fought against itself in reality. The Federation's present rejected its past. At a precise moment in history two possibilities had differentiated, and although the forces appeared immensely unequal, the weaker of the two had inflicted a first check on the stronger.

The jungle planet was not the final lair of Urzeit. The buoy indicated the contrary. It must lead to another world—any world, perhaps to Altair itself. After that world, perhaps there would be a third one, and a fourth, and so on, almost to infinity. Urzeit's genius passed for madness; but no one in the Federation, thought Jorgenssen, except them, knew exactly to what point he was mad. The four looked at each other, not needing to speak. Together, they went toward the buoy buried in the sand. The beacon shone like the eye of a cyclops, shining not only in space, but also in time. It defied immediate, apparent reality. It was the tangible proof of the existence of a reverse side to things, of an underlying network in which space, the present, the past, and the future were almost unreal projections.

All four of them, Jorgenssen thought, were in the act of discovering the true face of reality—not understanding it, since it was much too complex, nor even seeing it in its totality, since it was much too vast—but catching a glimpse of it as possibility, as a potentiality they furnished from their existence.

He lowered the hand-lever. The somber light caught them and swept them away. This time, they found themselves in the middle of a desert

Not a cloud in the sky... an immense expense of sand. Immediately, they recognized the sun, enormous and blue. Very low on the horizon, the two giant moons floated like balloons.

"The same planet" said Shan d'Arg in a low voice. "It's unheard of— we've moved in time, but not in space."

"What year?" Mario asked on his own account.

"Impossible to say," said Jorgenssen. "If our instruments worked, maybe, we could decide by studying this blue sun, or the composition of the soil. But now, we can't even tell whether we're before or after the jungle we left."

They were so excited that they didn't immediately realize the desperate nature of their position. The desert extended as far as the eye could see; the buoy had not accompanied them in their time voyage; they could no longer regain the jungle, much less Dalaam.

"This time," said Mario, "I think we're at the end of our rope." He studied his detector: no trace of a spatiotemporal door... not the least sign of a buoy. The instruments were dead.

"Maybe not!" cried Erin, with a sort of exaltation that surprised even himself. "Look! Don't you recognize anything?"

They looked in the direction Erin indicated. They saw in the distance, a scarcely visible, semi-circular cliff, which emerged from the sand like a crescent-rock.

"The terrain hasn't changed," said Erin. "That's where the waterfall was."

"Or where it will be," corrected Jorgenssen. The two possibilities were equally admissible. How long had been necessary for the jungle to give way to this absolute aridity, or for the desert to become peopled with the teaming life of the jungle?... Ten million years?... One million years?... Or only a thousand years? In the absence of any intervention, geological eras would have been necessary; but "they" had transformed the causal network, the structure of reality. Who then? Urzeit?

Perhaps the cabin survived at the foot of the cliff; the buoy was perhaps buried in the sand. It was an insane hope, but the colossal diverting of the river of time which had been accomplished on that world without a name was no less insane. And yet, thought Jorgenssen, all this must have a meaning... Balaam, the jungle, the desert. "They" didn't lead us into this maze without a reason. The sequence of events they had experienced must have had a profound significance, like a sentence composed of words.

But they didn't have the key to the words. In the depths of time, they had met the sphinx. If they solved the riddle, they would survive and new understanding would open the doors of a new universe to them. If they failed...

Ygone, the jungle, the desert: three stages in the evolution of life. On Ygone reigned cooperation between the forest and the city; struggle was the law of the jungle; but the desert knew nothing but the inanimate—it was anterior or posterior to life, incompatible with it.

Jorgenssen licked his heavy lips. He felt full of pity for his companions. It was a new feeling. Suddenly, he discovered he had affection for Mario, Erin, and Shan d'Arg, and that it was not merely a camaraderie of arms, but a deeper, more human feeling. He realized that they existed outside himself, that they were not merely objects in his universe. He realized that each had his own time, a personal past, future, and present, and that he had never really looked at them, although he had thought he knew them. He discovered that at the precise moment he became conscious of their individuality, he understood them better.

"I'm sorry I dragged you into this," he said. "I'm afraid our situation may be a dead end."

Mario smiled weakly. "We came because we decided to, that's all. You're not responsible. It would be best to try to reach the cliff."

Jorgenssen wanted to say "thanks," but only sighed and let out a laconic "fine." As he began to march, his boots stirred up dust and sank into the sand. All four, tiny points in the desert, attracted by the crescent cliff, dead tired, advanced along tiny dunes sculpted by the everlasting wind.

"I'm thirsty," said Erin. "I remember, last year I climbed mountains of lava on Circe. Millions of years earlier, they'd been nothing but torrents of fire. But after scaling a steep wall as smooth as glass, when I reached the top of a plateau, I saw a small lake at its center, with perfectly pure water falling down the eastern side in three cascades, as beautiful as sheaves of fire. At night, the stars were mirrored in the lake, like a second sky. And the water was cold as you could want it, almost glacial. It went down your throat like a sword. It was as clear as space. I'd like to see that water again."

The sand became finer and their feet sank deeper into it. As they marched, they talked as they had never talked before. They talked about the Federation and the worlds they had known, and about their past ambitions and secret defeats. Jorgenssen spoke of Ygone and said he hoped to meet Anema again, if he survived. Erin spoke of vertigo, and Shan d'Arg revealed his obsession with death, and Mario, his fear of time. And all at the same time, they experienced, in the intoxication of fatigue, the usefulness of frankness and the necessity of speech.

Then came the mirages.

Sometimes near, sometimes far away, furtive visions of the jungle were superimposed on the desert: a scent of water, a spot of green, an animal roar, the delicate design of a tropical creeper embracing a trunk.

Jorgenssen rubbed his eyes. The world was full of sparks of light. The beginnings of delirium, he thought, without despair. Beyond a suddenly transparent dune, he recognized the silhouette of Livius. A giant tree of Dalaam anchored its roots in front of him and disappeared. An abyss opened under his feet and closed again.

Disoriented, Jorgenssen stopped. The others seemed transparent, as if struck by a tremendous vibration. Their surprised voices came to him confused and distorted. Fragments of darkness extinguished the overwhelming sunlight. Hallucinations, he thought, but his eyes fell on the bewitched dials of his detectors, and within him, an immense terror sprang up, which Shan d'Arg's cry defined and crystallized.

"A time storm!" cried out Shan d'Arg.

Time—maltreated, deformed, violated—avenged itself. The forces which had kept distinct possibilities parallel gave way under the overwhelming weight of reality. A time storm—it was the cataclysm most dreaded by the teams. Sometimes, it happened naturally, in certain regions of space where energy discharges were so violent they came to affect the structure of the continuum. But most often, time storms arose from an abortive, blundering intervention. Time, locally, would collapse. Sprays of the past would come to slap the future. The present would collapse. A man touched by the rain of time would see his hand suddenly shrivel like that of an old man, or his whole body return to the fetal state and, in one last spark of consciousness, he would know the defied gods had avenged themselves. In the constellation of Cygnus, seven planets had been destroyed by such a catastrophe: a star had become a nova. Twenty billion beings had perished. The survivors had been plagued by madness until their deaths: they had caught a glimpse of something more terrifying than their own destruction—that of the universe.

The jungle. The desert. On that world without a name, in the light of a blue sun, conflicting interventions succeeded each other. Now, it fell into fragments. But the idea occurred to Jorgenssen that this chronoclasm was not accidental, that it was the final period of that logical sentence whose incomprehensible words were Dalaam, the jungle, and the desert—after that sentence came sterility, destruction. It was, at the same time, the clear image of the Federation's destiny: by manipulating time, it undermined the universe; by defending its present, it consumed its future. One fine day the galaxy in its turn would explode; and ten million stars would die fluctuating among ten billion possibilities; and without a sound, the flame of humanity would be extinguished.

Already the others' voices reached him only as absurd rumblings. He still saw them, like furtive reflections sent back by fragments of a mirror against the monotonous background of the desert. And he even saw Livius, Nanski, and Cnossos emerge from the void. An incredible chance or a subtle intervention had brought them into the time storm and thrown them onto that world. And again, the seven reunited, at once distant and near, struggled in silence against the fury of time.

Jorgenssen could see the seven silhouettes swept away by the more and more violent squalls of time as if he had been projected outside his body— Mario, Shan d'Arg, Cnossos, Erin, Livius, Nanski, and himself, staggering, struggling, trying to keep their eyes open in the whirling of the cosmos. At times, he could see all seven as they had been ten years before, and, instants later, as they would be ten years from then. He knew, in the space of an instant, that he would survive and see Anema again, and, a second later, that memory from his future was erased from his mind.

And behind the seven silhouettes, he could see seven others—paler, almost transparent—which followed them and threatened them, which were preparing to kill them. He could even recognize the killers' features, and they were those of the seven, launched into the eddies of time, pursuing themselves in an infernal hunt

He wanted to shout a warning, but what escaped him remained unintelligible. The two teams receded on the horizon. He closed his eyes and began to run, then fell, fell endlessly, without knowing whether his legs still carried him or whether space had opened under him. And the waves of time brought the thoughts of the others to him.

A particle of time crossed his mind, and forgotten memories rose again to consciousness. He remembered a dream he had had: In a circular public square, a man pursued him; and that man had his own face. And an immense crowd, the anguished crowd of Dalaam, watched his defeat. He tried to reach a sanctuary, the center of the square, and to touch a statue, a face of enigmatic stone, the only substantial point in that unrestrained whirling... but he knew he would never reach it

Anema's words came to mind again: If you remember the dream, you'll be cured. You'll stop hating yourself. He let out a cry of triumph. He had remembered the dream; finally, he had won. He had found himself again. And the face of his adversary changed abruptly. That other self walked toward him, his face calm, smiling, and offered him his hand.

And he knew the dreams of the others. He knew that in that same instant, each of them was experiencing what he had known in the heart of the Dalaamian tree, and that each had to resolve his own problem. He, a powerless spectator, was present at the mortal game that each of the six others played against himself.

Livius in his dream—or was it a reality produced by the eddies of time—found himself on his home planet. He was running through the narrow streets of a filthy city. Cracked walls, pierced by windows through which a million eyes watched him, rose up to the sky and surrounded him like a prison. He unsheathed his useless weapon and fired at random, and whole sections of wall collapsed. But he fled. He didn't know from whom, but he ran as fast as his legs would carry him, descending the tortuous stairs and making use of the covered passages penetrating the monolithic mass of tenements.

The paved ground was slippery and slimy. At a corner, he ducked into a side alley so narrow that he could have touched the opposite walls without even extending his arms. Silence. Then, like distant splashing, came the footsteps of his pursuer. Very high above Livius's head, in the dark wall spattered with stains, a tiny window opened— like a porthole whose only horizon was the other wall, the artificial cliff—and, raising his head, he recognized it instantly. It was up there he had been born, where he had lived the first years of his life in that suspended cave. A face appeared in the window, and immediately he saw it was his, and he let out a howl of rage and terror. The hunter's footsteps came nearer; and, from the corner where he was hidden, he could see his shadow grow on the surface of the alley. He also recognized the shadow and the walk... and they were his. The silence, excepting the hunter's footsteps and a disquieting clank of metal, was absolute. All the city's residents had burrowed into their lairs, had fled before the hunter, before Livius the wolf... and Livius was alone, facing his double.

He retreated down the alley. He slipped and lost his equilibrium. He wanted to get out of the city, to reach an open space. The sky above his head, reduced to a narrow, greenish hand, taunted him. He turned and started to run again. The alley was interminable, and he knew it had no other outlet except a loathsome network of narrow, dark passages. But suddenly, to his great relief, he emerged into a green meadow and recognized a park where, as a child, he had taken part in dangerous games and which, in his memory, was in a quite different part of the city. He went toward a grove of trees where he hoped to hide, as he had many times when the children of an enemy gang would search for him to give him a beating. To reach it, he had to cross a circular esplanade, its center adorned with a fountain.

A spherical stellar ship crossed the sky, and he lifted his eyes to look at it, surprised; then his gaze returned to the fountain and to the mysteriously smiling statue which crowned it

In front of him, the hunter emerged from the bushes —with his own features, his uniform, his hand weapon. Livius fired on the hunter; but he continued to advance with slow and implacable steps, a tall silhouette set on thin legs, and, meticulously, he raised his weapon....

Cnossos, in his dream, was exploring coral caves in the depths of the sea. A secret anguish filled him. A shadow passed over him, and, supple as an eel, he spun. Through the porthole of his mask, in the slimy darkness crossed by purple reflections of coral caught in the light of his frontal beacon, he saw that it was not a sea monster, nor a shark, nor a ray, nor a great annelid, nor a giant spider, but a man.

He recognized his double...

Erin was scaling a steeply cut wall and did not dare to look behind him, not fearful of considering the depth of the gulf above which he had raised himself, but fearful of discovering who was following him so stubbornly.

"Climb," said a voice which he recognized as his own. And he pulled harder with his exhausted arms. His bloodied fingers contracted on the stone. His fingernails tried to catch in the crevices.

When he reached the top of the cliff, his hands gripping the edge, he lifted his head and saw a massive, overwhelming silhouette which towered over him. It was he himself. The man's boot rose and fell again to crush Erin's fingers. He howled and released his hold, falling backwards; and he had the time to see that he fell toward the one who followed him, who had his face and who had resolved to kill him...

Mario pursued a woman in a city park of Enguerrand HI. In the distance, an invisible orchestra played ancient music, strange and sad. Sweat beaded on

Mario's forehead. He knew only that he had to overtake the woman and ask her a question, but he didn't know what. He didn't know her name. Night was beginning to fall.

The woman wore a long cape which flew as she ran; its color changed ceaselessly, and it concealed her up to her head.

He had to overtake her before she reached the place where the concert was being performed: a great, circular public square where a crowd pressed. The place was dominated by an enormous, glass sphere suspended above the orchestra, from which the sound reverberated toward the public.

He threw himself into the bushes to cut off her path. He lost her from sight for an instant, and when he saw her again, it seemed that she was running slower, and also that she had grown. Stupefied, still running, he saw her grow again and stop completely and turn toward him.

He stopped. He was afraid. The cape still entirely hid the person's face and form; but Mario was sure it was no longer a woman. The cape slid down slowly. He did not immediately comprehend who was before him.

He only knew one thing: he was going to die... at the hands of his double.... His double, dead in the ravine of Ygone, had returned and wished for revenge...

A stellar ship hurled itself toward Nanski's in a void without stars. Distressed, he wanted to call Nelle, his wife; but she didn't answer. He was alone on board. The strange ship grew monstrously on his screen. He saw a door open in the hull and a man go out into space without any protection whatever. The stranger walked in space and came so close that he filled the whole screen. Then, for a second, Nanski thought he was looking into a mirror. The man surged from the screen and fired his weapon...

In the arena of Tanatos, Shan d'Arg awaited his adversary. He knew the combat would be pitiless. The mob already roared on the steps, and the artificial vultures carrying telecameras wheeled in the sky, aiming their single, fixed eyes on him, gliding soundlessly on their black metal wings.

A tiny sun, a ball of fire floating above the arena, threw a harsh light on the sand. Shan d'Arg—the bow in his left hand, the three worn arrows in his belt, and the mass of the weapon in his right hand—stared at the distant door, an obscure half-moon from which his adversary would emerge.

For the first time in his life before a combat, he trembled. He saw the small silhouette of his adversary standing out clearly against the far end of the arena. The shouts increased. Shan d'Arg let the champion approach. Then he saw that the other had neither bow nor mass, but a ray gun which he leveled slowly. Shan d'Arg pulled an arrow from his belt, set it on the bow, and aimed... but one of the vultures swooped down and diverted the arrow.

The killer was quite close. Shan d'Arg recognized him. There were no two men in the galaxy who had that yellow skin, those flat cheekbones, and those narrow eyes set under black, thin eyebrows—except him...

Thus, under Jorgenssen's eyes, each had to meet with his double and his death in a dream. This was part of the labyrinth, and Jorgenssen knew that all were conscious of the others' dreams, and that each had to find a solution before dying, as he had found one himself. They could benefit from his experience and his success. The solution was simple when you knew it: accept yourself, eliminate all duality in yourself. But to attain that end, it was necessary for the personality to be entirely overthrown and recast; and only the approach of death could compel a person to put his entire personality in question.

It was logical. It was the issue of the labyrinth, if not its final point It was in view of this metamorphosis that they had been led there. Dalaam, the jungle, and the desert had been as many tests.

But who? The question remained unanswered. The labyrinth still included unexplored rooms.

Lull. The ground became more solid under Jorgenssen's feet. The time storm still raged, but he found himself in a zone of relative calm, the center of the cyclone.

He opened his eyes. He saw that he had progressed a great deal, or that the storm had brought him much nearer the cliff. The others were far behind, still prey to their nightmares.

The cliff reared up in front of him, so high that it blocked the sky. He saw the cabin almost buried in sand, the door open, choked with sand. Through the narrow opening which remained free, he slipped inside, where the calm was total. His eyes became accustomed to the darkness. The sand had almost reached the level of the table. The book was set there. He wanted to pick it up, but his gaze suddenly fell upon a white object which emerged from the sand, on the other side of the table.

A human skull. The upper part of a skeleton. A fine steel chain had caught on the vertebrae and a medallion hung between the disconnected ribs. He stretched out his hand to seize it, but he didn't have to know it bore the name of Arcimboldo Urzeit

Thus Urzeit had ended his prodigious life here. The labyrinth no longer made any sense; it only led to a dead man. Centuries before, perhaps, it had been constructed with a definite end, to protect Dalaam, and also to transform its possible aggressors. But it no longer corresponded to anything.

They would never know why. They had exposed themselves in vain. Jorgenssen was filled with despair.

He wanted to open the metal book, but in doing so, he must have released a mechanism, for the universe spun around him in a debauch of colors, and he knew he was entering the absolute Beyond and traveling in time.

VI

The social sentiment signifies before all else, the tendency toward a form of collectivity which one must imagine as eternal.
—Dr. Alfred Adler

The year? Undetermined.

The place? Nowhere. A garden under a blue sun... a paradise of great trees spreading their shade on vast prairies... gentle hills separated by water courses... rich, firm earth... green grass... limpid water, clear and light, like a flow of liquid diamond. Jorgenssen rubbed his eyes. A large, reddish-brown quadruped surged out of the foliage and looked at him, then withdrew nonchalantly. Birds twittered. The stream was peopled with silver flashes, almost-triangular fish that turned quickly in the backwaters.

It was no longer the jungle, nor the desert, but it was the same planet. He was sure he was on the same world, in another possibility of the same world. He held his breath to hear better. Only the sounds of the forest came to him. He called out. No one answered. The others had remained in the desert, or else the time storm had thrown them onto other planets, into other fractions of time.

He knew where he was. The water course led to the waterfall. It was the very same one which had permitted them to plunge into the jungle. Logically, the cabin, and perhaps the buoy, must have been at the foot of the cliff.

He walked with a light step. He felt completely sane, lucid. Now he knew the meaning of the labyrinth: it was a test and, at the same time, a treatment. The test had rid him of the prejudices of the Federation, and the treatment had made him mentally healthy.

Yet after a moment, he keenly felt a vacancy, an absence: Anema... his companions. He was alone, and a paradise is to be shared. But his solitude had nothing in common with what he had experienced for so long. It was no longer the solitude tainted with distrust that was common to the men of the Federation, but the simple verification of his physical isolation. From then on, he knew he would have to put all the resources of his being into play in order to find the others again, to integrate himself into a community.

As he walked, he picked a golden fruit.

A man appeared at a bend in the stream. He smiled. He was old and fat, almost bald. Watching Jorgenssen approach, his black eyes sparkled with intelligence. The thumbs of his plump hands were hooked in his belt. He wore a faded costume which must have been orange at one time. Stretching out his right hand toward his pocket, he took out a pipe which he lit carefully.

Then he waved his hand in welcome. "Greetings," he said placidly to Jorgenssen, who was abashed. "It's a fine day, isn't it?" Jorgenssen's appearance—his tom uniform, his face covered with dirt and sweat—did not seem to surprise him.

"Greetings," replied Jorgenssen. The man's bearing surprised him even more than his greeting. In the Federation, he had never seen an old man, much less a fat one, since the Federation's biologists could maintain a man at the peak of his form almost indefinitely.

The old man had expressed himself in Dalaamian, but he did not have the natural stateliness of the Dalaamians. Life had left sharp and deep wrinkles on his face.

"Is there a city near here?" asked Jorgenssen.

"I don't think so," said the old man. "In fact, we're the only two human beings on this world, at this moment."

Approaching, Jorgenssen saw that the old man was a good head shorter than he. He sucked placidly on his pipe, which sent scrolls of smoke into the air.

"By the way," said the old man, "I believe you were looking for me. My name's Arcimboldo Urzeit."

Silence. Jorgenssen caught his breath again. His limbs were like lead. The pipe in his mouth, his thumbs in his belt once more, Urzeit smiled. "I'm glad to see you're well recovered," he said. "I need your collaboration. You'll be free to decide, naturally."

"Pardon? What's it about?" choked Jorgenssen.

"The future of the Federation, that of Dalaam, and yours, of course." His voice was calm and good-natured.

Jorgenssen suddenly regained contact with reality. "You're not dead?" he said in a toneless voice. "That wasn't your skeleton?" He bit his lip.

Urzeit's smile became still broader. He agreed with a wink.

"That depends on the year," said Urzeit. "At the time you came from, I was in fact dead. But now, no. In the cabin in the desert, it was really my... my skeleton. But the desert won't exist for five or six thousand years. From here to there..." He made a broad gesture.

"And don't consider me a ghost. The theory teaches that we don't exist in relation to each other because I die before you would have been born, and that the two events are found on the same causal curve—the official theory of the Federation. I must say I contributed a little to its construction, but after my disappearance, I worked. Nothing like intellectual work to keep the suppleness of the arteries. As you see me, I still have twenty years to live."

He knows when he'll die, thought Jorgenssen. He's explored his future, even if it seems incredible. He's defied and conquered time. And he's not paralyzed by terror, by knowing the day and the hour. Then he said to himself: The Dalaamians aren't afraid of death either. They freely accept it. For a second, this seemed monstrous. Then he saw that the terror within him had vanished. Fear of dying and fear of living were the same thing. He who hasn't accepted death cannot live fully.

"The others?" he asked in an altered voice. He could not take his eyes from the blue smoke rising from the pipe, which evoked ancient times. Jorgenssen could not accustom himself to the idea that he had before him the mythical Arcimboldo Urzeit. Unconsciously, he had formed an imposing image of him: a giant with stem features, heavy, firm hands, well-knit fingers, and a deep, grave voice—a kind of super Daalquin—not this little, smiling man, pot-bellied and mildly comical.

"Your companions? Don't worry. I'll talk to you about them later. For the moment, I've got questions to ask you, explanations to give you. And you'll have to make a decision."

"I'm listening," said Jorgenssen in an inaudible voice.

"Relax. You're tired. You've passed the most brutal tests. You've left everything behind you... all that you were. You're completely new, like a butterfly scarcely out of its chrysalis. Your wings aren't dry yet, or even unfolded. Let them grow strong in the sun."

"I'll try," said Jorgenssen.

"Sit down on the grass. Eat that fruit Nothing's better than the fruits of the earth."

Jorgenssen obeyed.

"Good," said Urzeit. "We have time. What are five minutes compared to five thousand years? We juggle with time, don't we, you and I? We mustn't give the impression that we attach too much importance to it. That's why I smoke a pipe. It's a lost custom, and I really think its disappearance sounded the death knell of the Federation. Pipe smokers are placid and reflective people. It takes a lot of time to properly fill a pipe. The one I'm smoking at the moment was cut from a venerable briar root from Earth." He sighed deeply.

"Naturally," he said, "you've never known Earth. Most of the Federation's young people, even in my time, had only heard of Earth through historical novels. Most of the species you see on this world come from there; those I couldn't acclimatize, I copied, starting with native plants and eliciting controlled mutations. It's tremendous, what you can do genetically when you control time."

"On Ygone, it was you," said Jorgenssen in a low voice. He closed his eyes, thinking of the great trees whose foliage banished the night, whose branches spread out like protecting fingers over the city, of the giant trees that were the memory of Dalaam, and of that heavenly replica of Earth.

"I've always loved trees," Urzeit acknowledged ingenuously. "They firmly plunge their roots into the ground. They climb the sky. They grow in all directions, into the past as into the future. You know, the rings in a trunk are crystallized, set waves of time. Seasons pass, but trees remember. I'm very proud of my trees of Ygone. I don't think they have their equals in the universe."

"I don't think so either," said Jorgenssen, astounded.

"This garden has no equivalent either," continued Urzeit. "Its originality poses a problem. It's a riddle, a very important one. I'm going to play the sphinx. Let's see if you'll know how to solve it. You've encountered three conditions on this planet—the jungle, the desert, the garden.

But you couldn't date them. How must they be arranged chronologically, in your opinion?"

Jorgenssen was on the point of shrugging his shoulders. He hesitated. "I don't know... let me think. You yourself placed the desert after the garden—you said in five or six thousand years. And this garden is your work. Then the jungle existed before that. The jungle, the garden, the desert—there's your chronological order. But I don't see what that means."

"You don't see?" shrieked Urzeit. His teeth separated and he caught his pipe again on the fly. He leaned forward and pointed the stem at Jorgenssen.

"You don't see? Three aspects of the reality of a world flowing one into another, and you can't see their relationship to your mission? Everything you've experienced, then, has been for nothing. I could whisper it to you, but that would interfere with your future. It belongs to you. No one has the right to interfere in the time of an intelligent being, above all not with the intention of limiting his capacity to choose."

Jorgenssen reflected. There must have been an analogy somewhere which escaped him. The jungle, the desert, the garden.... The jungle, the garden, the desert. Between the jungle and the garden, a series of temporal interventions—exactly like those of the teams. And between the garden and the desert?... Nothing. The logical conclusion of temporal intervention was the desert.

The pieces fell into place: the universe before the Federation, then time travel, the management of the past, the work of the teams. The Federation was the equivalent of the garden, that was self-evident. And the logical conclusion of the Federation was the desert, decadence, the death of all civilization.

He, Jorgenssen, had to choose: the destruction of the Federation by executing Altair's orders, or the destruction of the Federation by opposing it. He examined the garden around him. It was a paradise, a dream oasis, and yet extremely fragile. A flaw somewhere in its subtle structure doomed it to a swift disappearance. Were the beauty of the garden, the richness of the Federation, not worth preserving for themselves, even if they were ephemeral? No, said a voice within him. No, echoed the six voices of Livius, Mario, Shan d'Arg, Nanski, Erin, and Cnossos. No, whispered the anonymous voices of the people of

Dalaam resounding in the luminous cavities of the giant trees.

There were things more important than beauty and richness, than order, than a civilization. There was life, all the species to be born, the future of mankind, all the civilizations not yet risen from limbo.

He sighed deeply. "I see," he said finally. He threw away the core of the golden fruit. He felt sick, nauseated. What does this garden lack? What does the Federation lack? he thought. Competition. All dangerous species eliminated from the garden planet... all possible threats erased from the Federation's future. He said it to Urzeit "I performed an experiment," said the old man. "You see, when I began to master time, I was almost terrified by the implications of my discoveries. I made plenty of experiments here and there. This garden is the result of one of them. You asked yourself what it lacks. No, it's not competition, nor the struggle for survival." He paused. "It's diversity, it's cooperation, it's a natural equilibrium in time. And likewise, the Federation is going to its destruction because it crushes all variety. I could maintain this garden in its present state maybe ten thousand years, maybe twenty thousand, maybe a million. But I'd have to intervene more and more often, deforming time more and more... leading to a catastrophe."

"And that's what the Federation's doing," said Jorgenssen. "I understand. The missions of the time teams are more and more frequent. But in the long run, the Federation doesn't have a chance; it's doomed."

"Exactly," said Urzeit, blowing a dense cloud of smoke through his mouth and nostrils. "I foresaw it. I told them that. They threatened me, prevented me from working, tried to kill me. They saw in the domination of time a marvelous instrument of power. They had a false, a perverse conception of time and of mankind. They thought on one track. Time's a complex thing—like a net, like a fabric, like a living tissue. It can be torn to pieces, and I didn't want it to be. That's why I created Dalaam. Ygone is an antidote to the Federation."

Jorgenssen stood up. He stretched. His body was fatigued again. "What do I have to do?" he said simply.

Urzeit's response came immediately. The small man's voice had never been so trenchant. "Decide for yourself. You're an adult, aren't you?"

They walked along the stream, going back toward the waterfall, toward the cabin where Arcimboldo Urzeit had watched the unfolding of his experiments, toward the time buoy which allowed him to control the past and future.

"Several weeks ago," said Urzeit to Mario, "you were incapable of deciding knowingly. You were a man of the Federation, even though you rebelled against it. An individual is always caught in his time and his society. It was necessary to tear you away from it. You had to be freed, given back to yourself."

"I understand," said Mario. "The Federation's madness had infected us."

"You had to get back in touch with reality, to become capable of directing yourselves."

"I see," said Mario. "You put us in such an uncomfortable situation that we had to think and change."

Urzeit's smile broadened. "I didn't do anything. I told you no one had the right to interfere in the lives of others by using his mastery of time. It's not just a matter of morality, it's also a matter of stability. Recall the garden and the desert."

"Then who?"

"Think. No one has the right to change the future or the past of another being. But your own..."

Mario remained silent a moment. "That means that we   "   He   stopped, astounded.

"Exactly," said Urzeit

They had come into sight of the waterfall. The banks of the stream were covered with moss. The cabin rose up on a lawn strewn with flowers, and a wood fire crackled tranquilly in an open-air hearth.

"That means we returned into our past, or rather, we were going to do it and we put our own equipment out of order, attacked ourselves," said Shan d'Arg. He had had time to get used to that idea. "But since it's already happened, we no longer have the choice. It's going to happen. We're going to start again. We don't have the power to decide."

"Yes, you do," said Urzeit. "Time isn't a linear series of events. If it were, it would be impossible to travel in time. Accessorily, it would be equally impossible to travel in space. Time is composed of a large number, maybe an infinite number, of possibilities of unequal probability. Each instant, a certain number of events can occur. Some are very probable, others are less so. Under normal conditions, the most probable possibility is actualized; but the others also subsist latently. And with time travel, the order of probabilities is upset. A very important possibility can take the place of a very probable one. I hope you follow me."

"I'm trying to," said Shan d'Arg.

"Observe that exactly the same thing happens with regard to displacement in space. The heavenly bodies follow the most probable trajectories, as do the water in rivers and the stones on mountains. Only relatively recently has man on occasion assigned them highly improbable trajectories, making rivers flow back to their sources, rebuilding mountains, moving planets.

"At this moment, we're in a rather improbable possibility, one not very real, if you prefer. We don't completely exist. At this very moment, if the expression has a meaning, in seven different possibilities seven Arcimboldo Urzeits are trying to explain to each of the seven team members the little they know about the structure of the universe."

"But the Principles?" asked Shan d'Arg.

"They're false," said Urzeit. "Or, more precisely, they're only partly correct. I know that better than anyone. I'm the one who laid them down, starting from the work of Horowitz. But at that time I only considered the case of a..." he smiled, "let's say, a restricted temporality. Generalization came later."

"Why don't they teach this generalization on the worlds of the Federation?"

Urzeit began to laugh. His cheeks shook like empty wineskins. "I told you the Federation was tinged with paranoia. The Arque did nothing more hastily than suppressing those ideas. In fact, it was from the moment I had the impudence to make them public, that I was considered a dangerous individual."

From whence, thought Shan d'Arg, the mystery surrounding the life of Arcimboldo Urzeit. The Archy wasn't so bold as to erase even the memory of his name, but preferred to turn it into a vague and inoffensive myth.

"Naturally," said Urzeit, "I drew the unavoidable conclusion, and I disappeared. I realized that I'd supplied the Federation with a formidable power, a power it wasn't capable of using for the best. It wasn't their fault. No, it was simply that the men of the Federation didn't know enough about what freedom was to weigh all the implications of the mastery of time. The tragedy was that now they had at their command an extremely powerful means of preventing all change... and it was I who gave it to them." Urzeit's face darkened.

"My responsibility is not total, though. If I hadn't made the discovery, someone else would have later. But I couldn't just do nothing. A civilization other than theirs was necessary for the mastery of time, but it could only spring from an experiment in time control. It was a vicious circle, and only time travel made escape possible. The future could help the past. I launched a counterattack."

Shan d'Arg smiled inside. The energy of the slightly grotesque old man had something amusing about it; but Shan d'Arg made no mistake. Urzeit was a real warrior, a man of courage and resolution, a thousand times better than the muscular gladiators that he, Shan d'Arg, had fought in more than a hundred arenas.

"I began by trying to create everywhere societies that would, in the long run, be capable of overturning the Federation's fine equilibrium. But each time, the Federation's teams intervened, sooner or later. They were more powerful and better equipped than I and could effectively protect the Federation. I had only one chance to succeed."

"You mean to say that for three or four centuries the time action teams fought only against you, without knowing it?"

Urzeit shook his head. "A good number of the expeditions, in fact, were against worlds where I'd intervened. There were others, of course. But the teams devoted more and more effort to fighting their creator. A beautiful paradox, isn't it? After several years, I'd had enough of seeing the teams destroy the worlds on which I'd built great hopes. I realized I'd taken a wrong path. It was necessary to set up a stable society capable of resisting the teams' efforts, and to secure myself the support of the teams themselves."

"Teams already work for you?"

"No. Chronologically, you're the first I've contacted. You're the first to have been sent to Ygone. But I can tell you, there'll be others. In a certain way, if you consider the scope of time—which is, by the way, on our side— you'll join a numerous host."

"That we'll help you assemble," emphasized Shan d'Arg.

"Exactly," said Urzeit. "But don't overestimate your importance. Whether you accept or refuse, that legion's probability will be scarcely affected."

"What's the most probable possibility?"

Urzeit did not answer directly. "It's always the one in which temporal intervention is weakest."

They went into the cabin. It was full of the furniture of all eras, apparatus constructed by Urzeit, and books stacked along the walls in the greatest disorder. Urzeit let himself fall into a leather armchair. On the other side of the steel table, Livius sat on a metal stool.

"Then," said Urzeit, "I created Dalaam. I was admirably equipped to study the development of human beings and human societies, since I could travel in time and compare, almost simultaneously, the different stages of evolution. But despite that, I wouldn't have been able to carry out the task alone. I was helped very much by the Institute of Theoretical and Applied Prospective."

"I've never heard of it," said Livius.

"That doesn't surprise me. It won't be founded for fifteen hundred years."

"Fifteen hundred years in the future?"

"Exactly," said Urzeit. "About nine hundred fifty years after the fall of the last Arque and the breaking up of the Federation."

"You talk about the events as if they'd happened already," said Livius.

"They're going to happen," corrected Urzeit. "Or rather, there's a strong probability they'll happen. And the Institute and I are doing everything to reinforce that probability still more. With your help, that possibility will become the most probable."

"A reciprocal influence between the past and future," breathed Livius, astounded. "I thought it was impossible. And you chose to destroy your own civilization."

"Don't be horrified. I told you there'd have to be another one." Urzeit reached over to the cupboard door, which he opened. "Taste this for me," he said as he poured a liqueur into a tumbler. He passed his gourmet's tongue over his rosy lips.

"I also told you," he resumed, "the Principles were inadequate. Contrary to what they maintain, it's possible to travel into your own past. It's possible to change your own history."

'To meet yourself, to kill one of your ancestors, to be your own father?"

"Yes," said Urzeit. "Or at least, up to a certain point. If you ran very fast around a tree, I doubt you could catch yourself. It's the same thing in time."

Livius emptied his glass in one gulp. The liqueur was stronger than any he had ever drunk in the most ill- reputed dens of a hundred planets.

"The Principles are only valid," said Urzeit, "if you consider a single possibility. If you only want to produce limited changes in that possibility, which would leave the present nearly intact, it's convenient to apply the Principles. But they aren't natural limitations. Nature is much richer. The Federation set up the Principles as absolute because it didn't want to see its present, its state, put in question. But reality can include everything, even paradoxes. Or, rather, in reali-

223

ty there are no paradoxes. In the future that'll follow the Federation, society constantly oscillates between several possible states. People are used to it. They even invented a word for it: they call it fluence. They have, simultaneously, several existences on different planes. Time no longer seems a linear succession of events, but a complex structure. Their physics includes a special idea, that of a kind of meta-time which contains all the lines of specific time, as space contains an infinity of geodesics.

"I see," said Livius. The world whirled around him. After all, alcohol was also a means of attaining fluence.

"There are traits of that kind in the Dalaamians," said Nanski, whose head felt heavy.

"In the embryonic state," acknowledged Urzeit. "Their tradition, for example, passes from one possibility to another. Dalaamian children know unconsciously what others in another possibility, on another plane, learn quite consciously. Do you understand what that means?... It practically multiplies the capacities of a human being by infinity... one personality reflected in a large number of extensions on different possible worlds, each devoting himself to the study of one field, the resolution of one problem, the acquisition of one experience... leading a thousand lives simultaneously."

"And the trees?" asked Nanski.

"They serve as mediators, as intermediaries," said Urzeit. "They plunge their roots into the earth, into time. In their hollows the possibilities cross each other, are superimposed on each other, meet each other."

"But the Dalaamians don't know all of the structure of time."

"It's too early for them to learn about it. The tradition has to progress slowly. What remains unconscious with them will become conscious in the course of centuries. The Dalaamians know enough to solve their problems. They bring their experiences to their doubles."

"I understand," said Nanski, and at the same time, the six others. The incomplete culture of the Dalaamians was explained: it represented only one facet of a vaster reality.

"In sum," said Nanski, "what you're asking us to do is to choose between the existence of Dalaam and the Federation."

Urzeit looked him straight in the eye. "You've understood," he said softly.

"It's enough for us not to intervene," said Cnossos, "for Dalaam to overcome. That ought to satisfy you."

"No," said Urzeit He seemed fatigued. He filled his tumbler and slowly emptied it. His features were drawn. His prodigious vitality was put to the test by his age, as much as by the effort necessary to exist simultaneously on seven different planes. His features had changed in a few minutes, and he was scarcely able to breathe.

"No," he repeated. "Remember, the most probable possibility is the one that's undergone the least temporal interference. There's a plane on which you accomplished your mission and which didn't undergo further interference."

"Then there's another in which no team set foot on Ygone."

"I don't exist on that one," breathed Urzeit. "Neither does Dalaam. Everything's connected. I need you... need you to help me. You have to..." He recovered his breath. "You have to erase all trace of your passage as soon as possible. You have to do away with the team at the very moment of its appearance on Ygone. That'll enormously reinforce the probability of favorable possibilities.

He gasped for breath. "You... you're free to decide."

Implacable, Cnossos extracted the lesson from Urzeit's words. "We have to kill ourselves."

"Exactly," said Urzeit. "You won't stop being yourselves—existing. You must believe me. You'll be free... free." He was pale, his face swollen.

Cnossos got up and went toward him. "Lie down. You're sick."

"No," said Urzeit, "I'm old. It's not the same thing. I don't have much time left."

Cnossos-Erin-Nanski bent over him. Jorgenssen-Mario unfastened his collar. Erin-Livius felt his pulse. All the faces blended with each other.

"In the cupboard," said Urzeit.

He made an effort and sat up straight again. He tried to estimate the time he had left. It was hardly more than a few minutes. They had been hard to convince, but he was almost sure he had succeeded.

"Your pulse is very weak," said Erin. "Your heart..."

"I know," said Urzeit "I'm going..."

"I can give you an injection. Tell me, where are..."

"Useless. I didn't tell you the whole truth just now. I still have twenty years to live, but not in this possibility. Here, I'm at the end of my rope. I've lasted as long as possible. This was the most convenient place to meet you. I've lasted beyond my time here." The words escaped his throat in rattles.

"I'm not really living here anymore. But you won't remain alone. I'll follow you."

Erin lifted the glass of alcohol to the old man's lips. Several drops slid down his chin.

"You've got to decide alone. You're free... free." Urzeit let the old man's head fall onto his chest.

"Dalaam," said Erin quickly. "Is it really the ideal form of society? Do you want to see Dalaams on all the planets of the galaxy?"

"Yes and no," breathed the old man between his teeth.

"Dalaam isn't the ideal city. Dalaam is a model... an experiment, you see."

Erin read anguish in the old man's eyes.

"Dalaam is a scale model of the society to come... after the Federation... when the traverse-materials will connect all the planets as the roads of Dalaam connect... and people will be free... space will no longer exist... and the entire galaxy... the entire universe... will be nothing more than an immense city... a single city.... They have to learn to live freely in the city whose lights are the stars."

The old man's eyes rolled back. Erin's hands shook when he saw the white orbs between his eyelids. But Urzeit was still fighting.

"It's terribly important that Dalaam survive. I can't do anything any longer. I'm worn out. It's a terrible effort to be seven at once... in possibilities of such low probability. You have to..."

Silence. Gurgling came from Urzeit's throat.

"They're my children, Dalaam. You understand, I love them..."

Erin thought it was only a figure of speech.

"In the cupboard, you'll find.... My children, I tell you. I had to know the genetic capacities and had to use a constant stock of chromosomes. Those of the natives weren't sufficient... introduced my own... succeeded in avoiding temporal interference." His head wavered.

"Stole at least three minutes' time. That means the probability's improving. I've won..."

His body collapsed. On a planet without a name, in the light of a blue sun, Arcimboldo Urzeit was dead.

Is it an illusion? wondered Jorgenssen. The flowers seemed to fade at the very instant of Urzeit's death, and the entire landscape took on a kind of unreality, a transparency. The probability of that possibility must have been very weak, and Urzeit's death must have diminished it more. What'll happen if it should disappear purely and simply?

Time hastened. He rushed to the cupboard and opened it.

He saw a complete time action outfit. Everything was there—strictly new—everything he himself had worn in leaving Altair. Where could it have come from? he asked himself. From a distant future? Or was it stolen from Altair?

He undressed and put on the suit and helmet. He adjusted the belt. With a kind of pleasure, his fingers glided over the weapons, the Ordzian ray detectors, the symbiotic complexes, and the field manipulators.

There was a supplementary apparatus that he examined with surprise. It was a spatiotemporal buoy, incredibly miniaturized. With it, he could travel in space and time. The buoy was set for a world and date which he could read at a glance: Ygone, Year Zero, and some numerical co-ordinates.

As he glanced at the old man's body, an idea came to him. Urzeit's death had not been a terrible accident; it had been calculated. Urzeit had said he would continue to live in other possibilities. He had chosen to disappear in this one to escape the members of the team. Even if they decided against Dalaam, they would not be able to use him as a hostage. He had foreseen everything, even defeat.

Jorgenssen would have liked to have buried him, but he didn't have time. That world could be obliterated any minute. The body would remain there, at that very spot. It would still be there six thousand years later, while the desert replaced the garden... awaiting him, Jorgenssen, as a skeleton emerging from the sand and dust.

"The skeleton of Arcimboldo Urzeit. That's the name of this world," said Jorgenssen-Mario-Livius-Shan-Nanski- Erin-Cnossos. It could have no other.

And the seven, confounded in the same movement, pressed the tiny button and swung into the absolute Beyond.

Ygone. Year Zero. The forest of fungi.

They found themselves facing one another. For a long moment, they didn't speak. They all knew the same thing, knew everything they were going to do. There was no hesitation possible. Or was there?

Anguish gnawed at the heart of Jorgenssen-Mario- Livius-Shan-Nanski-Erin-Cnossos. They stood at the brink of an abyss, balanced on a razor's edge: They had to choose.

The image of Urzeit's body came to mind. If they chose Dalaam, they would give more reality to the possibilities

Urzeit inhabited. Perhaps they would enable him to live longer in the paradise where they had met him.

Otherwise.... They didn't have to speak. Otherwise, in a few minutes, in the nearby clearing, sprung from nothingness, from Altair, would appear the team assigned to rectify the history of Dalaam. And they would disappear, would give way before their more real doubles. And the galactic city, of which Dalaam was a model, would never exist; the Dalaamians, born of Arcimboldo Urzeit's cells, would be erased from the map of the universe; and the galaxy, in a distant, undetermined future, would be a desert—with stars as dust.

They had a second to decide. All at the same time, they glided toward the empty clearing, their teeth clenched, hearts anguished, hands poised on the stocks of their weapons. With the same flick of a finger, they released the field-inhibiting circuits which would deprive the newcomers of all protection. This also deprived themselves of all defense, but they were confident. They would be faster.

A lightning flash in the clearing—seven men and a buoy—seven silhouettes dressed in white, deformed by their equipment. They recognized themselves instantaneously.

And fired—Jorgenssen on Jorgenssen, Mario on Mario, Livius on Livius, and so on, each on his double. They knew that in a preceding possibility they had already fought against themselves and that Mario had already killed Mario, and that this had been necessary to finally accomplish the achievement of time's liberation, which they had once evoked in dreams.

The seven silhouettes in the clearing, grouped around the spatiotemporal buoy, wavered like flames. In Jorgenssen's eyes, Jorgenssen could read surprise.

In the eyes of the dying Livius, the Livius who was to live detected a ferocious hatred which he no longer felt; Mario, in the eyes of the Mario who lost consciousness without noise or smoke, could see the end of solitude; Shan d'Arg, on the face of Shan d'Arg, the end of combat; and the others, on the masks of their doubles, could all hail the death of their obsessions and the birth of their freedom.

It was finished. The men of Altair and the spatiotemporal buoy had reached absolute nothingness. Ygone's sunlight seemed to shine more brightly.

Jorgenssen put away his weapon and wiped his forehead, where sweat beaded. "We've killed the old man," he said to Mario in a hoarse voice, "the old man in us. We're"—he hesitated—"changed."

Mario shook his head. "Have you ever thought," he said, "that others might be able to act on our future, as we considered doing for Ygone?"

Jorgenssen hesitated. "I see what you mean. But we're free. Urzeit did everything so we'd decide freely."

He turned from the clearing, and the others followed him. He wanted to go down to Dalaam, see Anema again, listen to Daalquin, and learn from the trees, if he could, the knowledge amassed for him by his other possibilities. He knew their destiny was all laid out: They would be the first, would travel in time, would fight against the Federation's teams, and would strive to win over the men of Altair. At long intervals, they would perhaps see Urzeit again. They perhaps would learn more of him.

But they would never know everything. That was one of the things that Urzeit had taught them, perhaps the most important thing. One could not exhaust reality. Freedom was choosing among several possibilities without knowing all the possibilities. In the future, that would be called fluence.

Dalaam had changed subtly. The city seemed closer, more real, to Jorgenssen. Was it perhaps an illusion, like the flickering of the landscape at the moment of Urzeit's death? Was this perhaps not due to his joy at having found Anema again? Or perhaps did Dalaam now exist on a higher plane of reality?

The question could wait, Jorgenssen decided. He walked along Dalaam's paths with Anema at his side. He wandered among the great trees. He fell upon a place he knew, a place he had discovered with Anema... long before... or just yesterday... a circular public square adorned with a statue, dominated by a fountain.

The marvelously fresh water glided over the statue. The statue's features were not entirely human, and yet reminded Jorgenssen of someone. The symbol was obvious: the water flowed over the statue as time flowed over beings... and eroded them. Nothing could stop it, or hold it back. It could be diverted, but it finally resumed its course, destroying whoever confined it.

Jorgenssen moved several steps closer to better examine the statue. He carefully scrutinized the features of the stone face, when a likeness, subtly altered by the sculptor's art, struck him like a blow. He regained his breath.

The statue's features were those of Dr. Arcimboldo Urzeit. He returned to Anema without a word.

LES TUEURS DE TEMPS

GILLES d'ARGYRE ★

★★ANTICIPATION★★

Editions
"Fleuve Noir"

THE MOTE IN TIME'S EYE

When God made Time, He made plenty of it.
Irish proverb.

I

The spaceship was approaching the end of a profitable 12-year voyage of exploration. It was halfway between the two Magellanic Clouds.

This had been the most daring expedition the human civilization of the Lesser Magellanic Cloud had ever sent forth. Its Supreme Magistrates had had great vision, believing that their interests required it.

Their forebears had come from the Prime-galaxy, 5000 or 6000 years earlier. They had quickly conquered new worlds and increased their population. In the year 27,937 (Universal Datation), when this story begins, the human civilization of the Lesser Magellanic Cloud consisted of about 6000 planets with an average population of roughly 250,000. On some worlds, there were almost 100 million people; on others, there were just a handful of families.

Men could still be comfortable in the Lesser Magellanic Cloud. They could continue to multiply at the same rate for another 20,000 years before reaching the limit of the stellar nebula. But this did not prevent them from going to see what was happening beyond their own systems. Their interest in unknown worlds tended to increase with distance.

The ship was spherical. It could travel one million light-years in one year. When it left Neo-Sirius, it had a crew of 6000. Twelve years later, taking into account births and deaths, it carried 7591. There was room for over 10,000 on board. The power of the ship's generators and weaponry was considerable; nevertheless, considering the distance and the obstacles, the *Vasco* was nothing but an eggshell in the ocean of space. There had been enormous risks, but the people of the Magellanics were adventurous. And the hold of the *Vasco,* packed with booty, was proof enough of the advantages of taking risks in space.

The last 18 months of navigation had proceeded without mishap, in known space. There was no mass of stellar importance to impede the ship's progress within a hundred light-years. The direction detectors had remained silent; had the robots been capable of boredom, they would have sounded an electronic complaint.

There was nothing on board the *Vasco* to indicate that it had been crossing the biggest battlefield in history for the last 1000 of light-years.

231

The ships which were in conflict—we'll call them ships for lack of a better word, but they bore practically no similarity to the sort of craft the *Vasco* was—lurked in folds of space where the *Vasco's* detectors could not reach. Although the battle had been raging for over 7000 years, its front was still spreading. In fact, the battlefield had shifted constantly throughout time. The war had started, as far as the *Vasco* was concerned, in a future so remote that its passengers could have no concept of it. The adversaries were two powerful civilizations from two different galaxies.

In theory, allowance had been made for the possible accidental incursion of ships foreign to both sides into the battlefield; the non-belligerents were not even supposed to suspect that they were going through a battlefield. But somewhere, a mistake had been made.

A series of unlucky circumstances had propelled the *Vasco* into the very center of the battle. First, it went through a zone in which a "cruiser" had exploded, thereby shattering the very structure of the space-time continuum.

Then, the *Vasco* slipped from "subspace," where it was traveling, into "multispace." There, it was immediately picked up by an unmanned robotic station which automatically proceeded to surround it with a minefield, as a standard precautionary measure. Had the *Vasco's* detectors been equipped to identify the mines for what they were, or had Captain Shangrin had any idea of the risks his ship was running, he would immediately have stopped the engines; but he had no reason to suspect that anything was amiss.

Nor did the station's "warning shots" alert him: the field which ought to have inhibited ordinary enemy generators was ineffectual against the primitive engines of the *Vasco*. Finally, the ship passed at less than one light-year from a mine and set it off. Without a sound, without a tremor, the *Vasco* was instantly projected into the past.

The robotic station immediately sent a report to its controllers that an alien ship of unknown origin had been withdrawn from the battlefield. The current state of the war in that sector was so preoccupying that the controllers decided to postpone an inquiry into the incident, since there were far more urgent problems that needed to be dealt with.

Nevertheless, an abridged version of the report was forwarded to Headquarters. But simultaneously, 16 million other reports, all from different sources, were pouring into their central computers, which were beginning to show signs of overload, and therefore did not pick out the *Vasco* incident.

This would not have been of any consequence had it not been for the rather eccentric nature of the Magellanites.

Captain Varun Shangrin was the Captain of the *Vasco*. The Supreme Magistrates of the 16 sponsoring planets of the Magellanic Cloud had hesitated a long time before hiring him to lead the expedition they were financing.

True, he came from a family which had explored many virgin planets. He had knocked about in countless sectors of space. He had always brought back his ships with their crews. This last was the deciding factor, for the Magistrates were terrified at the mere possibility of giving back to space the tremendous fortunes that they had wrenched from it.

But Shangrin was also reputed to be an adventurer, quick-tempered to the point of violence. His voice could make the stars quake. He was said to be a galley master rather than a captain, an eager warlord, a man who enjoyed life to the full. The Supreme Magistrates of the Lesser Magellanic Cloud trembled in their comfortable houses as they remembered Varun Shangrin's exploits and his laughter. Privately, they referred to him as a pirate, a space brigand, a pillager, and thought him the repository of all vices. But they knew they could launch him into the unknown, sure that he would come back laden with riches, fired up with new routes, his eyes reflecting the glories of new and fabulous worlds.

He made them nervous because he was a truly great leader and a better businessman than they were. He would walk into their elegantly appointed offices, helmeted, booted, trailing the chill of outer space and the smell of machinery, and then coerce them into risking their money in exchange for an uncertain hope. He would leave them panting for months and years, but he would come back unchanged, tanned by giant suns. He made them nervous because what he risked was his life; they risked only their fortunes. And they were afraid of him because he often made outlandish deals with mythical, inhuman beings whom they, the pale merchants of Lorne or Suni, Arno, Yorque or Neo-Sirius, would never know. Their ultimate fear was that, one day, he would loom out of the sky over their cities at the head of a hostile fleet.

They feared him as sedentary merchants have always feared their captains because they did not know him. They could not fathom the source of his laughter or of his strength.

But it was because they were afraid of him that they trusted him. He was invincible; the holds of his ships were always fuller than anyone else's; and he was never defeated. The rewards were enormous, even in proportion to the risks.

And so, when the Supreme Magistrates of the 16 cooperating planets interviewed other candidates, they were disappointed. This captain was too young, that one too timid. A good technician but a poor trader. Too rapacious. Too easy on his crew. Too tricky. Of doubtful courage. Too crippled by space diseases. Too old. Too unstable. Too mediocre.

Too something. The tall and handsome captains of the Lesser Magellanic Cloud filed past the Supreme Magistrates of the 16 planets, but none proved suitable. The assignment was too difficult for them and the stakes were too high. The Magistrates hesitated. They did not want to lose the *Vasco,* the largest, most powerful manmade ship in this part of the known universe.

Then Shangrin came in. He marched right up to them and said: "I will take the *Vasco.*" He burst out laughing when he saw the expressions on their faces.

As he looked over the handsome captains of the Lesser Magellanic Cloud, he asked the Supreme Magistrates if they wanted children or a man.

So he got the assignment and the *Vasco* was his. It meant, of course, new worries for the Magistrates, new wrinkles, new ulcers, palpitations in their old hearts, but also—in the future—even greater prosperity. Along with the *Vasco*, they let him have an army of scientists, technicians, astronauts, soldiers.

And a mountain of recommendations.

They also gave him a first mate named Gregori, a reliable young man whose fame would perhaps someday equal Varun Shangrin's, and who might be able to bridle the Captain's impetuousness.

Since they were a cautions lot, the Supreme Magistrates took an extra precaution: they made Gregori into a safety mechanism.

But as they were also discreet, they did not tell him. Nor Shangrin. So Shangrin and Gregori plunged into intergalactic space with their ship and its crew, both their hearts yearning for conquest, but with secretly implanted, strange devices in the latter's mind, unknown to both of them.

The *Vasco* and its crew were now on the way back to the Lesser Magellanic Cloud and the devices within Gregori had remained unused so far. They would have remained so if…

Captain Varun Shangrin was calmly raising his china tea cup when a sudden gesture of his first mate made him drop it. The tea spilled all over his red beard, the cup rolled on to his knees and shattered on the floor. Shangrin's blue eyes flashed. His heavy fists came down on the metal table, making it tremble.

"Have you no respect?" he shouted. "At least for this superb Lenqsen tea, if not for me?"

"The stars!" said Gregori.

"Well?"

The Captain's eyes flew to the collection of screens which covered one wall of the room. His face, which had been flushed with anger, became ashen; his eyes bulged.

"The stars vanished for a second, then, they came back—but they're not the same ones! It all happened very quickly. If I hadn't been looking at the screens at just that moment, I probably wouldn't have noticed anything. Except the new positions of the stars."

"Never saw anything like it."

Shangrin stood up, looking a lot like a bear. He leaned forward, hunched down, then suddenly he was erect, slightly stooped. He weighed 286 pounds, and was six feet six tall. Of his 67 years, 40 had been spent in outer space. He spoke with authority, was a good technician and a skilled trader.

He went to a screen which gave an excellent impression of transparency and depth.

"I don't know a single one of those constellations—not one. We must have made an enormous jump for the starscape to change that much. Look at the relative positions of the stars."

"Could the computers identify any of those constellations and find our location?"

Shangrin closed his eyes to think better and snapped his huge fingers two or three times. But no inspiration came.

"The crew and the passengers have noticed something, Captain," said Gregori. "They're beginning to worry."

Red lights were popping up everywhere. Almost all the posts on the ship wanted to communicate with the Captain. Then the shrill ring of priority bells was heard. But Shangrin did not stir.

"What are you looking for, Captain?"

Shangrin slowly looked up from under heavy lids.

"Something to say to them, young man. After all, we're lost, as far as I know. What I'm trying to figure out is how to make them think this is an opportunity and not a disaster."

"That's going to be tough."

"In the long term, impossible. But I think I can keep them pacified for ten minutes. You'll see."

Shangrin ran his fingers along a keyboard. All the red lights went out; only one green light remained, the one connecting the Bridge to Navigation.

"Cut all contact between Navigation and the rest of the ship," ordered Shangrin. "All private conversations are forbidden until further notice. All crew members will remain at their posts. They are not to answer questions from the passengers. Is that understood?"

"Yes," answered an anonymous voice.

Shangrin cut the contact with a flick of his finger. Then he turned on the master switch. Seconds later, his voice echoed in all the corridors, public rooms, dining halls, dormitories and cabins of the *Vasco.*

"Captain Varun Shangrin speaking." He cleared his throat and winked at Gregori. "I have an announcement to make. First Mate Gregori and I have been researching and performing experiments in instantaneous teletransportation. We've just tried one out. That's the reason for the sudden change in the stellar horizon. We're going to take advantage of this side trip to visit this new region of space. This will not delay our return—quite the contrary."

He disconnected the speaker.

"Is that the best you can do?" asked Gregori. "They'll be on our backs in an hour."

"A lot of things can happen in an hour. By then, we may have no cause for worry. Or we may have found out what happened. Or even—"he winked again—"within the hour, I may really have found the secret of instantaneous teletransportation. Or you will."

"Neither of us is a scientist, and I doubt if the words 'instantaneous teletransportation' mean anything."

"Frankly, I don't know," said Shangrin. "I know we're not scientists and that we can't possibly make such a tremendous discovery, but we'll dream up some other story for them. That, at least, is well within our power." He gave his loud laugh.

"The essential, obviously, is that no one panics," admitted Gregori.

"Can't be done," said Shangrin. "It's bound to happen sooner or later. There are already two people on board whose insides are tied up in knots."

"Who?"

"You and me. Let's go see the Navigators. Maybe they know something we don't."

"OK," Gregori said hesitantly.

He knew how well the Captain could bluff. He had seen Shangrin talk his way out of tight spots hundreds of times, spots others could not even have shot their way out of. But that he would try to lie to the crafty Magellanites, his own people, was unthinkable.

The *Vasco,* however, had already done the unthinkable—it had gone beyond the stars.

Henrik, the bald little Chief Navigator, was jumping up and down with surprise and fury.

"But it's illegal!" he protested. "You have no right to forbid all communication between Navigation and the rest of the ship. You cannot take away from the crew the right to be kept informed. You should be—"

"Mr. Henrik," thundered Shangrin, "I have piloted ships when the Captain was the only one with any say-so on board. Times have changed, I know, but I haven't. Anyway, in unusual circumstances such as these, I am allowed to assume full control. Now, let's get down to business. Every minute counts."

Swallowing his rage, Henrik led them into the control room. It was spherical, surrounded by limitless space. The walls were transparent—invisible. Stars shone in the dark. Sometimes larger spots would loom up: nebulous, distant little islands of stars; sometimes a nova would flare up, like a lighthouse set up to guide navigators in a billion-chambered labyrinth of the universe.

The vast cabin where the navigators operated floated in the center of the sphere, reached by a light, transparent walkway. Henrik, Shangrin and Gregori climbed up.

Visible space was an artificial creation. Stars were not directly visible in subspace, where the *Vasco* was traveling at a speed many times greater than that of light. Furthermore, normal space was subject to transformations in subspace which altered the relationships between distances. For this reason, complex instruments reconstructed on the wall of the navigation sphere an image of space such as might have been seen by a hypothetical traveler going through it on the same trajectory and at the same speed as the *Vasco*.

The navigation room was a superb and costly piece of equipment. Its usefulness during long cruises was questionable, for most operations could be better performed automatically by computers. But the Magellanites liked it because they preferred human control to mechanical control. It gave them a maneuverability in stellar clusters that was envied even by the pilots of Prime-galaxy who had better, more sensitive, but still automatic instruments.

"Where are we?" Gregori asked under his breath, as though speaking to himself. "I don't recognize any of the position of the stars."

Henrik raised his arms.

"I don't either. Nothing is familiar. Absolutely nothing. And I know this sector like the palm of my hand. The sector we were cruising in before this accident, that is. We'll never find our way home. Never."

"If I hear you say that again," roared Shangrin, "I'll wring your neck and throw you out into space. We'll get out of here—and with something to show for it."

"Very well, Captain," Henrik replied with obvious restraint.

"What do the computers say?"

"Nothing yet. I started an analysis at once. I thought, at first, that we'd made an unexpected jump through subspace for some unknown reason, and that we didn't recognize the stars anymore because our perspective had changed. I have the computers systematically comparing the positions of the stars that can be observed with the information available in our databanks, but up to now, they haven't identified a single constellation."

"I see. A topological analysis. Good. And there's no nova, no known nebula?"

"Nothing in the way of novae. The computers haven't been programmed to identify nebulae yet. Only star clusters that are relatively close to the Clouds. By the way, have you noticed anything unusual?"

"Yes. The stars here are clearly more numerous than in the space sector we've just left," Gregori said.

"Quite right. We'd just finished crossing the chasm separating the Lesser Magellanic Cloud from the Greater, where stars are relatively rare. Here, they're distributed more densely—much as in a local cluster of small size."

"I see," said Shangrin. "When do you expect a definite answer from the computers?"

"Maybe in a minute; maybe never. Of course, we could ask them for an approximation at anytime."

"Go ahead; do so," said Shangrin.

Henrik gave some orders. The men bending over their control panels got busy. The synthetic voice of the computer could be heard, muffled, throbbing.

"…There is no known star system consisting of more than twelve units, within a probability of point zero five. In approximately 12 hours, it will be possible to determine the general outline of the stellar cluster surrounding us. However, initial analysis indicates that its shape is different from the one we have just left. Three distant galaxies have been observed: these could be, respectively, the Prime-galaxy, Andromeda's Nebula and the Swan Cluster. However, it should be noted that they seem to be significantly nearer to each other than they ought to be according to the databanks and that their light—"

"Shut it off," roared Shangrin.

Henrik gave a signal. The computer stopped intoning.

"Of course I don't believe a word of your story about 'instantaneous teletransportation.' It's nothing but a lie."

"I know," said Shangrin. "So what? I tried to preserve the calm and I've succeeded for the time being. What did you expect me to tell them?"

"The truth."

"In other words, that we are lost and we'll probably never see our own homeworlds again?"

"Maybe."

"You think that would have made them more likely to forgive me?"

"I don't know," said Henrik. "But I know you're finished. The ship's Council will fire you."

"You'd like that, wouldn't you? But you'll have to wait a while. This being an emergency, I'm taking over. I'll dissolve the Council if I have to."

Henrik choked.

"You can't push us around. The Guardians will take steps."

"I'm not afraid of the Guardians."

Henrik flailed at the air with his thin arms as though he were struggling for breath. Gregori dragged the Captain out.

II

"You have a terrible disposition, Captain," Gregori said cautiously, feeling as though he were walking on thin ice.

Shangrin did not answer. There were little drops of sweat on his forehead. He could be silent for hours on end; for as long as his anger lasted.

Gregori thought hard. The situation was serious—physically and psychologically. Physically, it had not yet become critical. True, they were lost in an unknown section of the universe, but the *Vasco* had enough supplies to continue its cruise for ten, 20, 100 years! Psychologically, however, a crisis loomed. People wouldn't like to be on a trip that, figuratively, went nowhere. The Captain was sure to be dismissed by the Council within a matter of hours. He would put up a fight, of course, and his admirers would find excuses for all his tricks, all his bluffs. They would follow him, if need be, to the very ends of space. But he also had enemies who did not care for his highhanded ways. A struggle would almost certainly ensue between the two factions. The unavoidable close quarters, even on a ship the size of the *Vasco,* tended to fan enmities more than to create friendships.

If Shangrin were to resist the Council, the Guardians would intervene—but that was the X factor. It was general knowledge that, on all ships, there were Guardians charged with maintaining order in case of an emergency, in accordance with the laws of the Lesser Magellanic Cloud. But no one seemed to know anything about them. Were they human agents infiltrated secretly on board? Or cybernators designed to do police work? Rumor had it that the Guardians were nothing but a myth made up to intimidate the crew to stop them from mutiny, and the Captain, to compel him to obey the Council and the laws.

Gregori reminded himself that the Captain had deliberately precipitated the crisis. With his tale of "instantaneous teletransportation," he had knowingly unleashed a wave of anger which would surely lead to his dismissal by the Council. But he must have foreseen this... He was stubborn, short-tempered, impulsive and arrogant, but he was also intelligent. Why had he stuck his neck out? For a few more minutes of peace? Nonsense. One doesn't use a nuclear weapon to squash a fly...

Gregori stared at the screens. They showed a cosmic landscape similar to hundreds of millions of others he had seen. Why did it seem so strange? What was the distance between these stars and the Lesser Magellanic Cloud, with its prosperous cities, its ships, its factories, its museums, its women? The length of a universe? Infinity?

The instruments quietly went on with their work, observing, translating, noting, measuring, recording, in a whirlwind of infinitesimal flashes, sealed into the irregularities of a chunk of crystal. Time and space mattered little to them.

However, they did to men. After traveling for 12 years, the passengers were looking forward to returning to the welcoming ports of the Lesser Magellanics and enjoying their share of the rich booty of the expedition. Instead of that, they were being offered a new lease on space.

Why had Shangrin spoken of "instantaneous teletransportation," Gregori wondered, and why had he put himself in the limelight? Because he thought that it was the only possible explanation for what had actually happened to the *Vasco?* Very unlikely. He could just as easily have intimated that the ship had fallen into a deep space pocket, and could have added the comforting thought that they could reverse direction. This would have been the easiest, most obvious explanation for the accident.

Gregori looked at the Captain out of the corner of his eye. Shangrin, his eyes closed, appeared to be asleep. But he was thinking, fast and hard. It was always when he seemed relaxed, free from any tension, at complete ease, that he was at his most dangerous.

He must have some idea in the back of his mind, Gregori decided. Perhaps he believed that somebody on board the *Vasco* actually knew the secret of "instantaneous teletransportation" and had tried to use it? Then, that somebody could easily sort things out, and Captain Varun Shangrin's reputation would remain undamaged. Shangrin had acted, Gregori thought, as though he were trying to cover up for someone.

Who could it be? A member of the crew? One of the physicists? One of the mathematicians? One of the psychomaticians who experimented with the fantastic powers of the human nervous system? No. Shangrin would not have thought twice about denouncing any of them. And anyway, why would a member of the crew have conducted an experiment of such magnitude in total secrecy?

There was only one person on board the *Vasco* both capable of successfully conducting such a surprising attempt and whom the Captain might want to protect. A shiver ran up and down Gregori's back. His neck became tense. It wasn't really a person—more like an entity.

The Runi.

Gregori tried to keep his hands from shaking. The Runi. That might explain everything—or almost everything. The pieces of the puzzle now fell easily into place. Who but the Runi would wish to head the ship in the opposite direction from the Lesser Magellanics? Who would possibly have the power to do it? And the Runi's presence on board was indeed something Captain Shangrin was very anxious to hide.

Gregori had not thought of the Runi before, because he just had not believed that such a monstrous creature could have such astonishing scientific knowledge. He remembered the night when he and the Captain had smuggled the Runi on board, in flagrant violation of the rules. It had been a strange experience to enter the ship under their command like thieves, to hoodwink the sentries and deactivate the alarms. Shangrin's reasons for introducing the Runi on board had always seemed rather obscure. But the Captain seemed to care more for that creature than for his share of the loot. Was it because the Runi seemed to enjoy their games of chess as much as Shangrin did? Or because he might have been the repository of an ancient and considerable body of scientific knowledge which Shangrin was hoping to use? But how could one tell, with that kind of creature, if he wasn't the one using you and not the other way around?

Gregori made a face. He had some pretty unpleasant memories of the Runi's homeworld. The xenologists had decided that the Runis were feebleminded creatures and everyone, except Shangrin, had taken their word for it. Shangrin had persisted in teaching one of them to play chess. The chessboard, with its 64 squares, had served to bridge the gap between the mental universe of the Runis and that of the humans. The xenologists had eventually revised their concepts and perfected a translation machine. Incoherent shreds of the Runis' knowledge had come through.

Very few of these had any parallels in human knowledge; only a few seemed to possess even a shadow of meaning. The question of how the Runis had penetrated certain secrets of the universe had remained unanswered. They had no apparent civilization, no language, no technology, no instruments. They seemed content to set up rows of pebbles or twigs in apparently meaningless patterns on the yellow plains of their world. Then, they would leave. A long time later, another Runi might pass by, touch up a detail and continue on his way.

It was like a series of endless games, which was what had given Shangrin the idea of teaching them chess.

Gregori took two steps toward the Captain and touched his shoulder.

"The Runi..." he said.

Shangrin growled and opened his eyes.

"You believe we owe this side trip to the Runi?" Gregori continued, accusingly.

"Yes," admitted Shangrin grudgingly.

"But he has no instruments, no source of energy, no—"

"They can do things we can't even imagine," said Shangrin in a slow, tired voice.

"And you think you can make him put us back on our initial course?"

"If I can still beat him at chess, yes."

There was a note of despair in Shangrin's voice. Gregori knew that the Runi had made tremendous progress with each game. At first, Shangrin could easily beat him just by himself; but he had played their last few games with the help of a computer, even though he had 50 years of chess playing experience behind him. The Runi had a phenomenal memory and his logic was flawless; very soon, he would be better than any human—any computer. He was not very quick—time was of no consequence on his planet—but it was not important for chess players either. Some games went on for months, years.

"Why don't we go ask him?"

"I was getting ready to," said Shangrin. "But first I was thinking out Eichenhorn's gambit."

Gregori knew how the chess pieces moved, although he did not share the Captain's passion. He preferred faster, more intense games in which the opponents' personalities were revealed more directly.

Shangrin got up heavily; his bearlike figure showed fatigue.

"You think all this is my fault, don't you? Because I saw a potential gold mine in that Runi?"

Gregori did not reply.

"You're right, but not entirely. I've been traveling in space for a long time and it's given me a couple of ideas. The chief one is that man's expansion in the universe is a miracle. Incredible and fragile. Thirty or 30,000 years ago—I'm a little vague—Mankind lived on only one planet in the Prime-galaxy, which they called the Milky Way. During that time, they secured a foothold on three or four other galaxies. We ourselves are only an outer limb, easily detachable from the parent tree.

"As men conquered the stars, they experienced numerous setbacks, but there was never any serious question about the power of their destiny. It's a miracle, I tell you, Gregori. In-credible luck. Sooner or later, it might come to an end. No one can win all the time. Sooner or later, something might happen. A cataclysm. A meeting with another species more powerful than ours, but just as domineering. It will never amount to anything more than a slight hitch in the history of the universe, but for mankind, it might mean the end of all that is.

"Of course, if we could bring another ally, another race into play, it would be quite a trump card. The Runis represent such an opportunity for Mankind. Whatever they know, whatever they can do over and beyond what we know and are capable of, could raise our own abilities, increase our power to match our ambitions. But there is also an element of risk in this strategy: someday, the Runis may turn against us, or drop us at some crucial point in our history. That's why I agreed to him coming with us—but perhaps that was a mistake…"

"You never told me all this before," said Gregori.

"What good would it have done? This is such a solemn speech that it might sound hollow. Personally, I like reality, things that are concrete and clear. Most people think of me as nothing but an old bully, and they're right. I like money and power. I can be overbearing and my ideas belong to another generation, but that doesn't stop me from being farsighted."

He put a huge hand on Gregori's shoulder.

"You, Gregori, are of a different breed. You're not afraid of the gods, nor fate, nor space. Perhaps that will come with age. I can't remember now how I felt when I was your age. But if you give in to this fear, then you'll make mistakes too."

His hand dropped and he stroked his beard pensively.

"Let's go ask the Runi what he thinks."

Was he sincere? Gregori wondered. It was impossible to tell. But if the old Captain had been trying to get at him through his better self, he certainly had almost succeeded.

III

The Runi occupied a stateroom cluttered with a heap of machinery and instruments designed for his survival and communication with humans. He looked like a big, furry crab. An orange shell protected the part of his central nervous system which was encased in a fur-covered cylinder. That cylinder was made up of seven rings of approximately the same diameter as a human body. The Runi could stretch his length to four yards, or compress his rings to less than one. He rested by coiling up. There were about a dozen small, articulated limbs where the body and the shell joined. They looked like surgical instruments and served as sensory organs, fingers and tools.

The Runi, coiled up on the floor, looked like a crab resting on a huge bail of wool. Next to him was a chessboard. His body was connected to various instruments which enabled him to communicate with the Captain.

When the two men came in, the Runi quivered and the instruments tried to interpret this in human language.

"Godgodgodgodgod when will you take me back to my own planet godgodgodgodgod."

"That's enough of that," Shangrin said curtly. He put his hands in his pockets and considered his passenger. The Runi's little organs were quivering—a repellent sight.

"Enoughenoughenoughenough," the Runi started up.

He stretched out slightly. A shiver ran over his orange fur. *He's completely stupid*, Gregori said to himself. *The xenologists were right. I don't know why Shangrin persists in thinking these creatures have any intelligence at all.*

"Listen, Runi," said Shangrin. "You admit that I beat you fairly?"

"Truetruetruetruetrue," said the Runi.

"Good. And you agreed to the terms of the deal we made. If you had won, I would've stayed on your planet for ten years, teaching chess to your people. But if I won—which I did—you were to spend ten years on *my* planet. Plus, that deal was to your advantage because I can't expect to live more than 150 years, whereas two or three millennia are like nothing to you."

"Truetruetruetruetrue."

"Damn it," said Shangrin. "The translation machine has broken down again."

He leaned over the instruments and checked the wires. He made a delicate adjustment.

"There. I think that will stop that infernal stuttering."

So it had been the automatic translator's fault, Gregori thought. He ought to have worked it out for himself. When such a chasm separated two species that they had to rely on a mechanical bridge to close it, it was always possible that any mutual misunderstandings might be caused entirely by the machines. Perhaps the xenologists' mistake had been to trust too blindly in their equipment? But without the machines, how could one ever truly know what the other was thinking? On the other hand, the machine might inject something extraneous into the message it is supposed to translate. It might only be a false interpolation, but in the long run, the entire message could be wrong. Communication was more than just words, semantics, but also involved attitudes, infinitesimal movements of members, vibrations of hairs… Without properly assessing all that, how could one ever be sure of what the other was trying to convey?

Automatic translators were not enough. Intuition was needed, good old-fashioned, reliable intuition, of the Varun Shangrin kind.

"You haven't stuck to our deal," said Shangrin. "I suspect you've tried to cheat, Runi. You've set off some kind of space-time disturbance that I don't understand so that you can return to your planet. You had no right to do this. You're going to take us back to where we were, Runi."

Could a non-humanoid life form have any sense of honor? Gregori wondered. Had the Runi any concept of honesty? Friendship? Pain? Could any of these concepts be understood by that strange-looking furry crab?

The Runi stretched out his body to almost its full length; the orange carapace balanced on the fur-covered cylinder. The articulated paws were wriggling frenetically.

"Not true, not true, not true," answered the translator. "We are lost, lost, lost…"

Silence followed. Then, suddenly, the machine said in a louder and clearer voice:

"That is not true. We are lost in the continuum. But it is not my fault. Runis cannot do anything like that."

A blue vein on Shangrin's left temple began to throb.

"Where are we, Runi?" he shouted.

The Runi's head almost reached the man's. Thousands of threads, finer than hair, connected it to the translating machines and formed a sort of metal halo around it.

It can't be, thought Gregori. *He has no way of locating us in space. He has no instruments, no radio telescope, not even a screen on which he can see the stars.*

But the answer came very quickly.

"We are still in the same location," said the Runi, "taking into account the movement of the ship. We are not in a different sector of space, nor with noticeably different coordinates."

"That's impossible, Runi," said Shangrin. "We don't recognize any of those stars. We can't find a single familiar constellation. Even the galaxies are different. You're lying."

245

"Nononononono, I am not lying. I don't know what happened. Something caused a change in the environment. Mass has consumed Time. Inertia is perpendicular to Phase. C has increased. I repeat, C has increased."

"The translator has gone all wonky again," said Gregori," or else the Runi has."

"I don't think so," said Shangrin, "The Runi is trying to to tell us something, but the translator isn't really programmed to express it. The Runi says more in one second than you could in a month, but the machine translates only what makes sense to it. We must appear feebleminded to the Runi. The questions we ask him are deplorably simple."

But he plays chess slowly, Gregori thought. Then, the explanation came to him in a flash. It's because he explores all the possibilities, and also because he is mentally working on all kinds of other operations we know nothing about.

"It is not a leap in space," the Runi went on, "but a leap in time. As I understand it, your selves do not have a direct connection to the space-time continuum, so you were not immediately aware of it. Your ship has jumped back through time. Into the past. Two hundred million of your years."

"I think the translator is on the blink again."

Shangrin shot Gregori a disgusted look.

"Quiet. Can't you see he's telling the truth?"

Gregori began to tremble.

"But he can't be."

"I can prove it," the Runi went on steadily. "The inertia of a mass depends upon the age of the universe. It decreases with time. It has suddenly increased. Your instruments must have registered it."

There was a shade of pity in the Runi's speech—or perhaps the translator had added it? It was impossible to tell.

"The universe, considered as a closed system, loses some of its mass as it ages," the Runi went on. "This phenomenon can be looked upon as an effect of expansion, or, conversely, the expansion can be looked upon as an approximate expression of that process. Time consumes Mass. It would seem that the relationship is reversible. Mass has now consumed Time. I have no means of telling whether the incident has an artificial cause. Somewhere, there might be an entity that controls time and that has projected your ship into the distant past. If my supposition is correct, this entity cannot be beaten in chess. Indeed, the game can be of no interest to it."

The Runi's last statement might have seemed like a non sequitur, but it wasn't, Gregori said to himself. Before the arrival of the *Vasco* on their planet, the Runis had probably never suspected that there were other thinking species in the universe. Then, the game of chess had seemed to them to be the necessary intermediary between two such species. It was, therefore, an enormously important tool.

It all pointed to one thing: the Runi knew the humans infinitely better than they understood him. And, for the first time, they were dependent upon him. That might give him ideas.

"Two hundred million years," said Shangrin, blinking. He turned to the Runi. "Is there some way of getting back to our time?"

"I do not see any," said the Runi. "I am not equipped to understand the problems of time. I merely noticed that we had passed, with no transition, from one state of the universe to another. If our displacement was the result of the will of a living entity, it surely can transport us back to our own time."

"How can we make contact with this... entity?"

"I do not know," replied the Runi. "But I want you to understand one thing. Even though our worlds are relatively far apart in space, they are neighbors in time. At the period where we now are, neither your race nor mine was yet in existence. I am just as lost as you are. I want, just as you do, to get back to my planet and to my mate. The force of circumstances is making me your ally."

Shangrin seemed to be deeply moved.

"We see eye to eye, Runi," he said in a deep voice. "We'll get out of this together. What are you going to do? Do you need anything?"

The Runi resumed his resting position. Slow undulations ran up and down the fur on his orange rings.

"No," said the automatic translator. "I'm going to go back to studying the moves of the knight."

Shangrin appeared to have lost the game. But Gregori saw that he was smiling.

"It's going to be a tough fight," said the Captain.

And Gregori wondered if Shangrin was referring to his ongoing game with the Runi, their confrontation with time and the unknown entity who had transported them through it—or the crew of the *Vasco*.

IV

The robot-usher was going down the concentric corridors of the *Vasco*. Its metal body had been painted in the traditional black. There was a little golden scale suspended on its chest from a gold chain. When it was wearing that symbol, humans had to obey its orders. More rarely, a small golden sword swung on its black thorax, displaying to all that it had been authorized to use deadly force.

It always followed a well-defined itinerary on its way to meet someone who was not expecting it. It entered an imitation park. The robot-gardeners had completely transformed it during the night, doing away with the lake, creating a river, setting up hills and planting trees. They had also changed the artificial color of the sky and chosen a nostalgic shade with grayish tones. The grass was green, tall and prickly. There were flowers scattered on the slopes. The robot-gardeners changed the imitation parks as often as possible to keep the humans from getting bored with familiar landscapes. They undertook these transformations at irregular intervals and without warning, so that when the humans went to the park, they never knew what they were going to find. That was apparently enough to keep them happy.

The robot-usher knew all this, but was complete indifference to it. It even knew that the name of this particular setup was the Prime-galaxy. For it, the Prime-galaxy was only a fabulously distant cluster of stars and the source for a large body of regulations it was supposed to enforce. It was just capable of realizing that the Prime-galaxy must have consisted of a large number of worlds and that they probably did not all look like this landscape. On the other hand, it was totally unaware that the hills, the river, the grass and the trees corresponded to the mythical image of a specific world which had been the cradle of the human species.

And yet, it was aware of the odd and exotic qualities of the landscape.

The humans were equally aware of it, for they strolled about, giving little exclamations of surprise. Some of them were already stretched out on the grass. A group of children played on the river bank, supervised by a human teacher. The robot-usher disapproved of human educators. It thought this was a task unworthy of humans. Indeed, it considered all tasks as unworthy of humans. It saw in the presence of the teachers in the fake park the regrettable influence of modem ideas.

The robot-usher walked resolutely toward the teacher, leaving no trace in the grass for the excellent reason that he glided along in the air a few centimeters above the ground.

It examined the teacher more closely. She was blonde, 30 years old, wearing blue trousers and blouse. She had a tanned oval face band very light blue eyes. She was smiling peacefully and seemed very sure of herself.

The robot-usher rose a little and went up to her. It was not really supposed to dominate over humans in this way, but it thought it was more dignified and this increase in dignity would be automatically reflected on humans. It was an expert at rationalizing.

"Norma Shundi?" it asked.

She turned quickly.

"What do you want?"

"You are required to attend a Council meeting. It will start at 8 p.m. On the agenda is a motion for the immediate dismissal of Captain Varun Shangrin."

She gave a start.

"Dismiss the captain? Why?"

"The motion cites an alleged overstepping of authority."

"Oh! You mean, the accident? But we don't even know what happened. Wait a minute. Does the motion concern the Captain only?"

"His first mate is automatically implicated."

"Gregori! Oh, Gregori!" she said with the hint of a sob in her voice. "I'm afraid I can't go."

"There is no choice. You are not sick. You have no valid reason to refuse."

"I've never attended a Council meeting. I don't know what to do."

"Most of the members who will be there tonight are no more experienced than you."

"Isn't there any way I could decline?"

"None," said the robot.

"But it's absurd to pick people out at random."

"That is the rule."

The robot-usher turned on its heel and left. It was strange how differently people reacted when he brought them the news that they had been selected to attend the meeting. Some were obviously flattered. Others, on the contrary, seemed to be concerned that they wouldn't be up to it. Only a few showed complete indifference, but even they would go to the meeting. There were penalties for staying away without valid reasons, although these seldom had to be applied. The robot's small golden sword with its chain remained, more often than not, in a drawer.

It had five more humans to notify. The list had been drawn up by the ship's computers, selecting names at random from the adults on board the *Vasco*. This democratic system prevailed on all ships of the Lesser Magellanic Clouds, and was the final outgrowth of the ancient system of public opinion polls. It had been common knowledge for a long time that one could learn the opinions and wishes of a great many people by questioning only a small segment of the population. The next step had been to invest power in that small segment. On board the *Vasco*, the Council met at irregular intervals, whenever there was an important problem, at the request of the Captain or of a given number of passengers. Anyone was liable to be selected, except for a handful of specialists and

249

crewmembers whose neutrality in matters of ship's governance was considered essential, such as members of the fighting squadrons.

The difficulty inherent in such a system was keeping any single person from controlling the composition of the Council. This was one of the responsibilities of the robot-ushers.

Norma Shundi looked for Gregori as she entered the Council Hall. The platform was still empty. The motion listing the charges against the Captain was displayed on a lighted board: abuse of power, etc., actions which could endanger the ship and her passengers, resulting in his immediate dismissal, if passed.

The motion was anonymous, as prescribed.

Who had dared? she wondered.

She settled herself into an armchair and looked up at the black ceiling on which could be seen the milky and irregular trail of the Magellanic Nebula. *Where are we now?* she asked herself. There were rumors than an accident had taken them way off course, but she was unconcerned. She was rather happy on the *Vasco:* she liked looking after children and she particularly liked Gregori.

She saw that Henrik, the Chief Navigator, was making an ostentatious entrance into his box. The robot-ushers finally arrived and the hall began to fill quickly. One of her colleagues, a silent, withdrawn young man, sat down next to her.

One of the ushers made a few stock pronouncements and formally declared the meeting open. Only then did Varun Shangrin sit down at the raised platform. Gregori followed close behind. There was total silence for one full minute. Norma scanned Shangrin's face, then Gregori's. The Captain towered over the Council; Gregori looked almost puny next to him.

A murmur of voices rose. Shangrin did not move. There were stacks of documents on Henrik's desk and he checked through them feverishly. From time to time, he darted an anxious look at Shangrin.

The Captain stroked his red beard.

"I want the floor," he thundered.

The murmurs slowly died down, then a sudden silence settled on the assembly.

"And I'm taking it," he said in a quieter voice. "So, some of you thought you could take advantage of the situation and demand my dismissal. Unfortunately, that will not be possible."

He looked around at his audience.

"I have just resigned."

One of the men on the Council stood up.

"We cannot, under present circumstances, accept it," he said. 'We want some details first."

"Yes, yes," came a chorus of voices. "We want to know what happened."

Gregori was smiling. *He can't be worried*, Norma said to herself. *He must have something up his sleeve.*

"What do you think happened?" Shangrin asked the man who was objecting. An usher intervened.

"The questioner must identify himself."

"Peer Nardi," said the man, "xenologist." He was tall and slender and his iron gray hair gave him an air of distinction. He spoke clearly and somewhat sharply.

"I've heard a great many rumors today," he went on. "It seems that, for some unknown reason, the ship made an enormous leap in space and that we are now in parts unknown. On the other hand, Captain, I heard your claim that a method of instantaneous teletransportation had been discovered, and that you had conducted an experiment. I confess I find it hard to believe in such a discovery. I don't like nebulous claims either. What are you keeping from us?"

Another man got up. Norma knew him by sight. He lived in the same section as she did, and often seemed to watch her admiringly.

"Jal Derin," he said, "metrologist. My field is precision instruments. I've noticed certain aberrations. I tried to get in touch with the physics section of navigation to find out whether something similar had been observed, but I couldn't get through. This is an outrage."

He looked put out.

Henrik began to stir behind his table.

"I had orders," he said.

"Orders from whom?"

"The Captain."

"Have you any idea where we are?"

Henrik hesitated.

"Yes, but it's so fantastic that—"

"I order you to keep quiet," shouted Shangrin, standing and looking menacing. He gave the impression of intending to strangle Henrik if the latter spoke.

"You have no right!" shouted someone.

"Yes! Yes!" said the crowd.

Shangrin ignored the shouts.

"Is that all?" he asked.

"No," said a woman. "Dora Norte, biologist. There is a rumor that our trip will last at least ten more years, possibly more, before we get back to the Lesser Magellanics. Is that true?"

"I don't know, ma'am," Shangrin replied in a voice that had suddenly become honeyed. "Personally, I should be happy to travel in your company for another ten years."

There was laughter, quickly smothered. *He's clowning*, Norma said to herself. *Is that his only trump, to gain time by playing to the gallery?*

"I protest the silencing of Henrik," Jal Derin said.

"Objection overruled," a robot-usher said calmly.

"Henrik can speak later for as long as he wants," thundered Shangrin. "But he'll have to wait his turn. Right now, I'm going to tell you what happened."

Silence followed. The two men and the woman sat down again.

"It happened at 7:38 p.m.," the huge man began. "Without any warning, the sky changed. Anyone looking at a screen could see this…"

On the screen behind him, the text of the motion against him vanished and space, as it was now visible from the fore of the *Vasco,* came on.

"We were lost. I didn't recognize a single one of the visible constellations. I had to give Navigation time to try to establish our position. I wanted to avoid a panic. I forbade all communication between Navigation and the rest of the ship. I announced that I was fully in control." He took a deep breath. "It wasn't true."

He paused, but no one spoke. His trump card was the unvarnished truth.

"I thought that we could speedily determine the causes of the phenomenon and that we could then sort things out, but it proved impossible."

Voices rose again.

"Resign! Resign!"

"I have."

The robot-ushers flitted about the hall to reestablish silence.

"I studied those stars carefully," said Shangrin. "And an idea came to me. I asked Henrik, in Navigation, to try an experiment."

Henrik stood up.

"It's fantastic," he said. "With the help of the computers, I—"

Shangrin interrupted.

"Show us the map of the sky I asked you to make up."

"But…"

"Go on. You can talk later."

A screen which had been blank until then was lit up above the one that showed the present view. Stars shone in a blank sky. A quick comparison was possible. There were great differences, but the general disposition of the constellations was the same. In the chart below a few luminous points showed as novae which were missing from the one above.

"This map," said Shangrin pointing to the original, lower screen, "shows a section of the sky actually around us now."

He gave a signal and a third screen at the top of the rail was lit up.

"This one shows the *Vasco's* horizon before the phenomenon."

His voice became dramatic. He raised his head and stared at the members of the Council.

"The middle map is the result of Henrik's labors. It is something quite special. It represents the same region of the sky as the one above, but with one difference. It shows the state of that region of the sky as it was *200 million years ago!*"

He gave a crushing smile.

"As a matter of fact, a little more: between 215 and 230 million years, to be precise. Your turn, Henrik."

Henrik shuffled his papers frantically. His bald pate reflected the light. His agitation was caused more by the discovery than by fear.

"The similarity between this chart and the portion of the sky actually before us is striking. There are numerous details missing which correspond to cataclysms that left no trace. But, in general, the constellations correspond."

"Which means," said Shangrin, "that we have not traveled in space but in time—a leap of 200 million years into the past. We are still headed toward the Lesser Magellanic Cloud, but it now looks the way it did long before it was settled by man. In fact, the way it looked 299 million years ago. We've jumped squarely into the past."

"Dear God!" a woman's voice whispered.

"We'll never see home again. You must get that firmly in your minds before you come to any decision." He added quickly, "The meeting is recessed for 20 minutes. The members of the Council may not communicate with anyone else on board during the recess."

He turned on his heel and left the hall. Gregori followed. Voices rose but fell almost at once, as small groups quietly started to discuss what Shangrin had told them.

This can't be happening; it's incredible, thought Norma as she headed toward the corridor. The ship seemed so real, so calm. Nothing had changed. There were a few lights in the sky that had barely moved. Two hundred million years! She didn't feel one second younger. The stars said that the universe which contained them was 200 million years younger than the one in which they had been born—surely the stars were lying. She stopped at the threshold of the Captain's office. Gregori's back was turned to her. He was sitting in front of a screen that showed a picture of the sky. There were seven luminous dots slowly moving amid the stars. She moved up silently and placed her hands on Gregori's shoulders.

He flicked off the light on the screen.

"Norma," he said without looking around. "He's next door," he added with a flick of the head towards the control room.

"That was quite a performance he gave. You, too," she said.

"I didn't say anything."

"That doesn't matter. You seemed so sure of yourself."

"It was just an illusion."

"They won't dismiss him, will they?"

"I don't know."

He got up and took her in his arms, but his mind was elsewhere.

"You shouldn't have come," he said.

"I know, but I had to tell you that it makes no difference to me if I never see Suni or Lorne or any of our other planets again. As long as you're here, I don't care."

"We can't live on this ship forever. We'll have to land somewhere."

"And there is no human being anywhere in the universe except us? I don't care."

"That's not what I meant. Anyway…"

"Anyway?"

"Nothing. You'll find out later."

She didn't insist. She snuggled closer to him, but he gently pushed her away.

"Not now."

Disappointed, she pulled back.

"Will he actually resign? I really hope so—then you would be free."

"You're crazy," he said. "Anyway, I don't know what he's going to do. No one ever knows what he's thinking, but, no, I think he likes power too much to resign."

"He's playing with them," she said. "I'd like him to be dismissed, but at the same time, I'd like to see him succeed."

"He knows how to manipulate people, all right," he admitted, "but it's a close thing."

"Are things as bad as he says?"

"Worse."

"I don't believe it."

The shrill ringing of the bell announcing the end of the recess could be heard down the corridors, echoing on the metal walls. They heard Shangrin's grumble, and then his heavy tread, behind the door.

"I'll see you tonight," she said from the hall.

The three screens behind the platform were dark. Henrik, gnome-like, was struggling with a barrage of questions. The Council members were beginning to take in the full impact of recent events. They were thinking that they, too, would soon have to field worried questions. The truth would spread like wind in the great ship. It would blow through the living quarters, the imitation parks, the recreation centers, the factories, the laboratories. It would run along waves and wires to reach the ship's periphery; the scouting craft and observation posts. It would be whispered, shouted, printed, read. In an hour or two, the ship would be nothing but a ball of worry rolling along the unknown depths of the past.

"You've had time to think about our situation," Shangrin said. "Are there any questions?"

At first, no one stirred, then a man who was almost as old and massive as Shangrin stood up.

"Arno Linz, warrant officer. Do you know the reason for the phenomenon?"

Everyone knew Linz. He had been in charge of the first shuttlecraft to land on the planet of the Runis. He was a tough, hard man, a loner with a long background of adventuring. He had discovered more new worlds than anyone else on the *Vasco*. He had also collected more scars.

"I don't know," said Shangrin. "And yet..." He stroked his beard and paused for a moment. "I've thought a great deal about it and I don't believe the catastrophe was brought on by natural causes."

"The phenomenon was induced?"

"I believe that a voyage in time constitutes a violation of physical laws. I think it was an artificial phenomenon."

There was a general hubbub.

"Induced by someone on the *Vasco?*"

"That's not what I said. I think it was an external act of aggression."

The noise doubled in volume. Norma gripped the arms of her chair so hard that her knuckles hurt. Henrik stood up and pointed an accusatory finger at Shangrin.

"Where did you get that idea?"

"I've been thinking."

"Listen, Shangrin, you've got some pretty peculiar ideas right now—accurate ones, too. Whose idea was it to ask me for a chart of the sky as it was 200 million years ago?"

"My intuition."

"I'm not questioning your intelligence, but not one of us thought of a jump into the past. It was totally illogical. It's not the sort of idea that just comes naturally. Where did you get it?"

"No comment."

Peer Nardi stood up.

"Varun Shangrin," he said, "I demand that you, as Captain of this ship, answer the question. You have no right to keep to yourself a piece of information that concerns us all. You speak of aggression. You seem to know a lot more than what you're saying about what has occurred. I accuse you of complicity with our aggressor."

Silence.

"I've spoken of the possibility of aggression," said Shangrin, "and I think it's our best bet."

"Why?"

"Because an aggressor can be forced to repair the damage he has caused."

He was so majestic, so Olympian, that Norma relaxed, leaned back in her chair and closed her eyes. Were they really at war? Wasn't it bad enough to be lost in the depths of the past?

"Frankly, I'm not sure of anything," said Shangrin. "But, right now, we may be in possession of a part of the answer."

A screen was lit up. Seven luminous dots in regular formation moved about against a background of stars.

"These are ships. The method of propulsion is primitive, probably inadequate for long interstellar runs. These ships are visible in a radius of a few light-years. And they were built some 200 million years before man had left the planet of his birth."

The Council members were riveted, perhaps with fear, or perhaps they realized the drama of that instant. Norma could not make up her mind.

"These craft were spotted less than an hour ago by Detection. They're moving toward us, but we're not their target."

He was looking at her, Norma thought. He was staring at her with those enormous, almost globular, china-blue eyes. Did he know about her and Gregori? He would have disapproved. He had high hopes for Gregori and he insisted that a leader must be alone.

"I would like to ask Zoltan, our distinguished biologist, a question," Shangrin threw out. "How old is the human species?"

The biologist got up. He was a young man with a disproportionately high forehead. He was so thin that he was ugly. His hands were never still; they ran up and down his shirt like yellowish spiders.

"About one million years."

"Could there have been one or several other species before that?"

The biologist shook his head.

"It's a moot question. During the course of their expansion throughout the universe, men have occasionally come across similar humanoid species. Give or take a few million years, they are not very much more ancient than man himself."

"And other species?"

"Officially, yes. We have found traces of life that are at least five billion years old."

"Intelligent life?"

"We don't know. I don't think so, but there may well have been civilizations more than a billion years ago."

"So we could run into a non-human civilization?"

"Yes, I think that's at least possible."

The biologist's hands betrayed his uncertainty. He blinked. He couldn't see what Shangrin was getting at.

"And a human civilization?"

"No, positively not. The most valid theory to account for the appearance of various similar species, outside of the one of common origin, postulates that forms of life succeed one another in great waves which each correspond to a well defined stage of development of the universe. We belong to the carbon cycle; all the species of this cycle appeared more or less simultaneously and generally followed the same stages of evolution. It leads to man. Perhaps beyond him."

Shangrin then addressed the members of the council.

"Zoltan is one of the finest biologists of the Lesser Magellanics, the man who developed the concept of biological eras, of vital patterns that succeed one another in the universe like waves. He has just stated that those ships cannot possibly be piloted by humans."

"I didn't say that," protested Zoltan. "I only said that it is my belief that man has not yet made his appearance in the universe."

"Very well, we'll ask the opinion of the head of the Xenology Department, Smirno."

A murmur ran through the Council. Smirno was Shangrin's most determined opponent, almost a personal enemy. Their fight over the Runis had made the *Vasco* tremble. The xenologist's box had remained empty during the first part of the meeting. The Council members had assumed his absence was caused by his animosity toward the Captain. He had just come in quietly. He seemed reserved and thoughtful.

"You've examined those ships?"

"Yes," replied the xenologist. "I know their general lines, their means of propulsion, but less than an hour's study is not enough to..."

"It's your first impressions we want."

The stars and the moving dots disappeared from the screens. An enormous alien ship appeared in their place, enlarged so greatly that the details were blurred. But its spindle shape was clear. All sorts of appendages, masts, propellers, perhaps armaments stuck out from what was the hull.

"That ship was built by humans, or at least humanoids," commented Smirno.

"Is that an opinion or merely a certainty?"

"A near certainty. There are close ties between the technology of an intelligent species and its physical aspect. All the characteristics of an object are conceived in relation to its user. I think we should have no difficulty in manning one of those ships were we to capture it"

"That ship is less than five light-years away," Shangrin interrupted. "Five light-years ago, it was cruising in these parts. Since then, it probably reached its destination. But the civilization that produced it still exists. It's waiting for us."

He pointed to the ghost ship on the screen.

"Zoltan maintains that no humans can sustain life in this era. He is probably right. Smirno says that this ship was probably built by men. We know how competent he is. At first glance, their opinions seem incompatible."

Shangrin smiled broadly. He was skillfully setting the stage.

"But there remains our voyage in time. Zoltan and Smirno could both be right—if the men in command of those ships come from the future. And if so, they control time!"

"Do you want to make contact with them?" Nardi asked.

"Certainly. As soon as we detected those ships, I stopped everything. We have given up intergalactic operations in favor of interstellar speed. In a few minutes, we'll reemerge into normal space. We're headed for the system from which those ships appear to have come. It consists of six planets, two of which seem to be habitable. If those people have the secret of time travel, we'll squeeze it out of them. If they're the ones responsible for dragging us from our time period, we'll make them regret it. If they want to be friends, we'll trade with them. If they want to be enemies, we'll wage war."

"Shangrin," said Nardi, "you're awfully sure of yourself. You know things that no one else knows, and now you are proposing to fight people who have a power we don't possess and which represents a fantastic knowledge of physics. And you still haven't answered my accusation."

"There's nothing to be said against a monstrous absurdity," bellowed Shangrin. "You're more experienced than I am, Nardi, but I have one skill you do not possess: I am a chess player. Because of this, I can recognize a superior intelligence when I meet one. It has given me, even here, an invaluable ally. I won't keep from you any longer that it is to *him* that I owe the few bits of information which have surprised you so much."

Something came in. The Council had some difficulty at first in recognizing what it was. It looked like a metallic contraption holding up something that moved—a huge orange crab set on a gigantic ball of wool.

A woman screamed. Several men got up, threateningly.

"Quiet," Shangrin shouted. "This is my ally. The Runi. I didn't know, when I surreptitiously brought him on board, how useful he would turn out to be. I ask you to give him a warmer welcome. He's our only hope for getting back to our time."

The Runi was too strange to be frightening, Norma thought. A chess-playing monster. There was really nothing human about him... How could he help them? Except that he, too, was lost in the past and wanted to get back to his own world. *Without us, he hasn't the slimmest chance of getting there,* she thought. She saw Smirno get up, but she paid little attention to what he was saying.

"In the present circumstances, we could censure Captain Shangrin as easily as we could reaffirm our faith in him. He has broken the law in every conceivable way. But it could well be that his very lack of respect for the law is now our salvation. Whatever my feelings toward him, I suggest that, in the interest of the ship, we confirm the mandate of the Captain and of his first mate."

"I object!" shouted Nardi.

But his voice was drowned out in the general uproar. The robot-ushers emitted a strident whistle that was agony to the ears. Silence was restored.

"Have you anything more to add, Captain?" asked an usher.

"Just this," Shangrin replied calmly, almost solemnly. "A piece of advice to my young and explosive opponents: the best way to win a war is to cooperate with the enemy, to win his help. That's all."

The voting procedure was brief. Eighty-seven percent of the Council members confirmed Varun Shangrin's mandate and trusted him to deal with the crisis. Shangrin, once more, had gotten his own way.

V

The most surprising thing was the normal, almost familiar, aspect of the alien ship. An abyss of time separated its builders from the Magellanites, but their ancestors had piloted ships similar to that one in the Prime-galaxy. And, according to legend, they had crossed the intergalactic void on ships scarcely more powerful during the course of incredibly long voyages.

Shangrin, ensconced in his large command chair, was carefully filling his teapot. Smirno nervously looked at the navigation charts. Gregori dictated orders to a robot.

"Eighty-seven ships in action in the stellar cluster we have just entered."

"That's not very many," said Shangrin.

"It's obviously a civilization still in its infancy," answered Smirno. He was plainly trying to cooperate, to conceal his hatred for the Captain as well as he could. "It's just starting on interstellar travel. I very much doubt that they have the knowledge of time travel."

The cluster was made up of seven stars relatively close to one another. There were less than 12 light-years between the most distant of them; the closest ones were separated by less than one light-year. All of these stars were surrounded by planets that were habitable and at various stages of their evolution. These conditions were ideal for a quick discovery of space travel. This civilization must have gradually progressed from interplanetary voyages to interstellar expeditions. If tradition was to be believed, there had been no need for a technological revolution such as humanity had required.

"I don't think they know how to travel in time," agreed Shangrin. "But I believe that they, too, were brought there and that they can probably lead us back to whoever's pulling the strings."

"Do you think they're our contemporaries, or do they come from our own future? And why should they know more than we do? They could have been projected here, just as we were."

Gregori stopped dictating.

"Maybe we've been caught in some kind of time-trap. Just imagine a powerful civilization in our distant future setting traps all over space and time. All those who fall into them are transported headlong into the past. If their technology is sufficiently advanced, they survive. They might regress for awhile, but then progress again. They start the whole process of colonizing the planets around them all over again." He indicated the mobile dots on the screen. "They may very well not know where they come from. As for us, it was a close call. Without the Runi, we would never even have known that we'd traveled through time, not space."

Shangrin objected.

"Not right away, but eventually, we would have found out. Derin, the metrologist, was on the right path. The mass of the universe—of each object—had changed. We would have discovered the truth."

"Yes, but these people might not have. On the other hand, a powerful civilization isn't necessarily going to examine in detail everything that falls into one of its traps. Just imagine a gigantic war between several galaxies. A myriad ships tumble into the moats that protect their cosmic fortresses. Who then would give a second thought to the frogs and mosquitoes in the same moats?"

"Maybe," Shangrin conceded. "But I'm more inclined to believe that these time masters keep a close eye on what they collect in their traps, and that they come and check it out every so often. I'll find a way to track them down, if it's humanly possible, and buy back our freedom."

"Providing you have something they want," the xenologist interrupted.

"I didn't have anything to sell the Runi either."

The xenologist made a face. He didn't like to be reminded of the Runi—especially when the reminder came from Shangrin. He pretended to examine the alien ship, now less than a quarter of a light-year away. It might not even have reached its destination, since this particular image had become detached from it and had traveled in space to reach them.

"The portholes are clearly visible," he said. "That means they have not yet conquered subspace. Everything fits."

He turned to Shangrin.

"What about those broadcasts we heard so much about?"

"They're going to be transmitted, any moment now, as soon as the image becomes clearer."

The xenologist stared at Shangrin. He was aware of the sarcasm that underlay the Captain's every word. You're an expert, Shangrin seemed to imply, but nothing else, and I'm making use of you.

The xenologist looked at Gregori, who was poring over star charts. He thought that ambition was written all over the first mate. Smirno's own talent lay in uncovering people's passions and their weaknesses, the cracks in their armor, their breaking points. Gregori wanted Shangrin's position, Smirno surmised, and when he attained it, he would be just like him. More cautious perhaps, less overbearing, but even craftier and, fundamentally, just as despotic. And in Shangrin's Olympian face, the xenologist could detect greed and a taste for power as well. That was the way they were. They were both powerful men, and he did not like them.

And what was his own passion? He wondered and found no answer. Science? Not even that. He enjoyed life, to be sure, but unlike most Magellanites, he did not believe in happiness. He was bored and growing old. He was tired of being carted about in the *Vasco*. He rather envied the two men because their activity seemed to satisfy them. His prime passion, he recognized, was jealousy.

261

What is a xenologist? Smirno asked himself. A fifth wheel, a man who went along on cosmic expeditions and who, nine times out of ten, served no useful purpose. That tenth time, suddenly, he was obliged to shoulder a tremendous responsibility: making contact with another form of life, with another form of intelligence. He knew a little bit about everything, Smirno acknowledged, but possessed no deep knowledge of anything, because his field was too broad. He had a mountain of files: all the data available on alien life and non-human civilizations. A xenologist was a gentleman who endlessly compiled information and, if he was lucky, would add a few nuggets of new knowledge to the mountain of data that his predecessors had already gathered.

The functions of xenologists in the data centers of the home planets were entirely different. They pored over information and built up new theories. Now that, Smirno felt, was passionately interesting and gave a new meaning to life. That was more than just making a hodgepodge of linguistics, biology, psychology, physics and intuition—plus a large dose of imagination—for the formulation of some theory about a species of which nothing positive was known.

The standing joke among space explorers was; what is xenology? Answer: a bastard art form—an opinion that was unfortunately all too often justified. A good xenologist ought to sniff out the unusual, be suspicious of abstractions, except on the home planets. There, Smirno thought again, a xenologist could really use his brain. If he ever got back to the Lesser Magellanics, perhaps he would get a research post. But he no longer hoped to return. They would never be able to cross over 200 million years; he would never come into his own.

He picked his words carefully.

"Listen, Shangrin. I agreed to work with you because of circumstances. But if by any chance, we do get back to Neo-Sirius, I'll lodge a complaint against you. I'll tell them everything you've done."

"Perfect!" said Shangrin sarcastically, sniffing the steam escaping from his teapot. "You make just about as much sense as the Runi."

"There they go, they've hooked up the telecast," Gregori exclaimed.

Smirno welcomed the diversion. He was powerless against Shangrin; the Captain, on the other hand, would never stop reminding him about the Runis. He simply would not let go.

To the right of the alien ship on the screen, they could see a blurred image crackling with flashes of lightning. It grew steadier, shimmering every now and then. A man wearing a strange uniform was speaking heatedly. He had a short black beard that outlined his thin, cruel lips. His clothes seemed to be woven of metal thread. Oddly enough, a dagger in a scarlet sheath hung from his belt.

"Barbarians," said Gregori.

"No preconceived notions," interrupted the xenologist.

"Can you understand what he's saying?"

Smirno shook his head.

"I'm not a linguist, but I think I recognize some of the roots. The sound of this language is not very different from ours. It could be a parallel form, or a more developed one."

"The semantics experts are studying the problem," Shangrin said. "I think they'll be able to start translating in a couple of hours. I just wanted your opinion."

Smirno turned angrily.

"You're trying to make me look like a fool."

"Not at all. I have a higher opinion of your capabilities than you have. You don't like me; that's your privilege. It makes things easier for me, but it's unimportant. I need your expertise. We are going to make contact with those people—tomorrow."

"You're going to board one of their ships?"

"No," replied Shangrin, staring at the golden tea in his cup. "No, I'm going to land on one of their worlds. And possibly conquer it."

Basically, thought Smirno, he hated the Captain because of his own mistake with the Runis. But knowing that did not soothe him. It did not do away with his hatred for Shangrin and his smugness any more than knowing the causes of a wound did away with the pain.

The *Vasco* dropped from the skies onto the surface of the planet. It circled several times, like a fiery star, before heading toward its objective, a vast plain near the equator. On the screens, space changed color from black to a lighter and lighter blue. The stars were extinguished, then lit up again, then disappeared once more, while the ship, in a spiraling movement, traversed day and night.

Then came the familiar excitement of seeing a new world with its continents shrouded in clouds, its high mountains covered with white lace, oceans sparkling in the sun like sheets of metal, inky black at night. There were lights of cities here and there on continents otherwise plunged in darkness. Air traffic was not very heavy and the *Vasco* paid little attention to it. Henrik, Shangrin and Gregori kept a close eye on the spherical navigation screen. It looked like a giant map unrolling evenly.

"You're taking a stupid risk," Henrik said. "Why didn't you put the ship into orbit and send out a reconnaissance shuttle? You haven't the slightest idea about their defenses."

"I want to impress them," said Shangrin. "And anyway, I do know about their weapons. They're nothing to worry about."

"Besides which, they apparently protect only their cities," observed Gregori.

"Then why have they refused to communicate with us? We've been signaling them on their own frequencies, and they've been sending rockets." Henrik was obviously nervous.

"They're at war... They might have thought it was a trap. Smirno is study-ing the photos we've taken of their cities and their plains. Has he made anything of them?"

"He's trying to get some idea of their social structure. But tell me, Shangrin, I thought he disliked you so much because of the Runi affair. How come he's helping you as though nothing had happened?"

"He hates me, all right," said Shangrin. "I know that, but it doesn't matter. He's a cool customer. He won't try anything against me in our present situation. He'll wait until we've gotten out of it."

"If I were you, I wouldn't trust him."

"Why? He's doing his job, that's all. He's the best xenologist on board, and one of the best in Lorne. He has a team of experts that I need, so I trust him. I've noticed that the people who hate me serve me better than those who admire me."

"Xandra, that planet's name is Xandra," said Gregori.

He didn't like the way the conversation was headed, but nothing ever kept Shangrin from finishing his thought.

"You don't like me either, Henrik, you'd like to be in my shoes. At your age, I had already been in command of a ship for eight years. You must dream about it. You can see yourself master of the *Vasco,* directing this metal tub be-tween those stars you know so well...."

"Come on, Varun. I've never..."

"I know. But you'll never be captain, Henrik. You're not ruthless enough. I am ten years older than you and I have twice your energy. I know how to roar, you don't. My mind is subtle; yours is only tortuous."

Henrik's bald pate became purple, a symptom of his fury. Shangrin liked to bait the officers under his command. When he could no longer rouse their anger, when they became indifferent, that would be the end for him. He would lose his hold over men and, consequently, over things. Then he would die.

Smirno's eyes, red-rimmed with fatigue, turned to the screen for the 20th time. The image was poor and the light too glaring, but if he turned it down, details would be blurred and details were what he was feverishly studying. They would provide a clue to the level of civilization of this people, of their technolo-gy, skills, perhaps even their way of thinking.

The screen showed a city, one of the planet's 100 or so, which was not re-ally very many for a civilization that was beginning to deploy itself into space. The buildings, barely visible on the screen, were crowded together inside tall white walls surmounted by massive towers. The cities were, in fact, fortresses.

This was rather peculiar, Smirno thought. The walls could in no way serve as a protection against aerial attack, yet the inhabitants of the cities were obvi-ously afraid of this possibility since they had launched primitive rockets with nuclear heads. The missiles had exploded in the upper atmosphere long before reaching the *Vasco,* unleashing huge fireworks.

Smirno had seen the rockets climbing toward the screen like a bundle of fine glittering needles at the top of a column of smoke. An invisible finger stretched out from the *Vasco* and dispersed them. They exploded in sudden inferno. The temperature reached one million degrees; the light was equal to one sun's. But there was nothing to destroy in the mesosphere of Xandra.

The cities had not sent out a second salvo. They must have realized they could not do anything to the spherical ship falling from the sky.

Plains and mountains were filing past on the screen. Smirno was surprised that the cities were still so crowded within their walls at this stage of civilization. He would have expected the people to have cultivated the surrounding land, built roads, established means of communication. But that wasn't the case: these cities looked like small autonomous islands, heavily equipped for defense against the plains and jealously guarding their independence. Was there a war going on below? Were armies being deployed in the plains, occupying fortifications, harassing the cities?

It was up to him to discover all this, and he was sure of almost no single fact. If there were indeed armies down there, they used no advanced method of communication; they had no truly modem weapons; they were not composed of units sufficiently large to be visible on the march or in combat. Could the war be taking place beyond the limits of the planet? Of the whole System? Perhaps the cities were only advance posts of an army determined to conquer Xandra? The ships Smirno had seen on the screens as luminous dots could easily have been in the midst of a battle. The *Vasco* had paid no more attention to their movements than an eagle does to a swarm of flies. An empire might be in the process of being created or undone; the most frightful anarchy could be reigning on Xandra and in all surrounding space and Smirno know nothing about it. He was in the position of a man studying the activity of an ant hill. He understood nothing.

Decoded messages piled up on his desk, but they were not enlightening. The meaning of most of them was too limited to be of interest to him—they referred to people and events he knew nothing about. There was some question of empire, however, or something of the sort, and without exactly knowing why, Smirno had a feeling, from reading the messages, that it was threatened.

The ship stopped 20 meters from the ground in hissing steam, shrieking wind and a howling storm. It floated like a perfect sphere, a polished mountain more than a kilometer high. It was beautiful and strange. No one had ever seen anything like it on Xandra. It was a miracle.

Shangrin burst out laughing.

"We're there. We're going to get a closer look at whoever wanted to tickle us with their atom bombs."

Smirno droned on: "It looks as if a state of war, at least a latent one, exists between the inhabitants of the plains and those of the cities. I'm not a historian, but the unusually massive fortifications of the cities tend to indicate that their technological superiority does not guarantee them control of the planet. This theory needs—"

"Easy does it," Gregori ordered, "Put down the gliders of groups seven and nine. Not so fast. Easy. Don't break anything. Give them room. How many times must I tell you not to shut off the force field all at once?"

"Radar shows a cavalry group in operation, north-northeast, less than 100 kilometers away. It seems to be headed in this direction."

"I'm not a biologist," Smirno continued, "but from the looks of the flora and fauna, we can deduce that a truly agricultural society has been in existence on this world only since—"

"Everyone on alert, Plan C. No one is to leave the ship under any pretest whatsoever, except the crews who have their orders. Open fire only in defense. Gliders will be armed as usual."

"Courage, my boys," shouted Shangrin. "Gold, loot, trade. You won't be sorry you came."

The *Vasco* was like a hive. Every member of the crew was at his post. Navigators scanned the sky. Biologists and geophysicists were trying to determine in what way Xandra differed from a type-T world. Message Control intercepted transmissions which cryptoanalysts decoded. The men of the defense groups were getting armed.

Shangrin put on his blue dress uniform. His red beard, against the dark background of his outfit, gleamed almost as brightly as the large medallion hanging from a chain on his chest. His head and hands were uncovered: he hated protective devices that shielded him from reality, suppressed smells, gusts of wind and the beat of the sun.

The great hatches on the *Vasco's* underbelly opened up and the gliders were let down on the ground. Each of the vast oblong skiffs flew a flag with the Lesser Magellanic coat of arms. The Captain's flew his colors, crimson and black.

He filed past the men in formation. Although this was a frequent occurrence, the Magellanites always celebrated their arrival on a new planet with a certain pomp. They saluted him with hurrahs. He had lost none of his popularity with them—he probably never would. Someday, though, he would leave their world and take his place among their legends.

VI

Lo Alabulo saw the first gliders. He was on scout duty, riding his hexapod unicorn, a bow in his right hand, a vronn resting on the leather pad on his left shoulder. The chitinous wings of the vronn vibrated against his bearded cheek, making the air resound with a shrill death chant.

He closed his eyes halfway in order to see more clearly the shadows which raced over the plain at incredible speeds. They floated in the air. They flew; like vronns, although they had no wings—and they were flying straight at him. There were seven of them.

Lo Alabulo pulled in the reins suddenly. His mount reared, turned about as he spurred him on, bolted away. The vronn on Lo Alabulo's shoulder unfurled his wings and steadied himself against the wind of their course.

"Foreigners," Lo shouted to the Sar. The Sar raised his lance in combat position. The foreigners had arrived in that bail of fire from the sky. The Sar looked upon everything that came from the sky as being inimical except, of course, the ships that mysteriously seemed to obey the Ulsar. They brought arms to fight against the cities. But those ships were as pointed as arrows and they gave out signals in the sky before landing. These foreigners had made no such signals. They were probably allies of the city dwellers and were, no doubt, coming to their rescue. But the fearsome weapons lent to the Ulsar by his allies would take care of them. The Sar was sure of it. He had already destroyed several of the cities' great ships which had either accidently fallen on his land or which had, with foolhardy temerity, come to challenge him.

The speed of the approaching vessels worried the Sar. The hexapods' strength lay in their mobility but, compared to these skiffs, their speed was tortoise-like. The aircraft seemed to be animated by a frightful wind which made the grass bow down.

The Sar gave the order to attack. His horsemen dispersed and Lo Alabulo resumed his scouting post. The vronn, sharing his master's excitement, made his wings vibrate harder. The Sar, in his chariot, smiled as he fingered solar grenades capable of melting rock and annihilating any enemy.

The gliders stopped three arrow-lengths from Lo. He had expected them to dive-bomb him so he had drawn his bow, keeping the arrow in his teeth, ready to release the vronn. When he saw the men in the skiffs, he shouted insults at them. He made his hexapod rear and pivot to show them he was not afraid, that he was ready to sacrifice his life. The gods had ordered the destruction of the demons who ruled the cities; this was the price the plains people had to pay for their freedom.

He released the vronn. The insect shot out like an arrow, catapulted by Lo's powerful wrist. It climbed high and circled twice. Then, having selected its prey, a red giant in the front of the biggest skiff, it dived down, wings immobile, legs folded under, fang ready to dart its poison.

The vronn's sting was fatal. It injected almost a quarter of a liter of a poison so strong that the game it killed was inedible. Vronns were used exclusively in warfare.

The vronn stopped suddenly in mid-flight and plummeted to the ground. Someone from the skiff had killed it with an invisible weapon.

Lo was overcome with anger and grief. The vronn had been like a brother to him. It had saved his life in many a battle. Lo Alabulo gave a bloodcurdling shout and spurred his mount to a gallop, releasing an arrow as he rode. He had the satisfaction of seeing a man in one of the skiffs collapse. He turned around and saw the Sar following with his men. A volley of arrows sailed over his head as he reloaded his bow.

A volley of fire hit him full in the chest, raised him from his mount and threw him on the ground. He heard the hexapod scream and saw it writhe in the flames. Then pain was joined to anger and grief and Lo Alabulo, his bow broken, rested with his gods.

"Barbarians," said Smirno. "They're going to attack."

"Not yet," answered Shangrin. "I know how to deal with them. Don't move."

The barbarian closest to them was executing a senseless maneuver with his mount. Suddenly, he stretched out his arm and something flew off his shoulder. They could not quite make out what it was.

"A rocket, some mechanical contraption?"

They let the thing come closer.

"An insect," said Gregori. "A giant insect."

Smirno agreed.

"They must train them for hunting. I've seen men on other planets use birds in the same way. I'm sure that a stinger that size can kill a man."

Gregori pulled out his weapon and shot. The giant insect was felled, hitting the ground with a dull thud.

Almost immediately, they heard a hissing sound. They ducked instinctively. Behind them, one of the men cried out and fell.

"An arrow," someone said.

"He's dead."

"Look out," yelled Gregori.

Defense fields were instantly drawn and tidily blocked off the volley of arrows. Only the first ones had penetrated to the gliders, wounding and killing a few men.

The Sar, from the top of his chariot, saw with astonishment the arrows of his warriors flattened against an invisible barrier. He did not believe in the gods, but he knew that men from space had strange powers. He smiled. Everything gave way before the solar grenades. He singled one out, patted it, pulled the pin, then hurled it.

Gregori tried to guess the intentions of the motionless horsemen. Only the archer had been shot and brought down before Shangrin gave the order not to retaliate.

Night was drawing near. On the horizon, the endless stretch of grass was becoming lavender-tinted. The soil was spongy, which explained the scarcity of trees.

"They surely don't know how to travel in time," Gregori said.

Shangrin turned toward him.

"You think so? They look straight out of the past."

"It's going to be difficult to approach them now that there have been casualties."

"I know," Shangrin answered curtly. "What are our losses?"

"Four dead, seven wounded."

"They were brave men," Shangrin said.

"If we had taken more precautions, they would still be."

Shangrin shot him a surprised look.

"You don't trust me anymore?"

"That's not it; only those deaths were unnecessary."

"One can never take all possible precautions. Whoever tries to protect himself all the time gets nowhere. Was I less exposed than those men?"

"No," admitted Gregori.

He saw a shining sphere rise above a war chariot drawn by two animals that certainly seemed to have six legs. It did not hesitate the way the insect had, but aimed straight for its goal.

"Screen," said Shangrin. "An atomic grenade."

He was not sure the protective screen would hold so he pushed aside a gunner and grabbed the controls of a heavy weapon. The cannon spat out a tongue of fire to meet the grenade. Other shots framed it.

It exploded. The sky became white, the color of overheated metal. The protection field attenuated the wave of the shock and deflected it back toward the barbarians.

The Sar was hurled from his chariot. The shock had thrown the animals and perhaps killed them. The chariot had lost its wheels. It was a miracle that he himself had not been killed.

He got up painfully, drew his small sword and looked about him. Some of his men were fleeing toward the north. Others were trying to keep their mounts from running away with them. Others still had broken a limb or so in their fall and were groaning.

It was a disaster. The grenade had exploded much too soon. Usually it didn't explode until it had hit its objective, but the invaders' fingers of fire had touched it and its mysterious mechanism had gone off.

The Sar blamed himself for having allowed Lo Alabulo to act. He could perhaps have made an alliance with the foreigners and thus brought credit on himself with his clan. He might even have lowered the credit of the Ulsar, who had become insufferable since his allies from other worlds had taken him into space—he now claimed that the gods had spoken to him.

And now the fingers of fire were going to touch him, the Sar. The gliders approached slowly, floating in the air like boats upon water. The Sar raised his sword to fight. The skiffs could run him over, but he would die with his sword in his hand.

A huge voice burst over him. It spoke the language of the cities, a language quite similar to that of the plains people except for a different accent. Long ago, that shade of difference had indicated caste and it could still anger the Ulsar.

But the voice spoke of peace. It praised the courage of the plains people and asked for an alliance with them; it promised riches.

Surprised, the Sar stopped. Then he looked at his sword and he began to laugh.

Shangrin's voice thundered and rolled in the wind with the majesty of the sea. It swelled and climbed skyward, then became soft and persuasive and slipped through the grasses. It said glorious, imperious, threatening, friendly things.

"We are merchants," Shangrin said. "There are many worlds in the sky and we go from one to another, and everywhere, always, we bring happiness and wealth. We come from powerful worlds and we control powerful forces, but we are peaceful men. We do not want to take either your possessions or your lives."

The Sar hesitated. This could be a pack of lies, but these men could already have struck him down if they had wanted to. He was wearing amulets, but he did not believe in their efficacy. Lo Alabulo had also worn some and he was now dead. The Ulsar did not wear any and he was feared and respected. In any event, the Sar was now at their mercy.

He threw down his sword and walked on the grass toward the skiffs. Then the largest of them landed and a door opened, like an eye in its side. A large man with a red beard came down four metal steps.

He too walked in the grass toward the Sar and put out his hand.

The Sar couldn't believe his eyes. Surely that enormous sphere come down from the sky was a star, but it was cold to the touch. He had looked for a long time at the stream of men pouring out of it, then being swallowed up again, before making up his mind to set foot inside. The red-bearded man urged him on. In the end, he had given in. He wanted to know what the inside of a star was like.

And he had seen gold, weapons, grenades more powerful than those of the pirates. He had seen the men from the star look after their wounded companions and bring some back to life—even those he would have ordered finished off.

He had been questioned.

He had distrusted them. Why did they want to know if his group was alone, the location of his camp, who was the Ulsar, with whom they were at war, if other men regularly came from space?

He had been plied with gold. A stronger sword than the one he had left in the grass had been hung by his side. He had been given a pistol like the ones the men from the star carried, an odd sort of weapon which induced sleep rather than death.

He had burst out laughing and, during the banquet, he had answered all their questions.

No, he was not alone. His group was part of a large army under the command of the Ulsar. The Sar was one of his lieutenants. He thought the Ulsar was the commander-in-chief of the planet. Yes, he was a hard, pitiless man, but he was fair. He was trying to wipe the cities off the face of the planet. It was a necessary war. Once upon a time, the cities had enslaved the plains people.

Long ago?

The Sar dug back in his memory. It was before he was born. There were stories old warriors knew, and the Ulsar had told them to his troops to urge them on. In olden times, the Sar wasn't sure when, people had been happy on Xandra. They had cities and cultivated the land, but hunting was their chief occupation.

Then men had come down from the sky, another breed. They were not numerous, but nothing could stand against their weapons. They had forced the inhabitants of Xandra to build cities for them and serve them.

This had gone on for a long time. Rebellions had broken out but they had always been suppressed. As the years went by, though, the people in the cities had become careless. They took in slaves and sometimes even raised them to their level.

Weapons had been stolen. A new rebellion had broken out and almost succeeded. The army of the first Ulsar captured three cities and razed them to the ground. The Ulsar was exceedingly able: it was said that the gods had helped him. He had spared some interplanetary spaceships and had forced their former captains to pilot them for him, venturing out toward the stars. He had never returned from his last trip, but it was said that some of his ships had become pirates and merchants. It was these ships which supplied arms to the present Ulsar, who had entered into strange and terrible alliances in the countries of the suns. The Ulsar even said that, in other worlds, there was the same sort of struggle as on Xandra, and that, someday soon, all the former slaves would unite and hunt down their oppressors to the ends of the universe.

"What do you think about all this, Smirno?" asked Shangrin.

The xenologist was looking at a screen on which bright lights shone, some steadily, some intermittently: city and airplane lights.

"We'll have to meet that Ulsar," he said. "The Sar is only a warrior. The other seems to be a man of stature, a statesman."

Shangrin nodded.

"I'm going to see the Ulsar; I'm going to propose an alliance."

"I doubt if he knows anything about our problem. The arms suppliers might, but it's a long way from interplanetary navigation and nuclear grenades to travel in time. Why not get in touch with the city people instead?"

Shangrin made a face.

"They know less than the Ulsar. They are losing momentum and, besides, I don't like them. Have you seen the snapshots that the scouts brought back?"

"No," said Smirno.

Silently, Gregori handed them to the xenologist.

They had been taken with a powerful telephoto lens. They showed part of a thick wall. At the foot of the wall there were pyramids of human skulls.

Smirno shuddered.

"Genghis Khan," he said. "Hitler. Tarn."

"I don't know those names," said Shangrin, "but I can tell a genocide when I see one."

"They're barbarians," said Gregori.

Smirno shook his head.

"No, they're not barbarians. They're worse—they're civilized. They erect those pyramids for the same reason we dress up a scarecrow. They either despise or insanely hate their former slaves. Or both."

"Do you want to know what I think?" asked Gregori. "Xandra was settled in population waves. A long time ago, perhaps several thousand years, a giant spaceship, or a fleet of spaceships, landed on this world, possibly after having been transported back in time the way we were. The passengers survived, settled down and started off almost from scratch. Almost. You've noticed that the Sar had a certain familiarity with astronomy and that he knows something about nuclear explosives."

"His people may have learned those things in the cities."

"Maybe, but I don't think so. I think, rather, that they form part of the oral tradition of the plains people and that they are now becoming useful once more. But to come back to my theory: a long time after this first catastrophe, a second wave of immigrants settled on this world. They, too, must have come from the future, probably accidentally and with no hope of return—they would not indulge in an uncertain war otherwise. But they preserved their technology. And they found, in the very presence of the first wave of settlers, the means of preserving it: slave labor to build cities and forge arms. All they needed to do was help themselves. Then they took on the mentality of their slaves and decadence set in."

Shangrin put his hands on Gregori's shoulders.

"Good for you. Someday, if you drink tea, you'll be as clever as I am. But you missed the most important point."

"What's that?"

"We're the third wave."

Stunned, Gregori looked at Smirno, then back again at Shangrin. He noticed that over his usual clothes, Shangrin was wearing a tunic woven of fine red metal. *What an odd idea*, he thought.

"What are you going to do now?" asked Smirno.

"I've told you. Enter into an alliance with the Ulsar and take all the cities one by one. Conquer the entire planet."

"And then what? That won't give us the key to time travel."

"Then there's space. You've left out a second point in your analysis, Gregori."

"The other worlds," said Smirno.

"Precisely. There are two empires at war, Gregori. One is rising from its ashes and shaking off the yoke of the second one which had destroyed it. But within the memory of the one or the other, behind the one or the other, there surely lies the secret we are after. We'll buy it, or we'll snatch it."

"Two empires," said Gregori.

"No, at least three," Shangrin corrected. "Two empires plus the Magellanites."

VII

He took a deep breath, but the air of the imitation park did not have that odor of earth and water, of wind and night, which pervaded the atmosphere of Xandra. The perspective was also all wrong: the sky was too low; there was no depth. Before, during the long trip, Gregori used to come into the imitation park to try to establish contact with nature, to get a feeling of space. After coming out of a narrow stateroom and a rectilinear corridor, the imitation park had given him the feeling of open space.

He saw Norma among the children. She liked looking after them. After they had returned to Lorne, perhaps he would marry her, but he hadn't the courage to mention it until the crisis was over. He thought about the children. What would happen to them if the *Vasco* did not manage to get back across those 200 million years? How many generations would it take before they reverted to a barbaric state?

She caught sight of him and ran toward him. He held her in his arms and kissed her.

"Not in front of the children," she said.

He began to laugh.

"When can we go out, Gregori? I'll be so happy to be in the open air again. I'd like them to know what a real planet is like."

"Not now. The planet is unsafe. Its inhabitants are barbarians."

"So I heard. But are you going?"

"I don't have any choice. Anyway, they're not too dangerous."

"What is *he* going to do?"

"The Captain? He wants start a war."

She shot him a horrified look.

"He wants to attack the cities—he thinks he'll find the beginning of a solution to our problem there. The inhabitants refuse to communicate with us."

She pulled away, looking at the children.

"He put on quite a performance at the Council meeting," she said, "but he frightens me. I don't like his laugh. And why did he drag in that creature?"

"The Runi? I helped bring him on board the *Vasco!*"

"Why?"

"Because Shangrin wanted it. And you just don't argue when he gives an order."

"But it was illegal!"

"Not for him. And the Runi could have meant a huge profit."

"Gregori! How can you balance a profit, no matter how sizable, against the safety of the entire ship?"

"The Runi is no threat to the ship," he said. "On the contrary, he may be our only hope of salvation."

She did not pursue the point, but looked at him with her light blue eyes, appearing surprisingly young and determined. He knew she was not a scientist, but that was not what he was looking for.

"And this war?" she asked. "Has he any right to start it?"

"What does it matter? The laws that would forbid it won't come into existence for another 200 million years."

"But it matters to me. Are you going to go along with his plan?"

"I think so. There's no alternative, and Shangrin's a brilliant commander."

"I'm going to try to stop you, Gregori, if you go too far. All this means more casualties, more suffering."

He was unable to repress a smile. The girl's indignation was characteristic of that of all the women of the Lesser Magellanics: they were self-assured, representing order, security and the rule of law; they acted as surer brakes to the daring of their men than an army of judges or policemen. Nonetheless, they brought out the best in the men, as they intuitively fought for their children, for the future of the race, against blind greed.

Shangrin and Norma... The struggle seemed uneven, but it wasn't. Maybe someday, some woman might be able to sway the old loner who had triumphed over space and alien races, avoided the ambushes of strange new worlds and made questionable deals—and who had now taken on the very Masters of Time.

It took them four days to reach the Ulsar's camp. The gliders could have gone across the grassy plains and reached the foothills of the mountains in a few hours, but Shangrin preferred to go at the slow pace of his allies' mounts. He felt it would be a poor idea to show off his power. Furthermore, he was flattering the Sar.

The horsemen were in front. Shangrin and the Sar rode in the middle. The Captain was mounted on the beast of a dead warrior; he wore his red metal tunic and carried a fine steel sword, looking as though he had, at last, found his place in the scheme of things. One might have guessed that he had spent his life traveling over the great plains, sword in hand, red beard flying in the wind. The Sar had abandoned his wrecked chariot and refused Shangrin's offer to have a new one built for him. He had, however, accepted the tungsten sword which the foreigners had forged for him in atomic fire.

The gliders followed, carrying Shangrin's men, Gregori, Smirno, and two combat groups. It was a delegation of 30 men. They all wore mail tunics and swords, but they had more deadly weapons in their pockets. Shangrin trusted no one absolutely.

They rode for four days without Shangrin's showing any signs of fatigue. The Sar was impressed that the use of machinery had in no way impaired the strength of these foreigners as it had that of the city dwellers. For hours on end, the Sar talked with Shangrin and he conceived tremendous respect for the powerful civilization which had produced such a man. He told himself that he had finally met a man whose personality was stronger than the Ulsar's. Had Shangrin asked him to follow him into space, he would unhesitatingly have done so.

They went northward on a complicated itinerary through a marshy labyrinth. For one whole day, the animals were chest-high in water; floating grass got caught on the riders' spurs, creating a green wake. Then the ground hardened and they crossed narrow gaps dug by violent winds thousands of years earlier, when great glaciers had overrun the plateau. Around noon of the fourth day, they reached the rocky hills. It was hot and dry, and the blue thickets were teeming with game. They made a wide detour to avoid a nest of wild vronns. They spotted it because the hill was too symmetrical; one could guess, despite the distance, that it consisted of chambers, corridors, and wells. It was a spongy mixture of rocks, soil and sand piled up by the saliva of the killer insects in chitinous armor.

The thin smoke of fires in the Ulsar's camp made stripes in an evening sky whose smooth purity was like fine silk or polished metal. Banners bearing the Ulsar's monogram floated at the top of tall poles. A lookout struck a gong and blew into a huge bullhorn. All at once, everything went into motion. The weapons of the warriors glistened above the camouflage. The Sar gave an arm signal and, in response, a standard in his colors was hoisted up a pole. Double wooden doors opened and a cloud of children ran toward the newcomers.

Shangrin signaled to the glider pilots to cut their engines. Studying the Ulsar's city through field glasses, Gregori saw palisades covered with vegetation, concealing interior arrangements. The flags lent a military aspect to the place, but the city still looked more like a temporary camp than a settlement. The Ulsar's supporters must be semi-nomads. There had once existed warlike civilizations of that sort in the dim recesses of the history of humanity. By and large, they had left unpleasant memories behind.

Gregori said to himself that perhaps this was the result of prejudice. History had always been engraved on stone or written on paper by city people who had no sympathy for nomads. From an objective point of view, cities were surely no more civilized, nor less cruel, even if their technology was superior. In this world, however, they did seem to be more savage, which probably stemmed from the numerical inferiority of their inhabitants.

Shangrin, riding abreast the Sar, went into the camp. He saw a sort of crater, with perfectly aligned tents filling the bottom. The limits of the camp were marked off by other tents and wooden structures. It must have been huge, for a corral near the crater walls seemed to hold myriad hexapods. Beyond it, the crater looked even deeper. Perhaps there were deep caves or gullies.

A man dressed in especially bright colors was watching their approach from the midst of a small group of warriors. The Sar jumped off his mount and prostrated himself before him. Shangrin decided it must be the Ulsar.

He betrayed none of the disappointment he felt. He had expected a large man, confident of his strength, prepared to challenge him to a fight, verbally or physically, ready to annihilate him with a word or a blow.

The Ulsar was a small, brown man with bright, nervous eyes. He carried no weapons. A cuff from one of the giants around him could have felled him. He must have been outstandingly smart to wield so much authority over a people for whom brute force had lost none of its power. He wasn't even of the same race as the warriors around him. He might be an extraordinary case of atavism, Shangrin considered, or he might have come from a city. Perhaps he had switched sides, leaving behind the race of conquerors. History had often seen liberators recruited from the ranks of the oppressors.

"Greetings," said Shangrin without dismounting.

The Ulsar smiled. It was neither a disquieting nor disagreeable smile. It was just an intelligent, almost friendly one.

"Welcome," he said.

Two guards helped Shangrin dismount.

"I come from up there," he said, pointing emphatically to the sky.

"From the stars," said the Ulsar.

"Yes," said Shangrin, somewhat taken aback.

He signaled to his two escorts, who jumped down from their hexapods and handed him some boxes.

"Your Sar told me of your power," Shangrin said. "We are merchants. We want to do business in a peaceful way with this land. We want to be your friends."

Shangrin spoke clearly and politely, with no trace of obsequiousness. He opened the boxes.

But the Ulsar did not put out his hand. He said coldly, "Gifts establish friendships between equals. Are you the leader of your people?"

"I am the leader of my people," Shangrin said quickly. "We are many. We live in a ship that has been traveling through space. The Sar has seen it and can describe it."

"I believe you."

Shangrin gave the boxes back to his men. The Ulsar was certainly the first chieftain who did not throw himself on the gifts offered to him: the Ulsar was no barbarian. Shangrin wished that Smirno were there, but the xenologist had remained with Gregori.

"I'll see you tonight," said the Ulsar. "You'll sleep in my camp."

He stopped. His bright black eyes stared deeply into Shangrin's and, it seemed to the Magellanite, somewhat sardonically.

"Why don't you tell those of your men who stayed outside to bring in their machines? They can easily park them in here. Unless they're afraid of hexapods and children?"

Shangrin showed signs of irritation.

"The gate is too narrow."

"I've taken a close look at those contraptions," said the Ulsar, blinking. "I'm sure they can fly over the walls. After all, they went through space, between worlds."

"I think they can," said Shangrin, "but we did not come down from the stars in these..."

"No," said the Ulsar. "No. You came in that large spherical ship."

Shangrin bit his lip. Was the Ulsar telepathic? Was that his hold over his men? If he could read Shangrin's mind, that was only the beginning of complications...

"I'll send one of my men with a message," Shang capitulated.

"Oh," said the Ulsar, "I think you've forgotten the little gadgets for communication at a distance which men from the stars always carry."

"True," said Shangrin.

He put his hand up to his mouth and whispered a few orders to Gregori. He did not want to give the Ulsar the impression that their entire conversation had been bugged, if the Ulsar did not know it.

"We'll talk some more tonight," said the Ulsar. "The Sar will show you to your tents."

He turned on his heel and left. But after taking a few steps, he stopped and looked over his shoulder.

"You may keep all the arms you want. I trust you. I want you to feel that you are my guests."

Shangrin turned to his men with a helpless look. The shadows cast by the great gliders passed silently by, then the sky cleared and the wind they had made died down. They came down gently in the square outlined by the tents.

This was going to be tough, thought Shangrin. And if it was a trap, they were certainly in it.

The tents were luxuriously appointed. Crystal decanters containing precious liquors were placed on fine tables made of rare wood. The floors were covered with furs; weapons hung from bone stands; leather saddle-shaped chairs formed a circle around an engraved copper hearth.

Shangrin, Gregori and Smirno were thoughtfully warming their hands in front of the fire.

"His manners are those of a barbarian, but he's too knowledgeable," said Smirno.

"He's traveled through space," Gregori reminded them.

"What I'd like to know," said Shangrin, stroking his beard, "is where he really comes from."

There was a teapot warming by the fire. Shangrin was keeping a careful eye on the boiling of the water. He picked up the teapot and threw in a pinch of aromatic herbs.

"I don't believe it's a trap," Gregori said. "He seems to be sizing up our strength pretty accurately. He knows that, even if he were to wipe us out, here, he would still have to contend with the ship—which is just about indestructible, at least to him, and capable of destroying the entire planet."

Smirno agreed. "He knows he's vulnerable; that's why he was so haughty. He wants us to know he's not afraid of us. I think that's how he became the Ulsar. I wouldn't put a penny on him in a fight against one of his warriors."

Shangrin was sniffing his tea.

"Who knows? I looked him over closely. He gives every appearance of being frail, but I'll bet he's strong, and only about 40 years old. If he knows how to fight, if he has some knowledge of human anatomy and the nervous system, he can kill an opponent twice his size. Barbarians usually don't know how to fight. You have to know what's under the skin to fight properly."

"Where could he have learned?"

"We keep coming back to the same question: Where does he come from? But you're right. He was suspicious and he wanted to show that he was not to be outmaneuvered, that I couldn't count on him for the conquest of the cities."

"He wanted it made clear from the start that he is your equal. The initial impression was that he was doing you a favor, but actually, he was making it plain that he was your equal, that a scruffy leader of a small army of barbarians was as good as a space captain."

"He's hardly a scruffy leader," said Shangrin with an ambiguous smile. "I was expecting a sort of martial lightning bolt, with quick reactions, and I find a crafty diplomat. I wonder how he would do at chess?"

"Why not teach him?" asked Smirno. "It would be an excellent ground for understanding."

"Or for misunderstanding. No, I might be beaten. It's the Runi I'd like to see here. His advice would be valuable—he's a profound thinker."

"About the physical universe, perhaps," said Smirno. "But about humanity…"

"He's a chess player. And humans are the pieces on the chessboard of the universe."

"His presence might irritate or even frighten the Ulsar," said Gregori.

"Do you think so?" Shangrin asked sardonically, sipping his tea. "I rather think he is the Runi's blood brother."

The Ulsar's dinner went off in the best barbarian tradition, Smirno thought. It was almost too ostentatious. Serfs had set up tables under a huge tent. The

Ulsar's table, to which the three Magellanites were escorted, dominated the banquet hall from a dais. The Ulsar had not yet arrived. His chieftains, in brightly striped, rustling silk tunics, their embossed and jeweled daggers suspended unsheathed from their necks by leather thongs, had sat down in the midst of great noise. They had brought with them heavy pewter tankards, and the serfs—probably captured in raids on the cities—filled them with a light wine.

There was a sudden hush as the Ulsar came in. Slaves, bending under the weight of great coffers, followed him. When he had settled himself in a wooden chair draped with spotted furs, the slaves opened the coffers and set the table with gold plates. On a tripod table at the foot of the dais Shangrin's gifts were displayed: an enormous, finely cut diamond which had lain for a long time in the veins of an asteroid, a set of fine weapons and a mysterious box, set with stones, which Shangrin directed be brought to him. He pushed a spring and the box played sweet music. The Ulsar's barons were filled with wonder, and even he seemed overwhelmed. He filled his goblet, toasted his guest and emptied the remains into a brazier, invoking the gods as he did so.

Was this a trick? wondered Smirno, watching his host clap his hands as course succeeded course. The Ulsar devoured a haunch of venison, grabbing it with both hands. He issued orders and dancing girls appeared. Was all of this nothing but a performance—this vulgar display of barbaric luxury, this excess of everything: colors, sounds, foods, wines, primitive and exciting dances? A girl came and drank from Smirno's cup. He did not doubt her intentions; she was trying to please him. She was beautiful, so he did not repulse her, but he couldn't help wondering if this was all an act. The Ulsar was behaving like a real savage chieftain, talking loudly, clapping his hands, draining cup after cup, laughing and joking with Shangrin, nudging Gregori. Shangrin, splendid in his iridescent tunic, kept up with him. He certainly was playing a part. He was playing it so well that Smirno thought a latent streak of barbarity had been awakened within the Captain. Perhaps so. The noisy pleasure he took in the banquet was a natural reaction for him, but nonetheless Smirno knew Shangrin remained himself, clever, alert.

The Ulsar's liege men were very noisy. Some of them had disappeared under their chairs. Others had climbed up on the tables, their boots clattering against tankards, and were chasing dancers too nimble-footed for their clumsy steps. The Ulsar and Shangrin were talking about hunting. Gregori seemed a trifle withdrawn. Smirno saw him furtively pop a pill into his mouth: a remedy against drunkenness. The Captain, although he had drunk as much or more than his host, seemed to be holding his own with no outside help.

Every so often, one of the Sars who was not too drunk would get up from the lower tables and vanish for a few moments. Smirno had a fair idea of his intentions: the human stomach had its limits, whereas during a feast the appetite of a barbarian had none. Then a serf brought the Ulsar a gold basin and the latter stuck two fingers down his throat to vomit. Smirno was unable to stifle a shiver of nausea. He saw with pleasure that Gregori had felt the same revulsion, instantly controlled. Shangrin was superb. He imitated his host's gesture and swept a rapid but angry look at his two cohorts when they declined the slave's services with brief but imperious gestures.

Adjustment. That had ever been the motto of merchants. When in Rome, do as the Romans do. Change your spots. Share. But there were limits, Smirno decided. Supposing the Ulsar was gulling them, pretending, for their benefit, to be a savage chieftain?

The conversation between the Ulsar and Shangrin was taking a different turn. Gregori entered into it every so often, and he almost always sided with the Ulsar. Clever work. Subtle. But the Ulsar was giving nothing away. Shangrin's questions were becoming increasingly direct.

"You're already doing some trading with spacemen?" Shangrin was saying.

The Ulsar smiled slowly.

"We buy arms from dealers. This enables us to fight with more or less equal weaponry against the cities."

"But the cities control space trade. Deliveries must be rare and irregular."

"I should certainly be happy to buy arms from you," said the Ulsar.

"That would ensure you a quick victory over the cities. You have numbers on your side, haven't you? But the cities remain pretty impregnable."

The Ulsar's face contracted fleetingly.

"That's true."

His speech was slightly thick.

"On the other hand," said Shangrin, "we won't be able to do much trading with this planet as long as the cities retain control over space travel." He leaned toward the Ulsar and whispered: "They launched rockets against us. Obviously, they missed."

"You were prepared to negotiate with them," accused the Ulsar.

Shangrin shook his head.

"We knew nothing about the political situation here. The cities have their own interplanetary trade routes. They would not have allowed us to compete with them." He laughed loudly. "I never meddle in the politics of the worlds with which I trade. It's a principle. But, in a way, I'd like to see you win."

"Really?" said the Ulsar.

He clapped again and a decanter once more hovered over their cups.

"We're brothers, aren't we?" He patted Shangrin's shoulder affectionately.

"Allies," said the Captain. "Yes, I think I'd be happy to see you defeat the cities."

"Bullies," said the Ulsar, his head nodding.

"I think I'll give you what you need for victory."

"Cowards."

"Naturally, I expect to have some share in the looting of the cities. And, provisionally, a monopoly on trading with this planet."

"They won't last long now."

"And contact with your suppliers. Perhaps we could put together a fleet and conquer neighboring space? I think we could control the whole system. Spread beyond. The cities would retreat everywhere."

"Lots of space pirates," the Ulsar muttered.

"We'll make corsairs out of them," said Shangrin, warming up. "Mercenaries. I can pay them."

Very slowly, the Ulsar straightened out.

"What exactly is it you are looking for?" he asked in a cold, controlled voice that held no trace of drunkenness.

Shangrin pretended to be surprised.

"Oh! Profit," he said in a boozy voice. Smirno kicked him under the table.

"No," said the Ulsar imperiously. "You have something else in mind."

So, it *had* all been an act. He was perfectly sober.

"Power, of course," said Shangrin. "The important thing is to have allies against the cities. It's been a tiring day and a large meal. We'll talk some more tomorrow."

He gestured broadly at the bacchanal unfolding before them. They were almost forced to shout to make themselves heard.

The Ulsar smiled shortly.

"You are no more drunk than I am. Nor are your friends. Waiting is poor counsel, and we're both in a hurry; isn't that right?"

"Yes," Shangrin conceded.

Gregori nodded approval.

The Ulsar stood and clapped, his hands making a brittle sound in the tent. The noise died down and silence ensued. Those in condition to do so turned toward the head table; the dancers stood still. A slave, taken unaware, dropped a goblet that smashed, spilling the wine all over the floor; it made a dark puddle under the torch light.

"Out," said the Ulsar loudly. "Get out, all of you!"

VIII

There was a mad rush for the exits. The guests still able to stand staggered out, assisted by the dancers. A horde of slaves rushed toward the others and carried them from the tent. A few came to, protesting, but their voices were drowned out. The girl kneeling at Smirno's feet looked up at him questioningly. He signaled to her to remove herself and she fled.

A second wave of servants cleared the tables by rolling up the tablecloths.

At the head table, the astonished Magellanites looked at the Ulsar. This had been a display of power, to show that he might rule over a gang of barbarians, but he himself was not one. Swallowing a pill to ward off intoxication, Smirno told himself that it all came back to the original question. When they were alone and the Ulsar had sat down again, a look of intense curiosity and also amusement on his face, Smirno was happy to hear Shangrin ask it without beating around the bush.

"Where do you come from? You're not one of them."

"I might ask you the same thing," said the Ulsar. "I've heard about most of the civilizations in this sector of space and you don't come from any of them."

Stalemate. Shangrin placed his hands on the table.

"It's enough that we share a common interest in the defeat of the cities. You want to rule this planet and I hope to find certain information there."

"I don't expect to govern this world," the Ulsar said. "I just want to free it from the oppression of the cities." He added, smiling, "If we are to be allies, we must be frank with one another. But in order to be frank, we must be allies. It's a vicious circle, isn't it?"

"No," said Gregori. "We can find what we want somewhere else, but you'll never defeat the cities without our help."

"Perhaps," said the Ulsar. "Perhaps you don't need me."

He raised his cup and looked at it, amused.

"Whoever keeps his wine cannot get drunk," he said, then added, "No, I don't come from here. I wasn't even born on this planet. You suspected as much, didn't you?"

Shangrin nodded.

"You see," the Ulsar went on, "the political situation in this region of space is pretty confused. Some years ago, a powerful empire stretched out over 30 odd planets. It particularly bore down on this planet."

"The empire of the cities," said Smirno.

"If you like. We simply call it the Empire. It included a ruling class made up of the descendants of the invaders, and a proletariat, infinitely more numerous, made up of slaves, who were the most ancient people of these worlds. The cruelty of the ruling class was unbelievable. Rebellions broke out here and there but were always ruthlessly repressed. The oppressed peoples of the various planets had no space fleets at their disposal and did not even know, most of the time, of the existence of an intersidereal empire. A revolution, to be successful, must break out simultaneously in several places and the rebels must have a fleet and good communications.

"However, in spite of apparent difficulties, isolated groups in certain worlds did manage to keep going and get properly organized. They even succeeded in infiltrating cities, learning snatches of technology, hijacking ships. There were bitter struggles among them for the ultimate control of the revolutionary movement. One; organization survived and won out. When conditions became favorable, it gave the signal for revolt. It sent men to the largest planet of the Empire to foment dissatisfaction and provide leadership in the movement. A war started; it was to be fought in a limited way in space, but, for the most part, on the planets themselves. In the two centuries that this war lasted, the Empire has steadily lost ground. The freedom movement will destroy the oppressors."

The Ulsar's face hardened.

"I belong to this organization—I was sent to Xandra over 20 years ago. My job is almost finished. The ruling class is hanging on only in the cities; in a few decades, Xandra will be free."

"And then, what will happen?" Smirno asked.

"I'm not in charge," the Ulsar said curtly. "The battle is now being fought on some 65 planets and I am only a cog in the machinery that controls this one. Two or three worlds have already been almost freed. Naturally, we have a plan. We want to set up a federation of the planets formerly controlled by the Empire and reawaken a sense of civilization in these people who have returned to a barbaric state."

"It's a worthy program," said Shangrin, "but you seem to have rather direct methods."

"We have a war to win. Then we'll see. With your help, we can expedite things."

"What forces in space do you command?"

"Oh, it's simple. The Empire has the better fleet. We ourselves have a few ships through which we deploy agents and distribute arms. And we keep in touch. But the war has given rise to all sorts of other traffic. Some ships that were once owned by our side have more or less turned to pirating. Neighboring federations send out their representatives to distribute arms indiscriminately to the cities or to us. There are easily 30 or 40 flagships running into one another in space. The Empire is in the process of collapsing, but we are not yet strong enough to take over."

Interregnum, Smirno thought. Looting, anarchy, wars, murder, instability. Bloody battles were being waged in the space through which they had just traveled, confident of their power and speed. Compared to the supreme power of the

Lesser Magellanics, these were mere skirmishes. But men were dying nevertheless.

"They don't know that, do they?" asked Gregori.

"My people? Yes. I tell them the truth a little at a time."

"They think space people are gods."

"That encourages them to face up to the city demons."

Smirno cleared his throat.

"They are not at war for themselves, are they?"

"I'm afraid not," said the Ulsar. "They'll never know peace. They're fighting for their descendants. And you—why would you fight?"

"I've already told you," Shangrin began.

"I don't believe you," the Ulsar interrupted violently. "Skip the rigmarole about profits. It won't stand up. You're not pirates. You don't belong to any neighboring civilizations."

"We come from quite a distance," said Gregori.

The Ulsar banged on the table with his fist.

"I'm not asking you where you come from! I'm asking you from what period in time. Time is what concerns you, isn't it?"

Shangrin whistled through his teeth.

"So you know that, too? You know about people traveling through time."

"Do you think this war would be lasting such a long time if we could control time? Listen. Neither the conquerors, the inhabitants, nor any of the surrounding civilizations originated here. The scientists of the Empire know it, although they have lost all traces of the time when their ancestors were born. But some of our legends tell of men who traveled across centuries as if they were rivers. By chance, or perhaps according to some plan, ships appeared out of nowhere, in space, every few centuries. They each came from different eras. You're the most recent and you're trying to get back to your own time. You're hoping that the cities hold a key to the mystery. And because they refuse to give it up, you want to wrest it from them."

Shangrin made a face.

"And you're not trying to make contact again with the future?"

"What for? We belong here. We have a war to fight. Later, perhaps."

Perfectly logical, Smirno said to himself. They were born in this period of time; a long chain of generations would have gone by since the arrival of the men who had been thrown backward into time.

But that made for a depressing conclusion. The Empire and its opponents knew, or guessed, what their own origins were, but they knew nothing about time traveling. Forcing open the gates of the cities would serve no purpose.

The Captain got up.

"I'd like to drink a little tea," he said gloomily. "Shall we go back to my tent?"

The kettle was bubbling peacefully. For a fleeting moment, despite the barbaric splendor of his surroundings, Shangrin thought himself back in the control room of the *Vasco*. Then, all at once, he felt hemmed in by the ghosts of long-ago ships, the remnants of oppressive empires brought to ruin by their own victims. He felt deafened by revolutionary slogans and oppressed by the cold, brutal logic of the tyrant who claimed to be fighting for freedom.

In some respects, the Ulsar seemed to have put himself at Shangrin's mercy. He wondered if this was another subtle trick to try to influence his decision. He had to take the chance. He might make a wrong move, but even the greatest miscalculation could not make the *Vasco's* situation any worse than it was.

In any event, he felt it was better to throw themselves into the battle. If the *Vasco* did not succeed in getting back to its own time, at least its passengers would be better off for being on the winning side. The days of the Empire were numbered. If the *Vasco* helped the rebels win, then the Magellanites would be able to play a decisive role in the organization of the future federation, perhaps even a dominant one.

He shook his head.

He knew perfectly well what would happen. The disparity between the technological knowledge of the *Vasco's* crew and that of the rebels was so great that the Magellanites were sure to come out on top. A new form of tyranny would take over in this sector of space, possibly more subtle and less crude than the old one, but a few centuries hence, another revolution would break out. And a second *Vasco* would arrive...

"And so a great many ships have come from the future," said Gregori, turning toward the Ulsar. "Did some of them have non-human crews?"

The Ulsar had hesitated imperceptibly, Smirno was almost sure. It was difficult to read on a foreign face the emotions of a civilization he hardly knew, but Smirno told himself that this was the first question to catch the Ulsar unprepared. Then he began to doubt, but he never again let his attention wander from the would-be barbarian.

"What do you mean?" said the Ulsar. "I don't see what you're getting at. I don't know of any civilization that is not human."

Was there really a touch of regret in his voice? Smirno wondered. He felt this might provide a hint or a clue to something the Ulsar was hiding. Only a lie detector could tell them for sure.

Shangrin put his hands on his piping-hot teapot.

"Yes," he said. "We've run into some. One of them has become an associate of mine. He has tremendous powers. We shall need his help in our fight, of course, so I'll have to consult him. As a matter of fact, I can't commit myself without asking him."

"A nonhuman?" The Ulsar seemed to be experiencing difficulty in getting used to the idea. "What's he like?"

Shangrin turned to Smirno.

"Why don't you describe him? After all, that's your specialty."

Smirno made a face but did not retort.

"He calls himself a Runi," he said. He described the alien minutely, but he kept certain details to himself. He did not mention the highly developed tactical sense of the Runi, nor his extraordinary powers of perception. He did describe him as a furry crab endowed with a keen intelligence, which was, after all, accurate.

The Ulsar seemed to be thinking.

"He isn't dangerous?" he asked.

This time, it was Shangrin who answered. "No, he's completely trustworthy. He has already been very useful to us."

"And what does he expect in exchange for his help?"

"Nothing. It was scientific curiosity that made him accompany us."

"Oh!" said the Ulsar.

Shangrin poured the tea into little earthenware pots. The Ulsar tasted the burning liquid and made a face.

"The Runi belongs to your time period?"

"Yes," said Shangrin.

"Have you and his species been on good terms for a long time?"

I could lie, Shangrin thought, *but what good would that do?*

"We were the first to come into contact with his planet."

"I see," said the Ulsar. He swallowed some more tea. "I prefer wine," he added.

"Tea is less harmful."

"To what period in time do you belong?"

This could be a harmless question, but Smirno made a mental note of it. What meaning could a date have to the Ulsar?

"The year 27,937 of our era," said Shangrin, "roughly 230 million years from now. Naturally, all sorts of adjustments have to be made. Time does not elapse in the same manner on board an interstellar ship as it does in the worlds which it visits."

"I know that," said the Ulsar.

He seemed inexplicably relieved.

"I think that the origin of our people is located in your future," he went on. "The legends are vague, but you seem to come from a time period located near the very beginning of our own era. The first ships that landed on Xandra must have come from 200,000 or 300,000 years in your future. The ships of our oppressors came from an even more remote future."

"So we are, in a way, your ancestors," said Shangrin

"Regression has smoothed out the differences. Actually, in many ways, you are more advanced than we are. Time is a complex thing."

"Do you think that some of those who arrived here came of their own free will?"

The Ulsar raised his eyebrows.

"You really want to know if there's any chance of your getting back to your own time, don't you? Well, yes, there is. It's a small one, but it does exist."

"As long as we fight on your side, is that it?"

The Ulsar smiled. "Maybe. You're awfully suspicious."

"I'm used to deal-making."

"You're right."

The Ulsar closed his eyes and his face suddenly looked old and tired. Deep lines were etched on his forehead. His cheeks had become hollow. He was flinching under the burden of his responsibilities. Normally, he wore a mask of confidence and energy, but he had just taken it off, in front of strangers.

"We're just toys," he said. "How do you account for the fact that so many ships have been thrown back into the past and ended up stranded here?"

"We have no precise information," said Shangrin. "In our case, it happened very suddenly. It was pure chance that we even realized what had happened. As I see it, there are two possibilities: it could be a natural phenomenon, some kind of vortex almost unimaginable in its magnitude which swallows up ships at some point in the space-time continuum and hurls them into another point of that continuum. Elementary particles are occasionally subject to such phenomena, but on an infinitely smaller scale."

The Ulsar shook his head.

"But we have another theory," Shangrin went on. "We think that, in some fabulously distant future, there is a race which has mastered the secret of time. We believe it's playing with our ships, projecting them into the past or into the future, either to protect itself or to carry out a plan about which we know nothing. It may even be a game. This space sector seems to be a privileged place: so many ships at several centuries' intervals have ended up here. Since these time masters treat us like pawns, they must be anxious, whatever their plan, to control our movements. It must be possible to make contact with them, perhaps even negotiate with them."

"They really do exist," said the Ulsar. "I'm sure of that. And I think they are in direct contact with some of the empires around us. I am not sufficiently high in my group to know exactly what it covers, but in the early days, it did receive help from some secret organizations. Even today, we still receive, via a complex chain of intermediaries, weapons that no one in this region of space could possibly manufacture. And out in space, there is talk of god-like, powerful entities lurking in the shadowy recesses of space and time which can shape history like clay. The Empire, for its part, receives other support. It's as if another struggle—an invisible one—was taking place behind the façade of our war, perpendicular to our space, on the battlefield of time."

Shangrin leaned toward him.

"Have you any proof?"

"Yes," said the Ulsar, "I do. But I must reach an agreement with you before I give it to you."

"Out of the question," objected Shangrin. "I buy only what I see."

"Listen," said the Ulsar, "if we defeat Xandra, if the federation is achieved,
if my organization wins out, you may be able to follow the leads I will mention
to you, perhaps even reach the time masters. Faced with such an upheaval, they
might show themselves. They're very near. It may be your only chance."

"I want to see," Shangrin persisted.

"Very well" The Ulsar seemed to have come to a decision. "I'm going to
tell you a secret that no one on this planet except me knows. You'll make up
your mind when you've seen it. I'm almost sure what your answer will be."

He got up and raised the hanging over the door. The fatigue on his face had
vanished, replaced by a strange smile pulling at the corners of his mouth.

"Follow me," he said, plunging into the night.

The camp slept. Torches splattered the darkness along the walls; silent
watchmen glided along the edges of the palisades. At the end of a row of tents, a
wavering voice sang, echoed by a drunken group. An occasional bark or the
long sonometric howling of a hexapod tore through the night.

The tent behind them was like a dark monolithic mass. On the square, they
could make out the shapes of gliders whose polished metal caught flickering
reflections. Inside, the men from the Magellanics slept and guards kept their
watch.

The Ulsar clapped. An armed giant stepped out of the shadows.

"Take a torch and follow me," said the Ulsar.

The giant did so.

"We have searchlights," said Shangrin.

"No good. Anyway, I shall need him."

They went across the field under the dancing light of the torch. It revealed
the clashing colors of the tents and the banners stuck in the ground. The sounds
of soft voices reached them, but there was absolute calm and peace. The Ulsar's
discipline must have been pitiless. Or perhaps his soldiers, inured to the long
tyranny of the Empire, had never lost the habit of going to ground at night. The
Magellanites saw weapons that were in startling contrast to the armor and
swords of the warriors—long rockets. Although they were not the product of a
high degree of technology, they could not have been manufactured in Xandra,
except, perhaps, in the cities.

"Have you ever captured any arsenals of the Empire?"

The Ulsar turned toward Shangrin.

"No, almost never. They're mined and explode as soon as we get inside.
These rockets come from space, but they are useless against the cities—their
force screens are impenetrable."

Smirno studied the man who carried the torch. He had harsh features and massive bones. Where did rockets fit in his primitive universe? For him, the explosion of atoms could only mean the rattle of divine swords: the gods fought above his head. He helped them as best he could, but had no illusions.

What's the difference between him and us? Smirno wondered. Above their heads were stars, and among these stars mysterious entities who had mastered time...

They were quietly going down toward the bottom of the crater. Their footsteps made stones roll. Shangrin, very much on the alert, thought that this crater was in an odd position strategically. Its sides were not sufficiently high to hide the camp from sight or protect it from direct hits. They must, in fact, have made it perfectly visible from space. Then he remembered that he had seen nothing, suspected nothing, which was strange. The camp might have escaped human observation, but the computers should have picked it up. One more mystery.

The crater was not circular and its walls, dark edges against a light sky, were of uneven height. They were much higher in the direction toward which the men were headed. The crater was in the shape of an asymmetric ellipse. One end, where the walls were low, was wide and round. The other end was narrow and pointed and the raised rock was like a spur. It was at the end of this spur that the crater plunged into the planet's crust.

Although certain fragments seemed to have been vitrified by tremendous heat, the rock was not in the least lava-like, nor even like a granite outflow. The walls of the crater were not of volcanic origin, but were made of the same sedimentary deposits as the surrounding plain.

It appeared as though a monstrous projectile had struck the surface of the planet at an angle of just a few degrees, almost tangentially. As the meteor—or whatever—had penetrated the ground, it had dug up layers of rock piling them up in front of it, forming a spur; it had hurled other mounds of excavated material behind it.

The slope became steeper and they had to slow down. The soldier hesitated and stopped; the Ulsar took the torch from him. Terror and respect were mirrored in the large man's face. Shangrin guessed that these emotions were aroused by something more than the person of the Ulsar.

"We are going to see the gods," said the Ulsar to the warrior.

The other's face lit up.

"I shall cross the threshold of Heaven," he said in a rasping voice. "Thank you, oh thank you, Liberator."

He flung himself down on his knees and kissed the Ulsar's hands in front of the astounded Magellanites.

"Forward," said the Ulsar.

The man got up, took back the torch and went off with a lighter step. They passed a low barrier made of white stones that shone in the starlight. There must have been some taboo on the unguarded depths of the crater, like a forbidden frontier. The credulity of the barbarians made an inviolable temple of it.

The path was dug into the crater along a spiral that hugged the walls. On their right, the bottom of the crater was a shadowy chasm. Did it shrink down into the size of a well? Gregori wondered. Had the Ulsar finally set his trap, against all their expectations? His hand automatically slipped into his pocket and caressed the butt of a weapon.

Soon the spur loomed high over them as they moved under the rock overhang. In the torchlight they could see stratifications like a signature of fire; awesome energies had been unleashed for the space of a flash. The crater suddenly disappeared under them in the wall at an oblique angle. They remained suspended along the narrow path between the mountain and a circular abyss so vast that the light of the torch died before reaching the other side. Gregori resisted the temptation to turn on his searchlight and direct it at the bottom.

IX

The path narrowed clown until they had to walk in single file. The warrior went first, lighting up the shadows with his torch. The Ulsar followed with a light step. Shangrin went next, then Smirno, who was having a hard time keeping up. Gregori brought up the rear. As they plunged deeper into the crater, the stars disappeared one by one.

The barbarian and the Ulsar stopped at a point where the path seemed to widen and end. Shangrin's eyes searched the darkness, unable to see on the side of the chasm anything to explain the purpose of the expedition.

The Ulsar turned toward the rocky side; the Magellanites now saw that a narrow passage had been dug under the mountain. It was walled in by a heavy, crudely rounded block.

The barbarian put his torch into a fissure in the rock; trails of smoke on the stone were proof that others had been there before them. He put his entire weight against the rock, as the Ulsar instructed him. It hardly budged.

It was a strange sort of door, Shangrin thought, surprised that the Ulsar had not provided another one. Then he noticed that the stone, despite its natural appearance, fitted the passage like a key in a lock. It would have required powerful explosives to move it unless one knew exactly where to push and in what direction: rudimentary but efficient.

The stone finally pivoted, almost soundlessly. It barely moved, then found a new balance. A gentle push with a finger would suffice to return it to its original position. At a sign from the Ulsar, the warrior went into the subterranean passage and the rest followed him wordlessly.

The tunnel wound down steeply. It had apparently been dug out of the mountain rather crudely, for the traces of tools were still visible on the wall: they were like thousands of insect tracks.

It was warm. The men sniffed the air, detecting an odor of ozone. Were there power installations, a factory below?

The torch-bearer stopped suddenly. Shangrin very nearly ran into the Ulsar as a fresh wind brushed his cheek. The soldier raised the torch and the men saw below them a subterranean chamber, large and dark, probably the bottom of the crater. Titanic forces must have been unleashed in the heart of the hill for, here and there, the rock had crystallized and caught reflections of light from the flame. Smirno realized that he had seen other deep caverns like this one— caverns which had resulted from the explosion of stellar bombs lodged in the crust of a planet.

They all stood at the edge of an abyss from which no light emanated; there was only a gentle breeze, like a current brushing against the walls of the grotto, which went out through the gaping mouth of the crater, into the depths below.

"Throw away your torch," the Ulsar said to the soldier.

Shangrin was about to protest, but he decided the Ulsar knew what he was doing. He was more at their mercy than they were at his. The torch went down, slowly, like a flower, and whirled about as the flame spread in the wind of its fall.

They thought it would continue to drop endlessly, but far, far below, a twin light came on, like a reflection in a looking glass, and the looking glass lighted up slowly, like a fire that is catching, and until the light owed nothing more to the torch. A soft bluish stain was spreading, like waves consuming the darkness. The walls of the chamber were already emerging from the night. The light reached the edges and showed fallen stones and the torch, burning itself out. They could see, next to the torch, tiny, whitish objects.

The warrior threw himself on his knees.

"Look," said the Ulsar.

Then the man muttered unintelligible words that seemed imbued with fervor. All this took place before the Magellanites could make a single gesture.

The Ulsar pulled a sharp stiletto from his belt and plunged it quickly and expertly into the nape of the barbarian's neck. The man crumpled up without a sound. The Ulsar extracted the weapon and blood began to flow—very little. The Ulsar shoved his victim into the crater and the body struck the fallen rock with a sickening sound. The Magellanites saw what the whitish objects were: human bones. From that distance they looked like the remains of insects. There were a great many.

The Ulsar sacrificed one of his men at each visit. ("We have a war to win.") A shiver ran up and down Shangrin's spine. So the Ulsar was a liberator, was he?

The Magellanite did not protest. He knew it would have been useless, and he was too experienced in the ways of worlds and men. Besides, the Ulsar would not have understood his indignation. It had been a natural, obvious gesture for him, entirely without cruelty. The secret had to be kept, that was all. And perhaps the rebel from Xandra had wanted to demonstrate to the spacemen the importance of the secret he was revealing to them.

An enormous oblong object rested on the bottom of the cavern—a spaceship. It might have fallen from the stars one century or one millennium ago; it had made the atmosphere hiss and roar with a red wake of fire and a white foam of steam, and it had perforated the ground, digging the crater, throwing earth hundreds of yards up, clearing a passage for itself toward its final resting place, its prison.

The shock must have been a violent one—the object had traveled at least 300 meters under the surface of the planet before finally stopping and letting the torrents of unleashed energy spend themselves—but the object had sustained no visible damage. There was not the smallest knick, the slightest scratch along its surface. The most durable of the Lesser Magellanics' cruisers, under similar circumstance, would have been reduced to a few shards of scattered metal.

"May we go down?" asked Shangrin.

The Ulsar nodded and smiled sardonically. He leaned over the edge of the abyss, took a deep breath and jumped. He remained suspended for a brief moment, a dark spot above that lake of bluish light, then went down slowly toward the bottom, like a spider on the end of its thread.

Halfway down, he looked up and signaled them to follow.

"An anti-gravitational field," whispered Shangrin.

"I'll go first," Gregori suggested.

He hesitated briefly, then jumped. He saw the bluish stain rise up so fast that he thought he was going to crash, that he had to save himself. Then his fall was suddenly halted; he remained suspended in the air, as if he had run into an invisible elastic mattress. He looked up and saw the outlines of Shangrin and Smirno silhouetted against the dark rock. He immediately began to rise back up slowly and jerkily: subconsciously he had wanted to be close to them.

Below, the Ulsar was making strange signs. Gregori struggled against the fear that was invading him and thought: I want to go down. His theory was proved correct. He went down slowly and came to rest on the blue surface.

He saw that Shangrin was calling to him, but the Captain's voice was muffled as it reached him; it was shapeless, unintelligible. The microradio was no longer functioning either, as the alien ship was surrounded by a halo of energy that disturbed the order of physical laws. The perfection of the anti-gravitational mechanism was unbelievable: its operation was attuned to the thinking of whoever wanted to reach the machine. Gregori deduced from this that its builders must be human, or at least not too different from those of his own race. The machine's detectors must be capable of recognizing and registering infinitesimal muscular contractions and discharges of nervous influx.

It was likely that the apparatus did not entirely rely on the principle of telepathy, but that it limited itself to interpreting orders given by the entire nervous system of the body to go up or come down or even move laterally. It did not try to deal with problems posed by the use of the words *up* or *down*. Consequently, any being more or less like a human could use it. Perhaps even a superior animal.

Gregori wondered what would happen if the Runi were introduced to the machine. He wanted to go back up to explain to Shangrin what had happened, but the two men were already coming down at moderate speed.

The Ulsar, from the other side of the cavern, was signaling to them to come close so they started to slide along the rounded, smooth surface. It was not uniformly blue, but showed something like a network of small veins, some lighter, some darker than the background, and constantly changing so rapidly that the eyes registered the phenomenon as a flutter. The cavern more or less complemented the shape of the ship. In some places, rock touched the blue hull and in others, a gaping passage remained free. Toward the rear, the vault was low and apparently prevented any exit through the crater. Probably a fall of stones had blocked the way.

"How long has this been here?" asked Gregori.

"Not very long," said Smirno. "Otherwise the crater would be stopped up and its walls eroded. A few dozen years at most. Probably less."

The voice carried badly, as if the air were too thick. Radiation curtailed the vibrations. The space was glutted with energy.

The Ulsar gestured that he wanted to take them inside. They reached the opposite wall of the cavern and went down by a passage dug out of the rock. They moved along the gigantic hull like so many worms along a fruit, looking for a place to get in to suck the juice. An oval opening appeared, breaking the uniform surface of the hull. It opened to a narrow corridor bathed in green light. They entered and crossed bare, mysterious rooms, lined with empty niches. The men guessed they might be means of transportation and communication, transmitting posts or launching pads permitting instant projection from one point to another in the ship, or perhaps to the outside, to other corresponding niches scattered throughout the cities and ships of an unimaginable civilization. The ceilings of the rooms were covered with mobile, luminous designs that opened with jerky pulsations, then slowly vanished only to reappear. Nowhere did they find instruments or instrument panels, levers, weapons, quadrants, books, logs, detectors. But looking for them was probably as futile, Shangrin thought, as a barbarian from the heroic ages exploring the *Vasco* and looking for a sail, a sextant, a tiller, a rudder.

This ship had traveled in time; not only in space. It was as different from the *Vasco* as the *Vasco* was from a sailboat.

They soon finished exploring the open passages, certainly less than one-hundredth of the ship's total mass, without seeing a trace of a door that might lead to the rest. And Shangrin had no illusions about the possibility of breaking down the partitions: the ship's resistance exceeded the properties of matter. It was the result of certain subtle alterations of space, perhaps even of time. In fact, these two aspects of things were inextricably linked here.

When they had finished exploring, they stopped in a vast triangular room whose walls must have been imperceptibly curved, for the angles were wider than prescribed by Euclidean geometry. In addition, the corners of the room seemed to be in a continuous flow which side-tracked and tired the eye. The Ulsar stretched and floated up. The Magellanites instantly followed suit, merely thinking their desire. There was no necessity for constant effort to continue floating, once was sufficient.

"There you are," said the Ulsar. "This ship appeared from nowhere a few years after my arrival on this world. At the time I was in another section of the planet and the news took a long time to reach me. I didn't immediately realize its importance. Neither, for that matter, did the cities, for they made only feeble efforts to locate it and they did not succeed."

He stared at them, wearing his customary smile.

"Yet the shock had been extraordinarily violent. It was heard for miles and miles around—it had shaken the ground. But the crater remained unnoticed by the squadrons of the Empire. I found it because I was moving slowly, close to the ground, instead of soaring proudly in the air."

He pivoted. This made the men feel slightly uneasy, and vaguely disquieted. The Ulsar seemed perfectly at home here despite his barbaric garb. He was the owner. Shangrin strode out aggressively, face to face with him, as though he had conquered the ship, but he was still an outsider. He was sure of his strength, of his rights, he did not feel remotely intimidated, but he was still an outsider. Gregori was no more than his shadow. He would doubtless accomplish great things in the future, for his mind was open, but he lacked the weight of maturity. As for Smirno, he was only a curious, weary, and sometimes vindictive onlooker, a recorder. It was in an alien place like this, outside of time, that personalities stood out most clearly, that the details of hum-drum existence vanished, allowing the naked substance of the being to show through. An almost imperceptible aura surrounded Shangrin. An equally faint green light that matched the walls of the room bathed the Ulsar. Gregori and Smirno had no lights.

"The crater is not visible from the sky," the Ulsar went on. "That was all. And what was underground could not be detected. Some sort of contraption enclosed the space on itself, deflected light rays. I don't know about those things. You know them better than I do. As one approaches along the ground, on certain days, as one gets nearer the crater, there is a noticeable shimmering of air that is attributed to heat. But it is no such thing. It is a contraction of space and perhaps of time.

"Slaves who had run away from the cities had taken refuge in the crater. They had noticed the Empire ships stopped pursuing them when they arrived here. Much later, I learned why. From the sky, only a continuous plain is visible. This may be an image of the past held prisoner by this machine and eternally projected above it like a shield against the passage of time. But, at the time, I could only see two things: the enigma and the potential power that this ship represented, and the asylum which the crater offered."

"Has it remained inviolate?" asked Shangrin.

"Yes. Twice we had to wipe out ground expeditions from the Empire which had ventured too close, probably by chance. They were only insignificant patrols and the cities did not undertake any searches. They had enough to do on other fronts."

"And the ship was accessible?"

"No. When I arrived, the crater had already become a sacred place. A religion was taking hold. The fugitives who lived here believed in the protection of the gods. Some of them had gone to the bottom of the crater and had seen a blue, supernatural light through the cracks. Some had tried to reach it. They never came back.

"I discovered what had happened to them—they had reached the stern of the ship. There is a violent blue whirlwind there which defies description. It is not very large, and it is insubstantial, but it is fatal to anyone who touches it or even comes close to it. I've seen it swallow men whole. It's something like a blind, voracious god. I think of it as the incarnation of time. There, seconds are counted, ground up and destroyed. Anyone who plunges into the whirlwind is projected into the ultimate future or the absolute past, or into emptiness. I had the crater plugged up with rocks, and this path dug out. I've discovered a few things about this ship, but I don't know where it came from, nor when, nor what civilization built it. I'm positive that it was conceived by man, or at least for men. I think it comes from a distant future because nowhere, in all the space around us, is there comparable technology. And we know that one can be propelled involuntarily out of the future. My theory is that this ship came voluntarily, that there was an accident and its crew disappeared; the ship ran into the planet by chance, by a miscalculation in its course that brought it too close to the planet. There are other possibilities. I don't know. Only the silence is discernible. But this ship is full of knowledge; I often come here to think. My people say that I come here to listen to the gods, that I am the only one allowed to come back from the underworld. Look at the ceiling."

They did so. The ceiling at first looked smooth except for the more or less luminous network palpitating under its surface; then it gradually became crowded with shapes, colored, intertwined, superimposed shadows. They clashed, then dissolved into a kaleidoscopic succession of abstract events. It could have been no more than an illusion, the result of optic fatigue, but it was too real. There was an innate logic at work which the mind could perceive without understanding. Could it be writing, or perhaps mathematics?

"I understand some of this," said the Ulsar. "How can I explain? It has made a new man of me; it has altered my thinking, made it disciplined, clearer. Perhaps there's no meaning really, or maybe it's a map of time, the shifting, interlacing of inaccessible roads connecting periods in time. Perhaps it's really only a game. But at least, this helps me better understand those who built this ship." His voice grew louder. It was devoid of passion, but it became more vibrant, more urgent. "And what this ship has done, others can do again more successfully. I think some of them are sailing in space around us. I believe that, when our power has become sufficiently great, they will make contact with us, or they will no longer slip through the meshes of our net. They are very near, there, behind the web of things."

"Could I bring my technicians here?" Shangrin asked.

The Ulsar shook his head.

"Their instruments won't work. I've brought scientists here from the cities, prisoners. They were so eager to solve this mystery that they would have done anything, even remained here, had they been given the chance. They were unable to find a clue. I had to have them killed.

"So there's your proof. The road to the future does exist. This is a lock—now find the key."

"We'll find it in victory," said Shangrin. "Ulsar, I'm with you. We'll take the cities. We'll liberate space. We'll bend time to our will."

"Time is an inconstant ally and an eternal foe," said the Ulsar with a smile.

Having left the strange ship, they retraced their footsteps along the rocky path and reentered the tunnel. After they had rounded the first bend, the blue light grew dim and went out. As they left the cavern, they climbed back into darkness because their searchlights did not work; just as well, for their eyes needed to rest before facing the brightness of a dawning sky. And so they left the cavern of night.

X

Rockets were raining down on a city named Tczila. From the Magellanites' headquarters, they looked like a volley of silver arrows. They shot out from the mountains in clusters, climbed so high in the atmosphere that no sound betrayed their upward passage and then aimed, hissing, at the town.

But the rockets never reached the city. At a few kilometers' altitude, they ran into an invisible obstacle and exploded. Radiation and heat glanced off the energy field that protected the city. Sunlight filtered through, however; Shangrin could see clearly, through his field glasses, heavy, massive buildings. The rocket explosions created clouds which were slowly dispersed by the wind, that was all. Not enough for Tczila to worry about.

This was why the outcome of the war was still in doubt. The rebellions of the plains beat upon the walls of the city like the waves of a stormy sea, but were powerless against the fortifications. The soldiers of the Empire were not sufficiently numerous to control all of the plains, nor were they equipped to do so. The opposing sides came face to face only by prearrangement, and the war had lasted so long that these meetings had become rare and uncertain.

To be sure, one or two cities had fallen as the result of internal revolts. But Tczila was sheltered from these tremors: the skulls of slaves suspected of harboring thoughts of revolt served as decorations for the gruesome pyramids at the gates.

And that was why, Shangrin said to himself, swords had survived the advent of rockets, why hand-to-hand combat, the bow and arrow and the cavalry, had outlasted weapons of mass destruction, such as rays, gliders and tanks. He could see, through his field glasses, the columns of the Ulsar as they made their way toward the city. His own men were ready to intervene with primitive arms that hurled projectiles instead of disintegrating rays. The latter was a technique that had completely escaped the Ulsar and the Empire and which might have been enough to transform the war, if it had worked.

From the very beginning, Shangrin had been opposed to the direct use of the *Vasco;* he wanted to keep his ship uninvolved as long as possible. He had put only his skill and combat troops at the service of the Ulsar.

The Magellanites' customary weapons had proved to be inoperative. The field that protected the city had made them explode. Shangrin had listened skeptically to the Ulsar's explanations until the rebel had ordered a march on the city with his barbarians carrying nuclear grenades and radiant pistols. They had vanished without so much as a flame. Shangrin had grown livid, but had not belabored the issue. The Ulsar's demonstrations were always to the point.

And yet he was not inhuman, Smirno thought now, as he watched with the liveliest interest the preparations for the forthcoming battle. This was the first time he had witnessed a battle from such close quarters. It was also probably the first time such strange armies confronted one another. The city was too far away for him to make out evidence of agitation amid its population, but every so often a group of barbarians would disappear in a cloud of smoke as one of the small rockets backfired.

Fires ravaged the fields. The besieged were using thermal rays. In the sky, flying low and protected by their invisible rampart, large black airplanes were circling like so many birds of prey. They were powerless, though. The city could not launch nuclear projectiles—the force field would have exploded them as soon as they were launched. This was a strange war indeed.

Gregori was waiting to give the signal to release the planelets. The strategic problem involved in the capture of the city boiled down, in the long run, to the neutralization of the energy rampart. The Ulsar could not bring it off but the *Vasco* technicians believed they had found the solution.

The force field protecting the city was of a subnuclear type. It was made up of much less massive particles than those which normally accompanied electromagnetic vibrations, and, correlatively, the wavelength of the rays which set it in operation was much greater, somewhat on the order of intersidereal distances. Consequently, the energy level of the field was quite low, almost negligible. It worked only indirectly, by interrupting the structure of space and intervening at a subparticle level on the connection between matter and energy. This was enough to cause the explosion of nuclear arms and radiant pistols or their derivatives.

Paradoxically, the Magellanites were unable to produce that type of field—it was the result of a more technologically advanced era than theirs. But its generator was probably extremely simple, and this explained why the Empire had managed to safeguard its secret, while having seemingly forgotten its principle.

The Magellanites could not cancel out the positive field by creating a negative one, but they could weaken it by draining energy from it. A simple antenna casts a shadow in an alternating electromagnetic field because it absorbs energy. In general, the consumption of energy thus salvaged on radio waves is negligible compared to the amount transmitted. But, in theory, it was possible to absorb all the energy.

The problem was simplified in the case of the subnuclear field because it had well-known limits. Once past these limits, it decreased in proportion to a square of a square of the distance. It was practically annulled within a few centimeters.

Hence Operation Planelet.

Gregori studied the dial of his watch. It was shifting from yellow to red and numbers were appearing behind small shutters. These were signals from units announcing, one by one, that they were ready.

The dial turned black... Gregori gave an order. Dozens of technicians, spaced all around Tczila, set off their contraptions.

300

Several million planelets, scarcely larger than birds, flew close to the ground toward the city, like a moving multicolored rug. With their long shining wings, they looked like a swarm of dragonflies.

They reached the energy field and immediately started to gain altitude. Horizontally, they never went closer to the field, but stayed exactly at its limit. As they climbed, they created an unwavering crown along the city's invisible protective field, some joined up at the top, forming a gleaming hemisphere that covered the city like a thick cloud of insects. Their metallic antennae drew off energy from the field itself and that energy kept the engines going. Not only could the planelets fly as long as the field lasted, but they were also weakening it considerably. In fact, almost all it could now do was refuel them. They sometimes collided, destroyed one another and fell in clusters, but there were millions of them and technicians kept sending in new flights.

The sky within the city must have been darkened by them. The psychological effect was not the least important factor.

A faint hiss startled Gregori, who turned to look. The Runi's floating egg was directly overhead. The primitive idea of the planelets had been his. The technicians and robots of the *Vasco* had carried it out, but he had found the solution to the problem as soon as it had been put to him. It was a theoretical solution: the Runi produced nothing, his civilization knew nothing about tools. He was only a problem solver.

The protective egg had also been one of his inventions. He had decided he needed to be mobile in order to follow Shangrin. He had given the specifications for the contraption and the physicists of the *Vasco* had built it. The egg was completely transparent and hermetically sealed. It contained, besides the Runi, all the necessities of life for him and for communicating his thought into human language—including a chessboard set up right in front of him. An anti-gravitational generator allowed him to move through space. He looked, in his transparent egg, like an enormous orange larva, pregnant with unfathomable metamorphoses.

The first rocket to cross the barrier of the planelets fell with a creaking of metal and exploded instantly—inside the city. It had crossed the wall of energy; the city was virtually destroyed. The Runi's tactic had worked.

But Gregori knew that things would not be quite so simple. The greater part of the installations must have been buried deep. Furthermore, there must be other parts of Tczila. An enormous cloud of smoke rose, shoving aside the planelets. The wings of a number of devices melted, others left the field and crashed after whirling around. When the cloud had been dissipated, only about a quarter of the planelets were still flying in the weakened field. They plummeted to the ground just as a second rocket roared by. For a second, Gregori was able to believe that the first explosion had destroyed the field's generator, but the second rocket exploded in mid-air: the field had been reactivated. The last planelets had not yet touched the ground before they rose again. The field was again drained off and they fell, finally, to the ground.

The defenders of Tczila took countermeasures. The Magellanites sent out another swarm, but they scarcely had time to mount an assault on the invisible hemisphere. Only one rocket out of a dozen got by.

"Men are dying," said the Runi.

It was a simple statement uttered in the Runi's synthetic monotone, devoid of warmth. It could have contained surprise or understanding or even compassion. Or even satisfaction?

A sudden violent hatred welled up inside Gregori because of that statement. Until that moment, he had felt dispassionate about the events unfolding around him: the cloud of smoke, the giant mushroom which wafted, with no apparent reason, at an altitude of several kilometers. The Runi had brought him back to reality. There were men dying, not just the cruel citizens of the Empire, but their slaves also. He glanced at Shangrin. The Captain did not seem to share his doubts. He was barking orders and carrying on as though the battle had been quite close.

"Synchronize the launching of rockets and the releasing of the swarms," said the Runi.

Of course, thought Gregori. He wasn't the only one who was thinking.

He gave brief orders. The rockets and the planelets flew off at irregular intervals. Most of the rockets exploded in mid-air, but a few got through. That was enough.

The city, ten kilometers away, was a bonfire.

It had become the core of a sun, a burning brazier, a heap of ashes; metal and stone fused, swimming in an ocean of steam.

From the scorched plains, columns of barbarians and Magellanites were marching on the city. The rockets stopped falling. The planelets that were still intact returned to their launchers. Only a fraction of them remained.

The battle was virtually over and won, although fighting would probably continue for several days in the underground of the city—battles between rats, of no importance. The most powerful city of the planet had been taken. For the first time in over a century, the balance of power had been destroyed. It had taken only three hours.

Shangrin jumped off his glider and rushed toward the Ulsar.

"Tonight, the city will be in your hands," he shouted.

"I know how much I owe you," said the Ulsar. "But in the next battle, we'll have to try to save the spaceships. We'll need them later."

"We'll conquer space. No one can stop us."

No, no one, thought Smirno. We've roasted them in their dwellings like so much poultry. He felt weary, nauseated. He hated Shangrin's brutal joy, the icy impassivity of the Ulsar. He hated all men of war. The sight of the bombs falling on the city had aroused feelings of cowardice within him.

When the men from the Magellanics and the rebels of Xandra entered the city, wiping out erratic fires, they were surprised at the manner in which the buildings of Tczila had withstood the nuclear fallout. Light shadows on burned walls bore witness to destroyed lives. Steel and concrete had flowed in the streets in incandescent rivers which were cooling off, but in the very heart of Tczila, huge and blind buildings were still standing like rocks. Their walls had taken on the polish of enamel; their doors had all been soldered by the heat.

They searched all these caverns. In the bottom of one of them, they found a chained man who was still breathing. They carried him outside. He had just enough strength to breathe, to say "Thank you." Then, he died.

After that, they looked for doors leading to the underground shelters of the city, opened them, went down and showed no quarter. The vronns had their work cut out for them.

After Tczila, it was the turn of Azultl, then Xiotl, Shipar and Nuss. The first two cities fell before the Empire had made a concerted effort to regain control. Then the cities undertook to support one another and a few rare spaceships came to back them up. When one was destroyed, the others fled; thereafter, they limited themselves to watching over the planet, providing weapons to the cities now and then. Shangrin did not pursue them; he had better things to do.

The cities fell one by one, and of some of them there remained only ashes, melted rock and a fine dust that rose to the edge of space. It would take years for it to fall down again. Others surrendered almost intact, which spared many lives. The chains changed bearers. On the maps, the troops of the Ulsar and Shangrin were so many colored trajectories which soon covered most of the planet like a net. The Ulsar conquered other tribes of barbarians. Once, they crossed an ocean to take revenge on a city that was showering rockets on them.

That took months. In its cavern, the ship from another time continued to sleep. The *Vasco* had returned to space and orbited about Xandra. For those who did not take part in the war, it was as though their long voyage was merely continuing

Men changed, or became even more set in their ways. The Ulsar was more enigmatic than ever, more unyielding, even more self-assured. There seemed to be no limit to his dreams. He wanted to carry the war into space and take the capital of the Empire as soon as possible. But Shangrin was not giving in to him; he tried to slow down the involvement of the Magellanites and to interfere as little as possible with the Ulsar's politics. After all, he was a businessman, not a power-hungry politician. Yet, he liked victories. He was the first to enter a city once, sword in hand, at the head of a troop of barbarians. Fire and blood left him unmoved, but the death of a Magellanite put him into a black rage. He would demand his share of the loot, but would put it into the *Vasco's* common treasury. He was great in the manner of captains of old, half trader, half pirate.

This fascinated Gregori, who was nauseated by the bloodshed. He thought all that destruction was pointless. He would have preferred reaching their goal more slowly, more subtly, more cautiously.

But this was not an era when people were concerned with refinements, Smirno thought. It was a period when the strong reigned until the weak unexpectedly rebelled. Until this moment, he had contemplated from afar the rise and fall of civilizations, their struggles. In the end, massacres and fires were reduced to a few lines on a data slip. He thought he had a clear view and thorough understanding of that type of misfortune, past or future, but Xandra was something new; it was reality. He could hear the cries of anguish, smell the odor of smoke and rotting flesh. And there was no remedy. None. No one could persuade the Ulsar or Shangrin, or the haughty officers of the Empire who faced death with an oath on their lips, that they ought to play at other games than war. This bloodshed and devastation was destiny to them. The enemy themselves were part of the conspiracy and Smirno hated them for this as much as he hated the others. He began to hope for Shangrin's downfall.

The Runi probably changed too, although no one could be sure of it, nor guess to what extent. The image of man in the secret torrent of his thoughts evolved, became clearer, without ever quite becoming set. The Runi's point of view, all xenophobia aside, was singularly like Smirno's. But whereas the xenologist was resigned in his role as a spectator, each day the Runi saw more clearly the threads that regulated the lives of those around him. The chessboard took up less and less of his time.

It was also in the nature of the Runi to play games and he had discovered that the pleasure derived from a game was a function of its complexity.

Like happy children, they forced open the gates of Cindra. It was an ancient city and its masters, who were all too few, had offered little resistance. They had been less cruel to their slaves than most of the citizens of the Empire, and consequently, the anger of the freed slaves had been less violent than elsewhere. A spaceship, taking advantage of the confusion, had escaped. Shangrin marched straight to the spaceport and his men were able to search the old patrician houses before the arrival of the barbarians. The libraries were crammed with books which recorded details and recollections of the world before the Great Transition. Those were the documents Shangrin wanted to preserve.

They took the spaceport almost without striking a blow. Shangrin, with the help of Smirno, was examining the captured ships when an old man, who said he was a historian, was brought to him. He wore a green silk tunic and appeared to be frightened and sick. Shangrin shrugged when he saw him. Until then, neither he nor the Ulsar had succeeded in extracting information of any value from the prisoners. The Empire was falling apart too rapidly. The rulers of Xandra knew little of what was happening on the other worlds, either because communication was faulty, or because the Empire had decided to abandon the planet to its fate, to encircle Xandra behind a sanitary cordon rather than recapture it. But what this man had to tell them changed everything.

"What's your name?" asked Shangrin.

"Hari Ilen Cindra," said the historian.

He belonged to the ruling family of the city, Shangrin thought, his interest aroused in spite of himself. The man seemed less arrogant than others of his caste, more open, more intelligent.

"What was your occupation?"

"I was studying history. It is a gloomy branch of learning. It allows one to foresee the defeats of the future in the victories of the past."

"Did you foresee your defeat?"

"Yes," said the historian. "I knew you'd come sooner or later."

"And you did nothing to warn your people?"

"I never stopped warning them, but they thought themselves masters of their own fate. You think you're the master of your fate too, but you're wrong."

"What do you mean?"

"My people believed that this was only a slaves' rebellion, and that it could not succeed. They refused to believe that they were only pawns and that the real game was not being played at their level."

"Why are you telling me this?"

"Because you won't believe me. You see, our struggles, our Empire, and your revolt, are unimportant. They're only small events—minor incidents in another, much greater war. We're not fighting for ourselves. We're struggling along an undefined frontline between two gigantic armies. I have noticed and observed many things during the course of years I've been examining the archives. I found strange things there, the story of entire nations displaced in time to pursue an endless war. I have guessed how the players will move the pawns."

"You speak about the time masters?"

"Yes. I don't know where you come from, but it's obvious that you don't belong to this world. Perhaps you come from the future. Perhaps you're only a mercenary, or even one of the secret masters who understand the hidden face of things. Perhaps I ought not to have spoken out."

Shangrin threw himself at the man, grabbed him by the throat and shook him.

"Explain yourself! I don't understand. I'm lost in time! I come from the future. Tell me what you know and I'll set you free."

"I've told you everything I know," said the historian. "Listen. Two great, unimaginable powers are fighting through time and space, but because of cowardice or exhaustion, they have chosen to do battle only through intermediaries. Thus, they wrangle over planetary systems without risking a single man. All they do is send one of their agents from place to place to set off a conflict; then, someone else from the opposing side does the same thing, and war begins. There is death and destruction. The line of demarcation between the two powers wavers and fluctuates. The battlefield moves. I know it is such an agent who is behind out confrontation."

"Not I," said Shangrin.

He had almost shouted it out.

"Then look for him. Perhaps he is in your retinue, but he's used you to defeat us. He is your real master."

"I don't believe it," said Shangrin.

But he was not so sure. They had taken and burned cities, found documents, questioned officers, followed clues, studied the organization of the empire; the Ulsar's promises had been empty. They had fought this war for nothing. Men and time had been lost, and now this historian from Cindra claimed they had been used... perhaps by the Ulsar.

Ever since they had left their own time, the shadows of great, unseen powers had loomed over them. Gregori had supposed they existed, the Ulsar had proved it. And now, this man... A flash of despair ran through Shangrin. The Xandran war was no more than the feverish activity of an anthill. Perhaps they had purposely been thrown here from the future in order to wipe out the Empire, to alter a delicate balance of forces... He took a longer look at the historian who answered his unspoken question.

"We lost because the gods abandoned us. They withdrew their support. We had become worthless to them. The front has moved; a few thousand worlds are going to change masters in one move. Then, the struggle will start all over again, step by step."

"But why?" asked Shangrin. "Why this struggle?"

"I don't know," said the historian. "Perhaps for fun."

"For fun," the Runi's voice echoed mechanically.

The transparent egg was over them. The Runi had listened to the man from Cindra. Then he left.

Shangrin had almost forgotten this interrogation as city after city fell and burned and revealed nothing, not the thinnest track to lead them back to the future, to their own time. The conversation had left a small impression, however, an indefinable feeling of unease. The Captain's recollection of it woke up all at once, opening like a flower when the Ulsar was killed.

It was just at the end of the war, after they had returned to the crater where the Ulsar had set camp. For several days, he had been urging the Magellanites to go into space. Shangrin was torn between his weariness of the war and his ambition: the thought of founding an empire went to his head like wine, then he would forget the future and Neo-Sirius and Lorne. The moment seemed propitious.

The Ulsar had become increasingly demanding, even insolent. He had, he said, the means to attack the Empire alone if Shangrin did not want to follow him. He was alternatively ingratiating and threatening.

The Runi, Shangrin and the Ulsar were alone in the Ulsar's tent. The Runi was silent, but suddenly, at a turn in the discussion, he said to the Ulsar: "I know now who you are."

And almost simultaneously he turned to Shangrin and gave an order.

"Kill him."

The Ulsar made a move, but Shangrin reacted at once. His weapon barked and the Ulsar fell to the ground. His clenched fingers still held a miniature energy weapon.

It had all happened so fast that, for a long time afterwards, Shangrin wondered why he had acted as he did. Perhaps the Runi held a hypnotic power over him? Then he told himself that his hatred for the Ulsar had slowly been growing up inside him until it had erupted in this single act of violence. It was made up of a thousand facts, doubts, hunches; it went back also to the words of the historian, to the secret knowledge behind the Ulsar's mask, which concealed more than the details of a revolution.

The Ulsar did not die at once.

"I made a mistake," said the Runi. "I ought never to have told you to kill him here. When he dies, the time ship buried under the hill will explode. There is a mechanism in it that is attuned to his life. I did not know. I have only just discovered it."

"The timeship is his?"

"Yes," said the Runi. "I have known almost since the start. He is not a pawn on the chessboard. Nor even a madman. He is one of the players."

"One of the players?"

The Ulsar was breathing with difficulty. Bloodstained foam oozed from his lips. Shangrin saw that he was trying to speak.

"We must get out," the Runi said.

Shangrin wanted to help the wounded man, lift him up, take him along with them or summon help.

"No," said the Runi. "There is not time. In any event, he must die."

As they left the tent, it seemed to Shangrin that the Ulsar was smiling in a sinister way. Stunned, the Magellanite automatically followed the transparent egg. The sharp outside air brought him to his senses and he shouted out orders. His men rushed to the gliders and the aircraft soon took off toward the south. Shangrin looked at the barbarians, then at the walls made of earth and grass. The palisades hid the tents. All at once, he sensed the Ulsar's passage over the threshold of death, for inside, he felt as though a page in his existence had just been torn up. Now everything was clear. He knew that the Ulsar had tricked him from the very start, just as he had taken advantage of the barbarians; he did indeed belong to that breed who were masters of time, who played with men as with pawns on a chessboard. Shangrin now understood that the foreign ship from the future could not, despite its fantastic resistance, have withstood the tremendous shock of impact—the crater was only a camouflage. But he had not made these discoveries, even though all this information had been accumulating in his subconscious over a long period of time.

It was the Runi who had provided the key. The Runi—a better chess player than Shangrin—held in his absurd-looking limbs the elements of another round of this game. Suddenly, Shangrin began to hate the entire universe. He understood the Ulsar's smile and the "for fun" of the historian, for his life now held no other purpose than to conquer and destroy in the impossible hope of reaching the hidden players and making them pay for the game.

"What happened?" asked Gregori.

"I've killed the Ulsar," said Shangrin.

At that very moment, the spur was slowly lifted and a thin red streak appeared at its base; it looked as though it was going to remain balanced there for an eternity and that these questions were no longer important. Then, they distinctly saw the rock splinter. There was a great flash of light, and space and time were chopped and mixed and a ball of fire sprang from the ground. They threw themselves down in the bottom of the gliders, their eyes watering and reflecting red lights. The wind caught up two of the gliders and dashed them to the ground.

The others miraculously escaped. Lava rose from the depths of the earth and filled the new crater.

XI

Shangrin had aged, but it only made him more awe-inspiring, Gregori thought as he came before the Captain. Now, it was as if there was a gap between him and the rest of the world, as if his words and deeds were of another period. He was living like a barbarian among barbarians. His beard was not as well kept as it used to be.

It would be difficult to get him to accept the fact that the passengers of the *Vasco* had had enough of war and of Shangrin's absurd and endless quest. Up there in space, in the company of Norma, the thirst for conquest seemed alien, monstrous. Everything seemed so peaceful in the spherical ship. A smell of spring floated in the ersatz parks. Here, it smelled of leather, oil, and metal.

"Well?" said Shangrin.

"They want you to stop. They demand your return and the gliders'. They say you'll never stop. They request a meeting of the Council and a reorientation of policy."

Shangrin got up. He moved slowly, hesitantly now. The bear inside him was tired.

"I've told you, Gregori, to let them know what my decisions are; you are not to take orders or advice from them. I know what I must do."

Gregori stiffened.

"They are not barbarians," he said. "They won't obey blindly. They are threatening to break off all contact with you, to cut off your supplies."

"I'll get along without them. I have my own fleet—32 magnificent ships powerfully armed. I can defeat an armada from the Empire, destroy its capital, capture the entire system."

Gregori stiffened some more.

"I'm afraid you don't quite understand, Captain. You are here alone. The exploration teams will probably follow you, but without the ship, you're lost."

Shangrin's head turned slowly, as if moved by an independent mechanism. Silver threads had slipped into his beard and hair, and his face had become deeply furrowed. His eyes were now less deeply set.

He raised his powerful hands as if to curse the passengers of the *Vasco*; Gregori noticed they were shaking slightly.

"Alone," grumbled Shangrin. "The Ulsar was alone, and just look at what he accomplished. Everyone is alone. I'm not afraid of being alone."

"They're talking of calling in the Guardians."

"I'm not afraid of the Guardians. I'm not afraid of anyone. I'm even willing to challenge the time masters themselves. I have 32 spaceships; I'm going to attack them and reduce them to dust."

The Magellanites had given Gregori the authority to arrest Shangrin and bring him on board the *Vasco*. They had decided the Captain was mad, and Gregori believed they were right. But he couldn't do it. After all, he was Varun Shangrin the lone wolf, Shangrin the bear, Shangrin the Great. And Gregori thought of Norma. He told himself that if he didn't make his choice now, he never would. He had worked with this man, undergone hardships with him. Shangrin had been like a father to him, and now something strange had happened to him, had broken him. The cracks were visible; Shangrin was no longer himself since the Ulsar's death.

"I'll never be alone," said Shangrin. "I have the Runi with me. And that's why you're handling me with gloves, isn't it? You're afraid of the Runi, all of you."

Gregori did not answer. It was true. Smirno had urged caution because of the Runi, because of the strange bond between a mad old man, obsessed with dreams of power, and a nonhuman creature of seemingly infinite intelligence. The others on the *Vasco* had sneered, but Smirno had urged prudence, and he, Gregori, was afraid.

Shangrin's triumphant laugh suddenly stopped.

"I killed the Ulsar," he said. "You know that, don't you? I've forgotten why I killed him."

His voice dragged woefully, then it rose, took on a new resonance.

"Did you tell them that I killed the Ulsar? I was walking in a labyrinth like a blind man and the truth was there, burning brightly before my eyes, like a flame. And I put it out. Oh, why did I kill the Ulsar? He was my brother."

"Take it easy," said Gregori.

He took the old man by the arm, but Shangrin pushed him back violently.

"I had to kill the Ulsar. He was tricking me, wasn't he? Don't you see that we are all walking in darkness, and that I want to destroy it, burn it with my war fleet? Do they want to die in the past, those people up there in the *Vasco?*

"They want peace. They're talking of establishing a colony on a virgin planet."

"The Runi told me to kill him, so I did. I wouldn't have gotten anything out of him anyway."

Smirno had told Gregori that if he couldn't persuade the Captain to come back, he should stay with him, trying to keep his trust. He had instructed Gregori to hurry up, but not take any chances.

"I see," said Gregori.

"We have to continue the struggle. The universe must be conquered. We must clear a path to the time masters."

"There is no other solution," said Gregori, giving in.

"We'll give you three months," Smirno had said. "If you haven't brought him back by then, we'll take steps."

"What steps?" he had asked.

"We'll try to destroy the Runi and bring Shangrin back on board the ship."

"He'll fight."

"Then we'll kill him."

"You're mad."

"No," Smirno had corrected, "*he*'s mad."

"Who is the leader of the opposition on board the *Vasco*?" asked Shangrin. "Henrik?"

"No," answered Gregori, "Smirno."

"They're wrong. They're all wrong. With the help of the Runi, we'll cross the time barrier. I knew you'd remain faithful, Gregori. Tomorrow, tomorrow, our ships will go back into space. In one month, the Empire will be ours."

He would do it, there wasn't a shadow of doubt, and Gregori had no way of stopping him. The barbarians were loyal to him. He had told them that the Ulsar had died in the bombing of the crater by the fleets of the Empire, and they had believed him. With the help of the rebels, and the *Vasco* technicians who also remained faithful to him, he might succeed. He might just conquer the Empire. But it didn't make sense. It was like the blind work of a giant mole, digging in the ground, stretching out its domain in the night, aimlessly. He was a machine gone berserk.

They vanquished the fleet of the Empire in the vicinity of a triple sun. They lost 14 ships, but the Empire's armada, which had been three times as big as Shangrin's at the start of the battle, was almost entirely destroyed in the raging floods of unleashed energy. There was nothing to keep Shangrin from taking the capital now.

And take it he did—but that changed nothing. The dumbfounded barbarians entered the megalopolis of 85 million inhabitants, the only city on the most densely populated planet of the Empire. Suddenly awed by the huge buildings and the grandeur of the city, they told the slaves they were free. Fires and shouts broke out here and there, with a colossal amount of looting. But the key Shangrin sought did not turn up. He decided to leave the megalopolis, perhaps because its great size reminded him too vividly of the peaceful cities of Neo-Sirius and Lorne. For a moment, Gregori hoped that he might return on board the *Vasco,* but Shangrin did nothing of the sort. He went through a period of feverish activity, questioning all the scientists and scholars of the Empire who were brought to him as prisoners, all the pirate captains who came to him, lured by the hope of gain, all the arms-traffickers, pale weasel-faced individuals, who came to beg for the right to loot the factories of the Empire. He spoke with members of the administration.

Following the Ulsar's lead, he placed his highest hopes in them. But all he saw were former slaves who had rebelled, war leaders, and politicians. He got nothing from them that he had not already guessed. It was possible that they had been infiltrated by men as important as the Ulsar, time agents from an unimaginable future, but he was unable to discover anything. Even the Runi was silent.

"You must help us continue the battle," Inoluno, one of the leaders of the rebels, said to him. "There's a lot more to be done. There are still a great many worlds which have not been liberated. The disorganization in space, where dozens of flags are floating, defies description. There are worlds to be reorganized, new societies to be created."

"That is no concern of mine," Shangrin invariably replied. "I've told you what I want."

"Yes, I know," Inoluno would answer wearily, "but we've told you everything we could. You wanted to know who was supplying us with weapons, what power was helping us. We've told you. But there are so many worlds and empires between us and those hypothetical time masters you want to reach, that we ourselves could never come face to face with them."

"Some of them have slipped into your ranks. Those are the ones I want. You think about it, for the sake of your future."

He could not be more explicit, nor Inoluno more sincere. Shangrin could not tell him that the Ulsar had been the secret agent of an empire in an unimaginably faraway time, which was why he had killed him. He could not explain how he felt a mesh, like a spider web, closing in on them. There was at least one agent per planet, Shangrin believed, perhaps more, and they were apparently linchpins in an organization secretly pursuing other goals. The sum total of what he could not tell anyone, not even Gregori, kept growing. He sometimes opened up with the Runi because the Runi was an alien and he understood everything.

But all these interviews did provide Shangrin with a better picture of the empires and the states surrounding Xandra, Powers unknown to him until then sprang out of the shadows, and could be located on his charts. Names took on meaning, substance. Horizons were lit up, peopled, animated. The population density was incredibly thin, but certain nations still maintained, more or less consistently, contacts of varying degrees of belligerency. Some traveled among the stars, others did not, illustrating the different levels of technology. Some of the neighbors of the defunct Empire were getting ready to nibble at its remains, as if their own under-populated planets were not enough for them.

As Gregori had once put it, frogs and rats were becoming active in the moats of the castle. This activity, laughable or formidable, depending upon the point of view of the observer, could well be the manifestation of a battle waged on an inconceivably higher level. But the manifestation remained inscrutable.

As time slipped by, a vacuum formed around Shangrin. There was a change in the men who came to see him. One day, Inoluno disappeared; the deep upheavals that shook the organization disposed of him—or was there another explanation? Perhaps someone had been afraid he would give Shangrin too much information? The men Shangrin now saw were less open with him. They hardly remembered what he had done. His questions were a nuisance.

Soon, he felt cut off from the rebel organization. He undertook operations on his own, on the basis of questionable information. He waged war, sold his fleet to one power, then to another. He refused, whenever invited to do so, to settle down, to establish a power base. He was, in a way, methodically putting into practice the plan he had outlined to Gregori: he was shaking up the universe. He was stirring up the mud deposits in the moats of the castle, hoping somewhere to destroy a balance, arouse the anger of the gods, until they came to confront him in person.

Three months went by. Gregori returned to the *Vasco* and obtained another postponement. He stressed the value of the loot Shangrin was piling up in the holds of the great spherical ship and promised some sort of settlement soon. They pretended to believe him, but he could see Smirno's power growing; the hour of decision was drawing near.

"Why is he fighting a war?" Norma asked.

Gregori's fingers were playing with the young woman's soft blond hair. He did not answer right away. He wore a grimace of sadness on his face, like a mask. He gently patted Norma's shoulder before making up his mind to speak.

"Because he does not want to give up his plan. He swears it will get us back to our own time."

"For a while, I believed him," said Norma. "But now, I think he's mad. He's refusing to look squarely at reality. He had a dream and he refuses to give it up."

"In his view, he is consistent," Gregori observed.

But he himself no longer believed it. He pleaded Shangrin's case with the *Vasco* people out of loyalty, but he pleaded the Magellanites' case with the Captain out of honesty.

"Why do you keep going back to him? Sometimes I wonder if you still love me."

It was an old, old question, one Gregori could not answer. He could only look at Norma and stroke her hair. He knew Smirno's influence on Norma was growing, and that she was doing everything she could to drive a wedge between him and the Captain.

"He may still be right," he said. "Since we're lost, we might as well try everything. And even if he fails, our power will be so well established that we'll be able to live a long time in peace on the planet of our choice."

"Do you really believe that?"

"No," he said, turning away.

For there was a wake of fear in the hatred Shangrin had sown. The *Vasco* could withstand any storm, but for centuries, its passengers and their progeny would be cursed in more worlds than could be seen in the sky of Xandra.

313

Then Shangrin scored a point and Gregori regained confidence. By checking and rechecking star charts, the Captain had discovered an artificial world in the void between two stars. It was where the pirate ships came to renew their supplies of all kinds of weapons. He captured it in a surprise raid and there, found only one man, who undertook to negotiate with him. The man claimed to be the representative of a distant stellar empire, but Shangrin did not believe him. He knew that he was, for the second time, in the presence of one of the time masters.

Shangrin lured him to his ship and brought him before the Runi. The man's expression changed suddenly.

"Traitor!" he shouted at the Captain. "You've made a deal with *them*!"

His face grew ashen and he collapsed. Shangrin had taken no precautions against suicide pills, and he regretted it bitterly. The huge, artificial world exploded, killing the crews Shangrin had left there to make a systematic inventory of its archives.

After this, Shangrin, accompanied by the Runi, asked himself some new questions. Was this second player on the same side as the Ulsar? Or did he belong to the Ulsar's adversaries? In view of the political situation, this was the more likely possibility, for the artificial world had furnished arms to the Empire, not to the rebels. But things were not so simple. A game of chess, even on a cosmic scale, would encompass sacrifices, gambits, strange reversals of strategy. Implicit in this game was the secret weakening of a faction that was being overtly backed. The rules and the stakes of the game had to be known before one could determine the psychology of all the players.

They found nothing unusual on the man—nothing, but a metal cylinder, no thicker than a finger. Shangrin was absentmindedly turning it over and over in his hand, gauging with his fingers the sharp vibrations which stirred the atoms of the metal. The gesture became habit and he was hardly surprised when a precise, clear voice, speaking in his own tongue, issued from the bluish cylinder.

XII

The explosion of the artificial world shattered not only the structure of space, but it reverberated like a wave along the strands of time. It finally reached the end of human history and the central computers trying to co-ordinate the trillions of basic events occurring on the battle lines through several hundred million years. Beyond the central computers, the destruction of the artificial world was also noticed by, and shook those who were the ultimate masters of time.

At first, it had registered only as a minor incident. But the disappearance from this sector of the space-time continuum of a depot of arms, even such a minor one, resulted first, in the loss of battles that ought to have been won; second, in the abortion of stellar empires that ought to have come into being; and third, in the rise of others which, in the original game plan, had not been figured to emerge from limbo. These unfolded like fabulous flowers against the black screen of the continuum.

The two antagonists—actually, there were more than two, but even they did not know it—saw their plans upset. The war, which had been fought openly on a 7000 years old front and covertly in a jungle of several hundred million years, came to a halt. The drawback of a tightly planned strategy was that it left no room for chance—unless it was of a purely statistical nature and, consequently, predictable within the framework of the laws of probability. The explosion of the artificial world, together with other elements, was the proverbial grain of sand that clogged the giant cosmic machine.

At least, for a while.

Naturally, the two antagonists had no illusions about the real origin of this accident, no more than they had about the real meaning of the war. But they knew the cause of the incident—an entity named Varun Shangrin—and what they needed to do in order to keep the chaos from spreading: either pull him out of the game, or move him to another square on the chessboard of time.

The high representatives of the antagonists, who were both human, at least in the sense of the word used at the ends of History, met on neutral territory, in a subuniverse that had been created in an absolute elsewhere especially for the purpose of conducting the negotiations. They were already acquainted with each other and had dealt with similar situations in the past, which explained the relative cordiality of their conversation, even though each power had, in theory, vowed eternal hatred toward the other.

"I have accepted this truce," said the Axelian representative, "because it is quite plain that the continuation of the current state of things can only harm us both equally. To be sure, the front has been moved, to your advantage, to several galactic clusters away, but you are undoubtedly aware of the instable nature of this temporary advantage. There is the risk that a long series of temporal oscillations will ensue. The economic principles which govern this ultimate war require that this absurd situation be terminated."

The Nirvian representative paused a moment before reacting. They were exactly alike and each knew perfectly well what the other was thinking.

They could see, through the portholes which looked out on the real universe, the profusion of intermingling colored ribbons which represented matter writhing like snakes in the fluid discontinuity of time.

"Because of this Varun Shangrin, we have lost an extremely able agent," said the Nirvian high commissioner. "You're the ones who threw him into the distant past, therefore it's up to you to bear the brunt of the loss."

"Just a minute," said the Axelian. "We ourselves have lost an arsenal which was turning out to be of prime importance for our local offensive. Besides, what happened was nothing but a simple accident. We never made the decision to send a ship of such primitive design back into the distant past Our central computer simply neglected to correct this stupid accident at its inception because, according to its projections, there was almost zero likelihood of its degenerating into a chaotic event."

"One cannot trust machines," the Nirvian said between clenched teeth. "That is why we refuse to use a mechanical contraption for central computing. Secondly, may I point out that you have endangered a ship which did not belong to any of the primary belligerents, and thus you violated the Charter of Conflict."

"We admit that," replied the Axelian. "We are therefore prepared to make reparation. We'll take that ship back to its space and time of origin. Of course, in order to do this, we shall be obliged to use stasis fields on a large scale, which is also forbidden by the Charter."

"Their use will be placed under our control," the Nirvian interrupted. "But there is another aspect of the question that seems to escape you…"

The Axelian, in his turn, paused. The colored ribbons in the unimaginable outside universe were reminiscent, in their mobile complexity, of a game of some kind, or a kaleidoscope destined for the amusement of a cosmic child. They represented, as they flickered, empires, trillions of beings, histories that were parallel as well as successive, dramas, struggles, suffering, solitude, stolen happiness, illusions and awakening consciences. At the level at which the two high commissioners sat, they could almost see the unfolding of the history of the Universe and make sense out of it. But they knew that, above them, were other entities playing with these colored ribbons and twisting them at will.

"The Runi," said the Axelian.

"Precisely," said the Nirvian envoy. "The main reason, the only reason, we are in agreement, is because of the presence of the Runi aboard the *Vasco*."

"And our common hatred for the Runis is even greater than our mutual hatred."

"Just so," said the Nirvian.

They both thought exactly alike:

Every time they had a chance to destroy a Runi, they had to do so. If they could have destroyed them by becoming allies, they would have done so, but that was impossible. The Runis pulled their strings, which was why the humans hated them. They forced the humans to play this stupid, subtle, brutal game known as war, because they were gamesters; because the Runis had discovered that the most fascinating pawns were human beings; and because they manipulated human empires on the chessboard of the Universe.

As soon as one game was finished, the two envoys knew, another one would begin. Or perhaps there was only a single gigantic game, continually improved, repeated and transformed to the point of perfection. By this means, the Runis had taken men to the limit of their capabilities and beyond; they had awakened in the human species capacities which were akin to dreams or mythology; they did not leave men in peace, and because of them, the humans experienced many new things. Thanks to the Runis, the brief flames of human life had been imbued with suffering, conscience, loneliness and existence. But men hated them because the Runis forced them to tear each other apart.

It took mankind a long time to find out who called the shots. When they did, they realized that their individual actions, any actions, would be of no avail: the Runis played the game according to the very rules of human societies. These rules were onerous and complex and could force men to act, in spite of their consciences, against their most secret or most fleeting wishes. The beings that the Runis moved on the chessboard of the stars were collective entities, such as empires, federations... Each man was nothing but an anonymous cell within these entities. Only a minority could try to pull out of the game, but even then, war caught up with them and forced them to defend themselves or resign themselves to be destroyed.

Only in the absolute elsewhere could men hope to escape the watchful eye of the Runis, because this was the edge of the chessboard. And that was one of the reasons why the high commissioners were meeting there, thinking such thoughts.

"He must be destroyed," said the Axelian.

"We cannot intervene directly," said the Nirvian.

"No. The Magellanites will give him up to us in exchange for return to their own space and time."

"I hope so," said the Nirvian.

"Don't you think the Runis will intervene to save him?"

"I don't believe so. They never interfere in a game. For them, it would probably be tantamount to cheating."

"I see that we are in agreement."

"Who is going to put the deal to them?"

"Let's draw for it," said the Axelian.

It fell to his lot. They were both silent for a long time, watching the ribbon game being played before them. A lavender fluorescence was winning out, then it burst and made way for a bluish fog whose convolutions for a moment seemed to dissolve the ribbons of light. The rules of this game were not intelligible to the men. Were they to become so, the end of the game would be near. Bt the Runis could manipulate and infinitely complicate these rules.

"One thing," said the Axelian. "I wonder what upheavals the disappearance of the Runi will carry in its wake. We have no way of calculating that."

"There is another worrisome point," said the Nirvian. "You have just seen the entire story of the *Vasco* and its Captain unfold before your eyes. We can't find out at once what its outcome will be because that would force us to intervene in the temporal plan and the Charter forbids this. But remember its beginning. It was actually the *Vasco* which made first contact with the Runis."

"That's right," said the Axelian.

"And it is the *Vasco* captain, that Varun Shangrin, who taught the Runis to play chess."

"I see what you mean," said the Axelian.

"But there's nothing we can do about it," sighed the Nirvian.

"It's too perfect a coincidence," insisted the Axelian. "It must be one of the Runis' tricks."

"You might as well stop speculating," said the Nirvian. "It will get us nowhere."

"Here is what we propose," said the clear, precise voice coming from the little bluish cylinder. "Your ship was hit—quite unintentionally—by a weapon which projected you into a period of time unfamiliar to you. You have caused so much trouble in the course of History that we are anxious to correct our mistake. We shall take you back to your own time and space. It is impossible, for technical reasons, to take you across time as easily into the future as into the past, but we can place you all in a stasis field. This will permit each of you to cross painlessly 230 million years. You will have to give up your ship and all your possessions, but you have our solemn promise that we shall replace them when your awaken; we will also watch over your safety during the 230 million years of your sleep. We are prepared to indemnify you for the physical and mental hardships you underwent, in the currency or precious metal of your choice.

"We make only one stipulation: you must give us the Runi you have on board, and whom you are treating like an ally. You must realize that the Runi is a monster, that all Runis are monsters and, as such, are hateful and must be destroyed by men everywhere they are. In the distant future, from which we are speaking to you, two entities are engaged in a struggle to the death. You are feeling the repercussions of this struggle, which is happening *for the sole amusement of the Runis,* to satisfy their monstrous appetite for games. In this distant future, which is the apogee of the human species, at the ultimate point of

History, men have become pawns for the Runis to move at will on the chessboard of the stars.

"We are sure you won't hesitate for a second. We ask for no reparation for the agent you killed and the artificial world you destroyed by forcing a high commissioner of our opposing faction to commit suicide—the only course of action open to a man worthy of that name when brought in the presence of a Runi... Death is preferable to submission. We only ask that you deliver the Runi to us."

"No!" shouted Shangrin.

Mingled fury and joy contorted his features. He threw the bluish cylinder on the ground, rushed up to Gregori and grabbed him by the shoulders.

"I've won," he shouted. "I've won! I've forced the gods to show themselves. The future belongs to us. I have unmasked the players."

"We are not the players," said the voice. "At least, we are not the ultimate players. Certainly, we manipulate your societies and your destiny, but we ourselves are manipulated by the Runis. We know that, but in the present state of affairs, we can do nothing about it. The only true players are the Runis."

"Are you going to take them up on the deal?" asked Gregori hesitantly.

He saw in Shangrin's eyes the familiar piratical look and he knew the answer. Shangrin had shouted it out... he was not a man to go back on his word. He belonged to a world where the given word was as good as a written promise, where no one ever complained about a deal once it was completed, whatever the harshness of the preliminary discussions. A long time ago, he had spoken of returning to their own time in exchange for some rare and desirable products from the time masters. But if he refused to pay the price they were asking, it was as if he had achieved nothing, as if all the struggles had been in vain. Smirno would have every opportunity to turn Shangrin's final victory into defeat.

"No," said Shangrin.

And this refusal was aimed at Gregori as much as at the anonymous voice from the cylinder.

"Think," said Gregori. "It's our last chance. Our very last chance."

"No," said Shangrin again.

The teapot was steaming before him in the control room of a primitive ship which had been captured on some spaceport of the Empire.

"I've entered into an alliance with the Runi," said Shangrin. "I told him we'd either get out with him, or stay on with him. He came on board my ship of his own free will, and he is the guest of a Magellanite. A Magellanite has never betrayed his hospitality."

The Captain looked up at a fragile goblet made of old porcelain. He placed it gently on the metal desk, looked at the alien stars shining on the navigation screen, and brought his fist down, smashing the goblet. All this was done almost noiselessly. He took the teapot in steady hands, removed the lid and sniffed the delicate aroma of the golden liquid. Then he threw the teapot into a comer of the tiny room.

"If I've succeeded," he said, "it's thanks to the Runi's help. Without him, we'd still be sailing in darkness. If they want him, let them come and get him. They'll have the cannons of Magellan to deal with."

"But suppose they can prove what they say, that the Runi is a monster?" insisted Gregori.

"I know what the Runis are," said Shangrin. "I don't know what they will become in the future, but I know *my* Runi. He is not a monster. He doesn't cheat at chess."

"And what will the passengers of the *Vasco* say? Do you think they'll give up their return to the Magellanics, that easily?"

"They will obey me," said Shangrin. And he got up and stretched to his full height. His hair and disheveled beard were now streaked with gray. He straightened up, firm and tall, all six feet six of his bear-like frame.

"You told me once that they wanted to colonize a virgin planet. I think it's a good idea." His voice became softer, persuasive. "I think it's a fine idea. I think I could sell it to them. And why should we believe what a metal cylinder says to us? Maybe we heard nothing. Maybe it was only an illusion."

"Then they'll never know you were right, Captain," said Gregori. "And I don't think that you'll be able to keep the truth from them. You cannot make a decision alone."

"There will be two of us to make it, Gregori," said Shangrin, "and you, at least, will know I'm right. Smirno, Henrik, Nardi, Derin, Zoltan, a bunch of technicians—their advice means nothing to me. It was in the name of everyone that I fought."

His voice swelled and rumbled; it was like the tumult of great comets howling through the atmosphere.

"I accept the reparations for the damage done to us, but I do not accept their other conditions. I shall continue the struggle. I'll bring those brazen masters of time to their knees. I'll make them roll in the dust."

The voice in the cylinder sounded thin and crackling after this thunderous outburst, but it was still clear and precise.

"There is no alternative to our bargain, Captain," it said. "If you refuse, we'll have your expedition wiped out by the very forces you've unleashed. And you are not in a position to decide. We'll put the terms of our proposition, which we consider fair and just, to the crew of the *Vasco*; they will decide. We'll give you time to get back on board so that you can be the one to announce what we have decided in the names of Axelia and Nirv, whose rival powers are united in this and thus cannot be denied."

The cylinder gave out a brief green light, shattered and disintegrated.

The door opened noiselessly. It was too narrow to allow the Runi's egg to get through, so it was floating in the narrow corridor.

"It is your decision," said the Runi in his level voice.

Then he left.

"Before you deliver the Runi, you will have to wait for us to have the necessary equipment in hand to destroy him," said the delegate from the future.

He was tall and slender. His eyes were cold, but strangely human as he addressed the Council of the *Vasco*. He had told them who he was, that he had come from the ends of History; that, after the passing of his own civilization, the fate of Man was only a fog of tenuous probabilities, an inextricable entanglement of parallel realities. He told them that he had assumed his present shape in order to not frighten them, and that, in any event, he was much closer to them than to the entities from the End of Time who had sent him. He had suddenly appeared at the appointed hour in the Council chamber. He might have been real, or merely a projection.

They felt in him the refection of an incomprehensible power and civilization. Even Gregori was fascinated by the envoy from the future, though he bitterly remembered the ovation that had greeted Shangrin when he had come back aboard, and the icy silence that had followed the announcement of his decision; he recalled the manner in which, in a split second, Shangrin had passed in the Council's eyes from the status of hero to that of a wild beast. Gregori felt Norma's eyes on him, a heavy, suspicious look. He had come to hope that Shangrin had failed, that the Runi had been wrong in his original theories about the existence of the time masters.

But the Runi and Shangrin, together, had been right. That, finally, was what the people on the *Vasco* held against them.

Gregori thought of the Captain's request to make things drag along. He wondered now if he should obey him one last time, not because he was the Captain, but because he had always known what to do and what not to do. Gregori felt he owed him this delay, even though he didn't know the reason for it.

He did not have any idea of what Shangrin was planning. And there was no one whose advice he could ask, not even Norma's, because he knew the answer would automatically be No. None of them had known Varun Shangrin as he had; they did not in the least feel bound by a madman's promise to an alien monster.

Gregori began to hate Norma with a violence that surprised him. He hated her because she no longer gave him the slightest support. He knew it would not last, but during that shattering moment, he was alone, in spite of her, because of her. He was alone as Shangrin had been alone. When all was said and done, he had become, willy-nilly, a reflection of Shangrin. It was Shangrin's decision he had to carry out.

XIII

"You have heard my proposition," said the envoy from the future.

The Council had heard it—and the Council accepted it. All eyes turned to Shangrin's empty seat.

"I think this formality was necessary," the envoy of the future went on, "because your leader will not agree to deliver the Runi to us. He apparently does not realize the monstrous nature of that creature."

"He's an old man," said Smirno. "Recent events have deeply affected him."

He was staring insolently at Gregori. And so he had his revenge, Gregori thought as he consulted his watch. His hands were shaking, although he held them flat on the table. Shangrin had asked him to make the meeting last until the end of the 14th hour. He had agreed, but his heart was broken.

Three more minutes. He sought comfort in Norma's eyes, but a new hope gleamed in the young woman's gaze: her children would be born on Lorne, or Suni, and not in this hideous past full of wars and barbarians. To be sure, the millions of years to be spent the stasis field frightened her a little, but she would have gone through fire to get back to her own time... They all would.

What was Shangrin be up to?

Two minutes.

"Let's move on to the vote," said Gregori.

"There's no point in doing that," objected Smirno. "Everyone agrees. The Runi will be delivered as soon as our friends from the future have the necessary equipment at their disposal. I hope Varun Shangrin will have no objection."

"*Captain* Varun Shangrin," Gregori protested.

"As you like."

Smirno turned toward the Council.

"I propose that the motion be amended to include the dismissal of Captain Shangrin. His refusal to deliver the Runi and his absence from our meeting betray only too well his state of mind."

"He has the right to be heard," Gregori insisted, even though he knew the game was lost. He hated Smirno but he could not blame him. The Runi had to be given up and, yes, Shangrin was mad—there was no more room for doubt. And yet, he had succeeded: he had taken them where he had wanted, he had opened the gates of time to them.

The results of the balloting began to appear on the board.

The hand on Gregori's watch passed the last second of the 14th hour. He had done what he could. So be it. Let the Runi be given up and let us sink deep into that sleep of 200 million years. Only let it happen quickly, he thought, before I go mad too.

Shangrin's voice yanked him out of his reverie. It was powerful, crushing. It was the voice of the Captain of former days, the voice of the man who had dared challenge the Supreme Magistrates of the Lesser Magellanic Cloud and the very Heavens themselves. It was a voice ten years younger, the voice of the bear, rolling like an ocean, cascading out of the speakers like an avalanche.

What it was saying stunned them.

"I refuse the forfeit," said Shangrin. "As long as I am alive, the Runi will not be given up. I refuse to have him put to death. He came on board this ship of his own free will and he is our guest. I would go down to the very depths of Hell rather than give up the Runi."

Gregori saw a strange smile forming on the lips of the envoy of the future. What were the real sentiments of a man who had come from the End of Time?

"Shame on anyone who would think of giving up the Runi," Shangrin went on. "He has done us no harm. On the contrary, he has helped us as much as he could. He cannot be held responsible for the harm that his species may someday cause to humanity. The Runi is my ally and I will defend him."

Gregori looked around at the appalled faces of the members of the Council. Smirno was ashen. He was listening, plainly frightened. Shangrin was only one man and they had all ganged up against him, but they had often given in to him before, and something of that old habit remained.

"Since I can't be sure that all the members of the crew wholeheartedly share my viewpoint," Shangrin grumbled, "I have taken certain precautions. During the two hours which have just elapsed, I have been locked up in the control room, from which I can control the ship's course. At the moment, it is set for extra-galactic space. In order to circumvent any attempt on my life, I must warn everyone on board the *Vasco* that the engine room and the navigation room have been cut off from the rest of the ship. The airlocks are closed and the partitions are in place. The corridors and quarters near this sector of the ship must be evacuated at once. Anyone found near here at the end of the hour runs the risk of death."

"You're mad!" howled Smirno.

The words burst out. His mouth was twisted with rage.

"Varun Shangrin, you are under arrest. You're fired. You have no right to give orders on this ship anymore. What you are doing is criminal."

Shangrin burst out laughing.

"Come and get me," he said.

"You've betrayed your crew. You've betrayed humanity itself! You're a monster!"

They all got up and started to shout. When he turned around, Gregori saw why: space had just appeared on the big screen. The ship was moving at fantastic speed. The stars went by like fireflies gone mad. The *Vasco* was going toward empty space—extra-galactic space—and already the stars were thinning out.

The envoy from the future waited for calm to be restored, then he looked at them coldly.

"It is not within my power to settle this affair," he said. "We are careful not to interfere in the affairs of primitive peoples when our interests are not directly at stake. It is up to you to handle this. I can only hope that these complications are only transitory. My offer still holds. In the present circumstances, I see no reason for remaining here."

He disappeared suddenly. The Magellanites remained for a long time looking at the place where he had been, as if they could find a solution there. Gregori thought their fury had abated.

It had not, but their hopes had flown.

The robot-usher was going down the ship's corridors. From a secret drawer, it had picked up, with its spidery metal fingers, a golden sword hanging on a thin chain. It felt self-important, but, at the same time, somewhat frightened. During 237 years of duty on various ships, it had carried the golden sword only three times, and each time, it had meant the death of a man.

The robot was not afraid for itself, but its usual instructions forbade it from harming a human being. The little golden sword suspended this interdiction for a time and for a definite assignment, but the almost unconscious memory of all those years' interdictions weighed heavily on its limited, computerized conscience.

It was progressing toward the center of the ship, carrying a heavy weapon that had been screwed like an eye into the center of its chest. Because of this, it was only able to go in the main corridors of the *Vasco* as their thick partitions could withstand the destructive proximity of nuclear energy.

The humans along his path stepped aside and remained silent. Nevertheless, the sensitive microphones of the robot-usher could pick up scattered words and fit them into the picture of the situation it was building up for himself.

"...always considered the Runi to be a monster..."

"...Major danger..."

"I can't understand why they let him on this ship where there are children."

"After all, those men from the future know what they are talking about, don't they?"

"Do you think that the *zotl* will slump, even taking into account our cargo..."

"That will depend upon..."

"To see Suni again..."

"I wonder if she waited for me..."

"...Hibernation, obviously..."

Then, there were fewer voices and, oddly enough, the robot-usher felt less worried. The hatred the men bore the Runi made it uncomfortable. They hardly mentioned Shangrin; his turn would come later. Right now, they did not dare talk about him. It was to Shangrin the robot was to deliver the summons.

"Captain Varun Shangrin, Captain of the *Vasco,* is ordered to present himself before the Council to hear the terms of his dismissal and the decisions taken concerning the alien being known as the Runi."

When he reached the limit of the evacuated quarters, the robot ran into a patrol of explorers who stared at him coldly. They had remained loyal to Shangrin. The Magellanics meant less to them than to others. For the time being, they were content merely to bare their teeth, but they would fight at a word from Shangrin. Their guardianship was ambiguous: they safeguarded Shangrin's mysterious plans and kept the *Vasco* passengers from venturing into the danger area.

The robot-usher wondered for a moment if they were going to shoot it, but the possibility that it might be destroyed did not really trouble it. The guards merely watched it proceed down the rectilinear passageway.

The robot could feel the torrent of energy coursing through the walls increase as it went forward. Sparks shot out from the thin gold chain and the end of the small sword. The discharge increased in intensity and framed it in a dazzling light.

It had nothing to fear from obstacles of energy. When it touched the first closed door, a flame leaped out and the paint on the door burned. The lock melted. It tried unsuccessfully to work the latch, then, carefully, with the help of its weapon, it cut a circular opening in the door. It entered the engine room. It was impossible to interrupt the generators without cutting off the energy supply for the entire ship, otherwise it could easily have annihilated Shangrin and deactivated the lethal walls.

The robot went through a second door and found itself in a corridor that led to the spherical control room. The now-rare stars on the huge curved screen danced crazily by.

The Council members followed the progress of the robot-usher on the large screen of the Council chamber. They saw him go up to the control room in the center of the sphere. They could see where Shangrin had linked up the various computers so he could more or less control the ship's progress. He was seated behind a bare table, next to which the Runi, in his egg, floated. The robot had barely begun his speech, "Captain Varun Shangrin..." when Shangrin's eyes took in the little sword. A flash of anger broke out on his face and he took aim with a heavy disintegrator. The robot-usher ought to have reacted instantly, but he had caught sight of the Captain's emblem on Shangrin's chest and had hesitated.

It was a fatal mistake. The golden sword had proved weaker than the symbol of the power of Magellan. Now, under Shangrin's blast, it melted and evaporated. The robot's armor resisted for a moment more before yielding. In less than a thousandth of a second, the superficial layers disintegrated, then the small juridical conscience of the robot-usher expired. Its ashes, the color of the void, fell forward on the screen, toward an artificial abyss gaping amid the reflection of the stars.

"The Guardians! Summon the Guardians," the Council members shouted in chorus.

The noise was deafening. Gregori grew pale and ground his teeth. By destroying the robot-usher, Shangrin had put himself beyond the law. He had irredeemably violated the Magellanic Constitution. He must have been mad. He could not hope to resist the Guardians—no one could resist them—that was one of the things taught in schools. They could deal with mutineers, utterly destroy, if necessary, the ship that carried them. They were the ultimate guarantee of obedience to the law of Magellan.

But they could not be called upon in just any circumstances. The innermost organization of the ship had to be in jeopardy. A special computer had been set up to evaluate the gravity of the threat and decide whether or not to summon the Guardians. Furthermore, in order to activate that computer, a two-thirds majority of the Council members serving their term at that moment had to insert, each of them, a special key in his or her balloting machine.

Gregori noticed that Smirno, up on the platform, had also grown pale. He was gesturing, but his words were lost in the uproar. Gregori thought he was hesitating about unleashing the Guardians. Actually, no one knew exactly what the Guardians were. They could be machines of an infinitely more fearsome power even than the robot-ushers, or they could be *Vasco* passengers, mingling with the members of the crew, disguised as ordinary workers. Should the Council so decide, power would be put entirely in their hands until the crisis had passed and law and order had been reestablished.

The robots emitted their strident whistle and calm was restored.

"I ask you to weigh carefully the decision you're going to make," Smirno said. "It is filled with consequences. Once the Guardians have gone into action, it will be impossible to call them off until they have completed their task."

"We want the Guardians," said a voice. Others echoed it.

"Very well," said Smirno.

His hesitation seemed incomprehensible, yet Gregori understood it.

Eighty-nine hands inserted 89 keys into 89 locks. Gregori's hands remained on his knees. He saw that Norma, having inserted her key, was looking at him. He did not stir. He could not betray Shangrin... not like this.

But the stars racing by on the upper screen were themselves a betrayal. What could Shangrin hope to achieve by that flight? What could the members of the Council hope for from the Guardians? The two questions complemented each other and canceled each other out.

"The die is cast," said Smirno. "You've asked for the Guardians." His voice was the voice of doom.

On the middle screen, which had become opalescent again after the destruction of the robot-usher, there appeared the 16 stars of the central worlds of the Lesser Magellanic Cloud. It reawakened their homesickness. A deep voice came out of the speakers, at once familiar to them: the voice of someone who was not to be born for another 230 million years, and who was the President of the Navigators' Guild.

"Men and women of the Lesser Magellanic Clouds," said the voice, "you have called upon the Guardians because a great crisis threatens you. During the 60 centuries of the history of our civilization, only 47,000 ships are said to have called upon the Guardians. There probably have been others, but they have never returned. I hope you will be luckier than they were.

"Men and women of the Lesser Magellanic Clouds, the Guardians have taken many shapes in centuries past. I am perhaps the only one who has known them all, because this final recourse to the law must be adapted to the individual needs of each ship.

"I am now going to tell you what this means for you. The master doors which cut off the various quarters of this ship are closed and only the Chief Guardian can unlock them. That leader is among you. He has been chosen on the strength of his experience and capabilities. Should he die during his tenure, he will be replaced by another who will remain nameless for the moment.

"Gregori, are you in this room?"

Gregori got up, ashen, knees buckling. His answer was almost inaudible.

"Yes, I'm listening."

His reply had been unnecessary, for the robots were all staring at him. Their sensitive cells allowed the computer to observe him from its hiding place somewhere in the depths of the ship. It had remained inactive, blind, deaf, powerless, until this moment, when it had been suddenly activated by the insertion of 89 keys into their narrow openings. They had set off the voice of a man, not yet born, who was ordering everything in accordance with a law as yet unwritten. There was no possible escape.

"Good," said the voice. "You have been conditioned for the task you are going to undertake, but you did not know this. In their great wisdom, the Chancellors of the Navigators' Guild have decided to remedy human weaknesses as regards the law. Gregori, you are only the arm of the law and you will continue to be only this. That arm must be steady and strong; let no consideration of sympathy or interest stop you. That strength and that steadiness have been foreordained, and the knowledge of this law has been graven in your mind, as have many peculiarities of this ship, which will make of you the sole master of the situation. A hypnotic block had been set up in your subconscious which prevented you, until now, from having access to this knowledge. It can be removed by a machine, several replicas of which are located in various places on board this ship. The robot-ushers will lead you to it."

"I refuse," said Gregori dully.

The computer, known informally as the Invisible Chancellor, appeared to hesitate for a moment. In the precautions taken, Gregori recognized the attention to detail typical of the commercial sharpness of the distrustful rulers of the Lesser Magellanics, and he felt a mounting nausea at the thought of the labyrinth into which he was being propelled.

"You have no choice, Gregori," said the voice.

The Chancellor must have chosen from among the various possible registers the tones of the man who was not yet born. Deep down in its metal entrails, all sorts of answers must be lying dormant, ready for every possible question.

"You have no choice. The robot-ushers are henceforth detailed to force you, if necessary after 12 hours, to undergo the treatment which will free you from hypnotic suggestion.

"Don't be afraid, Gregori. As soon as your mission has been accomplished, you will be returned to your normal self; you won't remember anything of what has happened. You must rise above yourself, above your personal prejudices, and become, for a time, the embodiment of Magellanic justice.

"To assist you, you will have the robot-ushers with the golden swords. Any men you choose will undergo psychological training. No one can refuse what you ask.

"Your adversary, whoever he may be, will not be able to escape your justice. This is the law and it must be carried out.

"If something happens to you, someone else will take your place. Done under my seal, I, Arno de Lurve, Archon of Suni and Lorne, Merchant Prince of the Lesser Magellanic Cloud and Chairman of the Navigators' Guild, so order."

The voice was still.

"I can't do it," said Gregori.

But he could scarcely be heard. The robot-ushers bowed to him and formed an honor guard around him. He felt a hand groping for his; he turned and saw Norma's blond hair, her clear blue eyes and bloodless lips.

"You must," she whispered. "You must."

He pushed her aside and cleared a passage to the exit; the robots followed him. Questioning looks turned toward him. He straightened up and forced himself to walk slowly, realizing that there was no escape; the robots would stick close to him and guard him against any possible mishap, against his will, if need be.

He had 12 hours left.

A man got up and beckoned to him. It was Arno Linz, the boatswain, Shangrin's old companion, the toughest man on board.

"Gregori, you're not going to let them put this over on you. Nothing is lost yet. My men are holding the center of the ship and they won't let—"

"Arno Linz, you are under arrest," said a robot-usher.

"Come and get me," retorted the warrant officer, pulling a weapon from his pocket.

A blinding ray struck him between the eyes. He collapsed, his body falling like a puppet against the back of a chair. A small dark spot over the bridge of his nose began to bleed.

This was the first bloodshed… There would be more. Each robot-usher now bore a small golden sword on its chest.

XIV

The news was alarming. The Space Exploration sector had just announced that no one would be allowed near the control room except by order of Shangrin himself. His men were ready to open fire. They would not give way to the Guardians.

"Is this a civil war?" asked Norma, looking up questioningly at Smirno.

"I'm afraid so," said Smirno. "They have heavy weapons at their disposal. They can resist for a long time unless Gregori is willing to give in and then, somehow, manages to make them see reason. Meanwhile, we are getting further and further away."

"I don't want anything to happen…" said Norma in a voice which suddenly broke.

She started to cry and turned toward the wall as sobs shook her.

"Stop it," said Smirno.

He wanted to appear tough, but he only succeeded in being disagreeable. He himself felt shaken by what had just happened.

Henrik came into Smirno's office

"Listen," he said, "something must be done. Gregori must be forced to accept, at once. Not in 12 hours. We are moving away at full speed from the stellar cluster of Xandra, and as most of Navigation's computers are disconnected, we'll never find our way again. We could become lost forever."

Doubly lost, thought Smirno. Lost in time—and space. Lost between irresolution and revolt, between loyalty and the law.

"I have tried to get in touch with Shangrin," he said. "He refuses to listen to me. He says he will turn the ship about when we have changed our minds."

"Who is that?" asked Henrik, pointing to Norma.

Smirno shrugged.

"Norma Shundi, Gregori's fiancée, or something of the sort."

Henrik's bald pate quivered. His eyes grew round.

"If anyone can sway him, she must be the one. Why haven't you sent her?"

"She refuses. She is afraid for him."

"Is everyone here afraid?"

"Aren't you afraid?"

"I, I…"

"Well then, keep quiet."

The Runi must love this, Smirno said to himself. What a complex game this was, with chessmen moving in every direction. He went up to Norma and put his hands on her shoulders. He hated himself for what he was about to tell her.

"You're going to find Gregori," he said dully. "You're going to convince him he must undergo the treatment. Otherwise, he will die. Otherwise, in less than 12 hours, the robots will kill him, and someone else will be chosen."

She turned slowly and stared at him as large tears welled up. He said to himself that she must have seen through his lie, but he read on her lips, in her mute cry, that she believed him. He looked away.

Supposing it's true, he thought. *Supposing I am on the list. If I was next in line, what would I do, what would be my reactions?* An icy shiver ran up his spine. *Would I accept, unhesitatingly, the operation that would turn me for a few hours, for a few days or for eternity, into an infallible engine of destruction, the ultimate incarnation of Nemesis?*

It could happen to him.

The thought of his possible sacrifice went through him like a burst of fresh air, like a promise of peace. He could take Gregori's place, he thought, and all would be well. Perhaps he would survive and, for once, he would have been Smirno, the chosen man, the man of action. But it wasn't possible. It was unlikely that he was on the list—he had probably never been properly conditioned. And the Invisible Chancellor would probably not let him take Gregori's place. Each one had to fulfill his own destiny. A man is replaceable only when he must be replaced, because he has disappeared.

"Go find him," he said.

He spoke through clenched teeth.

"Yes," she said at last.

He looked up and saw in her eyes a determination so ruthless that even Shangrin might have paused.

"I don't want to see anyone," said Gregori into the speaker.

"Not even me?" she asked.

"Not even you."

"You don't love me anymore?"

Pause.

"I don't know." Then: "This is hardly the time."

She forced herself to say very quickly; "Gregori, you can't wait there. Gregori, you don't want our children to live in this horrible past. Oh, Gregori, you don't want me never to see Suni and Lorne again, the gardens of Lorne where I met you? Gregori, you can't hesitate. On one side, there is only an old man and an... an alien. You can't weigh them against thousands of children, women, men. Gregori, you have no right to do so! You're like Shangrin. You are now his successor and he has never let his people down. He has always come to their rescue. You must do as he has always done... you must save them, even against him."

He did not answer. She stared hard at the screen and tried to read in his face that he had heard her, but he seemed deaf. His eyes were unblinking. Only his upper lip trembled imperceptibly where minute drops of sweat were gathering.

"Gregori," she said.

He saw the woman's lips flatten against the screen, her features distorted, then her hair brushed against the screen as though she were trying to reach him physically through that technological thickness.

He turned off the switch. The screen grew dark.

He had to speak to Shangrin; he had to get to him before he turned into a machine. He felt that he could at least put as much energy into speaking with Shangrin as he would use up later in trying to bring him around. He turned and saw the robot-ushers: a black swarm, outlined by the sign of the slender sword.

He had to escape them first.

The great ship plowed through the void or, more precisely, through subspace. Shangrin's alterations in his navigational system had dangerously weakened the margins of safety. The *Vasco* was brushing against chronal aberrations that could wipe them all out of the continuum without so much as a bang.

"They're complaining that you're doing nothing," Henrik was saying to Smirno. "They are beginning to form combat groups. They've raided an arsenal and found weapons; they're breaking through main doors. They say they will wipe out the explorers, get to the navigation sphere and capture Shangrin."

"Who is their leader?" asked Smirno. "What are the robot-ushers doing?"

"I don't know who their leader is. It's rather an anarchic movement. There are several gangs operating separately and they'll attack anybody, including the robots. The robots, in the absence of orders to the contrary, don't dare use lethal weapons, so they are being destroyed one by one."

"Who could stop them?"

"I don't know. I tried—I didn't succeed. Gregori, perhaps."

"You ought to try."

"You think like I do, don't you?"

"They're going to get themselves massacred."

"Yes. They don't know how to fight. The men in the Exploration Sector do. Only Shangrin can stop the mess."

Henrik stroked his bald pate.

"He can't be reached. He doesn't answer anymore."

"I'm going to try to speak to them."

Smirno juggled with the switches of the communicators. He tried to clear his throat but couldn't relax the lump that paralyzed his vocal cords.

"Stop and listen to me," he said in a voice squeaky with emotion. "I am talking to you, men of the Exploration Sector who want to defend, over and beyond the call of duty, a man who has condemned you to a fate without issue. I am also addressing those who have seized weapons illegally, in a desperate, disorganized, futile and murderous attempt. The situation is bad enough without adding..."

His voice trailed off and broke. Like an undertow, like a long murmur of the sea, he could hear from all over the ship the boos that greeted his speech: hatred, terror, violence in their purest state.

He consulted his watch. He had ten hours left. He still had half the ship to cross, the gangs of armed mutineers to avoid, the barrages of the exploration crews to surmount and death lurking in the walls to escape.

He undressed, took out of a closet a well-insulated spacesuit and put it on. He hesitated a second, then picked up a weapon. The robot-ushers watched him without making a move. They would intervene only if he turned it against them.

He grabbed a phone and dialed a number.

"Smirno?" he said. "Can you hear me?"

"I hear you," said Smirno.

"All right. I am going to try to get in touch with Shangrin, make him change his mind. Is there some way of talking to him? I couldn't do it on the normal circuits."

"Neither could I. He must have short-circuited the wires."

"Well then, I am going to go there," said Gregori. "I'm going to try to get through."

"Why don't you accept the treatment?"

"Because," said Gregori.

"Well, I see your point in a way. What can I do to help you?"

"Do you know how to reach the control sphere?"

Silence.

"Henrik says that you can try Simili Park Number three, and go from there by the canal system in the bottom of the lake. You will reach the cooling circuit of the generators. If you manage to make an opening in the right place, you'll come out right next to the sphere."

"And the lake will empty into the generators?"

"No. The breach will be closed instantly. But there is radiation. You have one chance in a thousand to get out."

"I'm going to risk it," said Gregori. "One more thing. How can I get rid of the ushers?"

"I don't see how," Smirno admitted.

"All right. I'll find a way, otherwise they won't let me go on to the end."

Smirno hesitated.

"I... I wish you luck, Gregori."

The door opened in front of him. He glanced down the corridor. It was empty. He went slowly up to the great radial artery of the ship. He could see, at the end of the tube, silhouettes darting between cold flashes of light.

He turned his back to them. He hurried along and went off diagonally into one of the secondary corridors. He was looking for a well that would lead him to the Simili Park. He carefully examined each doorframe before going on. He kept turning around.

He came without difficulty to a well. His heart was pounding as he un-locked the well and contemplated the cylindrical shining depth stretching below him. Wells were not normally used for moving from one place to another in the ship, but they did connect the different levels and, in an emergency, allowed passage from one to the other in a minimum of time.

He jumped. The degravitational field slowed his fall. The well was so per-fectly smooth and even that it was difficult to see if he was actually moving.

When he heard voices rising from the bottom of the well, he realized he had made a mistake—he was landing in the middle of a group.

He saw at a glance that it was a gang of mutineers. Their weapons were varied and they seemed to be without a leader. He had taken them by surprise, but he didn't stand a chance of escaping them, and he had no time to waste in explanations.

He lunged into the only empty space. A hand grabbed his shoulder and, pushed off-balance, he pivoted. That saved him, for a beam went by his head. He rolled up into a ball and tried for the shelter of a wall. The Simili Park was a few steps away but he had to cross open terrain to get to it. He heard the others shouting questions and orders. He had been recognized—they were after his blood. The mutineers seemed to think that if he was killed, his successor would have less hesitation in submitting to the treatment, which would solve the crisis more rapidly.

He slipped his weapon from its sheath, aimed carefully and pulled the trig-ger. The radiant beam cut through the metal of the ceiling, which collapsed in a cloud of sparks. Live cables short-circuited and fire began to spread. The sprin-kling system went into action instantly in the thick smoke. He leaped from his shelter and rushed toward the park.

The smoke made him choke. He fought his way through a welter of shapes that must have been the men looking for him, so close he could have touched them. He took advantage of their confusion to reach the Simili Park.

It consisted of a landscape of sand and dunes, set up only the night before. Wide palm trees shed clear shadows under a torrid sun.

Men leaped out from groves of trees. They did not shoot immediately as they tried to figure out from whom he was escaping and to what side he be-longed. Then his pursuers shouted something and the new arrivals tried to cut him off; he had been identified.

A spotlight picked him up just as he was going over the crest of the dunes sloping down steeply toward the lake. He rolled into a ball and tumbled down the length of the slope. A sharp pain shot through his ankle when he tried to get up. He saw along the top of the wall of sand his pursuers taking careful aim at him. He closed his eyes.

But death did not come. He heard shouts, but no finger of fire touched him. He sat up in the sand and started to rub his sprained ankle, then he looked up. He owed his safety to the robots who had followed him. They scattered the assailants before floating down toward him slowly and majestically.

This time, they would not let him go. He got up as quickly as he could and took a few steps toward the lake. The water was soon up to his thighs; he plunged in and started to swim.

The robot-ushers flew directly over him, plainly wondering how they were going to fish him out. He dived under to get away from them, trying desperately, under the lukewarm water, to adjust the breathing apparatus of his suit, but he didn't succeed at first and had to surface. He took a deep breath and saw the robots, like giant June bugs, dive-bombing him.

He plunged again and finally succeeded in adjusting the respirator. Then he swam with powerful, rhythmic strokes toward the bottom. He had to make a tremendous effort to remain on the bottom because he was insufficiently weighted.

A long black shape sped before him. It took him a moment to recognize it as one of the robots. They had not given up their idea of saving him; they could not, in fact, abandon him.

He was trying to follow the channels in the bottom of the lake. He finally saw in the clear water the large apertures, surrounded by small whirlpools, of the water intakes. They were covered with grids.

The robot-ushers stayed as close to him as a school of sharks. He struggled with the grate locks but, unable to open them, shot them out. The grids gave way in a maelstrom of vapor. He hid in the protective darkness of the channels, which were just wide enough for him to go forward. There, at least, the robots would be unable to follow him.

He let himself be carried by the current. The lake water was used to cool certain parts of the generators, but it was divided up among a great number of reservoirs and he had to keep from getting lost in that labyrinth.

At the first branching off, he placed his ear against the wall and tried to detect a vibration. He chose the direction from which the most noise came and groped his way about for some time in the total darkness of the ship's entrails like a monstrous fish lost in a cavern.

He finally realized where he was. Those enormous parallel tubes, he was sure, went through the engine room. But which wall should he cut through? Some of the tubes were dozens of yards above the ground. Others went right through the core of the generator. He had to keep as close as possible to the bottom and as far as possible from any sources of radioactivity. He tried to reconstruct mentally the plan of the labyrinth.

He finally grappled with the canal wall at a bend. It resisted for a time, then gave way all at once. He was pushed through by the rushing torrent and thrown to the bottom, barely a yard lower down. He remained stunned on the metal floor, which was already being dried up by pumps. A siren went off.

He pulled himself up on his forearms and smiled wryly. He had accomplished the first part of the opera-don. He consulted his watch: less than an, hour had passed since he had told Smirno his plans. Action-time was also relative.

The hardest part, if not the most time-consuming, still remained to be done—reaching Shangrin and, above all, persuading him.

XV

"Get up!" the guard shouted.

Dazed, Gregori stared at him. The guard had a tough face and a shaved head. He was wearing an explorer's outfit and handled his weapon as easily as a tool. He came up to Gregori and, seeing that he was not moving, kicked him.

"Who are you?" he asked. "Where did you come from?"

Gregori painfully tore off his respirator.

"Gregori," he said, "I've come to speak to Shangrin,"

He knew the guard. He feverishly groped for his name but memory failed him.

"Gregori," said the guard. "You've gone over on the other side. You had Linz killed, huh? And you're after the old man now. Well, you're out of luck."

He slowly raised his weapon. Gregori gestured frantically.

"Stop. Don't be silly. I've come to try to save him. Can you take me to him?"

The guard hesitated. Gregori remembered him as part of the expedition on Xandra, at that time under Gregori's own command. The other could not have forgotten.

"Do you really think I would betray him?" he asked.

"Don't move," said the guard. "I may be making a mistake, but I'll give you one chance."

He whistled. Several men came up, one of whom was a junior officer.

"You're crazy," said Gregori, getting up as they jointed their weapons. "You are under my orders. I'm second in command on board this ship."

"I follow only Shangrin's orders," said the officer.

But Gregori noticed that he was weakening. Old disciplinary reflexes were still functioning.

"Shangrin won't approve…"

"He asked us to stay here," said the explorer. "He gave orders to let no one through, neither man, nor machine."

"Tell him I'm here."

Gregori spoke clearly and with authority. His sprained ankle hurt so badly he could hardly stand up, so he leaned against the wall. He saw panic in the officer's eyes.

"We're no longer in touch with him—he's disconnected all the intercoms. He said he wanted peace and quiet."

Gregori shook himself. Water dripped from his clothing.

"I *must* speak to him."

"Have you undergone that… treatment?" the leader asked hesitantly.

337

"Do you think I'd be in this state if I had?" Gregori burst out. "Do something and do it fast! You'll be under attack any minute now."

"We're not afraid of anyone."

They were rocks of stubbornness.

"Do you really want to shoot Magellanites, kill Magellanites?"

They looked at one another. After a pause the officer made up his mind.

"Get rid of your weapon and come forward."

"Tell one of your men to help me. I can't walk."

They looked at one another for a moment, then the leader nodded. One of the men put down his weapon and came up. Gregori leaned on his shoulder and walked, wincing.

"Anyway, it won't do any good," said the explorer. "We can't communicate with the Captain."

"He's still in the control room?"

"He's retreated to the room behind the computers."

"Can I get within shouting distance?"

"Maybe. We didn't try."

"Let's go," said Gregori.

They were a strange procession as they went through the huge engine room.

"There is current running through all the walls of the control room, so don't touch anything."

"Thank you," said Gregori.

He went ahead, with the assistance of the guard, up to the circular door of the celestial sphere. He could see the navigation dome at the end of the narrow gangplank which looked as though it were suspended above a void. Beyond it was the opening of the corridor and, at the end, the cubicle where the computers reflected in silence on the ship's course. Shangrin had taken refuge with the Runi. A real rat hole.

"Shangrin?" he called.

His voice reverberated in the sphere as though it had been reflected by the stars, bounced back by the invisible walls of that fleeing universe. He filled his lungs.

"Shangrin!"

Then he listened. He thought he could perceive, beyond the narrow rectangle of light from the door, a rustling, as if a heavy mass were being dragged along the floor. He took a step forward.

"Look out!" said the guard, but Gregori paid no attention to him.

"Shangrin!" he shouted. "It's me, Gregori."

Shangrin's voice finally reached him, magnified by a megaphone. It exploded in that restricted space.

"Go away," Shangrin was saying. "Go back to your friends."

Gregori waited for the echo to die down.

"Come back, Shangrin, come back. The ship is a mess. You're surely not going to let your men kill each other. Come back, Shangrin, it's not too late."

He waited for silence. His words had to go across a sphere—a microcosm of the universe—and reach the little gods who had taken refuge on the other side of the ersatz sky, in a metal cave. All around them, in the rest of the ship, chaos had been rampant since their withdrawal. This was probably Shangrin's view of the situation from where he sat, deep in the heart of the ship, as it raced through the real universe at a speed steadily increasing in tune.

"It's no good, Gregori," said Shangrin. "I've made up my mind."

"But you have no way out."

He lowered his voice.

"Can the Runi hear me?"

Dead silence.

"Yes," Shangrin finally answered. "He's right next to me."

"I'd like to speak with you alone."

"Can't be done. I'll never come out."

"Very well," said Gregori. "Let the Runi hear what I have to say then."

He cleared his throat. His voice was already hoarse from shouting. Maybe he was shouting unconsciously because he wanted to be heard everywhere.

"You can't really sacrifice the *Vasco,* the men and women entrusted to you, to an alien. Come back. There's still time to straighten everything out. They'll carry you in triumph."

"No," said Shangrin. "Leave me alone. I'm too old, it's your turn now."

"Then let me come in. Let me take the *Vasco* back to its point of departure. You're losing us."

Shangrin roared in fury—but it was a weary roar,

"Do you think I'm mad too? All ask is time! I'm going to straighten this out. Don't you suppose I've asked myself all those questions?"

"Well then, what are you waiting for? What are you doing?"

The answer was slow in coming.

"I've made a deal with the Runi," Shangrin said slowly. "I'm playing chess. I proposed one last game. If I win, he will settle for his life; he'll run away at once and try his luck out there in space. If I lose, I shall have to do what I promised. I need time... I must win. Let me be, Gregori, tell the others to give me a few hours."

Gregori's shoulders slumped.

"He is mad," he said softly, to himself.

The guard heard him and looked at him, an unfriendly gleam in his eye.

Gregori made one last effort to reason with Shangrin.

"But if you win, we will have nothing to give to the time masters. You won't get your people back to their own time, like you promised you would."

"I'll never see the Magellanics again, Gregori. I know that. But my people will, unless I lose. But I won't lose... I am taking drugs to stimulate my mind. The Runi let me do it; he accepted the handicap. Go back to your friends."

"It's a fascinating game," said the Runi, his voice crystal clear.

"But why, why?" shouted Gregori.

"I have entered into an alliance with another race, Gregori. I shall fulfill my obligations, that's all. Is there a guard with you?"

"Yes."

"Well then, he must take you back to the Council. I forbid you to stay in this part of the ship."

The rectangle of light on the other side of the ship shrank and the door slammed.

"Come on," said the guard.

Gregori leaned on him and, filled with despair, left to find the exploration crews. The officer came up to him, sneering.

"The robot-ushers came as far as here," he said. "All they want is to take you away."

As Gregori looked at the robots, he realized there was a distant kinship between them and the Runi: they both represented the same inhuman, unfathomable side of the universe. They picked him up very gently as he closed his eyes and allowed himself to be carried through the deserted corridors.

Gentle hands slid along his body, absorbing the pain. He was lying down, eyes closed, thinking. Voices floated over him. They seemed to be raised in an incomprehensible prayer.

He was thinking about the game being played in the center of the ship between the Captain and his Demon; its only point seemed to be the concern of an old man for his own personal ethics. Or was there something deeper which Gregori couldn't put his finger on, but which he vaguely felt? The game could be the means of communication between two species; it had to be played to prevent a definitive misunderstanding between them. The consequences of the game could spread like waves in the fluid substance of time, along the series of moves alternately played by unimaginable players. The game, for Shangrin, could be the ultimate means of throwing light on the innermost nature of the Runi, and for the alien, the best method of gauging human nature in its infinite variety. Passion as well as reason presided at that game. The whole face of future history could depend upon this confrontation. There was a striking parallel between the game being played by Shangrin and the Runi, and the infinitely greater one being played by the Runis from the future who, according to the envoy, were moving humans, like so many pawns, on the chessboard of the stars.

Gregori clearly saw the stars reshape into a chessboard, then the board spun quickly and collapsed in the middle, and he fell into a well of gold and night as the whispers around him grew more audible.

He came slowly out of a deep sleep. He blinked and recognized Smirno, Norma and Zoltan looking down at him anxiously.

"I don't want the treatment," he said.

It was an obsession. He turned it over in his mind, then gave it up. A sort of curtain was torn inside him. He suddenly felt more mature and surer than he ever had before. He understood more clearly the *Vasco's* situation and he knew what he had to do. It was absolutely essential that Shangrin be protected, against his will, if necessary. He also knew more about the workings of the ship than he ever had before. He suddenly remembered the secret passages whose existence he had completely forgotten, and switches that could either cut or supply energy to the different parts of the ship.

"It's too late," said a cold and distant voice which he recognized as Smirno's. "You have just had the treatment. Successfully. How do you feel?"

"Well," he said indifferently.

He examined, logically, all the possibilities. He did not in the least feel inhuman; he did not hate Shangrin, nor anyone else. On the contrary, it seemed to him that he understood Shangrin better, and respected him more than ever. The mist in his mind shrouding his thoughts about Shangrin's actions had been dispelled. All the little secondary emotions which had hampered the exercise of his intelligence and sensitivity appeared clear to him, unimportant now. He realized that Shangrin was neither a god nor a hero, but a man, like him, and what he had done, he had chosen to do, as a man.

I am ready, he said to himself.

He got up effortlessly and looked curiously at the instruments surrounding him. They were simple: a tiny ball, glistening with light, revolving and jumping in a magnetic field. The eye could hardly follow it. It oscillated to rhythms engraved in the mind.

"I'll need 30 men," he said. "Volunteers only. All the others must surrender their weapons. I suppose they'll obey me now."

"Not the exploration crew, I'm afraid," said Smirno. "But are you sure you don't want to rest before starting?"

"He looks in first rate condition to me," said Zoltan, the biologist.

"I want the men to be ready in half an hour," Gregori said.

He tried his leg. It felt a bit weak still, but the pain had gone. He could walk unaided.

Then he had an idea. "How long have I been sleeping?" he asked.

"About seven hours," Zoltan said. "You didn't say anything in your sleep. All we know is that you got in touch with Shangrin. What is he doing?"

341

Gregori hesitated imperceptibly. Seven hours. The game must have proceeded in all its complexities; it might even be over. He could not tell them about the game... They would not understand.

"Nothing," he said. "He is waiting."

There were 31 of them, threading their way through the secret passages of the ship toward the central navigation sphere. Gregori was first. He was now familiar with a maze of wells, canals and manholes secretly built into the ship by the distrustful builders. They reached the cables which provided Shangrin the current to isolate his section of the *Vasco*. They disconnected them and, in the sudden darkness, went forward by the beam of their headlights, like strange glowworms headed for the conquest of an enormous artificial fruit

They reached the engine room. Gregori's voice burst out, reverberated in darkness filled with expectation and hatred.

"Surrender," he said to the exploration crew. "You can't win anymore."

Beyond them, he was speaking to Shangrin. He hoped he was listening, that he would answer, give the necessary orders. But he heard nothing except oaths and challenges. Then he gave a signal and a light, odorless gas issued from thin capsules. The volunteers waited for a few moments in silence in the dark, then they heard the thuds, occasionally muffled by distance, of falling bodies. The explorers had not had the time to understand what was happening to them and put on their masks. They were all fast asleep.

"Stay here," Gregori said to his men.

He groped his way forward, alone in the dark, not daring to light his torch and show himself as a target for any guard who might have escaped the gas. He glided slowly to the door of the sphere, knowing that he was silhouetted against the stellar horizon. He waited. The shot he expected did not come. Then he called again in his radiophone.

"Shangrin? Shangrin? Listen to me."

The stars fled, disguised as slender rays of light. He felt utterly alone.

"I've come back, Shangrin."

Silence. A nameless anxiety gripped him. He tried to imagine what had taken place between the old man and the Runi. The Runi could not make his escape from the center of the ship.

"Shangrin!"

The door at the end of the gangplank remained obstinately closed, a deadly current still flowing through it. He couldn't neutralize the power without, at the same time, cutting off the energy source of the computers, which would have caused instant disaster to the entire ship.

"Shangrin?" he called.

He took a step forward. He heard a sort of rustling in the silence.

"Wait," said a voice. "Wait, give me another minute."

He did not recognize it at first, but it could only be Shangrin's voice. It was weak and worn out, as old as if it had come from a toothless mouth. It was redolent with the weariness of a million years spent traveling through worlds.

Gregori knew what worries had haunted it, what drugs... drugs which stimulated the brain but exhausted the nervous system, lowered the reaction time but wore out nervous cells, consuming their medullary sheaths... drugs which made a mind work a thousand times faster than normal and then shriveled it up.

"Shangrin?" he shouted.

"Give me a few more minutes," the voice whispered. "I... I'm almost through."

"Check," said the Runi.

Gregori stiffened. The nape of his neck grew icy. He wanted to call out again, but it was senseless now. It would be just as senseless to hurl himself against the lethal door, to cross the bridge over the stars. He strained to listen. He heard something like a gurgle and he thought he heard the sliding of wooden pieces on a chessboard, but it was only an illusion, perhaps only the song of those imaginary stars following their unimaginable trajectories.

"Checkmate," said Shangrin.

And in the sound of that word, there was something of Shangrin's former overbearing attitude, his biting irony, his arrogance, a shadow of his former haughtiness.

"Shangrin?" called Gregori.

"Just a few more seconds, just a few," the voice implored.

Metallic noises emanated from the silence, the sound of springs being broken or stretched. He had said he'd let the Runi go, here and now, Gregori thought, but how? Did he want to clear a passage to one of the space docks of the *Vasco,* put the Runi in a shuttle and let him loose in outer space? He wondered what his men, left behind in the dark, were thinking. He had come alone, not to accept the decision of the gods, but to force them to give in, and here he was, waiting. He was the only one who knew what he was waiting for, and he would remain the only one.

Gregori told himself that he could still risk everything, rely on his insulated outfit, force open the door, keep the Runi from...

He went forward on the narrow gangplank almost up to the door and started counting. He could afford to give these moments to Shangrin. He could take it upon himself to grant them to him, because they were no longer of any importance. If Shangrin took too long, he would not hesitate any more.

"You may come in now," said Shangrin's voice, faraway, weary, weak.

XVI

Gregori put his hands on the door, half-expecting a deadly shock to put an end to his life, shrivel him in a flash, not even giving him time to scream. It didn't come, the door was inert. The torrent of energy had been stopped. He pushed harder until the door gave. He went through the dark control room, then through the corridor, forcing himself to walk despite a sudden and frightening exhaustion. The light bulbs had burned out when the walls had been electrified. The light he had seen the first time came from the corner where Shangrin had retired. It was strange to go forward, groping one's way, through the familiar corridor; it was like rediscovering it as one's feet and hands parted the darkness and brushed against the partitions on either side.

A door at the end of a corridor. He shoved it with his foot and it pivoted. The first thing he saw in the blinding light was the Runi's egg. Empty. Spread all around it was a profusion of wires, the whole tight and complex network which had imprisoned the Runi and allowed him to talk like a man.

That reminded him of something. He remained still for a moment, trying to keep his balance and struggling with his memory to dig up a recollection. Then it came to him: that gold and silver complex, those subtle feelers, looked altogether too much like a lie detector. Why hadn't he thought of it sooner? The Runi's translation system worked exactly like a lie detector. And the Runi must have known it.

This threw a worrisome light on certain events. He made an enormous effort and again searched his memory, he remembered circumstances when the translating system had seemed out of whack, when the machine had stammered.

He saw, in a flash that the Runi had been lying, that he had forced the machine to disguise his thoughts. Gregori tried, but he hadn't the strength to recall those occasions. It was of no avail anyway, since the Runi had gone, but perhaps he had lied from the very beginning. Perhaps he had always played a solitary game, carefully, diabolically. And now, he had fled. Even the secret of his flight belonged to him, possibly a way of vanishing in the imaginary space of fictitious stars. Or he might have known the secret which allowed the envoy of the future to appear and disappear in a flash? It did no good to speculate, since there was no one now who could answer. The Runi would probably never find his own people again, nor return to his own time.

Gregori shook his head. He wanted to laugh, a weary, sad, bitter laugh. The Runi could have been lying and a good man, a great man, a man rare in the history of the Magellanics, had been destroyed because he had placed his trust in the alien. It was a bitter and final irony. There remained, however, a shadow of doubt. The Runi might not have acted perversely, but because it was his nature to be a gamester, a liar.

Just as it was the nature of Captain Shangrin to be loyal beyond all expectation. Gregori turned to the Captain, who appeared to be sleeping, sprawled in his chair, his head forward but his eyes open. He decided to say nothing to him. There was a world where games had rules and players abided by them—Shangrin's world. And there was the real world where rules did not exist. The Runi and Gregori and Smirno and all the others lived in this one. Shangrin was considered crazy because he did not know this, and he would continue not to know. The most important thing in the world for Gregori now was that Shangrin should continue to remain in ignorance.

Very gently, he raised the Captain's head. His beard was limp and the lines in his face were so deep that he might already have aged those 230 million years he had so desperately tried to win back by gambling. But his eyes remained clear and childlike. There was not the slightest trace of hardness in them, nor had there ever been. They were a mirror of Shangrin's soul.

He moved his lips and a deep gurgle came up from his lungs. All his muscles seemed flabby, worn out. Finally, words formed on his lips, so low that Gregori had to put his ear to the old man's mouth.

"I cheated," Shangrin whispered. "I cheated to beat him and he didn't notice."

The eyes were clear but, as Gregori looked, horrified, they slowly turned up and stared obliquely at the ceiling. Varun Shangrin had died. Gregori wept.

They were going home, over the abyss of time.

They were leaving Shangrin behind, sole master of his ship, prepared to navigate through time, even though time no longer mattered to him. They were leaving him behind, and it was fitting in a way. It did not imply oblivion, disgrace, condemnation or revenge, or any of those human passions which, in the end, he had mastered. They were leaving him behind because they had to travel another road and, in their course through time, they could not take the dead with them, nor a ship. They were leaving him behind in the largest, most complex, costliest sarcophagus in the history of humanity. In the misty memories about the legendary planet on which man had first appeared, there were stories of Kings who had been buried under huge pyramids, and of emperors of the sea whose mortal remains were carried by ships with crimson sails into northern mists, in the land of ice. Varun Shangrin would take his place in a long line of such legends...

They left him, uncontested master of the past, because the future was opening before them just as the envoys of the time masters had promised. They had come back, two of them this time, so alike they might have been twins. They had wordlessly accepted Gregori's version of events. They had accepted, without batting an eye, the Runi's escape. They were certainly skilled players, good at hiding their reactions.

They had recognized the good faith of the men of the Magellanics and had offered them, this time with no strings attached, return to their distant future. Perhaps they were afraid, Smirno thought as he witnessed their satisfaction when Gregori accepted, that the turbulent men and women of the Magellanics would again upset their plans. They said what had to be said and did what had to be done. They arranged a rendezvous for the *Vasco* on the planet they had chosen to shelter, in great crypts, the stasis field. For 230 million years, the almost 8000 passengers of the *Vasco* would sleep, in a perpetual present, outside the movement of molecules and the intimate dance of matter.

For three days, a continuous stream of men flowed from the *Vasco*. Gliders filled with passengers filed out, one after another, toward the giant crypts dug out of the mountains of a small planet in an almost starless region of space. During the long nights, the sky remained almost black, and with the day, the light from the distant sun barely pierced the icy clouds which floated in the high atmosphere.

Smirno was the last to leave the ship. He watched Gregori and Norma go off on the rocky ledge toward the last glider. The first mate of the *Vasco* and the young woman were walking side by side, silently. For a long time, the memory of Shangrin would remain between them, the shadow of madness and greatness. Then, perhaps, time and happiness would heal the rift. It wasn't sure, Smirno said to himself. There were the makings of a Shangrin in Gregori. Sooner or later, he would set forth again, defying space and time and, if need be, the law itself, in response to an inner necessity.

What was that necessity, Smirno wondered, which plucked men from their worlds, their womenfolk, and threw them into the abysses of time and space? Did the time masters know? Perhaps what they termed the end of History corresponded to the disappearance of that necessity. What can happen to a man in a world in which all planets are known, all destinies understood?

Shangrin had sought the answer, with the Runi, in the game of chess. In one sense, Smirno told himself, Shangrin had found it. As he watched, the enormous, deserted *Vasco* rose high in the atmosphere, like a gigantic bubble, its shadow on the ground growing smaller and finally disappearing in the gray expanse of the sky.

Shangrin had found it whereas he, Smirno, was still seeking it. As he looked into the sky long after the *Vasco* had disappeared, he thought of the identical ship, promised by the envoys of the future, which would take them home.

He had hoped to find peace once the doors of the future had been opened to him. He could again cherish the thought of becoming a xenologist for the central worlds, one of the men who formulated theories and plumbed the mysteries of life and intelligence. He had been successful, after all. He had even had his revenge on Shangrin, for he had been right. But peace eluded him.

The bitterness lingered and, with it, anxiety. He knew now that he had been jealous of Shangrin, of his strength, daring and vitality. He had won, but he had paid dearly for his victory.

He boarded the glider and looked at the arid plain speeding by below them. A few tufts of lichen clung precariously in the interstices of the rocks. He saw the mountains rise in front of them as though they were growing out of the soil. Then, silently, the great doors of the crypt closed. Now they were going forward in the immense cavern whose walls had been honeycombed into thousands of cells. A Magellanite slept in each of the niches, bathed in cold bluish light. If ever some more complex form of life, groping its way toward intelligence, were to appear in the lichen, this place would appear to it like an underworld, an Elysian field where the gods waited, as they slept, for a rebirth of the world.

He went to his niche. Looking over his shoulder, he saw Gregori and Norma kiss and separate. One must go through time alone, he reflected, and yet he knew that billions of creatures would haunt his dreams. One could not glimpse the veiled face of the future with impunity. All the men who would be born one day were now his neighbors—all the men destined to live until the Universe was full of them. And not only men, but all races... the Runis as well as others, the players and the pawns. Perhaps this was what Shangrin had glimpsed.

That completed the picture marvelously, Smirno said to himself bitterly. Just as the sum total of history told a tale, so humans and Runis complemented each other. Without Runis, humans would probably not have achieved only one-tenth of their potential. The Runis had momentarily been the ultimate challenge to human civilization, or civilizations, forcing men to surpass themselves.

And war itself, as he now understood it in its multiple variety, need not be murderous. There were infinite ways of waging war, economic, cultural, social, other forms he could not even imagine, with only one point in common, hatred. And he, Smirno, was incapable of judging humans or Runis because it was his nature to be an outsider, an observer, an outcast; in short, a xenologist.

He was sure of only one thing: that for hundreds of years to come, no one would openly question the purpose of the Runis. For a human to do so would be considered worse than murder.

This was the crime which, up to a certain point, he had taxed Shangrin with. He had won out over Shangrin, but it had been an empty victory. He himself was only a bit of flotsam to be washed about by the waves of time for 230 million years.

Such were his thoughts as the stasis field gripped him and froze his nerves, for a fraction of eternity, in the blue light. Shangrin had led them to the edge of the regained future, but because he had questioned the gods—and glimpsed something greater and more important than man and Runis together—he had not been allowed to cross the threshold of time. Had he been their victim, their pawn, or had he deliberately chosen his fate? He may have thought he was giving the Runis a handicap by playing his own game, according to his own rules. And he had acted accordingly. He had freed himself, alone, from their hold.

In that respect, at least, Shangrin had won.

Time passed. An invisible finger moved a piece on the chessboard. Gregori stirred. His lips opened and he murmured:

"What time is it?"

In a boundless universe, humanity had just appeared.

THE MONSTER

Night was ready to fall, just in equilibrium on the edge of the horizon, ready to close like a lid over the town, releasing in its fall the precise clockwork of the stars. Metallic curtains fell like eyelids over the shop windows. Keys went into locks and made the bolts grate. The day was over. A rain of footsteps beat upon the dusty asphalt of the streets. It was then that the news ran through the town, leaping from mouth to ear, showing itself in dazed or frightened eyes, humming in the copper telephone wires or crackling in television picture tubes.

"We repeat, there is no danger," the loudspeaker said to Marion, sitting in her kitchen, hands on her knees, looking out the window at the newly cut grass, the white garden fence and the road. "Residents of the areas around the park are merely asked to remain at home so as not to interfere in any way with the movements of the specialists. The thing from another planet is not at all hostile to human beings. It's a historic day, this day when we can welcome as our guest a being from another world, one undoubtedly born, in the opinion of the eminent professor who stands beside me at this moment, under the light of another sun."

Marion rose and opened the window. She breathed the air charged with the scent of grass, a spray of water, and 1000 sharp knives of cold, and stared at the street, at the dark and distant point where it detached itself from the high cliffs of the town's tall buildings, and spread itself out, widened among the lawns and the brick houses. In the front of each house, a light burned in a window, and behind nearly every one of these windows Marion could make out a waiting shadow. And these shadows leaning on the sills disappeared one by one, while men's footsteps echoed in the street, keys slipped into oiled locks, and doors clicked, shutting out the day that was ended and the nightfall.

"Nothing will happen to him," Marion told herself, thinking of Bernard, who would be crossing the park, if he came as usual by the shortest and easiest way. She glanced in the mirror, touching her black hair. She was small and somewhat round, and soft as melting vanilla ice cream.

"Nothing will happen to him," Marion told herself, looking toward the park, between the tall illuminated checkerboards of the building fronts, seeing the dark, compact mass of trees enlivened by no other light but that of passing autos' headlamps; "probably he's taking another route;" but in spite of herself, she imagined Bernard walking down the gravel paths with an easy stride, between the clipped shadows of yews and the quaking of poplars, in the thin moonlight, avoiding the low fences that bordered the lawns like iron eyelashes, carrying a newspaper in one hand and whistling perhaps, or smoking a half-burned-out pipe and blowing little puffs of thin smoke, eyes half closed, his attitude faintly insolent, as if he could fight the world. And a big black claw moved in the bushes, or a long tentacle coiled itself up in a ditch, ready to flick through the air like a whip and snap, and she saw them, with her eyes closed, on the point of calling out and screaming with terror, and she did nothing because it was only an illusion brought on by the confident words of the radio.

"All necessary precautions have been taken. The park entrances are being watched. The last pedestrians have been escorted individually as far as the gates. We ask you only to avoid making any noise and preferably any light in the vicinity of the park, in order not to frighten our guest from another world. Contact has not yet been made with the being from another planet. No one can say what its shape is, or how many eyes it has. But here we are at the entrance of the park itself, and we'll keep you up to date. Beside me now is Professor Hermant of the Institute of Space Research, who will give you the results of his preliminary observations. Professor, I'm going to turn the mike over to you…"

Marion thought about that thing from space, that being, huddled and lonely in a corner of the park, crouching against the wet ground, shivering with cold in this alien wind—staring up through an opening in the bushes at the sky, with its new, unknown stars—feeling the Earth shake with the footsteps of the men who were surrounding it, the throbbing of motors, and deeper down, the subterranean rumbling of the city.

"What would I do in its place?" Marion wondered, and she knew that everything would be all right because the radio voice was solemn and untroubled, assured, like the voice of a preacher heard on Sunday, whose words hardly broke the silence. She knew the men would move forward toward that creature trembling in the light of the headlamps, and that it would wait, calm and trusting, for them to hold out their hands and talk to it, and then it would go to them, quivering with anxiety, until, listening to their incomprehensible voices—as she had listened to Bernard's a year ago—it would suddenly understand.

"Our instruments have barely scratched the surface of the immense spaces around us," said the professor's voice. "Just imagine, at the very moment I'm speaking to you, we're hurtling through cosmic space, between the stars, between clouds of hydrogen…"

He paused for breath. "Therefore, anything at all might be waiting for us beyond that mysterious door that we call space. And now, we find that a being from another world has pushed open that door and passed through it. Just one hour and 47 minutes ago, a spaceship landed silently in the park of this city. It had been detected an hour and a half earlier, when it entered the upper layers of the atmosphere. It appears to be small in size. It is still too early for any conjectures about its method of propulsion. My distinguished colleague, Professor Li, is of the opinion that the device may be propelled by an effect of oriented spatial asymmetry, but the research undertaken in this direction—"

"Professor," the announcer interrupted, "some people have advanced the idea that it isn't a ship at all, but merely a creature capable of movement among the stars. What do you think of that theory?"

"Well, it's still too soon for any definite opinion. No one has yet seen the object, and all we know is that it seemed able to direct its flight and arrest its fall. We don't even know whether it actually contains a living being. It's possible that it's only a machine, a sort of robot, if you like. But in any case, it contains a message of the highest scientific interest. This is the greatest scientific event since the discovery of fire by our remote ancestors. We know now that we're not alone any longer in the starry immensity. To answer your question: frankly, I do not believe that a living creature, in the sense you mean, could survive in the conditions of outer space—the absence of atmosphere, of beat and gravitation, the destructive radiation."

"Professor, do you think there's the slightest danger?"

"Honestly, no. This thing has shown no hostile intentions; it's simply stayed in a corner of the park. I'm amazed at the swiftness with which the necessary precautions have been taken, but I don't think they will accomplish anything. I'm more concerned with the possible reactions of people when they meet an absolutely alien being. That is why I ask each person to remain calm, whatever happens. The scientific authorities have the situation in hand. Nothing unfortunate can happen..."

Marion took a cigarette out of the drawer and lit it awkwardly. It was something she had not done for years, since her 15th birthday, perhaps. She inhaled the smoke, and coughed. Her fingers were trembling. She brushed a little white ash off her dress.

"What shall we have for dinner tonight?" she asked aloud, reproaching herself for her nervousness. But she did not have the courage to take a frying pan from the cupboard, or even to open the refrigerator.

She put out the light, then went back to the window, and drawing on her cigarette like a little girl, tried to hear a sound of footsteps in the road. But there were only the voices in the peaceful houses, a strain of music, muffled like the humming of bees in a hive, and the purring of words in the loudspeaker.

"Keep calm," she said in a loud voice, biting her lips. Thousands of people have gone through the park tonight and nothing has happened to them. And nothing will happen to him. Things never happen to people you know, only to gray faces with unlikely names in the newspapers."

The clock struck 8 p.m. "Maybe I could telephone the office," Marion thought. "Maybe he'll be there half the night." But they had no telephone, and it would have meant putting on a coat, going out into the darkness and running through the cold, going into a cafe full of curious faces, unhooking the little black dead humming beast of the phone, and calling with a changed, metallic voice while she crumpled a handkerchief in her pocket. That was what she should do. That was what a brave, independent woman would do. But she was not, she told herself, filled with shame—either brave, nor independent. All she could do was wait, and look out at the glittering city with eyes full of night-mares.

"Thank you, Professor," said the radio. "We are standing now not more than 400 meters from the place where the creature is hiding. The men of the special brigades are moving forward slowly, studying every square centimeter of the ground. I can't make out anything yet—oh yes, a black shape, vaguely spherical, on the other side of the pond, perhaps a little taller than a man. It's really quite dark, and... The park is absolutely empty. The ambassador from the stars is all alone now, but don't worry, you'll be able to make his acquaintance very soon..."

Marion dropped her cigarette and watched it burning it-self out on the clean tiles. Bernard was not in the park. Perhaps he was strolling toward it, or perhaps he was prowling around the park fence, trying to glimpse the visitor from the stars. In 15 minutes, he would be here, smiling, his hair sparkling with the microscopic droplets of the mist.

Then the old anxiety rose up out of some internal cavern, purple and damp. "But why don't they move on faster?" she thought, imagining the men working in darkness, measuring, weighing, analyzing, moving soundlessly through the night like moles above ground; "why don't they move on faster if there's no danger?"

And it came to her mind that something was being hidden behind the calm screen of the loudspeaker and the words embroidered with confidence. She thought suddenly that perhaps they were trembling as they spoke, perhaps their hands were clenching convulsively on the microphone while they pretended to be sure of themselves; perhaps their faces were horribly pale in spite of the red glare of the dark lanterns. She told herself that they didn't know any more than she did about things that might be wandering outside the atmosphere of Earth. And she thought that they would do nothing for Bernard, that only she could make the least gesture, even if she couldn't think what it might be: perhaps run to meet him, throw her arms around his neck and press herself against him, per-haps take him far away from that loathsome star creature—or perhaps simply weep in a white-metal kitchen chair, and wait, motionless, like a silhouette cut out of black paper.

She was incapable of thinking about anything else. She did not want to hear the voice from the radio any more, but she dared not turn it off, for fear of being still more alone. She picked up a magazine and opened it at random, but she had never really liked to read, and now she would have had to spell every-thing out letter by letter, her eyes were so blurry; and anyway, the stale words had no more meaning for her at this moment. She tried to look at the pictures, but she saw them as if through a drop of water, or a prism, transparent, strangely dislocated, broken along impossible lines.

Then she heard a step; she got up, ran to the door, opened it, and leaned out into the night, toward the dim wet lawn, and listened, but the footsteps dwindled suddenly, paused, receded, and died out altogether.

She went back into the kitchen and the sound of the radio seemed unendurable. She turned down the volume and pressed her ear right up against the loudspeaker, listening through the curtain of her hair to that minuscule voice, that insect rubbing against a vibrating membrane.

"Look out," said a voice at the other end of a long tube of shivering glass, "something's happening. I think the creature is moving. The specialists are maybe 200 meters away from it, not more. I hear a sort of voice. Maybe the being from another world is about to speak... it's calling out... its voice seems almost human... like a long sigh... I'm going to let you listen to it."

Marion crushed her ear against the radio, her hair imprinting itself into her skin. She heard a series of clicks, a long wordless buzzing, a sharp whistle, then silence; then the voice came into being in the depths of the loudspeaker, hardly audible, deep as the heavy breathing of a sleeper.

"*MA-riON*," said the voice, nested in the hollow of the loudspeaker, huddling in a dark corner of the park.

It was Bernard's voice.

She sprang up; the chair toppled behind her with a crash.

"*MA-riON*," murmured the strange, familiar voice. But she did not hear it. She was running down the road, leaving behind her the door wide open and all her anguish dead. She ran past two houses, then stopped a moment, out of breath, shaking with cold. The night was everywhere. Hairlines of light barely escaped from the drawn blinds of the houses. The street-lights were out. She began to walk down the middle of the road, where she was less likely to trip over a stone or fall in a puddle.

An unaccustomed silence hung over the neighborhood, punctuated from time to time by a distant bark, or the metallic uproar of a train. She met a man who was singing as he walked, as black as a statue carved from anthracite. She was about to stop him and ask him to go with her, but when she got near she saw he was drunk, and walked around him.

It seemed to her that she was lost in a hostile city, even though she knew every one of these houses, and had criticized the curtains at every window a hundred times, out walking with Bernard in the daytime. She ran between the tall buildings as if between walls of trees overhanging a forest trail. And she was certain that if she paused, she would hear the breathing of a fierce animal behind her. She was crossing a desert place, a concrete clearing, which the night had roofed over with a canopy pierced with pinholes that were the stars. She came to the edge of the park and began to run along the fence, counting the bars.

Her heels struck the asphalt with the clear ringing of a hammer falling on the keys of a xylophone. Fear ran over her skin like an army of ants. She held her breath. The Moon cast a tenuous, impalpable shadow before her.

353

She whirled, her skirt flaring. There was nothing behind her but the row of nocturnal walls, without form or tint, like great mounds of obsidian devouring all light and all color, turning the night into a gulf and the edge of the sidewalk into a tightrope along which she had run, weightless and numb with her anguish and her cold. She was alone with the night.

A hand touched her arm, made her turn around. She cried out. The hand released her and she backed away to the park fence and pressed her shoulders against the bars, throwing up her hands.

"Sorry, ma'am," said the policeman in a-heavy, stumbling voice that was strangely reassuring. "Everybody was asked to stay home. Do you have a radio?"

"Yes," Marion whispered with an effort, not moving, not breathing, not even really moving her lips.

"Want me to take you back home? There isn't much danger here, but..." He hesitated. His face was pale in the darkness. A tic jumped at regular intervals in his cheek. "... A man was caught just now, and it would be better..."

"Bernard," said Marion, her spread fingers pressed against the folds of her dress.

"It wasn't pretty," the policeman muttered. "It would be better if you came with me. And now the thing's calling out. Hurry up, ma'am. I've got my rounds to finish. Hope you don't live far. I don't usually patrol by myself, you understand. But we're short of men tonight."

With the tip of his shoe he crushed a half-smoked cigarette, swollen with water; the paper tore apart and the tobacco scattered.

"My husband," said Marion.

"Come on, let's go. He's waiting for you at home."

"No," said Marion, shaking her head, and her hair fell across her face like a net of fine black mesh. "He's there in the park. I heard him."

"There's nobody in the park." The tic appeared again, deforming his cheek. Marion saw that his jaw was trembling slightly. His left hand rubbed his leather belt and his right hand touched the polished holster of his revolver. He was more frightened than she. He was afraid for himself.

"Don't you understand?" she cried. "Don't you realize?" She threw herself at him, seized him by the arms. She wanted to claw that pale, trembling face, that human façade, as white as the façades of the city were dark. "My husband is in there calling for me. I heard his voice on the radio. Why won't you let me alone?"

Without warning, she felt tears running down her cheeks. "Oh, let me go," she moaned.

He tipped up momentarily on the square toes of his shiny black leather shoes. "Maybe," he said hesitantly, "maybe. I don't know." Then, more gently, "Sorry, ma'am. Come with me."

They walked along the fence. She ran ahead of him on tiptoe, paused to wait for him every four or five steps.

"Hurry," she said, "for God's sake, hurry."

"Don't make too much noise, ma'am, it's not so far away, and it seems it has sharp ears. Pretty soon now we'll hear it."

"I know," she said, "it's my husband's voice."

He looked at her fixedly, in silence.

"It ate him up," she said. "I know it. I saw it. It has great big pointed teeth all made of steel. I heard them click. It was awful."

Suddenly she began to cry again. Her body shook with her sobs.

"Calm down. Nothing's going to happen to you."

"No," she admitted. "Not anymore."

But her voice was broken with hiccoughs and tears blurred her eyes as she ran. She slipped and one of her shoes flew in the air and she kicked the other off hastily and went on running in her stockings.

Suddenly she heard the monster's voice, and she saw Bernard's lips moving. It was a prolonged, tranquil sound, not at all frightening, but so weak that she would have liked to cup it in her hand to protect it from the wind.

She saw the men in dark uniforms who were guarding the park entrance. She stood still and waited through the exchange of questions and the muttered, tight-lipped answers. She went into the park. She saw the web of copper wires they had woven, glittering wires in a circle, surrounding the strange thing that spoke with Bernard's voice. She felt the dampness of the grass under her feet.

"Who are you?" breathed a voice.

"I came to..." she began, but she heard the voice in the distance: "*MA-riON. MA-riON.*"

"Don't you hear it?" she said.

"I've been hearing it for an hour," said the man. He turned the beam of his flashlight on Marion. His teeth and the buttons of his uniform gleamed. His thin mustache made his mouth seem forever smiling, but his eyes, now, looked desperate.

"It makes human sounds, Earth words it found in that poor guy it caught—words without any connection or sense. At first, we thought it was a man calling out. Then we realized no man in the world has a voice like that."

"It's Bernard's voice," she said. "Bernard is my husband. We'll be married a year next month."

"Who are you? What's your name?"

She let herself fall on the grass and wrapped her arms around her head to shut out the voice.

"*MA-riON,*" the voice repeated insistently. It could not be the voice of a man, it was too penetrating. It seemed to come from the bottom of a pit, or from the inside of an oven. It flowed along the ground and seemed to issue from the earth, like the voice of plants, or the voice of insects, or the voice of a snake gliding through the damp grass.

"You'd almost think it was waiting for somebody," said the man. He sat down beside her. "Tell me your name."

"It's me he's calling to," she said. "I have to go to him."

"Don't move. What's your name? What are you doing here, in that dress, on a night like this?"

"Marion," she whispered, "Marion Laharpe. That's my name."

She thought of her name, that fragile bubble, floating away in the time it took to put a ring on her finger, blown up again in the time it took to run to a park invaded by the night.

"My husband was"—she hesitated, then made up her mind—"eaten by that thing, and he's calling me and I have to go to him."

"Don't excite yourself," said the man. His narrow mustache quivered. "No one's been eaten. And even if they had, how could you be sure it was your husband?"

But his voice shook, cracked apart like a wall about to tumble down; it had a quality of uncertainty, fear, and pity, all mixed together and weighed down by anger.

"Don't lie," said Marion. "I recognize his voice and that policeman that came with me said a man had been killed, and he had to go through the park, and he didn't come home, and I heard the voice on the radio, just now, and it was calling me. A million people heard that voice. You can't say they didn't."

"No," he said, "I believe you." His voice faded as he spoke, and seemed dead, the syllables dancing like ashes in the breath of air from his lungs. "There was nothing we could do. We shut the gates too late. We saw him come out of a path, and just like that the thing was on him, covering him. It happened very fast. I'm sorry. If there's any way I can help…"

Then his voice hardened. "We're going to kill that thing. I know that won't bring your husband back, but I wanted to tell you. We're not going to take any unnecessary risks. Look."

The long tubes of flame-throwers shone like tongues on the grass, like sound teeth in a rotten mouth. They lay on the lawn, on the other side of the glittering network of electric wires. And beside each of these lances a man seemed to sleep, but from time to time a shudder ran over his back and his head turned as he tried to look through the tall weeds and the leaves of bushes and probe that hostile, ambush-filled area in front of him.

"No," said Marion in a loud voice. "Don't touch it. I'm sure it's Bernard."

The man shook his head. "He's dead, madam. We saw it happen. The monster may be just repeating his last words, over and over, mechanically. He died thinking of you, that's certain. The professor can explain it better than I can."

"The professor," said Marion. "I heard him. He said there was no danger, that we should keep calm and that he knew what he was doing and that it was a historic event and..."

"He's human like the rest of us. He yelled when that thing attacked your husband. He said he didn't understand. He said he'd been waiting all his life for a friend from the stars. He said he'd rather have been eaten himself than see that."

"He kept quiet," she said bitterly. "He said everything was all right. He said we mustn't lose our heads, and he knew that Bernard..."

"He did what he thought was best. Now, he says we've got to wipe that vermin off the face of the Earth and send it to hell. He's sent for some gas."

"*Marion*," softly called the voice without lips, the voice without ivory teeth, or fleshy tongue, from beyond the gleaming copper tubes.

"I want to talk to him," she said into the silence. "I'm sure it's Bernard, and he'll understand me."

"Very well. We've tried that too. But it doesn't answer."

She grasped the microphone in her fingers like a stone curiously polished by the sea.

"Bernard," she breathed. "Bernard, here I am."

Her voice spurted from the loudspeaker like water from a fountain, strangely altered, distilled. It rebounded from the tree trunks and scattered among the leaves, ran along the stems like a noisy sap, crept among the twigs and weeds in the hollows of the ground. It flooded the lawn, soaked into the shrubbery, filled the paths, disturbed the surface of the pond with undetectable ripples.

"Bernard. Do you hear me? I want to help you."

And the voice answered, "Marion. I'm waiting for you. I've been waiting for you so long, Marion."

"Here I am, Bernard," she said, and her voice was light and fresh, it soared over the children's sandbox, glided between the swings, the merry-go-round, the seesaws, between the rings and trapeze that hung from the crossbar.

"He's calling me. I have to go," she said.

"It's a trap," voices called behind her, "Stay here. There's nothing human in there."

"What do I care? That's Bernard's voice."

"Look," said someone.

A spotlight came on like an eye opening and pierced the black air like a tangible bar of light. And she saw a mass of darkness, sparkling, bubbling, foaming, made of clusters of big bubbles that broke at the surface of a sphere of flabby, viscous coal. It was a living sponge of jet, breathing and swallowing.

"Filth from outer space," said the solemn voice of the professor, behind her.

"I'm coming, Bernard," said Marion, and she dropped the microphone and threw herself forward. She dodged the hands that tried to stop her and began running down the graveled path. She leaped over the copper-meshed web and passed between the gleaming tongues of the flame-throwers.

"It's a trap," called a deep voice behind her. "Come back. The creature has absorbed some of your husband's knowledge—it's using it as a lure. Come back. That isn't human. It has no face."

But no one followed her. When she turned her head, she saw the men standing up, grasping their lances and looking at her, horrified, their eyes and teeth gleaming with the same metallic light as the buttons of their uniforms.

She rounded the pond. Her feet struck the cement pavement with soft, dull sounds, then they felt the cool, caressing touch of the grass again.

She wondered even as she ran what was going to happen, what would become of her, but she told herself that Bernard would know for her, that he had always known, and that it was best that way. He was waiting for her beyond that black doorway through which his voice came with so much difficulty, and she was about to be with him.

A memory came suddenly into her mind. A sentence read or heard, an idea harvested and stored away, to be milled and tasted now. It was something like this: Men are nothing but empty shells, sometimes cold and deserted like abandoned houses, and sometimes inhabited, haunted by the beings we call life, jealousy, joy, fear, hope and so many others. Then there was no more loneliness.

And as she ran, exhaling a warm breath that condensed into a thin plume of vapor, looking back at the pale, contracted faces of the soldiers, dwindling at every step, she began to think that this creature had crossed space and searched for a new world because it felt itself desperately hollow and useless in its own, because none of those intangible beings would haunt it, and that she and Bernard would perhaps live in the center of its mind, just as confidence and anxiety, silence and boredom live in the hearts and minds of men. And she hoped that they would bring it peace, that they would be two quiet little lights, illuminating the honeycombed depths of its enormous, unknown brain.

She shuddered and laughed. "What does it feel like to be eaten?" she asked herself.

She tried to imagine a spoonful of ice cream melting between her lips, running cool down her throat, lying in the little dark warmth of her stomach.

"Bernard," she cried. "I've come."

She heard the men shouting behind her.

"Marion," said the monster with Bernard's voice, "you took so long."

She closed her eyes and threw herself forward. She felt the cold slip down her skin and leave her like a discarded garment. She felt herself being transformed. Her body was dissolving, her fingers threading out, she was expanding inside that huge sphere, moist and warm, comfortable, and, she understood now, good and kind.

"Bernard," she said, "they're coming after us to kill us."

"I know," said the voice, very near now and reassuring.

"Can't we do anything—run away?"

"It's up to him," he said. "I'm just beginning to know him. I told him to wait for you. I don't know exactly what he's going to do. Go back out into space, maybe? Listen."

And, pressed together, inside a cave of flesh; surrounded by all those trees, that strange grass, and that hostile light, cutting like a scalpel into that palpitating paste of jet, they heard the approaching footsteps, distinct, stealthy, of the human killers who ringed them, fingers clenched on their copper lances, faces masked, ready to spew out a lethal grey mist... a broken branch, a liquid rustling, a stifled oath, a click.

PARTY LINE

The two telephones rang at the same time. Jerome Bosch hesitated. An annoying coincidence which often occurred, but never at this hour, never at 9:05 a.m. when one has just arrived at the office and has only the dreary outlook outside—a long gray wall, with just a few spots, so abstract, so dim, that they didn't even allow the starting point for a daydream.

At 11:30 a.m., yes, the time when people began to feel well, quickly finish their business with the idea of saving some minutes for lunch, feeling more at their ease, when the lines are busy or all the telephones ring together, mostly when the telephone centers in their cool caves begin to vibrate, to smoke, to melt.

He knew a few solutions to the problem. Take one of the phones off the hook, answer, and let the other ring till the caller got tired and decided to call five minutes later. Take the receiver off, ask the name, say you're sorry. Take the second line, ask the name, ask them to be patient. Choose the most important name, or the longest, listen first to the woman, if there is one, rather than the man. Women in business were more concise. Or take the two calls at the same time.

Jerome Bosch seized the two phones. The ringing stopped. He watched his right hand, and the little cold black halter which weighed next to nothing at the end of his arm. Then looked at his left hand and the other twin halter. He had a desire to crash the one against the other, or to kindly place them next to each other on the desk right side up so that the two callers could talk to each other and, who knows, maybe make some sense out of it.

But nothing to do with me in any case. I'm an intermediary. That's what I am. Listen and repeat. I'm a filter between a receptor and a microphone, a hearing aid between a mouth and an ear, an automatic pen between two letters.

He put the receivers next to each of his ears.

Two voices:

"Jerome, bas someone called already?" "I'm the first, isn't that so?... Answer me..."

A precise, clear voice, a disturbing voice, at the border of hysteria. They made an echo, curiously alike.

"Hello," said Jerome Bosch. "Who am I talking to please?"

The ordinary formula, prudent, impersonal, but why don't they give their names?

"It would take too long to explain... the communication might be cut off . . . . pretext...	"... don't... don't you mustn't...you mustn't I am

difficult to get... Listen well,   no... not...
it's the chance of a   ....
lifetime. You have   ....
to say yes and go..."   ....
(*Click, static, noise of*   ....
falling sand on metal.)   ....
" ... don't hesitate."   ....

"Who are you?" cried Jerome Bosch into the two phones.

Silence.

A double hissing. To the right, it was the rubbing of metal. To the left, the rattle of a machine. To the right, a tiny noise of eggshells being crushed. To the left, the light sound of a grater on a bed spring.

"Hello," Jerome Bosch said in vain.

Click. Click. Buzzing. Silence. Buzzing. Silence. To the right, to the left. A double busy signal on the lines.

He hung up the phone on the left. He waited a minute for the other phone, lying in the palm of his right hand, pressed next to his ear, listened to the sad mechanical music which sang on two notes, noise and silence, noise and silence, which like a siren of absence moaned at the bottom of its plastic shell.

Then he put the telephone at his right on its hook.

Through the open window, he scrutinized the sky where a few dirty city birds and black sparrows drifted above the weather-glazed wall which blocked a good part of his horizon. Then, inside near the window he regarded the artistic calendar offered by an electronic calculating machine company, which presented a careful reproduction of a baroque painting for each day: *Visit to the Rhinoceros*. The Rhinoceros, with an air of annoyance, turned its back on his visitors, probably to better show himself to an art amateur. On the other side of the fence, quite low, a woman in a long dress with a mask on her face, a harlequin, and two children tied with ribbons amused themselves with the beast.

It was the same voice. But how could someone talk at the same time into two different phones, and, in spite of that, speak different words, simultaneously, on two different lines.

He knew the voice. He had already heard it somewhere.

He thought back on the voices of his friends, his clients, the voice of people whom he had relations with, without being especially friends or without selling them something, the voice of businessmen, doctors, tradespeople, taxi-telephones, all the voices one hears at the bottom of a phone without being able to add a face, oily voices, arrogant voices, dry voices, sprightly voices, laughing, metallic, harsh, hoarse, contracted, distinguished, mannered, vulgar with a husky accent, suave and almost perfumed, gloomy, tight, precise, pretentious, bitter, or sardonic.

He was sure of only one thing. He had heard on the two sides a man's voice.

They'll call back, he said.

He'll call back, because it concerned only one and the same person, even though at the left the voice had been clear, assured, exacting, and almost triumphant, and at the right smothered, terrified, and almost whining.

It was incredible what one could learn about people simply by listening to them on the telephone.

He began to work. A ream of white paper, a small box of clips, three colored pens, and all kinds of samples of formulas next to him. He had to prepare a letter, complete a document, fix up a report, and verify some columns of figures. That was enough to take up the morning. The writing of the report would have to be taken care of in the afternoon. He would take care, before going to lunch, of the difficult problem of choosing to eat in the office canteen or in one of the little restaurants in the neighborhood. He would go as usual to the canteen. The first two years, he chose regularly one of the two small restaurants, because the canteen depressed him. It reminded him that he lived in a universe he hadn't chosen, and as long as he could try to escape it, even if only symbolically, he held on to the impression that his stay was only temporary. A bad moment to pass, like school or military service. Not so bad, however. Work was often interesting and his colleagues were intelligent and cultivated. There were some who had even read his books.

Someone wanted to play a joke on him.

Things like that were possible with a tape-recorder. There wasn't even any conversation. He had just listened, called out hello, and asked for names. A joke without the punch line. He began to work. The strange thing was that, when he worked, he couldn't help thinking of the stories he wanted to write, that he had to write, and of the one he wrote with difficulty, the evening in his apartment, lit from one end to the other, where he walked from one room to the other because he could not stand the night. And then, not less curious, he thought of his work in the day; he could not keep from worrying about a certain affair, and how would so and so take the explications—a little flimsy—would the final document come out on time, everything which should have been blotted out in the silence and left him in peace with his dreams. A man, it was said, could not keep up with two different activities. He would end up by developing two different personalities, which would fight and destroy each other. He had started down the double road of schizophrenia.

He picked up the telephone and dialed an interior number.

"Mrs. Dupont? Yes... Bosch here. How are you?... Fine, thank you... Will you bring me the Marseilles report? Thank you."

One day, one day, he'd write full time. But at this idea a sudden terror made him lose his breath. Would he be capable of writing, to invent stories, to put together other words than those of accounts and letters? There was a knock on the door. "Come in," he said. The young woman was attractive. She had a round face and a small, pointed nose. What would she like to do, he thought, if she weren't weighed down with paperwork and typing? Paint, sew, read, walk, increase her sentimental relationships? It was a question he'd never ask. But somehow, he thought, it should be the subject of an inquiry, the only inquiry worth taking. It should be taken in the streets, the cafes, in the movies, in the theaters, in vehicles, and right into homes to ask people what they would do if they were completely free, how they would choose to spend that rare commodity which is called "time," in what sort of bottles they desired to pour the numbered sand of their lives. He could imagine the hesitation, the incredulity, the reserve, the panic. How does that concern you? I don't know, no really not, I never thought about it. Wait. Maybe I…

She saw that he was reflecting, put the document on the desk, and, without saying anything, left.

He took the document and opened it.

The phone on the left rang.

"Hello," he said.

"Hello, Jerome Bosch?"

It was the precise voice.

"I called you two days ago. The contact was bad. Can you hear me better now?"

"Yes," he said, "but it was a little while ago, not two days. If this is a joke…"

"For me it was two days ago. It isn't a joke."

"I believe it, nevertheless," said Jerome Bosch. "Two days or a little while ago is not the same thing. And why are you so familiar?"

"It took me two days to find the combination, or rather to arrive at favorable conditions. It's not so easy to telephone from one time to another."

"Excuse me," said Jerome Bosch.

"From one time to another. I prefer to tell you the truth. I'm calling from the future. I'm you, older than… It's better you don't know too much."

"Look, I haven't any time to waste," said Jerome Bosch, his eyes fixed on the open document.

"This is not a joke," pleaded the voice, calm, reasonable. "I didn't intend to tell you the truth, but you don't want to listen to me. You always need explanations and precise reasons."

"You also," said Jerome Bosch, entering into the game, "because you are me."

"I've changed a bit," said the voice.

"And how are you?"

"Much better than you are. I'm working at a job that interests me. I have all my time to write. Quite a bit of money, at least from your standpoint. A villa at Ibiza, another in Acapulco, a wife and two children. I'm glad to be alive."

"Felicitations," said Jerome Bosch.

363

"All that is yours, naturally, or will be yours. It's just necessary not to make a mistake. That's the reason I've called you."

"I see. The stunt of tomorrow's newspaper. The stock market or next week's lottery…"

"Listen," the voice said, annoyed, "at 11:58 a.m. this morning you will receive a telephone call from a very important man. He's going to make you a proposition. You must accept. Don't hesitate to leave the same night even if it's to the end of the world. Have confidence."

"I hope at least it's an honest proposition," said Jerome Bosch ironically.

The voice on the phone seemed hurt.

"Very honest. It's what you've been waiting for, for years. For God's sake take me seriously. It's the chance of a lifetime. One you won't have again. This person often changes his mind. Don't give him the time. It will be the beginning of a brilliant and stimulating career."

"And why have you called me, since you have succeeded?"

"I won't succeed unless you decide. You so often have the habit of hesitating, of equivocating, and then…"

The telephone to the right began to ring.

"They're calling me on another line," said Jerome Bosch, "I'm going to hang up."

"Don't hang up," cried the voice frantically, "don't…"

He had put the phone on the hook.

He waited a moment, listening to the other phone ringing, and time suddenly opened up. The ringing stretched out over miles of seconds and the silence was like an enormous cool oasis of repose. Ibiza, Acapulco. Names on a map. White and red villas hanging on the sides of steep hills. All the time to write.

He remembered the day when he had heard this voice. It came out of the speaker of the tape-recorder. It was his own voice. The telephone naturally had changed it, impersonalized it, smothered it, but it was his own voice. Not the one which he had the habit of hearing, it was different, re-stored by being registered. The voice which others heard.

The telephone on the right rang for the fourth time. He picked it up. He thought at first that there was nobody on the other end of the line. He only heard a false silence full of hissing and echoes, of mechanical scratchings as if the line picked up the sounds emitted in a great cave buried underground, full of microscopic noises, feeble drippings, raspings of insects, and tiny landslides. Then he heard the voice, even before understanding what it said, or rather like an indistinct singsong.

"I hear you very indistinctly," he said.

"Hello, hello, hello, hello," said the voice, now a little more distinct. "You mustn't go… under any circumstance… Jerome, Jerome, do you hear me? Listen to me, for the love of God. Don't leave…"

"Speak louder, please," he said.

The ridiculous voice shouted, strangled:

"Refuse... refuse... later..."

"Are you sick?" said Jerome Bosch. "Shall I let someone know? Where are you? Who are you?"

"Yyyyy... " said the voice. "You."

"Again?" he said. "But the other voice said that."

"...am in the future... don't leave... that's how it is... understand..."

There was a timid knock on the door.

"Come in," said Jerome Bosch, lifting the phone from his ear and mechanically putting his hand over the microphone.

The new office boy came in. It was his first job, and the men and women shut in their offices, who blackened sheets of paper all day long, impressed him. He blushed easily and he was always impeccably dressed. He put the newspaper and letters on the edge of the desk.

"Thank you," said Jerome Bosch with a nod of his head. The door closed.

He put the phone back against his ear. But the voice was gone. It was lost in the labyrinth of wires that covered the world. A click. Then the dial tone.

He hung up the phone, thoughtful. Was it his own voice like the other time? He wasn't sure. Yet the two voices, the one at the right and the one at the left, had a familiar air. Two moments of the future, two different moments that tried to reach him.

He opened the letters. Nothing important. He annotated them and put them in a box. He threw out the envelopes. Then he tore open the band on the newspaper and rapidly scanned the pages to look at the financial section. Like every morning, his glance wavered over the page and then fixed on the weather report. He looked without interest, as usual. The map pinpointed with symbols caught his attention.

He read:

Weather cool and humid over region of Paris.

His eyes skipped two or three lines.

The cyclical perturbations in the Antilles are moving toward the northeast, above the Atlantic Ocean. There might be...

His attention wandered to the top of the page and flickered diagonally over the stock market and the leading values. Stocks strong, but not many transactions. Rise on silver. Light fall on cocoa.

Nothing but the usual business. He folded the newspaper.

He began to read the first document in his file.

He reread the first paragraph four times without understanding it. Something was wrong, not in the paragraph but in him. A drunken squirrel turning in a cage that resembled a telephone dial.

He took the phone at the right and dialed the switchboard.

"...I'm listening," said an arrogant voice.

"A little while ago I had two telephone calls. Can you tell me if my callers left their numbers?"

It was the habit of the switchboard operator to note down all the communications, not like a policeman, but to be able to easily establish a broken communication.

"Which extension?"

"Four one three," said Jerome Bosch.

"...go see... don't leave."

He heard the indistinct voices at the end of the line.

Another voice, feminine, friendly:

"You haven't received any calls this morning, Mr. Bosch. At least not from outside."

"I've been called four times," said Jerome Bosch.

"Not from outside, Mr. Bosch, at least not on your extension."

"I haven't left my office."

"I can assure you..."

He cleared his voice.

"Can a telephone call from outside reach one without passing through the switchboard?"

The switchboard operator waited a moment

"I don't see how, Mr. Bosch."

Uneasy: "I haven't left my post."

Polite but cool: "Shall I call the main office?"

"No," said Jerome Bosch. "I must have been dreaming."

He hung up and passed his hand over a moist forehead. It was a joke. They had used one of the secretary's tape-recorders and they hadn't even taken the trouble to use the outside line. They must be screaming with laughter in the office next door. Melchior was a specialist at imitating voices.

Silence. The staccato of a typewriter stifled by the thickness of two doors. A distant step. The clamor of the city swallowed up by the open window, drilled by escaping rumblings.

He looked at the two telephones as if he had never seen them before. It was impossible. The two telephones were supplied with two distinct bells. A piercing one for the exterior, a muffled one for the interior. The ringing that had preceded each of the four strokes of the telephone still echoed in his ears.

He got up so abruptly that he almost turned over his chair. The hall was empty. He pushed the partly opened door of an office, then a second, then a third. They were all empty; there wasn't even a scrap of paper on the polished surface of the tables as a reminder that they were used. In the last office he picked up the phone, pressed the corresponding button for the inside office, and composed his post number. A muted grumble came from his office, filled the hall. Nobody had reversed the lines of the bell system.

He crossed the corridor, knocked, and entered his secretary's office. She waved her fingers in the air over her machine.

"There's no one around this morning."

"It's vacation," she said. "There's only the assistant director, you, and I... and the office boy," she added after a moment.

"Oh," said Jerome Bosch, "I forgot."

"I'm leaving next week." She pointed in the air. "Don't forget. Will you need someone else?"

"I don't know," he said helplessly, "see personnel."

He leaned against the frame of the door.

"Do you think the weather's going to be good, Mr. Bosch?"

"I have no idea. I hope so."

"The radio this morning announced a cyclone over the Atlantic. We'll probably have rain."

"I hope not," he said.

"You need to take a rest, Mr. Bosch."

"I'll leave soon. Two or three little jobs to finish. Oh, by the way, did you hear the phone ring this morning in my office?"

She nodded her head affirmatively.

"Two or three times. Why? Weren't you there? Should I have answered?"

"I was there," said Jerome Bosch, ill at ease. "I took the calls, thank you. Where are you going?"

"To the Landes," she answered, watching him curiously.

"Well, I hope you have good weather."

He left, closing the door after him, and waited a moment in the empty corridor. The staccato of the machine began again. Reassured, he returned to his office.

He picked up a letter.

The telephone to the right began to ring.

He looked at his watch. It was 11:58 a.m.

"Hello."

"Mr. Bosch," said the operator. "A call from out of town. One minute please."

Click. He heard the distance, the waltz of electrons crossing frontiers without passports, waves leaping across space, sent over oceans by the intercontinental rackets of satellites, bounding along cables posed on the bottom of the sea.

"Hello," said a man's voice. "Mr. Bosch. Jerome Bosch?"

"Speaking," said Jerome Bosch.

"Oscar Wildenstein on the phone. I'm calling you from the Bahamas. I just finished your last book, *Within a Long Garden.* Very good, excellent, very original."

A male voice assured, vibrant with a light foreign accent. Italian, maybe American, or a little of both. A voice that had an odor of expensive cigars,

367

dressed in a white tuxedo, speaking from the edge of a pool, under a clear blue sky from which hung a torrid sun.

"Thank you," said Jerome Bosch.

"I read it all night. Couldn't tear myself away. I want to make a film with Barbara Silvers. You know her? Well, I want to see you. Where are you now?"

"I'm in my office," said Jerome Bosch.

"Can you get away? You have a plane that leaves Paris-Orly at 4 p.m. local time... Wait... it's 4:30 p.m... I'll get you a ticket. My agent in Europe will take you to the airport. No point taking anything with you. You can find everything in Nassau."

"I'd like to think about it."

"Naturally, think it over. I can't tell you everything over the telephone. We'll discuss the details tomorrow over breakfast. Barbara is very excited over the idea of meeting you. She's going to read your book. She'll have read it by tomorrow. I'll translate the difficult passages. Natasha wants to see you, also. And Sybil, and Merryl, but they're just extras."

The voice became distant. Jerome Bosch heard feminine laughter, then the voice of Wildenstein, a little fainter but very distinct, so distinct he might have been speaking from the room next door: "No, you can't speak to him just now."

"They're completely crazy. They want to talk to you immediately. It's not possible. I told them to wait until tomorrow. Harding or Hardy—can't remember his name—who is my representative in Europe, will take care of you. It was very nice to talk to you. Tomorrow. *Domani. Mañana.*"

"Good-bye," said Jerome Bosch in a weak voice.

What time is it there? he asked himself.

6 or 7 a.m. He had read all through the night. A novel not possible to adapt for the movies. Except, maybe by him. After all, I know better than anyone else how to adapt it. He understood that all the screenwriters would break their backs over it. A brilliant and successful career. Two houses, one in Ibiza and one in Acapulco.

There was a knock on the door.

"Come in," he said.

The secretary stood in the doorway, a strange expression on her face. She held a small piece of paper in her hand.

"There was a call for you while you were on the other line, Mr. Bosch. I was given the call."

"Well?" said Jerome Bosch joyously.

"I couldn't hear very well. The transmission was terrible, really bad. He must have been calling from far away. I'm sorry, Mr. Bosch."

"And what did he say?"

"I couldn't understand except for two of three words. He said: TERRIBLE... TERRIBLE... two or three times, then... ACCIDENT... or OCCIDENT. I wrote it here."

"He didn't leave his name?"

"No, Mr. Bosch, or his number. I hope he'll call back. I hope nothing bad happened to your family. An accident, Heavens, it's so quick to happen."

"I don't think there's anything to worry about," said Jerome Bosch, taking the little square of paper. His glance wavered over the stenographic hieroglyphics and stopped over: TERRIBLE … TERRIBLE … ACCIDENT.

The A of ACCIDENT was underlined and above it was marked an O.

"Thank you, Mrs. Dupont. Don't worry. I don't know anyone who could have had an accident... No one."

"Maybe it's a mistake."

"Certainly it's a mistake."

"I'm going to have lunch."

"Very well, enjoy your meal."

When she had closed the door he wondered if he should wait for her to come back before leaving the office. Usually he arranged it so someone was there to take the urgent calls. But it was vacation. There wouldn't be any calls.

Unless the two voices called back.

He shrugged his shoulders and threw an oblique look at the Rhinoceros. The real question was what to decide. It was vacation time, after all. He could leave for a week without having to give an excuse. The Bahamas. Maybe Wildenstein's agent would show up. Maybe it was a millionaire's whim. As soon as said, forgotten. Someone in the Bahamas had read his book or heard it talked about and wanted to hear the sound of his voice, verify that he existed.

He put the newspaper in his pocket. He stared at the telephones as if he was waiting for the ringing to start again while he crossed the corridor with its threadbare rug, stripped with parallel lines, and walked down the large stone stairway. He listened, almost surprised not to be stopped by a loud ring. He crossed the courtyard into the street.

He took the street to the little Basque restaurant

He went up to the first floor, where few people came in this season. He looked at the menu purely from habit, as he knew it by heart, and ordered a tomato salad and a Basquaise chicken with a small bottle of red wine. It was almost one o'clock. In the Bahamas, Wildenstein was having breakfast with Barbara, Sybil, Merryl, Natasha, and a half a dozen secretaries under a clear blue sky in the shade of exotic palm trees, and while eating called the four corners of the world with his assured male voice echoing around him, speaking in three or four languages of all the books he had read at night.

Jerome Bosch opened his newspaper. He had just started on his salad when the waitress came over to him.

"Are you Mr. Bosch?"

"Yes," he said.

"There's a telephone call for you. The person said that you were upstairs. The phone is downstairs next to the counter."

"I'll go," he said, suddenly anxious. Was it that faraway voice, indistinct, covered with static? Or was it the other voice, which phoned from Ibiza or Acapulco? Or was it Wildenstein's agent?

The telephone stood between a counter and the kitchen. Jerome Bosch squeezed into a corner to let the waitress pass by.

"Hello," he said, trying to protect his ear against the rattle of dishes.

"I had trouble finding you. Oh, I knew where you were, naturally. But I couldn't remember the number of the restaurant. To tell the truth, I never knew it. It's not so easy to find a number when you don't know the name or the exact location of the restaurant."

It was the voice to the left—precise, clear, but more nervous than in the morning, it seemed.

"Wildenstein, did he call?"

"At the exact time," said Jerome Bosch.

"Are you going to accept?"

The voice was anxious.

"I don't know yet. I have to think about it."

"But you must .accept. You must go. Wildenstein is an extraordinary man. You'll get along great. From the first minute. You'll do big things with him."

"And will the film be good?"

"What film?"

The adaptation of *Within a Long Garden.*"

"It'll never be done. You know it's completely untranslatable. You'll speak to him about another idea. He'll be thrilled. No, I can't tell you what. It's necessary... It's necessary that it will happen."

"And Barbara Silvers? How is she?"

The voice softened.

"Barbara, oh, Barbara. You'll have plenty of time to get to know her. All the time. Because... I can't tell you."

There was silence.

"Where are you calling from?"

"I can't tell you. From a very pleasant place. You must not know your future. It would upset a lot of things."

"Someone called me this morning," Jerome Bosch said abruptly. "Someone who had your voice or mine, but broken, tired. I heard it very badly. He told me not to do something. To refuse something. Maybe Wildenstein's proposition."

"Did he call from the future?"

"I don't know."

A silence. Then:

"He spoke about an accident."

"What did he say?"

"Nothing. Just one word. Accident."

"I don't understand," said the voice. "Listen, don't worry. Go see Wildenstein. Go ahead."

"He called several times," said Jerome Bosch. "He'll certainly call back."

"Don't get scared," said the voice, anxious. "Ask him the date when he phones, understand? Maybe someone is trying to keep you from succeeding. Someone who is jealous of me. Are you sure he had our voice? One can imitate voices."

"Almost sure," said Jerome Bosch.

He waited a moment because a waitress was behind him.

"Maybe he's calling about *your* future," he continued. "Maybe something will go wrong for you and he wants to let me know. Something which began with Wildenstein."

"That's impossible," said the voice. "Wildenstein is dead. You... you needn't know. Forget it. It doesn't matter. In any case, you don't know when."

"He... he will die in an accident, isn't that it?"

"In an airplane accident"

"Maybe that's it. You... you have something to do with it?"

"Absolutely nothing. I can assure you."

The voice became nervous: "Listen, you're not going to ruin your future over this story. You don't risk a thing. I know what's happened. I've lived through it."

"You don't know your future?"

"No," said the voice. "But I'm capable of taking care of it. I'll watch out. Nothing will happen. And even if something happens, I'm much older than you. No, I can't tell you my age. Let's put it that you have a good ten years ahead of you. Really good years. I wouldn't let the opportunity go, even if I had to die tomorrow!"

"Die tomorrow," said Jerome Bosch.

"Just a way of speaking. It's a lot, ten years, you know. And I'm fit as a fiddle. Much better than at your age. I promise you. Accept. Leave for the Bahamas. Don't tie your-self down to anything. Promise me you'll accept."

"I would like to know one thing," Jerome Bosch said slowly. "How can you talk to me? Have they invented a time machine in the future? Or have you done the job yourself?"

The voice began to laugh at the other end of the line. A laugh a little forced.

"It exists already in your era. I don't know if I should tell you. It's a secret. Very few people know about it. Anyhow, you wouldn't know how to use it. Nobody knows how it works, even now. You need luck, the right set of circumstances. The machine is the telephone."

"The telephone," repeated Jerome Bosch, surprised.

"Oh, not the combination you hold in your hand, but the network, the whole network. It's the most complicated thing done by man. More complicated than the calculating machines. Think of the thousands of miles of wires, the millions of amplifiers, of the inextricable tangle of the centers. Think of the millions of messages which go around the earth. And everything is connected. Time and again something unexpected happens in this jumble. Time and again the phone connects two moments instead of two places. It might become official one day. But I doubt it. Too many unknowns. Too many risks. Only a few are in the know."

"How did you do it?"

"You will have very intelligent friends in the future if you accept Wildenstein's proposition. But I'm talking too much. You don't need to know everything. Accept. That's all."

"I don't know," murmured Jerome Bosch as he heard a click at the other end of the line.

Someone was waiting behind him

"Oh, excuse me. I was very long." He tried to smile. He walked up the stairs holding on to the railing. The chicken had been served. It was almost cold.

"Do you want me to reheat it?" asked the waitress.

"No, that's all right."

They didn't have a machine to travel in time but they had discovered a new way to use the telephone.

The telephone.

It covered the entire planet. It ran along roads, railways, suspended over linear forests. It plunged under rivers and oceans in a rubber coat. It formed a thick and spiderlike bail at the same time. The wires crossed and intercrossed. Nobody would be capable of drawing a complete diagram of the telephone System. And in ten years? And in twenty years? The system would be more complex than the human brain.

He tried to imagine the cool, dark caverns of the great centrals where, in silence, impalpable impurities drowned in a crystal heart, oriented innumerable voices. And the networks were in one sense living. Men spread it all the time and meticulously repaired it. The networks were nerves. Automatic calculators cutting messages into small pieces so as to be able to cross and fill the silences. What would be: so surprising if the telephone should be capable of another miracle?

He remembered stories—maybe legends—that one told about the telephone. Numbers one could dial at night that would put you in contact with unknown voices. Not only one voice, but anonymous voices, bodiless, which exchanged between them their own talk, playful, joking, who profited from the situation and said things which wouldn't be quoted under cover of a known name or face. He remembered ghost voices, which, they said, wandered without stopping in the line of the network and always repeated the same thing. He remembered automatic Systems answering when you lifted the phone.

Sooner or later, everything in the universe found a means which it hadn't been made for. So with man. A million years ago, he ran through the forests gathering game and fruit with his bare hands. And now he built villas, wrote poems, threw bombs, and phoned.

So it was with the telephone.

He pushed away his plate, ordered a coffee, drank it, paid, and left. The Sun had chased away the clouds. He turned toward the pier. But just loafing was impossible since cars were all over. Even the fishermen had given up. I'm just turning around he said. I know all the streets in this neighborhood by heart. I work, I inhabit one of the most fantastic cities in the world, and it has ceased to move me. It says nothing to me. I'd love to get out of here.

He looked at his watch. Almost 2:30 p.m. The time to go back and finish what I couldn't do this morning. The walls and windows, always the same, were gray and almost transparent, used by the insistent and excessive stare of eyes.

Then there were the girls who the seasons, the change of work, and the tourist buses renewed. But this year's crop was very bad. He hadn't seen a good-looking girl for over a week.

In the Bahamas, Barbara, Natasha, Sybil, and Merryl were splashing in a pool under the satisfied eyes of Wildenstein. He was right. I should accept. It was a chance not to be repeated.

The secretary's door was open. She was waiting for him. A new call, he thought anxiously.

She leaned toward him.

"Someone is waiting for you in your office, Mr. Bosch." He stopped short, a lump in his throat. He didn't have an appointment. Who could it be? Have they managed to physically cross over into time? Wasn't it enough for them to call him? He took his courage in his two hands: no, they couldn't do anything except telephone through time. He opened the door.

A man who didn't look like Jerome Bosch waited, seated on a corner of his desk, one leg hanging, the other on the worn rug. His face was long, his features fine. His dark hair was long but carefully cut at the collar. He was dressed in a gray suit with large checks, with lots of pockets—the one over his heart had a colored handkerchief artistically creased—and the narrow lapels underlined the fantasy. He wore a striped shirt, a tie with polka dots, black shoes with complicated designs, and red socks. Next to his right hand, a small suitcase of black shiny leather. He looked English from the tip of his toes to the end of his nails. He got up.

"Mr. Jerome Bosch? I am very pleased to meet you."

The voice was cultivated, serious, with a strong British accent.

Jerome Bosch nodded his head.

"Fred Hardy," said the man, holding out a beautifully manicured hand. "Mr. Wildenstein called me before coming here. He hoped that I would take care of all the details."

He opened his suitcase and spread out on the desk a handful of papers.

"Here's your airplane ticket, Mr. Bosch. Here's a special visa that you just have to put in your passport. You have a passport, don't you? This wallet bas 50 pounds in it in travelers' checks. You just have to sign. I think that will be sufficient for the voyage. And here's a letter to give to customs at Nassau. The governor is a personal friend of Mr. Wildenstein. You don't have to handle anything. Mr. Wildenstein is probably not in Nassau but someone will be at the airport and conduct you to Mr. Wildenstein's island. I wish you a very good trip."

"I haven't accepted yet," said Jerome Bosch.

Hardy began to laugh politely.

"Oh, naturally you're free. I've prepared all this on the assumption of a favorable answer."

"You've done it very quickly," said Jerome Bosch, astounded, contemplating the plane tickets, the visa, the wallet, and the envelope. "You live in Paris?"

"I just arrived from London, Mr. Bosch," said Hardy. "Mr. Wildenstein likes efficiency. Mr. Wildenstein recommended that I accompany you to the airport. Moreover, my plane leaves a half hour after yours. These schedules are practical between Paris and London."

The telephone to the right began to ring. Hardy put his case under his arm.

"I'll wait for you in the corridor, Mr. Bosch. The taxi is downstairs. We have plenty of time."

He smiled, showing his large, immaculate white teeth. The door closed after him.

Jerome Bosch picked up the phone.

"Hello," he said.

Nobody. The echo in a cave, a long tunnel, a well.

"Hello," he said, louder. He had an impression of not hearing himself. He had the impression that his voice was swallowed up by the phone, smothered, stifled.

Without conviction he said:

"Where are you calling from, what do you want?"

He held the airplane ticket close and leafed through it. The ticket, Paris-Nassau via New York and Miami. One return-trip ticket. Hardy had done things thoroughly. It wasn't a trap. No matter what happened he could return. And Hardy had come from London just for this. Let's see. Wildenstein had called him at 10:30, maybe 11 a.m. He had taken the 12 p.m. plane. At 1 p.m., he was in Paris. At 1:45 p.m. in the office of Jerome Bosch. It was very simple. He lived in a world where you jumped from one plane to the other, where one wore apparently sober suits but which in reality were quite extravagant, shoes made to order, where one was invited to governor's dinners and was to telephone from the four corners of the globe. *I can't let him down before he goes back to London*, thought Jerome Bosch.

It was a first-class ticket. On the upper left-hand corner of the cover was a stamp. V.I.P. And someone had added Fm. WDS.

Very Important Person. From Wilderstein. Made out by Wildenstein.

He was in a state. I couldn't just tell him: Tomorrow if you like, but not today, I must think it over. He'd laugh at me. No, he's much too well bred. He'll say Mr. Wildenstein will be sorry, he hopes to see you tomorrow morning. He would bend over and put the ticket, the visa, the 50 pounds, and the letter from the governor back in his case and then he'd return to Orly to wait for his plane. What time is it? Almost 3 p.m. In an hour and a half, the plane would take off. Nassau via New York and Miami. They had no intention of letting the plane wait 15 minutes just for him.

"Hello," said Jerome Bosch into the dumb phone. He opened a drawer of his desk, the only one that locked. He picked up official papers and found his blue passport, drew it toward him with one hand and opened it. An old photo of three or four years ago. He was almost good-looking then, much thinner. He looked alert.

"Hello," he called for the last time, and hung up. His hands were damp and trembling. I don't have the experience for this type of situation. I don't know what to do. In his right hand he put the passport, ticket, visa, the wallet, and the letter. With his free hand he opened a large drawer in his desk and threw in papers, documents, pens, and the box of clips.

At the end of the corridor, Hardy was waiting, smiling, not even leaning on the wall, holding the suitcase nonchalantly by the handle with two hands.

Jerome Bosch knocked and pushed open the secretary's door.

"I have to leave for a few days, Mrs. Dupont," he said, "this man…"

"It was an accident, wasn't it?"

She seemed frightened. What must she imagine? He thought. But I can't tell her the truth. I can't say that in an hour I'll be in the sky on my way to the Bahamas.

"No," he said in a sudden hoarse voice. "Not an accident, on the contrary. A… Personal affair. I'll be gone for a few days. I think it's better to get a temporary helper. To answer the telephone. I'll send you a postcard."

She finally decided to smile.

"Have a nice trip, Mr. Bosch."

He must leave and recover.

"If… if someone calls me, say I'm on vacation, I haven't much time. This man… You'll explain all this the codirector… all right?"

"Don't worry. Enjoy your trip, Mr. Bosch."

"Thank you."

In the corridor, Hardy took a cigarette from a red and gold box. He tapped the end against his case, then slipped the cigarette into his mouth, the lighter from his pocket squirted a flame, he inhaled a puff, and exhaled the smoke in a thin line almost without opening his lips.

"A cigarette, Mr. Bosch?"

"No, thank you," he said. "I... I... smoke a pipe."

He felt his pocket, but he knew that his black briar pipe, the one which was split—its life would be short even though he preferred it to his others—wasn't there. He had left it at home this morning. Moreover, he never took it to the office. He didn't use it except while writing or reading in the tranquility of his apartment with all the lamps lit.

"Mr. Wildenstein will be very pleased with your decision, Mr. Bosch. He'll be very happy to see you. He likes people who know how to make quick decisions. Time is so precious, isn't it?"

They went down the large stone stairway.

"Do you have to let anyone know, Mr. Bosch?" said Hardy. "You can telephone from the airport."

He looked at his watch.

"We don't have tune to go to your home, but it doesn't matter. Mr. Wildenstein is about your size. He has an enormous wardrobe. You can find everything in Nassau. Mr. Wildenstein likes to travel without baggage."

The pebbles in the courtyard cracked under their steps.

"Your taxis are so convenient in France, Mr. Bosch. I only have to telephone from London before leaving and a car is waiting for me at Orly. Radio-taxis, isn't that so? Our taxis are so out-of-date in London. And in New York, it's so difficult to find a driver who will wait for you. It's a nice day, don't you find it so? It rained this morning in London. It's even better weather in Nassau. But the sky doesn't have this shading, this soft color. I want to talk to you about your book, Mr. Bosch, but I must admit I haven't had the time to read it yet. My knowledge of your language is very incomplete. I hope it will be translated soon. You'll like Mr. Wildenstein. He's a man with a lot of personality, or, as you would say, character."

"Well now, Baron," said the driver when they were installed in the back of the car, "where are we going?"

'To Orly," said Hardy.

"By Raspail or by Italie?"

"Take the Boulevard Saint Germain and the Boulevard Saint Michel," said Hardy. "I like so much going along the Luxembourg Gardens."

"As you like, but it will be longer."

The streets were almost deserted. The traffic lights before them turned green almost as if the driver had telecommanded them. It only needed, said Jerome Bosch, that the car have a little flag and a siren. No, a siren would have destroyed this deep silence. Real power bas a great deal of discretion. No noise, baggage. Invisibility. Only a name used as a passport.

As they were going along Luxembourg, the radio began to ring. It was an old telephone model. Without slowing down, the driver unhooked the phone and hung it at the side of his head.

"I'm listening," he said.

A voice breathed a few words.

The driver looked in the rear-view mirror.

"Are you Bosch?" he said. "That's me," said Jerome Bosch.

"It's not regular, but someone wants to talk to you. It must be important if the station gives it to you. This isn't a telephone, it's a taxi. Go ahead, take the tube, because they want to talk to you. I've never seen anything like this. And I've been driving for over 20 years."

His throat dry, Jerome Bosch took the apparatus. He was obliged to fold himself almost in two on the seat because the cord was too short. His chin pressed against the worn velvet.

"Hello," he said.

"Jerome," said the voice. "Finally I found you… difficult… Don't leave, for the love of God. There's going to be… Don't…" Static. Cracklings.

"Where are you calling from?" asked Jerome Bosch with a voice which he tried to make firm and keep discreet.

"Why, why, why?" said the voice plaintively, the voice broken, complaining. "From… tomorrow… or after… don't know…"

"Why mustn't I…?"

He stopped, thinking that Fred Hardy would hear him. He had come from London just to put him on the plane.

"Accident," said the voice. It was nearer than it had ever been. But it sounded more miserable, more worn for being clearer.

"Who's talking?"

"Yyyy… you," said the voice to the only Jerome Bosch. "I have already…"

"Your voice sounds so low… isn't it?" asked Jerome Bosch abruptly.

"I'm so far… so far," said the voice as if explaining.

The car went faster. They rode on the left side of the autoroute.

An intuition hit Jerome Bosch like a blow.

"You're sick…" he ended.

He didn't dare say any more. Not in front of the driver and Hardy.

"No, no, no," said the voice, "not that… not that… worse, it's terrible. You mustn't… I… I… I wait…"

"I mustn't what?"

"You mustn't leave," said the voice distinctly, and immediately it disappeared as if it had accomplished a last terrible exhausting effort.

Jerome Bosch remained overwhelmed for a moment, bent forward on the seat. The perspiration dripped from his forehead. The apparatus slipped from his fingers, bounced on the cushion, then hung at the end of the line, hitting the driver's knee, ringing on the metal.

"Is it finished?" said the driver.

"I think so," said Jerome Bosch, breathless.

"So much the better," he said, hanging up.

A jet plane passed very low overhead.

"You seem nervous, Mr. Bosch," said Hardy.

"It's nothing," said Bosch, "nothing at all."

He thought: I haven't left yet. I can change my mind. Say I've been called back. A very important affair. Leave it till tomorrow.

"The air in Nassau will do you a world of good, Mr. Bosch," said Hardy. "The agitation of big cities is wearing on the nerves."

"Departures or arrivals?" asked the driver.

"Departures," said Hardy.

The car stopped beside the sidewalk. Jerome Bosch looked in front and saw that the amount registered on the meter had three digits. Hardy paid. The glass doors opened automatically in front of them. They kept away from the lines in front of the booking office and went to the entrance of a small discreet office. Jerome Bosch put his hand in his left pocket, which contained the passport, ticket, wallet, visa, and the letter. They took care of the formalities.

"No, not there," said Hardy as Jerome Bosch went toward the large stairway. He conducted him to a narrow hall. The marble was covered with a large rug. A door opened without noise.

"Back already, Mr. Hardy," said the elevator operator.

"Alas, yes," said Hardy. "I can never take advantage of my stay in Paris."

They were now in the upper hall.

"You have plenty of time to buy newspapers, Mr. Bosch, or a book. It's a ten-hour flight to Nassau including the stops. There is a direct flight from London, but only once a week."

I can still refuse, thought Jerome Bosch. *Thank him, wait with him for the plane to London, promise to leave tomorrow. Say I had forgotten something. Through what did he call me? From where did he call? Why did he say tomorrow? How could he call me through tomorrow? Tomorrow I wouldn't know more than today how to telephone across time. Who is he?*

He let himself sink little by little into the atmosphere of the place.

"You haven't given me time to fetch a coat," he said.

"Useless, in Nassau, you won't need one. You rather need a light suit. You have the best English tailors in Nassau, the best London houses."

On the other side of the glass wall, giant planes waited, immobile, frozen. Others rolled slowly on belts. Another warmed its motors at the end of a runway, pushed ahead, refusing to leave the ground, then suddenly breaking its headway, lifted and rose. *I am in an aquarium. Even sounds don't come through this glass prison. On the other side, above, in the blue sky, freedom begins.*

Jerome Bosch let his eyes wander over to a young woman printed in two copies. Twins. Exactly the same. Long honey-colored hair, same faces, a little dull but exquisitely fresh. Their legs were long and thin. They each carried a small shoulder-strap bag of red leather. They are either in the movies or models, thought Jerome Bosch, at bottom surprised not to discern between him and them the thickness of a window or the impenetrable depth of a movie house, or the photographic varnish of a magazine page. The story of a man in love with one of the twins, either one; which should he choose, A or B? He chooses A. Very quickly she shows her nasty character. He understands that he should have married B, who is sweet, affectionate, and who loves him in silence. What should he do? Divorce and marry B. That would never work. She loves her sister too much. He discovers a method to call through time. He telephones himself the day he makes his decision. Marry B, he cries helplessly to his undecided past. What will the past do? And if B should become in time nasty also? *Completely idiotic*, said Jerome Bosch to himself.

"The Berthold sisters," said Fred Hardy. "They pretend they are Swedish, but in reality they are Austrian or maybe Yugoslavian. Mr. Wildenstein wanted to use them. But they don't know how to act. Nothing to be done. Not the least stage presence. As if one was the reflection of the other and vice versa. In Hollywood, Jonathan Craig pretends that they have only one shadow for two. They are going to act in a small French film."

"Do you meet the same people all the time in the airports, Mr. Hardy?"

"No, but you fall sometimes on well-known personalities. Especially on the Paris-New York line. Like a suburban line. London is the suburb of New York today, Mr. Bosch."

"Isn't it dangerous to travel by plane?" Jerome Bosch said impulsively and naïvely. He heard the voice: Accident... accident.

"Certainly, Mr. Bosch," said Hardy, "but less dangerous than traveling by automobile. There are statistics. I take the plane three times a week generally. And Mr. Wildenstein belongs to the millionaires' club. You've heard it talked about. That means that he has covered more than a million miles by plane. Never a single accident. Have you ever taken a plane, Mr. Bosch?"

"Yes," said Jerome Bosch, suddenly humiliated by his cowardice. "I've been to London two or three times, and to New York, to Germany, and also to Nice. But I don't care for the taking off and landing."

He had a desire to tell how he had seen a helicopter burn in Algeria during the war. The plane hesitating like a large fly, then slipping, gliding a few feet from the ground, and for an unknown reason turning over. A sudden light of magnesium. A thick cloud of smoke, no explosion, it only burned, the sirens, the fire engines, a shroud of snow, carbonic suds on a ridiculous block less than a yard from his side, the motor, all that remained of the helicopter.

"The weather is splendid, Mr. Bosch," said Fred Hardy. "It will be an excellent flight. Look, your plane has just been announced."

Jerome Bosch turned toward the flight panel and read: FLIGHT 713 B.O.A.C. PARIS - NEW YORK – MIAMI - NASSAU. SALLE 32.

"We have plenty of time," said Hardy. "Really, you should buy some newspapers, a book, a pipe, tobacco. Or maybe you'd rather think on the plane. Planes are really such quiet places."

PARIS - LONDON 5 P.M. AIR FRANCE FLIGHT A SALLE 57 FLIGHT B SALLE 58

"Your plane," he said.

Fred Hardy examined the panel.

"Oh, it's been doubled."

"Which one will you take?" Jerome Bosch asked abruptly.

"It doesn't matter," said Hardy. "If there's no room on A, they'll put me on B. They arrive at the same time, I think."

But, thought Jerome Bosch, *if plane B had an accident, wouldn't it be better to take plane A? The chances, are they mathematically equal? How to choose?*

"They are calling you," said Fred Hardy.

"Who, me?"

"The microphone," said Fred Hardy. "Maybe it's Mr. Wildenstein."

He smiled, a cigarette between his fingers, his valise placed on the arm of a chair, leaning against his hip, impeccable, elegant.

"Mr. Jerome Bosch is requested to come to the courtesy phone," said the voice, asexual but feminine, angelic, too low-pitched, too smooth, too calm.

"Someone wants you," said Fred Hardy. "Here. Straight ahead. Do you want me to buy you some newspapers? A pipe? Meerschaum or briar? What do you prefer in tobacco? Amsterdammer or Dunhill?"

But Jerome Bosch had already gone, dizzy, staggering. Too much noise. Too many faces. A complicated itinerary. Where was it? The panels. Welcome.

He held on to the counter as if he were drowning. He understood. An idea flashed in his mind. Till now, it turned around like a fish in a bowl. Circular. It came to him. He believed everything.

"I'm Jerome Bosch," he said to a young woman with a smiling face and a gray beret placed across her head. Her eyes were too big, heavily underlined with black, and her teeth too large, also.

"Someone paged me," said Jerome Bosch nervously. I'm Jerome Bosch."

"Certainly, Mr. Bosch. An instant, Mr. Bosch."

She pushed an invisible button, said something, then listened. "A telephone call, Mr. Bosch. Booth three. No, not there. On your left."

The door closed automatically after him. Silence. The roar of the planes didn't sound here. He picked up the phone and without waiting:

"I don't want to leave."

"You're not going to give in now," said the voice of the left, firm and resolute.

"The other," said Jerome Bosch. "He isn't calling from your future. He's calling from *another* future. Something has happened to him. He took the plane and he had an accident and…"

"Are you crazy?" said the voice. "You're afraid to take the plane and you invent anything. I know you well, you know."

"Maybe I've invented you too?" said Jerome Bosch.

"Listen," said the voice, "I had a lot of trouble getting hold of you. I knew you'd hesitate. I don't want you to give up this opportunity."

"If I don't leave," said Jerome Bosch, "you won't exist. That's why you insist."

"But then," said the voice, "I'm you, no? I've explained all this to you. Ibiza. Acapulco. All the time to write. And Barbara. And Barbara. Good God. I shouldn't tell you, but you're going to marry Barbara. You don't want to miss that. You'll love her."

"I don't know her yet," said Jerome Bosch.

"You'll meet her," said the voice. "She'll be crazy about you. Not right away. Ten years, Jerome. More than ten years of happiness. She'll act in all your films. You'll be famous, Jerome."

"Give me time to think about it," said Jerome Bosch. "What time is it?" He looked at his watch. "4:10 p.m."

"You must get on that plane."

"But the other voice that phones from I don't know when. It told me not to leave. Another future, another possibility. He said he called from tomorrow."

"Another future," said the voice, indecisive. "But I'm here, no? I took the plane and nothing happened to me. I've flown hundreds of times. I belong to the millionaires' club. You know what that is? And never an accident."

"The other one has had an accident," said Jerome Bosch stubbornly.

Silence. Cracklings. An abysmal insect devoured the line somewhere on the bottom of the ocean.

"Let's admit," said the voice, "you could run a risk, no? Look at the statistics. There are 99 chances out of 100 that you will arrive safely. More than that, 900…"

"Why should I believe you," asked Jerome Bosch, "and not the other?"

"…chance out of two…"

"Hello," said Jerome Bosch. "I can't hear you."

"Even if there wasn't," said the voice, which cried and died far away, which spoke from the other side of a partition of glass, which screamed from the interior of a closed box, "one chance out of two, you can't let it drop. You don't want to spend your life in an office, no?"

"No," said Jerome Bosch feebly.

A tiny voice at the end of the line as if the caller out there was sinking in the foam, falling in the infinite labyrinth of telephone wires.

"Hurry up," said an insect, "you'll miss the plane."

Click.

"Hello, hello," cried Jerome Bosch.

Silence. Dead phone. He looked at his watch. 4:14 p.m. He was one or two minutes slow. Hardy must be asking what he was doing. *I'll miss the plane.*

Should I leave? Jerome Bosch asked himself.

"It's time," said Fred Hardy, smiling. "I bought you a briefcase. A meerschaum pipe. Mr. Wildenstein prefers meerschaum pipes because it's not necessary... how do you say *de les culotter*. Three packages of tobacco. *Le Monde* and *Le Figaro,* the New York *Times, Paris-Match, Playboy,* and the latest *Fiction.* That's the French magazine where you publish your short stories, isn't it? I bought you a toothbrush. A flask of whiskey. Chivas. You like Chivas, no, Mr. Bosch? We just have time. No, not there."

The policeman smiled, greeted Fred Hardy, and made a sign.

The customs officer let them-through.

"Tell Mr. Wildenstein that everything is all right in London, Mr. Bosch will call him tomorrow. No, Mr. Bosch, here."

Loudspeakers diffused soft music.

They advanced into an infinite corridor, limited at the end by a large mirror which threw back their images as they hurried toward it. But they didn't reach it. Fred Hardy took Jerome Bosch's elbow and turned him a quarter way around and they walked immobile down the lower story on a little mechanical escalator.

The waiting room was divided into two parts. To the right, a line of people. Jerome Bosch wanted to join them. But Fred Hardy took him toward the other door. There was almost no one there. A gray suit with a weather-beaten face who held in his hand a shiny leather briefcase, and a woman, very tall, very beautiful, whose long pale hair touched her shoulders. She didn't look at anyone.

There was one more door to go through,

I don't want to leave, thought Jerome Bosch, pale. *I'll pretend I'm ill. A forgotten appointment, I have to get a manuscript. I won't say anything. They can't hold me back. They can't kidnap me.*

"Here," said Fred Hardy, handing him the briefcase. "I hope you have a nice trip. I would have liked to go with you, but the London office is waiting for me. Perhaps I'll be in the Bahamas at the end of the month. I am very happy to have met you, Mr. Bosch."

The door opened. A hostess entered, smiled, looked over the three first-class passengers, took their red tickets, and left.

"Will you please take your place in the bus?"

"Good-bye, Mr. Hardy," said Jerome Bosch, moving away.

Jerome Bosch is almost alone in the bus, which carries the first-class passengers. The bus rolls slowly, following a complicated itinerary on an enormous surface of smooth cement which doesn't seem to be ground-lighted. Jerome Bosch feels nothing, not even the slight excitement which accompanies all his trips. He thinks that now nobody can reach him by telephone—here he fools himself. He thinks that no one will try to influence his conduct because that will not have any importance. The bus stops. Jerome Bosch gets off the bus, which leaves to get the batch of second-class passengers. He climbs the mobile stairway applied to the front of the plane. He hesitates an instant on entering the first-class cabin. He lets himself be conducted to a chair next to a porthole in front of the wings. He fastens his security belt under the hostess's vigilant eye. He hears some noise, the scraping of feet behind him, the second-class passengers settling down. He sees the hostess go forward toward the pilot's cabin and disappear for an instant, return, and unhook a micro. He hears her wish everyone welcome in three languages and recommend everyone to put out cigarettes and examine their seat belts. A panel lights up which renews these instructions. A basket filled with candies is served to him. He chooses one. He knows that it fulfills a rite, that these planes are pressurized and that his eardrums will not suffer even if he doesn't take the trouble to swallow, and moreover, he will have swallowed the candy even before the plane bas finished taking off. The plane rolls. It seems to Jerome Bosch that in the distance, near the waiting room, stands the tall, elegant silhouette of Fred Hardy. The plane stops moving. The motors roar and the universe hurls itself ahead and throws Jerome Bosch against the back of his seat. He tries to look out the porthole. The plane bas left the ground. A shock. The wheels have been drawn up into their place.

Jerome Bosch begins to relax. Nothing happens. He is given a newspaper, this morning's, and he opens it to the economic page and his eyes fall on the small weather map. He puts it aside. He opens the briefcase, looks inside and finds the pipe, examines it, superior quality, and stuffs and lights it. He is served a whiskey. He flies over the clouds. He asks himself if ephemeral, tiny civilizations are growing in the folds of these mountains of fog. He thinks he is beginning to forget the telephone. He tries to imagine Nassau. He begins to discover that he has left. He takes possession of the cabin. He makes his seat move. He questions himself on the possibilities of his two futures. It seems to him, but he isn't sure, that the voice from the left, the firm assured voice, Ibiza, Acapulco, and Barbara, has become more distant, become less clear, from conversation to conversation, and the other more present. Question of telephone lines. He is given something to eat. He is served Champagne. He looks at the hostess, who smiles when she passes by him. He asks for more Champagne. He drinks a coffee. He sleeps.

When he wakes up—but what time is it?—the plane is flying over the sea in a perfectly clear day. Jerome Bosch hasn't dreamed or he couldn't remember his dreams. He regrets rather absurdly, in looking at the sea, not having brought a bathing suit. Mr. Wildenstein certainly has a dozen suits. Jerome Bosch finally understands that the hostess is addressing him. She holds out a blue piece of paper intricately folded like a telegram. She seems surprised.

"A call for you, Mr. Bosch. The operator excuses himself but he could only understand a few words. There's static electricity in the air. He tried to confirm it, but without success."

He unfolds the paper and reads only one word scratched in pen: *Soon...*

Mr. Wildenstein, he thinks. But he can't be sure.

"Please," he said, "please could you find out what the voice was like."

"I'll go see," said the hostess, who disappeared into the pilot's cabin and came back in a moment.

"Mr. Bosch," she said. "The operator couldn't describe the voice very well. He begs to be excused. He said it seemed very near, that the communication was very powerful and he didn't think, in spite of the static, that there was any more to say. He asked for confirmation."

"Thank you," said Jerome Bosch, as he sees her leave, take up the microphone, take a breath, and say in a smooth voice:

"A second of attention, if you please, ladies and gentlemen. We are going through a zone of perturbation. Please fasten your seat belts and put out your cigarettes."

He doesn't listen anymore. He looks out the porthole at the bottom of the sky, otherwise clear, and sees that a little cloudy spot, almost black, is topped by an intense dark bubbling toward which the plane precipitates. Black, black, black, as an eye.

CIVILIZATION 2190

They hurriedly broke down the door with their boots. They entered. It was a large room, dark and cold as a cave, and the walls were lined with books. The air inside was a hundred years-old. Generations of spiders had woven thousands of webs in vain, before leaving or dying, but their work had remained intact and it settled on the hair and faces of the men of the Search for the Past group. There was a window, but it was dark and opaque, and when they tried to open it, the wood broke apart and the glass shattered. The wind rushed into the room, blowing between their legs and raising the dust; they hastily stepped back, rubbing their eyes and coughing. The light caressed the shelves and they saw vivid and surprising colors bursting out of the dark: the books.

Their steps left traces in an almost intangible snow of dust. Their fingers touched the back of the books, releasing them from their sheath of oblivion. Their voices awakened buried echoes. For the first time in a hundred years, the floor creaked. One heard something like whispers, crackles, rustles, the groans of doors, the clicking of locks, the shuffle of boots—in short: a presence.

They hesitated. The house waited. They relaxed. The house felt inhabited again. It was reborn.

Outside, the purple, flickering glow of the poisoned hills shone. From time to time, their counters clicked as if little insects were trapped inside. All around them, the Earth burned calmly and silently, with a cold, cold fire. In a millionth of a second, this house had turned into a blackened and charred block, then it had waited, for over a hundred years. Inside, amongst the books, reigned peace and the serenity of civilization. Outside, for over a hundred years, the purple flames of the desert had burned around the house and tried to consume it. For over a hundred years, luminous clouds had risen from the barren hills and dropped all their weight of radioactive rain on the house.

But the house had remained.

"I think we finally found what we were looking for," said the captain. "A library. The last library of the dead lands."

Some of the books were leatherbound. They shone under the lamps; they broadcast a friendly welcome, but their golden letters were so pale that they could almost no longer be read. Others shone with bright colors, bleached on the spines but still vivid on the covers, where they had been stacked against each other. The captain took a book, at random. Astonishment could be read in his eyes when he opened it.

"Paper books," he said. "Printed on real paper. These are surely items of extraordinary value. Maybe we'll finally learn who Shakespeare and Poe were, and Cervantes, Cicero, Goethe, Homer, Andersen and Pirandello, too... Perhaps all the works that enlightened the past rest here."

The technicians listened silently. Some had taken off their helmets.

Someone handed a box to the captain. He opened it.

"Illustrated books," he said. His voice trembled with joy. "Illustrations! All the museums of Earth were destroyed. We don't even know what paintings are like. And here are dozens of illustrations, hundreds even..." He flipped the pages. "In little panels, with the text in bubbles... It must be a catalog of all the art galleries of Earth. Here! We didn't dare hope to find such a treasure!"

He stared at the cover of the book he held in his hand for a long while. The illustration was strikingly realistic. The bright colors contrasted with each other with astonishing vigor.

"This is the strength, the barbaric beauty of primitive art," thought the captain. "God, how civilization has softened us!"

He painfully deciphered the old characters: *Saddle Justice*.

"What splendor, what genius, in the title alone! We have a lot of work to do. We will have to handle all these books very carefully."

"Who can be the author of this book?" he wondered. "I have never heard of it. But we know so little about the past... So little since the war..."

He began to read.

The brightly-colored covers of the books glowed like embers on the folding, metallic table they set up. They illuminated the entire room with a silent fire. Horses galloped and galloped, machine guns rumbled and killed, forests blazed, planes took off or crashed, men crumbled, their eyes bulging, beads of sweat dripping on their forehead, their mouths twisted in a silent cry, kisses were exchanged, bulls charged, ships sank, rockets flew to green planets, wars, accidents, fires, derailments unfolded in the great silence of the dead plains on the small and still stage of the covers.

A woman jumped out of a car in a panic, and rang a bell with all her strength while a man watched from the first floor, his eyes hard, a gun in his right hand and his left fist clenched, and the woman rushed into darkness, shouting when the door gave way, but someone appeared just at that moment and whispered, "Be careful, I'm the Killer." There was the sound of chains and a ghost coming out of a wall, and if we recoiled, we found our way blocked by a clammy wall that pivoted upon itself, revealing an unfathomable abyss where giant insects lurked. And all that without having to move an inch. It was just enough to sit and look at the covers. It was a wonderful swirl of life.

They worked all day. They moistened the dry, brittle pages so they would not crumble. They handled the books cautiously.

They counted them. They classified them. They copied them. They stacked them very carefully in sealed boxes that they loaded on helicopters.

The deserted hills were already shining with their own stardust when they decided that they were ready to leave.

"We are done here," said the first officer to the captain. "We have everything registered, numbered and packed."

At that moment, the captain was turning the last page of the book he had been reading. He remained silent for a moment.

"What a surprising book," he said. "It can compete with all the greatest works of the 21st century. It surpasses what our best authors have produced." He daydreamed for a second. "What type of men were they? We could not have taught them anything. On the contrary.

"Perhaps it would interest you to learn what we found?" asked the first officer.

The captain nodded.

"We did not find any Shakespeare, Dante, or Cervantes," reported the first officer. He seemed downcast and disappointed. "Neither did we find Hugo, Goethe or Homer..."

"I have Homer," said the captain coldly. "*The Iliad* and *The Odyssey*. It's not very good. This surely gives us the level of others whose names have come down to us."

"You have Homer? I didn't see it."

"Here, in the box labeled *Classics Illustrated*," said the captain. "The illustrations are very good—better than the text."

"This may not be the original text," the first officer said hesitantly. "It's a translation. Maybe it's a bad translation?"

"Why would it be a bad translation? Can you tell me why they would have published a bad translation? No, Homer just was not a great poet. Fortunately, the illustrations are beautiful."

"Maybe," said the first officer. "There were several similar boxes of books like the one you found. They were called: *Tales from the Crypt, Vault of Horror, Two-Fisted Tales*, and one that was somewhat peculiar, called *Mad*... They formed almost the entire library."

"What originality! What talent!" said the captain, smiling with pride. "This discovery will be a landmark in our history."

"But we didn't find any Shakespeare or Dante," said the first officer.

"What about the leatherbound books?"

"Something called *Comics Buyer's Guide, Coins' Price Guide, Sports Collector's Digest, The Big Book of Dogs* and *Sports Almanacs* with charts and statistics."

"Charts and statistics! What geniuses! Wonderful! What a discovery! A whole civilization reborn before our eyes. Perhaps Shakespeare, Dante and Goethe were only minor writers... Perhaps they did not deserve to be printed on invaluable paper. May I remind you that all these books we've found are on paper!

"It's must have been deliberate. A sign of the importance of this collection. I can well picture an old man, very well learned, gathering together here all the treasures of human culture, thinking of the world running towards destruction, looking out of the window watching the columns of fire, waiting for death. We now have the essential. The principal. All the great works of the past. We can praise the foresight of that long-deceased benefactor for having collected here the highest testimonies of the human race's genius."

"Nobody would have had the time to make such a selection," observed the first officer. "The war surprised everyone. Death was instantaneous."

"I tell you, it was a deliberate choice. It fits so well with what we expected of the past. It's wonderful!"

"I'm still not sure," said the first officer.

He glanced again at the empty shelves. There was nothing left. Absolutely nothing.

"Don't you understand?" said the captain. "Do you realize the importance of this legacy, which the twentieth century has gifted us? Are we truly worthy of this heritage? All of their civilization is gone, their great deeds erased, the memories of their achievements vanished... But thanks to this, we can now know what the twentieth century was like!"

The captain's voice rose and choked. Tears were beading at the edges of his eyes as he was deeply moved by the thought of this treasure, this wealth of culture.

They left. They climbed into their machines. The captain put the precious book on his lap. They flew over the dead plains that made their counters sizzle. The hot breath of their engines caused the burning walls of the now-empty library to flicker and collapse. The dead house sank and melted into the purple plain, glittering and cursed.

FULL STOP

I

He stood there, at the end of the corridor, his nose and hands pressed against the huge quartz window that blocked the torrent of dark emptiness. He stood there, wide-eyed, like the lookout on an ancient sea-faring ship made of wood, continuously staring at the stars, measuring their strands of light, discovering new solar systems. He stood there, inside the shiny starship, filled with the hum of a thousand sleeping engines, the mechanical gestures and sighs of hundreds of men who missed the Earth, lost in an endless ocean, with only tiny islands, glittering like birthday cakes candles in the vast, dark emptiness.

"Have you noticed? The stars are going out."

It was true. But after ten, twenty years, spent in space, searching for new worlds, at a speed where the light of known stars was devoured by black holes, he no longer cared. Meanwhile, the indifferent stars jumped from one square to another on the grid engraved on the quartz window.

"The stars are going out."

Not just the stars. Light was failing too, and colors as well. Even the thick black of emptiness was no longer the same.

He thought of summer on Earth, a summer evening, when all the colors become gray and blend together, when one doesn't know if one will soon fall asleep, never to wake up again.

"That's true. Look. The stars are turning pale."

"Don't worry, children. We're in a nebula, that's all."

"Do you believe that we will ever reach a new star, if they all go out?"

"Don't worry. There will always be more stars. And new heavens. Worlds without end. We're like those who seek the finest pearls in the depths of the ocean! Listen, even if we stay here, our children, or their children, will eventually go out into the dark, into untrod regions of the sky where new constellations shine. We can't stop it."

And thus, they traveled for ten years, twenty years, further into space.

"That's it! I'm done. I don't want to stay among the stars. I want to go back to Earth. Continue to your heart's desire, if you want, but my children will grow up on Earth."

"Everyone says that. Always. Then, when they got bored on Earth, they drag themselves to the spaceports to watch the rockets go, and they cling to the fences every time a starship rises on a column of fire, and they stamp their booted feet, and they imagine themselves strapped and crushed into a seat, and all of a sudden, bam, they find themselves inside a spaceship, all too happy to see the same old stars again."

There was the quartz window, with its engraved grid lines, the ever paler stars, and the emptiness that hesitated to grow dark again, and beyond it all, more emptiness, more worlds, but no more ships.

But eventually, there would be—so far away that men, from one side of their little pond to the other would no longer be able to meet face to face, and soon would forget about their origins, but continue to move forward like insatiable parasites, leaping from one star to the other, expanding from galaxy to galaxy, without being able to turn back, until there would only be one man per planet, then one per star system.

The shiny ship was traveling between the stars, but those aboard who might young enough to dare to dream of seeing Earth again were very few.

"I never heard that the stars could turn pale. Not even once, do you hear me? Maybe we've come to the edge of the universe?"

But nobody believed it. There would always be new worlds ahead, and men to visit them. Without end.

The detectors plunged their long, invisible tentacles into space. The lines engraved on the quartz window converted the void into small, quantifiable cubes. The analyzers were humming

"No dust cloud. No nebula. Unknown cause. Unknown cause."

The captain ignored the void. He only saw piles of metal disks, charts, psychological equations, and control dials.

"I wonder if that's what draws people to the void," he said. "No dust. No nebula."

He got up, opened the door, and went down the hallway until he discovered a large slice of void inside his ship. The sound of his boots resounded more softly on the metal, but he ignored it.

"Are the stars really going out?" he asked.

"I don'know," said an officer.

The captain became transparent. Through him, the officer could see the opposite wall and the cabins, and beyond it, the void, and the dying stars.

"I must be dreaming," said the captain.

For the officer was also a ghost.

And, through the fog of the walls, they saw the bewildered crew coming and going, but without haste, without slamming the doors, because of their airtight seals, without running, because of the gravity, and without being afraid, because of their long habit and old reflexes that had toughened and smoothed the exteriors of their minds and souls.

"We will not see the Earth again," said the officer.

"No," said the captain. "Earth does not exist anymore. And never again will there be new stars. Or more starships."

The scents vanished first. The odor of ozone, the smell of rubber, of clean skin and healthy bodies, of purified air, the vanilla-like fragrance of plastic.

Then the sounds.

Then, the ship faded noiselessly, with the sweetness of a sugar cane licked slowly.

The men fluttered for a little time in space; and then, they, too, melted very slowly, like sugar statues dipped into the black water of the void.

And someone, one by one, blew out all the candles of the splendid birthday cakes that had been the universe, further and further away in the cosmos, all the way to the Sun and the Earth.

II

He had reached the end of his story; he got up, went down the stairs, and paused for a moment on the last step, so that the grains of sand under his feet would stop crunching.

The smell of a warm desert, as one finds only in dreams, floated above the red tiles of the corridor. He felt empty, dry, and light, like the cartridge of a burned out flare. He was not sure why he was still alive. Normally, he should have fallen and disappeared.

He forgot about the image of the desert, put his hand on the cold latch of the door, and opened it; the sky, the sun, the exuberant shimmer of the grass, the leaves and the trees, the white pebbles, and the small, regular, round flames of the geraniums exploded inside the house.

There were lines of moss between the geometric slabs of the garden path. He took two steps forward, shouted, ignored a multitude of buzzing, golden flies which flew for a second around his head, and placed his feet with circumspection and delight on the thick turf. And then, in a flash, the moss and the slabs seemed to fade, sink behind blocks of fog, and abandon their comfortable feeling of dry dust.

The walls flickered and collapsed into bright, fragile fragments. They, too, slowly sank into nothingness.

The sounds became silence. The disks, the lamp posts, the mouths that had crushed, broken and fragmented the silence earlier, now rose in long smoke trails, all straight, all pure. There were no screams; only great peace and the murmurs of astonished questions.

Everything was disappearing; the curtains on the windows and then, the windows themselves, the stones on the steps, the tire tracks and the cars, the calls that choked in a confused gargle, the sparkles.

Everything was vanishing; the golden fruits that would not ripen, the tiles balancing on the top of the brick walls, and the book he had left on the bench in the morning, whose characters danced like gray flakes and turned into invisible ashes like a fragrance in a light wind.

The roofs cast a last red glow, then broke up, fragmented and melted away. Had they shouted or merely groaned? He couldn't tell. Behind the walls, unreal furniture descended slowly through the vaporous floors, or dissolved without moving, their subtle arrangement of trinkets, colors, crockery and linen that shimmered like hot air, disappearing into space, dying in barely luminous fires.

He bent down and picked up a stone. But it fell through the phalanges of his fingers, in fine streams of gas, interminably, never touching the ground.

Everything was ending. The pebbles became less and less real, the leaves still hid the ghosts of the trees for a short while behind their green essence.

Men evaporated in puffs, randomly.

Snow began to fall—a snow made of children.

"What is it? Was it a bomb? They still managed to complete their damned experiments. It's over now, huh? It's really over."

He did not suffer. He was not even scared. He slowly turned his head toward the person who had just spoken, as if he feared to break it and to spin it into increasingly fine fragments, which would scatter in the wind. The other man was not worried either. He only wanted to know.

"It had to happen, huh? It had to happen."

"Well, yes, and it has."

Truthfully, he did not know what had happened. He looked for answers in the fantastic heaps of engulfed shapes that were consumed as softly, as clearly and as completely as burning mountains of diamonds.

"Maybe we should run away?"

"No. It'll be the same everywhere."

They began to think.

They did not really want to leave; their pasts had piled up around their legs in piles of gray dust; they could no longer remember it, but they could not conceive of themselves without a future.

"...to act... no way out..." they thought.

The road was there; it ran soundlessly between the sidewalks and it led elsewhere than that square. It was winding between the places where street lamps and large, flat facades had already disappeared. There was now a desert on both sides of it, and a timid wind chased the sand away from the dunes.

He was ruminating over an idea, somewhere in the red fog of his brain. He wondered why everything had ended like this, even the sun that he guessed was made of pure crystal and floated into space, even the stars, even the void, all without a glitch. All the décors that had burned, melted pell-mell, and superimposed over themselves.

He would have liked a prodigious firework display. He felt frustrated. The idea grew and grew. The only thing that was getting stronger in him...

"I know what happened."

Blue spheres, green spheres, and pink spheres were falling everywhere, and when they touched, they burst noiselessly. Then the dreams of men faded away, fairies, dragons, amazing journeys, wonderful dolls, heaps of gold and jewels, a play, and sometimes pages of books never written. There were palaces, the skies of the South Pacific, an electric scooter, and many proclamations.

"Ah," said the other man.

It did not interest him very much. He had just understood that everything was gone. He did not harbor the secret desire to find the reason why.

"It is strange that nobody noticed it earlier. There was such a parallel between what's happening and what we did. He simply typed a full stop. Like I did. Like all the other poor saps."

He was breaking into soap bubbles from his cheeks as he spoke. He laughed because, deep down, it had the comical aspects of the weirdest of dreams, and, like dreams, it was all meaningless, illusory. Not even the death of humanity could darken the delicate humor of this ending.

"What? Who typed what? What full stop? I don't understand."

"I do not know who. Someone who just finished writing the story of man, and many other stories, perhaps, that took place in other parts of the universe and that we shall never discover now. Maybe he will start on a new story. But he's done with us. What would be extraordinary is that we would go on without him. Has that ever happened before?"

"What a bastard! He could have let us know! There are lots of things I could have done differently. Now, it's good night everyone!"

He did not really hate him. He was irritated because he thought they could just as well have gone on, rather than drown, dragged into a bottomless ocean.

Never again would the creations of men and the sand castles of children be; never again the peaceful homes and the gardens, the growth of which one liked to watch during in the empty hours of the day, and never again, either, the noisy and heavy rockets, the fire of which was stolen by the skies.

And never again, men.

"Have you ever thought about the fate of the characters from a book when the book is finished?"

They were almost alone. They did not know where they were, but it must have been in such a tenuous world that it could barely exist for more than a few seconds.

"I wonder if he was telling our story, if he was just daydreaming about it, or if he was actually writing it down? What richness of imagination, and so precise! What creative genius, down to the smallest details. Still, perhaps he could have come up with a concept that would have been kinder to us, in the course of time."

They floated alone, the last, perhaps because they thought intensely.

"Our bad luck is that we did not quite end our own story in line with the rest of his story. But it does not matter."

"But who is he?" begged the shadow of the other man.

The idea was expanding and expanding, with small branches of dream and reason abounding and crisscrossing. It already contained a vague notion of the answer.

"He may resume our story. In a long time. He may want to write a sequel. Maybe this has happened to us already? Do you remember?"

Time passed.

"I think I see him now... But what if he, too, is a dream, and so on to infinity?"

Their two puddles of fog had become almost white. They condensed in pale, elongated spots. It was getting harder and harder to breathe. And to move.

"Farewell."

"Goodbye."

One of the spots fluttered a bit because he wanted to say something again. But there were no longer any sounds or smells.

There was no space. Just a stop. A full stop.

Bibliography

(fiction only)

1955:
Le Jeu [*The Game*] (short story) in *Le Petit Silence Illustré* n°6 ; incl. in *Faiseurs d'univers, et autres récits sur le jeu*, Gallimard, Coll. *Folio Junior SF* n° 15, 1984.

Une place au balcon [*Room on the Balcony*] (short story) in Ed. Nuit & Jour, *Galaxie* n° 23; incl. in *Les Perles du temps*, 1958.

1956:
Civilisation 2190 (short story) in Opta, *Fiction* n° 26, ; incl. in *Les Perles du temps*, 1958.

Les Villes [*The Cities*] (short story) in Opta, *Fiction* n° 30 ; incl. in *Histoires comme si...*, 1975.

1957:
Le Bord du chemin [*The Edge of the Road*] (short story) in Opta, *Fiction* n° 45; incl. in *Histoires comme si...*, 1975.

Cache-cache [*Hide and Seek*] (short story) in *Le Petit Silence Illustré* n° 7; incl. in *La Loi du talion*, 1973.

Point final [*Full Stop*] (short story) in Opta, *Fiction* n° 40; incl. in Les Perles du temps, 1958.

1958:
Agent galactique [*Galactic Agent*] (under the pseudonym of Mark Starr) (novel) in Editions Scientifiques et Littéraires, *Satellite* n° 1, 2, 3, 4, 5 and 9.

Le Cavalier au centipède [*The Centipede Rider*] (short story) in Opta, *Fiction* n° 57 ; incl. in *Un chant de pierre*, 1966.

Drame de famille [*Family Drama*] (short story) in Opta, *Fiction* n° 57.

Démonstration (short story) in Satellite, *Les Cahiers de la Science Fiction* n° 2.

Embûches dans l'espace [*Ambushes in Space*] (under the pseudonym of François Pagery) (novel) in Hachette/Gallimard, *Rayon Fantastique* n° 53.

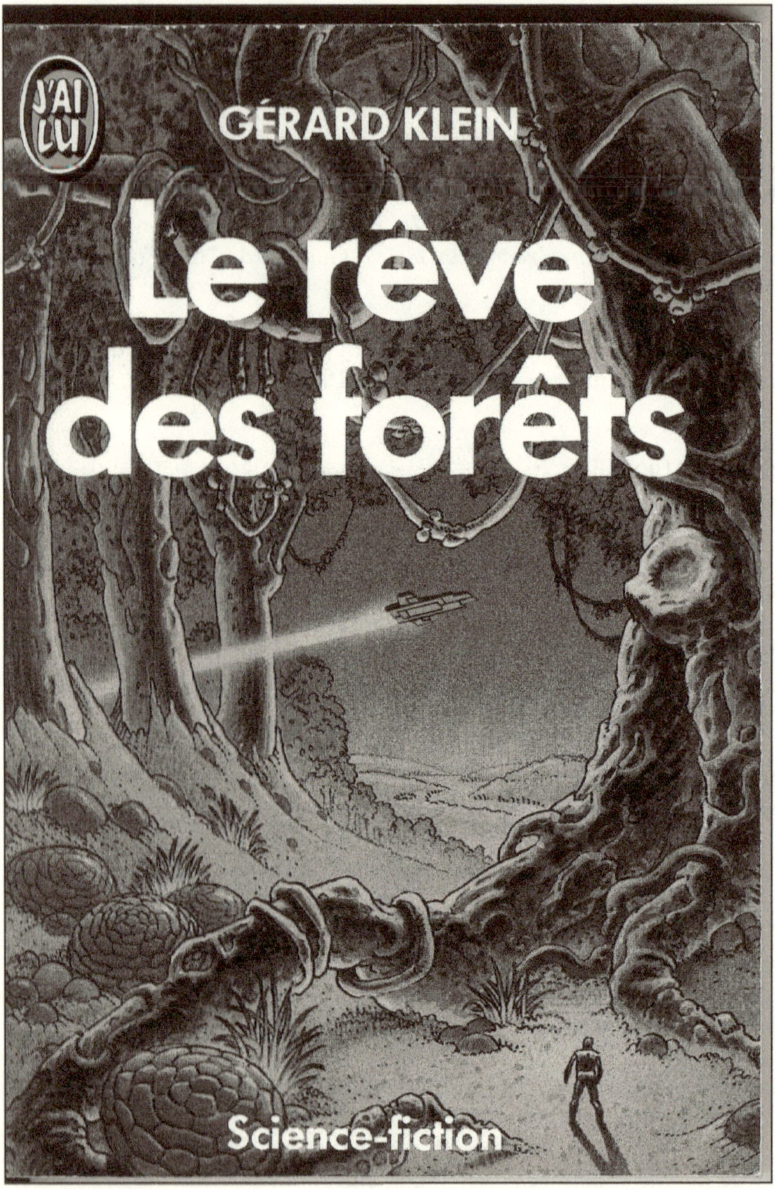
J'AI LU
GÉRARD KLEIN
Le rêve des forêts
Science-fiction

Le Gambit des étoiles [*Starmasters' Gambit*] (novel) in Hachette/Gallimard, *Rayon Fantastique* n° 62.

Le Monstre [*The Monster*] (short story) in Opta, *Fiction* n° 59; incl. in *Les Perles du Temps*, 1958.

Les Perles du Temps [*The Pearls of Time*] (short story collection) in Denoël, *Présence du Futur* n° 26.
    Prologue
    Tels des miroirs gelés [*Like Frozen Mirrors*]
    Le Monstre (q.v. 1958)
    Une place au balcon (q.v. 1955)
    La Vieille Maison [*The Old House*]
    En vacances [*On Holidays*]
    Les Abandonnés [*The Leftovers*]
    La Fête [*The Feast*]
    Les Hôtes [*The Hosts*]
    Le Grand Concert [*The Great Concert*]
    L'écume du soleil [*The Foam of the Sun*]
    Trois versions d'un événement [*Three Versions of an Event*]
    Les Voix de l'espace [*The Voices from Space*]
    Impression de voyage [*Travel Impressions*]
    Les évadés [*The Escapees*]
    Bruit et silence [*Sound and Silence*]
    Civilisation 2190 (q.v. 1956)
    Les Prisonniers [*The Prisoners*]
    Point final (q.v. 1957)

Le Plénipotentiaire [*The Plenipotentiary*] (short story) in Satellite, *Les Cahiers de la Science Fiction* n° 5.

Les Recruteurs [*The Recuiters*] (short story) in Satellite, *Les Cahiers de la Science Fiction* n° 9 ; incl. in *Un chant de pierre*, 1966.

Le Visiteur [*The Visitor*] (short story) in Opta, *Fiction* n° 53; incl. in *L'Habitant des étoiles et autres récits sur les extra-terrestres*, Gallimard, Coll. *Folio Junior SF* n° 18, 1985.

1959:
Le Condamné [*The Condemned*] (short story) in Opta, *Fiction* n° 65; incl. in *Histoires comme si...*, 1975.

Le Domaine interdit [*The Forbidden Domain*] (short story) in *Ailleurs*, Bulletin du club Futopia; incl. in *Histoires comme si...*, 1975.

L'Observateur [*The Observer*] (short story) in *La Première Anthologie de la science-fiction française*, Opta, Fiction-Spécial.

La Pluie [*The Rain*] (short story) in Satellite, *Les Cahiers de la Science Fiction* n° 14 ; incl. in *Histoires comme si...*, 1975.

Retour aux origines [*Back to the Origins*] (short story) in *Ailleurs*, Bulletin du club Futopia, 1959 ; incl. in *Histoires comme si...*, 1975.

La Vallée des échos [*The Valley of Echoes*] (short story) in Satellite, *Les Cahiers de la Science Fiction* n° 15 ; incl. In Un chant de pierre, 1966.

1960:
Chirurgiens d'une planète [*The Planet Surgeons*] (under the pseudonym of Gilles d'Argyre) (novel) in Fleuve Noir, *Anticipation* n° 165 ; rewritten and expanded as Le Rêve des forêts [*A Dream of Forests*] in Flammarion, *J'ai Lu* n° 2164, in 1987.

Rencontre [*Encounter*] (short story) in Opta, *Fiction* n° 80; incl. in *Histoires comme si...*, 1975.

Les enfers sont les enfers [*Hells are Hell*] (short story) in Opta, *Fiction* n° 84; incl. in *Histoires comme si...*, 1975.

La Planète aux sept masques [*The Planet of Seven Masks*] (short story) in *24 passionnants récits d'anticipation*, Opta, Fiction-Spécial; incl. in Un chant de pierre, 1966.

Vous mourrez quand même [*You Will Die Anyway*] (short story) in Ed. Opta, *Mystère magazine* n° 145 ; incl. in *Histoires comme si...*, 1975.

1961:
Le Témoin [*TheWitness*] (short story) in Ed. Opta, *Mystère magazine* n° 163, ; incl. in *Histoires comme si...*, 1975.

Lettre à une ombre chère [*Letter to a Dear Shadow*] (short story) in Opta, *Fiction* n° 95, 1961 ; incl. in *Histoires comme si...*, 1975.

Mode d'emploi [*Instruction Manual*] (short story) in Opta, *Fiction* n° 88.

LES VOILIERS DU SOLEIL

GILLES d'ARGYRE

★

★★ANTICIPATION★★

Editions
"Fleuve Noir"

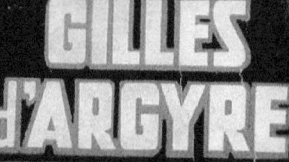

LE LONG VOYAGE

GILLES d'ARGYRE

Editions
"Fleuve Noir"

Les Voiliers du Soleil [*The Solar Sailors*] (under the pseudonym of Gilles d'Argyre) (novel) in Fleuve Noir, *Anticipation* n° 172.

1962:
Le Dernier Moustique de l'été [*The Last Mosquito of Summer*] (short story) in Opta, *Fiction* n° 106 ; incl. in *Un chant de pierre*, 1966.

Le Vieil homme et l'espace [*The Old Man and Space*] (short story) in Opta, *Fiction* n° 108; incl. in *Histoires comme si...*, 1975.

1963:
Un chant de pierre [*A Song of Stone*] (short story) in *Anthologie de la science-fiction française*, Opta, *Fiction-Spécial* n° 4 ; incl. in *Un chant de pierre*, 1966.

Le Temps n'a pas d'odeur [*The Day Before Tomorrow*] (novel) in Denoël, *Présence du Futur* n° 63.

1964:
Le Long voyage [*The Long Journey*] (under the pseudonym of Gilles d'Argyre) (novel) in Fleuve Noir, *Anticipation* n° 253.

Magie noire [*Black Magic*] (short story) in Opta, *Fiction* n° 130; incl. in *Histoires comme si...*, 1975.

1965:
La Tunique de Nessa [*Nessa's Tunic*] (with Luc Vigan) (short story) in Opta, *Fiction* n° 138; incl. in *Un chant de pierre*, 1966.

Les Tueurs de Temps [*The Mote in Time's Eye*] (under the pseudonym of Gilles d'Argyre) (novel) in Fleuve Noir, *Anticipation* n° 263, 1965.

1966:
Un Chant de pierre [*A Song of Stone*] (short story collection) in Eric Losfeld.
   Un chant de pierre (q.v. 1963)
   Le Dernier Moustique de l'été (q.v. 1962)
   Jonas (1966)
   La Vallée des échos (q.v. 1959)
   Les Recruteurs (q.v. 1958)
   Les Plus Honorables emplois de la Terre... [*The Most Honorable Jobs on Earth*]
   Le Cavalier au centipède (q.v. 1958)
   La Planète aux sept masques (q.v. 1960)

De la littérature [*Of Literature*]
La Tunique de Nessa (q.v. 1965)

1967:
Les Créatures (short story) in Ed. Le Terrain Vague, *Midi-Minuit Fantastique* n° 18-19 ; incl. in *La Loi du talion*, 1973.

Les Virus ne parlent pas [*Viruses Don't Talk*] (short story) in *SF made in France*, Opta, Fiction-Spécial n° 12; incl. in *La Loi du talion*, 1973.

1968:
Discours pour le centième anniversaire de l'Internationale végétarienne [*Speech for the 100th Anniversary of the International Vegetarian Society*] (short story) in Opta, *Fiction* n° 170 ; incl. in *Histoires comme si...*, 1975.

Un gentleman (short story) in Opta, *Fiction* n° 180; incl. in *Histoires comme si...*, 1975.

Le Sceptre du hasard [*The Scepter of Chance*] (under the pseudonym of Gilles d'Argyre) in Fleuve Noir, Anticipation n° 357.

1969:
Ligne de partage [*Party Line*] (short story) in Opta, *Fiction* n° 183; incl. in La Loi du talion, 1973.

Avis aux directeurs de jardins zoologiques [*Advice to the Directors of Zoological Gardens*] (short story) in Opta, *Fiction* n° 189 ; incl. in *La Loi du talion*, 1973.

1970:
Trouvé [*Found!*] (short story) in *Les Chefs-d'œuvre de la science-fiction*, Ed. Planète.

1971:
Les Seigneurs de la guerre [*The Overlords of War*] (novel) in Robert Laffont, *Ailleurs et Demain* n° 8.

1973:
La Loi du talion [*The Law of Retaliation*] (short story collection) in Robert Laffont, *Ailleurs et Demain* n° 21, 1973.
    Preface : Un instant s'il vous plaît [*A moment of your time, please*]
    Cache-cache (q.v. 1957)
    Ligne de partage (q.v. 1969)

Les Blousons gris [*The Grey Jackets*]
Les Virus ne parlent pas (q.v. 1967)
Avis aux directeurs de jardins zoologiques (q.v. 1969)
Réhabilitation
Sous les cendres [Under the Ashes]
Jonas (q.v. 1966)
La Loi du talion [*The Law of Retaliation*]
Les Créatures (q.v. 1967)

1975:
Acmé ou l'anti-Crusoé [*Acme, or the Anti-Crusoe*] (short story) in *Les Soleils noirs d'Arcadie*, Opta, Nebula ; incl. in Le Livre d'or de Gérard Klein, 1979.

Histoires comme si... [*Stories As If...*] (short story collection) in Union Générale d'Edition, *Collection 10/18* n° 924.
Rencontre (q.v. 1960)
Le Bord du chemin (q.v. 1957)
La Pluie (q.v. 1959)
Le Dernier Moustique de l'été (q.v. 1962)
Le Vieil homme et l'espace (q.v. 1962)
La Vallée des échos (q.v. 1959)
Discours pour le centième anniversaire de l'Internationale végétarienne (q.v. 1968)
Les Plus Honorables emplois de la Terre... (q.v. 1966)
Un gentleman (q.v. 1968)
Les Villes (q.v. 1956)
La Tunique de Nessa (q.v. 1965)
Lettre à une ombre chère (q.v. 1961)
La Planète aux sept masques (q.v. 1960)
Un chant de pierre (q.v. 1963)
Le Condamné (q.v. 1959)
Retour aux origines (q.v. 1959)
De la littérature (q.v. 1966)
Le Domaine interdit (q.v. 1959)
Les Recruteurs (q.v. 1958)
Les enfers sont les enfers (q.v. 1960)
Magie noire (q.v. 1964)
Vous mourrez quand même... (q.v. 1960)
Le Témoin (q.v. 1961)
Le Cavalier au centipède (q.v. 1958) de

Gérard Klein

Histoires comme si...

10 18

1978:
Tout conte fait [Said and Done] (Short short) in *Pourquoi j'ai tué Jules Verne*, Ed. Stock, Coll. Dire/Stock 2 ; incl. in *Mémoire vive, mémoire morte*, 2007.

1979:
Le Livre d'Or de Gérard Klein [*The Golden Book of Gérard Klein*] (anthology by Michel Jeury) in Presses-Pocket, *Le Livre d'Or* n° 5056.
    Préface by Michel Jeury
    La Tunique de Nessa (q.v. 1965)
    L'écume du soleil (q.v. 1958)
    Le Monstre (q.v. 1958)
    Les Virus ne parlent pas (q.v. 1967)
    Trois versions d'un événement (q.v. 1958)
    Discours pour le centième anniversaire de l'Internationale végétarienne (q.v. 1968)
    Ligne de partage (q.v. 1969)
    Acmé ou l'anti-Crusoé (q.v. 1975)
    Le Condamné (q.v. 1959)
    Les Prisonniers (q.v. 1958)
    Le Dernier Moustique de l'été (q.v. 1962)
    Le Cavalier au centipède (q.v. 1958)
    La Planète aux sept masques (q.v. 1960)
    Réhabilitation (q.v. 1966)
    Jonas (q.v. 1966)

1986:
Mémoire vive, mémoire morte [*Living Memory, Dead Memory*] (short story) in *Demain les puces*, Denoël, *Présence du Futur* n° 421, incl. in *Mémoire vive, mémoire morte*, 2007.

1987:
Le Rêve des forêts [*A Dream of Forests*] (rewritten and expanded version of *Chirurgiens d'une planète*, 1960) in Flammarion, *J'ai Lu* n° 2164.

1989:
La Serre et l'ombrelle [*The Hothouse and the Umbrella*] (short story) incl. in Mémoire vive, mémoire morte, 2007.

1997:
Pour en finir avec l'an 2000 [*To Be Done with the Year 2000*] (short story) in 1000 jours pour en finir avec l'an 2000, Libération n° 4939; incl. in Mémoire vive, mémoire morte, 2007.

Spéculons sur l'avenir [*Speculate about the Future*] (short story) ; incl. in *Mémoire vive, mémoire morte*, 2007.

2004:
Dernière idylle [*Last Idyll*] in *Le Dernier Homme*, Les Belles Lettres & Manitoba ; incl. in *Mémoire vive, mémoire morte*, 2007.

La Question (short story) ; incl. in *Mémoire vive, mémoire morte*, 2007.

2007:
Le Rôle de l'homme [*The Role of Man*] (short story) in Ed. du Bélial, *Bifrost* n° 46 ; incl. in *Mémoire vive, mémoire morte*, 2007.

Mémoire vive, mémoire morte [*Live Memory, Dead Memory*] (short story collection) in Robert Laffont, *Ailleurs et Demain*.
   La Serre et l'ombrelle (q.v. 1989)
   Mémoire vive, mémoire morte (q.v. 1986)
   Acmé ou l'anti-Crusoé (q.v. 1975)
   Le Monstre (q.v. 1958)
   La Fête (q.v. 1958)
   Les Abandonnés (q.v. 1958)
   L'écume du soleil (q.v. 1958
   Les Voix de l'espace (q.v. 1958)
   Impressions de voyage (q.v. 1958)
   Bruit et silence (q.v. 1958)
   Civilisation 2190 (q.v. 1956)
   Les Prisonniers (q.v. 1958)
   Tout conte fait (q.v. 1978)
   La Question (q.v. 2004)
   Spéculons sur l'avenir (q.v. 1997)
   Pour en finir avec l'an 2000 (q.v. 1997)
   Dernière idylle (q.v. 2004)
   Le Rôle de l'homme (q.v. 2007)
   Trois belles de Bréhat [*Three Beautiful Girls from Brehat*] (2007)
   Point final (q.v. 1957)